D0987119

WHISPERS OF STONE

Paperback ISBN: 978-1-952348-13-6
Hardback ISBN: 978-1-952348-14-3

Cover design by: Allegra Pescatore
Illustrations by: John Fisher
Interior formatting by: Ailish Brundage
Printed in the United States of America

Whispers
of
Stone
Allegra Pescatore

TABLE OF CONTENTS

Dedicated to those who live with chronic pain.

Drink some water. Don't forget your meds.

Be kind to yourself.

That cup of tea you made and forgot is probably cold by now, but that's ok.

You're doing the best you can and are not alone.

AUTHOR'S NOTE

Thank you for continuing on with *The Last Gift* series. Your support means the world to me. I wanted to take a brief moment to introduce *Whispers of Stone* and, hopefully, deepen your enjoyment of the upcoming story.

The Last Gift series is one of several in a collection called Project Ao. These books span multiple authors, worlds, and genres, but all take place within the same universe and are part of the same overarching plot. While each series may be read alone, they are best enjoyed together. *Whispers of Stone* will be the first novel in Project Ao where knowledge of the other worlds will come into play, so if you have not yet read *NACL: Eye of the Storm*, I encourage you to do so. For a suggested reading order, please see the next page.

If you're ready to move on to *Whispers of Stone* please be aware that it is the first half of a two-part story. It was a hard decision splitting the sequel to *Where Shadows Lie* in two, but in the end it was simply too large to print as one. As such, I entreat you to go into *Whispers of Stone* knowing that while it does stand on its own as a chronicle of the tumultuous first three days after the death of the Red Dragon, it is also only the beginning of a story that will conclude in *These Gossamer Strings*.

Whispers of Stone will pick up immediately after the events of *Where Shadows Lie*, so to avoid having characters rehash what they, and you, already know, there will only be a minimal amount of recap in the text itself.

If you've just read *Where Shadows Lie* and are ready to jump right in, feel free to. If, like me, you prefer a quick reminder of the events of the story, you can find it at the back of the book, along with a content warning, a glossary of all major players and Eldel words, a table of Gifts, and much more. This includes a bonus novelette *Solace of Memory* that sheds light on some of the events that shaped the past. Now, on to the story.

Happy reading!

PROJECT AO SUGGESTED READING ORDER

Branch One

Where Shadows Lie
NACL: Eye of the Storm
Solace of Memory
The Greatest Adventure
Whispers of Stone

Branch Two

A Bond of Thread
The Binding Day Truce

PROLOGUE

All These Little Lies

24 YEARS EARLIER

ARA & ROBIN

THE NIGHT WAS STILL, air heavy with the threat of rain. Outside the open bedroom window, the lights of the Academy were dim, only the most studious scholars still working. Those few, Ara hoped, would be too focused on their research to look up and see what she and Robin were about to do. She looked down at the bed, at the young couple she had talked to just a few hours earlier. Jonah and Estelle had been concerned for their safety. They had come to Ara and Robin because they trusted her, because Ara and her husband, more than anyone on this island, understood what they were going through.

Because they were family.

Where the half-dragon stood, Ara could have brushed away the lock of hair that had fallen across Estelle's face, or pulled the blanket back over Jonah's shoulders. They thought they were safe, here in this little room, on the Island that was supposed to be the sanctuary of the Gods themselves, never expecting that the haven that sheltered them would steal what they treasured most.

Ara would never be able to look them in the eyes again after tonight.

Forcing herself away from the bed, she parted the curtains between the two rooms just enough to slip through. From her pocket, she pulled out a small glass globe. With a silent command it filled the chamber with a diffuse golden light, the small surge of magic easing some of the tension in her muscles. She should have channeled off some excess power before coming here, but doing so would have been too much of a risk. If she needed magic tonight, better to have as much as possible at her disposal.

The light was dim, but illuminated the narrow room enough to see two cribs. Ara knew she had to hurry, yet she took a moment to look down at the sleeping children. The eldest rested fitfully, his small arms tight around a stuffed cat. The other was so very little, his dusting of brown hair shifting in the wind from the open window. She let her fingers trail across the downy fuzz and smiled, despite the horrible task at hand.

"Hello, Alexander. I'm sorry I have to do this, I really am, but I hope I can explain everything one day."

Jonah had looked so proud and frazzled at the meeting that morning, chasing after one toddling child while holding the other swaddled in his arms, giving Estelle a chance to talk. Ara had snatched the older boy up, making Alaric giggle and shriek as she tickled him. Later, when Robin had asked to speak to their parents alone, little Alexander had been placed into Ara's arms. He had stared up at her with those vivid green eyes of his and waved his hand towards her nose, then fallen asleep, safe and warm. The elder—equally tired after all the excitement—had curled up on Ara's lap.

One of these young ones was destined to change the course of history, to bring down kingdoms, unite empires, and crush Tirit Mindel's monopoly on the way. Ara had given everything to make sure of that, but it was impossible to know which child it would be until they were older. For there to be a chance of that though, they couldn't stay here. Too many wanted them dead, even on Ara's side. They would only be safe away from each other and the influence of court and the Colleges. She was doing the right thing; the people she would hurt just didn't know it yet.

And Gods help her if she was wrong.

With great care, Ara pulled two carefully measured vials of dacel from the pouch at her waist. She unstoppered one of the vials, poured the greenish liquid into the toddler's mouth, and gently pinched his nose to make him swallow. He squirmed a little, but soon the sleeping drug kicked in and Alaric stilled. She counted three breaths, then did the same with the infant. It made her nerves scream to watch their breaths slow, but having the children wake mid-kidnapping would only make this harder.

As Ara stood in the eerie silence, she could hear Jonah and Estelle's breathing and the rustle of the breeze from a small window as it played over Ara's clothes and scales.

The last silence before the storm.

When her nerves gave out, she strapped the older of the two into a back-carrier and made sure he was secure before placing the younger in a sling at her breast. She shifted uncomfortably. They were light, but so was Ara, and the backpack-like contraption rubbed against the base of her small wings. She looked around the room one last time, then down at the abandoned stuffed cat. Could she afford to take a keepsake? Both children had to become invisible after today, but would a little bit of sentimentality really hurt? Her fingers closed around the plush animal, but after a moment of hesitation she left it where it lay and turned off the light.

Nothing had changed in the main bedroom when she reentered. Estelle and Jonah were still asleep, the air in the room was still heavy, and Ara's heart still raced. Slowly, she inched forward and was about three feet from the door when her foot caught on a toy. It made a shrieking noise against the floor and she fell to her knees, unbalanced by the extra weight of the children.

"What was that?"

Ara pushed to her feet with a magic-fueled kinetic thrust, pulse racing.

"Stop! Estelle, the babies, they have the boys."

The parents scrambled out of bed, but Ara had already reached the door. She yanked it open, knowing that the light of the hallway would reveal her. There was no other half-dragon who knew Jonah and Estelle were there, and that . . .

No, no time to think about the implications. No time to do anything other than flee.

Ara pelted down the corridor to her left, praying that the guards were in the other direction. She could hear yelling behind her, then heavy footsteps. She focused on the balcony door mere yards away.

Safety. The pounding feet behind her were gaining. Opening the door with a kinetic push, she put on a burst of speed and lunged onto the balcony.

It was empty. Ara skidded to a stop at the rail.

"Where are you, Robin?" She hissed under her breath, searching the skies. "Where in the name of the Five are you? I need you here now."

"Stop!"

Damn it.

Ara turned to face Jonah Iaming, King of Seehana, and raised a hand, ready to rift. "I don't want to do this, Jonah, but if you take one more step, son of mine or not, I *will* blast you."

Did he know how painful those words were, after so many years of distance between them?

Jonah froze and behind him, so did Estelle, holding herself up on a column, one hand over her mouth as her eyes fixed on the baby in Ara's sling.

"Don't take them from us. Not like this," she pleaded, and Ara felt the pain in her words as keenly as if it had come from her own heart.

"I know what it feels like to have a child ripped from my arms, Estelle, and I'm sorry, but they won't survive the year if we don't hide them. You have to trust me." Ara heard the faint sounds of beating wings and took another step back. The base of her tail bumped against the balcony rail and she risked a glance skyward.

Any minute now would be great, darling, she sent magically to her husband.

Almost there, Robin replied.

"Give them back to us, Mother. We can talk. You don't need to do this." Jonah held up both hands in a placating gesture as he took a step in her direction. Ara didn't think, she just acted on a lifetime of training on Tirit Mindel.

A burst of energy crashed into Jonah's chest sending him flying backward into Estelle and leaving them sprawled on the tiled floor.

Here.

The form of the black mock dragon swooped down out of the

darkness. The man sitting astride it reached out a hand to her. Ara turned and flung herself onto the rail.

Their hands collided and Ara jumped.

With a flap of mighty wings, the mock flew upwards, pulling Ara towards the sky. Her shoulder screamed in pain, but she didn't let go of Robin's hand.

"Pull me up, I can't hold on."

Robin grasped her arm with his other hand and pulled. She grit her teeth to stop from crying out, the weight of the children unbalancing her as she swung her leg over the saddle.

Once astride, Ara wrapped one arm around her husband's waist and buckled her legs into the straps, then checked to make sure both boys were still secure and unharmed.

As they banked to begin the journey west, Ara looked down. Below them, two moonlit forms stood at the balcony rail.

"Ara, please, bring them back to us," Estelle called, her voice only a whisper over the wind. Ara closed her eyes and pressed her face into Robin's shoulders, biting back tears.

"Ara! *Mother!*" Jonah's voice was whipped away and with it the last shreds of Ara's self-control. She began to weep.

**Robin, tell me we're doing the right thing. Tell me again. This breaks every vow I've ever made. To them, and to my parents. This was the line we were never supposed to cross . . . **

We're doing what must be done, he responded, tone as heavy with sorrow as her own. **They'll be dead in a week if we let them stay, now that the secret is out.**

But what if it's a mistake? Her voice hitched.

Then everything that happens from now on is our fault.

The black mock dragon landed with a gentle thud on the damp grass. The silvery moon was at its zenith, undisturbed by clouds and in the gentle company of the stars. Ara unstrapped herself from the saddle, careful not to wake the sleeping child she cradled in a sling.

She jumped down and patted her mock's flank. "Stay close, Iro. I won't be long."

The mock's black wings unfolded and he took to the clear night sky. Ara stretched her flight-sore muscles, then began walking towards the solitary group of lights near the end of the long valley. The village of Nillenia spread out in the opposite direction, its windows gleaming like fireflies in the darkness. The baby in Ara's arms shifted in his sleep, a whimper escaping his tiny lips.

"Shh . . . it's alright, little one. You're safe and almost home. Nothing can hurt you here."

He quieted and she smiled. Her soft boots made hardly a sound on the narrow stone bridge as she crossed over to the other bank of the river. The flickering lights grew closer, illuminating the form of an ivy-covered cottage. Compared to what this child would have had, it was abject squalor, but at least he would have a chance of a normal life—or any life at all.

Despite weeks of travel, Ara paused a few yards from the door. Her arms tightened around the child. She looked down at him again, at her little Alexander, her sweet grandson. The boy who never should have been born, but who, along with his brother, carried so many of their dreams.

I could keep him.

There were ways to hide her draconic form—uncomfortable, yes, but maybe worth it. Having him with her these last few weeks as they'd flown across Lirin had hurt, but it was a good pain, one Ara would gladly embrace for the chance to finally raise a child instead of giving another one away.

Her fingers brushed against his pudgy hand and she sighed. What kind of life could she offer him? They would have to live in solitude, cut off from the people he might someday be called upon to rule. No. As much as it hurt, this would be better, even if Ara would never get to see his first steps or have any influence over who he grew up to be. Perhaps that was the price for her sin. She had taken Alexander away from parents who loved him and, in doing so, broken a promise to her long-dead mother.

"Never sink to their level, Ara," Corinne had said, as she'd passed

the torch of leadership to her daughter. "*The Silvarin Project murders babies and rips children from their parents' arms. That isn't our way. We cannot make the world a better place if we are not first better people. Whatever else happens, the children of the True Project should know their families and the people that they come from. They should choose their futures, not be forced into them.*"

This, Ara was sure, was not what Corinne had in mind when she made her request. Still, at least the boy would not be completely without ties to his roots. Besides, this speck of a village that no map even named was the last place anyone would look for him, which meant it was the safest.

She took the final steps up to the door and knocked twice.

The door opened. Another woman stood there, framed by the orange light of a fire. Ara had not seen her in many, many years, but she still looked the same: suspicious, proud, but with kind eyes.

"Talia, I've come to ask you a favor. This . . . is Alexander, and he needs a place to call home."

Robin got out of the coach and tipped the driver well. It was the middle of the day and the weekly market was in full swing. No one would notice one man arriving with a child and leaving without one.

The toddler was looking about with wonder, despite the gloomy, lackluster surroundings. North Island might not boast huge cities like Lirin, but it would be important for at least one of the boys to have a foothold here.

Robin strolled down the street into the market square. The crowds, dressed in heavy furs and moving with purpose, were so thick that he had some difficulty maneuvering them. Robin found the whole experience uncomfortably cold and claustrophobic, but the little boy loved it, babbling on in that peculiar language only they could decipher.

Robin had to ask directions once or twice, but he at last arrived at the address he was looking for. It was a large house, but not extravagant. It didn't stand out, being neither the grandest nor the poorest; it was exactly the middle-of-the-road sort of property the True Project's financiers favored.

"Robin? Come in, come in," his brother, Harrison, said upon opening the door.

"Thank you for having us. I know the risk you take, both being here and taking him," Robin said as he wiggled out of his coat and helped the child out of his.

"It's not a big deal." Harrison grinned wryly. "It's not like North Island would burn me as a heretic if they found out I was a rifter or anything." Harrison winked, then turned his eyes to the boy, weather-worn cheeks dimpling as he smiled. "So this is him? My little nephew?"

"Yes. This is Alaric Nameh, though we'll have to come up with another given name for him before you place him. Are you sure you'll be able to get him into the Patriarch's family?"

"That won't be a problem. They have half a dozen adopted children by now, what with their Tekomii 'rehabilitation' project," Harrison wrinkled his scarred nose in disgust. "I'll wait long enough that Estelle won't recognize him in the unlikely event that she were to visit, then arrange for him to join the Patriarch's brood. Leave the details to me and trust that I will watch over him and make sure he grows up with a more open mind than most of these people. My position as a tutor should make it easy to stay close. So, what do we call him? Whatcha think, little one? Got a favorite name?"

The child studied Harrison as if he understood, though Robin doubted he did.

"Noth!" Alaric suddenly exclaimed, reaching forward to tug on the old rifter's beard.

"I don't think that's a name, kiddo," Harrison replied as he offered his arms to the boy.

Robin handed him over without protest. "I'm sorry to hand you a baby and run, but I need to meet Ara in Hardor ahead of the birth of the Lirion Heir, and the longer I stay here, the more danger both of you are in. Just make sure nothing bad happens to him, alright? He might just be the most important person alive."

"You can trust me. I haven't let you down yet, have I?"

Robin smiled and shook his head. "No, you never have. Just make sure he gets the love he needs, and don't let the fuckers turn him into another xenophobic icecube."

That made Harrison laugh and the boy smiled in that unsure way that he was wont to do when grown-ups were talking.

"I'll be back to get him when he's ten. Send word whenever you can without risking your cover," Robin said, then bent a little to look Alaric in the eyes. "I wish you the very best of luck in your new life. May it be blessed, safe, but most of all happy."

With that, he pressed a kiss against the child's forehead and walked out of his life.

PART ONE

CHAPTER ONE

Survivor's Guilt

GABRIEL

It's the anniversary of Nillenia's destruction next week and I'm worried about Gabe. I think we should try to talk him into another Night Market expedition soon. He won't settle until he's found something to send his sister and had a good cry. Both of those are easier off campus.

—From a note passed to Fedrik Tellen, from Fayrian Avilor, during mathematics class at the Academy of Tirit Mindel, Fourth Year.

HAVE YOU COME FOR US, KEYHOLDER?

Gabriel startled awake, whispers ringing in his ears. For a moment, the silvery light of the moon filtering down from the high windows confused him. The soft bed, too, caught and held his wayward attention, incongruous with his dark, dank cell. Crimson and gold brocade, delicate lace curtains, a carved mahogany wardrobe in the corner. Why did the air smell of honey instead of death?

That brought a flash of memory. Light, blinding his eyes as he emerged from the consuming darkness of the subterranean torture chamber where he had been left to die. A sweet voice, begging him to live. Mari, clinging to him and missing both her hands. Then fresh air and . . .

The King. Elenor kneeling in front of him to kiss his ring. Fury, pain, darkness again.

Dread worked its way up Gabriel's raw throat like a scream wanting to burst forth. He scrambled to sit up, heart thundering, but only got up to his elbows before a searing pain tore along dozens of wounds.

"Easy. You're safe." A soft, firm hand pressed Gabriel back into bed as the scent of minty evergold filled his nose. Elenor Lirion stood over him, her blonde hair a damp, tangled mess, nightgown and robe plastered to her moonlit skin.

"What—" he began, but Elenor pressed a finger to his lips.

"Shh, Paul is asleep in the other room and I don't want to wake him. You're safe, Gabriel. No one can hurt you. I just came in to take some evergold for my legs before I go to bed. If I woke you, I'm sorry."

She pulled her finger away as Gabriel relaxed back into the cloud-like pillows. He looked around, at last recognizing the small bedroom where Elenor kept her poisons. A slow drizzle pattered against the large windows, a sound Gabriel had worried he would never hear again.

Safe.

His frenetic pulse began to slow. As it did, the pain crept back in. He grimaced and tried to adjust the pillows, but it didn't help, not when there wasn't so much as an inch of him not somehow bruised, burned, or cut. A twitch in the wrong direction pulled at new stitches along his back. He tried to draw in breath, only to have his lungs seize. Panic raced along his nerves and his magic flared to match it.

Cool relief followed. Gabe let out a long sigh, closing his eyes at the dizzying, pleasant feeling. "You said you came in here for evergold? If you have some to spare, I could really use a bit. Or maybe something stronger."

"Of course. I'm surprised you're awake. You were so . . . hurt. Are you still in pain, even with the magic?"

Elenor's voice hitched, making Gabriel's gaze fix on her. She shifted from foot to foot, tucked a strand of wet hair behind her ear, and looked anywhere but at Gabe. There was a scabbed-over gash along her hairline, framed by a swollen bruise. Her arm was in a sling, and her other hand was wrapped in bandages.

"How . . . how much of that did I do?" He gulped, more

fragments of memory fitting into place like frayed puzzle pieces. He could remember flinging his arms out, magic blasting towards the King with all the fury that had built up inside him. He also remembered seeing Elenor caught in that pulse of raw power and flung through the air.

The princess stepped towards the bedside table where bottles and medical instruments lay in a haphazard mess that would have made his Island professors wince. As Elenor poured out a dose of dacel—a strong sleep aid—and counted out two evergold pills, she answered in a murmur. "You weren't in control of yourself, and you saved my life. Father would have killed me if you hadn't intervened." She swallowed the medicine, then poured a second dose. "Try not to dwell on it. Daemon fixed me up, including my arm. It's just a bad dislocation and slight fracture. Nothing that will cause permanent harm. I can hardly feel it through the serindalla I took a few hours ago. Besides, I've been hurt a lot worse in the past."

Sure, because *that* made it better. "I'm sorry."

Elenor turned to him. "Don't. Don't apologize, because if you do, I'll have to apologize for letting you suffer like you did, and then you'll apologize for . . . well, you get the idea. It's too late for apologies."

She sat down on the edge of the bed, which was when her state of dress finally registered. "Why are you soaking wet?"

Elenor handed him the small glass, then admitted, "I like to twirl in the rain."

That answer was so far from what he had expected that it pushed the anguish over her injuries and his role in them from his mind for a blessed moment. He smiled. "That is the single most Lirion thing I have ever heard."

Her lips twitched up at the corners. "Well, you may have failed to notice, but I am, in fact, a Lirion."

"Oh, I noticed."

Elenor dropped the pills into Gabriel's other hand. "Here, this should help with the pain. I do have stronger medicine, if you need it, but Daemon said not to mix magic and laudanum."

He hesitated, looking down at the pills.

Elenor's smile faded. "My father's dead, Gabriel. He can't hurt you anymore. You can rest."

He's dead.

Gabe's hand trembled, almost spilling the pills all over the covers. Tears filled his eyes, and he tilted his head back to hold them in check. If he started crying, he had the feeling he would never stop. "I remember seeing him fall, but I wasn't sure . . . "

"It's over."

He brought the cup to his lips and drank, the bitter taste of dacel hardly registering above the dizzy relief. Elenor sat in silence but for the occasional droplet of water hitting the floor, giving him space as he processed his mess of emotions.

"Did you . . . Or did I?" he asked at last, as he reached up to press the palm of his hands against his burning eyes.

"Don't know who ended it. I poisoned him, you crushed him with magic, Daemon hit him in the head with a copper ball. We may never find out which one . . . "

A giddy, broken laugh tore from his lips. Then a choked sob. His hands fell away from his face and Gabriel met Elenor's eyes. "I'm sorry. He was your father."

Her bottom lip trembled, but she did not respond at once, expression steadily darkening until she asked, "Do you blame me?"

"Why would I blame you for killing the man who murdered my family?"

"No, not for that." She reached up to rub at bruises around her neck. Gabe hadn't noticed them before, but the moment he did, worry overtook the mess of emotions crashing around inside him. He couldn't remember leaving those.

Before he could ask her what had happened, Elenor continued. "I meant, do you blame me for all of it? For murdering Ian, for getting Wil and the Tellens killed, your arrest and torture? All of it. I know it's my responsibility. I'm not trying to shirk it, but I need to know if you, personally, blame me."

Gabriel bit back an impulsive reply. His head throbbed and, considering how sweaty he felt, the fever must still be running strong. Her question, though, merited thought. He pushed aside his own confusing mix of elation and grief, as well as his distress about those marks on her neck, to focus on his answer. She deserved an honest one. "Some of it, yes. I don't blame you for Ian, or for my arrest. I would have done the same to protect my family, but the Tellens . . . You knew. I told you what your father did to traitors; you saw it when he arrested me, but you chose not to believe it. Even when you witnessed what he was doing to me with your own eyes and after he killed the Tellens, you still weren't convinced."

She nodded, bottom lip trembling. "That's the part I keep coming back to as well. I should have known but I was too scared to see the truth. I got people I loved killed, then I dragged my closest friends into the same sort of treason that already claimed so many lives. I don't regret it—it was the right thing to do—but . . ."

Gabriel reached forward and placed his hand on hers, where it curled around the blankets. "I understand. I've seen a lot of friends die too. I am truly grateful for the help you've given me, and for freeing Lirin from your father."

Her shoulders shook and she squeezed her eyes shut but did not cry. She just sat there rocking and hugging herself, as though her thin, trembling arms could hold back the avalanche of emotion that only loss could conjure. Gabriel's heart ached for her, but he didn't know if it was his place to offer comfort, not with grief of such a personal nature.

Especially when her pain was his triumph.

As Gabriel began to feel the effects of the dacel, Elenor shook herself and sat up a little straighter.

"Can I ask you a question?"

"I'm sure it's more than one, but yes," he replied, hoping a little levity might make her smile. He was rewarded with the ghost of one, but it warmed him nonetheless. It was so much like Wil's.

"Could you tell me about your family and why it happened? You told me some of it before, but . . . I need more than just facts. I need to know the cost of his rule on people like you, and how things came to be this bad. My family broke Lirin, which means it's my responsibility to fix it, now more than ever. I can't do that without understanding the full scope of our crimes."

Gabe sucked in a breath, the action painful but necessary as he considered if he had the emotional fortitude to tell that story. The drugs pulled at his eyelids, promising the sweet oblivion of sleep, but he wouldn't be here if not for her. She had put herself and people she loved in danger to help Gabriel, and had killed the man who had terrorized Lirin for decades. If this was what Elenor wanted, he owed her that much.

"Are you sure you want to know? It might be better to hear it when you aren't exhausted and dealing with the death of your father," Gabe cautioned as gently as he could manage. "It could be needlessly masochistic for you to take this onto your shoulders right now, on top of what you're already dealing with."

Elenor shook her head. "I need to know, Gabriel. I don't think I'll be able to process his death if I don't fully understand why . . ."

She didn't have to finish. Gabe winced as he pulled himself up in bed to better stay awake. Elenor, too, shifted until she sat cross-legged. She discarded the soaking robe and pulled a wool throw blanket around her shoulders.

Gabe found he liked her better this way, face free of anger or distrust. Other than the dark bruises at her neck and brow, she looked like just another girl. Her damp blonde hair was starting to frizz as it dried. Pretty gray eyes stared at him without hostility, a kindred exhaustion mirrored in them. She looked like someone he could talk to without feeling like he had to tiptoe. Gone was the commanding young woman who had orchestrated both his capture and his escape, and in her place was just . . . Wil's little sister.

He could tell that girl about his family.

"Do you want me to explain the politics that lead to it? Because that might take all night."

"No. I think we can save that for another time. I want to know about the politics, I *care* about them, but I'm too tired to remember anything complicated."

"A Lirion who cares. I must be sicker than I thought. It has to be a hallucination," Gabe said, again trying to lighten the mood just a little. She needed to smile, and so did he. It had been far too long.

And smile she did. Elenor even chuckled, though it brought on a cough, the sound hoarse as she rubbed at her neck. The blanket shifted a little, revealing more ugly purple bruises.

His eyes narrowed. "Who hurt you? Was it your father? Wil never said it outright, but he implied that—"

"It wasn't him," Elenor interrupted, then sighed. "In a way, I wish it had been. This could prove worse in the long-run, but my problems aren't our topic of discussion right now."

Well, that was direct and provided exactly no wiggle room. Damn it.

"Alright. No politics, no questions about who hurt you. Got it."

That got another smile. Elenor had a pretty smile, one that went all the way to her stormy eyes and made a dimple appear on the right cheek. He had the sudden, near-compulsive urge to run his thumb over it. It was ludicrous and probably brought on by weeks without human contact, so to resist the temptation, Gabe focused on what she had asked him.

It was easier than usual to conjure the memories of that horrible day. He'd had a lot of time to think about it while locked up in the dark.

And then there was the magic.

He could feel it there, power far more vast than he remembered, except in those hazy, feverish days after his family had died. He had always thought he had misremembered, but this magic was familiar and wonderfully boundless. It would be so easy to just reach out and grab more of it . . .

With a start, Gabe yanked his attention back to Elenor, only to find her staring at him with eyebrows scrunched together.

"Are you alright?" she asked.

"Yeah. Sorry, I'm just tired."

"We can talk about this later if you want," Elenor offered, but Gabriel jerked his head in dissent.

"I don't know if I will be *able* to talk about this later. Right now everything is dulled and foggy. I might get through it without breaking down."

"Fine, but if you want to stop . . . "

He reached for her hand again and gave it a quick squeeze, this time not letting go. "I lost them a long time ago. It's alright."

"No. It's not. You don't have to pretend like it goes away, because it doesn't. I know that. But it does get easier if you say it aloud," Elenor whispered. "Though there are also things that can't be said, not for a long time. Truths and guilt that . . . are too big. You just went through something unimaginable, Gabriel. I shouldn't have asked. You need time to recover. I'm sorry." She sounded dangerously close to tears again.

"You did nothing wr—"

"I should have come sooner." The unabashed sorrow and guilt on her face made his heart lurch. "I knew what he was doing to you was wrong, but I was scared and you . . . you paid the price for that. You told me that my father was a monster. If I had believed you, Djina might still be alive—"

"Wait, what happened to Djina?" Gabe's attention sharpened, his hand around hers tightening. Elenor's lip trembled, and she didn't have to answer. "Shit. *Fuck*. I'm so sorry. She was . . . "

"She saved me and I killed her . . . or as good as. It doesn't matter that he wielded the sword. I've spent the last few days thinking about all the people who died because of my misplaced loyalty to my parents and I realized that I don't even know. How many suffered under their rule after I got sick because I lied to protect them? What about those who Wilam might have saved had I not derailed his plans? How many unjust executions have happened between the day you tried to poison them and today? I saved you and a handful of others, but . . . "

"No." It came out with more bite than Gabriel had intended and made the princess flinch. When she began to pull away, he tightened his grip on her hand despite the pain it brought him. "Don't torture yourself over death and suffering you had no hand in and didn't know about. Learn from them, choose to do better, but trust me when I say that *what-ifs* will eat you from the inside out if you let them. Do you know how often I've stayed awake all night wondering if I could have saved even one more person in my village if I had run to help instead of hiding? Or going over every failed plan to kill or depose your parents, wondering what more I could have done? Regrets don't bring back the dead or right the wrongs of the world. Actions do, and you have already taken steps to make Lirin a better place, haven't you? Focus on those."

Eyes glassy and nose a little red, Elenor inhaled deeply, then nodded. "I can try, though I don't think I've done enough." She sat back and looked up at the ceiling, sniffled once, then let out a long breath. "I need to get it together. I've done nothing but alternate between crying and taking foolhardy risks since Djina died."

Another pang of sorrow on her behalf shot through him, but other than giving her hand a squeeze, Gabriel did not reply. He had a feeling that if he asked about the details of the old doctor's passing, Elenor might crumble altogether.

After a few seconds, she wiped her eyes and into that silence, Gabriel began to speak. "I had a brother and a sister, Samuel and Riona. Sam had taken me and Riona to the lake to fish. Well, she mostly just crawled around in the sand, but it got her out of mom's hair for a few hours. Our house was at the very far end of the valley, away from the other farms and close to the paths up to the higher meadows. It was . . . wonderful. I can still remember how crisp the air was at night, and the smell of herbs drying from the rafters."

Even knowing what was coming, he couldn't help but smile. "My mother was a doctor, just like Djina. My dad tended goats. I can hardly remember their faces, but I think about them every time I eat goat cheese, and whenever I handle herbs and tonics. I think that's why I liked working at the clinic on the Island so much."

He was stalling, but didn't try to rein it in. To remember the dead, after all, was how their souls lived on, and his parents deserved to be remembered.

"They sound wonderful," Elenor said.

"They were. They both loved old stories, and would argue about which legends were true, and what versions of fairy tales to tell us. It was the only thing they ever fought about, at least in front of us."

He settled back against the pillows a little more comfortably, blinking away the heavy drowsiness of the dacel. "On the day it happened, I thought the shouts coming from town were some sort of celebration. I was annoyed that we were fishing when there was fun to be had. But then we started hearing screams. Sam told me to gather up Riona and go home to our parents while he looked into it."

Elenor's hand left his, rising to cover her mouth. "Was that the last time you saw him?"

Gabriel swallowed past the lump in his throat and inclined his head. "He . . . he was only sixteen. He seemed so mature, capable of protecting us from anything. I wanted to be just like him when I grew up. Then one day on the Island, I realized that I was older than Sam was when he died. I don't think I've ever cried harder than that, even the day it happened."

Fedrik had been the one to find Gabriel, curled up between his bed and desk, and had run to get Fay. The two of them had held Gabe for hours as he'd sobbed and talked freely about his family for the first time since they'd been killed. Even thinking about it made Fed and Fay's absence ache with a consuming pain deeper than any wound.

"How . . . how did Samuel die?"

Gabriel clenched his jaw and rubbed at his face. "Your father had a system by then. Surround the village. Shoot the ones who tried to fight back, line up the others, then slit their throats one by one and bury the bodies in a mass grave. I found Sam with a broken arrow through his heart under a pile of bodies, and a knife in his hand. At least . . . at least he died fighting. Most days, I wish I had too."

Elenor's face was steadily growing more ashen, twisted in sorrow that mirrored his own. "I'm sorry, Gabriel."

"I told you, it's not your fault—"

"I know. I'm not apologizing. I'm just sorry you went through it." She looked down, then back up at him, shoulders slumped. "I think about it all the time, about how different things would have been had I died instead of Wilam. You never would have been locked up and tortured to begin with."

"They have a name for this, you know? The doctors on Tirit Mindel, I mean. It's called survivor's guilt and it's a bitch."

Elenor let out a surprised snort of laughter, and without any more cue than that, began to cry. Gabriel, who had been holding onto his composure by a hair, felt his own resolve wobble. She wrapped an arm around her chest, as if in doing so she might be able to hold the pain inside, and Gabe decided he'd had enough of this.

With a grunt, he inched to the side. It made his head spin, but he shoved the pain away in favor of patting the bed next to him in invitation, one arm open. "Come here."

Her sobs halted, and she looked up at him with reddened eyes. "You're offering me a hug?"

Elenor sounded so baffled.

"You make it sound like I'm offering to dump a glass of ice water on your head. Yes, a hug. You're crying, hugs help," Gabe answered, arm still outstretched though it shook a little at the effort.

"But—"

"I'd forgotten how stubborn you are. Seriously, Lirion, you need a hug and so do I; accept the damn thing. I don't bite."

That made her snort. "I bit your hand once, if I recall. Maybe I'm not the one who should be afraid."

Why *was* she afraid? The idea bothered him, but Gabriel didn't ask and Elenor, after a few more seconds of sniffling, scooted forward just enough to press her face into Gabriel's shoulder. He wrapped his arm around her back and leaned his cheek against her hair with a sigh.

"Tell me honestly, just how bad are things? I know what I have to cry about, but you seem just as messed up. What else happened? How did you get those bruises?" Gabriel asked.

Elenor shuddered but didn't pull away. At last, she said, "I made some very bad decisions over the past month. Would you believe me if I told you that my father wasn't the enemy I was most scared of tonight?"

It *was* a little hard to believe, but he didn't contradict her, just held her, hoping that she would open up a bit more. What happened instead, much to his surprise, was that Elenor leaned into his embrace. Then, as if she needed this as much as he did, she shifted to curl up beside him and buried her face in his shoulder.

After weeks alone in the dark, the simple physical contact almost made him weep again. This had to be real, because even his most vivid hallucinations never felt this warm. "Must be pretty scary if you'd voluntarily cuddle up with a known criminal just to be able to talk about it."

That got a hoarse chuckle and her face emerged from hiding. "Maybe it's a ruse to poison you again."

"I could say the same in return, Princess," he said, pointedly glancing at the wardrobe in the corner. The break in tension, paired with the relief of feeling another's touch, made a bubbly, joyful lightness spread through him. It wasn't an appropriate emotion, given the topics they were discussing, but it just felt so fucking good to feel . . . normal, that Gabriel couldn't help but indulge it.

He wanted to laugh. To joke the way he used to with Fay, Fedrik, and Wil. None of them were there anymore. A month ago he would never have imagined that it would be Elenor Lirion, of all people, that he wanted to make smile.

Funny how fast things could change.

"Poisons and betrayals do seem to be our main sources of interaction. Guess it's just a matter of time before one of us tries it again," she snarked back, then pressed her face against his chest again and sighed. "Duncan Eurieha found me stealing the spare keys to the Subterranea and almost killed me on my aunt's orders last night."

Gabriel's smile faded as fast as a blown-out candle. "*What?*"

"Her children are in line for the throne after me. She's been trying to kill my brother and me since the day we were born."

Well, shit.

Wilam always said he and Elenor were in danger and that he wanted to keep her safe, but never once mentioned that the danger came from inside their own family. "How did you get away?"

She shook her head. "I didn't. I passed out and someone saved me, then we had to run and couldn't kill Eurieha. He's still alive, and he hasn't sent the guard to arrest me, which means he's got other plans. He knows I saved you and the only reason I can think of to not turn me in is if he plans to blackmail me."

"Then we take him down before he can," Gabe promised, words muffled against her hair. "You saved my life. If I can return the favor or help you in any way, I will."

"You don't owe me that."

"Whether I do or not doesn't matter. We could go back and forth, blaming each other or ourselves for what has happened and keeping score, but accounting every little debt is a Lirion thing. I don't do that. You saved my life and killed the man who murdered my family. Most of all, you want to make Lirin a better place and have the power to do it, so if I can help, I will. It's just that simple." He yawned, unable to fight it. Squeezing her as tight as his injuries would allow, Gabriel pressed his face into Elenor's wet hair. "Want me to go on? I don't want to heap more pain and guilt on you right now if you can't take it."

"I want to know. If I don't, I won't sleep."

"Alright then." It felt strange, yet oddly fitting to be holding the daughter of the man who had murdered his family while talking about it. For all their differences, both he and Elenor had lost family to Mark Lirion, and together they had avenged those deaths. She might not have been a friend when this had started, but after what she had done to help Lirin, she was now.

In a quiet voice and with his face pressed into her hair, he went on. "I honestly don't remember much of the run back home, only that my sister was crying. I heard my mother calling for us. She sounded scared, and that made me scared. When we got to the house, she pulled me inside and pushed a bookcase out of the way. There was this hole in the wall full of . . . stuff. I remember asking about it, but she ignored all my questions. She told me to keep Riona quiet and not come out until either she or Dad came to get me, then kissed us both on the head and closed the panel."

He'd never told anyone what her final words to him had been, and doubted he ever would. They still haunted his dreams some nights, mixing with the smell of smoke to make him feel as though he couldn't breathe. Gabriel shivered, memories of both the tiny crawlspace and the dark torture chamber closing in on him. Yet some combination of the drugs and Elenor's presence made it bearable. "It took over an hour before the soldiers came. I heard them searching the house. Other survivors of the razed villages told me that the King let the soldiers take anything they wanted. It was one of the perks that kept them from deserting. They were loud and Riona was scared, so I had to hold my hand over her mouth the whole time. I was worried I was going to hurt her, but finally they left. I thought it was over."

He tensed, old but never-forgotten pain tingling along the burn scars that covered the left side of his torso, back, and arm. "I heard the crackling before I smelled the smoke. I waited as long as I dared for the soldiers to be gone, then I tried to push the bookcase away. It was really heavy, though, and there wasn't enough space to get any leverage. It got harder to breathe and . . . so, so hot. Riona was hysterical. She was—" Gabe had to reach up to rub his stinging eyes. "Coughing and crying. I must have finally pushed hard enough to topple the bookcase because suddenly the panel fell away and we fell out. Everything was on fire. I landed in a pile of blazing wood and books, but I managed to shelter my sister from the worst of it. The door was barred from the outside, but we had a window nearby. I climbed out and fell straight into the goat's water trough. I'm pretty sure that's all that saved us from burning alive. After that, I just ran. I hid in a hollowed-out dead tree until I couldn't hear any more screaming."

The pain had been incredible. Only Riona's crying had cut through it, giving Gabriel a reason to fight. There was more to the story, like the agonizing hours of burning and chills inside that tree, the slog through the bloody snow on the mainstreet of Nillenia, looking for survivors, or the grueling walk to Garendor, but it would have to come another time. Gabriel's eyes were starting to drift shut, and he didn't want to fight the lure of dreamless sleep anymore. "Would you mind if I finished telling you about my family tomorrow? I don't think I can stay awake much longer."

"Yeah, I'm getting sleepy too. Thank you for talking about it. I know it can't be easy."

"No, but you're right. Some things have to be spoken aloud."

She yawned. "Would it be alright if I stayed here just a little longer? I don't want to be alone right now."

"Me neither," Gabriel whispered, pressing his face into her soft hair. "Stay as long as you like."

CHAPTER TWO
Deadman Switch
DAEMON

It has been two and a half decades since I broke my oaths to my mother and destroyed my relationship with my son. I did it for the boys, so they would live. Now, I question if I was a fool. We lost Alaric. Gabriel has lived a life full of suffering. Those we entrusted the boys to died to protect them, and for what? The world has grown darker. Our plans are in tatters. Now, a God is dead. If Fulsixia the Red can fall, how can we puny mortals think to save the world? We were fools to believe we could. Robin still wants to try, but all I care about now is seeing Gabriel again and making sure that he is safe. I cannot lose him too.

—From the journal of Ara Daran, Tirition of the College of Discipline.

THE HUM OF THE VILLA that usually lulled Daemon to sleep wasn't there. He lay in the cramped bed in his Hardor apartment, covers kicked to the bottom of the mattress. The windows were open to the rain-scented breeze, but it did little to curb the thick, clammy humidity sticking his skin to the sheets. While a simple rift could have fixed the unpleasant temperature, Daemon was far too shaky to risk using magic. His thumb trailed over the gold ring on his left hand for the thousandth time. It thrummed a slow, steady pulse that tracked the beat of Elenor's heart, the only stable thing left for him to cling to.

Circuitry diagrams lay scattered over the tables and workbenches of the single large room. Spools and sheets of copper, cerulean, and gold had been piled and weighed. His many devices hummed, beeped, and gyrated as they always did. Daemon was exhausted, eyes just as tired as when he'd fallen into bed, yet sleep eluded him.

His house was gone.

Fulsixia the Red was dead.

It felt surreal to think those words, but as he stared at the darkened ceiling, the new reality of this changed world continued to sink deeper into his bones.

Almost sixty years ago, Daemon had sat down with a young Tirit Mindel graduate over tea. Corinne Daran, who would go on to sit on the Council of Ten and become the Dean of Core Six training on the Island, had said something that he had never forgotten. Daemon had asked her which of the Gods she took comfort in, and why. She'd answered, *"I worship the Silver Who Was, because they were a God and are now dead. That means that the others can be killed, too. It gives me hope for a world where we are not bent and twisted to their whims."*

If only she had lived to see this day.

Part of Daemon wanted to go to Tirit Mindel to tell Corinne's daughter that her mother's dream had begun to come true, but with Ara so tangled up in the business of the Black Dragon these days, that would be most unwise. He was sure Robin would have told his wife already, and they were likely lying sleepless too, wondering how many of their plots and plans would have to be changed now that their world only had four Dragon Gods, instead of five.

Daemon idly rubbed at his wrist where four bracelets rested, the last tossed away as soon as he'd got here after finishing the complete evacuation of Ayre. None were blinking, and somehow Daemon doubted he would receive any more communication from the Green, the White, or the Black Dragon Gods. Xirra had drawn a line and all-but called for war. If they came to Daemon it would be to rid themselves of him.

Five hundred years of relative peace were coming to an end. The Hardor Accords would fall—it was just a matter of who broke them first, and how. When they did, Daemon had to be ready. So would the families of the Gods, because once the laws protecting them ended, every Lirion, Grau, Arlen, Silvarin, *jiakappa* tribesman and *daradeio* would be on the chopping block.

With a sigh, Daemon abandoned his futile attempt to sleep and rolled out of bed. He walked to the balcony and looked out over the rainswept city of Hardor, turning his mind back to the vast array of problems that required his attention.

Xirra would call him to her side again soon, to begin working on whatever plan she devised. Ayre remained in great danger from Kennotoza and Zorbennen, and if his patron found out about his island under the wrong circumstances, she could be an even bigger threat. Should he just tell her?

No.

A shudder coursed down Daemon's spine and he turned back to the room. Sleep might be impossible, but making big decisions while tired was beyond stupid. With a yawn, he rubbed his sore eyes, then looked around for something to distract himself with. Books lay spread out on every flat surface not otherwise occupied, but Daemon ignored the tomes on rifting and circuitry, on Gifts and theology. He walked to a large bookshelf in the corner. Fingers skimming the spines with the gentle touch of a lover, Damon continued along until landing on a thin volume.

He pulled the battered book out and settled in an overstuffed armchair. Daemon had just opened the well-loved poetry book when something buzzed from the darkened corner of the room. He froze, staring in the direction it came from, eyes narrowed. He was about to return to the book when it happened again.

Daemon put the volume aside and walked towards the sound. He stopped between pulses, moving when they came until he stood next to the wicker waste paper basket. Through the crumpled pages and apple cores, a dim light pulsed once more, accompanied by the low-key vibrating sound. Heart pounding, Daemon crouched down and dug through the refuse until his fingers found the thin bracelet he had tossed there hours ago.

It buzzed against his skin, the red gem at the center pulsing with light.

"What the . . . ?" His fingers wrapped around it and he squeezed his eyes shut. Could he be dreaming? To make sure, Daemon pinched his forearm firmly enough to yelp, but still the bracelet buzzed.

Impossible.

Could it be that the other Gods were wrong? That Fulsixia the Red still lived? No other being, God or man, had access to the circuit connected to his band, which he had built for her. If it had activated, that meant there was a message waiting for him, but why would Fulsixia contact *Daemon* if she were still alive?

Only one way to find out.

Daemon shot to his feet, exhaustion forgotten as he rushed towards the table that held the paired circuits. He had tossed his coat on top of them, but he yanked it away. A soft red light filled the apartment.

Daemon froze, hand already outstretched to the button. The last time he had come here and listened to the orders of a God, it had tossed him deep into trouble. What good could possibly come of doing so again, especially with the Red? If she was alive and the others didn't know, Dameon sure as hell didn't want to get mixed up in it. She had a whole damn desert full of minions. Dae owed her nothing, yet his curiosity raged and in the end, as always, won.

He pressed the button.

For a moment, there was only static. It lasted so long that Daemon's tense shoulders began to deflate, then he jumped as Fulsixia's voice came through loud and clear.

"If you are hearing this, it means that I am gone. I had one of my circuitry-adept *daradeio* build a deadman switch. If I did not take a deliberate action each night to stop it, this message would be sent to you. Tonight, it seems, a foretelling I received centuries ago has come to pass, and so I must carry out my final act as a Holder of Dracona."

Daemon's eyebrows scrunched together at the unfamiliar term, but the recording didn't pause to give him time to think back on whether he had heard it before.

"When I first met you, Jac, I chose not to Name you. You were a man between identities, not quite the Jac Drego you were born as, and not yet Daemon Indigo, the person you would become. Now, I make your Naming my last act, in the hopes that you pick up the burden I lay down today."

The Red paused, and in the breath of silence, Daemon could

almost feel the weight of her presence in the apartment. He closed his eyes, preparing himself for what truths she knew about him that he did not want to confront.

"You are no longer he who they called Jac Drego. You rose from his ashes as a being of a thousand faces and a thousand names, but it is the one you chose for yourself that matters most. It is a name out of a fable, a rifter who asked the Gods to return his family to him and, after trials and tribulations, was given the cruel gift of life everlasting. Those he loved would live on in his memory until the end of time but he, lonely and repentant, would never join them. Out of all possible names, you chose his: Daemon Indigo, the Magician of Eldale."

Dae sucked in air through his teeth and squeezed his eyes tighter shut, as if in doing so he could force out the memories of Julian cuddling into his embrace and asking him to read *The Magician of Eldale* just one more time.

"Names have power, Daemon. You chose the Ae Essence, the Mock: intrepid, supportive, loyal. Like the mock dragon that glides on the wind, you have distanced yourself from the world that bore you. As Jac, your calling was magic. It was discovery, invention, the relentless pursuit of answers. That calling started you on this path, but it was not the one that let you step out of the tethers of mortality. Jac raised a hand against a defenseless child and died. Daemon risked his life to pull that child back from the Plane and was reborn. On that day, with that choice, your calling changed. You will bear more names than there are stars in the sky, but these two are the ones that define you. They will pull you hither and thither, a war with no end between who you were and who you have become. Between Jac, the father of a loving son and husband of an ambitious wife, reckless master of magic, soldier, scholar, skeptic; and Daemon, the lonely servant of a vengeful God, careful builder of safe havens, patron of the lost, inventor, teacher, dreamer.

"Two names, two paths: that of power, and that of faith. On this, the day of your Naming, I ask you to reject the bonds of fate imposed by Gods and man, reject the notion that your future is limited to just one of these paths, and set your own course. Today, I hope that the man you were then and the one you are now begin to find peace with each other, for you will need all the ingenuity and loyalty that was Jac and all the tenacity and perspective that you have developed to survive the oncoming storm.

"You are, as I was, a protector of magic, guardian of the Gifted and the rifters of this world. It is your calling and your responsibility. Go to the desert and find its beating heart. I bequeath it to you, if you prove yourself worthy, for when I looked into your eyes and saw your name, it has and always will be entwined with that of the First Gift and the Last. When the time comes, Daemon, only you will love them enough to know what to do. This is why I trust you with that which I love most, on this, the day of your Naming and my demise."

Daemon stood, stunned and shaken to his core, as the last words echoed through the room and the device stopped glowing. He remained there for so long that the first light of the oncoming dawn shone through the blinds and over his blank face.

Protector of Magic.

Protector of Gifted and rifters.

All rifters? All Gifted? What about the ones watched over by other Gods? His racing mind circled back around to the reason he had not been able to sleep for days as his fingers trailed, once more, over the gently pulsing ring on his finger.

She had to be Gifted . . . and if he was meant to protect the Gifts and reject the bonds of the Gods . . .

Before he could slide further down that rabbit hole and go see Elenor, Daemon pinched his arm again. No.

No.

With a grunt of frustration, Daemon reached towards the circuit and yanked out the gold battery. He did the same to the communication devices for White, Black, and Green Dragons, leaving only the Blue. With the same frenetic pace, he ripped the bracelets from his arm, tossing all of them into a box of scrap metal.

I'm not falling for this again. I don't care what she left me. I'm not becoming another Dragon's pawn, especially not a dead one's.

Yet the Red's words kept circling him like vultures.

"You are, as I was, a protector of magic, guardian of the Gifted

and the rifters of this world."

What had she left him in the desert? What were the First and Last Gifts? Curiosity burned like a flame in his chest, mixing with the bitter fury at the White Dragon for what she had done, and his own self-loathing. He had known better. He should have just done what the Blue wanted and left both Lirion and Silvarin alone after killing Gabriel.

Zorbennen and Robin had rejected his offer of aid.

Kennotoza had destroyed what little he had left of his family.

Gullien couldn't pull his shit together if he tried.

And now Fulsixia—dead and gone—chose *this* moment to try to get his help? No. Daemon was done.

He was going to go to his patron and find a way to get revenge against those who had wronged him, settle his debts to her, figure out what the fuck Elenor Lirion was so he could purge this desire to be near her from his soul, and if all that didn't kill him, Daemon was fucking retiring.

Enough was enough.

"Go to hell, Lady Red," he snarled, and slammed the lid of the scrap metal chest shut.

CHAPTER THREE
The Dead God
NORTH

We have chosen to embark on this path together, Merihem. You told me the risks, and I accept them. If the worst comes to pass and I am gone when the Mother in Gold returns to us, promise me that you will help my people. They are resilient and strong, but until my final wishes are carried out, they are also vulnerable. Help them, old friend, as I once helped you.

—From a letter to Merihem "Moe" Crystal, from Fulsixia the Red Dragon.

THE LAMENTS OF THE BROKEN and the grieving did not end.

North Hillman stood on a ridge of sand, eyes closed and shoulder-length hair fluttering in the breeze as the sun rose on the first day without the Red Dragon.

There were so many questions he had wanted to ask of her, but he would never look into her eyes again. At least he had been able to once.

Quindo was waiting for him in the orchards, once his name was called. Up close, the Archivist looked tired. North didn't envy him the dark circles under his eyes, or the problems heaped on his people now that they had lost their Incarnate.

The moon was high as they walked out of the trees and over the dunes. This place felt so very foreign, so different from the verdant life of Ayre or the rough beauty of Namnia, yet the more time he spent here, the more North liked it. After a few minutes of silence, Quindo turned to him. "You are lucky, you know. Not many outside the daradeio *see Lady Red as she truly is, but your arrival is special to us."*

"Is it because you can't find the new Incarnate?" North asked.

The Archivist nodded. "Akaaron is talented and has identified many people of interest for us, some of whom we have high hopes for, but he can't tell a Gifted person from anyone else, nor can our other Namers."

"I'm sorry."

"Thank you, North, but it is not all bad. You are here and Baarin is here, which might lead us to the Incarnate in time."

They made their way down a dune and along the valley between them.

"Is that because you think he's a Gatekeeper?"

"Kaedy thinks so, but I am not so sure. Gatekeepers are not . . . not like other Gifts. It takes great force of will to control the Gift, usually only attainable through training and the balancing presence of an Incarnate. Baarin is too sedate and even-tempered. His power, to me, looks more like Rian's or that of a Quell. I have never heard of a Gatekeeper that took away power instead of killing."

"But I can see her Gift. I cannot see his."

Quindo stopped and turned to North. "It is a puzzle, but one that Lady Red will solve. She is waiting around this bend to meet you. She is a being of great power and many have a hard time adjusting to her presence. Take a deep breath."

"Alright, but how am I supposed to address her? Does she go by Veiled Wanderer, Lady Wanderer, Goddess-"

"Her name is Fulsixia, though most of us call her Lady Red. North, don't worry. She's used to people stuttering and going wide-eyed. Ready?"

North shook his head, but also said, "Never going to be, so yes. Let's do this."

Quindo gestured him forward. North hesitated a moment longer, then stepped around the bend and came face-to-face with a Dragon.

Blood-red eyes bored into North's and in them, he saw things he had no words for. He was blinded by shining lights, felt the humid heat and cool metal of a world beyond comprehension, the place where this creature before him—this God—had originated. Shining fields of stars, flat glass embedded with colors and symbols that shifted and moved too fast to follow, and light—blinding, beautiful, terrible light. The whisper that usually told him the power each person possessed thrummed with something new, and the calling that rolled off of this creature like waves was so complex, painful, and beautiful that it made North's breath leave him in a whimper.

His knees slammed into the sand, driven to bow before the majesty of this all-powerful being.

"There is no need to kneel, Alaric the Namer, trueborn Gifted of Dracona. You are welcome here, kin of my kin, Gifted by my heart. I have been waiting a long, long time to meet you. Rise."

North didn't think he could, but the command brought him up on shaking legs to face the greatest Namer in existence. "Lady," he whispered, voice cracked and hoarse.

Quindo took North by the arm and pulled him forward a few steps, each a struggle. The aura of information floating around the Dragon's head was just too immense and incomprehensible to wrap his mind around.

"What you are seeing, North, is the truth of our world. It can be a little shocking. Breathe deep. We are still waiting for one other. Breathe."

North obeyed, at least until another voice broke the night.

"I'm heeeeeere." All heads turned towards the top of the nearest dune as a lanky man with smooth black hair pulled into a long braid and an eye-jarring pink suit blinked out of existence then reappeared about an inch away from North's nose.

North shrieked and fell backward. As soon as he scrambled to his feet again, he took another look at this new arrival and his eyes bulged.

"You're—"

The pink-clad man held up a hand. "None of your business, I'm sure."

"But—"

"Shh—"

"Ah—"

"Trust me, kid, if you say what you want to say right now, there is a 99.7% chance you will die within the week. I wouldn't bet on those odds, would you?"

North was still sputtering but managed to clamp his mouth shut, trying to make sense of the dizzying information he was getting.

"Just call me Moe. That will do for now," the man said, and extended his hand to shake North's.

"Moe is an old friend of mine," Lady Red said with a chuckle that made the very ground rumble. "He is trusted and vetted, North the Namer, and what he is, is known."

Warning received.

The newcomer bounded across to the taloned feet of the Dragon and jumped up to sit on one, then rubbed his hands together. "Right then. Let's begin."

Salt. The taste suffused North's mouth as he stared at Moe. Salt and blood. Like staring at lightning in a dark sky, flashes of information shot across North's mind. He could not hold on to them, but even the afterglow was enough to make North queasy.

"Look away," Lady Red said, though even speaking softly, her voice boomed. "Your power will not work on him. He is . . . other."

North obeyed, and focused back on the Dragon instead. It was hardly better. With every breath, Fulsixia's nostrils flared and fire-hot dry air blew across him, fluttering fabric and blowing sand into spinning dervishes. He craned his neck, but North could not see how far the mighty Dragon extended into the darkness. Her skin was thick, shimmering reddish scales in every hue of fire and autumn.

Beautiful.

Moe clicked his tongue. North jumped, realizing too late that he was staring like a love-struck idiot and that it was probably a very rude thing to do to a God.

"Do close your mouth, boy. Flies will get in," Moe rebuked.

"You would know," the Dragon chuckled.

"Tis true. I ate a fly, once, but it was on a dare, so that hardly counts. Now, back to the business at hand: our lovely guest. Tell me, how do you feel about going Incarnate hunting? So many powerful people, so little time."

Well, that was straight to the point. With a gulp, North looked once more to the Dragon. "Is it a choice?"

"Of course it is. Everything in life is a choice, and what we choose defines us just as much as what we are. You, even with such great power, only see where a soul comes from, not where it is going. So, where do you wish to go, Namer?"

Good question. "I've never had a destination. Not really. Life just

. . . happens to me, most of the time. I haven't accomplished much, but I've tried my best to avoid causing harm."

"Oh come now, my boy. A bit of harm now and again keeps you young. Life gets so boring without the occasional forays into thievery, murder, and mayhem," Moe drawled and North turned to squint at him. That was some Daemon-level bullshit.

"A single life wasted is too many, and you took one of our brightest ones, Merihem Crystal," Quindo said from North's side, speaking up for the first time since Moe's arrival and calling him by what must be his full name. Not that North's Gift was working well enough to confirm it. "Do not minimize the cost of what you did when you sent Sidian away. This would not be necessary if you did not fill his head with your talk of the future."

"I am a Bode, that is what I do."

No you're not, *but North didn't dare say that aloud. Instead, he looked to the Dragon again. She had said this Moe was vetted. Surely, he could trust a* God. *Couldn't he?*

"If you are such an all-powerful seer, why is it that Sidian died?" Quindo growled, the open irritation in his tone at odds with his hitherto calm nature.

"Oh, I didn't tell you? You should have said something sooner," Moe replied, then reached up to his ear and tapped a sleek black device no larger than a thumb. "Note to self: tell people things more often."

"You were nowhere to be found and you know it. Just like always when you are actually needed," Quindo snapped.

"Oops, you're quite right, of course. Well, let me set your mind at ease, Quindo my dear. I sent Sidian to find poor doomed Wilam Lirion, the man destined to light the spark that would unite all the world of the Ao Collective and fuck it to hell in the process—not that most precognizants agree with me. But everything is going splendidly. Wilam and Sidian both died on schedule, which I'm sure has Kennotoza the White in a tizzy. Do you have any idea how annoying it was to have to pretend that I wanted Wilam Lirion of all people to get the Last Gift, just to stop her from interfering? Though it did make Sidian much more willing to believe me and collaborate, when I told him to leave ahead of schedule in order to be there in person to free the woman he loved."

"Do not minimize how much it hurt to deceive him, Moe. I know you grieved just as I did. He was a friend," Lady Red scolded in a deep, sorrowful voice.

Quindo looked ready to boil over.

Moe just shrugged. "Friends, tools, what's the difference? I warned him he would die so he could put his affairs in order and prepare Suela, didn't I? I was just fuzzy on the details. Anyhow, since Sidian died before passing on the Gift, the new Incarnate should be born within the next year, far too young for Kennotoza to snatch up and use in the next few essential months. I do so love denying my enemies their toys. Now all we have to do is find the correct baby by the time it's born, raise them right, and collect the supporting cast. I'm oh so excited to meet them all. Gotta love a good ensemble crew."

North's eyes went wide. He looked to Quindo, then Moe, then the Dragon. "We think Sidian passed on his Gift before dying," he said.

There was silence, then Lady Red turned her attention to Moe as he sprang to his feet.

"Merihem?"

Moe had his eyes closed, brow scrunched, then sprang into action. He ruffled through his pockets until he found a small notebook. Flipping through to almost the end, he let out a startled little gasp.

"Moe?"

"That must be why the probabilities have been so in flux. I thought it was because the Incarnate Gift hadn't settled on a new host yet. Which means . . ." Moe ran his fingers through his long black hair, tugging upon it before flipping a few more pages. Then he snapped the notebook shut. "Which means that Fedrik Tellen must be the Gatekeeper after all. He's what blows tonight, and I couldn't see it because his Gift keeps blocking my powers. Fuck. This is gonna be bad. Gotta start evacuations." The perplexing man looked past North and Quindo and into the Dragon's eyes. "You need to get your ass to Suela, Red. I'm sorry, but it's time."

"Wait, evacuations? *" Quindo yelled as Moe began to run back towards the party. "What's going on?"*

Moe paused halfway up the nearby dune and looked at what appeared to be a pocket watch strapped to his wrist. "You'll see in . . ."

He closed his eyes, brow scrunched as though thinking hard. His aura pulsed brighter, making North feel sick. "Seven minutes and thirteen seconds. We're in the bad *timeline now."*

Across countless miles of desert to the east, the light of day broke over the horizon, yet the cries of the broken did not fade. The light crept higher and higher, up past North's sandals, over the blood-splattered yellow linen of his pants and the rolled-up sleeves of his long red tunic. It reached his full beard, his sunburnt nose, his closed eyes.

North opened them and blinked as they adjusted to the refracted brightness of the golden sand. He heard a sigh from behind him.

"She always came from the east. I don't know why, but that is how it has been since the first time she arrived. The Veiled Wanderer: she comes from the east and disappears into the west, truth etched in every footprint," Akaaron said, stepping level with North. "How did you know where to look?"

"I didn't. I just thought last night would never end and wanted to feel the sun."

Akaaron did not reply at once. The *daradeio's* customary smile no longer graced his lips. When he did talk, it lacked either joviality or anger. "Suela is sending those who can be spared back to the Mother Rock. Our people must find out about . . . "

There was no reason to finish that sentence. North turned from the eastern sky and looked at the middle-aged man. "You mean your people. I don't belong at the Mother Rock to share in your grief. I hardly knew her and am not Mondaer except by a technicality, nor am I *daradeio*. I can remain behind to help with the broken. Or go help Fedrik wherever it is that Quindo took him."

Akaaron nodded. "That is a kind offer, but one we must refuse. They will need gentle souls like yours to tend to them, but without our . . . our Goddess, we need you more than ever. Until we leave, though, your continued help would be most welcome. Have you ever cared for one of the broken before?"

North shuddered and nodded. "The place I come from, North

Island, does not take kindly to the use of magic. If a rifter is discovered, they have the option of having their capacity ritually broken, exile, or death. I didn't have the first option."

"Barbarous." Akaaron said with a shiver, then grew silent.

"What will happen now?" North asked into that stillness, as yet another wail rent the morning peace.

The Namer beside him looked back over his shoulder toward the Deil estate. "I do not know. You and I, we are supposed to know things, to be some fragment of a fragment of Lady . . . Lady Red." Akaaron's eyes filled with tears and North placed a hand on his shoulder as he began to weep. It was not the first time that night, yet those unbroken by the magical blast that had killed the Red had been forced to mourn while helping those who had lost their connection to magic.

The dead had yet to be seen to. They would have to wait.

"I wish I could do something to ease your suffering, Akaaron. Being a Namer has never meant anything but pain to me, but if my Gift, or even just my hands, can be of service to you, I give them freely."

"She was our everything," Akaaron whispered, then pressed his face to North's shoulder and sobbed. "What do we do without her? Who will Name our children? How will we know who should lead us? H-how do we protect those who we have promised to shelter, without our Dragon?"

North had no answers, so he just reached up to stroke the back of Akaaron's bald head as the Mondaer man cried unabashedly.

Pop!

The sound made North's hackles rise. The man who called himself Moe appeared on the dune a few paces away, hands in his pockets. "Ready?"

"Ready for what?" North snapped, aware that perhaps the tone was unfair, but unable to modulate it. This lying snake reminded him too much of Daemon's self-important arrogance, and he wanted nothing more to do with men like that.

"For the next move. Do look up, Akaaron. You won't want to miss this."

Akaaron lifted his head and wiped at his eyes, then glared at Moe.

"Quindo said you knew this was coming. You knew the Gatekeeper would kill her."

"Incorrect. I knew that there was a chance that the Gatekeeper would lose control if Wilam Lirion didn't become the next Incarnate. It was Red's choice to sacrifice herself to save all of you. And she did. The boy's destruction spread less than a mile. Still an idiotic move, in my opinion, but she got what she wanted . . ."

North had to grab Akaaron to stop him from launching himself at Moe.

"How dare you speak ill of her?" the other Namer screamed. Moe didn't so much as flinch. He just smiled and nodded to the east.

Despite not relishing taking instruction from a man who would talk about a dead God that way, North glanced in the same direction and froze, just as Akaaron did.

A Dragon shimmered in the sky above the dunes.

It was gold, body lithe but powerful, scales glistening in the sun as she hung in the air upon beating, gargantuan wings. Her brilliance was blinding, but the voice that boomed across the desert was what made North fall to his knees. He slapped his hands over his ears, sand flying in every direction as a feminine voice thundered over them. "Fulsixia the Ruby Dragon, Holder of Dracona, Goddess of Namers, is dead. Those who killed her heed these words: Repent, or face the reckoning."

A flash of light tore over the sand and with an earsplitting boom, she was gone, leaving behind only a fierce ringing in North's ears and lights dancing in his eyes. Somewhere to his left, Moe began to laugh. It was a delighted, high-pitched, giddy sound, and it chilled North to the bone.

"Well, that was fun. Also my cue to finish up here and get going; have fun with the apocalypse, kiddos."

Pop.

North still could not get his eyes to clear, but he didn't need them to know Moe had gone. For several minutes, neither he nor Akaaron could rise. At last, they helped each other up, neither able to quite get to their feet unassisted. North's chest ached and ears stung, as if the voice had done physical harm to both.

"What . . . the hell was that?" He gasped upon his first full inhale.

"I don't know," Akaaron replied. Red eyes met green as they exchanged a scared, bewildered moment of confusion.

Shouts filled the air. Mondaer were running from the Deil estate towards them, but as North's vision cleared, he looked back in the direction where the Golden Dragon had appeared.

There was nothing but ominous empty skies and rolling dunes.

CHAPTER FOUR
The Missing Queen
ELENOR

The Eight Writted Noble Houses of Lirin have a long history of infighting. With only Houses Lirion and Ondai routinely holding their territories during the decennial Water Race, the other six have struggled to keep up. Every ten years, they are faced with moving their entire center of operations to a new province. This has meant that alliances matter more than land, and deals sealed in marriage are the most valuable commodity of all. The only thing more coveted than a generation of peace through marriage is a shot at the throne. Whether that be through love or violence is inconsequential.

—From the notes of Elehanna Ondai, before a lecture on Lirinian politics at the Tirit Mindel University of Garendor.

ELENOR'S HANDS SHOOK AS SHE WALKED. Three cups of coffee and a double dose of serindalla had cleared the haze pain meds and sleep aids always left behind, but she regretted them. The gardens were silent in the dim dawn light. Unfortunately, Elenor could already hear muffled voices raised in anger within the Throne Room.

"Chin up, *taale*," Paul said from behind her, placing a reassuring hand on her shoulder.

The guards who stood by the double doors made to open them, but Elenor motioned for them to stop. She reached up to straighten her coronet, then carefully rolled her shoulders, adjusted her arm in its sling, and smoothed the silk of her dark-blue dress. She took a deep breath. "You've confirmed Kallen and Eric are already here? I don't want to walk in there without allies."

"They arrived half an hour ago."

"And no news of my mother?"

Her *doena* shook his head. Elenor tried not to let the motion trigger another bout of anxious hyperventilating.

She flicked her fingers and the doors swung open. All the voices within stopped. Elenor placed her unbandaged hand behind her back so they wouldn't see it quiver, then walked forward. Each of her footsteps echoed off the marble floor as she crossed the cavernous room, her eyes fixed on the empty thrones on the dais.

The seven Writted House representatives on the King's Council were waiting for her, along with a number of aides, retainers, and lesser nobility. Elenor tried to smile at Kallen and Eric, but couldn't muster one. It wasn't until she reached the dais that Elenor realized she didn't know where to sit. Her steps faltered.

Eric, standing closest, must have seen the panic that flashed across her face, because he smoothly stepped forward and offered Elenor his arm. She took it, and with only a momentary stumble, let him escort her up to stand before her father's empty seat.

"If you don't take it now, they will never let you," he whispered, too low for anyone else to hear.

"Thank you," she mouthed. Her skin felt clammy and all Elenor wanted to do was run back to her room, hide, and hug herself while breathing into a pillow. Instead, she forced her back straight and resolutely sat down.

At once, people started speaking. Elenor held out her hand for silence, but it didn't follow.

"Where is Queen Lilian?" Lady Petrona asked. "Is it true that no one has seen her since last night?"

"Nevermind that. Is our King really dead? Did you—"

"Are you about to accuse Princess Elenor of—"

"SILENCE." The baritone yell boomed across the gathered nobles at a volume much louder than should have been possible. All eyes turned to Kallen Drego, who stood with his hands in his pockets. "Good. Do I have your attention? Now, I believe Her Highness called for quiet. Have you all lost your courtesy as well as your inside voices?"

Considering he had definitely just rifted to make his voice loud enough to shake the very stonework, that caused a few laughs. Also a couple of scowls, but the point had been made. All attention shifted back to Elenor, and they waited.

She gulped, mind going blank and her prepared statement along with it. "Um . . ." She began, scrambling to find the right words. "First of all, thank you for meeting at such short notice. I know it's early. I'm sure you have a lot of questions, which I will try to answer in a moment, but first I need to address the rumors you have doubtlessly already heard."

Elenor shifted on the uncomfortable throne, aware of how her feet only just touched the floor. Did she look like a child wearing their parents' shoes? Because it certainly felt like it.

Out of the corner of her eye, Elenor saw Claire slip into the room. Her lover's short hair glistened as though she had just showered, and she was buttoning the jacket of a formal suit in House Enica colors. Elenor felt a weight lift off her shoulders and sat up straighter.

Claire was back in Hardor.

With her best friend in the room and no longer in some unknown amount of danger wherever her Gift had taken her, Elenor turned her attention back to the impatient nobility. Along with Eric and Kallen, Claire's presence brought the number of Writted families whose alliance she could count on up to almost half. The other half of the room did not seem to include Duncan Eurieha among them to whisper poison in their ears, just a single younger man with a broach bearing the Eurieha turtle sigil to represent the minor house, so perhaps not all was lost. Elenor could do this. She had to.

"Lords and Ladies of the King's Council, nobles of Lirin. I regret to inform you that my father, King Consort Markus Miri-Lirion, passed from this world late last night during a mass prison break here at the palace."

Everyone began to speak again. The shouts bounced off the stone walls and echoed back, turning their voices into a veritable cacophony. Only Claire, Eric, and Kallen didn't add to the din, though Elenor noticed Claire whispering to her father, Lord Ludo Enica, and Kallen unobtrusively speaking into the bracer around his wrist. Who was he sending to? Were there other rifters at court?

That question was answered a few seconds later when the doors to the Throne Room swung open. For a brief moment, Elenor hoped it was her mother, somehow miraculously here to save the day. Instead, Robin Tirition strode in.

Elenor's heart sank.

"Master Robin, this is a meeting of the King's Council—"

"Forgive me, Your Highness." Robin bowed low, as though it somehow excused the interruption. "But I believe the King of Lirin is dead and the Queen missing, which would make it no one's council, since you are only heir presumptive of Lirin and do not yet bear a Water Writ. Am I incorrect?"

Elenor froze, uncomprehending.

"You are, actually," said the man with the turtle broach, stepping forward. He was perhaps forty, with a touch of gray along his temples but no stoop to his shoulders yet. Though he wore Lirinian clothes, his almond-shaped eyes and amber skin stood out in the crowd. Elenor vaguely remembered seeing him at court before, but could not recall his name.

Neither, it seemed, did Robin. "How so, Lord . . . "

"Daniil Eurieha, adopted son of Duncan Eurieha, standing in for my father as he recovers from last night's . . . excitement."

Oh no. This couldn't be good. Elenor reached up to rub at her neck, the bruises Eurieha had left there hidden under the high neckline of her dress and loose blonde hair.

"Ah, the Orthodox Ionist priest. Yes, I've heard of you and the trouble you stir up. Please, do tell me how I've misinterpreted Lirinian law," Robin replied, his voice calm. "I'm dying to hear it."

Daniil Eurieha stepped forward into the clear space before the dais and turned to Elenor, giving her a small bow. "With your permission, Your Highness. My father caught me up on all of the brave and selfless actions you have taken for our country of late, so I am sure you could defend your claim to the throne with accuracy and eloquence, but I am somewhat of a scholar in these matters. May I have the honor of correcting Master Robin Tirition in your stead?"

Fuck.

He might as well have said *I know what you did, and I can ruin you. Now shut up.* Elenor tried not to show her flash of terror and managed to nod.

Daniil turned to Robin and cleared his throat. "Master Tirition, you are correct in saying that an heir who does not yet have a Water Writ cannot step in to rule the nation. The Gods would not ordain such a ruler. However, Her Highness has, as of a few weeks ago, begun the process of petitioning for a Writ before the Gods, when she was named heir presumptive."

Had it only been a few weeks ago? It felt like an eternity since Elenor had knelt in front of the Altar of the White Dragon, pledging herself to this country and the task of swimming across the River Claire to prove her worthiness to rule.

Daniil wasn't finished. "The Queen of Lirin is missing. This is grievous news in light of our King's untimely demise. She has, however, been missing for less than one day. I am sure all efforts will be made to find her. In fact, I have already mobilized a large portion of the Palace guard and city watch to begin the search."

"Excuse me?" Elenor asked, interrupting him. "I wasn't aware the post of Head of Security was hereditary."

Daniil turned to her, eyebrows rising. "Do you disapprove of searching for your mother, Your Highness?"

"No, of course not," she backtracked, aware that some of the other nobles were looking at her oddly. "Sorry. Go on."

He smiled, bowing once more before turning back to Robin. "I am confident we will succeed in finding the Queen, but if the worst were to happen and Her Majesty were not found within thirty days, both her Writ and the Writ set aside for her daughter would be released to House Lirion for reassignment. Until then, Princess Elenor is still our heir presumptive and may attempt to complete her Water Rite, confirm her Writ, and be ready to take the throne at the end of those thirty days."

Thirty days? Elenor bit her lips to keep from showing her flash of terror. There was no way she would be physically prepared to swim across the river in a single month. She hadn't planned on doing it for at least half a year. Even thinking about it made her legs ache and burn. Her other injuries protested loudly too, reminding her of every sprain, burn, and bruise.

"Of course, until that happy day comes, Lirin must be ruled," Daniil continued. "As such, this Council of Writted Lords may no longer be the King's Council, but it *is* the temporary ruling body of Lirin. Normally, a neutral party, such as Tirit Mindel, would step in to represent the Lirion family during such a murky transition, but I do not believe that is necessary. We have an heir presumptive capable of conducting her Water Rite within thirty days, do we not? It is my proposal that we immediately vote to grant Her Highness Elenor Lirion temporary voting status and appoint her as regent pro-tempore of the Kingdom. I see no honorable alternative, assuming Her Highness does not object, and, naturally, that she is found to be innocent of the murder of her late father."

It had looked so good there for a second. Elenor carefully swallowed past the rising nausea in her throat. Kallen's expression darkened. Claire had a hand on Eric's elbow, holding him back from the outburst brewing behind his pursed lips. Daniil Eurieha might as well have said: *I'm making you my puppet.* He was going to give her power but hold back the proof that she had killed her father as blackmail. Worse, there was nothing Elenor could do about it.

"Murder?" Lady Adelina Lavarin asked, a hand rising to cover her mouth.

"I'm sure Lord Eurieha spoke in haste," Kallen began, but Daniil cut him off.

"I did not." He turned his back on Elenor, speaking to the other nobles. "My family is not Writted Nobility, but my father was the right hand of Mark Lirion, and Loren Lirion before him. You all know this, and know him. He was recently appointed Palace Head of Security, and the words he spoke to me last night before the surgeons put him under were grim indeed. He swore to me that Markus Lirion was murdered, and that the breakout was a plan to cover it up. I think it is our duty, as nobles of Lirin, to take his warnings seriously. As such, I propose two items for your council to vote on. The first and most pressing is to allow Her Highness Elenor Lirion regency pro -tempore, and the second that a full inquiry of the death of Markus Miri-Lirion begin, investigating all those present at the time of his death, including, regretfully, our heir presumptive. I would like to volunteer to run that inquiry, in my father's stead and under his supervision."

Well, at least Robin looked as dismayed as Elenor felt. Neither of them, though, were in a position to stop what was about to happen. Most of the nobles were nodding along, many with alarmed looks upon their faces.

Eric took a step forward. "As the representative of House Ondai, the second-place winner of the last Water Race after the Lirion, I am willing to bring the matter of Her Highness's regency to a vote."

"What about the inquiry into the King's murder?" Lady Lavarin asked. "That, too, must be dealt with."

"Perhaps, but not at present. The stability of Lirin is paramount, and the King is dead. How he died doesn't matter. We have a delegation coming in from Seehana as soon as *tomorrow,* people. Anything less than a united front will weaken Lirin to the eyes of the South. As much as it pains me, the why cannot be looked into at this time. It would make us look too unstable to our southern allies."

"And what of Miriel?" Lord Giles Amad asked. "He was a Miri before he was a Lirion. If we don't find the person responsible for his death and bring them to justice, we'll have more than Seehana to worry about."

"This is exactly why you need Island representation right now," Robin interrupted, stepping forward into the ring of nobles. "No offense to Her Highness, but she is young, injured, and has had little training in statecraft."

Why thank you, Robin. I really needed that ringing endorsement, Elenor thought, but didn't try to speak over the noise. Eric was shouting at Robin, defending Elenor, but he wasn't the only one. Every noble was talking, their voices layering with Robin's and Daniil's, each with their own idea about what should happen. Some, like Ludo Enica, were agreeing with Eric. Others shouted for the inquiry Daniil wanted, and a few, like Kallen, just tried to bring order to the madness.

Elenor sank further and further into the throne, but she couldn't get away from the noise. Her head was throbbing. Her breath came quicker and quicker, her uninjured arm moving to hug herself. Too loud. Lady Lavarin's shrill voice rose above the din, a bony finger pointing at Eric, screaming accusations that the Ondai had planned all this to get closer to the throne. Someone else, maybe Lord Amad considering the deep bass, was shouting about those old rumors that Elenor had died as a child and the Tellens had replaced her. That she had no place sitting on the throne.

And there was Robin, still arguing for Tirit Mindel control. And Claire, right up in his face, fighting back.

I can't do this.

Her pulse rang in her ears and tears sprang to Elenor's eyes, chest rising and falling so fast that it was making her lightheaded.

"Stop it." It came out as a choked whisper. "Stop it. Shut up, shut up, *SHUT UP!*"

The words rent the air and burned her throat. They rang in the sudden silence, all eyes turning to Elenor once more. She wiped the tears off her cheeks and sniffed, panic still coursing through her but joined by something else. It was familiar but foreign, like a friend she had always known but never met—a warming fire that started in her chest and traveled down the nerves to the tips of her fingers and toes.

Elenor pushed herself to her feet, tingles dancing across her skin, making even the smooth fabric of her dress intensely uncomfortable. They were all staring at her. Before her brother died, that would have been enough to make Elenor want to run and hide. She no longer had that luxury.

Through the milling nobles, Claire caught her eyes and her lips moved. Inaudible, they formed the words, "You've got this. I love you."

Elenor straightened her back, reaching to curl her fingers around the evergold pendant that sat atop her dress.

I will walk in the light, alone and unafraid. In shadows, I will find no fear, for they are fleeting and when darkness blocks my path I will not stop, for only challenged will I grow. It is mine to walk the troubled road where others dare not tread and speak the truth where shadows lie.

The litany of the Blue focused her racing thoughts. In a clear, carrying voice, Elenor spoke. "Is this how it happened? Were you all bickering amongst yourselves and jockeying for power while my father slaughtered whole towns? Where was this anger when he killed his own son right in front of you? Where was the vitriol when he imprisoned innocents and drove our people to rebel?"

Dead silence. Elenor clenched her teeth, her hands balled up into fists. "No wonder my brother turned to the Rebellion for help. You didn't even raise your voices when our late King killed a Writted Lord and Lady without a trial. You let the Tellens die without so much as a word, yet today, when we have a chance to begin to make things right, you stand here squabbling like children."

A kaleidoscope of different emotions showed on the upturned faces of the nobility. Accusation and approval from the representative of House Tellen, shame from several other Writted nobles, and a pleased smile from Robin. That unnerved her, but anger still flared in her chest. Elenor's nails dug into her palm as the Tirition stepped forward and bowed.

"That's exactly the point I've been trying to make, Your Highness. You are about to enter some very complicated negotiations with multiple other Kingdoms. Tirit Mindel can step in and be a neutral party, delaying any major choices until the nobility can calm down and Lirin is once more in competent hands," Robin said.

Elenor leveled a glare at him. "Master Robin, I may have a few bumps and bruises, but I am of sound mind and, I expect, much more likely to further Lirinian interests than a Tirition or Mindellion. You meant no offense and neither do I when I remind you that you were not invited to this meeting, and have no business here. This is a decision for the Lirinian nobility to make, not Tirit Mindel. *Leave.*"

Kallen was shaking his head at her, eyes wide as if trying to shut her up, but Elenor wasn't about to let Tirit Mindel walk all over her. Nor, for that matter, House Eurieha or anyone else. She hadn't killed her own father just to become someone else's puppet. She had done it to help Lirin and, damn it, she wasn't going to let a single person in this room stop her now.

There was only one way to make sure of that.

She turned away from Robin to look at the nobles of Lirin.

"Our country is broken, and I dare a single one of you to say otherwise. Our people are *suffering*, our nobility has been divided and turned against each other, and lies have piled up so deep we're choking on them. You can sit here throwing blame about until we crumble, but I won't. I plan to dig us out of this mess my parents buried us in."

"Bold words from a girl who has never set foot in a meeting of the King's Council, and whose only allies are western separatists and rifters," spat Lady Lavarin. She took a step up the dais, turning her back on Elenor to address the gathered nobles.

"Our King has been murdered and his own daughter speaks ill of him the very next day. Her brother tried to kill him not two months ago. How do we know she wasn't in on the plan and just finished the job?"

Elenor stumbled back a step, anger fizzling under a renewed wave of sticky guilt.

"Even if she did not, we don't need a youthful idealist with no practical experience in charge right now, but rather an experienced politician."

"Meaning you?" Eric snapped. "Whose family has done nothing but eye the throne like vultures since the last time you tried—and failed—to take it by force?"

"You have no grounds to speak that way, Ondai. Didn't your own parents die trying to secede from Lirin? Served them right to get buried with the common filth."

Claire and Kallen each grabbed one of Eric's arms as he launched himself forward. "How dare you?"

Lady Lavarin pulled herself up to her full height with a sniff. "I dare plenty, Ondai. They were traitors, and there are more in our midst, as Lord Daniil said. We will have Seehana's and Miriel's eyes upon us, so our first priority must be finding the criminal who killed our King. Do you think a populace who believes royalty may be murdered without retribution will hesitate to turn on the nobility? I don't know about you, but I don't want mobs beating down my door. We must put down those who have committed this heinous crime the way our late King put down the Western Revolts, and do the same to all those who supported them. If we do not, our allies will see it as weakness. Unlike some of us," she glared at Eric, "House Lavarin does not wish to be a province of Seehana."

"But you're fine parting your legs for Miriel? Because that's what Lirin has been doing," Claire yelled back, still holding on to Eric though she looked only slightly less mad. "You're nothing but a self-serving coward, Adelina. If you treated the people in your province decently, you wouldn't be scared that they would see this as an opportunity to rise up and behead you. Elenor is thinking about more than her own hide, yet you interrupt our heir with your squawking, you power-hungry toad."

"Ah, the lover speaks. You think none of us have noticed House Enica worming their way towards the throne? Why, I wouldn't be surprised if you and yours were responsible for either the King's death or the Queen's absence."

"She's not. I am." Elenor hadn't planned on shouting that in the middle of the Throne Room, but it left her mouth before common sense could stop it. Lady Lavarin, who had opened her mouth, shut it.

No one else spoke either, the quiet thick and heavy. Then Kallen bounded up the stairs to the dais and Elenor's side and took her by the elbow. He pulled her behind him, smiled wanly at the gathered nobles, and said, "Crazy thing, the love of a daughter for her father, right? It's so easy to feel responsible, even though—"

Elenor placed a hand on Kallen's arm. She appreciated what he was trying to do, but it wouldn't work. She could already see the delighted glee in Lady Lavarin's eyes, and the alarm in Daniil Eurieha's. Of course he would be worried. Blackmail, after all, required secrets.

The problem with confessing, of course, would be that Elenor would also likely be tried and found guilty of murder.

It's either that, or live a lie for the rest of my life.

She'd done that once already.

Never again.

So with gentle but firm pressure, Elenor pushed Kallen to the side. "Thank you, Lord Drego, but I am capable of speaking for myself."

"Elenor—" he protested.

"We serve the Blue, remember? Lies do not become us." She

faced Lady Lavarin, who looked like a child at Harvest with a pot full of candy. "You want someone to blame for my father's death? It's me. I'm not sure if I killed him myself or someone else did to protect me, but I *am* the reason he is dead."

"She admits it!" the noblewoman shrieked, but it did not raise the ruckus she seemed to have expected. Almost everyone was still staring at Elenor, who pulled herself up a little taller, even though she just wanted to curl into a ball and weep.

"Yes, I admit it. I didn't want to do it, I wish I had not needed to, but it had to be done. My brother knew that, and I just regret it took me so long to figure it out too. I won't lie to you, and I won't lie to the people of Lirin either. Honestly, I am too tired and in too much pain right now to mince words and play politics. You all know the truth, even if you have convinced yourself the lies are real: Markus Miri-Lirion was a horrible King who never gave a shit about any of you, or this country."

Elenor reached behind her neck to unclasp the button there, pulling down the fabric that hid the bruises on her throat. "Last night, I orchestrated the mass-breakout of prisoners wrongly held captive and tortured within these walls. While doing so, I was apprehended by Duncan Eurieha, who, while trying to strangle me to death, admitted he was acting on the orders of Sianta Miri, Queen of Miriel, the woman who will likely seize control of the Lirion family Writs if my mother and I both lose them. When he failed to kill me the first time, he called my father to finish the job. The King you so defend, Lady Lavarin, cornered me and threatened to turn those I love, including members of the Writted Nobility within this very room, into hostages he would torture or murder if I did not sign my Writ over to him as regent as soon as I got it. I suspect this is how he has controlled my mother for the entirety of their reign and seized her power to begin with." Elenor swallowed, then finished. "I chose not to let him do that to me. I chose my country over my family, and I would do it again. I will gladly face justice for it if that is the will of this council, but in the meantime, this pointless bickering *will stop*. My mother is missing, and the people who profit most from that, right now, are the Miri. So either you vote to arrest me where I stand or you vote to give me power, because I intend to find the Queen and fix this country, and you have wasted enough of my time already this morning."

Kallen coughed from beside her. "We will vote on the matters separately. All those in favor of trying Her Highness Elenor Lirion for the murder of King Consort Markus Miri-Lirion, respond aye. Those against, nay."

"Nay," Eric said, crossing his arms.

"Nay," Claire's father said, flashing Elenor an encouraging smile.

"Aye," Lady Lavarin snapped, "and she should be arrested at once for it."

"Aye," said Lord Amad.

"Nay," the representative of House Petrona said, surprising Elenor, whose pulse was thundering.

Her eyes moved to the Tellen representative. She didn't recognize him, but he wore the armband with the family crest, marking him as speaking for the House Elenor had once considered family. He took a half step forward.

"This is not the first time that Her Highness's actions ended in needless and reckless deaths. Whether she was the one to end the life of our King or not is immaterial to House Tellen. However, she must learn that her actions have consequences, thus, we vote Aye."

Tears pricked at the corners of Elenor's eyes, but she managed to nod in respect and turned to Kallen. His face was drawn as if in pain. He looked down at her, then slowly said, "I believe in the rule of law and that no person is above it. Based on what Her Highness has said in front of this gathering, I am afraid I must vote Aye, but on the condition that she *not* be arrested, and instead be presumed innocent until found guilty by a court of law, with no immediate negative repercussions or limits to her freedom of movement."

Lady Lavarin crossed her arms, scowling, but did not oppose the motion. Eric, though, looked like a kettle about to boil over. He shook off Claire's grip on his elbow and called for the second vote. "All those in favor of appointing Elenor as regent pro tempore of Lirin for the next thirty days?"

Around the vote went, the same lines drawn with Enica, Ondai, and Petrona on Elenor's side and Lavarin and Amad against, until it got to House Tellen and Drego.

"Aye," the Tellen representative said.

"Aye," Kallen declared. "Five to two. The motion passes. Princess Elenor Lirion is appointed regent pro tempore starting immediately, and will stand trial for the murder of King Consort Markus Miri-Lirion. So it is decided. All kneel for your new regent."

Elenor's knees wobbled. She slumped back onto the throne as, one by one, the nobles gathered sank to their knees in a bow. Well, almost all of them. Robin Tirition stood with his arms crossed and a knowing smile dancing on his lips, and Daniil Eurieha was nowhere to be seen.

CHAPTER FIVE
A Fear Of Falling
FAYRIAN

It is time to say goodbye, my old friends. I am sorry for leaving the way I did, but I would not have gotten off the Island had I not acted with haste once they found out where my loyalties lie. Quindo is meeting me at the border and I promise I will be safe. You know where to find me, and if you ever wish to visit, write to me at the Deil Trading Company. Already, I miss you. I am sorry our time for adventures is at an end, but if the fates are kind, we will be together again one day. Stay safe, my dearest friends. You have been my family for many years, and leaving you rips me apart.

—From a letter to her friends on Tirit Mindel, from Phoebi Tirition.

RIAN—BECAUSE WHY NOT ACCEPT THE NAME when this fucking desert had torn everything that was Fay from her—wiped the sweat off her brow, leaving a smear of blood behind. She rubbed at her eyes for what had to be the thousandth time that night, but the blurriness didn't fade any faster.

She could see better than a few hours earlier, when Fedrik had been taken from her, but the faces of the broken rifters she was helping were still fuzzy around the edges.

In a way, Rian was glad for it. There were *so many*. It was easier to see blurs instead of people.

She had been there to help her father in the aftermath of the last few razed villages in the Western Revolts, but while heartbreaking and gruesome, those attacks had left few survivors alive to suffer.

This explosion of power had not been so merciful. Out of the sixty-seven rifters who had been present at the Deil estate, only eight were unscathed. All of them were children. The man in the pink suit had walked into the wreckage of the party an hour after the Red died, leading all the missing little ones. By then, Rian had been too busy to pay the small mercy more than a passing glance.

Fifty-nine broken rifters, and, according to the man in pink, the ripples of the magical explosion of a God had extended much further than the Deil estate. Each time a rifter overloaded badly enough to break, their power rippled out in an explosive blast of their own. It was too early to know the total count of the dead and broken, but Rian had heard the man in pink estimate it at *hundreds.*

Eleven had died outright at the Deil estate, including one of Kaedy's brothers and two slaves. They had been the lucky ones.

"Please, just let me die," the rifter Rian was treating moaned, that plea all she had repeated for hours. The woman sat huddled beneath blankets, even as the heat of morning grew stifling. "I want to die."

"Well, tough luck," Rian said, adding another log to the fire, before going back to bandaging the jagged cut along the wrists of the unconscious man she was also working on. All the surviving rifters were bundled up and tied down securely. Well, the ones who hadn't succeeded in walking into the oasis with stones in their pockets.

Rian had been taught enough rifting theory while training with Ara and Robin to understand the basics of what had happened. Rifters grew dependent on magic. If they shattered the ring that allowed them to access it—their capacity—they were cut off for life. She had been warned, time and again, of the consequences of letting Gabriel's power flare out of control. He could hurt others, and if he pushed far enough to break his own capacity, could hurt himself.

"*Worse than any drug withdrawal, because it never ends. The magic is still in their well, pushing against a capacity that no longer exists. It's like being famished in a banquet hall, but unable to reach out to take so much as a single bite. That hunger and need will never leave, but the initial shock is the worst. If they can survive long enough to grow accustomed to the pain, they might not die, but they will never be the same again. Unfortunately, the average lifespan of a broken rifter is one year from the day of their breaking. Even if they do not seek out a way to end their lives, the will to survive is gone as surely as their magic is,*" Ara had said.

It had scared Rian enough to never let Gabriel get more than the smallest taste of his magic, yet all the theory in the world had not prepared her for this.

She finished tying the bandage in place and rocked back on her heels, raising a hand. "Done. Who needs extra hands?"

"Here," called an older woman kneeling next to a man who was rocking and sweaty. "He's going into shock and is going to pass out any second now."

Rian scrambled to her feet but didn't run, for fear she would trip on an obstacle her fuzzy eyes didn't see. There were plenty of those. Each fallen rifter had one or two people tending to them, and there was little order yet to where they lay. Rian zig-zagged around them, grabbing a spare blanket on her way.

At the side of the hyperventilating man, she skidded to a halt and knelt, reaching for his wrist. As expected, his pulse was erratic and too fast. Very much wishing she had Gabriel here or had paid more attention during their medical training at school, Rian helped the other woman lay the trembling man down and cover him.

"His skin is chilly. Is he pale?" Rian asked.

"Yes. Thank you for coming over. I didn't want to be alone if he ends up needing chest compressions," the woman said, with a remarkable lack of Mondaer accent. Rian vaguely recognized the voice, but could not place it.

"Well, let's see if we can avoid that being necessary," Rian replied, hoisting the broken rifter's knees up over one of her shoulders and rubbing his legs to increase circulation. "Stay with us, alright? Don't go getting any ideas that you can just slip away, because there are already way too many corpses to get rid of, and I don't want to lug your body around. Got it?"

"Charming bedside manner," the other woman snorted, as she rubbed along his arms. Her motions were oddly jerky and inconsistent, and her voice a little slurred and slow.

"You're not hurt too, are you?"

"Only my heart at seeing so much pain. Other than that, I am old and I have cerebral palsy, but neither of those facts change my ability to provide assistance."

Ah, this must be one of Kaedy's grandparents, the one that had sat near them at lunch a few days ago and asked Tellen all about Tirit Mindel.

"What was your name again?" Rian asked.

"Phoebi Deil, Tirition of the College of Academics, Gifted Razer."

Rian stopped her rubbing for the space of a shocked breath. The presence of another Gifted was no surprise, given that they had discovered the Mondaer had sat on a Gift that gave Gifts for generations, but *a Tirition?*

Had Rian really run all the way here to *still* be within reach of the Island?

"Patient first, Fay," Phoebi admonished.

Rian's hands began to move again, then she blinked a few times. "You used my real name."

"I've heard a lot about you from a dear friend. It just slipped out."

Who the fuck had been talking about her in the Mondaer? Though a more pressing question came out first. "I thought Tirit Mindel wasn't allowed in the desert?"

"Oh, it's not, but quite a few of us have had the same idea you did over the years. I came back here for good once the Island found out I was a Mondaer spy."

Any other time, Rian would have jumped on that. The thought of almighty Tirit Mindel not noticing a spy for even a single day tickled her pink, but the moans and wails of the broken cut through that glee. She returned her attention to the shaking man and gave his leg a gentle squeeze. "Keep breathing, my friend. It will get better, I promise."

They were empty words. There was a very real chance that it would *not* get better, but there was sometimes great comfort to be had in a well-placed lie. Rian opened her mouth to ask Phoebi to check his pulse again when a voice louder than the loudest thunder boomed over the desert.

"Fulsixia the Ruby Dragon, Holder of Dracona, Goddess of Namers, is dead. Those who killed her heed these words: Repent, or face the reckoning."

A flash of light followed, burning Rian's already stinging eyes.

New screams filled the air, ringing in her ears despite having clamped her hands over them. The man she was tending to spasmed and shuddered, then fell still.

The whole desert, in fact, quieted as the reverberations of that inhuman voice faded. Phoebi's hand reached out for Rian's and Rian found herself clutching it back, holding on to those frail fingers with all her might.

"What was that?" she gasped in a hardly audible whisper, throat dry and heart thundering wildly against her ribs.

Pop!

"HOLY BALLS!" Rian screeched as a man appeared less than a foot away from her.

"They are pretty holy, if I do say so myself. But to answer your question, my dear, *that* was nothing good and everything exciting, I expect," the pink-clad man who had just appeared out of thin air said, voice too casual for the field of broken and dead rifters. "Up you get, slowpoke. Time to be on our way."

"What—" Rian began, before he bent, hooked his arm through hers, and yanked her to her feet. "Hey. Get your hands off me."

"Moe, our Goddess is gone, a man is dead at your feet, and you look like it's your birthday. Show some damn respect," Phoebi said, reaching forward to close the eyelids of the man they had just failed to save. "Do you know what that voice was?"

"Oh yes, and you have a good chance of figuring it out soon. But why would I spoil a perfectly good mystery? You like puzzles, don't ya Pheebs? This one's gonna be a killer."

Rian tried to shrug Moe's hand off, but his long fingers were tight on her arm. "What do you want with me?"

"Not to use your Gift for the next . . ." Moe looked down at his wrist, where metal glimmered, "thirty-seven seconds."

Pop!

They were falling.

Rian screamed and threw her arms around Moe's neck as they appeared thousands of feet above the desert and plummeted towards the ground. Wind whipped at her hair and clothes. The biting cold clawed every inch of exposed skin. They were going to die.

Pop!

Water. All around them was cold, muddy water. Rian's head broke the surface and she gasped for air, limbs still tangled up in Moe's. She caught sight of the Hardor Palace, shining on its hill, then—

Pop!

They landed with a squelch in a hallway made of warm reddish stone, striated with glowing golden veins. The heat and scent of the desert slammed into her once more, and her heart sank. "Take me back."

That had been Hardor. How—

"Oops. Thirty-nine seconds. My bad," Moe said, hoisting Rian up as her knees wobbled. He straightened her sodden scarf, and pulled off the pigeon pin he had placed there the night before. "I'll be taking this back, now. Recordings must be recorded and studied, and all that. Not that I'd expected one quite this soon. Still, that was a good one. I should know; I'm a connoisseur of big booms. Must say, drowned rat looks great on you, darling. You should consider it as a fashion trend. Then again, you live in a desert. Don't worry, though; it won't be for long. Well, I've got a full agenda, so toodles."

He waggled his fingers at her, then *pop!*

"FUCK!"

"Language, girl," a stern, frail voice said from behind her. Rian swiveled around, recognizing it at once. Though she still could not make out her features, the woman who had ordered Tellen to be taken away stood in an open doorway. "I see Moe missed his mark again. Typical. Come in. I've been waiting for you. My name is Suela Alveara."

Rian did not reply, turning on the spot. Droplets of water splattered against the stone, turning the reddish rock crimson. "Where did he go?"

"Moe? Who knows. He'll be back, though. He always is, especially during times of calamity." Suela sounded as tired as Rian had felt before thirty-nine seconds of adrenaline-fueled terror.

"What's happening here?" Rian asked, still spinning around, mind trying to catch up to her very changed circumstances. She bent over as her breathing became shallow gasps. "We were . . .

falling. And then plunged into the Claire River. And now—Where am I? How . . . ?"

"Come inside, and I will tell you," Suela said, gesturing to the open door to a sunlit room.

Rian, though, wasn't even halfway calm enough to do anything but hyperventilate. "We . . . so high up . . . Hardor . . . "

Suela placed a firm hand on Rian's elbow. "You're scared of heights?"

"We were *falling.*" Everyone should be fucking scared of that shit. How—

"I see," Suela said, voice clipped. Her skin was wrinkled and dark, like leather left out too long in the sun. Her graying hair fluttered around her shoulders and she wore robes of deep red, belted in black. Her most noticeable feature, though, was the bandage that covered her eyes. Rian fixated on that, both because the lighter color was a good focus for her blurry eyes, and because her scrambled mind needed *something* to focus on.

Now, if only she could actually formulate a coherent question.

"A God is dead," Suela barked. "These little fears will not serve you and we have no time for them. You will banish the fear."

"You can't just 'banish' fear. Fear isn't a fault." Robin had drilled that into her head for years. *"Follow your instincts. If you're afraid, look for the cause. Your fear will tell you what your eyes do not. It will keep you alive."*

Suela was shaking her head. "Fear is the first kiss of death. It kills you before you stop breathing."

Despite her age and the heavy way Suela leaned on her cane, the *daradeio* was surprisingly strong as she dragged Rian forward. Rian was so intent on staring at the old lady and trying to wrap her mind around what had just happened that she did not see them approach the ledge.

Rian's belly bumped up against a railing. She looked down and felt her stomach lurch.

The drop seemed to go on forever, down and down the side of a monumental pillar of carved red stone to a sky-blue lake, beyond which lay an enormous city. Rian gripped the railing with both hands, her knuckles white as vertigo assailed her.

The wind gusted through her auburn hair, and as Suela pushed further, she involuntarily let out a yelp of terror.

"Face your fears, Rian. You're scared of heights, so you need to face the heights. Only by facing the fear will you be able to move past it. Don't close your eyes. Look down. Think about how long of a fall that would be, how your body would break as you hit the water, how your bones would crack and skin split open. Imagine slipping, flailing, screaming as you tumble through the air."

"Let me go!"

"Or what? No one is going to save you, Rian. Our Goddess is dead. There is no one to help you just because your eyes are now red. If I decide you will not serve the Mondaer well, there is no one to punish me for ending your life. Look down or fall."

Her whole body shook. She felt nauseous and dizzy, vertigo making her hands sweat, but she forced her eyes open. Suela's bony fingers clutched her neck in a vice-like grip, holding Rian just on the brink of falling. Panting, she struggled with the desire to scream again and curse her captor, instead trying to face her fear like this crazy witch wanted her to. Yet she was unable to stop picturing the fall Suela had described. Tears welled in her eyes, the brutally fast wind whipping them away. Rian *hated* crying, but could not make it stop once it started, her vision blurring more as she sobbed out her fear. The hand on her neck did not loosen. It shoved her further down, causing her feet to skitter on the floor for balance and another scream to rip from her lips.

"Please, please don't—" Rian begged, not recognizing her own voice. When had she ever sounded so desperate and pitiful? She had faced death a hundred times, so why couldn't she now?

"Face the fear, Rian."

"I can't! I can't breathe!"

"Yes, you can. You're still jabbering, aren't you?" Suela pushed forward once more and Rian's knees buckled, thudding against the rails.

This was too much. She couldn't do it, not after everything else she had gone through over the last few months. Not after losing first Wil, then Gabriel, and then the Rebellion, after running from Tirit Mindel and becoming a slave. Especially not after being ripped away from Tellen and spending all night among the dead and dying. It was just too fucking much. She had no more fight to give.

Rian closed her eyes and went limp, giving up any semblance of struggle.

Suela's fingers let go.

For a panic-inducing moment of wild flailing, Rian lost her balance, then Suela grabbed the back of her dress and yanked her to safety.

Her butt hit the stone floor with a thud. Rian looked up at the sadistic *daradeio,* eyes still wet with tears but heart too exhausted to fight back.

"Why am I here?" she whispered, voice a hollow husk of what it had been.

"To learn to face your fears and walk into the fire to save us all," Suela answered.

"You have the wrong person. I'm loud, not brave. I failed and ran away from the people who needed me. If I couldn't stay to fight for those I love, why would I do so to save a place I fucking hate? You're wasting your time."

The tip of Suela's cane poked Rian painfully in the shoulder. "And what gives you the right to wallow in self-deprecation when there is work to be done? I faced both my greatest fears, have survived the gauntlet, yet am still standing strong. Until you do too, you have not earned the right to this piteous drivel. Now, on your feet and follow me." Suela spoke calmly, her voice emotionless.

Rian wilted, her shoulders slumping in defeat.

The fucking witch just impassively waited, a tapping foot her only sign of impatience.

It took Rian an embarrassingly long time to pull herself up to her knees, then her feet. When she was at last steady, Suela led her out of the room. The *daradeio* walked with none of the hesitations of the blind—these corridors were obviously places she had memorized—but with some of the shuffle of the elderly. Rian followed without argument. She didn't even look around, just kept her eyes on Suela's feet.

It didn't take long to reach a staircase lit by bright sunlight streaming from above instead of the dim glow of the gold-striated walls. They exited onto a tiled roof and despite her numb exhaustion, Rian swore under her breath when she realized they were on top of a giant mesa, the whole desert spread out before them.

"What is it with you and heights?" Rian muttered, not expecting Suela to catch it.

A poke in the side with the end of the old woman's cane made it abundantly clear that she had. "Why do you think I made you face your fears down there? I didn't want you having a fit on the roof, girl. I'm not a nice person, but I'm not needlessly cruel."

I disagree, Rian thought.

Despite not having any interest in revisiting the drop, she couldn't help but look around. The top of the mesa was easily a quarter-mile across, the stairwell she and Suela had exited not far from one of the edges. Most of it was covered in low buildings and tiled walkways, mock dragons landing and taking off, and *daradeios* dressed in red running about. People were smiling as they worked. Easy banter, even snatches of song, carried over the breeze.

"They don't know yet, do they?" she asked Suela.

"No. I will tell them soon, but we must have measures in place to keep ahead of the panic. To first lose my Sidian and now Lady Red . . . It is a nightmare turned real, and will shake my people to our foundations."

Beyond the edge of the enormous mesa, a city easily twice the size of Hardor lay glistening in the morning sun. Her stinging eyes couldn't make out individual buildings, but the sprawling mass of whites and blues merged into a riotous mosaic. Past the last straggling neighborhoods, the desert stretched for miles and miles of rolling dunes, interrupted only by long roads packed with travelers. If the people here panicked as badly as those at Kaedy's estate, then Rian had to admit Suela had reason for caution.

Yet, even the prospect of being in the middle of a nation in turmoil didn't take away from the wonder of this view. Fedrik would have loved it. Gabriel would have been right up at the edge of the precipice, grinning like a madman. Yet it was Rian who was here instead of them and it made her heart ache.

"Where . . . are we?"

"This is Aina Brisbhan. The Mother Rock and our greatest city."

"How did I get here? We were days away." At any other time, that alone might have been enough to terrify her, but in a world where Gods weren't just real but could be killed by someone she had known for years, what point was there in being surprised?

"What does it matter?" Suela asked, echoing her thoughts. "Rian, our Goddess is dead."

"I fucking noticed."

The old woman clicked her tongue. "You could swear a little less, girl. The word fuck isn't particularly eloquent, nor does it endear you to me. Do try to be more creative, if you must use profanity."

"I'm not trying to be endearing. That's not who I am."

"I'm already tired of hearing what you are not," Suela said tersely. "You are not endearing. You are not brave. You are not interested in our plight. These are not insightful or pertinent facts. Tell me about what you *are*, Rian."

Fucking hag. Rian shifted from foot to foot, annoyed that she didn't have an easy retort. "I thought we were supposed to leave everything we were behind when we crossed the Wall."

"Ah yes, Leo brought you in. That boy takes things much too literally. No, Rian. A line of stones does not erase who you were, it simply allows you to begin anew, bringing with you only the parts of your past that you wish to hold. It did not negate your Gift, did it? It did not lessen the destructive power that your friend held within him?"

Rian's chest actually ached as she spoke of Fedrik. "Where is he now? Where is the Sandhewn City?"

"You were paying attention, I see, not just screaming and fighting like a wounded beast. That's good. The Sandhewn City is one of our oldest temples, a monument and a warning of what a Gatekeeper can do. Baarin—"

"His name is Fedrik. Fedrik Tellen." They could not take that little bit of him from her. It was all Rian had to cling to.

Suela shrugged. "Baarin, Fedrik, it does not matter to me or, I'd guess, to the people he killed. He is not the first of his kind to leave a path of devastation in his wake, nor will he be the last. Though none in our history have committed quite so heinous a crime as killing a God." Suela's stern tone wavered on those last three words. Rian knew that deep, heart-rending grief, and for a moment she even felt sorry for this woman who had seen Tellen destroy something she loved.

Rian had watched him do the same to her father.

That shred of sympathy vanished when she remembered how Suela had called for Fedrik's blood. "You said you would kill him once you find this Incarnate person."

"And at the time, I meant it. Yet I was wrong. I spoke from fury and grief, instead of reason. Lady Red taught me better than that. She showed compassion for me when I was first coming into my powers as a Gatekeeper, but I was too overcome with anger to do the same. It is an insult to her memory, and a shame I will always carry."

Rian scrambled away from the woman so fast her feet slipped on the tile and she fell on her ass. "You're a Gatekeeper?"

"I was. I am not any longer. But what are *you*, girl?"

Still on the ground, back pressed against a low wall, Rian looked up at the wizened old woman. "I'm a Ghoster. I drain people and the air around me of magic."

"And what else?"

"What do you mean?" Feeling oddly touchy and vulnerable about the subject change, Rian didn't try to stand again. It wasn't as though Suela could see her, right? Pulling her knees to her chest, she looked out over the desert once more.

"Are you only your Gift? You are Tirit Mindel trained, yes? And Akaaron told me you were a rebel in Lirin, working alongside my Sidian. So what else are you?"

There was that name again. Sidian. She had thought it was a coincidence the first time she had heard it, for while she had known a red-eyed rebel who went by Ian and had often spoken of the desert, she always just figured his eyes were a fluke, kind of like Gabriel's startling green.

Oh how she missed him. Even now, after all these miles and weeks, the engagement bracelet Gabe had left her was in her pocket. Rian's fingers brushed against it and she was so distracted by her grief that she didn't see Suela's cane swing until it bonked her on the head.

"Hey! What was that for?"

"For daydreaming when we have work to do. Now, answer my question. What else are you?"

"I don't know, alright?" Rian snapped.

"Unacceptable answer."

Rian bared her teeth, which provoked no reaction. Ah, excellent. If verbal sass wasn't going to be allowed, at least she could make faces and gestures at the blind bat. "Introspection isn't my thing."

The cane moved again, but this time Rian was ready for it and grabbed it from the air. She yanked it out of the old woman's grip and threw it with all her might towards the edge of the mesa. It sailed over the ledge and fell out of sight. The giddy satisfaction was abruptly cut off when Suela calmly said, "I see you have the manners of a beast, not just the lack of control. There are eleven thousand, two hundred and ten stairs from the bottom to the top of Aina Brisbhan. We shall see if you are still this contrary when you have climbed each and every one to retrieve that."

"The fuck I will. If you don't want to lose your cane, maybe don't hit people with it."

Suela shook her head, lips twisted. "If you don't want to be hit, don't act like a selfish, petulant child. You will get respect when you earn it, and not a moment sooner. You may think on that while you are retrieving my cane. When you return it to me, you will do so with an apology, and an explanation of why what you did was wrong. Until then, you will not be eating. If you think that you can out-stubborn me, girl, you are in for an unpleasant surprise. Now, before you begin, answer my question."

Rian's teeth ground audibly. Much to her annoyance, the mention of food also made her stomach grumble, a stark reminder that it was breakfast time and she had spent all night running from patient to patient without much pause.

"You are deeply dislikable."

"Is that supposed to offend me, Rian?"

"It's Fay. That's what your precious Lady Red said. Faerian with an Ae and an Ia Essence," she snapped, "but if I get a choice, I'm spelling it with a fucking *y* the way my parents wanted. If you want my cooperation, we can start there."

To her shock, that made Suela smile. "Good. That is something you are. Tell me more, Fayrian-with-a-Y."

Fay took a shaky breath. Her hand once more closed over the bracelet in her pocket and words she had pushed down since the day the Rebellion fell bubbled up without her consent. "I wasn't being stubborn when I said I don't know who I am. I don't. All I've ever been is part of someone or something else, but that was ripped away from me. First, I was my father's reason to keep fighting, then I was charged with controlling my best friend's magic to save his life, then I was the Rebellion's leader. They all depended on me having my shit together and giving everything to keep them going. Even when I came here, I had Fedrik. I could define myself by how much I resented him, and how much I hated this place, because I don't fucking know how to live any other way, alright? I've never had a chance to figure out who I am without them, but now . . . now they're all gone."

Suela seemed to consider this, then slowly inclined her head. "I believe that may be the first genuine thing you have said to me. I understand what it means to be lost, Fayrian. My Goddess is dead, my Incarnate gone, my Gift torn from me. It seems as though the darkness will not end, that there is nothing to cling to, but feel what is around you. The sun is up, the world still moves forward, and now both you and I are at a crossroads.

"You say that you have always been defined by others. Take this as a chance to make a choice for yourself. You are now a *daradeio*. Quite possibly the last that will ever bear the red eyes of our God. Like all *daradeio* initiates before you, it is your decision what you will do with your life, and who you will apprentice under. As such, what I ask of you today is a choice, not an order."

Suela leaned on a nearby railing, the breeze playing in her long white hair as she faced north over the rolling dunes. "My Sidian is dead. Another bears his Gift. My own gift passed to your companion.

Had I stopped Sidian from returning to Lirin, perhaps Fulsixia the Red would still live, but we were told that it was the only way. We were promised that if we made the sacrifice, our Mother in Gold would return to us, and we would get a chance to right our past mistakes. But it didn't go to plan. He was supposed to pass his Gift to Wilam Lirion. Instead, his Gift is lost and your friend's power grows.

"As soon as our brethren find out how our Lady in Red died, he will be a target of their anger. It usually takes years to learn to control the Gatekeeper Gift. He may only have weeks, and his Incarnate is in just as much danger. Without their other halves, their powers will blossom unchecked and unbalanced. I cannot do anything for the holder of the Last Gift at present, but with your help, I believe we may yet be able to save Fedrik Tellen. It will require you to apprentice with me and heed my orders, for this path will be both difficult and dangerous in ways only I may be able to recognize. Even so, you may die, or you may suffer worse than death.

"Knowing that, will you help me stabilize your friend, find his Incarnate, and deliver them both back here where they can train in safety?"

It was very nearly the exact same deal that Robin had once offered her. Rian's stomach twisted and she almost refused on principle. A day ago she would have, but she had promised Fedrik she would watch his back. What would her father, who believed in the litany of the Green to uphold every sworn oath, say about her if she walked away from him?

Three are the oaths to which I hold, sworn anew each day. First, to freely share that which I have with those in greater need. Second, to stand for what is right, even if I stand alone. Third, to bear the weight of every choice I make, and pay the price of each mistake.

Fay may have lost everything else, but no one could take away what her father had taught her. She'd ignored his advice far too often of late, and it had only gotten her mired deeper into this fucked-up reality.

Just because she was going to accept, though, didn't mean Fay had learned nothing from the last time she'd negotiated with someone who needed her skills. "Both of us go free. No slavery crap, no ten year apprenticeships, nothing. We work for you until you have your precious Incarnate back, then we stay or go as we please with your full support. I heard all that bullshit about working for the right to resources. The way I see it, keeping Tellen from blowing anyone else up is worth some protection, especially if I might die. Give me that in writing with no small print or loopholes, and I'll help you. I swear it."

Fay had expected Suela—stubborn as she was—to argue. Instead, the old woman whipped around and held out a hand. "Agreed."

Shit.

I should have asked for more.

INTERLUDE
A Last Awakening
ALEHAN

ALEHAN SILVARIN SURGED AWAKE, wheezing and choking.

The wind off the mesas around Gold City was hot and dry in his lungs as he gasped for air, hands fisted in the silken sheets. Panting, he struggled to breathe, coughing as the numbness he always felt upon these awakenings began to fade.

"Hello, Alehan," said a voice he had last heard what felt like mere hours ago, but could have been decades. Aleh whipped around, halfway to his knees before his brain caught up with his ears.

An old man sat in the chair by his bedside, leaning on a cane. His face was wrinkled, hair that had once been a lustrous brown, a dull, wispy gray. Even his eyes had changed, sunken and clouded instead of bright and enticing.

"Nash." The name felt thick in Alehan's throat. In the five centuries since the Gold Dragon had plucked him from the jaws of death, Alehan Silvarin had only spent a few dozen years awake. Each time, he had been given just long enough to get to know and care for people like Nash, only to be put into a deep sleep again for decades. This wasn't the first time he had woken to find someone he had cared for aged and weathered, but it never got easier.

"Not how you remember me, I take it? You're exactly as I remember you." Nash leaned back in his chair with a low groan. "It makes me feel all the years since they put you into stasis. I never expected to see you again."

Alehan didn't reply. What could he say? That it was easier to wake up to every person he knew being dead than to be shown so plainly what the gods had stolen from him? That seeing Nash this way was torture?

Releasing the tensions in his limbs, Aleh moved to the edge of the bed and extended his arm, brushing Nash's cheek with his fingertips, allowing tears to well up in his eyes.

Nash briefly leaned into the touch, closing his eyes with a sigh. Then he pulled away. "I know you hate this. You don't have to look at me if it makes it easier. I'm not as easily heartbroken as I was when I was young."

Alehan stood and, a little unsteadily, stumbled to the balcony of his room to look out over Gold City. Was it bigger? The sprawling metropolis didn't seem to be—at least not by much. Of course, for Nash to look as he did, no more than fifty years could have passed.

Directly below and far above them, the massive bulk of Sarthia's golden temple made the city feel small, but the sight did not fill Alehan with the same awe it had when he was eleven. Then, he had thought that the Gold Dragon saving him from the unforgiving ocean's depths meant that the nightmare was over. This was a new land, one where his green eyes were not a death sentence and Jac Drego did not lurk in the shadows to torture him to madness.

He had been a naive idiot.

The Gods never did anything except for their own gain.

Without turning from the city, Aleh rasped, "Why did they wake me? They usually wait until anyone I've formed intimate attachments to is dead."

"Our Lady wants to talk to you. One of the Exiled Gods is dead."

Alehan's grief at the lost years bled into cold disdain. He turned to look at his former lover again."So?" It wasn't as though there was a lack of Gods. Eighteen Dragons ran this world, and Alehan hated every single one of them individually and uniquely.

Nash flinched at the flippant remark. "The last time a Dragon died, the exile to Carinn followed."

"The last time I was in Carinn, my family and I were put on a boat to die and *the Exiled Gods* did nothing to stop it. I have no lingering sympathy for them."

"Our Mother in Gold saved you."

"I saved myself." His tone was biting. Nash didn't deserve this, but Alehan wasn't speaking to the soft-spoken, quick-witted acolyte he had known before he'd fallen asleep. He was speaking to a priest of the Goddess who'd imprisoned him. "Did she have you wake me because she thought it would make me more compliant? If so, she still doesn't understand how few fucks I have left to give."

Nash did not react the way Alehan wanted him to. Anger would have been easy to deal with. Instead, the elderly priest simply closed his eyes for a moment, then opened them again. In a steady voice, he said, "The Gold is expecting you."

"What for? Whatever this is about, I had no part in it." Alehan paced toward the bathroom, stripping off his shirt as he went. He wanted a damn shower. Waking from stasis always made his skin itch as though it had been pulled too tight. As soon as he caught sight of himself in the tall mirror, his shoulders tightened. Scars criss-crossed his shoulders, back, and chest, paling his light-brown skin. They had always made Alehan hate his body, but it was the fact that while in stasis someone had cut his hair that made him shudder. Could they not leave him even that much bodily autonomy?

"She's considering sending you back to Carinn."

That got Alehan's full attention, hands pausing at the waistband of his pants. "No. *Fuck* no."

"Careful. She does not like that kind of language."

Alehan stared at Nash in disbelief. "Let me rephrase. No *fucking* way am I returning to that *fucking shithole* of a continent. It screwed me over and literally put me in a boat to die of dehydration once we got tired of drinking our own piss. That is, if the storm the *fucking Gold* created didn't kill us first. Which it *fucking* did. Is that language clearer?"

"I see your slumber has not improved your vocabulary," Nash replied, still with none of the anger Alehan wanted. He could deal with anger, but he had always *hated* when people were patient with him. It reeked of condescension and pity. From someone he had once cared for, it chafed.

"I'm not going."

"That isn't your choice, unfortunately. It is for the Gods to decide. The Gold did say she would do so one day, and that just because she wanted to study you did not mean you could escape the fate of Carinn. You were the one who told me that." Nash shifted in his seat, eyes dropping from Alehan's. "The Gods want you to return to give the Exiles one last chance to repent. You have the opportunity to save all of them, a chance I and many others have fought hard to see materialize."

"Horrible idea. My track record of saving lives is even worse than hers. Only five out of eighteen of her underlings rebelled against her. *Millions* of my family's subjects rebelled, won, and threw us out of Carinn." This was idiocy. Aleh balled his fists and resisted the urge to turn everything in the room to shreds with magic. It might not be much, but this room was his. It held his life—a shitty one, but existence nonetheless. Carinn was a death sentence.

"Be that as it may, you are going if she sends you. And I expect she will, since she wants you to deliver a message."

Curiosity got the best of him, even though Aleh knew he would regret asking before the words left his lips. "What message?"

Nash took a deep breath. "It is still being argued, but our Mother in Gold is furious. She believes that the death of another God means that the Exiles are building a God-killing weapon and preparing to come for her again. The others are trying to quell her paranoia, but I am not certain it will work. If they send you, the message is either the Exiles fulfill the prophecy and promptly unite the continent under the Silvarin . . . or Sarthia considers the exile a failure and wipes the slate clean. You will have to rebuild your family's Empire, Alehan. If you do not, every man, woman, child, and God of Carinn may die."

Alehan had only one thing to say to that. "Serves them right."

Nash stood with effort, leaning on his cane. "On that, we disagree. Whether you like it or not, though, your days in Sitla are coming to an end."

PART TWO

CHAPTER SIX

In Djina's Shoes

GABRIEL

I'll keep this short, since I can't remember the last time I slept. Doubt I'll be able to, as we're all dosing ourselves with serindalla to keep from catching the fever while we help its victims, but I must try. It's horrific, Fay. Every hour is filled with screams, and even with the backing of Tirit Mindel, we just don't have the medicine, supplies, or manpower to help everyone. It breaks my heart. The fires for the dead burn around the clock. I miss you so much I can't stand it, but they need all the hands they can get. They've asked for volunteers to stay an extra week. Please forgive me for saying yes, even though it means I'll miss our first anniversary. I love you.

—From a letter to Fayrian Avilor, from Gabriel Navarl during the Mirielee wasting fever outbreak of 529AF.

**WE ARE WAITING. FIND US.*

The voice woke Gabriel from a fitful doze. He sat up with a start, panting as he looked around the empty room. "Who was that?"

No one answered.

"Hello?"

Nothing.

Rubbing the sleep from his eyes, Gabe swung his legs over the edge of the bed. He tried to stand, but his eyes swam with black spots and his head spun; the agony in his chest and shoulder became all-consuming before magic flooded his body. He hissed in relief, leaning forward to keep his vision from going dark from the heady rush of power mixing with pain.

A loud gurgle emanated from his stomach in response. Fuck, he was hungry. Not just hungry—starving. It was a deep, insistent, gnawing ache that, once noticed, drew his entire attention.

He was about to attempt to stand again when a door slammed in the other room, raised voices audible even through the closed door.

"How did you think admitting to your father's murder in a room full of the most important nobles in Lirin was a good idea?" a deep voice shouted. "Of course I had to vote in favor of a trial. It would have been a dishonor on the entirety of House Drego and the laws of this country if I hadn't."

"Are you trying to say that we're somehow unpatriotic for voting to *protect Elenor?*" another man demanded. "You'll want to watch your tongue, Drego."

"If I hadn't voted for the inquiry, I wouldn't have had the leverage to insist that Elenor not be imprisoned for the next month. Once Tellen voted against, I didn't have a choice. It would have been too close a win and wasting social capital placating Lady Lavarin wasn't worth it."

"Social capital? You really are a cutthroat banker, aren't you?" a woman asked. "Just when I was starting to not hate you, too."

"Lady Enica, whether you hate me or not is entirely immaterial to the politics at hand. In fact, *all* of your feelings matter less than a crushed ant. Or did you fail to notice, in all the bickering amongst the Writted Houses, that Elenor just *told a member of the Council of Tirit Mindel to shut up?*"

What the fuck had happened?

Gabriel carefully pushed himself to his feet, holding on to the nightstand, then the doorframe. Every movement was painful and his head spun, but this sounded important.

He cracked the door open, old instincts not lost, and peeked at the four nobles in the other room. He vaguely recognized the tall, long-haired man and the dark-skinned young woman from the night before. The last man had sandy-blond hair, fair skin, and a stocky build. His arms were crossed and brow furrowed in anger.

Elenor stood several paces away from the other three, eyes staring off into the distance and face as pale as ice. The others seemed too caught up in their argument to notice.

"He was trying to walk all over her. And don't forget he threatened all of Lirin. She was right not to give Tirit Mindel the time of day. He had no business—" the noblewoman began.

She was interrupted by the dark-haired man. "The fact that he has already threatened Lirin in the past makes her action worse, not better, Enica. Do stop to think before running your mouth."

Did Gabe know him? He seemed familiar. As he shifted, the Tirit Mindel medallion around his neck caught the light and jogged a memory. Kallen Drego. He had been in his final year of Core Six when Gabriel had started. They hadn't interacted much, but the Academy—for all its grandeur—was still a small, tight-knit community.

"Running my mouth? Who the fuck do you think you are to talk to me that way, Drego? Just because you went to the Island doesn't make you any better or smarter than the rest of us."

"Actually, it does. Literally. But that doesn't matter. How offended you are doesn't matter, and what we voted won't matter in a month—maybe not a day—if we don't work out how to pacify Tirit Mindel and the nobility, get Elenor off the hook for murder, and either find her mother or have her pass her Water Rite. Then, of course, there is the matter of her impending marriage. Her first act should be to enact a period of mourning for the King starting today. That will delay all non-essential business in the city. If we spin it right—"

"Do you three realize that you've just spent the last two minutes talking about Elenor as though she's not standing right beside you?" Gabriel asked, pushing the door fully open.

Every eye in the room but Elenor's turned to him. The princess's *doena* gave Gabriel an approving nod. The other guard, who Gabe recognized as the redhead from the prison, reached for her sword, eyeing him warily.

Which left the nobles, but their opinions weren't worth shit.

Gabe focused his gaze on Elenor and waited until her dazed eyes met his, then asked, "Are you alright?"

"No," she mouthed.

"Would you like to sit down, *idaa?*" Paul said, placing a hand on Elenor's shoulder. She nodded mutely and accepted being led to a couch. The other noblewoman reached out to touch the back of Elenor's hand, but she twitched away.

The pained expression that crossed the woman's face made

Gabriel feel bad, until he remembered the way they had all just been talking over Elenor while the princess was clearly not well.

Ignoring his own pain and dizziness for the time being—because, really, it was an improvement compared to the last few days in that cell—Gabriel crossed the room towards Elenor. Half-way there, the blond man came over to help support him.

"You must be Gabriel," he said. "I'm Eric Ondai, that's Claire Enica, and Kallen Drego. Thanks . . . for calling us out. We deserved that."

It was a pleasant surprise to hear a noble admit to being a jackass instead of throwing it back in Gabriel's face. Paired with the last name Ondai—the family that had tried to take Mark Lirion down at the start of his reign—Gabe's opinion of the man rose significantly.

When they reached Elenor, Gabriel knelt with a wince. He took her hand and felt for her pulse. He wasn't entirely surprised to find it racing erratically. "Last night you mentioned taking serindalla for pain. How much?"

"Huh?" Glassy eyes focused on Gabriel.

"I saw you take a dose of dacel well past three in the morning that was large enough to knock out someone twice your size, plus evergold. If you're awake right now, it means you either took quite a bit of sap, or drowned yourself in coffee. Which one was it?"

Serindalla sometimes brought painless sleep in very small dosages, but it was usually used as a stimulant. Gabriel had only once taken the powerfully addictive drug derived from the sap of the homonymous plant for any length of time, but a few students on the Island always ended up in the clinic during exams, high off their asses. Since exam season was usually when Gabe had pulled the most hours of work to get enough for the interest payments on his loans, he recognized this look.

"Don't remember," she whispered. Her fingers felt clammy, and Gabriel's frown deepened.

"Both. Mostly coffee," Paul supplied. "She takes serindalla daily, though. One grain of rice's worth at night, two in the morning."

"Daily?" Kallen asked, tone as shocked as Gabriel felt. Besides monstrously expensive, serindalla was, with a few rare exceptions, not usually a drug prescribed long-term. "You walked into that meeting *high?* No wonder—"

"Shut your mouth, Drego, or I'll sew it shut. And trust me, that would be messy. I don't have Elenor's delicate touch with embroidery," Claire warned.

Gabriel ignored the squabble, turning his attention back to the princess. "You need a nap."

"No time. Gotta . . . " She drifted off, staring past Gabriel.

"He's right, El-belle," Claire said, sitting on the couch next to Elenor and taking her other hand. "I doubt you've slept more than four or five hours in the past two days. You need your rest before you make any more big decisions."

Elenor shook her head. "I'm r-regent now. I need to—"

"Regent?" Gabe mouthed to Eric, who nodded.

"As of about ten minutes ago," he mouthed back, holding up that many fingers.

Well, no wonder Elenor was this shaky. Even without the unpleasant and cross-reactive mix of sedatives and stimulants, that would be a lot for anyone to absorb.

"What do you need us to do, Ellie?" Eric asked. "You tell us, and we'll divide it up and get started while you rest. Then in a few hours, we can come back, report, and you can take it from there."

"For once, I agree with Ondai and Enica," Kallen said. He had yet to so much as acknowledge Gabriel's presence. Probably thought Gabriel had overstepped his position by telling nobles off. Well, too bad for him.

Gabe's hand tightened around Elenor's, then he frowned and pressed the tips of his fingers to her forehead. Out of the corner of his eye, he saw Paul's attention sharpen, gaze following Gabriel's hand.

"Fever?" the *doena* asked.

"I think so."

"Shit," Claire hissed, then was on her feet. "Drego, Ondai, out. I'll pass along Elenor's orders."

Eric started protesting, and Kallen opened his mouth too, but Paul's cough and pointed nod to the door with a hand on his sword hilt got them both moving.

"Jozen, you too," Paul said, motioning to the redheaded guard.

"Stay outside and let no one in. Do not speak of what is happening. If anyone comes by to talk to Her Highness, tell them that she is busy and take down their names. I will deal with them later."

As soon as the door closed behind them, Claire hurried into the attached bathroom. She returned a moment later with a small jar. Gabe didn't pay her much mind, more concerned with the way Elenor's eyes were getting wider and more panicked by the second, chest heaving faster and faster. At least until Claire all but shoved him out of the way. It hurt like a bitch to catch his weight on his arm, but the fact that the limb—which he could distinctly remember being broken the day before—held his weight was startling enough to draw his attention.

It snapped back to the two young ladies when Claire opened the jar to reveal a sticky yellow sap and a small dosing spoon.

"El, sweetheart. I need you to focus on me for a minute, alright? I know everything is a mess, but I can't remember what dosage Djina said to give you at the first sign of fever, and I don't know how much you took already today."

Elenor squeezed her eyes shut, then opened them again, focusing on Claire. "I can't go through this again. Not now. I can't . . . "

"I know. Love, I *know.* But if you're running a fever we have to do this now, or it will get worse."

"What will?" Gabriel asked. "Serindalla isn't a cure-all. Too much could be dangerous."

"The alternative is worse," Paul said. "I should have thought to check your temperature this morning, *taale,* when you woke up so groggy. Forgive me." He squeezed Elenor's shoulder and leaned down to kiss the top of her head. "You doubled up your dosage with breakfast, yes?"

Elenor nodded.

"That was hours ago. How much would she have metabolized? The starter dose is important, isn't it?" Claire asked.

"It is. Djina had a formula, but I don't know that she ever wrote it down."

Gabriel was trying to follow, though he kept getting distracted by Elenor's obvious distress. Her eyes were glassy with unshed tears, hand in Claire's visibly trembling. She had saved his life not a day ago. Seeing her suffer was like a knife twisting through his gut.

"I know the formula for therapeutic serindalla titration," Gabe offered, "but I would need to know the reason she needs it. If it's just a fever, willow bark might be better."

Claire looked to Paul, as if asking for permission, but it was Elenor who answered. "I had wasting fever as a child." She tugged her hand out of Claire's and reached up to bite her clenched fist, eyes squeezing shut.

"How did you get wasting fever in Lirin?" Gabriel asked to try to distract her from her obvious panic. He looked around for a pen and paper, finally understanding the urgency, and why Elenor was shaking with fear. He would be too, if in her place.

Gabe had been one of the dozen or so students who had gone to help with an outbreak of wasting fever in southern Miriel during his final year at the Academy. Four weeks of around-the-clock screams and the smell of stale sweat while Gabriel and the rest of his team battled vainly to keep them alive had imprinted themselves on his memory with indelible ink. Those who could afford the life-saving sap usually survived, though they often lost significant motor function and lung capacity. The others died in a rictus of agony as their muscles wasted away, until their heart or their lungs gave out.

That month of never-ending death had been enough to convince Gabriel that he wanted to study medicine. It had also made him certain that no one, not even his worst enemies, deserved wasting fever.

"It doesn't matter how she got it," Claire snapped, pointing to a drawer.

"Maybe not, but I will need to know how long it's been since her last flare." Gabriel yanked open the drawer and found a pile of elegant embossed stationery, along with an ink pen. Each sheet probably cost enough to feed a family for a week. At the moment, though, that didn't matter. It had been years since he had done this math, but it wasn't the sort of thing one forgot. "What do you weigh, and when and exactly how much medication have you taken in the last twelve hours?"

Between Claire, Paul, and Elenor, he got the numbers he needed, but it was hard to concentrate with the aching hunger still gnawing at his stomach. As he attempted to focus, Gabe also became aware that he was still channeling magic. He tried to stop, worried that running low on power might be adding to the dizziness, but the moment he did so, the pain went from distracting to excruciating. He backpedaled fast.

Choosing to figure out that mystery later, Gabe chewed on his bottom lip and ran the numbers a second time, just to be sure. He almost reached for the jar, then realized how hard it would be to accurately measure out the correct dosage when his hands were still painful, shaky, and wrapped in bandages.

"If that's a half-milliliter measure, you'll need six and a half now, and three and one-fourth every six hours until the fever has been gone for at least two days. Then we can wean you back down to a maintenance dose. We'll need patience, too, if the pain starts to make you spasm too badly. Does that sound like the dosage you've had before, Elenor?"

"I think so," she whimpered. "I can't take this again. I can't."

Gabriel felt a pang of sympathy for her, because he knew exactly what came next. The serindalla, in such an astronomical dose, would keep her wide awake until she could either lower her dosage safely, or she became so worn out her body succumbed to a few fitful hours of rest. The drug would make her muscles twitch and shake, which would prevent them from wasting away while the other properties of the serindalla—to strengthen the body's ability to fight disease—worked. Some people chose the fever over the cure, and Gabriel couldn't blame them.

Tears spilled out, rolling down Elenor's cheeks as she kept her eyes squeezed shut. "It's too much right now. I can't."

"You can and you will, *taalida*."

"Not without Djina. Not—"

"Elenor, look at me," Claire said. "Open your eyes and look at me." The princess did. "I know it's a lot. You've got all of Lirin depending on you, your mother is missing, and a whole lot of people are dead. Everything is on fire. Nothing is alright. But guess what? None of that matters. Do you know why?"

Elenor shook her head.

"Because I fucking love you, silly, and I don't care how many noble heads I need to knock together, or how much legwork I have to do if it means you have the time you need to kick this fever's ass again. Flares are never as bad as the original illness, remember? So you're going to take the drugs, and then you're going to tell me what you want me to do, and then you will *lie the damn hell down* and give yourself room to deal with the grief and stress that's eating you alive. You're going to let Paul pamper you. You are going to eat and drink something that isn't sugar and coffee. You are going to *get better,* and we'll worry about the rest afterwards. Seriously, El-belle. If someone else was half as mean and hard on you as you are on yourself, I'd punch them in the face."

Elenor let out a surprised and snotty laugh. She wiped her tears away, then held out her hand for the jar.

Carefully, Claire measured out the correct amount, Gabriel checked it, and Elenor placed it gingerly under her tongue. As she made a face and waited for it to dissolve, Gabriel nudged Claire and held out a hand. "Hey, I don't think we've actually been introduced. I'm Gabriel."

"Claire," she replied, taking it and squeezing tight enough to make his mending bones grind together. Gabriel winced, eyes watering from the pain. "That's for kidnapping my girlfriend and locking her in a wardrobe." Then Claire reached forward and gave him a quick peck on the cheek. "And that's for giving her a reason to get out of bed after Djina died. I owe you one." She turned back to Elenor. "Now then. Bed, food, water. You too, Gabriel. If you're stepping into Djina's rather big shoes as the person with the knowledge to keep my Elenor alive, it would be best if you stop looking like you're on death's door yourself."

CHAPTER SEVEN
Coin Toss
DAEMON

The Gold Dragon appeared in the sky above the desert today. How much longer do we have, Kennotoza? Are we out of time? I hate to even postulate it, but could Xirra be right when she says that another war is inevitable? Does Zorbennen have a Silvarin candidate? Are we all about to die?

—From a message to Kennotoza the White Dragon,
from Gullien the Green Dragon.

DAEMON WOKE UP AROUND NOON to his one remaining bracelet buzzing. Rubbing the sleep from his eyes, he heaved himself out of bed and over to the table where his patron's message was waiting for him.

"The war has begun. It is time that you know who our true enemy is, and the battleground that we must fight on. Meet me in the shrine below my lair at dawn in two days. Find out who killed the Red before then. We will need every weapon at our disposal for the coming struggle."

Daemon pinched the bridge of his nose and turned away from the table. "Sure, that's easy. Just go to the desert and find out who killed a God. Piece of cake, Xirra. Fuck you."

Continuing to grumble, he got dressed the mundane way—even though doing so in the Plane would have been faster—and made a pot of coffee. It was only then that he noticed that the ring which tracked Elenor's pulse was racing.

"Shit."

All annoyance at the strange draw the princess had on him forgotten, Daemon tried to reach the Plane. Sleep broke his connection to it, but most days it only took a minute or two of concentration to re-establish. He tried to relax and clear his mind, but every time another hurried heartbeat pulsed against his finger, that calm burned away.

When ten minutes had passed and the source of magic still eluded him, Daemon snarled, grabbed his raincoat, and left on foot. Located in the Old City, his apartment was on a narrow street of towering townhouses only a few blocks from the palace on one side and the Hardor branch of the Tirit Mindel University on the other. Many of the buildings had been split into rental apartments for the less well-to-do nobility that still wanted a foothold in the heart of power and politics. Technically, the whole townhouse still belonged to House Drego, but Daemon had buried it so deep in his birth family's accounts that no one would find it. For Daemon, it was now the only home he had left.

It only took him fifteen minutes to walk to the Palace through the neatly-cobbled streets. That was more than enough time to clear some of the panic from his head and start thinking clearly.

Turning down a deserted alley, Daemon removed the distracting ring from his finger and tried again to reach the Plane. As soon as the connection formed, he opened a doorway and stepped through. Dae had one hand up, ready to open a window into Elenor's room when the reality of what he was doing stopped him. "Damn it."

Kennotoza had made her line clear. Daemon had every intention of crushing that line and the Goddess who had drawn it, but he didn't know how yet. Ayre's inhabitants had all been evacuated, scattered around the continent where Kennotoza could not get to them in one swoop, but Daemon had no doubt she would find a way if he pissed her off enough.

So instead of opening a doorway into Elenor's bedroom, he peeked into the room where Gabriel had been recovering. No one was there. Daemon expanded the door in the air and stepped through, feeling for the sources of copper in the next room over. Selecting one, he opened a reverse-sending connection. Voices came over it at once, the sound waves transported from the copper to the air near Daemon's ear.

" . . . priorities must be stopping the Euriehas from causing more trouble, taking charge of the search for my mother, and getting ready for this trial."

"What about the press? You'll want to control how the story breaks," Claire Enica said.

"Add that to Eric's list. If the Ondai Tribune runs with our version first, we can distribute it widely. I know Father had control of the city papers, so we'll have to find out who he was working with and take that over if we can. Send Tomaz to figure that out. They won't talk to an Ondai. Oh, and if he can't work out how to steer the story the way we want, we'll need a bigger one," Elenor said. Her words were oddly rushed, spilling end over end with very little pause for breath. Daemon frowned in concern, then cautiously opened a small planar window in the darkened corner of Elenor's room.

She was pacing back and forth, dressed in the same ratty yellow robe she had been in the night before, but with her hair still done up for court. Her cheeks were unnaturally flushed, and the hand not bound by a sling was tapping against her thigh as she paced.

"If you try to distract them, they'll just spin that to make it look like you're covering up that you killed him," Gabriel said, from where he sat on one of the couches by the fire. He looked much more awake and aware than the previous night. There were several empty plates stacked up on a tray on the coffee table. Good. With enough fuel, Gabriel's magic should take care of his injuries within a few days. After that . . . Well, Daemon would worry about it then.

"I don't know if we can stop that narrative. Elenor did admit to murdering him in front of the whole court," the princess's *doena* said in a calm tone, though Daemon noticed his eyes never left his ward, worry written in the deep creases of his brow.

"Blame it on me," Gabriel offered.

Elenor stopped her pacing. "What?"

The young rifter shrugged. "I'm a well-known rebel and an escaped prisoner. You already spun the break-out to look like the rebellion was involved. So blame me. It's like you said: we don't know if you killed him, or if I did, or if Daemon did. Blaming him isn't an option as people will just assume you made him up, but I'm right here."

"He has a point, El-belle," Claire said. She was sitting at a small writing desk, a pad of paper in her lap. "I don't know that you'll be able to avoid *all* the blame, but spinning it to look like you were working with the Rebellion to avenge your brother is a solid angle."

"I don't know how wise that is," Paul interjected. "Confirming that you were allied with a Tirit Mindel graduate and rifter may anger your father's allies further, *taalida*."

"But give hope to those who have been oppressed by his anti-rifting laws if you don't have me slapped back in irons," Gabriel countered. "You have the chance to fix what he broke, Elenor. You said yourself that you want to start making Lirin better."

"I don't know that confirming that a rifter killed our King will ingratiate the public to the idea of rescinding anti-rifting laws," Paul pointed out.

"But it would shift the attention off Elenor, which is the point," Claire reminded them. "What do you want to do, love?"

The princess hesitated, then in the same rushed tone as before said, "Get Tomaz to draft an article about Wilam, announcing that his name is no longer taboo. I told the truth in the throne room this morning, but I have the feeling it's going to get twisted up very fast if we don't get it out ourselves. So we will. We tell the papers everything. About Wil, the Rebellion, the Tellens, Djina, what he was doing to prisoners, how he was forgoing due process, all of it. End it on what happened last night, including his threats to take my power away through blackmail and threatening members of the nobility and the country at large. We tell the public that it's unclear who killed him, but we don't make that the focus of the article. Instead we imply that he was blackmailing Mother the same way as he tried to do with me, and that this is all a Miri set-up. We can't know that for sure, but I'm willing to bet on it. If the city papers won't print it, the Ondai Tribune will. Tell Eric I will cover the cost of this printing and to make the paper free. I want the truth in as many hands as I can put before the lies get there."

Claire scribbled that down, then looked up at Elenor. "Good. Better this way. Do you want to include what Eurieha did and his Miri connections?"

"What he did, yes, but the connection to my aunt, not yet. I need to talk to some people before I do that. Bad enough I told the nobles. This could end in war with Miriel if we tread wrong, and as much as I want to have nothing to do with them, we can't afford that. I'll need to talk to Tirit Mindel, so make me an appointment with Robin Tirition for tomorrow."

"You're piling too much on your plate, *taale*. You need to rest if you don't want this flare to turn into another full bout of the fever. I won't allow you to work yourself to death," Paul chided, crossing his arms.

Daemon, who had been caught up in the politics despite himself, froze. In a rush, Elenor's elevated pitch, her flushed cheeks, and the way she couldn't seem to hold still connected.

He swore under his breath, then closed the small window so he could curse a little louder. Almost, he burst in. If she was suffering from a flare of wasting fever, she needed to be in a hospital, not directing a country. That would be meddling with her life, though. Kennotoza had said that even interfering to save her wouldn't be tolerated.

But he couldn't do *nothing*.

Taking a calming breath, Daemon pulled on a small thread of magic to send his words to the air right next to Gabriel's ear. "Don't act startled. Excuse yourself and come back into your bedroom. We need to talk."

"Gabriel? Are you alright?" Elenor asked, from the other room. Daemon resisted the urge to smack himself in the forehead.

"Ah, yeah. Fine. Just . . . need to take another dose of pain meds. Be right back," the fool boy said, with exactly zero ability to bluff. Great—a Silvarin who couldn't lie. Just great.

A moment later, Gabe slipped into the room, closing the door behind him. Daemon put up a sound barrier around them, just in case.

"How did you get here?" the young man asked.

Daemon leaned against one of the posts holding up the bed

canopy. "Like I get everywhere: none of your business."

Gabriel scowled, but it vanished almost as soon as it had appeared. The young man studied Daemon, then said, "I saw what you did last night. You saved her. And then you saved me. I remember feeling like I would . . . "

"Explode outward in an uncontrollable burst of magic?" Daemon ventured, crossing his arms.

Gabriel reached up to rub the back of his neck with fingers that were no longer bandaged. His magic was working even faster than Daemon expected. How powerful *was* this boy?

"Yeah. Elenor said you helped patch us both up, too. I still don't know why, or how you're involved with her, but . . . thank you."

Why did he have to look so much like Alehan? The same light-brown skin and green eyes, though Gabriel's hair was straight where Alehan's had been a riot of curls, and features closer to those of the Mondaer than the Jia.

Those words of thanks slashed deep. Dae had to take a steadying breath just to reply, "We can talk about why later. Right now, tell me how she's doing. She sounds like she's on a high serindalla dosage. Do you know how much?"

"I used the standard equation, adjusted for her weight and magical status."

"Show me your math," Daemon ordered.

Without argument, Gabriel pulled a piece of paper from his pocket and presented it to Daemon. He checked the numbers over, nodded, and folded it back up.

"Is that right?"

"Yes. I am begrudgingly impressed, which is a first when it comes to you. Are you monitoring her temperature?"

"Hourly," Gabriel replied, a little terser than before. "Is there anything else we should be doing?"

"I'll be back with something later today that will help. Make sure she rests. Now you. How are you?" Daemon looked the young man up and down, noting the way he stood and which bandages were still there. "How are your magic reserves?"

Gabriel's eyes narrowed. At once, the prickle of ambient magic increased tenfold in the air around them. Daemon's breath caught. He took a step back before he'd consciously decided to.

"What do you know about my magic?" the young man asked, tone icy where it had been calm seconds before.

He was *still* oversaturated. That shouldn't have been possible with how much physical improvement had already taken place. Then again, he *hadn't* exploded Hardor last night, which meant it was plausible that the dent to his reserves wasn't enough to pull him back from the edge.

"Easy, Gabriel." Daemon held out his hands in a placating gesture. "Take a breath. I can answer your questions, but you need to calm down first or you'll be a danger to everyone in this palace." That did nothing, so working on a hunch, Daemon added, "a danger to Elenor."

Gabriel's whole posture changed. He stumbled a half-step back, looking down at his hands which were pulsing with raw magical power—invisible, but bright to Daemon's senses. "W-what's happening to me?"

"You're coming into your adult magical potential for the first time."

Gabe shook his head. "No. That's not how magic works. It doesn't grow. Not like this. Not past adolescence."

Daemon did *not* want to be the one who told him about Fayrian Avilor's Gift. That was Robin's mess. So instead, he stepped forward with care until he stood right in front of Gabriel. "There is a lot your education hasn't taught you about magic. I understand why you're scared. You've been through a terrible ordeal and this isn't an enemy you can fight. I can help you understand your power, but first we need to get it under control. Can you tell me how you're feeling? Strangely energetic for how injured you are? Having a hard time focusing on more than one thing at once? Really want to cuddle Elenor?"

That last one seemed to catch Gabe's attention. He squinted at Daemon, lips pursed.

"I'll take that as a yes," Dae said. The boy had fixated on her last night too, when his magic was slipping out of his control. Something about Elenor drew people in, and it seemed to be worse during oversaturation. If Gabriel felt it as well, it gave weight to Daemon's theory that she had to be tied to magic. "Right now, you're oversaturated. It's making all your emotions much more intense. I can show you how to fix that, but you'll have to trust me."

Gabe's hands balled into fists. "I *don't* trust you."

"And that makes you smart, but also very stupid. You know I can take your magic by force if I wanted to. I did it before, but I'd rather teach you how to take care of this yourself."

"Why? Why are you helping me? Who *are* you?"

Before Daemon could answer, the door behind Gabriel was yanked open. Paul Marek stood on the other side, one hand on the hilt of his sword.

Damn it. He must have felt the ripples in the ambient magic too.

"You again," he growled.

"Shit."

"Daemon?" Elenor asked, appearing over Paul's shoulder.

Damn it!

"I have to go. Marek, teach Gabriel how to vent power into gold right now. He's still oversaturated."

Elenor was already ducking under Paul's outstretched arm. Every part of Daemon wanted to stay, but he forced his feet to carry him backward. A sweeping hand gesture opened a doorway in the air.

"Wait—" Elenor began, her voice cutting off as Daemon snapped the portal closed behind him.

It took Daemon a full twenty minutes of pacing to clear his head and stop wanting to run back to the Palace. It wasn't even just Elenor who made him itch to return. The lure of Gabriel's magic was equally strong. Ideas for circuits raced through his mind. There were projects he had always wanted to try, but that were impossible without a sufficiently strong rifter.

Robin had been right. Daemon *wanted* to train the boy. It was a challenge with the potential for near-infinite reward. The problem was Elenor. In future, Dae would have to bring Gabriel to him, not the other way around, or there was no way he could ignore the desire to see her.

Oh, and the other little problem: the Goddess he served still expected Daemon to kill Gabriel. Well, unless the death of the Red had changed things. Daemon certainly hoped it had.

As he continued fretting, Daemon worked. By the time his mind had stilled enough to get on with his day, a small box lay on the table. Inside was a pretty white and yellow knitted shawl in an evergold pattern. Daemon had seen something like it before, so it had been easy enough to walk into the Plane and will it into existence. The harder part was the small circuit that clung to the underside. Thin copper wire ran along many of the strands of yarn, all coalescing on a strip of gold and small cerulean chip.

On top of the shawl was a letter addressed to Paul Marek.

I know we have not yet been formally introduced, and I am certain you do not trust me, but I have your ward's best interests at heart. This circuit will suck in heat excess to normal body temperature, helping control her fever. Make sure to empty the gold at least once a day, or when the device stops working.

Please tell Gabriel that I will be back soon to speak with him and help him with his magic. Until then, I have enclosed several gold bars along with the shawl. Have him fill them for you; it should balance out his power temporarily. Keep them with my compliments. I am certain you will use them in defense of Elenor.

-Daemon

The *doena* probably didn't like or trust him, but he seemed the most sensible of that lot. Given what Daemon had seen on the night when all this had started and Paul had torn through the Rebellion's headquarters singlehandedly in pursuit of his ward, he also had the magical know-how to be useful. Daemon certainly wasn't about to trust an oversaturated rifter or the girl who had tried to brain him with a rock.

With a sigh, Dae placed a lid on the box and opened a window to place it on Gabriel's bed. He didn't try to make contact this time. They would find it eventually. He couldn't meddle in Elenor's life again until he had made a few arrangements. Besides, before he went gallivanting off to find the person who had killed Fulsixia, he had to make sure that his own people were safe.

The door he opened was not to Ayre. The city had been deserted, a hollow husk that hurt to look at. Instead, he walked into another house in Hardor, where Obri, Tsiihsi, and a handful of other Ayre Island residents gathered around tables full of circuits.

"Hey, Daemon," Obri said, waving but not looking up from his work.

"How's it going? Is everyone settling in?" Daemon walked over to the center table, where a giant circuit was spread out. It was shaped like a map of Carinn, small pinpricks of light in clusters around it.

"Well, considering we just uprooted about five thousand people over the course of a couple days, no. But we're managing." Obri finished what he was doing and walked over to Daemon, patting him on the shoulder in greeting. He pointed to the cluster of lights inside Hardor. "We're working on integrating as many people into Hardor as we can since it's a neutral zone."

"For now," Daemon cautioned. "The Accords will break eventually."

"Yes, but Tsiihsi had an idea about how to stay safe. Hear her out. It's kind of brilliant."

Daemon turned to the young Eldel woman, who was sitting at a desk with a pile of talismans. Daemon recognized them at once. He gave one to every resident of Ayre once they'd proved themselves trustworthy enough to return to the outside world and not spill his secrets. Tsiihsi had pried one open, and was studying the circuitry inside.

"This is the locator beacon, right?" she asked Daemon.

He leaned against the desk, holding out his hand. "Yes. It tracks your location on the map. When you need help you twist and press the button at the center; it breaks this copper wire, which transmits a signal to the paired cerulean circuit. Then backup shows up and takes care of the problem."

Tsiihsi frowned. "Assuming they can get there. That was fine when you spent most of your time on Ayre, but we rely on your ability to make portals. I don't suppose you could teach someone else how to do th—"

"No," Daemon interrupted, tone brooking no argument.

"I thought not. Well, I don't have a solution for how to keep us connected while you're not around, but I do think I have an idea for protecting us from the White Dragon. You explained how her predictions work. She needs to track our movements to find us. Spreading out helps, but I think randomness will help even more."

"Explain," Daemon said, crossing his arms.

Tsiihsi turned her chair to better face him. "Well, assuming there is a way to add something into these talismans to warn us if we have a Dragon coming our way, I think we can become invisible to her. It's quite simple." She pulled a coin from her pocket and flipped it. Catching it in mid-air, Tsiihsi held out her hand. "Heads or tails. It's random. I *think* that all we would have to do to avoid her is to base all our movements on chance. You give us the signal, and we all start walking. At every turn, we flip a coin. I know she's a God and all, but there are a *lot* of us, and that becomes millions of variables quite fast. We can do the same when and if you figure out how to kill her. If she doesn't know where or when the blow will come from, she may not be able to stop it."

Daemon reached out to take the coin, and gave it an experimental flip. A smile twitched at the corners of his lips, then bloomed into a full-blown grin. He closed his fingers around the coin. "I like it. It's ballsy and clever. Hold down the fort while I go test it out. Time to steal something from the White Dragon."

"Wait, what?" Obri cried, but Daemon already had a portal open to the icy glaciers outside Kennotoza's lair. The frigid wind whipped against the exposed skin of his face and neck. His jacket billowed around him, snow catching in the dark fabric to form swirling dervishes. Dae squinted against the gale.

No reason to be stupid. This exercise was about leaving his actions to chance, but pure randomness would get him eaten. He would just let the coin decide between equally good options.

Before him stood a pair of massive double doors made of thick, intricately carved ice. Shimmering blue eyes watched him from all sides, the furry coats of the white mock dragons indistinguishable from the snow.

Heads: open a door to the Plane in the shadows to the inner right of the door. Tails: inner left.

Daemon flipped the coin and opened his doorway to the left. He held his breath as he stepped through, careful to put his foot down slowly, lest the crunch of snow echo.

The entry hall was deserted. Colored threads and ribbons swirled in mesmerizing striations along every surface, frozen between layers of crystalline ice. Each one, Daemon knew, represented a possible future of a single unlucky soul. The White could not track every person who was born or died, so it was bad luck indeed to be singled out.

He looked down at the coin.

Heads: find out where Kennotoza is working. Tails: steal the first valuable thing you find.

Heads.

Rolling his neck to ease his tension, Daemon began to walk. Light suffused the gargantuan halls from deep within the ice. He passed out of the entryway and into the huge cavern where he and the White had sat down for tea. She wasn't there.

Even so, Daemon tried his best to be noiseless as he crossed the wide open space, big enough for a dragon in its natural form to slumber. He could still feel draconic eyes on him. In the shadows, the swoosh and slither of the mocks that guarded Kennotoza's lair mirrored Dae's every movement.

White mocks were sweet creatures for the most part, but they were guard animals equal to none. If something was theirs to protect, not so much as a fly could get by them.

Whatever he stole to prove Tsiihsi's theory, he would have to be quick and have a portal ready or Daemon might well lose a limb or two in this impulsive venture, even if Kennotoza never noticed him.

There were four hallways off of this chamber. Two flips of the coin sent him down the third. At every branch, Daemon flipped the coin and proceeded, the mocks following but not attacking . . . yet.

No sign of the Goddess. On and on Daemon went, deep into her lair until a lucky turn brought him to the edge of the spherical room where Kennotoza had shown him the end of all futures.

There she was.

Kennotoza the Bode stood on the walkway, staring at a golden starburst caught in ice. In her hand she held dozens of dull, burnt-looking threads that might once have been yellow.

She was muttering to herself, though Daemon was too far away to catch more than the occasional words.

"Damn you Moe. You've left me no other choice . . . But how many must die besides her . . . ? At least fifteen of the eighteen before the end, except . . . Alehan will complicate everything, but there's no avoiding that now. He must return soon or they'll never be ready in time. He is the catalyst, but he must be contained. It will have to be the girl. She's the only one close enough to Lilian. The cost to be ready in time, though . . . "

Daemon's whole body stiffened, his breath caught in his throat. What had she just said? *Alehan?*

Heads: shake some answers out of her. Tails: back away before getting eaten, and find out after *panicking.*

Tails.

Inch by inch, chest aching with confusion, Daemon backed away, until he could turn a corner and press himself against the frigid wall.

What had she meant, *"He must return soon?"*

Alehan was dead; Daemon had seen him drown five centuries ago. Could the White mean a different Alehan? Or some kind of symbolic return of the Silvarin? But then why name Alehan and not Alexander?

A low growl from one of the mocks drew his attention from his burning questions.

He had to get out of here. First, though, he had to finish his task. Kennotoza was a dragon like any other. She didn't like what was hers being stolen. If she wasn't there, ready to stop him from taking something dear to her, then this method worked.

He wouldn't bet the safety of his people on it, if it did not.

Going back the way he had come was not an option with his

mock-shaped, growling shadows. A right turn brought Daemon into a stretch of winding tunnels where all the threads were ashen and dim. He couldn't be sure, but Dae thought these might have been bright last time, which meant that futures were still dying. Whatever Kennotoza was plotting, it wasn't working.

More uneasy with every step, Daemon hurried onward. The hallways were, for the most part, bare. The few rugs and lanterns scattered around seemed more utilitarian than valuable.

Where was Kennotoza's wealth? Xirra collected powerful people, Gullien talent and beauty, Zorbennen knowledge, and Fulsixia . . . whatever it was that she had cared about. Strays, maybe?

He had always assumed that Kennotoza, too, would have something of worth hidden here—though probably not people, given the cold. But as the tunnels went on and on into the glaciers, Daemon began to have doubts.

He was about ready to call it quits when he came to a door. The coin told him to open it, but the moment he reached for the handle, a growl tore through the silence.

One of the mocks slunk out of the shadows. Large for a white, the mock dragon had short, powerful legs and a long, sinuous body covered in thick white fur. A mane of the same soft hair framed its feline face, and wide wings spread out to either side of the beast, filling the corridor.

It might have been cute, if not for the bared teeth and low, rumbling growl of a mock with something to protect.

Daemon tossed his coin. *Heads: leave empty handed before getting eaten. Tails: open the door, grab the first thing I see, and bolt.*

The coin fell and he caught it, knees bent and ready to spring into action.

He pulled his hand away, the coin glistening in the refracted light of the ice.

Tails.

Both Daemon and the mock moved at the same time. The dragon lunged. Dae threw open the door with a huge burst of magic and launched himself inside. Blindly, he flung open a planar doorway with one hand and reached out with the other.

Anything would do at this point, even if it was only a teapot.

His fingers connected to something small and fluffy. Not stopping to look, he tightened his grip and yanked. The momentum sent him and his prize flying through the doorway onto the sand of Ayre Island. The portal winked out of existence behind him.

Three long, stiff whiskers floated to the sand, shorn from the muzzle of the mock dragon who had been half a second too slow.

For a while, Daemon lay in the sand, his heart trying to pound out of his chest. Then he jumped, shrieking as the soft thing he held in his hand started to buck and screech. He let go out of reflex. The moment he did, a mouthful of tiny sharp teeth dug into his hand.

"Ow!" Daemon screamed.

The small, fluffy, pure white and very angry baby mock bit down harder.

"Get your teeth out of my hand, you little—OW. Shit!"

He tried to shake it off, but the minuscule dragon locked its jaw and refused to let go. Shock abating and sense returning, Daemon wedged the thumb of his other hand behind the creature's molars and leveraged its mouth open.

That got a hiss and thrash, but his hand was free. Before the mock could bite again, Daemon picked it up by the scruff of its neck, staining the white fur red. "Fierce little beast, aren't you?"

The baby continued to wriggle and snap, but it—no, she—lacked the angle to bite or scratch him anymore.

Out of all the treasure to steal from the White, he had not expected one of her house-pets. What was he supposed to do with another baby mock? Ayre was already having trouble housing the hundreds it had, and the evacuations had only made it worse.

Dae certainly didn't need or want a guard-mock who didn't like the heat and who still looked ready to bite his hand off. For a second, he considered returning her, but if Kennotoza got a whiff of his blood on her . . . Too risky. A piece of treasure he could have buried and forgotten, but even Daemon wasn't heartless enough to harm a creature this young.

While he considered her fate, the mockling grew distracted. Her long, fuzzy tail swept through the sand with a swish. Then again. The third time, she sent a shower of sand straight into Daemon's face. Spluttering, he held the creature further away. "You are trouble."

She looked up at him with wide, calculating blue-gray eyes. Daemon sighed, shaking his head and gingerly swapping which hand held her. "And you know it, too. Don't you? Don't think I'm going to trust you near my extremities again."

He got to his feet, shaking out the bleeding and smarting hand the mockling had mauled. Another glare in her direction faded as he looked down at the cat-sized dragon. "Damn, you're cute. Dangerous for my health and too pretty for your own good." Dae let out a long sigh and shook his head. "Yeah, I know exactly where to take you."

CHAPTER EIGHT
Aina Brisbhan
NORTH

You are our heart of beating gold, the bridge between the earth and sky. You are our compass, pointing home, our end and our beginning. Aina Brisbhan, mother of stone and wind, shelter us in your shadow. Water us from your springs. Let us fill your halls with our voices raised in song. You are ours, and we are yours, from the first breath to the last.

—From the writings of an unnamed daradeio, found tucked into a crevice deep within Aina Brisbhan.

NOT TWELVE HOURS after the great Gold Dragon had appeared in the sky, Quindo came to fetch North. He was sitting next to Kaedy, whose vacant eyes had been so full of life and love just the night before. She sat huddled in blankets, her son—blessedly unbroken—asleep in her lap. He was too young to understand why his mother didn't respond to his requests to play, but intuitive enough to know that the best place he could be was in her arms.

"You'll get through this," North said for the thousandth time. "It hurts now, but it will get better."

She did not answer. He knew Kaedy could hear him, because she responded to simple commands. At no point had she spoken, though. That was, honestly, one of the better reactions. As of yet, she had not tried to walk off a rooftop. Her heart had not stopped beating on its own.

On her other side, one of her grandmothers, Phoebi—Gifted, like so many in this desert—sat gently petting Kaedy's hair. She looked up as the Archivist entered the small room. Quindo had dark circles under his eyes, sweat staining his shirt, and the imprint of flying goggles on his cheeks. He must have returned from taking

Fedrik Tellen to the Sandhewn City, wherever that was.

"My love," Phoebi said, extending a tremulous hand to him. Quindo took it and brought her knuckles to his lips. "Is it time?"

He nodded. "All the broken, all the *daradeio,* and all the Gifted. For once, Moe isn't gallivanting off before the work is done. He is taking us to the hospital in Aina Brisbhan, and we can make our way to the Mother Rock from there. Most have already gone."

He crouched down to Kaedy's level. "Did you hear that, my darling? You will be at the Stone soon. It will shelter you and Daari from this storm, daughter of my heart."

She seemed to look right through him.

North could almost see the blow land on Quindo's soul, and felt sorry for him. Most of his family were rifters. Of those, all but Daari were broken or dead.

Carefully, the old Archivist extracted Daari from his mother's loose grasp, hoisting the two-year-old up to his hip. "North, would you help with Kaedy? I cannot carry them both."

"Of course." North's eyes clouded with tears for the thousandth time as he hooked his arms under Kaedy's knees and behind her back, then got to his feet. She did not resist, and while her eyes were open and chest rose and fell, she was dead weight in his arms. "Where to?"

"The courtyard. We will be transported to the hospital directly. We are the last . . . except for the dead."

"What about my mock?" North asked, nodding to Bard who was asleep in a corner of the room, curled into a tight ball.

"He may come too."

A whistle had the young mock on his feet. He trotted behind North as they exited the house.

In the darkened courtyard where Akaaron had woven his tapestries, row after row of bodies covered in red cloth were laid out. At the center, Moe stood, still in his pink suit, though no longer laughing.

His gaze fell to Kaedy, and he let out a long sigh. "I liked her. She was full of spirit."

"She will be again," North countered.

Moe gave him a pitying stare, shaking his head. "Believe that if it brings you comfort, but unless she finds a handy Incarnate lying around, there's an 83% chance that she'll be dead within six months. Ready?"

Moe held out a hand to Phoebi, who took it, and put her other one on Quindo's arm. The Archivist grasped North's shoulder, and Moe touched his elbow to complete the circle.

"Call your dragon; he must be touching one of us," Moe directed. At the word 'dragon', Bard's attention fixed on Moe. He bounded over to rub himself against Moe's legs with a happy chirp. The gangly man looked down, shrugged, and said, "That'll work."

North was about to ask what they were doing when a loud *pop* rang in his ears, and the whole world shifted. One second they were standing in the Deil estate, the next they were in the busy atrium of a hospital.

North stumbled, arms tightening around Kaedy so as not to drop her, a strange, salty taste filling his mouth.

Moe steadied him, then let go. He stepped away, giving a wide-eyed and alarmed-looking Bard a pat on the head. "Aren't you the brave little fellow? Alright, clear the area. I'll be back with the dead."

Pop!

He was gone. North looked down, eyebrows scrunching together at the ring of salt the strange man had left behind, which Bard was sniffing.

"I know it seems impossible to move from one place to another so fast—" Quindo began, misinterpreting North's confusion.

"It's not that. He just doesn't do it the same way I've seen before."

Before the Archivist could respond, a voice North recognized broke through the hum of the hospital atrium around them.

"Quindo!" It was Leo. The young man looked as weary as North felt, though it was the dust of travel, not the blood of the dead, that covered the *daradeio* from head to toe. "I just got here. They said a rifter exploded at the estate. Where's Vea? Is that Kaedy? What *happened?*"

He rushed over, though with the wincing gait of someone very saddle-sore. Akaaron had sent him ahead to the Mother Rock. North wasn't entirely sure how far that was from the Deil estate, but he must have been far enough to avoid the burst of magical energy that had broken so many.

Thank the Gods for that.

"Your *doena's* capacity was broken along with that of most of the rifters at my estate, but she is among those coping well with it. She is sleeping now, but I promise I'll send word to you the moment she wakes," Quindo reassured, though he sounded exhausted. "Leo, would you take North to the Mother Rock? We need to convene a meeting with Suela. Find her and send word back to the hub rifter here with the time and place. North, do not speak of what happened with anyone but Leo and Suela. I must tend to my family, but will join you as soon as I can. I'll let Vea know you made it and are fine, Leo."

A team of people hurried over, holding a stretcher. They set it down and North laid Kaedy on it.

"Where's Daari?" she asked through cracked lips, the first words she had spoken all day. "Where's my son?"

"He's right here, Kaedy. He's alright," North said, squeezing her hand. He looked up to Quindo and Phoebi, pointing to the little boy. "See, he's right there. Your family is here with you."

Behind him, North heard Leo let out a shaking sob. The stretcher was lifted, and Quindo placed a hand on North's shoulder. "Thank you for your help and your compassion. Try to get some rest."

As they walked away following the stretcher, North stood. Leo came over to him, and offered him a hug when the tears he had been holding back all day finally spilled over. North didn't try to hold back. If this wasn't reason enough to cry, nothing was. Leo pressed his face into North's hair and rubbed his back, the other man's shoulders shaking too.

Bard sidled over and nuzzled his head against his owner's leg, trilling low in his throat. He was such a good dragon; he might not understand what had North so upset, but he knew when to offer comfort.

Leo stood silently as he held North, simply offering a handkerchief when his unabashed tears turned to sniffles.

"Thank you."

"Let's get out of here. You look like you could use some air, and maybe tea," Leo suggested. One arm still around North's shoulders, he led him towards the hospital doors. Behind them, a loud *pop* sounded, but North did not have the heart to look back and see Moe return with the dead.

The exterior of the Mondaer hospital would have put a Tirit Mindel temple to shame. Carved and tiled in intricate geometric patterns and bright colors, it shone even in the dim moonlight. At another time, North might have marveled at it and the city beyond, but not this night.

Leo led him down a side street and into a cozy tea shop, open late.

"Weren't we supposed to go find Suela?" North asked, as the *daradeio* tugged him down to sit on cushions on the floor by a low table. If the owners of the shop had any issue with the small black dragon at North's heels, they did not say so. Fortunately, Bard had gotten most of his energy out earlier in the day and seemed quite content to curl back up to sleep the moment North sat down, instead of wreaking havoc.

"That can wait for one cup of tea. You need tea after tears. It's the rules."

"Whose rules?" North asked, wiping his eyes and blowing his nose.

"Tavea's. My *doena* is very wise, and deals with a lot of distressed people who just crossed the Wall. Tea almost always helps." Leo held up two fingers to the shop's attendant. A moment later, beautiful glass cups of steaming mint tea were placed on the table.

The desert's chill night air had cooled North down enough that wrapping his fingers around the cup felt good. The tea was sweet and strong. As they drank in silence, North's breathing steadied out and his cheeks dried.

Only then did Leo ask, "What happened?"

"We shouldn't speak of it here." North didn't want to talk of it at all, but definitely not in a busy tea shop. How would this city react to the news their Goddess was dead? "How far are we from the Deil estate?"

"About two week's travel on land, four to five days by air. Three and a half if you're me," Leo replied, smiling. It wasn't as bright and exuberant as the last time North had seen him, but it was still nice. North hadn't spotted a smile all day.

They finished their tea and Leo paid. Back out in the

street with Bard dragging his feet behind them and yawning, the *daradeio* led North around the hospital. They arrived at a large yard, where dozens of red mock dragons and a smattering of blues and blacks were settled in for the night in magically warmed sand wallows.

"We could walk to the Mother Rock, but trust me when I tell you that you *don't* want to have to take the stairs up to Suela's office. During the day we have lifts, but at night it's either mocks or legs. Let me see about borrowing a dragon. I don't think my Aisha is moving for a year." Leo nudged his deep crimson mock dragon as they passed her. Aisha didn't so much as alter the timber of her snores.

Fifteen minutes later, a youthful male mock dragon had been saddled with a double-seater, and North and Leo were strapped in. Bard was staring at North with deep betrayal, but flapped up to follow when Leo signaled their dragon into the air.

By the time they had cleared the rooftops, North understood why it had only taken Leo three and a half days to make it here. Obri and Tsiihsi flew like sane people. Kaedy, when North had gone up with her, loved doing loops and aerial maneuvers, but in a sedate, playful way. Leo flew like the earth and the sky were his playthings and the air his lover. Their legs were strapped into the saddle, but where most took that as an added precaution, Leo seemed to take it as leave to be upside-down and sideways as often as possible.

They rose into the sky at a speed that made North dizzy. No sooner had they reached the open air, though, than Leo swept them back down, the dragon's wings brushing the rooftops before catching a spiraling updraft.

"I think I'm going to be sick." North shouted, over the roar of the wind.

"No, you won't. That's why I had you drink mint tea," Leo shouted back, voice nearly lost in the roaring in North's ears. Still, North's words seemed to garner some amount of pity, because they leveled out a moment later in a steady upward climb towards the huge pillar of stone that was the center of the expansive city.

"Is that the Mother Rock?" North asked, not having to yell quite as loudly since they weren't racing forward anymore.

"Do you see any other giant rocks around here?"

North could hear the raised eyebrows in Leo's tone. To be fair, it had been a stupid question. Unlike other rocky areas they had passed on the trip from the border of the desert, the area around Aina Brisbhan was flat for miles, turning to rolling dunes at the horizon. The center of the city was entirely taken up by the pillar of stone that rose unnaturally out of a large lake of open water.

The lake shone indigo blue in the moonlight, and the city's white-washed houses were bursting with greenery in defiance of the desert beyond. It was simply stunning, so much so that despite North's desire to have both feet on the ground and never leave it again, he let out a sigh of regret when they reached the apex of their ascent and began to dive towards the top of the Mother Rock. As the angle of their descent steepened, North squeezed his eyes shut and clung to Leo with all his might, the other man's joyous laugh mixing with the wind whipping through his hair and the screech of pure panic that was ripped from North's lungs.

They landed with less of a thud than he had expected. The young dragon was already large for a red mock, but was still one of the breeds that were most prized for their grace and speed. When Bard was full grown he would likely outweigh him by a significant margin, but he would never have the lightness of wing that the desert-born creature did. Right then, though, the little black mock was still flapping his way towards them. If a dragon could fly sulkily, Bard was doing it.

Leo was unstrapped and out of the saddle before North, but waited to help him down, grin wide on his face as North wobbled. North's feet nearly slipped on the smooth tiles that made up the flat top of the mesa, wind blowing through his hair and making him squint.

"Vea taught me to fly. Says it was the biggest mistake of her life."

"How do you do that? It's like you and the mock were one, and he isn't even yours. I didn't feel you directing him with your legs." Even Obri had to wrestle obedience out of Kita on occasion, and they had been flying together for over a decade.

Leo patted the rippling flank of the dragon, fingers sliding over reddish scales as a strange look crossed his face. "We don't use legs or prods here. Those who can't use magic have whistles. Those who can, subvocalize and send our whistles to their ears. It's very little magic, but much more precise than kicking them."

North blinked a couple times. "So all the mocks are trained with the same commands?"

Leo grinned. "Makes them easy to ride and hell to steal, if outsiders try."

Before North could ask more questions, Leo handed the reins to an attendant and grabbed North's hand. He yanked North towards a stairwell, allowing him only a second to marvel at the view from up here.

At the bottom of a short flight of stairs, Leo stopped in front of a door where a man in white robes stood. "New arrival for check-in. Blue, please."

The man, presumably a slave but who held himself with a regal bearing, nodded solemnly and opened the door. "In here, please."

North hesitated, but complied. The white-clad man followed him in, but Leo remained out in the hallway.

"Please strip and remove all metal from your body. Your clothing and possessions will be returned to you when you leave," his escort said, bowing his head politely but not taking his eyes off North.

Frowning, the Namer looked around for a screen or something to undress behind. There was none, so, with a shrug, he pulled his shirt off, then his pants. There was a bracelet Obri had given him and the pendant on the braided grass cord that Tsiihsi had made. The man gestured down to North's shoes, which he removed, then had him turn in a circle, pull back his shoulder-length hair to show he had no earrings, and even open his mouth.

When the slave seemed satisfied, he walked over to a cabinet and pulled out a pale-blue robe and cloth belt. "You may wear this while you walk our halls. It will mark you as one of the Gifted, and a guest. When you are ready to leave, *daradeio* Leo will bring you back here. Welcome to Aina Brisbahn, Gifted one." He bowed his head again, and when North had dressed, escorted him out of the room.

Leo was waiting there with Bard, leaning up against a wall and grinning from ear to ear. "Looking good," he said, with a whistle.

North scowled at him. "You could have warned me about the strip search."

"And have you get clever on me? Never. Besides, what fun would a warning have been?"

North shook his head at the smirking *daradeio* and looked around. "So, what now?"

The hall they were in made North feel . . . off. The ceilings were too low, and the reddish walls seemed to tilt just a bit in opposite directions, making North want to lean to the left and hunch his shoulders.

Leo must have noticed his discomfort because he chuckled. "You get used to it after a while. Most of the tunnels here are wind-shaped. We expand some and connect others, but Aina Brisbahn mostly built itself . . . with a bit of help from the Veiled Wanderer and the Mother in Gold, of course."

The smile vanished from North's face. Leo must have noticed, because his faded too. "What happened at the estate, North?"

"The . . . " North swallowed past the lump in his throat. He was about to try again when a group of *daradeio* turned the corner. "Later."

"Alright. This way to Suela's office." Leo started walking. For a fairly short man, Leo had some legs on him and seemed insistent on taking stairs two, three, and sometimes four at a time. North's height advantage should have made it easy to keep up, but instead, he spent most of his energy just trying not to run into walls in the oddly shaped corridors.

They headed down, away from the outer walls with their windows and into the core of the mesa. He had expected some sort of torches or even magic lights, but instead as they walked deeper in, the walls—which had seemed just plain red stone with yellow striations—began to glow. Light seeped from veins of what he realized was metal, making the corridors radiant.

"Is that gold in the walls?" North asked, reaching out to run his fingers along it.

"Gold and copper, but mostly gold. It glows because of us. The *daradeio* store our excess magic here, and there is so much stored up now that it seeps out. Isn't it beautiful?" Leo asked with a pleased sigh, his fingers caressing the stone as if it were an old friend. "It is one of us, as much as our home. Much like the desert is for our people."

North didn't reply, unable to think of anything that wouldn't ruin the depth of feeling in those words. He could almost sense the love Leo felt for this place pulsing off the man as if it were tied into his true calling as inextricably as a mother to her child. The desert was a part of Leo, which made North wonder if the same would be true of other *daradeio*. These they passed in greater and greater numbers as they got deeper into the mesa, even this late at night. Each of them had those distinctive dark-red eyes, but a surprising number had lighter skin like Leo.

When his guide noticed his constant double-takes, he explained, "Slaves get chosen all the time, too. The *daradeio* comprise one-fifth of the population, give or take, and with no regard for station in life—only potential. You're Gifted. Had you been born among us, you would be a *daradeio*. If you choose to stay with us, the Veiled Wanderer will mark you as *daradeio*. It is the way it's been since the time of the Five."

Guilt once more assailed him, but North just didn't have the heart to break it to Leo that the Veiled Wanderer was gone. Instead, he jumped on that last sentence. "The Five? As in the Five Gods?"

Leo snorted, "Mother, no. We have no quarrel with Ionism and the worship of the Gods, but to us, they are not mythical beings of infinite power. They are mighty and worthy of fear and respect, but they are people at their core. They are fallible and petty and make mistakes just like we do. Our Five are just one of our legends: five friends who shaped the Mondaer into the people we are now and won us the protection of the Veiled Wanderer. We don't worship them, but they are remembered, always."

At that, he stopped for a moment and held out his right hand, pointing out the symbols that were tattooed below the knuckles. "The Beetle is for Baarin and his Perseverance—your friend's name was chosen based on this—the Mouse is for Nessei and her cleverness, the Snake is for Deon and his honor, the Goat for Amelia and her bravery, the Owl for Kaia and her wisdom. They are why the Mondaer family consists of five adults. We are each, in a way, a piece of one of them. When I form my own family, these roles will ceremonially fall to us. For the first night of our marriage, we will *be* the Five, remembering and honoring their memories and the lessons we learned from them, until dawn finds us united."

A blush crept along North's cheeks, and Leo must have noticed for he reached up to pinch one. "Get that pretty head out of wherever it went. Not *every* Mondaer family is just one big pile of panting and moaning bodies. That is pure myth and only represents *most* of our family units." His eyes were sparkling, and North's mouth felt unexpectedly dry as Leo turned away from him and continued along the hallway, whistling.

North was saved from having to respond when they turned a corner and almost ran right into Fayrian. North reflexively braced, because the look on her face screamed *murder.*

Fay held a gnarled cane with a death-grip and looked ready to bludgeon someone to a pulp. Her hair hung in frizzy, half-dry ringlets around her face, red tunic and pants likewise damp. North was surprised she wasn't steaming, what with the glower that could have boiled ice.

"Hello, Rian."

"Get. Out. Of. My. Fucking. Way," she snarled, baring her teeth.

"Are you . . . alright?" Leo asked, taking a few steps back from the fuming young woman.

"No. I am fucking not. There are too many *fucking* stairs in this slave-blood-soaked, gold-gilded, piss-smelling giant dragon dildo."

Leo started coughing, but North, who had survived half a year of Obri, just asked, "Piss-smelling?"

Fay cracked a grin. "Yeah. I peed in a corner."

"Charming," North said, crossing his arms. "Why are you wet?"

"Better question, why isn't he crying like a baby?" she asked, pointing the cane at Leo.

Oh no.

"Because there was a magical explosion?" Leo asked.

Fay's lips curled into a smile, and before North could stop her, she turned to Leo and in the least tactful way possible broke the news. "Because your multi-eyed freak of a deity is dead."

CHAPTER NINE
The Sandhewn City
FEDRIK

We head to the Sandhewn City today. I am nervous, but Suela is terrified. I know she worries that she will not be strong enough to control the Gatekeeper Gift. I would offer to swap, to take the darkness so that she may have the light, but it doesn't work that way. I have been chosen, and I trust none more than the woman who trained me in the ways of the desert to carry this burden by my side. All I can do now is gather my strength to see my doena through the next six months as our powers grow. She will hate me, so I will have to carry the love for both of us, until she comes out the other end . . . or we both die.

—From the journal of Sidian Tailor.

WHERE AM I?

Fedrik felt cold stone against his back, covered by a gritty layer of sand. The scent of dust filled the air and when he opened his eyes, the dim moonlight made his head throb. It filtered in through two small, high windows in the thick walls of the room in which he lay.

Other than a half-broken chair in the corner, the wicker torn and faded, the room was bare. The walls and ceiling had once been painted, but Fedrik couldn't make out the faded designs in the low light.

With a groan he rolled onto his side, then jumped and yelped when a hoarse voice said, "You're awake. We were starting to worry."

"L . . . Leo? Where—"

"Up here. No, no, to your left a little." Leo sounded like he had been crying, or maybe as though he were only just holding it together.

Fedrik's eyes scanned the room but didn't see anyone.

"Higher," Leo said, and Fedrik turned his gaze to the ceiling, then scuttled backwards until his back slammed into a wall when a small floating orb began to softly glow.

"What the hell is this? A sending circuit?"

It bobbed a few feet towards him. "Of a kind, yes. I will not get closer than this, to avoid being caught in your field. Hold tight. I'm going to get Suela. I've been watching you sleep while the important people talked."

"Wait . . . how long have I been out?"

A pause. "More than a day. A lot's happened and I'm not the right person to tell you any of it. You need Suela."

There was a strange, distant sound of shuffling, then a different voice emanated from the sphere—feminine, harsh, and vaguely familiar. It actually reminded him a little of Fay's clipped tone, but there was a creaky, elderly, almost nasal quality to it. "There you are."

Fedrik squinted in an attempt to get a better look at the floating orb, but the strange way it shimmered made it hard to focus on. "Who are you?"

"My name is Suela Alveara. We met once before; I am the one who sent you here. Know that you are safe where you are, at least for now."

"What do you want? And where am I?" Both seemed pertinent, as the last thing Fedrik could remember with any clarity was standing in a clearing on the Deil estates, talking to a Mondaer woman with shrouded eyes. Wait, had her name been Suela? Was that who had spoken out of the orb?

But where was he? No lemons scented the air, and where was Fay? Every joint and muscle of his body was sore, but Fedrik heaved himself to his feet and stumbled to the doorway.

"Easy there. You're bound to be a bit wobbly," a different voice said.

"North?" Fedrik asked, knees weak.

"Yes, I'm here. You should sit down."

He ignored the caution and trudged to the opening, where he promptly stopped, staring in horror and awe at what lay beyond.

It was a city, or had been, but nothing moved in it. Homes, streets, empty plazas and buildings were carved into the sides of a huge canyon. Like Hardor's Crescent but several times the size, reddish sandstone rose for hundreds of feet, ending in a narrow band of starry sky far above. The moon shone in from that uneven crevice, beams of dusty light filtering down to a narrow stream at the very bottom of the ravine.

He stumbled forward a few more steps until he hit a low wall and clutched it for support as his eyes roamed over the vast, deserted mass of buildings. "Where *is* everyone?"

The sphere floated into his peripheral vision, always maintaining the same distance. "No one has lived here for thousands of years," Suela said. "It is one of the oldest relics of the world, one that survived the Decimation and now serves only one purpose."

Fedrik couldn't break his gaze from the crumbling ruins to look at the orb, but her response prompted his next question. "What purpose?"

"To keep each new Gatekeeper away from anyone they could harm until they have their power in check."

With that single word—*Gatekeeper*—memories flashed before his eyes. Fedrik squeezed them shut and clenched his fingers around the reddish stone.

What did I do?

He could remember his Gift tearing away, rending him apart from the inside out. Then a woman's face, veils blowing in the wind and . . . *Elenor.*

A gasp passed his lips and he leaned forward, bracing against the railing with shaking arms. Within him, the Gift that he had almost lost flared to life, pounding in his head and curling around his thoughts as her face sprang to the forefront of his mind.

With it came fury.

He screamed, the roar of anger and pain echoing off the deserted streets and sheer walls of the Sandhewn City. Ten feet away, the sphere fell from the air and shattered into a thousand crystalline pieces.

When his lungs were empty the sound stopped, but it still drummed inside his skull, ricocheting and rising in volume until rage was all he could feel. There was something at the center of all that anger. As it roared through him, Fedrik sank into the ire, intent on crushing the source. He reached the center of his fury and felt a tug. It pulled him to his feet and made his eyes spring open as his body oriented itself towards the north-east and began to move.

Down wind-worn steps and across deserted streets, up winding inclines and along walkways with sickening drops, Fedrik followed that pull. He had to find the source. *He had to.* The pain in his head and fury in his heart would ease if he could just find the other end of this thread that tugged at him, and crush it.

For hours he wandered, up and down and up again. Nothing else moved in the still morning except for the occasional scuttle of a mouse or lizard as he searched for a way out. Hours passed, each more frustrating than the last. His feet began to ache and his mouth grew parched.

The needs of Fedrik's body finally started to divide his attention. He stopped at the bottom of the ravine to take a drink of the cool water and rest his aching legs, then continued his search. Each dead end added to the exhaustion and as the moon began to set, Fedrik sat down on the wall of what must have once been a garden, out of breath and close to tears.

"Feeling better?" came Suela's voice. Like before, it came from above. Fed was too exhausted to look around for the sphere, but it bobbed into view a few seconds later.

"The globe shattered."

"There was a second receptacle, but only one, so try not to break this one, will you? They are hard to replace, since some of the components come from other worlds."

That made no sense, but Fedrik was too tired and distracted to care. "Go away."

"Oh, for fuck's sake, let me sit down," a much more familiar and welcome voice said, though it was distorted and distant.

"Avilor?" Fedrik shot to his feet, looking around.

"Up here, you dolt. I think I'm talking to you out of some kind of disk or something? I can see you from here—well, kind of. My eyes are all sorts of fuzzy. Can you wave?"

Feeling utterly foolish, Fedrik held up his hand and awkwardly waved.

"So this thing lets them communicate with new Gatekeepers at a safe distance. They got quite pissed when you destroyed the first one, so try not to do it again. Suela is going to talk to you now. She's a bit of a sadistic bitch, but has agreed to help protect you. She's going to let me come to you if you do what she wants. Try to not kill anyone else till I get there, alright?"

"Wait, Avilor."

"Yes?"

"You . . . I didn't hurt you, did I?"

A brief pause. "Not me, no. Lot of people are broken, though. You really know how to make enemies, don't you, asshole?" Did she sound . . . tearful?

Fedrik ached to see her, but didn't ask when, not wanting another blow to his shaky calm if it was far off.

"I'll see you soon, Fed. Listen to Suela."

There was a moment of strange, crackly noise, then the female voice from before spoke. "Ready to talk? I know it's difficult, but the faster you learn to focus, the faster you will gain control over yourself."

The orb drifted a little closer and Fedrik wearily turned his head in its direction. "Answer me this, then. How do I get out of here?"

"You don't. That's why you were brought here. The Sandhewn City once had magic-operated lifts. Now it is only accessible by mock. It is a place where you can rage and pace to your heart's content without accidentally murdering anyone. Again."

Fedrik closed his eyes and tilted his head up, so that the last rays of the moon could bathe his face before it disappeared beyond the lip of the canyon. "Can you make it stop?"

"Only your Incarnate can make it stop."

Fedrik bit down until his jaw ached as the anger reignited in his chest. *His Incarnate.* Was that the source of this driving fury? If so, Fedrik had to find them and kill them so it would stop. He just had to get out of this damnable city and he could—

"You should eat before you get lost to the bloodlust again. Food was left for you by the river while you stalked around."

His stomach growled and as his attention shifted, Fedrik realized that he was, indeed, starving. Even so, it was harder than he cared to admit to turn toward the river instead of up towards the lip of the ravine where freedom lay.

Tomorrow. Tomorrow he would find a way out of here.

With weary steps, Fedrik made his way to the bottom of the city. The orb followed along at a distance and some of his irritation shifted to his new jailor. That annoyance was so light and pleasant in comparison to the soul-eating fury that had consumed him all night that Fedrik welcomed it. "So, is this it, then? I stay here forever, now?"

"Oh no. The city is a training ground. Normally, you would be there with your Incarnate, but we are in uncharted territory with you. When I arrive, I will do my best to make sure you understand what it means to be a Gatekeeper and why you must learn to control the impulse to find your Incarnate and kill them," Suela replied, bobbing ahead of Fedrik as the orb led him downstream.

The river wasn't very deep and boulders dotted its course. Fedrik stopped to take off his shoes and walked in the shallow water by the sandy shore to ease the blisters that had formed over the course of his desperate search for a way out.

"Fayrian said I broke people . . . Who?"

"Are you sure you are ready to know?" Suela asked.

No, he wasn't, but maybe concentrating on that would cut through the burning drive to murder with his bare hands. "Yes."

"You killed dozens of rifters and broke many more. You set off a chain reaction of breaking capacities that we are still cataloging, but the death toll has topped a hundred already. More egregiously—but no more your fault than any of the others—you have done something only one other Gatekeeper ever has before, and become a God Killer."

"What do you mean, God Killer?"

"That our Lady in Red, Fulsixia the Ruby Dragon, Goddess of Namers, died yesterday at the hand of your Gift; for only the second time in history, one of the beings that made us has themselves been unmade. Don't you remember?"

Fedrik tried thinking back, but all he could recall was pain, and a face, red veils shifting as his power exploded outward. That had been a God?

He had killed *one of the Five*?

Fedrik's knees buckled and he splashed into the cool water. He was not sure how long he remained there, first too shocked to move, then unable to stop shaking as the implications began to hit.

Fulsixia the Red. What were her words?

Though born a seed, I will sink roots and rise towards the sky. No storm can break me, for always will I bend and grow. May all be welcome in my shade, where side by side we craft a better world. Let our names live on in our creations.

A keening cry filled the air, and it took Fedrik minutes to realize that it came from him. Unable to do anything but rock in place, the words of the dead Goddess circling him like vultures, Fedrik hugged himself and squeezed his eyes shut. "Why is this happening to me?"

"I do not have an answer to that, but crying isn't going to fix it. Do you know what will?" The voice from the orb did not sound entirely as unsympathetic as her words would imply, not in the gentle way that she asked that last question.

It was that hint of kindness that drew Fedrik's eyes to it, though it looked no different than it had all day. "What?"

"Figuring out what to do with the power and fury you have been given. There's no going back to what you were before, but that doesn't mean that the road ahead is written. I was in your shoes once, confronting the monstrosity of my existence. It is difficult and painful, yet within the suffering you have the opportunity to find strength you never knew you had. So you're a monster, a murderer, a God Killer. Some of the best people I've known have been monsters, too. What matters isn't how destructive your power is, but how you use it."

Fedrik wanted those words to bring him more comfort than they did, but the aching pull to the north whispered exactly what and whom it yearned to destroy, and it filled him with a dreadful certainty that this was not something he was strong enough to control, even if he wanted to.

As if sensing his despair, the orb floated a little closer. "I'm not saying that it will be easy. You're supposed to have a partner in this to balance you out, and it's likely that you will kill again without meaning to before you learn to control your Gift, but don't get so caught up in the power that you forget that there's a person underneath. You know what the difference is between the ones who learn to wield the power given them instead of letting it wield them?" Suela asked.

Fedrik shook his head.

"A goal."

That made him laugh, the sound choked and hollow. "What goal could I possibly have that excuses my continued existence? I killed a God. If given my freedom, I will kill the Incarnate. The Mondaer should just dispose of me before I can do more harm."

"If I were there, I'd smack you. I didn't ask you what you would do if you were free because, obviously, no one is going to let you out of there until you have a handle on your Gift. I asked you for a goal. What objective burns bright enough that you're willing to put in the work? Something that you're willing to sacrifice everything for, even your despondency and hopelessness."

A face flashed before his eyes. Not the one that haunted his dreams and made his fingers ache to close around a pale throat, but rather a strong face and a riot of auburn curls. With that image, so came her words: *I need something outside myself to focus on, Fed, something worthwhile, or there's nothing but this—an angry, petty, vengeful asshole.*

He couldn't leave her alone, not after she had already lost everyone else. It wasn't a grand cause, but as he thought of Fay, a little of the murderous ache faded, and even the despair lifted a little as he reached up to rub his still-tender nose from where she had punched him.

"What about keeping someone else alive and happy? Is that a good goal?" Fedrik asked.

"It will do for now. That's what I sacrificed everything for too, a long time ago," Suela replied. "Are you ready to begin learning to master your Gift?"

Fedrik took a deep breath and raised his eyes to the clear night sky and the bright dusting of stars. Somewhere out there, that same light would shine on Fayrian and all the trouble she was doubtlessly already causing. He had promised her that she was his only priority and that he would never leave her or hurt her again, and he'd be damned if he broke yet another oath to her.

More than that, though, these stars also shone on another woman, one his heart ached to see torn apart. Fedrik's fingers twitched and he licked his lips. Two reasons to live. He could cope with the gnawing anger if there was an end in sight, and working with the Mondaer offered him a way out of here. He would cooperate, find Fay, and together they could kill the Incarnate.

If it was who he thought, Fedrik doubted Fayrian would object.

"I'm ready," he said aloud.

"Then get on your feet, boy. We have a lot of work to do before Fayrian and I come to the Sandhewn City in person."

CHAPTER TEN
The Best Fish Pie in Hardor
ELENOR

For the perfect fish pie, choose a goodly mix of oily and flaky river fish, with no more than one-third salted cod. These must be well-cleaned and the salt soaked out, then patted dry. The crust must be half-and-half rice and wheat flour, brought together by melted lard and boiling water, with only a small pinch each of salt and thyme. Raise it and fill with the fish well-browned in oil, currants soaked in rice wine, a handful of field herbs finely chopped, and a gravy made from fish-bone stock, onion, celery, carrot, and peppercorn, thickened with rice. Seal and pierce the tops, then apply egg wash generously.

—Directions for the baking of Hardor Fish Pie, as dictated by Mari Baker.

TEARS RAN SILENTLY DOWN ELENOR'S CHEEKS as she lay in bed, muscles twitching, eyes stinging from exhaustion. Claire's steady breath against her shoulder grated against her oversensitive skin, and the light nightgown was torture. Yet she tried not to move, despite the constant ache in her wrist and tickle of her burns against the bandages, yearning to be itched.

It was well past four in the morning and Claire had only just fallen asleep. Paul, too, was sprawled out on the couch snoring gently. Elenor didn't want to wake them. It had been hard enough to convince them that staying awake in solidarity wouldn't be helpful the first time. Elenor doubted she'd manage it again.

She squeezed her eyes shut and pulled the shawl Daemon had left for her tighter around her shoulders. It was cool to the touch, sapping away the heat rolling off of Elenor's body. It did nothing for the discomfort, but any relief was better than nothing.

It was pointless to try to sleep. The serindalla made every thought and emotion magnify and bounce. Years of daily microdosing had let Elenor forget how excruciating this mix of fever and sap was. At least the discomfort and the growing pain in her legs was something to focus on. It was easier to cry because she was tired and sore than for the other things squeezing her chest like a vice.

Claire had told her to take time to process, but how was she supposed to *process* the loss of her father or the worry for her mother, when Elenor had yet to even properly mourn Wil? It had been less than two months, and in that time her only moments of stillness had been the numb disbelief after Djina's death.

A quiet knock came at the door. Elenor considered ignoring it, but instead pushed back the covers and slipped out of bed, murmuring an apology to Claire. Pain shot up her legs as her heels touched the floor. With a small wince, Elenor reached for the crutch leaning by the bedside and hobbled across the room as quietly as she could.

"What are you doing here this late, Eric?" she asked, as soon as the door opened enough to reveal her cousin's face in the crack.

"I need to talk to you."

"At four in the morning?"

"It's urgent."

Elenor sighed but nodded to the guards watching her door, who moved to give the two nobles a little privacy. Normally, she would never dream of having an important meeting in the middle of a hallway. Considering that everyone else who lived in this stretch of corridor was either missing or dead, though, Elenor wasn't as worried about being overheard.

"What is it?"

Eric reached into his breast pocket and pulled out a folded letter. "I was looking through your father's office like you asked me and Drego to, and found this. Kallen wanted to wait to tell you until tomorrow, since you aren't feeling well. I've just been staring up at the ceiling all night regretting it, so I finally came back up the hill. Your parents might already have told you, but if not . . .

well, I thought you ought to have as much warning as possible." He passed Elenor the letter.

Her fingers curled around the glossy paper, pulse thundering in her ears. "More bad news?" she asked, quietly.

"Considering the last time it came up, you were hyperventilating for nearly three days, I think so," Eric replied, and just like that, Elenor didn't need to open the letter. Her whole body stiffened. The pain that had been hard to ignore before swelled like the crescendo of a macabre aria, where every note was a different, lingering anguish.

The little scar behind her jaw tingled.

"She's coming?" Elenor managed to whisper. "When?"

"She was going to meet the Iamings at the coast and finish the journey with them, so as early as tomorrow afternoon, depending on travel conditions."

A high-pitched, distressed whimper left Elenor's lips, despite her attempt to press them shut.

"Ellie, is your aunt the reason you got sick when you were little?" Eric asked. He had asked before, but there was none of his usual annoyed curiosity, just open concern. "Are you in danger?"

"I'm always in danger, Eric. Every hour, every minute. This just brings our timeline forward."

Her cousin frowned. She knew her obvious avoidance of his first question would annoy Eric, but telling him while the fever raged and she couldn't sleep felt impossibly daunting. He didn't press. Elenor could tell it was taking all his self-control by the way his fingers tapped his crossed arms and his brow scrunched. She reached out and squeezed his hand, which earned her a wan smile.

"You should get home to Beth," she said. "Tomorrow is going to be a long day and I need you sharp for it, because I won't be."

"Ellie—"

"Please, Eric. I promise I'll tell you, but I don't want to repeat myself. Have Tomaz and Kallen meet us here in the morning, and bring Beth too. I promise I'll go over all of it, but right now my head is both fuzzy and going at about a hundred miles a minute."

"And you can promise me that you'll tell me everything I need to know so you don't end up dead too?" Eric pressed.

"I'll try my best."

He shook his head, then reached forward to press a kiss to her brow. "Try to get some sleep, pipsqueak."

"You haven't called me that since I was twelve."

"I don't usually see you barefoot. Aren't you Lirion supposed to be all tall and majestic?"

Elenor snorted. "No, I'm pretty sure we're just supposed to be ruthless and bloodthirsty."

Eric smirked, then left. As soon as he turned the corner, Elenor slumped against the door, her fingers tightening around the letter, and smile falling from her face.

"Your Highness, are you alright?"

Elenor jumped and looked to her left, where Jo, the guard who had helped them during the escape, stood holding a spear. Paul must have put her on night duty after Elenor had insisted that Jo be given the promised posting as one of her bodyguards.

"You're kind of freaking me out with that thousand-yard stare," Jo said.

Elenor blinked, realizing that her thoughts had wandered again thanks to the serindalla. "I think I'm about to have a panic attack, to be perfectly honest."

"Is there anything I can do to help?"

Elenor looked down at the letter in her hand, then opened it and read the neat text in her aunt's handwriting, ice crawling down the back of her neck.

She looked up at Jo. "Talk to me. You said you were only hired on a month or so ago, right? What did you do before?"

"I was a constable in the city watch. They called us in to look for you when you were taken by the Rebellion. A week later, a whole bunch of us who got the closest to getting you back were offered jobs at the Palace when the guard was purged of people loyal to Lord Tellen. The pay was better, so I took it."

Elenor carefully folded the letter, then stuck it in her sling, safe against the tight bandages on her wrist. "Yesterday you changed sides for money and a promotion. Should I assume that you'd do that again? I promise that you won't be dismissed if you answer honestly. I just need to be able to trust my bodyguards right now. Things are about to go monumentally more to hell than they already are."

Jo fished around in her pocket and pulled out a small tobacco case. "Fun times. I can understand why you'd be worried, but that's a complicated question. I was about to take my break. Would you mind if I smoked while I answered?"

Elenor shook her head. After a quick word with her other guards—one of whom remained behind to tell Paul where she had gone—Elenor hobbled along after Jo. There was a stone bench near the path in the nearest garden. Elenor sat with a sigh of relief, the cool marble and brisk night air soothing to her overheated skin and racing nerves.

Jo remained silent while filling and lighting a small pipe. As she blew out a rather impressive smoke ring, the guard glanced over at Elenor. "Do you know who makes the best fish pies in Hardor?"

Elenor shook her head.

"I do. I was born and raised here, and you eat a lot of easy-to-carry food when you're working for the watch. Almost all of us have a favorite place to stop for a quick bite, but I've tried them all and can say for certain that the person who makes the best fish pies in Hardor is Mari Baker, off market square."

Elenor thought she recognized that name, but couldn't quite place it. Jo must have seen her confusion, because she continued without prompting. "Three days after starting here at the Palace, some of my old colleagues in the watch showed up with Mari Baker and her husband, and tossed them into separate cells on my level of the Subterranea. Both constables were all fucked-up about it, too, if you'll pardon my language, Your Highness."

"Swearing doesn't offend me."

Jo nodded and took another puff off her pipe. "Still feels weird to swear in front of a royal."

"Would it help if I told you that I was once grounded for a month for swearing in front of a roomful of foreign dignitaries when I tripped and fell into a fountain?"

Jo let out a surprised snort. "You know, I'm still not entirely convinced you're the princess. I thought you rich folks were much more . . . dignified."

"We like to let the common riffraff think that, yes," Elenor said, in a mockery of Lady Lavarin's nasal tone, which caused Jo to snort again and let out a surprised chuckle.

"I think I like you, Your Highness."

Elenor sighed, looking down at her hands. "It might be better if you didn't. People who like me seem to die a lot."

Jo's smile faded. "I heard about the doctor. The paper said she died of a heart condition, but rumors travel fast among the guards and servants. We all know what happened, and I'm sorry."

Elenor's fingers found the edge of the letter again. "Those condolences belong to her family, not to me. I'm the one who got her killed."

"Yeah, I've heard that too."

Elenor looked over at the guard, eyebrows raised. "You don't pull punches, do you?"

"No, not really."

"It's refreshing. Now tell me about Mari. I have a feeling you have a few more blows to land."

Jo hesitated, looking Elenor up and down. "Are you . . . feeling well enough for that? Your people have seemed mighty worried all day. I thought you were supposed to be resting."

Elenor shook her head. "Can't sleep, I feel horrid, and lying in bed fretting and panicking because I can't *do* anything is so much worse than this. I also just received about the worst news possible, and am this close," Elenor held up two fingers, "to having a complete sobbing meltdown, where I hide in my closet, shaking in terror for the next . . . year. *Please* keep talking, swearing, and being normal. You have no idea how much I need that right now. It's why I always loved Djina. She never let me get away with anything, so in honor of her memory, please don't censor yourself."

Jo gave Elenor an unsure-but-game smile. "If you insist. But it won't be entirely nice."

"I never expect nice, Jo. I haven't since I was six."

"Six? Well that's fucking tragic." She lit her pipe again. "Most people are, you know. Nice, I mean. Sure, there are the occasional murderers and assholes, but the majority of people will do right by others as long as they have the ability to. That was one of the first things I learned while working for the watch."

Elenor wasn't sure she believed that, but she stayed silent.

Another smoke ring drifted through the gardens, then Jo said, "Mari's husband was killed in front of her to get her to talk. I was the newest hire, so I got to deal with the body once that doctor of yours pronounced him dead. Mari hardly had a scratch on her, but Kyle was seriously messed up. Missing limbs, face cut open, burns everywhere. Your boy in there," she gestured back in the direction of Elenor's suite, where Gabriel slept, "had it easier than most, until the end. There was a standing order that none of the damage to him should be too visible, since the Island was asking after him. Most of the others didn't have that kind of protection. Two days after Kyle was buried, they chopped Mari's hands off."

Finally, Elenor remembered. She must have been the older woman Gabriel had been so distraught over during his rescue. Not for the first time, shame flooded her, and Elenor pulled her knees up to her chest, pressing her face into them. "I never checked on the others. I never asked Djina about who else he might be torturing. If not for Gabriel's suggestion, they would all still be there."

Jo reached out and patted Elenor on the shoulder. Her too-sensitive skin sent zings of pain along her back and arm, but she tried not to let it show.

"That's pretty shitty, but don't be too hard on yourself. Seems like you're the kind of girl who takes all the blame on your own shoulders, but guess what? I had the keys to every one of those cells and didn't do squat. That doctor of yours kept them alive to be tortured more. The guys ordered to do the torturing came to work every day. Good people can be part of a bad system. The man your friend blew up? He had five children and brought baked goods when we had weekend shifts. Does that justify what he did? Hell no. Does it make the fact that he was killed for doing his job alright? Also no.

"Shit's complicated. Even I know that, and I'm literally just talking to you because I was in the wrong place at the right time and got caught up in the whirlwind. You're just one person, Your Highness. Maybe you were late to the game, maybe Gabriel suggested it, but you're who freed them. Now, whether that's good or bad in the long run is above my pay grade. If we're playing the blame-game, you're now responsible for the slew of petty robberies and bar brawls that will come out of all those criminals being back in the streets. The city watch is going to be pissed as all hell at you, that's for sure. But as far as I'm concerned? Your father cut off the hands of the best baker of fish pies in Hardor, and you saved her. So no, Your Highness. I'm not going to jump ship."

Elenor let out the shaky breath she had held for most of Jo's monologue. "You said you weren't going to be nice."

"That's your definition of *nice?* Five above, you're a bit messed up, aren't you?"

"You have no idea," Elenor replied, then turned to look at Jo. "Thank you. For being honest with me, I mean. I've spent so much of my life cut off from any . . . normalcy. It's nice to speak to someone who knows where to buy the best fish pie in Hardor. Or . . . used to be able to."

Jo tapped the last of the ashes from her pipe and put it away, then reached into her pocket. She pulled out a scrap of paper. "Here. This might serve you better than me." She passed it to Elenor, who unfolded it to see a recipe, written in a scratchy shorthand.

She looked up at Jo, who shrugged. "I asked Mari for the recipe, so that if she died and was buried, I could pass it around to remember her by. It wasn't much, but it was what I could do. She doesn't need to be remembered now, thanks to you, and I know she'll find a way to get back to baking, hands or no hands. So keep it. To remember the little people down here at the bottom, and that what you do matters. Just do your best, Your Highness. Even if you fuck-up a few times along the way, it will be better than not trying. As I said before, most people are nice."

Elenor folded the scrap of paper and held it to her chest, closing her eyes in a moment of quiet reverence. "Thank you, Jo. This helps more than you know."

"Sure better, because I just used up my whole break talking to you. I expect a raise if this is going to become a habit."

Elenor let out a surprised laugh. "Actually, I had another idea about how you could get a raise. I have a proposal for you, Jo. How do you feel about helping me fix our country?"

INTERLUDE
Legacy Of Ash
RIONA

THE ROOF TILES WERE SLIPPERY and the drizzle relentless. Not that Riona minded—a little rain had never killed anyone and the goings on in the plaza beneath her were far too interesting to be missed because of the weather.

She could always tell Garendarens from other folk. Even in Lirin—a country named after the rain that poured incessantly from fall to spring—most people still complained about it. But Garendor was a city of water, sprawling out across the coastline of the temperate south-westernmost corner of Lirin. No Garendaren worth their sea legs was bothered by silly things like getting wet. Of course, Priestess Katrin wasn't from Garendor, so she would probably scowl and put Riona in detention for 'taking foolish, unnecessary risks and getting water all over the floor.'

It would be worth it.

Riona gripped two heavy pouches tighter, their contents sloshing audibly even over the pattering of raindrops. She leaned, cautious but determined, over the lip of the roof, watching foreign lords and ladies walk down the street. They were dressed pompously in fine silks, each with an umbrella shielding them from the weather. Riona giggled. All these nobles coming to Garendor to view their famous colors and cheer. Well, they'd be leaving today feeling very . . . colorful.

She had done this, or things like it, enough times to have the timing down to an art. With a small push, she nudged a pebble off the shingles. It dropped right onto the umbrella of one of the passing ladies. Just as her victim looked up, searching for the source of the unexpected rock, Riona released the first bag. It opened on the way down, scattering dozens of little cloth pouches. The woman shrieked, suddenly covered from head-to-toe in sticky, vibrantly colored paint. At her shock, others looked up, just as Riona dropped the second bag and scooted out of sight, clutching at her side to stop it from hurting while she laughed herself silly at the shrieks, complaints, and angry curses from below.

By the time the constables reached the roof, panting and unbalanced, Riona was long gone.

The way over the rooftops of Garendor wasn't hard. It almost felt as though the rambling buildings, tight alleys, oddly placed stairwells, and frequent chimneys were made for the spry-footed youths of the city. Of course, not many were quite as willing as Riona to risk life and limb scrambling over them in the pouring rain, but the opinion of others had never slowed her much.

She knew that the moment Priestess Katrin heard the commotion, she'd come looking for Riona. The young woman wanted to be sitting in her room—wearing a neatly pleated uniform and doing her schoolwork—when the old grouch barged in. Maybe she'd even pretend to be studying for her final exams. That was sure to stop the Priestess's heart.

Riona had left her window propped open, but knew better than to clamber in and leave a puddle. Instead, she stood on the wide sill and removed her clothes and shoes first. Her window faced a boring stone wall. It was a dull view meant to encourage studiousness. The one and only time another student had seen her naked on the sill, she had just smiled and waggled her finger, and he hadn't been able to look at her without blushing for two months. It had been glorious.

Completely divested of everything but her hat, Riona reached for the cloth sack she kept for just such occasions and shoved her clothes and shoes inside, then tied it to the drainpipe so it would dangle out of sight.

Once in her room, she pulled her hat off and flung it under the bed, letting her dark brown hair tumble in mostly-dry waves down her back. A clean uniform was already waiting for her on top of the covers, just where she had left it. It was a simple gray wool tunic and skirt over a white linen chemise. Belt, shoes, hairband, done.

When Priestess Katrin came bursting through the door with a look of triumph on her face, she found the seventeen-year-old diligently working on her theology paper.

"How . . . ? That's not possible."

"What's not possible, Priestess?" Riona did her best to keep the grin off her face as the tall Priestess stammered.

Alas, the moment was over too soon. Katrin Mindellion was not easily flustered, and always recovered quickly when she was. "Riona Angler, I take it you know nothing about what just happened in the plaza?"

"No, ma'am, what happened?"

Katrin frowned, her bushy eyebrows almost meeting above the bridge of her nose. She huffed quietly and clasped Riona's shoulder, pulling her to her feet. Surprisingly, her grip was gentle. If anything, the Priestess looked more perplexed than angry. Riona stood and let herself be guided out the door. No reason to resist, especially since she was actually being allowed to walk, instead of being dragged to Katrin's office by the ear.

"Where are we going, Priestess?" Might as well try her luck. Either she was being taken to be punished regardless of proof, because—to be fair—past experience was probably proof enough, or something else was going on.

"My office." Punishment then. Well, it had been a long shot that she would get away with her latest prank. This wasn't unexpected. Riona just hoped that Priestess Katrin never realized that for her, extra chores were never a punishment. Being bored, now that would be terrible. "There's someone who wants to see you."

That caught Riona's attention. There was a tension in the Mindellion's voice and posture that she'd rarely seen except when awaiting for the twice-yearly Tirit Mindel test results. But it wasn't time for the tests, so who was it?

Curious now, Riona found her steps springier, and soon the Priestess quickened her stride to keep up with Riona instead of the other way around.

Just outside her office, Katrin stopped her. "Listen to me, Riona." She took Riona's chin between her fingers and forced the girl to meet her eyes. "This is a very important individual. I will not accept any of your sass. If you so much as sneeze out of turn, you will be asked to leave. He insisted that this meeting include you, but I still decide if you stay or go, understood?"

Staying or going? What did Katrin mean? "Priestess Katrin, there has to be a mistake. I age out of the orphanage in a month. Why would anyone take me now? I have *plans*."

Katrin's eyes softened. "They'll have to wait, I'm afraid. Now, shoulders straight, eyes down." She opened the door.

A man with long black hair going white near the temples and spindly glasses sat in one of Katrin's office chairs. He stood as they entered, Tirition robes in the black color of the College of Academics brushing the floor. His belt, though, Riona noticed, bore all six colors—a sign that he was part of the faculty of Tirit Mindel's Core Six Academy. Other than that, he certainly didn't look important. He wore no jewels and ink stained the tips of his fingers. What did Priestess Katrin know that Riona didn't?

"What's going on?" Riona asked, deciding to cut to the chase.

Katrin's eyes shot open, then narrowed on Riona as the hand the Priestess had on her lower back turned into a reprimanding poke. "Manners," she hissed.

"What's going on, *sir*?"

The man chuckled. "She's just as spirited as you said, Katrin. Thank you kindly for your help, but I am used to children at the Academy. I promise you, a little attitude won't ruffle my feathers." He stopped for another chuckle, but if it was meant to be a joke, Riona didn't get it. He must have noticed her scowl, because he extended his hand to her. "My name is Robin Tirition."

Ah. Robin. Bird. Feathers. Riona cracked a smile. "I'm Riona."

"No last name?"

Riona shrugged. "On the books it's Angler, but they just gave that to me at random when I was dropped off at the orphanage. I don't answer to it."

"I apologize, Master Robin. I did try to warn you," Katrin began, but Robin held up a hand to silence her.

"Thank you, Katrin. If you don't mind, I would like to speak to

Miss Riona in private. Could you give us a few minutes?"

"Of course, Master Robin," Katrin replied, bowing low. Considering this was *her* office, Riona was surprised to see her capitulate so quickly. It made Riona give Robin another once-over. Nothing. She was used to seeing Tiritions and Mindellions around the Temple, so the pendant that hung against his chest hardly impressed her. What made this man different from any other Island faculty? Riona had seen a few of those over the years, mostly around testing time. She was much too old for this to have anything to do with admittance to the Academy, though. That boat had sailed many years ago.

As soon as the door closed behind Katrin, Riona crossed her arms. "Listen, I don't know what this is about, but you should know that I'm not interested in a job with the Island, I'm not looking for a new family, and I have final exams to study for. So whatever you're selling, I'm not buying."

Robin's smile did not fade. If anything, it grew wider. "You are the spitting image of your mother."

All the wind dropped out of Riona's sails. Her eyes went wide, arms falling limp to her sides. "What did you say?"

"You have Talia's hair, and her eyes. Her spirit, too, it seems. I knew her well. We were in the same class at the Academy many, many years ago."

"My . . . mother went to Tirit Mindel? You *know* who my mother is?"

Robin gestured to the chair in front of him. "Why don't you sit down, Riona? You look a little shaky. I understand this must come as quite a shock."

Normally, that would have made Riona lock her knees and stand on principle, but she wasn't sure that would be smart right then.

Once they were both seated, Robin handed her a folder. Riona opened it, then her hand rose to cover her mouth.

There, atop a small pile of documents, was a pencil drawing of a woman.

"Her name was Talia. She was born to an important Seehanesian family, and I met her on the ferry to Tirit Mindel on our first day of school. We were inseparable for six years; even after we went to different Colleges, we spent most evenings together. I knew everything there was to know about her back then, and will be happy to answer any questions you might have."

It really was like looking into a mirror. Talia's face was oval and pretty, just like Riona's. She had long hair done up into hundreds of small braids and neatly piled atop her head. The picture captured her mid-grin, mischief sparkling in her eyes.

Riona reverently trailed her finger across the edge of the paper, wanting to touch the first portrait of her mother she had ever seen, but not daring to smudge the charcoal. "What happened to her?"

Robin let out a long sigh. "There is no easy way to answer that, so please forgive me if this hurts, Miss Riona. Talia died when you were about a year old, along with your father and the elder of your two brothers. They were living in the village of Nillenia when it was razed by order of King Mark Lirion. You and your other brother were the only survivors."

Riona leaned back in her seat, trying to absorb that. Her eyes never left the drawing, at least not until Robin carefully flipped it over to reveal another. This one was of a man and two boys. They were kneeling together amongst a flock of fuzzy goats, the younger of the two children holding a kid and the elder leaning on their father with a wide grin.

"A friend visited briefly the summer before they passed away. She drew these. This was your father, Rioden, and your eldest brother, Samuel. The younger boy is Gabriel, who I've had the pleasure to know in the years since your family's death."

Riona swallowed back a distressed sound which was not at all *her.*

Talia. Rioden. Samuel. Gabriel.

Her *family.*

Her mostly *dead* family.

All but Gabriel.

"I never knew his name, but I always hoped he was alive. He's the one who left me here, wasn't he? I was too little to remember, but I've asked Priestess Katrin a thousand times. All she knew was that a little boy handed me to her and ran away before she could offer him a place at the orphanage too. I've received a lot of small gifts over the years, but none of the letters were signed. Do you know why? Or where he is?"

Robin smiled, though his eyes were sad. He once more flipped the page, to show Riona a thick piece of shiny paper. In it, with a realism that took her breath away, was a young man in a Tirit Mindel Academy uniform that must have been Gabriel, sitting under a willow tree with two other students. "It's a photogram. One of the College of Science graduates has been perfecting how to capture images with a circuit. That's Gabriel when he was my student at the Academy, not long before he graduated."

"How long ago was that?"

"Six years," Robin said. "He never confided in me, but I believe the reason he did not come for you or allowed you to know him was that he wanted to protect you. Gabriel has been trying to take down the man who killed your family since he left you here, Riona. Regicide is a dangerous path, considering the families of those who have risen up against Mark Lirion were often his next targets. By distancing himself, he kept you safe."

Riona's hands balled into fists. "Didn't it ever occur to him that if he was trying to avenge our parents, I might want in?"

"You were a child."

"So was he." She looked down at the photogram again, at Gabriel's youthful face, trying to see the boy holding the goat in it. The same dimple softened his cheek, but even laughing with his friends, the young man in the photogram had harder eyes. "You never answered. Do you know where he is?"

Robin raised an eyebrow. "Planning to storm off to find him?"

Her cheeks flushed. Had she been that transparent? Well, might as well lean into it. "I'm of age in a month. My plan was always to go looking for him. Now I have even more reason to do so."

"Actually, you don't. The news hasn't spread this far yet, Riona, but King Consort Markus Lirion died yesterday. While I can't confirm it was your brother who did it, he was involved."

A confusing mix of emotions washed through Riona at those words. She tried to parse them out and process them like her teachers had instructed over her years of theological study, but they were piling atop one another too fast. "This is a lot," she said, as the silence stretched on too long and Robin's face scrunched in concern.

"I can imagine. Unfortunately, we don't have much time. I am returning to Hardor in a few minutes."

That strange sentence pulled Riona out of her thoughts and gave her something to focus on. "No boats leave this late."

She should know. She had been poring over the barge schedules heading east for weeks.

"I'm not taking a boat. Thanks to my employer, I have a rather faster way to get around. Which brings me to why I am here today. I would like you to come with me, Riona. I need your help with a project that is very dear to my heart, which, if successful, will see you reunited with your brother. He's in a dangerous and precarious position right now, but I am confident that with your help, we can turn the person who is his greatest threat into an ally and perhaps save the whole of Carinn while we are at it."

"Save Carinn? From what? I didn't realize it needed saving," Riona said.

"Not many do, but we are on the precipice of destruction. Your brother may be the only one who can stop it, but he will need help. *Your* help."

Riona wanted to agree, she really did, but she wasn't stupid. She was a Garendaren, and she knew a sales pitch from a mile away. "You're being awfully vague, Master Robin. I'm not interested in getting tangled up in Island business. What aren't you telling me?"

"Truly Talia's child. Alright then, Miss Riona. I'll make a deal with you. I would like to offer you a job. You come of age in a month, yes? Work for me for those thirty days to try to save your brother. Do everything I ask of you, even if it doesn't make sense or seems counter-intuitive, and—"

Riona held up her hand, palm out. "No way. I've had quite enough of people having carte blanche power over my life."

"Let me finish," Robin chided, an amused smile back in place. "What I was about to say was: give me those four weeks to prove to you that the work I do is worth continuing, and that I mean the best for you and for your brother. All on a trial basis, of course. If I have not won your loyalty in a month, you will be free to go with an ample severance package for your time, your educational loans forgiven, and all the protection the Island can offer. Or you may stay, and continue the work I do at my side. Either way, you will get a chance to know your brother. If I do something that you do not believe to be in his or your best interest, you will be free to tell him. I am not trying to trick or deceive you, Riona. I would require your obedience not to control you, but to protect you both. The players in the game your brother is immersed in are dangerous. When they find out about you—and it is when, not if—they will come for you. They will use you. If they cannot, they will kill you. This is not hyperbole or exaggeration. I have seen the bodies lined up and have lost people to this fight that I still mourn. For Talia's sake, and to avoid more needless bloodshed, I will do everything in my power to spare you and Gabriel from that fate."

"You're still talking in circles, and I don't like it. Why would people try to kill me? Why is Gabriel in so much danger, and how is he supposed to save all of Carinn? From whom? You talk a lot, but you're not very good at answering questions. Cut the Academics bullshit and tell it to me straight."

It was rude. Riona didn't care.

Fortunately, if it bothered Robin he did not show it. He leaned back in his chair and steepled his fingers. "I'm speaking in circles because you haven't agreed to work for me yet. As soon as you do and swear you'll keep the secrets I tell you for the next four weeks, then I will answer all your questions."

"You just said I could tell Gabriel anything. If they're such important secrets, why should I believe that you'll just let me blab? How do I know you're not one of the ones trying to use me, and who will kill me if I'm not useful?"

That got a chuckle. "You are wise to be so distrustful. Fortunately, this question is one I can answer: I don't care if you talk, because after the next month, all my secrets will be out. We have come to the precipice of all my plans. Either they will work, or everyone on this continent will be dead. Perhaps not so soon as one month, but within a few years. When everyone around you is a dead man walking, only the petty and cruel would try to add to the misery. I am many uncomplimentary things, but I am *not* petty, nor do I enjoy cruelty. You are safe from me, Riona. It is the rest of the world that is dangerous."

She looked down at the folder once more, flipping through the three pictures. "You're not going to tell me where Gabriel is if I don't agree, are you? I've noticed you haven't told me my real last name, either, so I won't be able to look him up on Island records. His name probably isn't even Gabriel. I don't have a choice, do I?"

"Of course you do. If you don't want to help, I would be happy to provide you protective custody. Or you may leave here and forge your own fate. Talia would never forgive me if I did not offer you safe haven, but all I can do is *offer*. The choice is yours. I do not want a reluctant and despondent assistant. I want Talia's daughter, a girl who, from what Priestess Katrin has told me, is too smart for her own good, unwaveringly stubborn, and sticks up for what she believes to be right at every turn."

Had Katrin really said that about her? Riona glanced towards the door, then back up at Robin.

She should say no. Even if there was truth to his warnings and people wanted her dead, Riona could disappear into the streets of Garendor and never be found. She knew every alley and house boat. It would be stupid to risk her own safety for a brother she had never met.

Good thing that doing stupid, risky things was Riona's primary area of study.

Robin stood and held out his hand. "Have you chosen?"

She didn't take his hand, but Riona closed the folder with a decisive motion. "You have one month. Not one day more."

A smile tugged at the corners of Robin's lips. "Then for the next thirty days, welcome aboard the True Project, Riona Navarl."

PART THREE

CHAPTER ELEVEN
Protector of Magic
DAEMON

I hear Alehan's name spoken as a curse as I walk through the camps of men I used to call brothers. I wear another face now, so they do not mince their words. The little boy I tortured to madness is being called a monster for the people he broke and killed, but Jac Drego is listed as a martyr. This is how the history books will be written, the lies that will pass from generation to generation as truth. I cannot change that without revealing myself, but I must do something. There's a little grouping of islands at the southern tip of the Island Union. I'm thinking of turning them into a refuge of sorts, a place where rifters who have done horrible things or wish to never be used as weapons may live in peace. It seems like the least I can do, after the harm I've caused. I just have to make sure that I do not become too invested. I must never become a force that wields those I choose to protect, or how am I different from Tirit Mindel, the Silvarin, or the Lirion?

—From the early journals of Daemon Indigo.

DAEMON LET A COIN-TOSS DECIDE the hour when he opened a window into Elenor's room. It was just past six in the morning, and unsurprisingly considering her condition, she was awake. The princess looked the picture of misery, her arms wrapped around her knees, eyes scrunched up in pain, and rocking gently. Claire Enica was asleep in the large four-poster bed, the *doena* on the couch by the hearth. There were papers strewn on the table in front of Elenor, but she had pushed them away. From his own experiences, reading anything with a high dose of serindalla in one's system was next to impossible. The letters just blurred together.

The shawl Daemon had given her was wrapped around her shoulders. Even from a shadowy corner he could see that, despite the relief it provided, her hair was damp with sweat and cheeks flushed with fever.

"Elenor," he sent in a whisper. "Come out to the garden."

She jerked in alarm, but without more than a moment of hesitation got up. The stiff, ginger way she put her feet on the floor told Daemon all he needed to know about her health. Textbook flare of wasting fever. Not the screaming, life-ending affair that the first occurrence tended to be, but still painful and potentially life-threatening.

At least she was one of the upper class. She would hopefully never have to choose between eating and the drug keeping her alive, like so many Daemon had known.

He opened a doorway into the gardens just as she slipped out of her room. The desire to reach out and pull her into a hug was near-overwhelming, but Daemon held back. For one thing, it would hurt her if skin oversensitivity was part of her current symptom set. For a second, he didn't entirely trust that the White Dragon wasn't about to show up again, coin toss or no.

"Daemon," she whispered. "Is this another one of those visits where you show up out of the blue, only to turn my life upside down and disappear? Because I don't know if I'm up to that right now."

That made him smile, which felt damn good after the past few days. "You *have* looked better."

"Are you saying I don't look pretty?" Elenor asked, one eyebrow raised.

"I don't know. Are overripe tomatoes pretty? Because your cheeks are about that color."

She let out a snort of laughter. "Tonight has had a refreshing lack of people trying to compliment or coddle me. I think I like it. Thank you for the shawl, by the way. It really does help."

"You're welcome."

Even though they were standing about ten paces apart, Daemon itched to reach out and check her temperature. He kept his feet planted, though. To avoid his earlier blunders, he had drained his magical reservoirs almost dry before coming here. It helped. Dae still *wanted* to be near her, but it wasn't the near-compulsion of the night of Djina's passing.

"So why are you here? Not that I mind, since sleep is about as elusive as a greased eel right now and you're much more pleasant to talk to than my own psyche, but you all but bolted from me yesterday. I'm just trying to piece together your motivations."

If only I knew anymore, Daemon thought. Instead of answering her question, he leaned against a nearby ivy-covered wall and crossed his arms. "Sorry about yesterday. Let's just say that you have someone looking out for you who gets very grouchy every time our paths cross."

"Well, can you tell them from me that if they're trying to help, they're doing a piss-poor job? My life is a wreck right now." Elenor sat down on the bottom step down to the garden with a wince and a groan. Her knuckles dug into the muscles on either side of her knee, face twisting into a grimace.

"I'll pass that message along," Daemon promised, before crossing the distance between them and kneeling in front of her. "May I?"

Elenor's eyebrows knitted together and her lips pursed, but she nodded. Careful to move slowly, he placed his hands over where hers had been and began to rift. First, Daemon absorbed some of the heat emanating from her skin, the small tendril of power flowing into his mostly empty well. That same crumb of magic became a gentle, pulsing kinetic pressure against her leg. Dae never touched her skin, aware of how sensitive wasting fever could make it. Instead, the pressure was even, cool, and controlled.

Elenor let out a little whimper.

"Too hard?"

"No. It hurts, but in the good way. Are you using magic?"

Dae looked up at her, surprised. "Doesn't your *doena* do this for you?"

She shook her head. "Magic is forbidden at the Palace. I know he drains it into gold, but until a few days ago I don't think I've seen Paul rift more than half a dozen times in my whole life."

It was difficult not to let his frustration show. "Magic isn't evil."

"Isn't it? No offense, but I've seen it do quite a bit of harm lately. I don't think rifters deserve the sort of mistrust and hatred my father had for them, but you're . . . dangerous, aren't you?"

Could he really deny that? Moving on to her calf, Daemon replied, "We are, but no more so than your lover is, or your father was. There are different kind of dangerous, and I don't believe rifters are the worst of them."

"Then who is?"

His eyes met hers. "People with nothing left to lose."

Elenor studied him, head cocked to the side. "Is that what you are, Daemon?"

"I used to be. Sometimes I'm scared I will be again. Right now, though, I still have a great deal I could lose, and am working hard not to."

"Yeah, me too." Without warning, Elenor reached forward and tucked a strand of his hair behind his ear. The brush of her fingers against the side of his face made Daemon's whole body stiffen with the now-familiar thrill of her touch. The princess's forehead was still scrunched up tight, her head tilted to the side. "Your hair looks different from a few days ago."

Was it? Daemon didn't pay much attention to those little details when adjusting his appearance in the Plane. He usually existed somewhere on the spectrum between the man he had been when he'd first became immortal, whose sharp features had been tempered with a little gray near his temples, and the smoother, more symmetrical and beautiful face he wore for his patron. The people of Ayre got used to his ever-shifting features, but Elenor didn't know he could change his appearance at will yet.

"Got it cut."

"But it's longer."

Oops. "Remember how you don't get answers about how I open those doors in the air?" he asked, with a forced smile.

"Remember how my life is a flaming trash fire of awful because people kept secrets from me?" she retorted, though he thought he saw her lips twitch up at the corners.

Daemon caught her hand in his, bringing her knuckles to his

lips. "How about this: every time you see me, you get to ask one question. About me, or the world, or anything you want. I promise that I'll tell you about it if I know the answer."

"And in return?" Elenor asked, not missing a beat.

"In return, I was hoping you'd help me with a little problem of mine. I've recently come into the possession of something that doesn't suit my lifestyle, but that I think you might enjoy. I was hoping you'd accept it as a gift."

Her eyes narrowed, and, much to Daemon's pleasure, Elenor reached up reflexively to wrap her fingers around the evergold pendant. "You've given me a lot of gifts and assistance without asking for anything in return. It smells fishy."

"Darling, this is Lirin. It *always* smells fishy here."

She laughed, and it was so genuine and unabashed that if Daemon had retained any doubts that he was falling for this girl despite his best efforts, they would have shattered.

"Alright then. Let's see this problem you want to foist on me, and then I'll decide if we have a deal."

Daemon grinned and bounced to his feet, worries momentarily forgotten. He disappeared into the doorway that still floated in the air behind him. A few seconds later, he reappeared with a large wooden box that had several slats pried off. It was rocking and hissing.

Elenor leaned back, posture clearly conveying *'what the fuck is that?'* Daemon's grin grew wider. He set the box down in front of her, then pulled a bag out of his pocket. "So, about fish . . . "

"What about fish?" Her voice was high-pitched and concerned. "Why is that box growling?"

"Here." Daemon handed her the bag, which did, indeed, smell strongly of fish.

Elenor took it between two fingers, wrinkling her nose.

"Take out a fish and hold it to one of the holes. Don't worry. You probably won't get bitten."

"I don't like the 'probably' in that sentence," she squeaked.

"Trust me."

As if to disprove him, the box took that opportunity to rock and hiss again. Elenor did not seem convinced, but she reached into the bag and pulled out a glistening sardine. "Ew."

"Don't tell me you don't like fish. You're a *Lirion*."

"I like fish just fine when they are alive or already cooked. It's just the in-between bits that are disgusting."

Daemon knelt and took hold of her wrist, guiding Elenor's hand forward until the sardine hovered an inch from one of the holes in the box. For a second, nothing happened, then a white muzzle full of sharp little teeth snapped from the darkness and yanked the fish out of her fingers.

Elenor yelped. "What is that?"

"Another fish, please. She's hungry."

Hesitantly, the princess presented a second sardine. This time, the little beast within already had her nose pressed against the crate. By the fourth fish, there was no more growling, just a plaintive whine each time Elenor reached back into the bag.

"Alright. This time, keep your hand there after she takes it. Let her smell you."

"Are you going to tell me *why* I'm risking my fingertips?" Elenor asked, but she did as instructed. When the little one finished gulping down the offered food, her muzzle reappeared and with only a momentary pause nudged the girl's hand.

Elenor jumped, but didn't pull her arm back. "Her fur is so soft. Is it a dog?"

Daemon shook his head. "No, not a dog."

He waited a few more seconds, watching as the black nose sniffled against Elenor's hand, a long tongue darting out to lick her palm.

When he was reasonably sure that the little demon wouldn't maul her, Daemon unfasten the latches holding the lid on. "Get another fish ready."

Once she had one in hand, Daemon inhaled, readied himself to magically catch a baby mock dragon if necessary, then lifted the lid. For a second, nothing happened.

Elenor leaned forward. A fuzzy head popped up over the edge, then shoulders, front paws, and extending wings.

"*Itsadragon*!" Elenor squealed, all-but smacking herself in the face with the sardine as she covered her mouth in excitement. The mockling's eyes followed the fish, body coiling.

Daemon snatched her up into his arms before she could spring right at the princess's face. "Elenor, meet the pint-sized problem that I hope you can help with. Little Miss Bitey, meet Elenor, giver of fish."

At the reminder, Elenor held out the fish, which the mock extended her neck to snatch, wiggling in his grip. Daemon knelt in front of Elenor, arms full of mockling.

"You're giving her to *me?*"

"If you want her. White mocks are very loyal and protective creatures. Once they bond with you—typically through food—they will defend you from anything or anyone who would do you harm. It seems to me that while you have a lot of people watching out for you, you might find some use for a several-thousand pound ball of fluff and teeth in your corner. Plus, I'm really not supposed to come visit as often as I do, and this little one does *not* like me. I'm hoping she might be a deterrent."

Elenor's gaze was glued to the mockling, who was leaning towards her, sniffing and kicking Daemon's stomach with her back paws. Without a word, the princess reached out her arms.

"Careful with the wings. They are very delicate when they are this young," Daemon cautioned, as he passed the small creature over. The mock twisted almost upside down as she tried to get to the unattended bag of fish. Elenor laughed, shifting her grip so that she could reach into the bag for another sardine. "Here you are, precious. Five above, you're soft."

It was love at first sight. Daemon knew that tone of voice. He had heard it again and again on Ayre Little as each new arrival to the island got to know their own mock. He was entirely forgotten as Elenor fed the dragon fish after fish, giggling as though she didn't have a care in the world and wasn't in the middle of a painful and exhausting flare of one of the worst diseases in Carinn.

He pulled a thick envelope from his inner coat pocket and placed it on the step next to her. "Instructions on how to train and raise her. I would hire someone for the training since you have a busy month or two ahead, but make sure to be the one to feed her at least twice a day. If you let her sleep with you for the first few weeks, all the better, though you want to break her of that by the time she's as big as a large dog. White mocks grow particularly fast. She'll be her adult size within ten months, and reach her adult weight within a year after that."

"Can I teach her to bite people I don't like?"

Daemon laughed. "I heartily endorse this plan."

Elenor looked up from the baby curled up in her lap, calmer than Daemon had yet to see the mockling, though that could have something to do with the fact that she had not slept or eaten much since he had picked her up. "What's her name?"

"Doesn't have one, though I would suggest a name with a double vowel. She comes from the far north, where the Tekomii tribes live. There, they believe that mocks, like people, have souls, and a creature without a double vowel in their name has had theirs stolen."

Elenor smirked. "Guess someone took mine. You seem to have yours, though."

That made the smile fade from his face. He knelt in front of her again. "No, I'm fairly certain I stole someone else's." He reached out to stroke the little dragon's fur. She hissed at him, but didn't try to bite this time. "I would suggest the Ee Essence. I know it means something else to the Mondaer and the Jia, but to the Tekomii it is the Essence of the arctic fox, who guides those who are lost and in need of food and shelter to safety in snowstorms. That, to me, seems like a fitting companion to someone with the weight of a kingdom on her shoulders and who looks rather lost right now."

Elenor's arms tightened around the fuzzball. "Thank you, Daemon. Are you leaving again?"

He inclined his head with a long sigh. "Alas, I have to go to the desert."

"Why?"

"I can't tell you that."

"Don't I get one question each time I see you for taking this adorable problem off your hands?"

He chuckled, shaking his head. "Remembered that, did you? Alright, then. One question, smartypants. Sure you want it to be that one?"

"Yes. But let me rephrase. Why are you going to the desert when you don't seem to want to?"

Damn, she was annoyingly perceptive. Daemon considered how to answer, and settled on honest, but vague. "I've been ordered to find out who killed someone there. I don't want to because long ago, I did a very bad thing and the Mondaer people have never forgotten it. Also because the person who was killed made a request of me that weighs on my mind, and I'm scared that going to the desert will force me down a road I'm not sure I want to tread."

"Not a follower of the Blue, I take it?" she asked, referring to the section of the litany of the Blue Dragon which said *I will walk the troubled road where others dare not tread.*

If only Elenor understood how ironic that question was.

"Not as much as I used to be."

"What was the request?" Elenor asked, her chin resting on the mock's fuzzy head as the small dragon's eyes drifted closed.

"That can be your question for next time. For now, why don't both you and your little friend try to get some rest?"

Daemon stood on a dune overlooking the vast and beautiful city of Aina Brisbhan. At the center of the sprawl of whitewashed buildings, the eponymous rock itself towered over the landscape, shining in the morning sun. Even at the height of his immortal hubris during the first century of his life, this was as close as Daemon had ever dared venture. The Mother Rock had been Fulsixia's domain, and she had defended it ruthlessly.

Now she was dead, and had left Daemon a responsibility he had never asked for. After his talk with Elenor, he had begrudgingly pieced the circuit that held Fulsixia's final message back together for Obri and Tsiihsi to hear, since they had agreed to accompany him. While Daemon wanted nothing to do with the task she had bequeathed him, the fact that a Goddess had made plans for after her death meant that there could be unforeseen dangers lurking in the desert. That, and whatever she had left him might be useful in ridding the world of Kennotoza the White.

Daemon wore the face of a nondescript Mondaer man, dressed in the loose linen robes the desert dwellers preferred. At his side, Tsiihsi wore much the same, though her clothes bore Jia markings as well. Obri stood a few steps away, looking around with curiosity at the endless rolling dunes. Since there was no hiding his light skin, the Bode had begrudgingly agreed to wear white, with a carefully painted impression of a scar on his inner arm so he could pass as a Mondaer slave.

"So, where to?" Daemon asked Tsiihsi as the wind blew from the city, ruffling his shoulder-length black hair and carrying with it the scent of smoke and spices. "You're in charge of directions today."

Tsiihsi tilted her head, eyes tracking across the city. "Is she really gone, Daemon?"

"You heard the message," Obri said. "Honestly, I don't see why you're so upset, Tsii. It's not like we're planning to desecrate some sacred temple. We're finding out who killed her, and besides: she *told* Daemon to come here."

"That's not what I'm upset about. She was one of *my people's Gods*. She had words I believed in. They weren't *my* words, but they were still important to me. Just because you think faith is stupid doesn't mean it is, O," Tsiihsi said, crossing her arms.

"Faith and superstition lead to nothing but wars and oppression. So the Gods are real and powerful. Big deal. That doesn't mean they're worthy of worship any more than Daemon is. He has power over every single aspect of my life, and you don't see me bowing to him or fetishizing his sayings."

"Except that you kind of do," Tsiihsi snapped back, though she did flash Daemon an apologetic expression.

Before Obri could dig himself deeper, Daemon interrupted. "Every minute we spend here is dangerous. This argument can wait for later. Where are we going, Tsiihsi?"

The young Eldel woman turned away from a scowling Obri towards the Mother Rock again. "She said the 'heart' of the desert, right? There's an old legend among the Mondaer that uses that phrasing. It's from before the Empire fell, when Lady Red did not yet take in all those who came to her border."

"You mean enslave, I'm sure."

"Obri, I know pushing people's buttons is your main form of entertainment, but could you stop for a few minutes? I'm actually hurting over this, asshole," Tsiihsi snapped. Obri's sneer faded. He walked up to Tsiihsi and placed a hand on her arm. No more words passed between them, but after a few tense seconds, Tsiihsi exhaled and relaxed. Obri wrapped an arm around her shoulders and gave her a squeeze, then stepped away again.

"Alright. Old legend, right? What does it say?" the Bode asked.

"Can't remember. I never paid much attention to them. But I know someone who would know. Daemon, I've never asked: can you open up those doorways anywhere, or does it have to be somewhere you've been before?"

Daemon had been staring at the Mother Rock again, but turned his attention to the young rifter. "I can open one anywhere. I usually try to scout a location from the air before going in lest I accidentally open a door in someone's chest. But if you show me where to go on a map, I can make an approximation and adjust from there."

Tsiihsi crouched down and with a long finger drew the outline of the desert in the sand. She pointed to a spot near the north-eastern corner. "There's a large oasis with huge citrus orchards somewhere around here. That's where we're going first."

That sparked a memory. Daemon frowned, remembering the night with Claire Enica, and the way the air had smelled of lemons when they landed on the dune overlooking the party. On impulse, he opened a doorway to that same spot. Tsiihsi's gasp confirmed he had the right spot, and his frown deepened.

That's not a coincidence.

Claire had taken him on four of those little jaunts of hers, and two of them were places Daemon had now returned to: right here, and the lemon orchard. The last—a long valley in the mountains, by a lake—had been all-too familiar as well, though it had taken Daemon a while to realize he had been right on his patron's doorstep.

Was there anything special about the cliff she had taken them to after trying to brain him with that rock?

"This the spot?" he asked, just to confirm.

"Yes. That's their house. Get me a little closer, and I'll go ask after my friend."

He did as instructed. Twenty minutes after Tsiihsi vanished into the mass of sprawling buildings, she returned, face ashen.

"This is where it happened, Dae. This is where Lady Red died. I spoke to one of Kaedy's uncles. He said that all the rifters who were here were broken in the blast, and that another Dragon—a golden one—appeared in the sky early yesterday morning."

What?

A *golden* Dragon?

Sure, Daemon had heard the legends. North Island and the Tekomii both worshiped a long-lost Gold Dragon in their own ways, and he had read enough Eldel mythology books over the centuries to have a basic understanding of their legends about the breaking of the world, but none of that lined up with a living dragon in the sky. Then again, if a magical blast large enough to kill multiple rifters had swept through here, maybe they had hallucinated it. Even non-rifters sometimes were shaky after that kind of event.

"Daemon, we need to go back to Aina Brisbhan. My friend was among the broken. She's at the main branch of the city hospital. I need to see her."

Tsiihsi's words yanked Daemon out of his reverie. "I'm so sorry, Tsii. Of course we can go. First, though, did he tell you how the Red died? I know it was one of the Gifted, but—"

"No."

Daemon narrowed his eyes. She had said that awfully quick. Obri, too, must have noticed, because he challenged her. "You sure?"

"I'm sure. He said that there was a Gifted who might have done it, but they didn't know what Gift he had, or where he is now. They did not see him after it happened."

"Probably dead, then. Too bad," Obri replied, but Daemon wasn't so sure. Tsiihsi was shifting from foot to foot, and when he tried to catch her eyes, she wouldn't meet them.

She was hiding something, but now was not the time to remind her of why that was a bad idea. "Where's this hospital?"

Ten minutes and several planar windows later, they stepped into an alley near a large, mosaic-covered building of reddish stone. Tsiihsi took the steps two at a time as she raced to the wide-open doors. Daemon followed at a more sedate pace, mind whirring. Obri, too, held back.

"This is a long way to travel in a day. How did they get here?" the Bode asked in a hushed tone.

"I was asking myself the very same question. I only know of one current Gift that could do it, but she's in Hardor and doesn't have much control yet. Something isn't right."

They entered into a large inner courtyard, surrounded on all sides by covered walkways. Tsiihsi was already talking to an attendant who sat at a desk by a gurgling fountain. By the time Daemon and Obri reached her, she had a room number written on a scrap of paper.

The wing of the hospital where they ended up was eerily quiet. When they reached the ward where Tsiihsi's friend was, Daemon understood why. In bed after bed, men and women lay in gentle but firm restraints. Had Daemon not seen broken rifters before, he would have questioned why the bindings were necessary. None of the patients thrashed or pulled. They lay there, some sleeping, others staring into space as if life had already left them.

So many.

Daemon shuddered, taking an involuntary step back into the hall. Obri placed a hand on his shoulder and squeezed, but, unlike North, the Bode didn't know the story of why a roomful of broken rifters would send Daemon into a spiraling panic. He didn't *want* Obri to know how he had tortured a child to the breaking point, sending out a shockwave of magic that had killed and broken hundreds, because . . . Because then Obri and his other handful of dear and trusted Ayre Island friends might look at him the way North had. Ayre knew him only as Daemon; he never wanted them to meet Jac.

Tsiihsi moved towards a bed at the far end, but Dae backed further into the hallways and slid down the nearest column, until his head was between his knees.

"Go with Tsiihsi, O. I can't—can't go in there."

The Bode didn't move. "What's wrong?"

Daemon shook his head, lips pressed shut. Obri studied him for some time, then walked across the hallway to sit next to Daemon. With a long sigh, he slung an arm around Dae's shoulders. "Tsii can take care of herself. I'll stay where I'm needed."

Within the room, Tsiihsi began to cry. It was quiet and muffled, but it made Daemon's chest ache. "Broken rifters . . . always get to me."

"Well, you are a protector of rifters and Gifted, aren't you?" Obri asked.

Daemon squeezed his eyes shut. "I've hurt too many rifters and Gifted to carry that title, my friend. Hurt, killed, and broken. I'm going to find the Gifted who did this, then leave these people alone. They're better off without me."

But what would he do with the Gifted who had killed a God and broken all these people? Daemon had seen the hatred and vitriol that had spread through Lirin after Alehan's explosion of power. To this day, anti-magic paranoia still popped up from time to time. How much worse would it be for a man who had killed a God?

I'll take him to Ayre. Even if he's alone there until I can find out how his Gift works, at least no one will be able to hurt him. I wasn't able to do that for Alehan, but maybe I can do better this time. Even if it angers Xirra, it's the right thing to do.

The decision lifted some of the weight from his chest, but not enough. Minutes turned into a half-hour. The occasional quiet whimper of the broken rifters scratched at his soul like razor-sharp nails. Each wound was tolerable, but they stacked atop each other, layering guilt and memories on so thick it became unbearable.

Obri quietly passed him a handkerchief when Daemon started to cry. He still hadn't stopped when Tsiihsi appeared at the door to the ward, supporting a short-haired young woman with red eyes rimmed in dark circles. She was wrapped in a thick robe yet still shivered, despite the heat. Even though she bore no visible injury, her movements were pained and leaden.

"Dae, this is Kaedy. Kaedy, this is my rifting instructor, Daemon," Tsiihsi said, looking towards him in concern.

Daemon wiped away his tears and pushed himself to his feet. He extended his hands to Kaedy, wrapping both around hers when she held it out. "It is nice to meet you, Kaedy, though I wish it were under better circumstances. I'm sorry for what you have lost. For *all* you have lost."

The young woman looked up at him slowly, the motion stiff. "Thank you. Tsiihsi told me about the message Lady Red left you. You are welcome here, chosen of Fulsixia."

Daemon's grief was momentarily shoved aside by annoyance. He pursed his lips, sending a quiet message to his apprentice that only she would hear. **I didn't give you permission to share that detail. Communications like that are private. Don't do it again.**

Tsiihsi huffed audibly, but replied, **If you want my people to help you, you'll have to give them a reason. Besides, I think I have a lead.** Out loud, his apprentice said, "Kaedy has agreed to take us to the Mother Rock. She says there is a chamber there known as the Heart of the Desert, where her grandfather just went for a meeting about what should be done with the Gifted who killed the Red. If we hurry, we might get there as it begins."

CHAPTER TWELVE
The Love of a Father
ELENOR

After the death of King Loren Lirion and his Queen Consort Sora Ondai-Lirion, Queen Lilian Lirion rose to the throne. At only eighteen years of age and with the Crown deep in debt after her parents' many investments into Lirinian infrastructure, the young Queen bought both money and security by arranging a double marriage with the two princes of Miriel. She married the younger, Markus, and her little sister Sianta was sent to Miriel to marry its heir, Warren. In doing so, all four ended up on the throne. While this may have been a good political move, neither of the marriages appear to be happy ones.

—From the private historical notes of Robin Tirition.

ELENOR STOOD IN THE PALACE CHAPEL as the dawn light crept across the tiled floor. Her wheelchair sat at the base of the stairs up to the altar of the White Dragon, Paul beside it, but it somehow felt right to stand for this, despite the pain.

Her father's body lay on the altar, covered in a thin white shroud.

"He looks like he's sleeping," she said, to no one in particular. "Do you remember when I caught him sleeping and drew hearts all over his face? How old was I?"

"You were almost six. It was just a few months before . . . everything changed," Paul replied, tone somber.

"I don't recall if he got angry." Elenor reached out, her fingers brushing over her father's straight nose.

"No. He never did back then. He took the day off since he couldn't make the ink fade enough for court, and took you riding in the countryside. You came back with strawberry stains all over both of your clothes. Wilam was inconsolable."

Elenor bit her bottom lip, fingertips trailing up to his bushy eyebrows. "I wish I knew why he loved me more than Wil. And why he stopped. Did Wil or I do something wrong, Paul?"

"No, *daareesha.* Never think that. You were both children and did nothing more than try to love your parents. It is not your fault that they were . . . difficult people. Whatever his reasons, *taale,* you are not responsible for the hatred that led him down his path."

Elenor wasn't so sure. Her hand cupped his cheek. "Almost everything from the night he died is fuzzy, but not those last few seconds. When I knelt and begged for his forgiveness," she swallowed the lump in her throat, "as I got ready to . . . to end his life . . . I saw his eyes soften. He looked sad, not angry. I hate him for what he did to Djina and to my country, but . . . " Elenor trailed off, unable to finish. Tears welled in her eyes and she did not try to wipe them away.

"Power has a way of complicating what should be simple," Robin Titition said, emerging from the shadows where Elenor knew a door to the priest's quarters stood. "Like the love of a father for a daughter, or that of a little girl for the childhood hero who turns out to be a villain."

Elenor looked up at the Tirition as he stepped up to the altar on the other side. She cleared her throat. "Thank you for agreeing to meet so early. I know you are busy, but this was the only time I had in my schedule."

"You need not thank me, Your Highness. You are, at present, the leader of the richest and most powerful Kingdom in Carinn. Even the Council of Ten bends to your schedule—at least on trifling matters such as an early morning meeting." Robin's gaze trailed along Elenor's features, and as always with this man, she felt like he was seeing more than she intended to share. "Forgive my impudence, but you look tired."

"I am," Elenor replied. There was no point in lying, not with the dark circles under her eyes and the way the serindalla still made her muscles shake. "And I'm afraid that is a state that is likely to persist for some time. If we finish our business swiftly, though, I may be able to fit in a nap, so I would appreciate brevity." A nap which she might actually be able to sleep through, curled around the fluffy warm ball of wings and fuzz that Claire and Gabriel were presently watching.

Robin inclined his head, eyes falling to the late King. "Brevity suits me as well. If you would indulge one question, however, I would like to know why you chose to meet here?"

Elenor, too, looked down at her father again. "Because I wanted to see him one last time before the Palace was inundated with visitors. When we light the pyre to release his body to the Gods tonight, I will have to be there as Regent of Lirin, not his daughter. Everyone will be watching. I wanted to say my goodbyes now."

Robin cocked his head to the side. "To the man who you claim to have killed?"

"No . . . not him. I have nothing left to say to him. It's the father I recall from long ago that I wish to remember, not the monster he became. Those memories are why I will not declare him forgotten, despite his crimes." Elenor pressed her palm to the cold marble of the altar. "He is a reminder that I dare not forget."

"A reminder of what?"

"Of what I can never allow myself to become." Elenor met Robin's gaze. "He was petty, vengeful, and proud. I cannot be, so I think I should start this conversation by apologizing about how we last met. I acted like a bully . . . like him. I don't want that to be the way I rule."

"Admirable sentiment, Your Highness. Not enough to make up for the damage you might have done if things had not turned out in your favor, nor a wise position to take going forward considering the obstacles in your path, but I will weigh it in the balance. Will you take me to Gabriel?"

Elenor hadn't really expected the Tirition to fold and accept her apology, but his reply still made her sigh. "No."

The affable smile Robin always wore faded. "So an empty apology, then? You still do not plan to cooperate. Have you forgotten the danger he poses to this city?"

"Frankly, Master Robin, I am not sure that he would be any less dangerous in your hands than mine. Daemon has promised to train him to use his magic—"

"He has?" Robin asked, sounding genuinely surprised.

"Yes."

"Hmm. Fascinating."

Elenor waited for him to say more. When Robin did not, she

chose not to press, continuing where she left off. "I want to know what you intend to do with Gabriel before I let you near him. The last time we met, you threatened Lirin, Master Robin. How can I call myself regent of this kingdom if I handed you a potential city-destroying weapon after that? Not to mention, he is one of my subjects. Gabriel has gone through too much already because of my decisions. I will not hand him over to you, only to have you put more wounds on his soul."

She expected Robin to be angry at her refusal. Instead, his smile returned, as did that maddening twinkle in the Tirition's eye. "What are your demands, Your Highness?"

"Demands?" Elenor asked, genuinely confused. "I asked what you wanted with Gabriel. I don't have demands."

"Of course you do. You requested I be brief, so let me speed this up. You asked what I want with Gabriel. That is none of your business, at present. When I say that, you will make demands, in exchange for giving me permission to meet with him. I have a few guesses at what they will be. First, you are going to ask for my assistance in the matter of the upcoming visit with the Miri. You fear for your life and your throne, and are clever enough to know that Tirit Mindel's power could protect you. Second, you will ask for information about your mother, because the Island sees everything and she and I had business together. Third, you will ask me to assist you in the upcoming trial to determine your culpability for the death of your father. Am I close?"

Elenor tried to school her face into something that wasn't disappointed shock, but must have failed, for Robin chuckled. "Don't worry, Your Highness. It is not that you are particularly transparent, simply that your situation is dire. I listed what I would ask for, were I in your shoes."

"And? Will you help with those things?" Elenor asked, bracing for further disappointment.

"That depends."

"On when I let you see Gabriel?" Elenor ventured, exhaustion heavy on her shoulders. She hated playing this game, but too much was at stake to just let this man get his way.

Was this why her father had always looked exhausted? Even

in death, the wrinkles on his forehead were deep furrows. He had hated the Island and the rifters it trained. Elenor wasn't sure how she felt about magic these days, but she didn't blame him one bit for not trusting Tirit Mindel. Even over the corpse of her own father, Robin was playing Elenor for a fool. She still had a few strings to pull, though. "Don't forget our deal, Robin. I could turn him against you, if you don't help me."

The Tirition shook his head. "You mean the deal we made with your boot against my throat? The one you just apologized for? You cannot have things both ways, Miss Lirion. Is this a negotiation between allies or an exchange of mutually destructive threats? I can play either role, though I prefer the former."

Elenor's hand slipped off the altar so she could ball it up without the Tirition noticing. "Gabriel deserves to know that you manipulated him, and that a woman he trusted was draining him of his magic at your command. Don't try to paint me as the unethical one."

"Aren't you? If you were as ethical as I think you wish to be, wouldn't you have already told him, instead of holding back because I might be useful to you?" Robin asked. "No, Miss Lirion. You are not as good-hearted as you believe yourself to be. Not yet, at any rate. I am not surprised, given who raised you, though I had hoped Djina had taught you better."

Had he really just . . . ? "How dare you say that? You didn't even know her. She was—"

"My sister."

Elenor's anger fizzled in shock. All she managed to stammer was, "What?"

Robin reached into his pocket and pulled out a small framed drawing, holding it for Elenor to see. In it, a young woman with Djina's face but none of the wrinkles or worries held a boy of three or four on her hip.

"Half-sister to be precise. She was already an adult when I was born and we were never as close as siblings should be, but that does not mean I did not know her. Tirition is a title that takes the place of my last name, but it was Grau before that. My loyalties always and forever lie with the family of the Black Dragon."

The what? Elenor's confusion must have shown on her face, for Robin smiled. "I see you do not understand. It is a pity your education did not prepare you for this battlefield, but I would not be able to call myself a teacher if I thought less of someone for needing to learn. There are five Dragon Gods, yes? Or six, if you count the Silver That Was. Each of these Gods has a family that is their bridge to the mortal world. Your family, Miss Lirion, is such a one. It is not merely fanciful speech when the Lirion are called the family of the White. She is both your patron deity and your direct creator. Zorbennen the Black is mine, as he was Djina's. The Grau have fallen from prominence over the last few centuries, but we remain, as ever, united in our cause."

"And what cause is that?" Elenor asked, still reeling.

"Remembering the past and dreaming of a better future. You ask what I want with Gabriel, and it is that. He is part of the future I have dedicated my life to: one where our world is united in peace, and where mine and Djina's families no longer have to hide in the shadows for the crime of not wanting to forget the past."

What did that mean? It *was* a crime to remember those deemed taboo, but not one that was often punished. How could a judge prove a memory, after all? It was only when people wrote or publicly spoke of the Forgotten that the law came down on them. Did the Grau family keep records, or something?

Elenor asked none of that, though her curiosity burned hot. Robin always seemed to use her words against her, and Elenor did not trust her muddled mind to win a verbal duel.

When she said nothing, the Tirition finally got to his own demands. "I am willing to help you, Miss Lirion. In part because I think our goals could be aligned, and in part because my sister cared for you. My priority is still Gabriel—and if you try to poison him against me my good intentions will evaporate—but if you are willing to cooperate, I shall assist you with your troubles."

"What do you want in return?"

Robin smiled at the bite in Elenor's question. "I'm glad to see that spirit survived the last few days. It is not a large request, but one that I expect you might be uniquely suited for. You see, your mother was searching for a specific document, of which only three copies were ever made. One is likely in the hands of one of your enemies if it is not already ash. Until recently I had one in my possession, but it was destroyed. The other is . . . lost. I want you to find it."

Behind her, Paul bristled. Elenor pursed her lips, attempting to contain her annoyance. "I don't have time for a scavenger hunt, Master Robin. I am a bit busy, if you haven't noticed."

"You would have been less busy if you had allowed the Island to step in as an intermediary in these upcoming negotiations, but alas . . . "

"I really don't like you," she spat.

He laughed. "But I like you, Miss Lirion. You have a will to greatness and the tenacity to see it through, though it's been buried under quite the pile of, forgive my language, bullshit."

Bracing her weight on the altar because her legs were starting to go numb, Elenor continued to glare at Robin. "What's so important about this document? Why would I have more luck finding it than you? And does it have something to do with where my mother is?"

More pressing but too dangerous to say aloud: *Do you have her?*

Robin looked down at Elenor through his spindly glasses, and she wasn't sure how to read the expression that crossed his face. His lips still turned up, but his eyes seemed mournful.

"It may, or it may not. The document is important because it opens a political shortcut that several factions are either counting on or fear. It is a rather thick envelope, closed with a special wax seal."

Out of a pocket of his robes, Robin pulled a ring, passing it to Elenor. She trailed her thumb over the raised metal, brows scrunching. "I don't recognize this. It's the Lirion heron, but the mountain behind it looks like the twin peaks of the Miri."

"Quite similar, yes. Here is what I know of the location of the document. I wrote it for Warren Miri in December of 518 on Tirit Mindel. One copy remained there with me, another went home with him. A third was entrusted to someone he didn't think would be targeted. I expect that someone was Djina. She never confirmed or denied it, but I would start with her office here at the Palace. What I *am* certain of is that it came to Hardor eventually, because if it had gone back to Miriel, I doubt you would have suffered so. It will be close to you, perhaps even in a place you've seen before, so I need you to think carefully."

Elenor's already narrowed eyes squinted further. "My uncle Warren wrote it? And I think you might be mistaken. I was born in December of 518, and Djina delivered me. Why would she be on Tirit Mindel?"

Behind her, she heard Paul cough. Elenor looked back at him, puzzled. Her *doena* approached. When close enough, he bent to whisper in her ear, "She was there, *talidaar*. I can confirm it. It was the very end of December, a few weeks after you were born."

How did *Paul* know that?

"Is there anything else you can tell me? Are you sure it even still exists?" Elenor asked Robin.

"I hope so. This is my deal, Miss Lirion: Find that document and read it, then bring it and Gabriel to me. Give me one hour to talk to both of you. Agree to that, and I will provide all the help I can. You don't even have to give me the document. All I need is your attention and an open mind."

Elenor's mouth was dry as she considered her options. "And if I cannot find it?"

"Then, frankly, you are of no further use to my plans."

Damn it.

"Then we better hope I find it quickly."

"Indeed, we better."

Robin placed the ring on her father's chest, inclined his head to her, and slipped out of the chapel the way he had come.

Elenor picked up the ring and looked at it again. "I feel like I've seen this before."

"You have, many times. Come with me . . . when you're ready," Paul murmured, gesturing to her father.

Elenor looked down at him one last time, then reached into her pocket and pulled out a sprig of evergold she had picked in her garden on the way here. She carefully lifted the shroud and tucked the little yellow flower in his beard, like she had so often as a child.

"Goodbye, Papa." She bent to kiss his brow. "I'm sorry."

CHAPTER THIRTEEN
Shadows of a Dead God
NORTH

You dared to take my son. Now, I have killed yours. You and Aislin broke every oath you swore to me and to the Empire. This is your reward. I hope you live a long life, Jac. A bitter and lonely one with time to contemplate how your actions killed your wife and boy. Would they be dead today if you had not come to the desert to steal Alehan from me? They suffered, before the end. You should know that, as you search for where I buried them. Now return our son to us, before the rest of your wretched family joins Aislin and Julian, you two-faced bastard.

—From a note to Jac Drego, from Alexander Silvarin.

LIGHT REFRACTED OFF THE RIPPLING SURFACE of the underground lake, painting ever-shifting patterns on the walls of the cavernous temple. Every drop from the stalactites sent a crystalline echo drifting through the air. It smelled of cool earth. Of lichen. Of reverence.

North shivered and pulled his thin blue robes closer, wishing that Bard had been allowed to come down here with him. He could use the comfort and distraction of his mock.

The temple was deep within Aina Brisbhan, the great rock extending nearly as far underground as it did above. Every winding, nature-wrought hallway looked the same to North, though in truth no two were even of equal height, let alone shape or direction. This cavern, too, lacked the clean lines and symmetry he was used to, but there was no doubt that it was a temple to a God.

In the center of the great underground lake, a huge statue of a red dragon loomed over the water. Time and moss darkened each crevice and shadow of her majestic body, giving the statue a depth and realism that art alone could not have. If North had not seen Fulsixia the Red in the flesh, he might have believed that the statue was the Goddess herself, about to open her eyes.

"This place is creepy," Fayrian said from beside him. He knew he should call her Rian, but his Gift still gave him the name she was born to. That detail had bothered North more and more of late. How much could he trust his Gift if all it gave him was beginnings?

"It is beautiful," Leo replied in an awed voice. "And it is sacred."

Fay snorted. "It's a damp cave."

"You are being purposely contrary, Fayrian," Suela scolded, tone sharp. "Follow."

The old woman walked past them, cane lightly moving across the floor in front of her. At the edge of the lake, a narrow path led to a small island in the shadow of the great dragon. There were words carved into the sandstone. As North got nearer, he recognized them as the words of the Red.

"'Though born a seed, I will sink roots and rise towards the sky. No storm can break me, for always will I bend and grow. May all be welcome in my shade where side-by-side we craft a better world. Let our names live on in our creations,'" Leo recited, catching North looking at it. "The Litany of the Red."

At the base of the statue, five short podiums stood in a circle, a pillow upon each. Other cushions were placed to form an outer ring, but it was clear that this space was primarily for five to meet.

As those invited trickled in, those five became apparent. Suela, Quindo, Akaaron, and Moe. One spot remained empty, and North noted that while Suela leaned on her pedestal, she did not sit upon it.

Other familiar faces joined them. Phoebi Deil arrived with Quindo, along with the news that Kaedy had been sleeping when they left the hospital. Tavea also came with them, huddled in a thick sweater and without her customary poise, but doing better than most of the broken rifters North had seen. Leo hurried over to aid his *doena* cross to the little island.

"No one who wasn't at the estate is here," North mentioned as they took their seats. "Is it because no one else knows what happened?"

"Indeed," Suela answered. "We will tell the other *daradeio* at today's gathering, but before we do, we must discuss how to break the news and what we will do with the Gatekeeper who took our Goddess from us. His life will be in danger, and we must be prepared to protect him."

North had formally met her when they had spoken to Fedrik through a huge and complex circuit high in Aina Brisbhan, but she still made his senses itch almost as much as Moe. Suela's name registered to North's Gift, but where there should have been a calling and magical status, there was only static.

It would have been enough to give North a headache on its own but, next to Moe, it was almost pleasant. Every time North's eyes traced over the strange man, flashes of pain ripped through him, leaving a salty taste in his mouth.

"Shall we begin?" Quindo asked.

Moe pulled a battered notebook out of his pocket. He had changed out of the bright pink suit at some point and wore a completely different style of trousers and an aggressively pinstriped shirt in teal and orange. The pants were tight and ripped over the knees in a way that looked oddly deliberate, and the top of his scuffed, lace-up shoes shimmered silver. Flipping through a few pages he nodded, glanced down at a pocket watch, then put the notebook away. "Not yet. We're waiting for a guest. He should be here any second—"

The great doors at the end of the cathedral opened, drawing everyone's attention. Kaedy stood there, shoulders hunched but a determined look on her face. That was not why North jumped to his feet, though. It was not even the shock of seeing Tsiihsi's arm around Kaedy's shoulder, or Obri standing behind them dressed in a slave's white. No, it was the unfamiliar man who walked in between them, whose face might be different but whose name, according to his Gift, was Jac Drego.

North marched across the bridge, past all the puzzled faces, right up to the man who had sentenced him to death under the harsh Mondaer sun. Without stopping to think it through, he pulled back his arm and punched Daemon square in the nose, beyond caring about the consequences. "Get out."

The rifter must not have seen it coming, because the blow landed and Daemon stumbled back, a hand to his now-bleeding face. Behind him, North thought he heard Fay whistle and clap.

"How dare you come here?" North bellowed. "Out. GET OUT! You have no business in this place."

"North?" Tsiihsi and Obri both exclaimed, her in surprised pleasure, him in shock. Under any other circumstances, North would have been overjoyed to see them again. Right then, all he could see was Daemon.

Daemon, who had sent him here, who had once come to the desert to steal a child from his bed and tortured him until he broke, turning himself immortal in the process. North hadn't forgotten the story Laitika the Lusion had shown him of how the Incarnate Gift first came to the desert as payment for that crime. The Mondaer thought Jac Drego died when Alehan exploded magically, but North knew the truth.

Daemon was a monster from their histories, alive and back to cause more havoc. But North wasn't going to let him meddle here. Akaaron kept saying that North was Mondaer, right? Time to protect his people. Daemon *could not* find out about the Gatekeeper and Incarnate Gifts. "You are not welcome here, Jac Drego. You will never be welcome here after what you did."

"Did you say *Jac Drego?*" Quindo said in alarm. "Akaaron? Can you confirm this?"

"It's impossible . . . " the other Namer gasped, his shocked whisper bouncing off the stone and still water.

"How could he possibly be Jac Drego?" Phoebi asked. "Wasn't he a rifter at the time of the Empire's fall? That was five centuries ago."

"North, you're a dead man," Daemon threatened, quietly enough only North could hear. He might have said more, but Suela's voice broke through the din of questions.

"Servant of the Blue, our brother speaks truth. You are not welcome here in Fulsixia's domain. Leave. Kaedy Deil, you had no business leading the servant of another God to this holy place. You are newly broken and your actions therefore forgivable, but we will have words."

Kaedy flinched, her once jovial face devoid of anything but the hollow pallor of pain and grief. "I accept your chastisement, but I would not have done so if it were not importa—Woah!"

With a loud pop, Moe appeared behind Daemon.

"What the—" Daemon cried as he stumbled back from Moe.

"Enough chit-chat. Running a little late, aren't we? I'd expect better from another Planar adept." A hand shot out to grab the back of Daemon's shirt and North's shoulder, then—

Pop!

North stumbled as they landed, and so did Daemon. Moe had no trouble pushing the rifter down onto the open seat in the circle of five. "You go here. Since there's a stupidly high chance she's going to trust you one day, you can speak for the new disaster-Incarnate—"

"The what?" Daemon asked, but was ignored.

"And you, girl—yes, you with the red hair—you go sit next to Suela and speak for the God-Killer. Suela, do take over for me, darling. I'm very behind schedule, so let's make this quick," Moe said, clapped his hands, then turned to North, who took an involuntary step back.

Pop!

Moe was an inch in front of North's nose. "You don't like him, do you?" he asked, pointing at Daemon, who still looked stunned. "And don't trust him?"

"Not at all."

"Good. In that case," Moe leaned in close and whispered something into North's ear. "Got it? Need me to repeat?"

"No, but—"

Moe turned back around to the gathered crowd and sank into an extravagant bow. "Good people of Dracona. I, Merihem Crystal—but please do call me Moe or I'll be forced to kill you—am, as a good friend would say, 'done with this bullshit of a planet.' Lady Red left me a message for him," he pointed at Daemon, "to be given only if he proves himself a friend to the desert and a person of good moral standing. I am not an expert in those things—though don't tell my fans—so since I am very late for my own bloody uprising and need to go figure out how to untangle the mess you fuckers have tied yourselves in, let me give you the short version."

He gestured toward North. "This kiddo knows the answers you're looking for, Mr. Indigo. Don't kill him. Suela my sweet, you got team murder munchkins in the bag? Yes? Good. Miss Fayrian, consider carefully where your loyalties lie. They'll be important later on. Quindo: stay your grumpy self and hold the desert together until things shake out. You'll have a lot to teach the Exiles soon. Akaaron, time to spill the beans about the kid. And speaking of inanimate objects, you . . . " Moe spun, pointing a finger directly at Daemon's chest. "The question you should be asking isn't heads or tails, but how many sides does a coin have?"

"What?" Daemon spluttered.

"Well, I think that's my cue to leave. I have other places to be, you know. Toodles. I'll see you after the fireworks." Moe waggled his fingers and popped out of existence.

"I hate that man so much," Quindo snarled through the dead silence.

"Who *was* that?" Daemon asked, for once sounding just as confused as North felt.

Good. He deserved it.

"That was *Moe.* He's been visiting the Mondaer since the breaking of the world," Suela replied, in the same even voice she usually used. "All of you, take your seat. *No arguing.* Kaedy and those by the door, come here and sit *in silence.* It's too late to keep you out of this."

Whether from shock or curiosity, everyone obeyed. In a matter of minutes, Daemon, Fayrian, Suela, Quindo, and Akaaron sat on each of the pedestals, with everyone else in attendance on the floor behind them, though not before some choice words between Suela and Quindo about whether Fay should be allowed to be one of the five. They concluded that she would be, but only permitted to chime in about the Gatekeeper. Daemon opened his mouth, but Quindo held up a finger. "Suela speaks first, then we will go around in a circle. You will not talk out of turn. For those in attendance, you will not make a sound unless you are invited into the circle. Understood? This has been our way since our people came to be, and it will be the way in this trying time as well."

Daemon glowered, crossed his arms, but did not speak. North

itched to, but just as he started opening his mouth, Tsiihsi reached out to take his hand.

North looked over at her, and saw her mouth, "I missed you." Obri, on her other side, was also looking at him with a wide smile.

The anger inside North softened, and he squeezed Tsiihsi's hand. "Missed you too," he mouthed back.

"We will begin with the business of this incursion," Quindo said. "North the Namer, please enter the circle. I have questions for you."

North obeyed, walking to the center and facing Quindo, though he angled himself so as to keep Daemon in view. "What do you want to know?"

"I'd like to start with who this man is."

North squared his shoulders, turned to Daemon, and without breaking eye contact said, "He is Jac Drego, known now as Daemon Indigo. Five centuries ago he kidnapped and tortured Alehan Silvarin to the point of breaking, and was rendered immortal in the act. He is a murderer, a manipulator, and the person who left me in the desert to die."

"Suela?" Quindo asked.

The old woman raised her unseeing gaze from her lap, giving the disquieting impression that she could see them all through those bandages. "He is the servant of Xirra, the Blue Dragon, the Gatekeeper of the Gods. I believe he has no place here, but we likely do not have the means to stop him from observing us, were he to want to. As such, I would rather hear what he has come to say."

Servant of Xirra, the Blue Dragon, the Gatekeeper of the Gods.

North shuddered, many pieces to the puzzle that was Daemon slipping into place. If Fedrik was a Gatekeeper and had killed a God and broken hundreds, how much more horrifying could the God of the Gatekeepers be? And who else would hold Daemon's leash? If it was the Blue who had given Daemon his order to kill Gabriel, North would never bow to her oath again.

Quindo turned to Akaaron, who, with a wobble to his words, said, "I don't know how, but it is as they say. He is Jac Drego, firstborn of Jakan Drego and Lucina Arlen, born five centuries ago in the time of the fall of the Empire and the establishment of the Charter.

That makes him the man who broke into our sacred Aina Brisbhan and stole Alehan Silvarin from our care. He has no business on this pedestal, especially speaking for the Last Gift."

North couldn't help but smile in satisfaction. The other Namer understood the horror of Daemon's presence in this sacred space.

Akaaron, though, was not done. "Safety for the last of the Silvarin was one of the founding principles of the Charter. He is a proven danger to that line. As such, another Naming must be made. First, though, Rian." Akaaron looked to Fay, then leaned in to whisper something in her ear.

She nodded. Fast as blinking, Fayrian reached over and touched Daemon's hand.

The rifter screamed.

He tried to pull away from Fay, but the steely-eyed redhead snagged his wrist and twisted it behind Daemon's back. By the time she had him bent over, his whole body was shaking and limp.

"Got him." She stepped away, leaving the rifter clutching at the edges of his pedestal and visibly clammy. It took North a few more seconds to realize that she must have drained Daemon's well of magic.

"He'll be able to refill with the heat in the air," North warned, remembering the lesson he had witnessed.

"You're going to regret—" Daemon started.

"No, she won't, and no, he won't refill," Leo said, voice colder than North had ever heard it. The air, too, grew chill, until North had to hug himself to keep from shivering. His breath fogged, taking him back to his childhood in the far north. Leo wasn't finished, though. He sat up tall. "No one will draw blood in this sacred space, while a single *daradeio* lives to defend it. Say what you must say in safety, *doena* Akaaron. I will aid our sister Rian in keeping magic at bay."

"Well spoken, and thank you, Leo," the older Namer said, then Akaaron looked to Daemon. "You may remain to speak and listen until the end of this meeting, but whether here or beyond our borders, he whom you know as North Hillman is under our protection. I heard your threats and warn you now: if you touch him, neither magic nor might will save you, for in his blood runs that of

Moira Silvarin, first of the Mondaer bearers of the Last Gift and last child born of Cianira Marzi of the Jia and Alexander Silvarin of the Exiles. By the tenants of the Eldel Charter—"

"And the Hardor Accords," Suela interjected.

"You may not harm him, on pain of death," Akaaron finished.

What?

As North reeled, trying to absorb those words, Daemon raised his head, dark hair falling in front of his bloodshot eyes. His shoulders still shook, and his face had grown haggard from having his magic forcibly drained away. He met North's shocked gaze and started laughing, low and just a little hysterical. "I should have known."

"I don't understand," Fayrian said, looking between North and Akaaron. "What are you saying?"

North took a step back, then another. "That's . . . not . . . "

"He's a Silvarin," Akaaron clarified. "His parents are Estelle Nameh, who descends from the Silvarin hidden away by Tirit Mindel, and Jonah Iaming, whose line traces back to Moira of the Last Gift. He's—"

"Gabriel's brother," Fay gasped.

CHAPTER FOURTEEN
Of Blood and Gold
GABRIEL

Keyholder, Keyholder, where did you go? Keyholder, Keyholder, what do you know? The halls are so silent, the walls made of stone. You've left us in darkness, abandoned your throne. But we will remember, we wait for your call. You'll come back to guide us, and rise from our fall.

—From a Valora Chant of the Third Century of Darkness.

"HOLD THE GOLD BETWEEN YOUR HANDS, like this," Paul instructed Gabriel, as they sat by the unlit hearth. The *doena* had one of the thick gold bars that had appeared along with the shawl for Elenor the day before. Paul was holding it level with his heart, right hand under the bar, left on top. "Imagine that your well of magic is your heart, pumping both magic and blood through your veins. Now, breathe in, and picture magic flowing from your heart into your left arm, all the way down to your palm, where it presses against the gold. Think of the metal like cheesecloth. Your will and magic pass from your left hand into the gold, where the magic remains, but your will passes through into your right hand and back along your arm to your heart."

"Like a circle," Gabriel ventured, closing his eyes and taking the same pose Paul had.

"Yes, exactly. Or, more technically correct, a circuit. A loop of focused purpose. Magic follows the mind's command, so if you do not succeed in pushing all of it into the gold, you want to visualize an alternative path. If you do not, it is liable to act on your erratic and passing fancies. A rifter must always be calm, focused, and prepared. Thus: a circle. Breathe with it. Exhale and let the magic flow down your left arm into the gold. Inhale and bring your focus up your right arm and back to your well. Then repeat."

"How did you learn all this, Paul?" a pregnant woman Elenor had introduced as Bethany Rinelisi, Eric's wife, asked. She sat with her husband, Claire, and Elenor on the rug by the garden doors. Between them, the little white mock dragon Elenor had been curled up with when Gabriel and the others had woken that morning was batting at a piece of ribbon.

"I was raised in the Cerulean Guild in Miriel," the *doena* replied. Though he spoke calmly, his voice held an undercurrent of annoyance as he looked over at the little mock dragon. Gabe couldn't blame him. He didn't like the way Daemon kept appearing out of nowhere either. So far, it had always been to help him or Elenor, but Gabriel wasn't convinced that would continue. He still remembered the bread and soup the mysterious rifter had given him in that hellish cell, and how he had called it the most expensive meal Gabriel would ever eat.

At some point, this generosity would come due, but telling Elenor that when she was smiling, despite her fever and the weight of Lirin on her shoulders, would be both pointless and cruel.

Next to her on the floor lay her brother's long rapier. As Gabriel watched, she picked it up for the hundredth time, examining the guard, where a heron atop a mountain was wrought in fine filigree.

"It's just a symbol, Elenor. Your father was a Miri, your mother a Lirion. It makes sense Wil would have included both when he commissioned this," a black-haired nobleman—Tomaz Catoali, scion of one of the minor, unWritted Noble houses—said from the bed, where he sat with a lap desk, taking notes.

"But the exact same design? And why would my *uncle* use this symbol? He was the King of Miriel."

A poke to Gabriel's arm yanked his focus back to Paul and the bar of gold.

"Focus."

"Sorry."

Gabe closed his eyes and inhaled, trying to visualize the circle Paul had explained. Both his hands were free of bandages now, bones and joints still sore but usable. He hadn't missed the sour looks Elenor kept directing his way as she gingerly maneuvered around in a sling. They made him feel guilty, but he had already asked Paul if he could use his magic to heal her and been given a stern lecture as to why that did not work.

"Magic isn't a cure-all. It follows will. Your brain understands your own body and can fix it, but you cannot do the same to others without decades of intense study. Even then, it is one of the most dangerous things you could ever attempt, requiring pinpoint precision. Never try."

"Focus!" Paul snapped.

Gabe made a face. "I'm trying. It's hard."

"Of course it is. You're oversaturated. That's *why* you need to focus."

Gritting his teeth, Gabe attempted to tune out the conversation going on between Elenor and the nobles, and focus on his magic.

Once he did, it was hard to pay attention to anything else. His well—which has always been a distant, difficult to access reservoir—was brimming with power. Gabriel pulled a small thread of it as he inhaled, pushing it down his left arm as he exhaled. The pain from the bruises faded at once. He let out a startled gasp, the magic slipping from his control.

"*Small* amounts, Gabriel. Not half your damn well," Paul chided, shuddering. "The ambient magic just went up several degrees. And don't even think of checking that for yourself. The last thing you need is to accidentally absorb even more power."

Gabe leaned back on the couch with a huff. "That *was* a small amount."

"No, it wasn't. Try again, but with one-tenth that much, if that."

Out of the corner of his eye, he caught Elenor looking at him. She seemed concerned. As soon as she caught him looking, she turned her attention back to the small mock dragon, who had crawled into her lap and was yawning.

"Gabriel," Paul snapped, yanking his attention back to the other rifter.

"Sorry." Annoyed at his wandering focus, Gabe sat up straight and tried again. This time, he pulled a thread so small and tenuous that he feared losing it. He sent it along his arm with supreme concentration and got all the way to the elbow when an itch on one of his scabbed-over wounds made him twitch. The thread of magic fizzled, and a sharp pressure flicked at the offending itch. Gabe jumped, his hand going to the spot on his ribs. Nothing was there.

Paul reached forward and lightly cuffed his ear. "That mock dragon has more focus than you, boy, and she can't be more than a month old. Clear your mind."

If it weren't for the fact that Paul had a sword and Gabriel only had a bar of gold, he might have snapped back. Instead, Gabe scrunched up his face and bit the inside of his cheek, trying to force his many distractions away.

"She really is the most adorable thing I've ever seen," Claire said, from near Elenor. Gabe cracked one eye open to see the mockling stretch, fuzzy white belly exposed.

He closed his eyes again. *Focus.*

"So when are we starting this meeting? Playing with her is fun and all, but we have a country to fix and a delegation of Miri and Iamings arriving shortly" Tomaz said.

Gabe ground his teeth. *Clear mind.*

The door opened. "I'm sorry I'm late. I transferred the funds you—"

His magic flared along with Gabriel's annoyance. His arm burned as the circle he had been trying to focus on caught the outburst of power. It flowed into the gold, and before he could control or stop it, the bar in his hands exploded.

Crack! Claire disappeared.

Everyone else screamed or yelped as shards of metal burst outward, becoming finer and finer as they flew. It was sand by the time it hit anything other than Gabriel's hands and a few nearby pillows.

"What the fuck just happened?" Eric gasped.

"Did he just *explode* gold?" Kallen demanded, where he stood by the open door, gaping at Gabriel.

None of their words registered over the searing pain in his hands. Gabe clutched them to his chest, blood pooling to the surface of the mauled remains of his palms.

"Shit. You're hurt," Elenor cried, pushing herself to her feet. It wasn't graceful or coordinated, but she had taken a few steps towards Gabriel when Tomaz grabbed her.

"Stay back!"

They were all looking at Gabriel as though he were a snarling beast. Blood was freely dribbling down his forearms, running in rivulets and dripping off his elbows to the floor. The room began to spin. Instinctively—and because he knew it would dull the pain—Gabe reached for his magic again. His well was less full than before, but it still ached with the need to use the power housed within. He let that energy enter his body. Focus wasn't hard this time. The pain was all he could concentrate on.

The moment the magic began to flow, the pain eased, becoming no more than a distant throb. More of a tingling, uncomfortable pressure than real agony.

"What messed-up, backwards method of charging gold are you teaching him, Marek? Why didn't you stop him when the gold was close to capacity? He must have been filling that thing for hours if—"

"He started when you walked in, Lord Drego," Paul replied, interrupting the irate nobleman. The *doena* brushed a speck of blood away from a shallow cut on his cheek. "It took him less then five seconds to overload that ingot. I've never seen anything like it in all my days."

Elenor tugged free of Tomaz's grip and stepped towards Gabriel, only to be stopped by Eric grabbing her waist. Pulling his cousin into his lap, Eric huffed, "Elenor—"

"He's as much of a danger to me here as from up close, Eric. And he's bleeding."

"Which is something you don't need to take care of personally," Eric shot back, tussling with the princess while getting to his feet. He stared pointedly down at Elenor until she slouched in surrender, then turned to Gabe and gasped.

"What?" Gabriel snapped, as one by one more of the nobles developed the same dumbstruck expression. Had they never seen blood before? Gabriel's head was spinning, the magic dulling the pain and slowing the blood loss, but not doing much for the dizziness.

"The floor," Beth whispered. "It's glowing.

Gabe looked down. At his feet, where several large drops of blood had fallen onto the floor, lines of glowing metal wove through the intricate stonework.

"That looks like circuitry," Kallen said, still standing by the door. Carefully, he closed it behind him and walked over, kneeling next to Gabriel to trace one of the glowing lines. "Yes, this is definitely copper, it's just made to look like grout."

"Um, could someone get me a towel or something," Gabe ventured. Circuitry was fascinating and all, but *his hands were bleeding.* These nobles had a very backwards sense of priority.

"For fucks sake, let me through," Elenor barked, finally disengaging from her friends and hobbling to the bathroom. She returned with a towel and brought it to Gabriel, sitting next to him on the couch. Paul opened his mouth to argue, but a sharp look from his ward shut him up.

Gently, Elenor pressed the towel to Gabriel's sliced-up palms, apologizing as he winced. "This looks bad."

"So did his back, yesterday, and that's all closed up," Paul noted. "I wouldn't be too worried, *talidaar*. Being a powerful rifter comes with some advantages."

A loud crack sounded in the room and Claire Enica appeared, drenched up to the waist with foul-smelling mud.

Everyone made exclamations of disgust when the smell hit them. Everyone other than Elenor, who jumped up and asked, "You made it back here in less than five minutes? How did you do that?"

Claire, who looked about ready to retch, shuddered. "Still just luck I think. This room is one of the ones my Gift likes to take me to again and again. It's better than some of the others. Ew, ew, ew."

"Where did you turn up?"

"City sewers."

"That's not mud, is it?"

"*No,*" Claire said, in a high-pitched moan. "I'm going to go shower now. For a year."

By the time servants had been brought in to clean the mess, Gabe's hands had been bandaged, Claire was out of the shower, and the glow was fading from the floor. Kallen had traced the copper lines to a wall, but there they disappeared. After a few minutes of fruitless searching, Tomaz had drawn the Mindellion into a discussion about the likely tactics the prosecution would employ in Elenor's upcoming trial.

Once they were again all gathered—this time with the bars of gold well out of Gabe's reach—Elenor called their little meeting to order.

"Whatever just happened will need to wait. The delegations from Seehana and Miriel have been spotted on the river. They'll be here by mid-afternoon. We have a lot to do between now and then," she began, having taken a seat next to Paul on the couch opposite Gabriel. Claire was sitting next to him, Beth in a large armchair with her feet up, and Eric, Tomaz, and Kallen on chairs dragged over from a small table. To Gabe's surprise, the redheaded guard from the prisons was also present, leaning against the wall by the hearth.

"What's the plan?" Tomaz asked.

"We proceed as though everything were normal," Elenor replied, her chin resting on the head of her mockling, who was fast asleep. "The arrangements for their arrival were already set, and I see no reason to change them beyond the necessary."

"Except for the fact that the Queen is missing, the King dead, and half of the Writted Nobility wants you tried for murder. That calls for a few changes, Elenor," Kallen said, leaning forward in his chair.

"I said we wouldn't change the arrangement for their arrival, not that I intend to do nothing," Elenor snapped back. Almost as soon as she did, she reached up to rub the back of her neck. "Sorry. I haven't slept in . . . a long time, and I'm very tired. I apologize for being prickly."

"Get it out now, lovely. Better here than in front of your aunt," Claire said, smiling at the princess. "We don't want a repeat of your eighteenth birthday."

"What happened on her eighteenth birthday?" Gabe asked, as every noble but Kallen winced.

"I'd like to know as well," the Mindellion added.

Elenor buried her face in her mock's fur and muttered something unintelligible.

"What our sweet, polite Elenor is trying to say is that she punched the Queen of Miriel in the middle of a crowded dance floor and very nearly started a war. It was great fun to watch, but I don't think it wise to repeat the experience," Eric explained, eyes somehow both alight with mirth and dark with worry.

"Oh, I heard about that. *Why* did you punch a foreign monarch, though?" Kallen asked.

"She won't answer that," Eric said, before Elenor could even attempt to. "She's been hiding something about her aunt for more than a decade. Every time someone asks, Elenor promises she'll tell us next time. It never happens."

"That was mean, Eric," Beth chided.

Her husband shrugged. "It's true, though."

"Elenor is allowed her secrets," Claire said, but before she could continue, Elenor held up a hand.

"Don't. It's time they knew, Claire. My father isn't here anymore, and for all I know my mother could be dead too. I need my allies to know the full story." It took Elenor some time to gather her courage, or perhaps to decide how to share her secret, but when she finally spoke, it was in little more than a whisper, fingers still tight in her mock's fuzz.

"Every other year my Aunt Sianta or my cousins come to visit. On the off years, my brother would go to Miriel. I was never sent. I don't know why, exactly, but my brother always came back thin and wouldn't leave his room for days." There she stopped and looked to Kallen, who nodded in confirmation of her story.

"He would never speak of it. Then again, we were not particularly close. We just ran in similar circles."

No one else said anything, so Elenor continued, "I was six, and Sianta had just arrived. I was walking by my father's office. Honestly, I can't even remember why, but then—"

"You were chasing your cat," Paul said, voice quiet and haunted. "You had a white cat called Petal."

"Right . . . the one who ran away."

"We told you that because you kept asking for her. Your mother asked me to bury the body in the gardens."

Gabriel watched what little blood was left in the princess's face drain away. Beth tried to take one of her hands, but Elenor jerked her head in refusal, jaw tight and breath coming quick, so Paul continued the story. "It was a few months after Warren Miri had died. Elenor and I were right outside the door when we heard raised voices. The King, Queen, and Sianta Miri were arguing about something. We only caught the tail end—really, it was mostly just Elenor's mother swearing at her sister, and the King yelling at both of them to keep their voices down—but Sianta slammed open the door and caught sight of Elenor. She just stopped in her tracks, staring at us—well, at Elenor, I don't think she even noticed I was there—but I saw this smile start to form on her lips. It vanished when the Queen stepped into the doorway. She told Elenor to go to her room. Elenor said she was looking for Petal, and Sianta asked who Petal was. Elenor loved that cat, so naturally she started talking about her at full tilt, Sianta glued to every word."

As Paul spoke, he wrapped a long arm around Elenor's shaking shoulders. Her eyes were squeezed shut, bottom lip caught between her teeth as if fighting back tears. Her hands were digging into her mock's soft fur hard enough that Gabriel was surprised the dragon hadn't woken.

"Lilian told Elenor to go to her room again, but Sianta stated that she wanted to hear all about Petal, and invited Elenor to come with her for a slice of cake and tea. Elenor, of course, accepted. What child would refuse? Sianta took her hand, and I was turning to go with them when I saw the Queen almost launch herself after them. King Mark grabbed her arm, shaking his head, then they followed along without saying a word. We went to one of the parlors, and the four of them sat down for tea and lemon cake. Halfway through eating her slice, Sianta turned to Lilian and asked if she had reconsidered. The Queen shook her head and then—"

Elenor reached up to squeeze one of her *doena's* hands, stopping him. Carefully, she pushed back her hair and placed her finger next to a little scar on her neck.

"Later, they made me say I had caught wasting fever by chance, but I didn't. The syringe my aunt used was full of blood infected with it, along with a whole host of charming, painful poisons meant to make me suffer. My parents just sat there while her men held Paul back and she injected it right into my neck."

In the stunned silence that followed her pronouncement, Gabriel could hear the pulse of his own blood in his ears.

"What the *actual fuck* is wrong with your family?" he asked.

"More important, why aren't we at war with Miriel over this?" Eric burst out at the same time.

Elenor held up her hand to forestall further questions. "It happened nearly fourteen years ago. None of that matters anymore. What's important is how it applies to our current problems. My parents saw my aunt poison me and did nothing to stop it. They watched me fall and start thrashing. While I was being carried away—instead of telling me they loved me—they ordered me not to disclose that I had been poisoned. Since then, Sianta has tried to have me killed dozens of times. Sometimes it's poison, other times it's assassins. Whatever she thinks I overheard that day, she wants me dead for it. Now that I am all that stands between her children and the Lirion throne, we must assume that she is coming here prepared to finish the job."

"And you can't go public about this, can you?" Tomaz asked, having remained mostly silent. "Because if you did, even if the nobility believed you, it would be a declaration of war. But there is a good chance they *wouldn't* believe you, since it would be your word against hers, and you're already under investigation for the murder of a Miri. Even though it's true, it would look like something you made up to excuse a war of aggression."

"Exactly," Claire said, frowning. "On the flip side, the reason a war *didn't* break out over her punching her aunt was probably because the Miri don't want this getting out."

"This is way past messed up and all the way into appalling." Gabe couldn't understand why none of the others, save perhaps Jo by the door, looked suitably horrified.

"Welcome to Court, Gabriel," Eric sneered, "where everything you say is a tool for someone else to use to take you down, and everyone you think you can trust is probably working behind your back to do it."

No one contradicted him.

Gabe crossed his arms, leaning back on the couch. "Well, obviously she needs to be taken out."

"Why is your solution to everything regicide?" Elenor snapped, head emerging from the bundle of fluff.

"Because it generally works," he said, annoyance flaring. "She nearly killed you. Your father was a Miri and nearly killed Lirin. Obviously these two things are connected, even if we don't see how yet. I'm sure it's a fascinating mystery, but we have to be practical. If she's going to be here tonight, we need a plan to keep Elenor safe, and one to take Sianta Miri out before she makes her move."

"I'm not going to murder another family member, Gabriel. One has already gotten me in more trouble than I can handle."

"You don't have to. I'll gladly do it," Gabe offered.

"He's right, cousin. She needs to be dealt with." Eric came to his aid, but it didn't make a difference.

Elenor's jaw had that stubborn set that Gabe was starting to recognize as the expression that messed up his plans. "I'm not going to start a war out of revenge. I hate her, but Lirin means more to me than settling a score. I just want to survive. That will be victory enough. Can we work on *that* plan?"

Gabriel leaned back against the couch, arms still crossed and temper simmering.

It was Kallen who answered. "She isn't the only one we have to plan for. You have an intended on his way. What do you want to do about that? Now, more than ever, an alliance abroad might not be your best move. Lirin needs to rise under strong leadership."

"Then again, if there's war brewing with Miriel, maybe a southern alliance wouldn't hurt," Beth pointed out.

Gabe snorted.

"What now?" Elenor asked, rolling her eyes. "Do you disapprove of the monarch of Seehana, too? Want to add them to your murder list?"

"I don't have a *murder list*. And no, I have no issue with Jonah Iaming. He gave most of his power over to a parliament of the people at the start of his rule, and as far as I can tell mostly stays out of running his country. It's his son I can't abide."

"Are you meaning to tell me that *you* know Cassian Iaming?" Eric asked.

"He does. They were in the same class on the Island," Kallen confirmed. "If I remember correctly, Cassian was a pretty typical self-important snotty-nosed princeling. You can do better, Elenor."

"I have to agree," Gabe said. "I don't know how he is now, but as a teen, Cassian was absolutely hateful. He once left me at the bottom of a hunter's trap in the middle of the woods, with a broken arm. And he was *horrible* to Fay."

"The woman who threatened to cut me up into pieces if Fedrik wanted her to? I'm sure she didn't deserve it *at all*," Elenor grumbled

"Cut it out, you two," Claire said, interrupting Gabriel before he could retort. He expected her to come to Elenor's defense, but instead the girl turned her disapproving glare on the princess. "They're trying to give you a warning, El. Are you really willing to defend someone your parents picked for you? When have they ever had your best interests at heart? As much as it pains me to say it, I think Kallen is right. A southern alliance may not be wise. You haven't signed a betrothal contract yet. You should consider receiving the Iamings, explaining that the situation in Lirin has changed, and calling the whole thing off."

"Well of course you would say that, Enica," Tomaz said. "I'm certain your main intention is for Elenor to be happy, but it can't have escaped your attention that the south is much stricter about fidelity in their marriage vows. But guess what? Sometimes arranged marriages are necessary. My house wouldn't have a chance in the next Water Race if I hadn't married Stella. As much as I don't love her, we are stronger together and it was the right political move. Cassian Iaming might well be too. Lirin and Seehana united are stronger than Miriel. Lirin alone may not be. If there is a chance of war over the King's death, we *need* an alliance."

"With the right influx of funds to the army and the support of Tirit Mindel, Lirin doesn't need the south," Kallen said, catching all their attention.

All but Elenor's, who looked miserable.

"You're about to suggest I marry you again, aren't you?" she asked.

"You did promise you would seriously consider it after the aid I provided. I'm only asking that you fulfill that promise. *Consider it.* House Drego is the largest supplier of weapons and soldiers to the Lirinian army, and I work for the Mindel Bank. I'm not a prince expecting to rule kingdoms, just a citizen interested in the wellbeing of Lirin."

"Bullshit, Drego. You're an ambitious noble who wants the next generation of Lirion to owe their existence to House Drego," Eric said, venom in every word.

"Which is exactly what the Ondai did two generations ago. Don't pretend to be on some moral high ground," Kallen retorted.

Gabe's attention settled on Elenor. She was sinking further and further into the couch, and he thought he saw tears at the corners of her eyes again.

With a sigh, Gabriel straightened and coughed, drawing the arguing nobles' attention. "Why don't we take this day by day? Tonight, the delegation arrives, and your father's Passing is being held, correct? How about we just plan that far ahead?"

Slowly, each of them nodded. To his surprise, it was Jo who spoke next. "I've agreed to join the contingent of guards providing security to the Miris tonight. I'll try to find out if any of their people seem more suspicious than others, and let you know what I overhear."

"Thank you, Jo," Elenor said, face emerging from behind her dragon. "Tomaz, you were Djina's ward when you stayed at the Palace as a child, right? I would like you to go to her old office in the infirmary and her house if needed, and look for a letter. It would be sealed with a heron and mountain sigil. Beyond that, I need you and any professors you trust at the University to start preparing a case for my tribunal. We can't let that creep up on us, and you're the only one of us who knows Lirinian law well enough to head that part of this mess."

"Of course, Elenor. I'll be happy to do that."

"Beth, you can't move around much, but you can write. Keep publishing updates about the situation in the Ondai Tribune. I'll work with you about the theme of each article, but we have to get and keep the people's attention and trust. I can't afford to lose control of the city on top of having problems with the nobility."

"I can help with that, if I can reach the rebel network," Gabe offered.

Elenor nodded in thanks. "It would be nice to be sure I'm not in danger of rebel assassins, on top of the Miri ones. I'll try to arrange for you to get a message out. Please tell them that I want to see Lirin grow in the direction Wilam wanted, and that if they have specific grievances that they can voice them without fear of reprisal. I need to know what's wrong if I'm going to fix it."

"Spoken like a Queen. Power suits you, El-belle," Claire said with a smile. "Right, so back to tonight. What's your plan?"

"Try to stay alive, and stall for time," Elenor replied, her composure from a moment ago vanishing as she sank back into the couch. "And not make any big decisions while on high doses of stimulants and several sleepless nights. Right now, that's the best I can do."

CHAPTER FIFTEEN
The Agreement
DAEMON

I had always known there was a darkness in the heart of Jac Drego, but I never expected what happened. As I watched him stalk towards us with arms caked in dirt and the blood of his family, I think I saw him die too. The Jac I'd known crumbled, and when he rose and dragged Alehan away, I am ashamed to say that I ran in terror instead of stopping him. I could have. I am an Incarnate. I am the reason he fought in the war. A single word from me would have stopped him, but I feared, and now firmly believe, that I would not have survived trying. Alehan Silvarin now bears the scars of my cowardice, and always will if he survives this trip back to the desert to his parents. At least Jac died in the magical blast. I would fear for the world if he had survived. I created a monster. This Gift I carry did this, and he is not even my Gatekeeper, just a normal rifter caught in my aura, and who never questioned whether I was worth following. I cannot allow it to happen again. Whatever happens when we arrive in the desert, I will make certain that this Gift will never fall back into the hands of the Lirions. We are not worthy of it, and never will be.

-From the final journal entry of Gabril Lirion.

DAEMON HAD EXPERIENCED serindalla withdrawal a few times throughout his life. Days of shaking, vomiting, and paranoia. He would have gladly traded that for having his magical well so completely and unexpectedly drained. He didn't try to hide his fury as he shifted his glare from Robin's little ex-pet Ghoster to North, a bitter laugh still shaking his shoulders.

"I should have fucking known. The Silvarin family has brought me nothing but misery. Why *wouldn't* you be one of them?" he spat, then clenched his teeth in a snarl. "You know, I was actually reconsidering killing Gabriel, but knowing he's related to *you?* Maybe I really should rip his throat out. I've done it to your kind before."

"Remember the Accords. You may not touch a Silvarin," Suela said, in a raspy voice.

Daemon's eyes snapped to her. "For now. The rest of you are not so lucky. Your Goddess is dead. The Hardor Accords don't cover you red-eyed bastards anymore, and I doubt they'll protect anyone for much longer."

"The Hardor Accords name the *daradeio*, with or without the presence of our Goddess. Lady Red knew this was possible. She left contingencies, which, I take it, is why you are here," the old woman said, unfazed by Daemon's anger.

The vivid image of launching himself forward to rip the head off her leathery neck flashed through Daemon's mind, but he fought back that old, familiar bloodlust. His eyes scanned each face one by one, memorizing their features and imagining the ways he would kill them. Not even Obri and Tsiihsi were spared in the daydream, though their deaths were quick ones. Just a snap of the neck or a knife through the heart for witnessing Daemon's earlier vulnerability.

Fayrian, North, and the young rifter cooling the air were last. Daemon cocked his head to the side, studying each and deciding how, exactly, he would ensure that their deaths were as painful as possible. Unlike with Claire Enica, the pulse of his ring did not redirect his thoughts. If anything, it sharpened them, annoyance flaring hotter. He could have been in Hardor, figuring out more about Elenor's strange power. Instead, he was here, having his magic and plans pulled this way and that by a bunch of self-important, desert-dwelling fools.

Carefully, he reached for the Plane, but without so much as an ounce of magic to make the connection, it was like grasping at smoke. His attention fixed on North, still kneeling on the floor in the center of the circle, and he opened his mouth to speak. As he did, the ring on his finger began thrumming like the wings of a hummingbird, jerking his attention to it.

She's in trouble again. Can't she go two minutes without—?

In his moment of distraction, Suela spoke. "Daemon Indigo, do you intend to abide by the Accords, or are you going to continue wasting our time with idle threats?"

Idle threats? Who did she think he was? If he wanted to, Daemon could bring this whole fucking place down around them. Thinking that, he pulled together what little magic he could by sucking every ounce of heat from the stone under him and reached out to feel around for copper, since it was the fastest way to do just that if the situation demanded it. Daemon froze.

He had been so focused on Fulsixia's death that he hadn't been paying much attention to their surroundings. Kaedy had blindfolded him, Obri, and Tsiihsi as they'd walked to this temple—much to his annoyance since it would mean backtracking later to check what the Mondaer were trying to hide—but the moment he reached out to sense for magical metals, the whole building lit up like a pyre.

So much gold and copper.

The sheer weight of it, striated through the mesa above his head, made Daemon gasp, drawing everyone's attention to him. His fingers clenched around the edge of the pedestal, but no gold met his skin. Kicking off his sandals and completely ignoring the others, Daemon pressed his bare soles to the ground.

His face broke into a grin, as every rifter in the room lurched forward, letting out exclamations of alarm or dismay. With a mighty pull, Daemon grabbed hold of a thin vein of gold and ripped the magic from it. Gold discharged all at once, so Daemon couldn't absorb all of it, but he took everything his capacity would allow, stretching his ability to absorb to the limit as power poured into his well. In the same move, he swiveled and pointed one hand at Fayrian, the other at the meddlesome young rifter draining the heat. A blast of kinetic power hit them at the same time.

The young man went tumbling into the shallow water around the platform with a splash, and Fay thudded into the pedestal behind her with a pained grunt. Daemon let go of the kinetic push before it could do any real harm, in case the old lady was right about the Accords, and stood up to his full height. "The next person who thinks they can fuck with my magic is dead, Accords be damned."

The ring on his finger was still pulsing frenetically, but Daemon fought to ignore it as excitement bloomed within him. He extended his senses further, pushing out and out, but the heavy veins of gold and copper did not stop. They extended as far underground as they did above him, each one dense with stored magic.

The Heart of the Desert. The Mother Rock. Fulsixia's domain, where she had never allowed outsiders to come. This had to be it: what he had been sent to find. A veritable *mountain of gold* the Red had hidden. Daemon had heard the rumors, since the Mondaer were vocal about using huge magical bursts to dissuade invasion. Yet he had always thought it was mostly theatrics and perhaps a single gold vein. Not this.

And the Red had left it to *him*.

Daemon began to laugh. It burst out of him, loud and a touch manic.

North had scuttled away, staring at him in pure, unbridled terror. With Fayrian's help he stood, but as soon as he was up, he pulled the girl behind him. There was no need.

Daemon leaned back on his pedestal, still laughing. "Oh, calm down, you worthless piece of shit. I'm suddenly quite interested in the message that teleporting man left with you from the Red, so I'm not going to kill you."

"I don't trust you, and I'm not going to tell you."

Daemon raised both eyebrows. "You really don't get tired of getting in my way, do you? You *do* realize that eventually it will end up with you dead, right?"

North squared his shoulders. "Wouldn't if you had any decency or morals to speak of. Leave, Daemon. I don't care what you think you're doing here. This is a holy place, and you are as far from holy as there could be."

Another chuckle. "Holy. Right. That's laughable. No way I'm leaving now, kiddo." He turned his attention to Suela, hopping up onto his pedestal to sit. "Your Dragon left this whole place to me and named me her successor: the protector of rifters and Gifted. I have the recordings to prove it. So since it seems like this place now *belongs to me,* why don't we cut the crap and get to business."

Suela, who had yet to so much as twitch, turned her unseeing eyes in Daemon's direction. "You're the one who has been holding us up while in dereliction of your duty. Shoving one of our young rifters into the water is not protection."

"He's fine." Daemon waved her comment off, gesturing at the drenched lad pulling himself onto land with the help of several others. "Now, who killed Fulsixia?"

"This is not how we do this," the man called Quindo protested.

Daemon held up his hand and rifted, absorbing all sound waves around the man's head. Quindo tried to speak, but there was only silence.

"Anyone else?" Daemon asked.

"Dae," Tsiihsi said, standing up. "You're doing it again."

Huh?

She must have seen his momentary confusion, because she expanded. "Being a petty bully. Pushing people around because they disagree with you. The Mondaer have lost their Goddess. They are grieving, hurt, and in crisis, and you're making this about you. You said you would try to do better. Prove it."

Daemon's smile slowly fell away. Once more, his eyes tracked from face to face, all of them ranging from terror to fury. Even Obri—*his* loyal underling and as close a friend as Daemon made anymore—looked dismayed.

She's right. I am acting like a bully.

Part of him wanted to rip her to pieces for the temerity of calling him out in front of all these people, but Daemon fought it back.

Just because there are Silvarin and Lirion running around doesn't mean I have to be Jac Drego again. If I can't gracefully accept being called out for my bullshit after five hundred years, I don't deserve half the trust the people of Ayre put on me.

Taking a deep breath, Daemon inclined his head. "You're right."

Tsiihsi audibly exhaled, took a step forward, then bowed deeply to the Mondaer in the circle. "Please forgive my intrusion. You can continue. May peace be upon this place."

"Thank you," Suela said. "If everyone is quite done being dramatic, please resume your places. We have much yet to discuss."

There was a little shuffling, some angry gazes in Daemon's direction, and a bit of grumbling, but in a minute or so the group had returned to their previous arrangement. Daemon let the rift around Quindo's head fade and remained quiet, with something that felt unpleasantly like guilt churning in his gut.

"North, I am sure you still have many questions, but you may retire from the circle. Jac Drego, we would listen to this message from the Red."

Daemon nodded and motioned to Obri, who had the device containing Fulsixia's final words in a satchel.

When Fulsixia's voice filled the air, every single Mondaer visibly reacted. One or two started weeping, others gasped or whispered prayers. Through it all, Daemon's anger continued to dim, cloying shame taking its place.

Daemon played the recording twice, then stopped it. He cleared his throat, shifted from foot to foot, then said, "I . . . apologize for the way I acted, and for invading your meeting. I honestly did not come here with the intention of revealing this to you, or to take ownership of something that is yours, especially knowing how unwelcome I am among you."

"Why did you come, then?" Akaaron asked, tears still dampening his round cheeks.

"I came to find out how she died," Daemon replied honestly.

"And now that you have realized what our Mother Rock is?" Suela asked. "Will you abide by her dying request and help us protect it and the magic users who call it home, or will you use it selfishly and without thought of we who have poured ourselves into it?"

Daemon shifted uncomfortably once more. It would be so very easy to lie. The thought of *not* using a veritable mountain of stored magic for his own ends was downright painful, and he could not promise that he would not for the sake of a mere handful of red-eyed people who would all be dead in less than a century.

Tsiihsi coughed.

So subtle.

"I can only be honest in that I do not yet know what I intend. The last few weeks have been very full, and I have not had a clear head to consider my options going forward. I believe it might be time to do so."

North snorted. "Says the monster who was letting a man be tortured while having every intention of eventually killing him, just so he could ponder the ethical ramifications. Even when you're considering your actions, you still bring nothing but suffering. Tell me, is Gabriel dead yet? Or are you still waffling while he suffers?"

Fayrian gasped, hands rising to cover her mouth and gaze flitting between North and Daemon. "Gabriel? *My* Gabriel?"

Dae rolled his eyes at the Namer's theatrics and the girl's obvious distress. "Yes, the Gabriel you spent years lying to and stealing magic from. And for your information, North, I'm not actually the sadistic beast you think I am. He's alive and well."

North crossed his arms. "Sure he is. And for how long? Still planning on killing him and making it look like an accident?"

Daemon pursed his lips, fighting the impulse to turn North into shreds.

"Is this true? Do you plot against the tenets of the Accords?" Suela asked.

Dae let out an exasperated sigh. "Like everyone doesn't. The Accords are nothing but a paper-thin veneer of civility. Everyone knows that they are there just to prevent all-out war, not to keep the occasional assassin from slipping through. I dare you to say differently, or need I remind you of the time fifteen years ago when you lovely people enslaved and executed three soldiers from House Arlen? The Blue was *not* happy about that, you know."

"We didn't know who they were, which allows for an exception in the Accords," Suela barked back.

"Sure you didn't." Daemon smiled widely, then turned his attention to the redhead on the old woman's right, who looked about ready to explode. "*Yes?* What do you want to ask so impatiently?"

"Gabriel is really alive? Gabriel Navarl?" burst out of her.

"Yes. Do keep up."

"How is he? Is he hurt? *Where* is he? What—"

Daemon held up a hand to shut her up. "I don't have the time or inclination to answer a thousand questions. He's alive, he's recovering, and he's in the care of Elenor Lirion, the new Queen Regent of Lirin after the death of the King. Now shush."

Suela nodded along. "He is correct, Fayrian. This is not the time for personal questions. You are Mondaer now. Your life before crossing our border comes second, as do the affairs of the other Gods. We have a crisis to attend to. I would like to put forward that for the present time, due to the dying wishes of Lady Red, that Jac Drego, known as Daemon Indigo, be allowed temporary access to the Mondaer desert without receiving the brand, but that our secrets remain ours until such as a time as we deem him trustworthy. Does a majority oppose?"

North raised his hand, as did the soaking wet young man, and an elderly woman in the outer ring whose hand shook as she lifted it. Fayrian started to raise hers, but Suela must have heard the rustle of fabric for she smacked Fay's rising arm with her cane. "You're just voting to be contrary."

The Lirinian rebel scowled and crossed her arms.

Daemon leaned back against his pedestal and kept quiet. Whatever came next was sure to be interesting, and listening instead of talking would give him a few minutes to wrap his mind around the enormity of the gold stores around him. As everyone shifted and Suela started discussing the first order of business—how to tell the Mondaer that their patron deity was dead—Daemon started doing the math.

The vein of gold he had felt was enormous. It couldn't be the only one, though. And there was copper around him too, which was nearly as valuable. The problem was that it wasn't in a particularly useful form, since gold discharged all at once. This mountain would be excellent to have if he wanted to cause some serious damage, but it wouldn't significantly help with day-to-day rifting.

And then there was the problem of actually releasing the magic in that much gold. It would have to either be channeled through a rifter and therefore their capacity, or through the artificial capacity of copper. But copper degraded the same way capacities broke. It would take a staggering amount of copper to be able to actually take a blast this large.

Or one suicidal rifter.

Well, or one who didn't know what they were doing. Gabriel was pretty clueless about his magic, and he *might* even have a large enough capacity to survive it. Maybe. Probably not.

Might be worth the risk in a pinch.

In the meantime, the underwater copper perimeter of Ayre was probably big enough for one hit. If he connected Ayre and the Mother Rock through a planar doorway, and made sure to keep that connection open and ready, it might be enough to scare even a God . . . .

Considering how angry Kennotoza had been, and the fact that he had just stolen one of her mock dragons and had every intention of getting to the bottom of the mystery of Elenor's strange draw, it might be useful to have.

"So it is decided? We will speak to them at the next meeting, but not name Baarin as the Gifted who killed her? They will ask, Suela. We need to have an answer, as it is their right to know," Quindo said, arms crossed.

Who was Baarin? Daemon didn't think he knew of anyone by that name, but then again, if Fulsixia had hidden a literal mountain of gold in the desert, Daemon doubted that there weren't more secrets. Clearly, one of them had gone badly. Whatever Gift this man had, it must be a good one.

"It is not their right. Fayrian has bought his freedom, so he is neither *daradeio* nor our slave. He is nothing but a guest of hers. We will name him as Baarin at the meeting, but that name and who it belongs to should die along with our Lady Red," Suela stated, only a slight tremble to her voice as she spoke the Goddess's pet name.

Daemon's attention sharpened. This Baarin fellow was an outsider? "Who is he?"

"None of your business," Fayrian snapped.

Ah, so someone she cared about. He considered what he knew of her and how she had gotten here, both from his own observations and what Elenor had used to threaten Robin. There was an obvious conclusion. "Ah, so it's Fedrik Tellen."

"How—" Akaaron started, then snapped his mouth shut. It was enough of a confirmation for Daemon.

"So what does his Gift do?" Daemon asked, leaning forward with interest.

"We will not tell you that," Suela said. "Nor will we tell you where he is."

Daemon crossed his arms but didn't reply. He could find out on his own; it would just take a little more time and effort. And if he didn't like the answers he got, he could always carve it out of their flesh.

The meeting droned on. Daemon took note of the discussion about the magical explosion, but since it matched what Kaedy had said on the way over, he once again lost interest.

Elenor's heart was still thundering, and Daemon's thoughts kept drifting in her direction. What *was* happening in Hardor? At least she had a few rifters close to her, including Gabriel who was probably still oversaturated. If he was as fixated on her as Daemon had been when in that state, then he would protect her. He might blow up Hardor to do it, but hopefully Paul Marek had done what Daemon had told him.

Worst case scenario, Elenor had her vicious little lover, whose Gift was connected to danger. He had to trust that Claire Enica would get Elenor out of trouble if it got too bad. Daemon couldn't afford to be racing back to Hardor every two minutes while on a job for Xirra, or his patron would eventually notice and start digging on her own. That would only end in tears for everyone.

"Alright then, to the matter of Baarin," Suela said, bringing the conversation back to something Daemon was interested in. "Or, I suppose, Fedrik Tellen since no one here seems capable of keeping a secret. It is decided that we will protect him, for the sake of his other half. How will we accomplish that? He must be moved to a more secure location, but before that happens he requires training, and rifters cannot be allowed near him until we know he's under control. I would feel more comfortable if that training came from me."

She was dancing around the secrets they didn't want to tell Daemon, and he added that to the growing list of grudges he was building against this old hag. "I'll find out eventually, you realize."

"It's not for you to know," North snarled.

"Secrets never last. Not when I decide to uncover them. You might as well tell me. I'm willing to help him, if you are able to do me a favor in return."

"What favor?" Suela asked.

Daemon gestured around. "This place is as safe as any I've seen. I have some people I am trying to protect. If you would alow them stay here without enslaving them, I can help secure this mesa from . . . intrusions." Between the gold here and the circuitry around Ayre, Daemon was sure he could rig something up. It would take some time, and he needed to keep some of his people in Hardor to help with everything he was sure was coming, but for those most vulnerable, this might be a place where he could ensure their safety.

"We can protect ourselves," Quindo stated, arms crossed. "We have for as long as your people have hunted us."

"It's not people who are coming. It's Gods. Multiple, likely, if the Accords fail."

North was shaking his head. "It's probably some trick. Don't give him an inch."

Oh, how Daemon was starting to hate the Namer. Trying to keep the annoyance from his voice, he said, "I'm supposed to be the protector of rifters and Gifted, remember?"

If the boy knew what was good for him, he would slip back into ignominy where Daemon had found him, and never cross his shadow again. Not that Daemon would let that happen. Whatever Fulsixia had wanted him to know, North was keeping from him. Until he found out what that secret was, he'd be keeping a very close eye on North.

"And yet you have threatened many," the other Namer pointed out. Wait . . . In all the chaos, it hadn't registered to Daemon that Akaaron had been the one to identify him as Jac Drego and North as a Silvarin. Only one power could do that, as far as Daemon knew, but he hadn't seen two of the same Gift appear at once since the time of the Empire. The chances of two Namers existing simultaneously *and* finding each other were infinitesimal.

Daemon's back straightened and his gaze fixed on Akaaron. *What else were you hiding, Red? First a mountain of gold, now a second Namer. And is that Moe another Gifted? That's too many coming out of the woodwork too fast. What is going on here? What don't you want me to know yet?*

He would have to shake it out of North when this meeting ended.

In the meantime, Daemon was there on a mission. Xirra wanted to find the person who had killed the Red, and if he didn't accomplish it, he would have less leverage to make sure his patron didn't order him to do something he couldn't condone. Finding safety for Ayre was important, but it would come to nothing if the Blue decided to punish Daemon for insubordination. "I threaten who I wish, and usually succeed in carrying out those threats if I decide it is warranted. So think carefully before pissing me off."

"We are not defenseless, Daemon Indigo," Suela said, arms crossed. "And I am growing weary of your attitude. You stroll in here as though you own our most sacred spaces, and demand secrets that you have not yet earned. Lady Red may have named you as her successor to protect the magic of this world, but it does not mean you are entitled to our trust. You must work for that, which is something you have clearly forgotten how to do. Each and every *daradeio* would gladly die before revealing the most vulnerable of us to a man who cannot control even his own temper. You are older than every one of us by an order of magnitude, and yet even our youngest acts with more honor and strength of character, even after having your behavior pointed out to you. We are short on time, so please stop wasting it. What are you offering, and what are your terms?"

Well, then. That stung like a bitch. It made Daemon want to retaliate, but if he did, it would only prove her right, and he was far too proud to let that happen. After the way Robin had thoroughly condescended to his pleas for assistance from the Black Dragon, Daemon wasn't in the mood for another one of the Gods' minions getting the upper hand again.

Inhaling, Dae straightened up. "I have people to protect too. Specifically, rifters and Gifted, whom I believe the White Dragon may target because of their connection to me. If you can offer a safe haven for them, I can work with you to make this city as secure as my circuitry knowledge can make it, and give a place of safety to the man who killed the Red. I can promise you that it won't just be people coming for him. I expect every single God and their minions will be trying to take him out or turn him into a weapon. I know that's why I was sent, and I won't be the last."

"All the more reason not to trust you," Akaaron said, but Suela seemed to be considering it.

"He speaks the truth. We cannot discount the danger from outside the desert as well as within. Lady Red trusted him to protect rifters and Gifted if she fell. While I do not like trusting an outsider in this, we cannot determine the sincerity of his words if we do not give him a chance to prove it."

"He's not—" North began, but Suela prodded the young man with a cane.

"Your grudge against him might be merited, but it is as blinding as my lack of eyes. This is my counter-proposal to you, Daemon Indigo: bring your people here to safety. That will be our hand extended in trust. In exchange, swear to help us prepare for what is coming, and aid us in protecting our people and the magical citizens of our world. Do not snoop where you are not wanted. Do not bully and threaten us. Act with the honor Fulsixia bestowed upon you when she named you her successor. You will do this while having one or more of our people with you at all times, other than during meetings with your Goddess. Only when you prove to us that you are working hard and honestly for the good of all those you are bound to protect, will we entrust you with that which you came here for."

Daemon considered that, as Suela asked for four others to agree to those terms. Four was *all* she got, but it seemed enough to satisfy the Mondaer. North still scowled, arms crossed. No surprises there. It would be bothersome to have tag-alongs at all times, but did Daemon actually intend to do anything underhanded if the Mondaer were willing to help him protect Ayre?

"I agree," he said.

"Then so it will be. Bring your people here. Now, back to Fedrik Tellen. I will have one of our Gifted take us to him late today, after the announcement has been made to the *daradeio*," Suela said. "Quindo,

I will be leaving you in charge of keeping the *daradeio* focused on dealing with Lady Red's death instead of vengeance. It will not last, but the more time you can buy us, the better. North, you and Leo will be in charge of keeping eyes on our new ally. Kaedy, you too, when you are recovered. Call it the repercussions for bringing him here."

Daemon ground his teeth. Perfect. Assign him two lackeys he wanted to chop into little pieces, and one who he felt too sorry for to kill. Suela knew exactly what she was up to, and was definitely doing it on purpose. She probably wanted to be sure Daemon's temper wouldn't get the better of him.

The old woman wasn't done. "Fayrian will come with me, along with any Gifted or broken rifters who wish to assist. As soon as Fedrik Tellen is stable, I will send word. Akaaron, prepare a new expedition. I will send details when I get them. The God-Killer will know where we must go."

Daemon tapped his foot in annoyance at the obvious obfuscation, but did not speak.

"What of the creepy golden dragon who showed up the morning after the Red died?" Fayrian asked.

What was that? Daemon's attention sharpened.

All the Mondaer fell quiet, until Suela said, "Lady Red and Moe warned me of that, were this to ever happen. All we can do now is get control of Fedrik and make sure none of the other Gods follow in Lady Red's path. We may need their help before the end, as I fear that all that we are up against now may seem pleasant in comparison to what will come."

CHAPTER SIXTEEN
Don't Read The Fine Print
ELENOR

Poisons have always been the arsenal of the Lirion. Poisoned words, poisoned lips, poisoned cups of wine. They are the family of the White Dragon, resplendent in her glory and purity, so they do not often bloody their hands or stain their reputation for all to see. I often wonder what I ever saw in them, and how I was ever such a fool as to trust them.

—From the journals of Alexander Silvarin, after the fall of the Empire.

THE SUN WAS SETTING, but still high enough in the sky to make Elenor's sleep-deprived, aching eyes burn, and sweat pool at the small of her back. She stood at the top of the long flight of steps to the great carved doors of the Palace as the two delegations finished assembling and began climbing up towards them. There were well over fifty Southerners: all bedecked in the blue, white, and copper of the Royal House of Iaming. Banners of the same colors flew in the breeze, the setting sun glinting off the fine silk. Behind them, the Miri delegation in purple, black, and cerulean were likewise assembled. Even from a distance, the sight made Elenor nauseous.

She surreptitiously smoothed her crimson dress and glanced to her left, where Eric and Beth stood, both in colors that more closely resembled the Seehanesians than her own red, white, and gold. Catching her eyes, Beth smiled reassuringly and reached up from her belly to adjust her hair, eyebrows rising. Elenor mirrored the motion and found a strand of hair that had escaped her tight bun. With a nod of thanks, she turned back to the Seehanesians.

"Cassian is the one in the blue doublet, right beside the King," Kallen said, from where he stood next to her.

Elenor's eyes scanned the ascending party and rested on a young man with long brown hair and a smooth, handsome face. He didn't wear a crown or circlet, but two copper-and-gold cuffs circled his wrists, the South's sign of succession. She had spent the entire afternoon refreshing herself on the customs and traditions of Seehana while her maid and Beth had been getting her ready. The woman was a miracle worker. While Elenor still felt like she had been run over by a carriage, the thick layer of makeup hid the dark circles under her eyes and the flush of fever. Beth had even found an old, diamond-encrusted necklace of her mother's that covered most of the bruising on her neck. There was nothing she could do about the fact that one of her arms was still in a sling. That Elenor would have to swim across the river with a weakened wrist in less than a month and couldn't afford any setbacks was a more pressing concern at present than appearing uninjured.

As the party reached the top of the stairs, Kallen stepped forward and bowed. "Your Majesty, welcome to Lirin. May I present our Queen Regent and Heir Presumptive of Lirin, Her Highness Elenor Lirion. Your Highness, these are His Majesty King Jonah Iaming and His Highness Crown Prince Cassian Iaming."

The southern King was tall and slender, dressed in flowing robes that trailed on the steps behind him. He wore a crown of copper instead of gold, the warmer metal contrasting well with his dark hair and warm brown skin.

He stepped up to her and inclined his head. "Lady Elenor, you may not remember me, but we met when you were no taller than my knee. It's a delight to see what a lovely young woman you've grown into."

"I'm afraid I don't remember, but I do hope I never ran over your toes. I hear I was a terrible toddler."

Elenor's reply seemed to delight Jonah, for he laughed, the sound merry and surprised. "No, although I do recall being bullied into having tea with you and your dolls."

Elenor's cheeks flushed red. "I do apologize for that."

"No need, it was a delightful afternoon diversion. Thank you for receiving us amidst such troubled times. I am sorry to hear about your recent losses. When we set out, we had not yet even received news of your brother's untimely passing. Now to hear of your father's death as well fills me with great sorrow. You have my heartfelt condolences. I would like to pass them on to your mother as well, but she seems not to be present."

Elenor cringed. Kallen came to the rescue. "Queen Lilian has not been back to the Palace since the night of our King's death. It is our hope that she is simply in mourning and will be back with us soon."

A frown replaced King Jonah's smile, but he inclined his head. "I shall pray for her speedy return, then. Princess Elenor, may I introduce you to my son, Cassian." Jonah beckoned the young man standing a step behind him forward. That was good, because Elenor was tired of trying to sneak furtive looks at him when she thought no one would notice.

His features resembled his father's closely, but his skin was far lighter, and his long hair lacked his father's curl. Considering she was having trouble walking ten feet without tripping over her own numb feet, seeing Cassian move with perfect poise and grace as he approached her, bowed, and reached for her hand made Elenor want to curl up and hide. His lips were warm and soft against her skin, and as he straightened to look her in the eyes, she tried her best to keep the wild, nervous beating of her heart from showing on her face. Would he be able to tell that she was as excited about meeting him today as eating a spoonful of slugs?

"Princess Elenor, I've been looking forward to this day for a long time. Thank you for welcoming us into your home." Cassian's voice was sonorous and pleasant, but with a hard edge that his father's lacked.

"The pleasure is mine and my country's." While she kept her gaze on Cassian, out of the corner of her eyes she saw the Miri delegation approach. Elenor had to swallow back a wave of nausea as the many retainers peeled off to the side. *Where is she?*

A gentle poke in the middle of her back from Kallen snapped Elenor's attention back to the man she was supposed to be welcoming. "I'm sure you must be tired from your long journey, but I do hope you'd consider sitting with me tonight at the dinner in honor of your arrival, before we retire to the grounds for my father's Passing."

Kallen's suggestion on their way here had been for Elenor to make the offer before Cassian could. It would establish her as the dominant party, and although Elenor had little patience with such power games, this was larger than herself. This potential union with the south was a political negotiation to which she knew neither the stakes nor the rules. Elenor would need every leg up she could get.

Cassian's lips pursed, and for a moment a flash of something not quite friendly shone in his blue-green eyes. Still, when he replied it was polite and without any hint of bitterness. "It would be my pleasure."

That was all the conversation they got in before the Miri reached the top of the stairs. Elenor took an involuntary step back, bumping into Kallen as Sianta Miri, the woman that filled her every nightmare, finally emerged from her swarm of attendants.

The Queen of Miriel bore a striking resemblance to Elenor's mother. They had the same thin build and fair hair, though Sianta had hers up in an elaborate Mirielee headdress, her crown perched amid the dark purple fabric. Where Lilian Lirion's eyes were usually vacant and serene, her sister's seemed to see everything—a hawk amidst a sea of sparrows.

"Niece, how glad I am to see you alive and well. We were so worried when we heard the news," Sianta exclaimed as she reached the top step. With an angelic smile that made Elenor's knees quake, the Queen of Miriel opened her arms for a hug.

Elenor didn't move. It wasn't that she didn't want to. It would be better for the ruse they were trying to put on if she greeted Sianta with the same warmth as the Southerners, but she couldn't make her feet budge.

Sianta slowly lowered her arms, smile fading in sync. "Not pleased to see me, child? Where *are* your manners? Are they, perhaps, in the same place you are hiding my sister?"

"Surely you don't believe that Her Highness would intentionally keep her own mother away," Jonah protested.

Sianta gave a small shrug. Behind her, Elenor's cousin Silla reached the top of the stairs.

"There are so many astonishing rumors of late that I do not know which to believe," Sianta said. "Just today, for example, I picked up a city paper on our way through Hardor and what do I see but the news that our Elenor is not only being tried for the murder of her own father, but has a whole editorial *justifying* her actions. Why, it was practically a confession."

A distressed, high-pitched sound was trying to escape Elenor's throat. Telling the truth to the populace had seemed like a good idea the day before, but as Sianta pulled out a copy of the *Ondai Tribune* and passed it to Jonah, Elenor wished she had Claire's power to disappear with a thought.

"The situation is complicated," Kallen interjected, coming to Elenor's defense, "and better suited to a more private venue. Your Majesties, Prince Cassian, Princess Silla, we have prepared suites for you in the fourth circle of the Palace and arranged for a full contingent of staff and added security. If you would like to freshen up, the Queen Regent and I will show you there ourselves."

"Such a gracious offer is impossible to refuse," Jonah said, still jovial, although Elenor noticed his smile was not quite as broad as it had been before.

"Your Highness, would you walk with me?" Cassian asked, holding out his arm to her.

She nodded, and placed hers through his, keeping a polite distance. Kallen offered his arm to Elenor's cousin, and Jonah escorted Sianta in, already beginning to converse.

As they turned to the open doors of the Palace, Cassian leaned in and asked, "So, is it true? Did you kill him?"

Still shaken from her aunt's presence, Elenor had not expected the blunt, informal question. Her steps faltered, causing her to stumble and land wrong on her right foot. A squeak of pain left her mouth, and Elenor caught Silla looking back with a smile.

Sadistic bitch, just like your mother.

Silla had never outright told Elenor she knew what her mother had done, but she had implied it plenty. Her smirk said it all: *you're fucked.*

"Are you alright?" Cassian asked.

"Fine," Elenor mumbled, lying through her teeth. Having Sianta and her daughter so close made every muscle, bone, and sinew in her legs ache, and her fever was making her dizzy. Without Daemon's shawl, her temperature had climbed back up over the last half hour. Elenor just hoped she would be able to excuse herself quickly. "Just not feeling myself at the moment. The last few days have been a lot to take in."

A frown briefly flitted across Cassian's handsome face, but it vanished a split second later. "If I can be of any assistance, I would be honored to provide it."

"Thank you." Elenor wanted to ask if that included packing up and heading home, but kept her mouth shut. There would be time to discuss that. Until she knew why her parents had picked Cassian for her, it would be impossible to decide if the match was a wise move. To change the subject, Elenor asked, "How was your trip?"

"Long, but your country is beautiful in the late summer. Even so, I'm glad it's now autumn."

In front of her, Elenor saw Silla laugh at something Kallen had said. She was hanging off the well-built nobleman with the sort of attentive, fascinated attitude that Elenor had never mastered.

"Autumn's always been my favorite season," Elenor muttered, trying to divide her focus between the southern prince and the two Miri.

"And is Harvest your favorite as well?" Cassian asked. "I hear the celebrations are quite spectacular in Hardor. At home, it is still too hot by the end of September to do much. Midwinter is our largest event of the year." They were entering the fifth circle as he said that, and Elenor caught sight of the collapsed section of hallways where the final confrontation with her father had taken place. Her sprained wrist throbbed in response, and she pulled her eyes away and back to Cassian.

"Harvest is excellent here, yes. It's the one day of the year that the gates of the Palace are opened to the populace, and all may mingle as they please. We give out food and gifts to any who come, and the party continues into the early hours of the morning until the bonfires go out." Her enthusiasm rose as she spoke. Harvest had always been the night she looked forward to all year. For the last two, she had snuck away with Fedrik and Claire to roam the Old City, drinking mulled, brandied cider and dancing to the music in the streets.

"It sounds a lot like how it is celebrated on Tirit Mindel."

"I heard you went there," she said, jumping on the opening and yanking her attention to Cassian. No more getting distracted. "How was it, studying at the most prestigious school in the world?"

Robin's words from a few weeks ago echoed back to her. *I think you would have done well on Tirit Mindel had your parents allowed you to be tested.* Why hadn't she been? Elenor had never really thought about it before, but it seemed odd, considering that the declaration forbidding testing had only been passed five or six years ago. Then again, at the age most people took the test, she had been . . . indisposed.

Cassian frowned again, although like last time, the expression passed as fast as it had come. "Not as pleasant as one might think. It's a lot of hard work for minimal reward, and they let in many who have no business being there. I left after my core years were over. Being tied to the Island may be alright for some, but with a country to lead one day, I did not want to be under their thumb any more than all of us already are."

That seemed to be the popular opinion. She had to wonder if, in Cassian's opinion, Gabe had been one of the people they should never have admitted. Did Gabriel realize how much under the Island's control he still was?

For the rest of the walk, they spoke casually of Tirit Mindel. Elenor knew he must have caught her frequent stares at Sianta and Silla, but Cassian either didn't care or was polite enough not to mention it.

The Miri and Iaming guest suites were on either side of the same corridor. They stopped in the middle, the three pairs reconvening.

"Please take all the time you need to freshen up. Dinner will be in the formal dining room. You are welcome to join us for my father's Passing after that, but I would also understand if you wished to rest."

She let go of Cassian's arm, and once again he took her hand and brought it to his lips. "I'll be counting the minutes until I can support you in your time of sorrow. It will be an honor."

With a few more pleasantries, the Iamings retired to their suites to freshen up. Unable to avoid it any longer, Elenor faced her aunt. Paul stepped closer, as did a large man with an impressive blade slung on his back. Probably her aunt's own *doena*. She seemed to have a new one each time she visited.

"Lord Drego, may we have a moment with my cousin?" Silla asked, with a saccharine smile.

Kallen hesitated, but couldn't easily ignore a request from a visiting royal. He bowed, gave Elenor a concerned look, then retreated down the hall. While far from alone, his departure left her feeling fragile, her composure glass-thin.

"Elenor, come with me," Sianta ordered, gesturing to her suite.

"I have things to attend to," Elenor replied, not moving an inch.

"Girl, let me make this clear: what little protection your brother and parents afforded you is gone now."

Protection? If her parents standing aside while Sianta stuck a needle in her neck was protection, then Elenor was better off without it. How had Wil been protecting her, though?

"I'm not going anywhere alone with you. I'm not a fool."

Sianta laughed out loud at that. "I agree. You give fools a bad name, for not even a dullard would admit to aiding in the murder of a Miri in a public paper and not see that as giving Miriel grounds for retribution. The only reason I did not turn around and return with an army is because there is yet one way you might be useful to me. So I'll make it simple, since we have established you are a fool: do you want a war, or will you talk with me?"

Elenor hadn't expected her aunt to be that blunt. She had counted on a few days of pleasantries while she plotted behind Elenor's back. At the very least, she had hoped Sianta would have the decency to wait until her father had been returned to the Gods.

Apparently, that wasn't in the cards.

Elenor turned to Paul. "Please convey the situation to Gabriel and Kallen, and let them know that if they do not hear from you in ten minutes with news that I am safe, to assume that the Miri have moved against me and come here post haste."

"As you command, *talidaar*," Paul said, holding his wrist up to his mouth.

"Who is Gabriel?" Silla asked. "Another one of your secessionist Eastern friends?"

Elenor crossed her arms. "Gabriel is the man who blew up that section of the Palace we walked near, and who has the power to level this city to the ground. He owes me a pretty big favor, so do take that into consideration before trying anything. Now, shall we get this conversation started? I'm quite busy."

Anger was good. It was better than terror. Those two were the only emotions that had any chance of making it to the top of the quagmire at present.

"Less than a day sitting on your mother's throne and you are associating with rifters and threatening to take your country down with you? Your soul will be Forgotten for that, girl. This way," Sianta sneered, holding her arm to direct Elenor into the suite.

Paul remained glued to her side as Silla closed the door behind them, leaving the three women and their guards alone. At least, Elenor thought that, until a knock came and the only man who could have made this worse walked into the room.

Duncan Eurieha.

There were bandages around his head and he leaned heavily on his son. No one had seen the tall priest since the vote that had made Elenor regent. Her concern at seeing him was entirely eclipsed by the sight of his father, whose arrest she had ordered not two hours ago. That he was blatantly standing there meant he thought he was safe, and that was terrifying.

Her hand flew up to her neck, the bruises still aching beneath the intricate necklace she wore.

"Ah, Duncan. Thank you for joining us. I think we have some business to discuss?" Sianta said, walking around the nearby card table and sitting behind it like a desk. "Elenor, sit."

Seeing no reason to obey, Elenor remained standing.

Eurieha looked her up and down, but did not say a word. He hobbled over to the Queen of Miriel and set a large stack of papers on the table. "As you asked, I had my son remove these from Mark's offices and have them ready for you. All is arranged."

"Thank you, Duncan. You have been a loyal servant. *Elenor,* sit."

"No." Elenor's unsplinted hand came to rest on her hip. Hopefully, it would look defiant, but actually it was because the muscle there had just cramped, sending jagged lances of pain down to her heels.

"I don't think you fully understand what is happening, cousin," Silla said silkily, leaning against the doorframe, her purple gown slithering across the floor. "You are on trial for killing a Miri, and mid-power grab to take the Lirion throne. It's a tenuous position at best. Clever, getting rid of both your mother and father on the same night, but only going public about Uncle Mark. Not clever enough, but more than we expected from you."

Elenor opened her mouth to argue, but snapped it closed again. They didn't need to know that she didn't have a clue where her mother was. She couldn't see any situation in which giving these people more information would aid her.

"She still does not comprehend, does she?" Duncan Eurieha asked, sitting on a nearby divan with the help of his silent son.

"When has our Elenor interested herself in politics instead of fairy tales?" Sianta replied. "Look at her. Not one day in power and she's a mess. She's sweating through her makeup and is incapable of even a simple conversation with family. She is a dishonor to the Lirion name."

Elenor flushed. That all hit a bit too close to home. She had lived in denial about how bad things were for years before her brother's death, and for too long after. But if anyone was responsible for Elenor not having the formative education in politics she should have received, it was the Miri.

"What do you want? Your time is almost half gone. As soon as we're done, my guards will be here to take him," she pointed at Eurieha, "into custody."

"So impatient and deluded. Straight to it, then," Sianta said, pulling out a pen. "You're going to sign these documents."

"No."

The queen raised an eyebrow. "Not going to ask me what they are?"

Elenor shrugged. "Doesn't matter. I'm not signing anything you put in front of me."

"So you plan on not signing this marriage contract? Be warned, child, that if you do not, I will not bother unpacking. The Miri's financial assistance to the Lirion is conditional on many things, not least the political alliance to the south that your worthless cunt will buy us. If you wish to bankrupt your family and risk war with Miriel, feel free to continue being stubborn." Sianta leaned back in her chair, twirling the pen.

The threat might be idle, but it probably wasn't. Elenor dug her thumb into the back of her hip, hoping the sharp stab of pain would help shock her into thinking clearly.

It did not. Her head was pounding and her skin burned. A bead of sweat formed on her brow and ran into her left eye, making Elenor twitch.

"Time's more than half up, Elenor," Silla mimicked in mockery. "Sign or don't. My mother thinks you can still be useful to us, as long as you marry the south. I am not so sure."

"I need to read the contract first," Elenor said, trying to buy herself time.

Sianta laughed. "Then you should have asked your parents. Now come here and sign."

"Paul, we're leaving."

Elenor turned towards the door, took one step, then froze. Out of the corner of her eye, she saw Sianta pull out a syringe, placing it atop the pile of paper. Memories of her aunt looming over her, holding Elenor by the hair as she jabbed a needle just like that one into the side of her neck, made her knees feel like jelly.

Paul steadied her, but he didn't look down. No, her *doena's* eyes were fixed on the Queen of Miriel and there was murder in them. "You will not touch her again," he warned.

"Oh, you've made that very clear over the years, rifter. I don't know what cesspool of disloyal scum my late husband found you in, Paul Marek, but you have been the most lingering frustration he left me with. I managed to get rid of dear Wilam's *doena* within a few short years. You have proven much more difficult to kill."

An actual growl tore from Elenor's throat. She stepped forward, hands balling into fists. As she put her weight on her cramping leg, though, it buckled. Paul lurched to catch her, but then he let out a cry of pain.

Elenor looked up at him and saw something small and red protruding from his neck. Following the line to where the tiny feathered dart must have come, she saw Silla lowering a thin tube from her lips and slipping it back up her sleeve.

Paul yanked the dart out with a grunt, a small bead of blood dribbling down his neck. Without hesitation, he grabbed Elenor's shoulders, shoving her toward the door and putting himself in the way of more harm.

"Paul!"

"Out, *taale,*" he ordered, but she couldn't move.

Elenor turned to Sianta. "What did you poison him with?"

Sianta placed the pen down next to the syringe. "Different people require different methods of persuasion to make the correct decision. Mark wrote to me about the little trick that filthy rebel rifter pulled that made you craft a poison to kill your own family. It was enlightening. My sister has been willing to give up her own life and the lives of her children in the name of being difficult. It has been frustrating, but she has earned a certain amount of respect from me over the years. But you? You are softer. I hear from Duncan that it was a threat to your lover, friends, and *doena* that seemed to make you snap and kill Mark. He was stupid enough to threaten your friends and then trust you when you submitted, but I am not so shortsighted."

Paul was still trying to tug Elenor to the door, but now his other hand was up, rubbing at the reddening puncture.

"What did you give him?" Elenor repeated, voice breaking and high-pitched.

Sianta smiled and picked up the syringe. "As long as you cooperate, you will never have to know. Now let me explain how this is going to work. You will sign this marriage contract. Tonight, you will host the vigil for your father's Passing and announce the engagement to Prince Cassian. Every day after that until Harvest, you will focus all your meager charm on making that southern princeling happy and oblivious while I clean up the mess you left the family with. I would suggest spreading your legs for him. That usually distracts men well enough. I want you to be nothing short of a vapid, silly little girl about to be married. While doing so, you will ratify every proposal I bring before the Council, and, most of all, you will not be a nuisance under my feet. In exchange, once a day, your *doena* will receive one injection of the antidote. It won't be enough to stop the minor effects, but it will keep what we gave him from killing . . . probably."

"You fucking b—"

"Did I forget 'be polite' in my list? Ah well. That too. You should know that the first dose is the most essential. He probably has about, oh, five minutes before his muscles begin to seize and his heart struggles to beat. These papers require a *lot* of signatures."

Elenor turned her back on the monster in the room and grabbed her *doena* by both arms, dragging him toward the door. "Come on. We need to get to Dj—"

Then it hit her. Djina was dead. Fedrik was gone. Gabriel, for all his knowledge of her condition, had made it clear he didn't know much about poisons . . .

And Elenor had been too busy to replace her chest of poisons or her supply of bloodgold, which slowed most common deadly toxins.

Paul's knees buckled, and he blinked rapidly, his arms dropping from hers to rub at his chest.

No.

NO!

"Paul."

He looked up at her. "Run, *taale*."

Run? Run where? Silla still barred the door, and Daniil stepped in front of it as well. Paul coughed, then choked as though something blocked his throat.

"Time's almost up, Elenor."

Without pausing to think, Elenor lunged forward, reaching across the table for the syringe in Sianta's grasp. A large hand grabbed her by the back of her dress and tugged her back so violently the velvet of her gown tore. Her aunt's *doena* stood above her. He grabbed her hair with his other hand and shoved Elenor into the empty seat. She flailed, but her fever-weakened attempts didn't even budge him.

"Elenor," Paul called, crawling towards her. He hacked out another cough. "Don't do this."

"Tick tock, Elenor darling."

"My life is not worth—" A wheeze and gurgle.

Sianta reached over to press the pen into her hand.

"I wouldn't bother with the fine print, niece. I don't think you can afford the time."

I underestimated her again. It took her all of ten minutes to break me.

Hand shaking and tears making a mess of her makeup, Elenor raised her hand to the first page and began to sign.

CHAPTER SEVENTEEN
Family Ties
GABRIEL

I want to see them, Estelle. I know why Robin and Ara did it, and despite the pain I'm glad they took them, considering what would have happened if we'd still had the boys when the assassins showed up. Yet still, every day, I miss them. I want to know who they are growing up to be, or even if they are still alive. Cassian and Nora are a comfort, but even though I love my children with Nadia, they do not take the place of the sons I had with you.

—From a covert letter from King Jonah Iaming of Seehana.

GABRIEL, KALLEN, AND CLAIRE turned the corner at as close to a run as Gabe could manage just as Elenor stumbled out of a room supporting Paul. The door slammed behind her.

Her gown was ripped along the back, her hair and coronet lopsided, and tears rolled down her cheeks. The princess's *doena* looked worse. His lanky legs were doing a poor job of holding him upright, and his face was dead pale as he clutched at his chest.

"Paul!" Claire cried, running ahead. "El, what happened?"

"Help me. I need to get him to Djina's old office. He needs bloodgold." Elenor's voice was high-pitched and edged with desperation. Kallen, too, broke into a sprint. Gabe did his best to catch up, although the exertion pulled at his healing injuries and made the stitch in his side burn. By the time he reached them, Kallen had a shoulder under Paul's arm, and Claire supported his other side. That left Gabriel to wrangle Elenor, who seemed far too distraught to get herself moving.

"Are you hurt? Did your aunt—"

"She . . . she . . . "

Elenor looked like she was about to be sick, and her legs weren't cooperating. What the fuck had happened in there?

"Why were you alone with her?"

The look of terror on her tear-stricken face was familiar. He'd seen it on too many people in Lirin. It was the expression of someone who had lost a family member, or a home, or simply the last of their trust in a kind world. Gabriel didn't think Elenor had any illusions of a benevolent universe left, so what had the Queen of Miriel done in only a few minutes to drive her to this state?

"I . . . " Her skin was burning against his. Gabe's magic pulsed in response, pulling that heat out of the air and her skin, pouring it into his well as sizzling power. His own pain became less noticeable, the energy-turned-magic shifting to where the worst of his injuries were still knitting shut.

Elenor let out a startled gasp, stumbling into Gabriel. He caught her, magic sharpening his focus as it had every time he had used it of late. "Woah there. Ele—"

"Get your hands off her, Navarl, or lose them."

Cassian Iaming stood in the open doorway of a lavish suite, a thin, elegant rapier pointed in Gabriel's direction.

Acting on instinct, Gabe put himself between Elenor and his old classmate, even though the threat was clearly aimed at Gabriel.

"Prince Cassian," Elenor exclaimed. She tried to straighten and pull her composed court mask back into place, but her voice shook unconvincingly.

"I won't warn you again, Navarl. Get. Your. Hands. Off. Her."

"Oh, go fuck yourself, Cass," Gabriel snapped.

Elenor wobbled again, and he caught her with one arm, wrapping it around her waist and bracing his feet in a fighting stance to better support her.

"This isn't what it looks like," Elenor said. She wasn't even looking at Cassian, though, her eyes glued to where Paul, Claire, and Kalled had disappeared around the bend. "I need to go."

"I'll help you," Gabe offered, though he kept his attention on the point of Cassian's blade. "I'm not here for a fight, Iaming. She's not feeling well and needs to go to the infirmary."

"You spent six years boasting about how you intended to kill the King of Lirin, and you expect me to allow you to walk off with his daughter a day after you succeeded? After you were imprisoned for kidnapping her? Do you think me a fool?"

Still pulsing with the renewed rush of magic from the heat he was absorbing, Gabriel was about to reply in the affirmative when another man appeared in the doorway. He bore a crown on his head and a striking resemblance to Cassian, so Gabe had to assume it was his father, the King of Seehana.

"What is happening here? Princess Elenor, who is this?"

Elenor finally got her legs under her and let go of Gabriel, ducking under his outstretched arm and placing a hand on his shoulder. This put her directly in line with the tip of Cassian's sword, which had the pleasant side effect of the prince lowering it.

"Your Majesty, this is Gabriel Navarl. He's a guest of mine here at the Palace, and is providing me assistance. I'm sorry to be brusque, but I have to attend to something. Would you excuse us?"

How did she do that? Gabe would not have managed that much composure under the *best* of circumstances.

"Gabriel *Navarl?* The boy you went to school with, son?" the King asked, eyes growing wide as he stared past Elenor to Gabriel. It made Gabe deeply uncomfortable to feel that gaze on him. What was Jonah Iaming looking for?

"Yes, the insurrectionist street-rat. Princess, he is not an ally you want."

"I'll take that under advisement."

The King was still staring at Gabe, one hand rising to cover his mouth. He moved forward, and Gabriel involuntarily stepped back, dragging Elenor with him.

"Wait," King Jonah began, but Elenor interrupted.

"We'll see you this evening. Your Majesty, Prince Cassian." She curtsied, the motion uncoordinated and stiff, then grabbed Gabe's hand and tugged him in the direction her friends had gone.

He followed without argument, though he did look back and caught the King still staring at him, and Cassian turning to his father with a scowl.

"What was *that* about?" Elenor asked, as soon as they had turned the corner. "He looked as though he'd seen one of the Forgotten dead. Did you kill someone he knew, or something?"

"I don't go about murdering people at random, you know," Gabriel replied, trusting that Elenor knew where she was going. "And no. Cass and I had a bit of a rivalry while at the Academy, but I've never met his father before."

"A bad enough rivalry that he would draw a sword the moment he saw you?" Elenor asked. She was nearly running, which itself was worrying from the girl who never voluntarily ran.

Gabe was panting with the effort to keep up. Considering she was in the middle of a wasting fever flare, this pace had to be excruciating. "Slow down, Elenor. You'll do yourself harm. Kallen Drego is a Mindellion. Whatever aid Paul needs, he's qualified to give it."

"Kallen is College of *Finance,* not medicine."

He could have argued, pointing out that all Tirit Mindel educated students had training in every branch of the Academy, but he did not. Instead, Gabe slowed down, holding tight to Elenor's hand so that she, too, would be forced to pace herself.

This wasn't the middle of the night like the last few times Gabe had traversed the Hardor Palace. The wide, stately halls were teeming with nobles, servants, and clerks. They scattered to the side as Elenor passed, but he caught the surprised glances and murmurs.

"The first rule of politics is to never let the opposition see the cracks in your defenses." Robin's voice drifted out of memory. Gabe looked around, then tugged Elenor to the side, through the nearest arched doorway to the gardens between this ring and the next.

"Where—" she stopped as Gabriel drew her to a halt in a secluded alcove and shrugged off the light jacket he was wearing.

"Put this on. Let me straighten your hair."

Elenor complied, though with one arm in a sling she only draped the jacket over the torn back of her dress. Gabe looked over her ruined bun and decided that the damage was too great. Momentarily removing her coronet, he pulled out the pins holding her blonde tresses up, allowing them to tumble down around her shoulders. "Better. Now, is there a back way to where they've taken Paul?"

"Yes."

The way she led him zigzagged through servant hallways and across gardens. Elenor didn't speak as they walked, but she kept a measured pace, her uninjured arm looped through Gabriel's for support.

After a few minutes they arrived at the Palace infirmary. The small clinic was bustling, and Gabe realized with a start that the wounded from the fight with Mark Lirion filled the beds. The closest lay with bandages around the stump where her arm had once been. Gabe gulped and let Elenor draw him into a small office off the main room.

Inside, Paul sat in a chair, head rolled back and teeth clenched. Gabriel shut the door behind them as Elenor ran to her *doena*. For good measure, he closed the curtains over the two windows into the office as well.

Every wall was stacked floor-to-ceiling with shelves of supplies. Herbs, bottles of pills and powders, neat rolls of bandages, jugs of alcohol. It smelled like the Academy clinic, making some of the tension in Gabriel's shoulders dissipate.

Kallen was kneeling by Paul's side, taking his pulse.

"Elenor, do you know what they gave him? He said that it was from a dart, and that they administered the antidote before you left, but his heart is still racing and I haven't gotten much out of him."

Claire pulled up a chair for Elenor next to her guardian. The princess sat, taking Paul's other hand. "No, I don't know what it is. And the antidote won't be enough. She . . . she attacked him to control me." Elenor shuddered. "Did you administer bloodgold? That helps with most common—"

"It did nothing," Claire said, face hard. "El, this is your aunt. She won't have used something common. We need to find out what it is. I know you hate talking about her, but you need to tell us what happened."

Elenor shivered again, and Gabriel checked the clock above the mantle. It was nearing the time she should take another dose of serindalla, but he wasn't going to interrupt this conversation for it. Even so, the way she was fighting to keep her eyes open and focused on her *doena* concerned him. She hadn't slept for more than a few hours since the death of her father. How long would she be able to keep going at this pace?

"Elenor," he prodded, when she didn't answer Claire. "What happened?"

The princess—who had been entirely focused on Paul's face—blinked rapidly.

"Right. Yes." Voice shaking, Elenor recounted the meeting with her aunt, though she never took her eyes off her *doena,* and every time his breath hitched, her whole body jerked in response.

"Fucking Five above," Claire said, when Elenor finished by telling them how Sianta had administered the first dose of the antidote after Elenor had finished signing the marriage contract. "That woman is a monster. There has to be something in that contract that she doesn't want you to see."

"What worries me is that Daniil Eurieha was the one to propose making Elenor the regent. That is starting to feel like a setup," Kallen said, standing and going over to the wall of medicines. "The good news is that her blackmail is conditional on Paul staying alive, which means we have time."

"He's right, *taale,*" Paul said, speaking for the first time, though through gritted teeth. "The pain is not growing worse."

"It shouldn't be there at all. I never should have agreed to speak with her alone," Elenor said, leaning forward to press her forehead against Paul's shoulder. "Forgive me. I never wanted you to be hurt. I can't . . . I can't lose you too, Paul."

"Shh, you're not going to lose him, beautiful," Claire murmured, smoothing a hand over Elenor's loose hair. "We'll figure this out."

"Yes, we will," Kallen agreed. "Navarl, you seem to have spent more time studying medicine than I did. Do you—"

"I'm not the poisons expert. Most of my training was in field medicine. Fedrik Tellen might know from the symptoms what this might be, but he's not here."

"Elenor might be able to figure out what it is if she had a sample of the poison or the antidote," Claire said, speaking for the princess who was still bowed over Paul. "When Fed worked here, one of the first assassination attempts he blocked was poison. He made sure El could identify all the ones Sianta was likely to use."

"Then we need to get a sample. For that matter, we need to get our hands on that contract, too," Gabe replied. "Tonight is the King's Passing ceremony, right? I assume the Miri will be there, so their rooms should be empty. If you keep them busy, Elenor, I can sneak in and try to find both."

"I'll help," Claire offered at once. "And see if I can get at least Tomaz in on it too. You'll need lookouts, and he's the least conspicuous of all of us. Drego, will you go with Elenor tonight and not let her out of your sight? I don't see why the Miri would hurt her after blackmailing her, but I refuse to put anything past them at this point."

"She's going to kill me."

Everyone turned to look at Elenor, who glanced up at them with tear reddened eyes. "She wouldn't play her cards like this if she intended to let me live. I don't know what's in that contract, why she's drawing it out, or why . . . why she hates me so much, but she's going to kill me. I am sure of it."

"*Idaa*," Paul coughed, face twisted in pain. "The wardrobe in your spare room. Look . . . under it. My orders were to not give it to you until your twentieth birthday, but . . . if something happens to me . . . "

"Nothing is going to happen to you, old man. El is far too stubborn to let you die," Claire said.

Kallen crossed his arms. "We can't let this get around, and since we had to come through the halls, rumors will already be spreading. I'm going to go do damage control. The story is that your *doena* started feeling unwell while you were meeting with the Miri and we were all worried for his wellbeing, considering Elenor is already grieving the death of her father. No one mentions poisons or blackmail. Understood? The Iamings and the Writted Nobility will hear none of this. We can't afford more infighting until we have a plan in place to deal with it. Elenor, Paul will have to stay here in the infirmary at least overnight to maintain that ruse, and to make sure that if the antidote he was given proves ineffective, he has medical staff on standby to help. I'll see to making sure he is checked in and no questions are asked. You need to go get ready for this evening. You're a mess."

Gabriel squashed down his instinctive irritation at a nobleman giving him orders. Seeing Cassian had reminded him how much he did *not* like the attitude of the high nobility, but in this case, Drego's logic was sound.

"I'm not leaving him," Elenor said, squeezing Paul's hand harder. "He never left me when I was sick."

Kallen stepped closer. "Yes, you will, Your Highness. You have a country to lead, and I backed you because you seemed to want what is best for it. Forgive me for being blunt, but you have been regent for less than two days and you are already falling to pieces. I understand that part of that is your illness, but unless you want to lose Lirin in a month, you have to get your shit together."

"Don't you dare talk to her like that," Claire snapped, from where she still stood behind Elenor.

"Someone has to," Kallen replied. "You were there, Enica. She confessed to the murder of her own father, and now she allows a foreign power to back her into a corner within minutes of their arrival. I understand that this man is important to her, but part of being a leader is setting your personal needs and desires aside for the sake of your goals. So if your goal is to lose the regency and get charged with murder, Princess, then please do carry on blubbering over an injured servant who isn't even dying."

No one spoke. Claire glared at Kallen with scorching ferocity, and Elenor couldn't seem to look up at the irate nobleman, her shoulders shaking.

Gabriel stepped to the door and opened it. "Go do what you have to do, Drego. I'll make sure she's ready by this evening."

Kallen nodded curtly at him and swept out of the room.

Gabe closed the door, locked it, turned to the others, and said, "He's an asshole."

"I strongly agree," Claire stated with a huff.

"He's right, though," Elenor murmured, looking down at the hand she still held clasped around Paul's. "This is only the beginning and I'm already falling apart. What if I can't do this?" She looked up at her *doena's* face. Paul had his eyes closed, fists clenched around the arms of the chair. If Gabriel had to guess, he would bet money on the guard only holding in tears for the sake of his ward.

"Elenor, why don't you go back to your room with Claire? I'll stay here with Paul until he's admitted."

The princess hesitated, then nodded. She stood with difficulty, then bent to kiss her *doena's* brow. "Don't you dare die on me too, Paul. I love you."

"Never, *daareesha.* Do not worry about me."

She let out a broken, tearful snort of laughter. "The way you don't worry about me? Impossible."

He chuckled, the sound wheezing and strained. "Go, *idaa.* Remember, under the wardrobe. It's important."

It took several more minutes to pry Elenor away from Paul's side, but eventually Claire managed it. Even so, she hovered by the door of the infirmary until her *doena* was tucked into a bed, and even then Gabriel and Claire had to practically drag her out into the hall.

The trip back to her suite was hampered by several nobles trying to get Elenor's attention. Claire shooed them off more politely than Gabriel expected. In a way, the noblewoman reminded him a little of Fay, what with her brusque tone and how hard she seemed to have to work to be patient.

A pang of longing and worry tore through him, but he tried not to let it show. *Where are you, Fayrian? Did you run like Sebastin implied, or are you still here in the city? Are you even alive?* All questions for later, but Gabriel would have to find a way out of the Palace soon. If she was with the Rebellion, someone would know.

By unspoken consensus, they walked right through Elenor's rooms and into the one Gabriel occupied, disturbing the white ball of fluff snoozing in a sunbeam on a couch. Gabe helped Elenor sit on the edge of his bed, resting there himself after the exertion of walking around, while Claire went to the large wardrobe in the corner of the room where he had once stashed the unconscious princess.

"Still can't believe you got out of that while drugged and managed to stop me from killing your parents," Gabe said, as they waited.

"I wish I hadn't. It's only been a few weeks, and both my parents are gone anyway. If I had just let you do it, you wouldn't have been tortured, Djina would still be alive, and so much . . . so much would be better. I'm sorry."

Gabe wrapped an arm around her shoulders and squeezed. "We all make mistakes. I should have clonked you over the head and made *sure* you were out cold."

Elenor laughed. It wasn't a joyous sound, but it still brought a smile to Gabriel's lips.

"Got it." Claire was on her belly, one arm under the wardrobe, the other wrestling away the little mock dragon trying to join the fun, tail swishing over the carpet and nose scuffling against the ground. Claire wiggled back a few inches, then sat up, holding a thick envelope in her hands. "I wonder what it is? It looks like it's been opened. No, don't bite it, little brat."

"Show me," Elenor said, holding out a hand to take it. Claire sat on her other side, the mockling bouncing up as well and settling behind Elenor as she pulled a dry, crinkly piece of paper out of the envelope and a smaller, sealed packet of papers. Carefully, she unfolded the letter and together they read it.

To Princess Elenor's permanent doena, whomever you may be.

Thank you for taking on this duty and setting my heart at ease. My niece will hopefully never need your services, but while I dream of a safe and happy life for her, I am not naive.

Your presence by her side is what I can do from afar to care for her, so know that you have my undying gratitude. If there ever comes a time when you have need of me, consider yourself a friend to the King of Miriel.

Enclosed is a set of documents I drafted and ratified with my closest advisors and Tirit Mindel. They must remain secret until Elenor reaches the age of twenty, or she may become the target of a great deal of harm. I hope to give her my own copy of this document on that day and answer all the questions she will have. Alas, I know the woman I married, and fear that despite my best attempts, I may not survive this farce of a marriage. If I do not, Robin and Ara Daran—the Tiritions who drafted the enclosed document—have a copy and will bring it to light at the appropriate time.

Yet still, I worry. I have learned to have a contingency for every contingency. Even that, likely, will not be enough. As such, I give this third copy to you, on Elenor's behalf. If everything else fails, this is all I can leave her with. She may choose to go public with it, or burn this package and move on with her life. That is her choice, but it is a choice I wish to not be made for her.

Keep it safe, and never let on that you have it. Again, thank you from the bottom of my heart. Please also thank Paul Marek for his service, however temporary, as Elenor's first doena, and tell him to travel the world with my everlasting gratitude, and the funds I promised.

Sincerely,
Warren Miri
King of Miriel

"What *happened?*" Claire asked. "If Paul was only supposed to be temporarily assigned to you, where is his replacement?"

Elenor shook her head, the fingers holding the sealed package trembling. "What if this is it? What if whatever is in here is the reason she tried to kill me?"

"So open it," Gabe urged, curiosity burning bright.

Elenor looked down at the sealed bundle, then drew it up to eye level, staring at the faded wax seal. "It's the same symbol as Wil's sword. Same as this." She reached into the folds of her dress where a pocket must have been sewn and pulled out a ring. It looked far too large for her delicate fingers.

"Where did you get this?"

"Robin Tirition," she answered, eyes returning to the sealed envelope. "He . . . wants this. I think my mother did too, and it was here all this time with Paul."

"You going to open it, love?" Claire asked.

Elenor hesitated, then, mindful of the brittle paper, she broke the wax seal and unfolded the pages.

December 23th, 518, City of Tirit, Island of Tirit Mindel, recorded by Robin Tirition and Ara Daran.

I, Warren Miri, third of my name, King of Miriel, do attest to the paternity of Elenor Lirion, first of her name, and claim her as my daughter and sole heir to the Throne of Miriel. I renounce the claims of my children by Sianta Miri, stripping them of all royal titles and rights, and grant to them instead governorship of their provinces of choice.

Gabriel stopped reading. There were dozens of pages to go but Elenor's face drew his attention. Her lips were mouthing the word *daughter*.

He looked past Elenor to Claire, whose dark brown eyes were as wide as dinner plates. "Does that say sole heir to the throne of *Miriel?*"

"She wasn't Mark's daughter . . . "

Claire's hand rose to cover her mouth, the other reaching to squeeze Elenor's wrist. "No wonder the Miri have been trying to get rid of you. Holy shit. If Wil had lived . . . he would have taken Lirin, and you would have ruled Miriel. It would have been . . . "

"A complete and world-shaking shift in power and the end to Miri-Lirion hostility for at least a generation?" Gabe supplied, head spinning with the implications. "And now that Wil's dead, that makes her—"

"The legal heir of half the world? Yeah."

"Fuck."

Elenor still hadn't spoken. Neither did she seem to be reading, because her eyes were not moving, still fixed on the first paragraph.

They were quiet for a few seconds, Gabe's mind reeling. Then Claire said, "Your mother had to have known this existed. She was looking for a document a few weeks ago, from that Robin fellow. Something must have happened to it, or he wouldn't have approached you to find this." Then, to Gabriel, "He's been trying to corner Elenor just as hard as the Miri, and it makes sense given he witnessed this certificate." Claire reached up to pass her fingers through her thick hair, looking just as overwhelmed with the enormity of this as Gabe felt. "We need to hide this as soon as we're done reading. No one can find it. Were it to fall into the wrong hands or get destroyed . . . "

"He wasn't my father . . . " Elenor's voice was cracked and hollow. She passed the bundle of documents to Gabriel, then stood, pacing to the wardrobe. "He . . . wasn't my father."

"El-belle?" Claire said, lengthening every syllable. "Are you—"

Elenor's fist collided with the wardrobe with a thud that shook the whole piece of furniture. "He wasn't my *fucking father*."

She thudded to the ground. Gabe looked over at Claire, unsure what to do as the princess bit down on her now-bleeding knuckles and started rocking. Claire jumped to her feet but approached slowly, hands outstretched. The mockling, meanwhile, was hiding behind Gabriel, fur puffed up like a cat's.

"Beloved, do you need to vent, cry, or be left alone?" Claire asked, crouching down in front of Elenor.

In answer, Elenor leaned forward until her face was pressed into Claire's shoulder and screamed. It was muffled, too quiet to hear outside this room, but in it was anger and grief beyond words. Her hand reached up to clutch Claire's shoulder, and then the tears came. Big, heaving sobs that shook both women and made Gabe's chest ache in sympathy and old, familiar anguish. He'd cried like that once too—alone and deep in the libraries of the Academy where not even Fay or Fedrik knew to find him—because some fears and revelations were simply too large to put into words.

Gabriel shifted uncomfortably on the bed, glancing down at the papers again, trying to push down his own rush of emotions. He'd ignored those memories for decades. He could do so a while longer while Elenor needed him.

Had Wil known about this document? He had always said that Elenor was in more danger than he was. Was this why? If Robin wanted it as Claire had said, then it had to be valid. With Tirit Mindel's backing . . . "The Miri have been trying to disenfranchise themselves from Tirit Mindel for decades. I bet this is part of the reason."

Elenor looked up at him. "The f-first time my aunt sent someone to kill me I was two. It was a couple weeks after my uncle Warren died. He was young and healthy, but he died of a heart condition that came out of n-nowhere." Elenor glanced in the direction of the infirmary, but needn't have. The connection was easy to make. "Then a few years later, my aunt came here and said something to my father. There was a big fight. I remember because Wil came into my room to comfort me, and held his hands over my ears until I fell asleep. But then three days later was when she . . . "

Elenor reached up to rub the little scar at the base of her jaw. "And they d-didn't stop her. My father had always come to me when I was sick before then, but he never visited me after. Not . . . once. Not in the seven years I was away. Didn't it matter at all to him that he had raised me, even if I wasn't his? Didn't it matter that I loved him?"

Her eyes clenched shut, then opened and stared right at Gabriel. He had expected to see the same pain in her words mirrored there, but instead they were filled with determination and fury. "He knew. They all fucking knew and never told me why I was hurt. Sianta took my childhood, she took my uncle before he could tell me any of this, and she's responsible for taking my brother too. And my parents, they did nothing to stop it.

"No more. She's not going to fucking take a single other thing from me, especially not Paul. I never knew Warren, my mother is useless, and my father lost all rights to call himself that long before today. Paul's the only parent I've ever needed. I'll be damned before she kills him too."

"That's my girl." Claire pressed a kiss into Elenor's hair. "Let's take the bitch down."

"If you're going to do that, you need to get better first, which means another dose of serindalla," Gabriel reminded her, as he folded the document and placed it back into the larger envelope.

Elenor made a face, shoulders slumping. "I'm so tired."

With hair a mess and tears still staining her cheeks, she really looked it, but Gabriel wasn't worried. He had seen that flash of purpose. He had a feeling that once Elenor got her feet back under her, she was going to be unstoppable.

INTERLUDE
Rainclouds and Pine
ALEHAN

Alehan grunted as he landed on the dusty, darkened streets of Gold City and let go of the rope. It swayed in the breeze, trailing up hundreds of feet to an open window on the north-facing side of the Temple. He carried nothing with him. The Gods did not allow the subjects of their experiments to own things, nor had Aleh risked wasting time in order to steal. He would rather be a penniless beggar on the streets of Gold City than go back to the place where so many of his nightmares had been birthed.

Pulling the hood of his coat up to avoid stares, he looked around to make sure no one had spotted his descent. There were patrols of *her* soldiers, but Alehan had tracked those over the centuries and they never changed much. The priests of the Gold Dragon were powerful and deadly, but they liked routine. Just like their patron, they strutted around, high on arrogance and might, never realizing how much slipped through the cracks of their white-knuckled grip over the world.

Alehan looked up at the Temple one last time, vast edifices stretching as far as the eye could see both up and to the sides along the curving mesa it sat upon, then turned his back on it.

Never again.

He started jogging as soon as he reached the first turn, intent on putting as much distance between himself and the Gods as he could by morning.

Escape had always been a possibility. Alehan realized that the second time they woke him for their experiments. The Gold never let him leave the Temple and never kept him awake for longer than necessary, but over the centuries he had spent more than a decade awake and aware. Following the Gold's instructions yielded nothing but pain—disobedience even more agony or, at best, another long stint in stasis until the few humans he had grown to know were dead. The only comfort he could find during all those lonely days was to plan his escape.

The city smelled different from the Temple. It wasn't sterile and airy, but rather hot, dusty, filled with the scents of cooking, the sounds of laughter, the mess of humanity. It made Alehan's chest ache with the desire to stop at one of the bars and soak in the boisterous chaos, except he wasn't far enough away yet.

As hours passed, his pace slowed. No matter how much he exercised between bouts of stasis, his body always took a few days to recover from the long, God-induced sleep. His arms and shoulders still burned from the climb down the side of the Temple, and were his life and liberty not on the line, he might have wished for sleep.

Not tonight, though.

If the Gold was considering sending him back to Carinn, it was because she had decided he was no longer useful to her. This wouldn't be a holy mission or a rescue operation. It was a trap.

It was vengeance.

His thoughts whirred as he rounded another mesa, upon which one of the wealthier neighborhoods of Gold City had been built, and got his first glimpse of the sea, moon sparkling over the waves.

Get on a boat, change my name, disappear. They can't find me if I stay close to other people and don't use too much magic. I can do this.

He had once avoided detection within the Temple itself by shadowing another powerful rifter for nearly a week. Laronok, God of the Ciphers, could find almost anyone, but like all the Gods with knowledge-based Gifts, he had too many humans to sort through. As long as Alehan remained inconspicuous, he had a chance at freedom.

A seagull flew by overhead, shadowing him as Aleh began jogging again. With every breath, the scent of ocean air filled his aching lungs. Once, he had loved that smell, and if it got him out of Gold City, he would set aside the memories of being left in a boat to die with his family and love it again.

The docks came into view, the huge marina stretching for miles along the sweeping harbor. Streetlights illuminated the golden sandstone and the bustling business still going strong. The night markets of Gold City were a sight Alehan had wanted to see with his own eyes since first hearing of them, but this wasn't the time to casually walk amongst the hundreds of stalls.

He scanned the lively crowd, then headed in the direction of the shipyard as he rehearsed the lie he had to spin, so it would spill smoothly from his tongue.

My name is Matt Adema. I just lost all my money in a game of chance and need to get out of town. I'm looking to leave on the next boat out, and can work for my passage. I'm not picky about what the work is, as long as we're underway by dawn.

There was a recruitment office for one of the big shipping companies at the end of a row of shops. Aleh didn't know what the business traded in, but he had seen the distant red sails from his window for well over a century, so they were long-lasting. That didn't mean they were reputable, but all Aleh needed was a ride out of this city. He could figure out a long-term plan once he got somewhere that wasn't in the shadow of the Gold's Temple.

He got into line behind an obviously drunk woman and a group of young sailors. It took forever for the man at the window to get through each sign-up. Every second that passed made the hair on Alehan's neck rise higher, sweat beading on his light-brown skin as he tried not to look around him too often. Looking suspicious and jumpy would draw attention, and there were gold-clad priests in shining armor strolling through the markets. As one such pair walked by, Alehan overheard a snippet of conversation.

"All the Gods were called in. Schedules are going to be up in the air while they remain. I wonder what has them riled?"

"It is not for you or I to know the will or worries of the Gods. You should watch your tongue if you intend to speak so casually of their Divine Presences. Heresy is easy to speak if it exists in your heart."

"I was making small talk. I'm not a heretic."

"You are *a priest.* The standards are higher for those of us who have chosen Her path."

Alehan grimaced and tugged at his hood a little more, holding his breath until their voices faded into the hum of the crowd.

At last, the recruiter beckoned him forward. Aleh hurried up to the window, heart thundering.

"Name?"

"Matt Adema."

"What kind of work are you looking for?"

Aleh opened his mouth to answer, but froze as a cool hand settled on his shoulder, the icy touch seeping into his skin through his coat. Around him, people gasped in shock. Murmurs spread and the recruiter just stared, mouth agape, at the space behind Alehan's right shoulder.

Aleh closed his eyes, suppressing a shudder.

Not again. Please, not her again.

"You've been a very naughty boy," Raiyana, Goddess of Lusions, crooned in his ear, each sibilant word enunciated with slow, deliberate clarity. "Sarthia does not like it when her playthings run away, Alehan Silvarin. She has sent us to recover you and has allowed the finder their choice of punishment."

Her cadence, each syllable distinct, made Alehan ache to pull away and run. The magic in his well called from within, urging him to use it and blast this creature away as he had done once before, the first time she had punished him for his impudence.

But it would just end as it had then: a futile reprieve and a worse punishment. Was it worth the minute or two of freedom? Could he make a run for it and lose her? Or maybe just throw himself into the sea and let it bash him against the rocks?

As he stood, frozen with indecision, her body pressed against his back, her other hand trailing across his side and down his belly. Aleh couldn't move, thoughts staticky as the noises around him changed. The sounds of the market faded and the creak of leather and squelching of mud replaced them, the scent of pine and rain filling his nostrils. The crack of a stiff belt hitting flesh.

"So many memories I could use to make you weep. This will be our final session . . . though perhaps pleasure would hurt you more. It always did draw out more of your secrets than pain. If you tell me what I've always wished to know, I might be able to spare you from your fate."

Alehan tasted bile as she trailed her finger along the waistband of his pants. He didn't dare open his eyes, knowing full well what illusion she had conjured this time. She always liked mixing pleasure and pain. If he looked, he would see it again, see Jac walking towards him with tears streaming down his cheeks, arms coated in blood and dirt, and eyes dark with anger.

How many times had she forced him to relive it? How many more days would she spend tormenting him for the secret she thought he knew? The other Gods had each had their turn with Alehan over the centuries, trying to pry the secrets of his immortality out of him. Calendra the Fathom had once ripped him open from throat to groin just to watch him sink into that terrifying place where his body went when in agony. He had returned whole, writhing in terror more intense than any pain. None, however, was worse than Raiyana.

I should have jumped from the window instead of climbing down.

But he knew it wouldn't have given him what he wanted. There was no easy way out for him. He'd learned the hard way that there was no peace to be found, even in the hands of the kindest of the Gods.

Zaylla the Schism had been gentle with Alehan. She had asked him about his childhood in Miriel with his mother and Uncle Mathe, holding Alehan when he cried over their loss. He had still been a child at the time, unaware that everything with the Gods was a game.

Then Zaylla had questioned him further. About the day when Alexander had come to their crumbling mansion and pulled them out of poverty and into a life of vicious luxury.

Aleh had told her all of it. How, at six years of age, he had yearned to fit in at the Imperial Court. How his mother had struggled with a nobility who had taken one look at her Jia skin and decided it was a threat. He had talked for hours about his uncle, who, despite being unable to walk a single step due to a childhood bout of wasting fever, had thrived on Tirit Mindel, pushing music and technology forward by leaps and bounds, but never earning his peers' respect because of his connection to the scandal rocking the Empire: Alehan.

The bastard son of the reigning Emperor and a poor woman of Jia heritage. It hadn't mattered that Alexander had never claimed him. The resemblance had been too obvious, and Aleh's existence a threat the nobility would not stand.

On and on, the questioning had continued. She had asked about Jac and Aislin, who alone among the nobles at court had made Alehan feel at home. And about Gabril Lirion, Alexander's best friend, who Alehan had been in awe of. Who had taken him through the Hidden City, teaching Alehan all the best spots to hide, and telling him stories of Alexander's childhood. Alexander certainly hadn't bothered to do that.

Then, the night the war had started.

Waking up to his mother's hand over his mouth. Being rushed through the Hidden City, past the bloody corpses of the Valora who had died to protect the Imperial Family and the Silvarin they had been too late to save. The doorways being closed and rekeyed to Silvarin blood. Darkness.

His father holding Alehan by the hand as they walked in the echoing quiet. The realization that Alexander's presence didn't actually make him feel safe.

Then years of running. First to Tirit Mindel until the day the Lirion came. Then to the Mondaer desert, where he watched his parent's relationship disintegrate, leaving him to rock his new baby sister and promise her that he'd keep her safe, without realizing that it was a promise he could never dream of keeping.

All that honesty had bought him nothing, because when Zaylla did not get the information she wanted out of him, she had turned Alehan over to her more sadistic brethren without so much as an apology.

Raiyana's hand trailed down his chest, her breasts pressing tight to his back. He could feel her ephemeral breath against his ear, drawing a scared whimper from Aleh's lips. His knees shook, but what was the point in trying to hide it? Raiyana was the Goddess of Lusions. Obfuscating was her power; next to her, all were novices.

"Oh Alehan, after all we've gone through together, were you

really going to leave without saying farewell? You disappoint me."

Her laugh seemed to come from all around and nowhere at once as the dock vanished into a thick, impenetrable darkness. Even his awareness of her faded, though it offered little comfort. Like a spider in a darkened room, he knew she was there and that was enough.

A cool breeze ruffled his hair, the scent of pine and rain incongruous to the hot arid coastline. The air around Alehan grew frigid as he sucked in magic. It was pointless but instinctive, a vain attempt to avoid what would happen next. "What do you hope to learn that you haven't after all this time? I told you the first time and I tell you again: I don't know how it happened. I've never known. I was a child."

Something brushed against the back of his neck. Alehan swiveled around, a hand swiping at the empty air. "Stop it."

"I don't think I will. My dear Sel'Caronok has kept you away from me for so long, and after today I won't get another chance. Do you know how disappointed Sarthia has been that I never cracked your secret? Your obstinacy costs me her trust, and the Gold's trust is everything on Dracona."

A flicker of light appeared in the darkness. Alehan braced, though in all the times that she had done this, no amount of preparation had ever helped.

The light grew, grew, then—

Alehan stood in a wooded clearing, amid a forest of pine. Rainclouds hung heavy in the sky, the canvas of the nearby army tents damp from the constant drizzle. For a second, he was disoriented, the world at the wrong angle. One look down at his small hands confirmed that it was happening once more.

She was making him relive it *again.*

"Shall we start here, or would you like to skip ahead?" Raiyana's voice whispered in Alehan's ear. It was a cruel joke, because he couldn't respond. His head rose, looking up at the man standing behind him, one hand on each of Aleh's shoulders.

"What's happening, Uncle Gabril?" His voice was high-pitched and scared, playing out exactly as it had that cursed day.

Gabril Lirion's fair hair was plastered to his head, gray eyes staring into the woods where a mock dragon had landed not long before. "Nothing good. But don't worry. You're safe. Jac loves you like his own son. Whatever happened, you'll be safe."

Calm washed over him. Yes, of course he was safe. He was with Gabril and Jac. They had come and taken him from the desert, but it wasn't because they were going to hurt him. They had promised.

Aleh leaned closer into Gabril, the warmth of the man's body a comfort in the chilly morning. "I hope nothing bad happened to Aunt Aislin and Julian."

Gabril didn't respond, instead glancing toward the open tent door where Caibre, his youngest brother, stood with crossed arms.

As though the look summoned him, Caibre strolled over. "Having second thoughts, Gabril?"

"We never should have done this. It was a mistake."

"What are you talking about?" Aleh asked, looking from one to the other and reaching up to squeeze Gabril's hand. Caibre had always scared him with that intent, knowing gaze.

The adults ignored him. "I'm not sure we'll be able to control him, Cai. Jac—"

"Needs a push, if he's going to take on Alex. His hatred is all . . . academic and superficial. One doesn't murder one's prior best friend for stealing credit on a paper."

Alehan flinched with momentary panic. But no, he must have misunderstood. He was here so that they could talk to his father and put an end to the war. They must have been talking about someone else.

The part of his mind that knew how this ended was trying to scream.

"He's losing faith in our cause. I hope you aren't too, big brother."

"Of course I'm not. I know what my duty to the family is, but this doesn't feel right." Gabril was shifting from foot to foot, eyeing the treeline. His nerves made Aleh nervous too.

Caibre snorted. "I told Jonas that you didn't have the stomach to be the Incarnate. What good is the power to control rifters if you don't have the balls to do what must be done? When he gets here, just point him at Alexander and release his inhibitions. One little sentence: 'he deserves whatever you want to do to him'. Is that really so hard? If it is, you could always give the Gift to me."

"Not in your wildest dreams, Cai," Gabril muttered, then tensed as the underbrush ripped aside. Pine trees cracked and fell in a deafening roar. Between them, head bowed and shoulders heaving, was a man Alehan had never once seen angry.

Jac Drego's usually neat black hair hung around his face and clung to blood-streaked cheeks. His sleeves were rolled up to his elbows, forearms and hands caked in dirt. The rain had washed rivulets away, drops of muddy water falling from his cracked fingernails and the piece of parchment clutched in one hand.

But it was his eyes that struck terror into Alehan's heart and made him press back into Gabril as hard as he could.

"Give me the boy," Jac said, his voice incongruously soft as his chest continued to heave.

"Alehan? Why?" Gabril asked, his hands on Aleh's shoulder's tightening.

"Give me the boy."

Caibre stepped forward, holding up his hands. "Calm, friend. Why don't you tell us what happened? Wouldn't you like to know what happened, *Gabril*?"

The whole scene froze, with Caibre looking back at his brother with squinted eyes.

Raiyana's form appeared, stepping around Caibre and tilting her head to the side as she stared at Gabril. "Let's analyze, shall we? Here we have the powerless little brother—vicious, clever, and hungry—and the middle brother, their very own Incarnate. Correct?"

Aleh couldn't respond. He was trapped inside his younger self, staring at Jac and wishing his frozen feet to run.

"And Caibre, he wants Gabril to use his Incarnate Effect to calm Jac down like it has so many times before. Like he's using it on you to make you trust him, despite these men having kidnapped you from the only refuge you had left. Didn't you question it at the time? Probably not. That's the tricky thing with Incarnates. By the time you realize that your will isn't your own anymore, you don't care."

Aleh wanted to cry, but couldn't. He couldn't even hyperventilate or tense at what he knew was coming.

Time started again. Jac marched across the clearing, thrusting the crumpled letter into Caibre's extended hand. "They're dead."

Even though Alehan had seen this repeated hundreds of times, that didn't stop the physical sensations; the way the air had expelled from his lungs and his stomach twisted.

Jac's gaze was still fixed on him as he let go of the paper. "Read it yourself. I'm not here to explain, I'm here for *him*."

The scene froze again.

"This is always the interesting part," Raiyana mused. "See that little smile on Caibre's lips? It makes me wonder what was in that letter. Have any ideas? Oh, right, you may speak."

She waved her hand, and Aleh unfroze just enough to gasp, "I don't know. I told you that I don't know. I've never known why it happened." And it had haunted him for all the long years of his life.

"Well, if you want to be that way, let's continue."

"No—"

Too late.

"Gabril," Jac growled. There was murder in his eyes, a crazed, panicky rage that Alehan knew from experience was oversaturation. "Gods help me, I will go through you if I must. I need to understand why . . . why . . . " A heaving sob, then Jac lunged forward, grabbing Gabril by the lapels. Only Gabril's quick movement swung Alehan behind him, out from the path of the distraught rifter.

"Easy—"

"You swore they'd be safe. You *swore.* You told me this would make the world a better place and that you'd keep them safe, but now they're g-gone." His voice broke.

Aleh tried to squirm out of Gabril's grip, but the man's hold was too tight. "Uncle Gabril, you're hurting me."

"Taking vengeance on Alehan won't bring them back. It's the person responsible who should pay," Gabril said, a quivering brittleness to his voice.

"Yes. He will. He'll suffer as I've suffered. He'll lose exactly what he took from me. I don't care what it takes. *Give me the boy.*"

"Jac . . . "

Jac's fingers closed around Gabril's throat. He was taller than the blond man holding Alehan, the motion pulling Gabril onto his toes. "Think carefully about your next words, Gabril Lirion."

"Give him the boy," Caibre shouted, one hand on his sword. "For fuck's sake, Gabe. He's just a Silvarin mutt. He doesn't matter."

Gabril hesitated. He closed his eyes, and Aleh watched a tear slide down his cheek. But then Jac squeezed. Gabril reached up, hand closing around Jac's wrist. Caibre lunged forward too, but a flick of Jac's other hand and a surge of kinetic power sent the younger Lirion brother sailing through the air.

"Jac—"

A wheeze. Alehan stood too stunned to do anything. Too terrified to even cry out as Gabril writhed, bucked, tried to free himself from the rifter whose eyes held nothing but icy murder. Then, in a hoarse, breathless croak, Gabril cried, "Stop. The boy is yours. Do whatever you want with him. He . . . he deserves whatever you want to do to him. They all do."

Alehan screamed. Not through his child-self's lips but in his mind. Screamed and screamed for her to stop. Screamed in hopes that it might drown out some small part of what came next.

But then a voice boomed through the vision, shattering it.

"Get your hands off him, Rai."

Alehan gasped in relief as the cold touch disappeared, the vision vanishing, leaving nothing but the tears streaming down Alehan's cheeks. He cracked his eyes open. No humans remained anywhere nearby. Even in Gold City—where the Gods were patrons not just puppet masters—everyone feared the ones they considered dangerous.

Alehan knew better: they were all dangerous, and there was no point in running.

Sel'Caronok, though, was better than most. As Aleh turned his head, he saw the towering, glowing form of the God of Lucents standing between himself and his sister. Raiyana's form—near-translucent and shimmering, ready to take the shape of anything or anyone she wished—looked tiny next to Sel'Caronok.

The brilliant God held out his hand to Alehan. "We go now. You are in enough trouble as it is. Come, Alehan."

Like a dog ordered to heel. Alehan wanted to bolt, but anything was better than Raiyana.

He stepped up to his patron deity and took the offered hand. There were two Gods watching him. Even with his magic, Aleh could no longer hope to escape.

A shimmering door stood in the air. As always with this method of transportation, a cold sweat broke across his brow as they stepped through it into the familiar offices of Sel'Caronok's wing of the eighteen-sided Temple of the Gold.

As soon as the doorway closed behind him—leaving Raiyana on the other side—Sel'Carokok turned to Alehan and calmly said, "Did it not occur to you that I would fight to keep you here? It serves no purpose to send you back."

No, it had *not* occurred to Aleh, yet he knew better than to talk back. Even Sel'Caronok would not abide insubordination. Aleh knew his place within the shadow of the Labradorite Dragon, and it was that of an interesting keepsake, not a person with autonomy—no matter what Sel'Caronok's litany stated.

At least Sel'Caronok was better than Raiyana.

"Forgive me, I was scared. I don't want to go back to Carinn."

The glowing form of the God paced across the room, then came to rest facing Alehan, arms crossed over a muscular chest. "That might have counted for something earlier tonight, when I almost had the Gold convinced to spare you if she goes through with this insanity. Now, you have proven to her that all the obedience and devotion you've learned to shroud yourself in is a lie. She will not spare those who do not deserve it."

Aleh winced and resisted the temptation to hug himself. He tried to conjure up any small bit of leverage he had gathered on the Gods, but gave up as Sel'Caronok shook his head in dismay, or perhaps disgust. "You had a chance to remain here, Alehan, and even after all the freedoms I have given you, you did not trust me enough to take it. I want you to stay. I would have fought for you to stay, but you tied my hands when you ran. You lack faith, and you cannot exist in a world ruled over by the Gold Dragon without it."

Aleh looked away, but with a gentle touch Sel'Caronok cupped his cheek and brought his gaze back. "I wish it were not this way. You were a child and do not deserve the tribulations that life and the Gods have put you through, but I do not make the rules. Those who have broken Her rules have suffered crippling defeats and centuries of torment. I will not join them. You, now, likely must. Your best chance, Alehan, is to do as you are told and hope that you do it well enough to earn her mercy."

Aleh nodded, then whispered, "Will Raiyana get me again before I leave?"

Sel'Caronok turned away. "That is not for me to decide. That—as all things in this world—are the purview of Sarthia the Incarnate, our Mother in Gold."

PART FOUR

CHAPTER EIGHTEEN

Reunited

FAYRIAN

We saw an impossible thing today. A man seemed to appear out of a door in the air in the middle of our encampment. Despite the snow, he wore summer pants, an unbuttoned shirt, and sandals. He proceeded to burn down our entire camp—including Phoebi's wheelchair—take our circuits and circuitry materials, and disappear the way he came. Had Denzel and I not noticed the flames and flown over, we would not have seen it happen. None of us, not even Harrison or Phoebi, had ever heard of magic that allowed one to appear between one spot and another. Among the circuits he took was the one we'd found on that desert island in the southern Island Union, and brought back home to study. I have to conclude that he was the original owner, and that we may have stumbled on something much more dangerous than we bargained for. We have, one and all, voted to do our very best to avoid this rifter in future. We have too much to accomplish to end up dead.

—From the journals of Amandine Tirition.

FAYRIAN FOUND NORTH LEANING AGAINST the rail of a balcony with his small dragon sitting by his feet. She didn't move towards him, not wanting to see the sickening fall beyond the railing. Instead, she coughed. He turned.

"Suela and I are leaving to rendezvous with Fedrik in a few minutes. I was . . . wondering if you wanted to talk before we left?"

North turned tired eyes to her. "You want to know about Daemon, don't you?"

Fay shrugged. "I mean, if you want to talk about him, sure. That's not why I came to find you, though. I've seen enough powerful megalomaniacs to recognize one. No . . . I came to see if you wanted to know anything about Gabriel."

North turned to face her fully, and Fay sank down onto a bench, patting it. "I won't bite. I know I can be a bitch, but not today."

In the light of the evening sun, Fay could really see how much green was in North's hazel eyes. How had she not seen it before? He looked so much like Gabriel. Not in the big ways—North was taller and broader than Gabe, with shoulder-length hair and a full beard over skin a shade or two lighter—but the small details were near-identical. The way his nose met his brows, how his smile went all the way to his eyes, even the cadence of his voice as he answered, "Ah, sure. That would actually be very nice."

He walked over, sitting next to her with the huff of someone deeply exhausted. His dragonet slunk over, staring up at Fay with wide, hopeful eyes.

"Fine. Just this once, you lumbering pain beast," she said, reaching out to stroke Bard's silky scales. The mock wiggled excitedly but did not jump up on her. Thank fuck for that. Fay looked over at North. "So, you're his brother . . . and a Silvarin."

"No, I'm not."

She cocked her head. "But—"

"His brother, perhaps. I might even be descended from the Silvarin, but that's not the name I was given at birth. He was. It was one of the Namings I did for Daemon. When I look in the mirror, though, the name I see is Alaric Nameh, not Alaric Silvarin. Neither fit me, nor have I ever gone by them. No, my name—the one that matters—is North Hillman. It's the one I chose for myself, and this doesn't change that." He took a deep breath, then let it out along with the tension that had built in his shoulders as he spoke. "Do you . . . do you think he'll want to know me, if we both survive that long?"

Fay burst out into a peal of laughter. "Oh, kid, you clearly do *not* know Gabriel. All he's wanted, for as long as I've known him, is a family again. He wants about a million kids and to go find his little sister once the fighting is over. The moment he finds out you exist, nothing in this world is going to keep him from hugging the living daylights out of you."

North chuckled, leaning his head against the reddish stone of the Mother Rock. Beyond the balcony, the city sprawled across the desert, brilliantly lit in oranges, teals, and blinding whites by the setting sun. Fay didn't like to admit it, but the view was spectacular.

"What's he like? I only glimpsed him once, and his calling . . . was quite beautiful. I don't have words for it, but *good*."

"Yeah, that's Gabriel. He's always been the best among us." Fay pulled her knees up to her chest, resting her chin on them and letting her eyes drift closed as she searched her memories. "Gabe puts too much sugar in his tea and coffee. That's the thing I always think of when I remember him. It's a stupid little detail and there is so much more to him that that, but he *loves* sweet things. I think it's his magic, but I always teased him that the only reason he was so sweet to everyone was the steady diet of sugar."

North chuckled. "I hate overly sweet things."

"Bullshit. You voluntarily walk around with Leo. He's condensed sugar and optimism, wrapped in fucking sunshine," Fay retorted. "Gabe would probably like him too. I never really understood what he saw in me. I definitely didn't deserve him."

North wavered, then asked, "Did you know you were using your Gift on him? Daemon explained a little of it before I came to the desert, including how potentially explosive his magic could be because of you. I wasn't sure if you knew, though, and I wasn't sure if he was alive, so I didn't mention anything. It never seemed like the right time."

"Yeah, I'm still pissed about that. But yes, I knew." Fay opened her eyes, staring right into the setting sun. It seared her still-tender irises, but she deserved the pain for what she had done to Gabriel. "I did it deliberately. I hobbled his magical potential. I believed I had to for his own good, but after a while I couldn't bring myself to be honest, because the lies had piled up so high. I had the key to everything he wanted: power to get rid of the man who killed his family, the reason why his village was targeted . . . even just the answers to his many questions about his magic. It used to frustrate him so much that sometimes he could use little bits, and sometimes not. I should have told him all of it, but I didn't. I lied, and I kept him off the front lines even when it hurt the rebellion. I had all the information about his real identity locked away in my head but never whispered a single word of it. We were *in school* with one of his half-brothers, and I never told them even when they were at each other's throats. As I said, he deserved better. At least he's alive. I know I may not see him again, but it's a comfort to know he's still out there working towards the dream."

North cocked his head. "Dream?"

A flock of birds danced across the sky, swooping and falling like waves on the sea. "My father's dream. He wanted Lirin ruled by someone who put the people first. Ideally, a parliament like the one in Seehana, even if we still had a King or Queen. Gabe and I were raised on that idea. My dad would put us to bed with whispered imaginings of a country where we weren't forced to hide in caves and abandoned, burned-out husks of towns in order to fight for our freedom. If Gabe is alive, he'll find a way to see it realized. I just wish I was there with him."

"So you think he succeeded? You were trying to kill the King of Lirin, right?" North asked.

"Gotta assume it, yes. Why else would that whiny piece-of-shit princess be in charge? Daemon said he was under her protection, so maybe he managed to convince her to come around. If anyone could, it's him."

"Or Daemon could be lying. He does that a lot," North cautioned.

Fay frowned, not liking that one bit. "Do you think he's lying about this?"

"No," North said, after a brief pause. "I spoke to Tsiihsi and Obri briefly. Apparently he's been obsessing over the events in Hardor for weeks, and making enemies of Gods in the process. I don't know what it's all about, but they're concerned over his mental state, and after seeing him today, I am too. He's more unstable than ever. I wouldn't trust him on the best days. Do you . . . do you want me to try to get a message to Gabriel, if following Daemon gets me to Hardor?"

Fay considered that for a long while, then finally shook her head.

"Are you sure?" North asked. "What if he thinks you're dead?"

"Nah, no way. I left my gramps a message on my way here to

let my people know that I was safe and going to ground. They'll trust that I'll come back when it's the right time." It tore at her heart to not take this opportunity, but it sounded like the situation in Hardor was delicate. Gabriel, bless him, always put the people he loved ahead of politics, and their country couldn't afford that. "If he knew I was here, he'd storm across the border and get in a tussle with the Mondaer about letting me come home. Better that he believe I'm hiding somewhere and biding my time. Lirin needs him more than I do right now." Then she exhaled, shook out her hands, and changed the subject. "By the way, what did Moe tell you?"

What little mirth there had been in North's eyes faded, and he looked down. "I have no intention of voicing that aloud, ever. I've seen how Daemon works. For all we know, he might be listening in right now. Or he might have changed his face to look like you, and is tricking me. All I'll say is that it worries me, and I think it would be best if he never heard it."

"So you're not going to tell him?"

"I'll tell him if he proves himself, like the Red seemed to believe he would. I just don't expect it to ever happen."

From inside the building, someone called Fay's Mondaer name. She rolled her shoulders, then stood. "Well, sounds like it's time for me to go. You take care of yourself, alright? Not that I really give a shit, but Gabe will, so you just became someone I'd like to keep alive."

North smiled. "You're sweeter than you let people think, aren't you?"

"No way. I'm made of bitterness and teeth."

He laughed, and stood too, opening his arms.

Fay rolled her eyes, but stepped in to let the oaf hug her. It might not be as good as one from Gabriel, but she would be lying if she didn't admit to needing one. Unexpectedly, when he squeezed her tight and Bard butted his head between them to join in, Fay actually sniffled a little.

She pulled back fast, but had to reach up to wipe moisture away from her eyes before it could form tears. "It's been a long couple days."

"Yeah . . . it has. Take care of yourself, and keep Fedrik safe."

Fay shrugged, and put on a brave smile. "Keeping people with dangerous magical powers from going boom is kind of what I do. Tellen'll be easy. I don't mind punching him in the face, unlike Gabriel."

North chuckled, shaking his head. "Just don't punch Suela. I'm pretty sure she'd eat you alive. And Fayrian . . . good luck."

They were late getting to the house of the Gifted person who would transport them to the Sandhewn City because Fay absolutely refused to get onto a mock dragon. She had dug in her heels, but instead of being allowed to walk, Suela had said something in Eldel to her fucking dragon and the horrible beast had grabbed Fay in its talons and flown down off the Mother Rock dragging her like a doll. Fay had screamed the whole way to the outskirts of the city.

By the time they landed, her throat burned and her hatred for the old woman had grown tenfold, but she was far too shaky to do anything about it. Of the people at the meeting, only one had agreed to come along with them to help train Fedrik: the old woman named Phoebi. A few others planned to come in a few weeks, but until then, it would be the three of them, Tellen, and whomever they had flown to meet.

"On your feet, girl. Or are you going to lounge around all day?" Suela barked, poking Fay with the tip of her cane.

"I will break that instead of throwing it next time," she warned.

"I see one jog up the Mother Rock has not been enough to teach you to respect your elders. You are my apprentice, Fayrian. Do try to remember that you agreed to follow my orders."

Miserable old bat. Fay scowled, which earned a shake of the head from Phoebi, who still sat in the saddle of a very out-of-place white mock dragon, a wheeled chair strapped behind her, along with a pair of crutches and her bags.

"I'll follow any reasonable order. Getting on a flying lizard isn't one. There's nothing wrong with being scared of heights, and torturing me by pulling stunts like that is petty and mean," Fay retorted, though she did get to her feet, brushing off her pants and giving Suela's large red mock a nasty glare. In her mind, he was just as culpable as his mistress.

"You're a *daradeio.* The sky is yours to control, and the way to do that is on mockback. You will have to get used to it eventually," Suela said, then waved a hand, dismissing the topic. "Go knock on the door and tell them we have arrived."

Fay crossed her arms, thought about arguing, but swallowed it back. They were going to Fedrik. Delaying that would only be to her detriment.

With a grumble, she stomped over to the door of a tall Mondaer home with a large garden and a rather impressive pool of clear blue water beside it and gave three curt knocks.

As she waited, foot tapping in annoyance, a small green mock dragon appeared on the flat roof, looking down at her with intelligent and creepily hungry eyes.

"Don't even think about it, mister. I'm nobody's snack."

The dragon started scaling down the wall, clinging to window sills and metal rings pounded into the stone. Unlike any of the other species but the blues, it had only four limbs, with taloned but very dexterous claws at the tips of its wings that it used like hands to climb.

"Shanty, not food," Phoebi called from behind Fay, then clicked her tongue. "Try not to smell so scared. It makes you seem like prey."

Smell less scared? How was Fay supposed to do *that?*

She had just taken a few steps back, convinced that the mock was about to lunge and snap her head off, when the door flew open.

In the doorway stood a man she thought she'd never see again. He was old, but not bent or out of shape, with shoulder-length white hair that had been pulled into a messy bun, and a scruffy goatee. Even out of his Tirit Mindel robes, though, Denzel Tirition's face was one Fayrian would never have forgotten.

"Master Denzel?" It came out as half-exclamation, half-question. "But . . . you drowned. I was at your Passing!"

The ex-weapons master of the Academy gave her a wide smile. "Avilor? Well, I'll be. As for the death part, well, best way not to be disturbed in retirement is for everyone to think you're already dead. Though I see that doesn't stop you. What are *you* doing here? Never thought I'd see my most determinedly Lirinian student in *daradeio* reds."

"But . . . " Fay spluttered, still reeling.

Denzel looked past her and waved. "Pheebs, I thought I heard your voice. What brings you back to the city? Are you coming along on this expedition?" Then his face fell, as both Phoebi and Suela failed to smile. "What happened?"

"Best that we not speak of it in the open. Is Atia ready?"

"Yes. We have the circle set up out back. If you go around the house, you'll see it," Denzel replied, then looked down his slightly crooked, scarred nose at Fay. "Off you trot. We'll catch up later. Shanty, backyard."

Order given, the green mock stopped its creep down the building and dove. Fay yelped and ducked, but the mock didn't grab her. It swooped over her head and into the air, flapping its wings until it could turn and head over the roof of the house.

Master Denzel nudged Fay, then pointed in the direction the two mounted *daradeio* were headed. Fay followed, a little dazed. In the large courtyard behind the house, a copper wire as thick as Fay's thumb had been laid in a huge circle that comfortably fit the three mocks. A woman Fayrian didn't recognize stood next to it, dressed head-to-toe in red, but with a bright white belt.

"Atia was a slave before becoming *daradeio,*" Denzel explained, appearing behind Fayrian and making her jump. "She, like many others, wears white as a sign of pride that they worked for their place in the desert."

"And you?" she asked.

Denzel smiled devilishly. "I got in on Pheobi's credit. I'm far too old to do things the hard way."

"How is this supposed to transport us?" Fay asked. Atia was talking to Suela. While Denzel carried a bag, Atia did not. Fay had to assume, therefore, that it would be a party of four, not five, that would head to the Sandhewn City. "We're not doing to go high up, right? Because I've been yanked across half the world already this week, and met someone who I hear can open doorways in mid-air to anywhere."

Denzel's eyebrows rose. "Tall fellow with black hair and a nasty disposition?"

That described Daemon well enough, so Fay nodded.

"So you, too, have had a run-in with Sandals."

"Excuse me?" She spluttered.

"Sandals. That's what we used to call him, if it's the same man. Not long after I became a Tirition, a group of us accidentally stole a circuit of his. He found our camp, burned it to the ground, and probably would have killed us to get it back, if we hadn't been away at the time. I remember flying in on a mock and seeing him next to a floating portal in the air, wearing sandals and summer clothes in knee-deep snow. He left an impression, and not just on us. There are records of his sightings going back centuries."

"He's an asshole."

"You'll have to tell me all about it. For now, step into the circle. Atia has the Schism Gift. She can fold space with a copper boundary to transport those within it. Try to hunker down. The effect is uncomfortable at best."

Fayrian did just that. The mocks were commanded to lie down, then Atia knelt next to the copper ring. "I would suggest holding your breath and closing your eyes. You'll be less aware of being upside-down, backward, and folded on yourselves."

With no more warning than that, everything lurched. The description Atia had given was nothing compared to what Fay's Gift sensed when Atia's activated. Fay thought she might have screamed, but no sound came out as what felt like a building's weight pressed atop her. Before she could react, she was falling, but in every direction at once. The boom of her own pulse ricocheted inside of her skull. Her limbs seemed to fold in on themselves like the knotted dough Mari used to fry for Fay and Gabriel as children. Her Gift battered the inside of her skull, a riot of pain and information that tugged and battered her this way and that.

Then it was over.

They appeared on a large stone terrace in a similar circle of copper. The mock dragons were loudly bellowing their discontent, but all Fay could do was press her face to the ground and whimper.

Maybe dragonback wasn't the worst way to travel after all.

It took people and mocks several minutes to regain their footing. Even Suela seemed rumpled. "I wish we had a better Schism," she complained, rubbing at her neck and leaning heavily on her cane. "Girl, go find the Gatekeeper. We must update Denzel on what our mission is."

They wanted Fay to *move* after that? Every muscle in her body ached. The world still spun, combining with her blurry vision to make her queasy. Fedrik was somewhere here, though. That thought got her to her feet, but she didn't get far.

She had only reached the stair down from the terrace in the direction Suela had pointed when she saw the sickening drop, and the near-vertical city they had appeared in.

"Fucking hell." She backed away fast, panting breaths turning to hyperventilation. What was it about these people and heights? What harm was there in building things on the ground? Or under it? Really, anything other than straight up and down.

"Language," Suela called after her.

Fay gritted her teeth and edged down the stairs, back pressed against the opposite wall from the drop.

She had descended three staircases and walked along the roofs of two stone-hewn houses when she heard sounds of running feet. Fay stopped, seeing no need to walk further if he was willing to take the stairs. Her heart thundered with anticipation. There wasn't supposed to be anyone else, right?

"Tellen? That you, asshole?"

"Fayrian," he called back.

The tension in her shoulders eased. "I'm up here."

And there he was, bounding up the stairs, dreadlocks pulled back from his face and dressed in the same red tunic and pants he had worn at their Naming party. It felt like so long ago, even though only two days had passed. Despite the drop, Fay couldn't help but run forward too. They met in the middle in a tight hug. His arms wrapped around her shoulders and squeezed until Fay couldn't breathe. It might have bothered her, if she hadn't been doing the same.

When they finally pulled back, Fay jabbed Fedrik in the chest with her index finger, craning her neck to look him squarely in the eye. "You are in *so much trouble,* Fedrik Tellen. I am personally blaming you for every single minute of the *awful* couple days I've just had. It's going to hurt."

Fedrik took her hand and brought her knuckles to his lips. "That's a given, Avilor. Gods but it's good to see you."

He hugged her again, and much to her surprise, Fay was crying by the time he let go. "You really screwed up this time, Fed. There are people who want to use you and others who want to kill you. It's a mess."

His voice sounded a little hoarse too when he replied, "I think they might have good reason to. I . . . I killed a God, Avilor. *A God.* It's all I've been able to think about. And . . . I want to kill again."

She took a quick step out of his reach, which earned a weak smile. Fay scowled. "I'd appreciate you not hugging me while in a kill-happy mood."

"Not you, Avilor."

"Yeah, well, considering your current track record, excuse a little paranoia. How . . . " Fay paused, then asked. "How has your Gift been? You were out cold the last time I saw you for real, and I couldn't exactly tell through the communication system, but you look . . . rough."

Fedrik passed a hand over his hair. "That's a word for it."

He sank onto a stone bench and leaned forward, hands clasped and shoulders hunched. "I've been waffling between desperately trying to get out of here so I can find my fucking Incarnate and wring their neck, and wanting to throw myself off the nearest building to end this monster they turned me into. Rough doesn't begin to cover it."

Suela would be waiting, but Fay didn't feel the need to rush back. Instead, she sat down next to Fedrik and after a moment of hesitation reached out and covered his hands with hers. "We'll figure it out together, alright? I know a thing or two about wanting to murder people, and about guilt. I'm here with someone who knows a lot about Gatekeepers, and you won't believe this—*Master Denzel Tirition.*"

His head jerked up. "But he's dead."

"Nope," Fay said, trying her best to sound upbeat because she couldn't stand the sad, despairing look on Fedrik's face.

"You're pulling my leg."

Fay shook her head. "Not sure of the details since I literally only found out a few minutes ago, but he faked his death and is here. If anyone can whip us into shape, it's him. You're going to be alright, Tellen. I'm here to help, and I won't let anyone hurt you, or let you hurt anyone else. Deal?"

He hesitated, then leaned in to press his forehead against hers. "Deal."

Fay closed her eyes, squeezed his hands, and said, "One more thing, Tellen. I just found out that Gabriel is alive . . . and that he succeeded. Mark Lirion is dead."

CHAPTER NINETEEN
The Contract
GABRIEL

I'm saying this in a note because I don't think it will come out right if I try to say it aloud. I was hoping that you might consider coming to my birthday ball with me. I don't mean as a group with Eric, Fed and the rest. Just . . . you, and me. I know your parents won't approve, but honestly, I don't much care and neither do you. And I know you can't dance yet. I don't mind. I can help push you around in your chair on the dance floor if you want, and we can run over the toes of anyone who looks at you funny. Damn, I'm doing a pretty poor job of it on paper, too. Alright. Here we go. El-belle, my best friend, the prettiest, funniest, (clumsiest) girl I know, I am formally asking you to come as my informal date to the ball. It's fine if you don't want to. You don't have to say anything but no, and I'll drop it forever. I'm not sure you even like me that way, or like girls, or . . . I'm prattling on. Anyhow, I'll see you tomorrow. Write back?

—From a note to Elenor Lirion, from Claire Enica

GABRIEL LEANED AGAINST THE RAIL of the second-floor balcony that ran around most of the large ballroom. Below him, a sea of nobles milled about, waiting for the guests of honor to arrive. Though Gabriel had been to affairs this grand while a student at the Island, it had always been while shadowing one of his teachers.

He tugged at the collar of the Namnian suit one of Elenor's servants had laid out for him. Gabe would have felt much more comfortable in a Tirit Mindel uniform—or hell, a servant's simple pants and shirt—but the point was to blend in.

"Stop that. You'll mess up your tie," Claire hissed from beside him. "And don't even think about running your fingers through your hair. It's messy enough already."

"Everything is itchy." Even his hands, which had been raw that morning, were mostly scabbed and peeling. The infected, oozing lash marks on his back still stung a little when Gabriel moved too fast, and the bones that had been broken ached fiercely. Overall, though, the most distracting part of his injuries was the constant, gnawing hunger and the itchiness while his magic repaired his body at a speed Gabe still couldn't wrap his mind around. Every time he tried, panic would seize him, so until he had the time to properly freak out about it or shake some answers out of Daemon, Gabriel had decided he was just going to push all his questions aside. Elenor needed his help. That came first.

"I don't see why you're complaining. If Elenor is managing to walk around the Palace while her body is tearing itself apart, I'm sure you can put up with some itchy spots," Claire said, annoyance evident in her tone and the tightness of her shoulders. "Do you have any idea how much most people would give to be able to fix their bodies with magic the way you can?"

"Yes," he replied.

Claire looked over at him quizzically, so Gabriel elaborated. "My mother was our town's doctor. I can't count the number of surgeries that happened on my kitchen table growing up, but I remember how much it hurt each time she lost someone. I don't understand what's happening to me, but if this power were something I could give away to help Paul or Elenor, I'd do it in a heartbeat."

"Is that how you knew how to treat Elenor? Because your mother was a doctor?" Claire asked, leaning back against a slender marble column, one elbow on the balcony rail. Unlike most of the court ladies below, Claire had not opted for a dress. Instead, she wore a flowing pair of forest green pants and an elegant blouse in a rich gold color that paired well with her dark brown skin and short black hair. Considering their planned activities, it was a sensible choice, and looked much more comfortable than Gabriel's suit.

"We didn't have wasting fever where I grew up. Too far west. I know how to treat it because I studied medicine while I was on Tirit Mindel. My plan was always to go back and finish my education after . . . I got done with the Rebellion."

"You mean after you killed Elenor's father," Claire corrected.

Gabe reached up to rub the back of his neck. "Yeah."

She chuckled. "Thank you for that, by the way. I mean, if it was you. But even if it wasn't, thank you for helping. I know she feels conflicted about it, but between you and me, Elenor has always been far too nice for her own good. Her family is, for the most part, pretty awful. Even knowing what we do now, it doesn't excuse what they did to her." Claire gestured down to where a woman who bore a striking resemblance to Lilian Lirion stood in a small crowd of people in the purple, cerulean, and black regalia of the Miri. "Her, most of all."

"So that's Murder Auntie?" Gabe asked, eyeing the woman up and down.

Claire snorted. "I like that. Yes, that's her. I swear, if I ever come face-to-face with that bitch, I'm going to teleport her into the ocean and damn the consequences."

"Even though it would mess up Elenor's plans?"

Claire turned to look at him, face serious. "Honestly, I don't care much about her plans when they are panicked and reactionary. Oh, I'd die for her visions, for the Queen I know she'll become, but for this mess? No. All I care about right now is that she gets out of this safe and happy. That means saving Paul and saving Lirin. Not killing Murder Auntie isn't on that list."

Gabe chuckled, though it was forced. It was hard to laugh when a woman who might well be worse than Mark Lirion had just swooped in to take the King's place. "If only more nobles were like you. For a second there, you sounded just like Fedrik during his Tirit Mindel years."

"Well I should. We are cousins, after all. Me, Fed, Eric, even our darling El—and yes, I know I'm sleeping with her; she and I are on pretty opposite sides of the family tree. I don't actually think my family and the Tellens are technically related to El and Eric by blood recently enough to matter, but don't quote me. My point is that us younger western nobles . . . we've seen a lot. The reason we're all friends is because we were taken from our families and brought here as hostages right after the revolts. That's not something you forget. El was all that got me through those years, until my family was allowed to see me again."

"How long?" Gabe tore his eyes from the gathered nobles to look at Claire again. The noblewoman was still squinting at Sianta Miri and her daughter with an expression Gabe had seen before. It was the look Fay had worn each time she was about to do something stupid.

"I was a toddler when they brought me here. Elenor was the same age, so I got handed off to Paul to raise alongside her. Eric and Beth were thrown in with Wil and his *doena*, and Tomaz was shunted off on Djina. None of us saw our parents again for more than an hour or two at a time until we were teenagers. My friends *are* my family, even now."

"Same. For me it was Fedrik and Fayrian. All through school, we were inseparable. They were there for me at every turn, and it's killing me that I don't know where they are. They should be here helping turn Lirin into the country we dreamed of, now that the King is dead."

Claire patted him on the shoulder. "Hey, I don't know this Fayrian, but Fed's a smartass. He'll be just fine."

Gabriel cracked a strained smile. "I hope so. Oh, there's Elenor."

He nodded at the double doors to the large ballroom, stepping further into the shadows in case Cassian looked up. The southern prince strode in at Elenor's side, her hand on his arm. As he had always managed—even in standardized Academy uniforms—Cassian Iaming looked regal and elegant. Elenor, on the other hand, looked absolutely miserable. While she was dressed in a pretty gold and black gown with a high neckline to hide the bruising, her arm in a sling and lack of composure were rendered all the more noticeable next to Cassian's immaculate perfection. Her gait was uneven, and while she was making a valiant effort to hide the shaking from the last dose of serindalla, Gabriel could tell it was a struggle by the way her brows were scrunched together.

"Tell me honestly, Gabriel, how bad is Cassian Iaming?" Claire asked.

Gabe shifted from foot to foot. "He's . . . everything I loathe about the aristocracy. Entitled, arrogant, dismissive of those he thinks are beneath him, and possessive of what he thinks should be his. He's smart, too, which couldn't be said about Mark Lirion. I got to Tirit

Mindel already wanting to kill the King, but it was Cass who made me really *despise* the sort of attitude that makes a ruler think he's more important than the people at the bottom. The only good thing I can say is that Cass is loyal to a fault. To the wrong things, usually, but he keeps his word. Once, he said he'd make my life a living hell, and for six years he damn well tried his best to."

Claire crossed her arms, teeth working her upper lip. "No wonder her parents picked him for her. Some days, all I want is to take Elenor away from all of this. This place and these people have done nothing but try to kill her, break her spirit, or take away the things she loves. Now . . . " Claire reached up to rub the bridge of her nose. "If this marriage goes through, that might include me. The south is much more stringent about fidelity, aren't they? This Cassian doesn't sound like the sort who would accept that his wife has a lover."

Gabe shook his head. "No, I don't believe he would."

With a sigh, Claire turned away from Elenor to look at Gabriel. "I love her, you know. Not the light, casual way I pretend to for her sake, but with every fiber of my being. She is my light in the darkness, the air in my lungs. I've known since we started things that she would never be mine alone. I've made my peace with that, but I'm scared of what we'll find tonight in that contract. If Sianta Miri wanted her to sign it, it will be bad, and I know my Elenor. If it's good for Lirin, she'll consider doing it even if it makes her miserable. I can live with her married to another if he fills every day of her life with joy, but it would break my heart to see her turn into her mother."

Gabe reached out to give Claire's hand a squeeze. "Guess what?"

She cocked her head to the side. "What?"

"I've seen you poof out of existence a couple times now. Worse case scenario: I help you crash a wedding, you grab your girl, and run off into the sunset together."

Claire let out a loud laugh. "Oh, I like you. You can stay."

Gabe smiled, turning his gaze back to Elenor, where she had stopped to talk to her aunt. Her shoulders were so tense he was surprised she hadn't shattered yet. "Whatever happens tonight, she needs to sleep when it's over."

"If she doesn't agree, we can all dogpile on top of her like we did when we were kids and make her rest whether she likes it or not," Eric said, as he walked up to join them.

Tomaz was trailing along behind, nose in a book. He looked up when Claire snatched the book out of his hands. "Hey! I was reading that, Enica."

"You were about to walk into me, Tomcat. Need I remind you about the time you *did* walk into a pillar?"

"I was seven," Tomaz muttered.

"And twelve, and eighteen, and yesterday," Eric chimed in, reaching up to ruffle Tomaz's mop of loose black curls. "She has a point. Reading and walking don't mix well, even for soon-to-be lawyers."

Eric stepped up to the railing between Claire and Gabriel, looking down at the milling crowd waiting for Elenor to lead them outside to the pyre. While the colors and music were sedate, there was a marked lack of tears. Fay's father had once described the Passing of the last King and Queen of Lirin as a sorrowful event that had shaken the whole country. Loren and Sora had been loved. Mark Lirion, it seemed, less so, even by the nobility he had enriched.

With one notable exception.

Like the center of a vortex, tears and sorrow seemed to swirl around the Miri. Sianta, though, was smiling.

"Are we sure it's safe to leave Elenor with them?" Gabriel asked.

Tomaz nodded in the princess's direction. "Kallen is right there. He agrees to escort Silla Miri so he's trailing close. And Beth is with Paul, right? Elenor is surrounded by people. They won't do anything in public."

"Are we certain of that?" Gabe said, still uneasy.

"Yes," all three nobles answered.

Gabe raised his eyebrows, so it was Eric who clarified. "Sianta is a Lirion by birth. The Lirion *never* air their dirty laundry in public. Trust me, if they did, we never would have gotten away with half the trouble we caused when we were younger. Balls and parties were always the best time to make mischief."

"Ready to make some more tonight?" Gabe asked.

"Sure am. I'm not going to stick around to watch Elenor announce that she's marrying someone else, or wax poetic about her abusive asshole of a dad. Shall we get this started?" Claire asked, turning from the ballroom.

Gabe took one more look back at Elenor, worry churning in his chest, then followed.

They headed down a servant's staircase with Tomaz leading the way, since by his friends unanimous consensus he was the best at moving about unnoticed. Apparently, a childhood of being looked after by Djina instead of a noble minder had helped him get to know the Palace inside and out.

No one talked until they were out in the gardens, well away from the party, when Claire asked, "So, what's the plan?"

Tomaz and Eric sped up so they were walking close, letting Gabriel speak without fear of being overheard by a passing servant. "Jo is on guard duty at the back door of the Miri suite. If they left their own guards—which I'm sure they have—they will have to be distracted."

"I can do that," Eric volunteered.

"Good. We have to find that contract and read as much of it as we can. It's unlikely we'll have the time to get through *all* the fine print, so if you see a section that probably isn't going to be dangerous to Elenor, skip it. If you can, copy down anything relevant word-for-word."

"My memory is excellent," Tomaz said. "Let me read the sections that are important, and I'll copy them down when we're out. How . . . are we getting out, if we're discovered, by the way?"

Claire raised her hand. "Elenor told Jo to keep whistling a tune outside the door. If you hear her stop whistling, get close to me. I can get us out."

"What, exactly, do you expect to find?" Eric asked, as they neared their destination.

"I only have guesses, but I'd start with the sections discussing military aid to Lirin, and Seehana's relationship with Namnia."

"What does Namnia have to do with this?" Claire asked, but Gabriel held up his hand to silence her. They had arrived.

Hidden from view by a weeping willow, they could see the back door to the Miri's suite was guarded by Jo and another woman, standing under swaying wisteria vines on a low balcony. The garden was deserted, as Elenor had predicted, but Gabe still waited a full minute, head cocked to the side, listening for any sound of approaching footsteps.

When he was sure the coast was clear, he nudged Eric.

The nobleman reached into his pocket to pull out a flask, took a sip, spilled some on the front of his shirt, ruffled his hair and coat, then stumbled out into the garden. As he did, he burst into a loud, off-kilter song.

Gabe almost choked as the familiar verses of Fed and Fay's favorite tune rang through the gardens. Claire clamped a hand over his mouth. "Shh. Eric plays drunk very well."

She, Gabriel, and Tomaz waited in hiding as Eric stumbled up to the two guards. "Lemme in. Gotta," burp, "take a piss."

"Lord . . . Ondai?" The Miri guard asked. "These rooms are off-limits. I believe there's a restroom around the corner there—"

Eric waved her off. "I'm not usin' a servant's toilet. Who do you take me for? Common riffraff like you?"

"No offense meant, My Lord," Jo said, playing along.

"Either you lemme in here right now, or I'mma piss right here, you hear me?" Eric took another swig from his flask. "Our King's dead, for fuck's sake. Gotta drink to that, right?"

"Lord Ondai, if you would just go that—Oh shit. Ew! Stop that." The other guard howled.

"Did he just . . . " Gabe whispered, trailing off at the sound of liquid hitting armor.

"He's rich enough he can afford to do almost anything," Tomaz muttered, shaking his head. "And get away with it."

"Lord Ondai, please put your dick away," Jo said, with absolutely no inflection. "Listen, he's clearly drunk off his ass. Why don't you take him to a bathroom and change into something clean on your way back? I'll keep watch and won't mention it. This shift just started. I wouldn't want to stand here for eight hours covered in urine. I've had to do it with the watch, and it's never fun."

"*Thank you.* Ew. Alright, Lord Ondai, let's go find you a bathroom. Seriously, you *reek* of alcohol."

They walked away, Eric picking up his song again. Gabe waited until it became distant, then motioned the others forward. Jo was waiting at the door. As soon as they reached it, she said, "It's locked."

"Not a problem." Gabe knelt and pulled out the lock picks he had taken from Elenor's stash of less-than-parent-approved supplies. The muscles of his recovering hand were still tender, and kneeling wasn't exactly comfortable, but he gritted his teeth and started working the lock.

Claire leaned back against the wall next to the door, watching him, eyes narrowed. "What illegal cesspool did Tellen find you in originally, again? I take it you're the one who taught him to pick locks."

"The Academy of Tirit Mindel," Gabe answered, glancing away from his work for just a moment to flash her a grin. "And no, he taught me. I traded him for pickpocketing lessons."

"Seems in character," she grumbled, and then fell silent. Gabe started to sweat as he slipped the pins twice in a row. He really should have practiced this more, especially on complex locks like this one. Fedrik had always been the one with a knack for these sorts of things.

When he was almost sure that it wasn't going to budge, and they should just take the risk and break one of the windows, a lucky wiggle made the lock click and turn. He let out a relieved sigh. "Alright, you two in. Jo, start humming and stop if we need to bolt."

"Got it. It's weird taking orders from a prisoner I spent the last month guarding, but what the hell. The longer I'm around you folks, the more the weirdness seems contagious." She started to hum.

Gabe slipped into the darkened suite after Claire and Tomaz. "Pull all the curtains before turning on the lights."

Claire ran to deal with the drapes as the other noble hurried to a table piled high with papers. As soon as the room was plunged into darkness, Gabriel slid the lights on as low as they would go and still allow them to read.

"Tomaz, look for the contract. Claire, try to find the antidote Elenor told us about."

Several long, tense minutes of pouring over loose papers and through chests passed, each second marked by the large grandfather clock in the corner. Finally, Tomaz exclaimed: "I have it!"

Gabe hurried over, Claire close behind. Tomaz held a file of papers almost two inches thick. The nobleman put the bundle down, then frowned. "This is bad. Looks like the Iamings already signed, which means it's legally binding, and there's only one copy here. They must have the other."

"We couldn't have destroyed it anyways, not with Paul's life on the line," Claire pointed out, though her face looked drawn. "You two work on that. I'm going to keep looking for the antidote."

Tomaz gestured them over to a coffee table that was clear, and produced several folded pieces of blank paper from his pocket, along with pencils. Gabe knelt on the floor and took the pile Tomaz handed him. Outside, Jo continued to hum a tune he didn't know. He kept one corner of attention on the sound and turned the rest to the first page.

He discarded it almost immediately. It was doubtful that any subterfuge would be hiding in how many horses Seehana was giving to Lirin, or how much rice was being delivered south. Pages and pages of the same followed. Gabe kept his eyes peeled for anything to do with the military or Miriel, but almost all of it was mundane and uninteresting. Tomaz was the first to find anything of value.

"Seehana agrees to not provide military aid to Namnia, in exchange for Lirin agreeing to aid it in any conflict with the Mondaer Desert."

Gabriel had half been expecting it, but it still made him shudder. He had always been fond of Namnia, but there was no way the northern Kingdom could withstand the might of Lirin without Seehana threatening Lirin with a war on two fronts in the south, were it to attack. It was the obvious play by Lirin. "Copy that down and keep looking."

"I have something else. Oh fuck."

Gabe hadn't expected the quiet-tempered Tomaz to sound quite so angry. Before he could ask, Tomaz read, "'Elenor Lirion, upon marriage to Cassian Iaming, will live in Seehana, not to return to Lirin for more than one month out of every twelve.' It goes on for about four paragraphs about Seehana providing Lirin's military with copper in exchange for this concession and a sizable amount of cerulean. This is probably so that Elenor will be more likely to rule in Seehana's benefit as well, but what it looks like to me is essentially a hostage situation. How is that worth it for some copper?"

"Lirin doesn't produce much of any of the magical metals. If we weren't the breadbasket of the continent, we would be fucked economically. But what do the Lirion want with a magical metal . . . " Gabe said, scratching his head with the butt of his pencil.

"More importantly, *Elenor is going to Seehana?* How is that even feasible? She's Lirin's only heir," Claire hissed, from where she was rifling through the bedside table.

"Keep reading. If we found this in the first few pages, I'm sure there's more," Gabe said, voice cold and angry. Ten more tense, silent minutes passed, but for the ticking clock and humming outside the door.

"This is terrible," Gabriel exclaimed, eyes stopping on a line halfway down a page of amendments. "I was wondering why Seehana would agree to so many trade concessions. Listen to this. 'In the case of Elenor Lirion's death before an heir is born, this contract and all that lies therein will be offered to the next in line for the Lirinian throne. No alterations of trade, military or financial terms may be made without the consent of both parties. If a marriageable heir is not provided, Lirin will pay—well, I'll sum up. Lirin pays a whole lot." He took a breath, and summarized, "Seehana doesn't lose Lirin if she dies. That means they will have zero motive to keep her alive, other than the kindness of their hearts. The only one who loses is Elenor. I mean, the same is true in reverse if someone offs Cassian, but that bastard is a survivor and doesn't have the Miri out for his blood."

They kept looking. Gabe got to the end of his pile and started to go over it again, straightening the pages as he did. Claire had just moved to a large chest at the foot of the bed when Jo stopped humming.

They all froze. All but Tomaz, who was staring at the last page of his stack as though it was a live viper. He lunged for the pencil and the paper Gabe had used to transcribe everything.

A single tap sounded at the door. Gabriel's heart, which he could have sworn had stopped with the humming, tried to make up for it by attempting to pound out of his chest. "Claire, over here."

"I haven't found the antidote yet."

"Now," he hissed.

She bared her teeth but obeyed. She grabbed his arm and reached for Tomaz, but the nobleman pulled out of her reach, still scribbling.

"Tom, we have to go."

"One more sentence. El needs to see this tonight. We need to get back to her *now,* before she announces the engagement."

Gabe snatched the contract out his hand, scrambled to return it to where they had found it, then raced back. "You said you could memorize it. Write the rest on the way. Claire, we need to go."

She grabbed his arm and took hold of Tomaz's hand. "They'll kill us if they find us, right?"

"Definitely. Now's not the time to freak out about that th—"

Crack!

CHAPTER TWENTY
Under the Stars
FEDRIK

You asked in your last letter what it's like to hold the Gatekeeper Gift. Well, let's put it this way, Sidian: I want to chop you up into tiny pieces and feed them to my mock, and that's after three months of training and on a good day. It's constant, debilitating, and overwhelming now that the Gift has fully matured, but at the same time, I miss you. Sure you don't want to come visit? We're supposed to start training together soon, right? Seriously, though, don't you dare get anywhere near me, not until they take my eyes. I know you don't want them to, but I don't trust myself to never so much as look at you. Without this weapon on my face, I may still try to murder you, but I'll have to do it the old-fashioned way. I like your chances much better if I can't make your heart stop before you so much as touch down on your mock.

—From a letter to Sidian Tailor, from Suela Aveara, during their first year as Gatekeeper and Incarnate.

"YOU ARE MORE TROUBLE THAN YOU'RE WORTH, TELLEN," Fay grumbled as she lay with Fedrik on the warm stone balcony of an abandoned building. Her head dug into his collar bone, red hair trying to suffocate him. Despite it, Fedrik could breathe easy for the first time since waking up in this place.

Suela had retired shortly after dinner. He and Fay had remained by the fire for another hour, catching up with Master Denzel and getting to know Phoebi Deil, but both had gone to bed shortly thereafter. Despite their warning that training would begin early the next day, Fedrik was still wide awake. "More trouble than I'm worth? Funny, from the girl who literally cost me more than her net worth to bail out of prison once, and who never showed up at the trial."

"I paid you back," Fay said, jabbing him in the ribs.

"No. Wilam paid me back. You won a game of Seven Rivers for it. And you cheated by making Gabe play for you. Everyone knows no one can beat him at that game."

"Strategy and resource management isn't cheating." Fay let out a wistful sigh. "As soon as you get your Gift under control, we'll be able to go back to Lirin and find him. He's still alive, Fed. And Mark Lirion is dead. I'm still reeling. It feels . . . like I'm no longer drowning."

She sounded so happy, and Fedrik felt like a horrible excuse of a human for not sharing every ounce of her joy. Oh, he *was* happy. Genuinely, fully, and unconditionally relieved that one of his best friends was alive. It wasn't even the excitement in Fay's voice for her imagined reunion with the man she loved that was spoiling his mood. Fedrik had long accepted that in the world of Fayrian Avilor, Gabriel Navarl always came first.

It was the recounted story of the meeting with this Daemon that tore at his happiness and turned it to ash. *"He said Gabe was under the care of Elenor Lirion, and that she's the regent of Lirin now,"* Fay had said.

Quindo had mentioned something about Incarnates and rifters, hadn't he? That day when they had arrived at the Deil estate and the *daradeio* had told them about the Gatekeeper and Incarnate Gifts? Knowing what he did about Gabriel's magic, it worried Fedrik to think of his best friend that close to . . .

"Fay," he said, interrupting her continued relieved babbling. The tremble to her name must have caught her attention, because she stopped abruptly. "I didn't want to say anything in front of Suela . . . but I think I know who my Incarnate is. I think I've always known, I just didn't have the word for it."

"What?" Fay sat bolt upright, staring down at him. Her messy curls blotted out the light of the stars, casting her face into shadow. "Who? And why didn't you—"

"You can't tell them. They can't know I know, or—" *They'll keep me from her. They'll protect her, when she deserves to die for what she did to my parents and for going back to her father after I showed her the truth.*

His nails bit into the hard stone, threatening to crack. Fedrik squeezed his eyes shut, breathing heavily. No. That was just his Gift. He had to—

Be clever. Fay hates her already. She could be an ally.

With a grunt of frustration, Fedrik pushed himself up and walked to the edge of the balcony, where he knew Fay wouldn't follow. She had spent all evening bitching about the heights in the Sandhewn City, after all. "Avilor," he said, shoulders shaking. "I need you to promise me something."

Chancing a look backwards, Fedrik saw her sitting, weight propped on one arm. The red clothes and eyes only added to the impression she always gave of being part flame. Whether she liked it or not, Fay had been accepted by the Mondaer—by the Goddess Fedrik had killed. Despite Suela's promise of aid and training, Fedrik knew he would not be so fortunate.

"I've spent years dragging you out of danger kicking and screaming, Avilor. Particularly and especially from trouble you made for yourself, or were about to run into without any forethought. I need you to be the one who does that for me this time. I . . . I can feel this Gift changing me. I'm not who I was when we left Hardor, and it's going to get worse. I don't want to lose myself, and you're the only person here other than Denzel who really knew me from before, so . . . "

Don't do this. You know she can help you kill—

"Don't let me kill anyone else, Fay," he stated, resolute despite having to speak between clenched teeth. "Everything wrong in my life has come from the times I've killed. I don't want to do it again. I don't want to be the monster this Gift is trying to turn me into, or let that be what defines me for the rest of my life. Don't . . . " His nails were digging into the stone railing, sending jolts of pain up his arms. "Don't let me kill my Incarnate, even if you and I both want her dead."

"Her?" Fay asked, standing up. Carefully, she edged toward him, until she was standing behind Fedrik, as far from the drop as possible while still able to reach out and place a hand on his shaking shoulders. "Who is it?"

"Promise first."

"I promise. I already promised Suela, and, honestly, I'm not keen to deal with the fallout of another one of your murders. It's always a shit-show."

"This isn't a fucking joke, Fayrian." Fedrik turned to face her, expecting one of her usual smirks.

It wasn't there. She was dead serious, red eyes shining up at him in the moonlight. "I know it's not a joke, Fed. Think about it for a second, though. What have I spent my whole life doing for Gabriel?"

It took him a moment, but then some of his anger faded. "Keeping his magic in check, so he wouldn't be a danger to the world."

"Exactly." Moving slowly, Fay held out a hand to him. "I know how serious this is, Tellen. I was there when you killed my father, and I was there when you killed Lady Red. I was one of the ones carrying the bodies to the pyres each time, and I am not going to let it happen again. The same way I'm going to find a way to get to Hardor to keep Gabriel from leveling it to the ground. I know I've messed up a lot in my life, but this is the one thing that I *can* do well. Assuming you give me permission to knock your ass out if you get murder-happy," she added with the faintest twitch of a smile.

"I didn't realize you needed permission for that. I figured it was more of a hobby for you," he said, choked up with emotion. He hadn't actually expected her to be willing to take this obligation on, not after everything he had done to her and so many others.

"I can take pleasure in the things I must do, can't I? Call it the bright side of my entire sense of identity being tied to keeping the men in my life from becoming accidental mass murderers. Among the *many* reasons I dislike Suela is that she made me quite aware of how much of who I am has been tied up in Gabriel's magic."

A pang of guilt cut through Fedrik's relief, and he looked down at his feet. "I didn't mean to make it seem like you *have* to do that for me, too. I should have—"

She reached up to press a finger against his lips, then lifted his chin. "I'm volunteering, you over-emotional mess. Sulea gave me a choice, and we both know I'm perfectly capable of telling you no. The truth is . . . Robin never did. He cornered me. I'm not a child this time. I negotiated us a way out, Fed, and the only cost is watching your back and stopping you from doing something dumb. That's something I'd be doing no matter what, so the way I see it, we got a great deal."

"You always were a penny-pincher," Fedrik said, stepping away from the railing and closer to Fay.

She craned her neck to look up at him, and it might have been the starlight or her never-healing sunburn, but he thought her cheeks grew rosy. "So?"

"So what?" he asked.

"Who is it? The person you want to chop into teensy tiny pieces?"

"Fayrian, don't give my Gift ideas. Do you have any clue how *vivid* the fantasies are?"

"Blood, viscera, OW!" Fay scowled and rubbed at the spot on the back of her head that Fedrik had just cuffed. "What, you don't enjoy my mean and morbid sense of humor?"

"I enjoy many things about you, Avilor. Many of them quite . . . *viscerally.* Your joy at my pain is not, in fact, one of your many charming qualities." Quite happy to lose himself in her eyes, and with a shameless glance down at her full lips, Fedrik pulled her closer. It was easier than thinking about what he had to tell her.

"I don't know. It brings me *endless* enjoyment," Fay said, laughter in her voice, "so it must be a good thing. Fed—" Her words were cut off by a squeak as a loud crack echoed through the quiet city.

Fedrik spun around, one arm still around Fay.

There, across and a little below them on the moonlit opposite wall of the city, three people stood where none had before. They were in Lirinian noble's clothes and drenched from head to toe. Their sudden appearance, though, was not what made Fedrik's jaw drop and Fay tear herself from him to rush toward the edge of the balcony. Fedrik lurched to catch her, illogically scared that she was about to vault the railing.

"Gabriel!" Fayrian's yell was whipped away from the wind that blew through the gorge. She wasn't wrong, though. Even at a distance, there was no mistaking their friend. Nor, indeed, the other two: Claire Enica and Tomaz Catoali.

What the actual fuck . . .

"Gabe!" Fay was still trying to shout into the wind, and Fedrik added his own voice, waving and jumping up and down.

The three didn't look their way. Gabe and Tomaz were bent double, as though out of breath or hurt, and Claire was pacing, tugging at her short hair, mouth moving rapidly. Then, she held her hands out to each of the men, another deafening crack echoed across the canyon, and they disappeared.

"What—? How—?" Fedrik sputtered, but Fay was already half-way down the closest staircase. With a curse, Fedrik tore after her. He called for her to stop, but she did not. All the way down then back up the other side of the canyon, Fay took the stairs two, or even three, at a time. They were both gasping for breath by the time they reached the rooftop where Gabriel, Claire, and Tomaz had appeared.

Fay skidded to a stop, dropping to her knees by a puddle. "Shit. That was real. SHIT!"

"What—?"

"How was he here? Who was that woman, what—?"

"That was my cousin, Claire. She . . . must have a Gift." He panted, brain and lungs both trying to catch up. Kneeling beside Fay, he touched the puddle and brought his fingers to his nose to confirm the scent of seaweed that filled the air. Saltwater.

"Wait, is *she* your Incarnate?" Fay asked.

No, but neither did Claire have a Gift before I left. She never could have kept that secret. That means . . . she got hers the same place I got mine. Fay said she's seen multiple people travel great distances in moments over the past few days. If Claire can do that too, maybe I don't need to rely on the Mondaer to get me to Hardor. I could kill . . .

Fedrik punched the ground. Hard. Pain seared up his arm, and he let out a hiss. The burst of clarity that came with it cleared his head, though.

"Tellen . . . ?"

He looked up, and saw Fay staring at him with wide red eyes, a placating hand held out and hovering near his shoulder. "Easy. Don't go losing it, alright? Take a breath."

Curling in on himself and rocking, Fedrik tried to breathe through the urge to lie. To plot. To kill.

"Should I get Suela?" Fay asked, hands still held out as though she wanted to comfort him, but wasn't sure it was safe.

"No!" The shout was so loud it startled even Fedrik. Fay's face lost much of the color from the run, and she jerked back. He drew in on himself more, arms wrapping around his head. "I want to kill her. It's all I can think about."

"Who? Suela? She's a bitch, but—"

"Elenor." The name burned on his lips, a bitter, angry, vengeful hatred rising in his chest. "My . . . Incarnate."

"Oh shit."

Fay screeched as Fedrik launched forward and grabbed her by the shoulders. He had meant to beg her again to not let him murder anyone, but instead found himself with his face in a puddle, arm twisted behind his back.

Fay's whole weight kept him pinned. "You grab me while looking murdery, I break your arm. Got it, sunshine?"

Through a mouthful of saltwater, Fedrik gasped, "Yeah. Got it. Thanks."

"Stable enough to be let up?" she asked.

Fedrik just wheezed, which seemed to get the message across. Fay let go, and he sat up, rolling his aching shoulder. "I wasn't trying to attack you."

"Yeah, well, better careful than dead." Fay paused, then asked, "Are you sure? That it's Elenor Lirion?"

Fedrik started nodding, then shook his head, and finally reached up to tug at his hair. "Yes, no, maybe? She's all I can think about when I close my eyes. I keep imagining . . . horrible ways to kill her. It comes in waves. Sometimes it's all I can focus on, and others it's just this low, throbbing hatred. She got my parents killed, and she's in charge of Lirin now, apparently. I don't trust her. I want her punished for what she did. If . . . if she's really an Incarnate, then she must have gotten it from Ian, right? He was the last. That meant that when she fucked up Wil's plans and killed Ian, she got the power to give Gifts and made me into this. She benefited, and I'm left to bear the brunt of this constant fury. I hate everything about it. It's not me, Fay. I've never *wanted* to take a life before."

Fay was staring at him seriously. "It *was* a little odd that you hit her, right after bringing her to us for her protection. I honestly thought it was all some sort of sneaky ploy to get me to want to protect her, but I bet that was the start of it. And it would explain you almost strangling me in your sleep. Are you *sure* you don't want me to just get out of your way? She's not my favorite person in the world either."

Fedrik clenched his teeth and squeezed his eyes shut. "Don't say things like that. Do you have any idea how hard this is to fight? I'm serious. I hate her, I want to rip her apart with my b-bare hands." As he said it, his fingers involuntarily clenched and relaxed repeatedly against his knees. "But it's wrong. Underneath it all, in the brief moments of clarity I get, I know it's wrong. I want to see her punished, but if she dies, these Gifts pass to others, and they might be even less equipped than me. At least I have you, and people to help train me—giving me a chance even though I killed a . . . a God. I can't in good conscience make someone else carry this."

For several seconds, nothing moved except Fay's hair in the ever-present wind whipping through the city. Then she let out her breath and said, "Alright then. I'll do it. I'll keep you from killing her, even if it means helping her. Besides, unless she somehow leaves Hardor, her death might make your power explode like it did with the Red, and I won't let that happen to Lirin. You can count on that, if nothing else."

She was right: he could. Fay had always put Lirin high on her priority list, right along with Gabriel. Though, which came first, Fedrik had never been able to tell.

Looking up at her at last, he whispered, "Thank you, Avilor."

"I expect suitable groveling, for making me promise to protect a Lirion," she warned.

Fedrik's lips twisted up and, while he wasn't able to fully form a smile, it was close. "You are insufferable."

"And yet you like me," Fay replied, tossing her hair over her shoulder in a surprisingly good rendition of a prissy noblewoman.

No, I love you, Fedrik wanted to say, but didn't. She knew.

Instead, he stood with a grunt and held out his hand for her. "Proves what a fool I am. Come on, we need sleep. Training starts tomorrow, and we're both going to have to be sharp for it. Play nice and I might let you cuddle up. It gets *cold* here at night."

"Course it does. Why wouldn't it? Fucking desert," she grumbled, but accepted his hand and didn't let go as they walked away. Before leaving the terrace, though, Fay looked back at the spot Gabriel had stood. It was only there for a second, but the look of longing that crossed her face was one of the saddest Fedrik had ever seen.

CHAPTER TWENTY-ONE

The Sound of War Drums

ELENOR

There are only three ways a rifter may exist piously in society—of this I am most certain. The first is the least useful, but most expedient, and should be administered to all magical anomalies, such as those called 'Gifted' by the Island. This is, of course, death. The second, and far preferred, is broken of their magical potential. This allows the reformed rifter to return the magic they stole from the Gods for their own selfish use. The pain they feel is suitable punishment for their sin; only thus may they spend the rest of their life living as any other. The best way, of course, is for them to be registered and put to work. Only in complete and utter selfless service to society can they truly redeem themselves, for in serving the Gods through labor for their non-magical brethren, they may seek not only to be forgiven, but remembered as part of the machine that will build a new golden age of faith.

—from the writings of Sianta Miri.

THE FLAMES OF THE PYRE CRACKLED, pirouettes of sparks and smoke rising to the cloudy sky above the Palace grounds. Elenor stood beside Cassian, eyes fixed on the fire and back ramrod straight.

Her legs ached, but while there were seats directly behind them, Elenor refused to take hers so long as Sianta stood across the fire. Thousands gathered along the banks of the river, watching. If her aunt thought a little pain would be enough to make Elenor fold and symbolically lower herself beneath Miriel, she didn't understand Elenor at all.

The crowd on this side was mostly made of the nobility and the upper-echelon of Hardor, but across the Claire River, along the docks and up the steep roads of the Crescent, the common folk of her city sat witness to the Passing of a King.

Or perhaps celebrating the death of a tyrant. The faint sound of voices raised in song drifted across the sluggish waters.

One of the gathered aides who had worked for her father wrinkled his nose. "Despicable. A curfew should have been put in place tonight to keep the riffraff off the streets."

"I would appreciate you not calling my citizens riffraff," Elenor said icily, before returning her attention to the dancing flames, remembering the grief she had felt watching Djina burn. What was wrong with her for feeling nothing but numb exhaustion this time? Was it that document? No. If Elenor believed that only blood could be family, it would invalidate some of her closest and most treasured relationships. Mark Lirion had been and always would be the man who raised her, even if he had not sired her. It was just that she had already said her goodbyes.

Beside her, Cassian Iaming was frowning. He had tried to get Elenor alone all night, but Kallen had done a good job of interrupting them every time the Southern prince started leading Elenor away. Cassian probably wanted to ask her about Gabriel. That sounded like an exhausting conversation.

Surreptitiously, she raised a handkerchief to her watering eyes and used it as cover to slip a pea sized bit of serindalla into her mouth. The smoke was blowing in their direction, and thank the Gods for that. Elenor had never been good at faking tears.

The drug dissolved under her tongue as the fire burned on. Within a few minutes, Elenor found it hard to stand still. She clamped her good hand around the straps of her sling to keep it from shaking, but at least the heavy weight of exhaustion was pushed back. Blinking a few times, the world swam back into focus, the fire turning from a flickering red-and-orange blob to distinct flames.

Unfortunately, the pain in her legs and wrist also came into sharp relief. With it, the worries that had been drowned under the daze of pain and fatigue clawed back to the surface. Were Claire and the others alright? What would the Miri do to them if they were caught snooping around in their rooms? Had they found the antidote?

"Would you like a chair, your Highness?" someone asked from beside her. Turning, Elenor saw Daniil Eurieha. The priest had conducted the ceremony of Passing earlier in the evening, his eulogy for the fallen King eloquent and generous, while not outright untrue.

If not for the fact that he was clearly on the side of the Miri, Elenor might have been grateful. As it was, she shrank back, surprised to find him standing so close. "No. I'm fine."

Daniil inclined his head. "Then you will have no objection to walking with me? We should circle the pyre, so all may see that you witness your father's Passing with the tears of a dutiful daughter. Any less will hurt your chances in your upcoming tribunal. You would not wish that, would you?"

Elenor wanted to scowl, but did her best to suppress the impulse. "Of course not."

Daniil offered her his arm. Elenor turned to Cassian, promising to return shortly. Across the pyre, she caught her aunt smiling. Only Kallen's presence a few yards away, subtly trailing her, gave Elenor the courage to actually move her legs toward the woman who held Paul's life in the palm of her hand.

"Why are you and your father working for the Miri?" Elenor asked, as they walked at a slow, measured pace. "My family placed our trust in yours. Was that not enough?

"I do not work *for* the Miri, Your Highness. I work for the soul of our continent. If anything, one could say that both Sianta Miri and our late King worked for the dream my father and I showed them: a world where all are equal in the eyes of the Gods."

Elenor snorted under her breath. "Sure."

"You are skeptical. I can understand why. You have been the victim of people's personal grudges getting in the way of the cause. Please believe, though, that I hold no such innate anger towards you. I would rather see you as an ally, than a pawn with vengeance on her mind."

"Then you shouldn't have hurt my *doena*."

"No harm will come to him, as long as you cooperate. I was against the strategy, but after your actions of late, you have shown yourself to be an . . . unpredictable element. If you choose to work with us of your own volition, I promise all coercion will cease. Nothing would make me happier."

"I don't negotiate with blackmailers. Last time someone attempted to force my hand, he ended up with my heel digging into his throat. Don't try me," Elenor snapped, though she kept her voice hushed, lest the nobles they passed hear them.

Daniil gave her a tight-lipped smile. "I seek not to quarrel with you, Your Highness, at least not this evening. We are meant to be remembering the life of Mark Lirion. Would you like me to tell you what my father once told him? Perhaps, if you saw the dream he lived for, you might understand him better."

"If my aunt has bought in, I want nothing to do with it." Elenor itched to cross her arms or hug herself. They were passing by a contingent of House Lavarin. They were all staring at her in stony silence, their unspoken accusations clear. *Murderer.*

"So be it. I won't disrespect you by asking again, but if you ever wish to hear it, find me." They reached the Miri. Daniil bowed to Sianta. Elenor didn't so much as nod.

"Stand with us awhile, Niece," the Miri Queen said, gesturing to her right. Seeing no alternative, Elenor did so, Daniil flanking her on the other side.

"What's this show about, Sianta?" Elenor asked. "Haven't you already made your demands?"

"That southern boy does not look happy, Elenor. Fix that," Sianta said, glancing at Cassian. "The Iamings have received and approved the contract you signed. I am going to announce the engagement shortly. Make sure by tomorrow Cassian Iaming thinks it's because you were instantly taken with him."

"You're announcing it now? It's hardly appropria—"

"And when have you cared about that?" Sianta sneered. "This is what will happen. Tonight we will announce the engagement. Tomorrow, you will ask me to stand in as interim holder of the second Lirion Writ in all matters of state, then dedicate yourself entirely to the preparations for your wedding. That, acting the part of the pious, obedient young woman, and entertaining the Iamings is *all* you will do from tonight until you are wed. Understood? No more running through the halls of the Palace looking a mess and starting rumors."

Elenor gritted her teeth, yearning to point out that Sianta had been the cause of that, but nodded instead. "Understood."

"Good girl. Now trot-trot. Or did you want me to withhold the next dose of the antidote?"

Elenor's chest ached and eyes burned at the threat. The urge to cry rose in her throat, making the princess press her lips tightly together and nod. She waited a few minutes until her emotions were under control, then rounded the fire again.

"Queen Regent," Cassian said, bowing his head as Elenor rejoined him. "Could we perhaps speak for a moment—"

"Attention, everyone," Sianta said loudly, interrupting him. The Queen of Miriel rounded the pyre, her face a perfect mask of grief. "I wish to say a few words, with the permission of Lirin's regent, my dear niece."

Elenor inclined her head, hardly able to draw breath. Why had she taken that dose of serindalla? She should have waited, so that the pain might have drowned out Sianta's coming speech. Instead, the temporary alertness the drug gave Elenor meant she heard every minute shift in inflection.

Her aunt came to stand near Elenor and Cassian. Bedecked in the crown and jewels of a ruler, and half a foot taller than Elenor, the Queen of Miriel seemed to grow impossibly large as she neared, making Elenor feel like the terrified child she always reverted to in her worst nightmares.

"Friends, family, honored nobles of Lirin and welcome guests from Seehana. We gather tonight to remember Markus Miri-Lirion, a great king and proud father. He was not born to this country, but I was. While Miriel has become my home, my childhood was spent running through these gardens with my dear sister, and looking over the magnificence of Hardor. These rivers, this land, they are in my blood, no matter how far I've gone. I thought it would be frightening to leave it when I married as a young woman, but it was not. Do you know why?" Sianta paused for dramatic effect.

Elenor noticed, as her eyes scanned the surrounding nobles, that three distinct factions had formed. Houses Enica and Ondai stood to one side, and looked upon Sianta with thinly-veiled contempt.

The Lavarin and Amad were nodding along to the Queen's words, and huddled close to the Miri contingent. Finally, Houses Tellen and Petrona kept to themselves, but were notably close to one another. Only house Drego's representatives moved freely around the gathering, acting as intermediaries, just as Kallen seemed intent to. Elenor had asked him to keep tensions under control, and clearly, he had his people working hard on it.

"I didn't fear leaving," Sianta continued, "because I knew Lirin was in good hands. My sister and brother-in-law worked tirelessly to save the very soul of Lirin, and while his early death is a tragedy, I am certain his legacy will endure. He wished to see a country where no one lived in fear of the inborn power of rifters. A country where all were equal, their rank determined not by magic—a mere accident of birth—but rather by the hard work of generations of ancestors." She gestured around, indicating the gathered nobles.

Next to Elenor, Cassian stiffened, but did not speak.

"Today, we honor his life and mourn his death. We stand with his only child as she recovers from the grief and guilt of surviving her dear father, and not being strong enough to defend him from the rifter who killed him."

So that was how Sianta was spinning it. Ironically, it was the same way Elenor was planning to get out of these murder charges, but the very fact that her aunt was willing to blame Gabriel for Elenor's actions made her want to do the opposite. With Paul's life on the line, though, she dared not speak.

"Were Mark still with us, our arrival would be a day of celebration, not of mourning. I think it is fitting, therefore, to honor his life by celebrating one of his greatest political successes. It is therefore my great pleasure and privilege to announce the engagement of my dear niece, Elenor, to Crown Prince Cassian Iaming of Seehana. With their marriage, our two great houses and countries will be closer than ever before, cementing Mark's legacy as a bringer of peace and unity to the continent." Sianta continued, but Elenor tuned her out, ears ringing as the truth of her predicament sank in. It was done. Cassian had agreed, which meant they were as good as married already. Elenor didn't know him, didn't trust him, definitely didn't love him, and yet for the rest of her life, she would be in his power. Her whole body felt weak, as though her bones were made of brittle glass and her muscles of water. She didn't want to be here. Surely, if they did not intend to involve her in any of the decisions, they also didn't need her participation for the spectacle. Surely—

Her attention snapped back to the present when her aunt stopped talking, and Cassian took a step forward. He let go of her one unbandaged hand and with a careful, delicate touch, nudged her chin up. He hesitated for a second, as if allowing her to understand what was about to happen, and then kissed her. It was short, chaste, but surprisingly forceful. Elenor tried to step away, but Cassian pulled her forward just as she jerked back, making the attempt to flee look like a simple repositioning.

Then he lifted his lips from her, confusion in his sea-green eyes, and knelt. From his pocket, he pulled a bracelet with eighteen intricately carved gold beads strung onto it. One for each of the traditional eighteen days of a formalized betrothal. Most, of course, lasted much longer than that, but in this case, Elenor had no doubt that the wedding would happen before the month ended. Whatever the real reason her aunt had for rushing this, she was certainly being efficient with the hours. Elenor's hand was shaking so hard as she raised it from her side that she was sure everyone would notice, but as soon as Cassian took hold of it, he steadied the motion. With deft fingers, he fastened the bracelet around her narrow wrist. It weighed more than she had expected, and as soon as he let go of her, her hand dropped. She didn't look at it, or at him, or at his smiling father. Instead, she fixed her eyes on the dark waters of the Claire shining where it met the extensive lawn and tried to drown out the applause.

"May I have a word in private?" Cassian's question made her jump. He had gotten to his feet and was leaning in so that she would be the only one to hear. Elenor nodded, and as the nobles started moving—many towards the Queen of Miriel and King of Seehana—Cassian took her hand and deftly led her away from the pyre.

Elenor looked around for Kallen, but didn't see him. Nervous, but too dazed to find a good excuse for staying close to her allies,

Elenor let Cassian draw her away from the crowd. As soon as they found a secluded bench, the Crown Prince tugged Elenor down.

"What's wrong?" His face was twisted in what was either concern or disapproval. Without warning, he reached out and placed two fingers against her throat. She started, about to pull back before she realized what he was doing. "Your pulse is racing and you're burning up. Are you feeling alright? You've looked pale and unwell all day, and I felt you shake when I took your hand."

Tirit-trained. After getting to know Fedrik, Kallen, and Gabriel, Elenor was starting to recognize the telltale signs of their education.

"I admit I am not feeling my best," she said, not sure if showing weakness was wise, but not able to think of a convincing lie. "It's been . . . a rough couple of days."

He smiled reassuringly, but Elenor wasn't able to muster the will to return it as her aunt's voice ordering her to please him drifted to the forefront of her racing, cloudy thoughts. When she didn't smile, Cassian's began to fade, a frown taking its place. "What's wrong? Does this have something to do with how fast the contracts were signed? We were told to expect days of negotiations. As much as I'm pleased that you accepted my suit so soon after meeting me and agreed to so many concessions, I can't help but be concerned that it wasn't for the right reasons."

He was smart, Elenor would give him that. Still, she didn't dare tell him the truth, because smart rarely equated to trustworthy in her experience.

"I do want to marry you." It wasn't exactly a lie. She had never had any objections to a southern alliance on principle. It was how first her parents and now her aunt were handling it that scared and angered her.

"There was an implied 'but' in that."

"*But* I had hoped to have a chance to get to know you better than I do before agreeing to spend the rest of our lives together," she said, choosing an answer that was true yet harmless. Her aunt's threat was still an icy hand constricting the back of her neck. *Make him happy.*

"Then why did you sign?"

"Just like you, I'm the heir to my country first. This allegiance is good for us, and you seemed . . . nice." Elenor winced. That had sounded less than enthusiastic. Why was she so incapable of lying well tonight?

"Your aunt made it seem as though you were besotted when she came to finalize the terms," Cassian said, each word slow as though his mind was whirring, analyzing the situation. "Does this have something to do with the man you were with earlier today? Are you being threatened or blackmailed, Princess?"

Not by Gabriel, Elenor wanted to say, but didn't dare. Instead, she pressed her lips shut and shook her head.

"You looked hurt. Your dress was torn," Cassian pressed.

When Elenor still didn't respond, his tone hardened. "Listen, I know you've been through a lot, but we're going to be married by Harvest and you are clearly keeping secrets. I will not have that, do you understand? What is happening?"

Elenor could hear her pulse thumping in her ears. *Make him happy.* Her hands tightened around the fabric of her dress as the world wobbled. *Pull yourself together, Elenor. Paul needs you.* "Ah . . . I . . . I'm just . . . trying to do what my family wants me to. That's all."

"Then where is your mother? And why have we heard that you were the one responsible for your father's murder? If you are not, then what possible reason do you have for Gabriel Navarl being free and, if rumor is true, *living in your suite*? That man is dangerous. Has he hurt you?"

"No. I mean, yes, but that was before—No. He's helping me. And I don't know where my mother is." The whole gardens were spinning, the dose of serindalla she had taken liquid gold in her veins making everything too loud and bright.

"Mhm." By the way Cassian's lips had become a thin line, Elenor could tell she was failing horribly at placating him. "I'm trying to be delicate here, but clearly we aren't getting anywhere. My family and I have a lot riding on this alliance, so I'll be direct: are you fucking Gabriel Navarl? It would explain why you broke him out of prison and are defending him now, and perhaps why you are rushing into a marriage."

"No!" Where had *that* rumor started? Well, Elenor supposed her father had first raised the suspicion when she had returned from the Rebellion, but seriously? "Is that honestly what you think is happening here?"

"No offense, Your Highness, but I have no reason to give you the benefit of the doubt. You are on trial for the murder of a monarch and have a reputation for dalliances."

"I've had the same lover for three years, and she is quite incapable of getting me pregnant. So if your concern is the integrity of your line of succession, don't worry yourself," she spat.

Anger twisted his too-handsome features into something significantly less pleasant. "What I care about is the reputation of the woman I have agreed to marry. Seehana is a proud and moral country. I'm trying to gauge how much work I'll need to do to repair your social blunders and questionable history. Bad enough that you are assumed to be unhealthy and might be incapable of producing heirs—something I was willing to dismiss as rumor until I watched you blatantly lying about the fact that you are clearly feverish. I had hoped you'd at least endeavor to minimize other potential embarrassments, considering the risks we're taking coming here and accepting you, so I do not appreciate this unhelpful attitude."

"Accepting *me?*" Elenor asked, anger sparking higher. "I'm the Heir and Queen Regent of Lirin, a country three times larger and significantly wealthier and more powerful than yours. You're lucky I agreed to a union with *you*, Prince Cassian." It took effort to stand without help, but Elenor managed it with only a slight stumble. She was about to march away, done with this farce, when she caught sight of Daniil Eurieha standing on the outskirts of the gathered nobility, staring her way.

Freezing in place, Elenor met the priest's eyes and knew, without the shadow of a doubt, that if she walked away from Cassian now, Paul would die. Taking a deep breath and screaming inside, she turned back to the southern prince and curtsied. It took every ounce of self control she possessed to crush down the fury and soften her voice. "Please . . . forgive me. I spoke out of turn. Saying goodbye to my father has hit me harder than I expected, and I unreasonably took my frustrations out on you. You are, of course, right to be concerned. Forgive my outburst."

Cassian stood too, taking Elenor's hand and bringing it to his lips. There was still anger in his eyes, but none in his tone as he said, "I share part of the blame. It was insensitive to bring this up on the night of your father's Passing. I admit to being quite tired from my travels as well. Perhaps we should take this up tomorrow?"

"Thank you." Could it be that she had jumped to conclusions about him, just as much as he had about her? "Would you mind returning without me? I need a little space, but will be there momentarily."

"Naturally." Cassian let go of her hands and bowed, then walked back the way they had come. Elenor had no sooner sighed in relief when a hand reached out of the darkness to grab her arm. Looking to the side, she saw Kallen.

"Are you alright? I saw you go off with him and I got worried," he said, drawing Elenor behind a tall ornamental hedge. He must have spoken to her trailing bodyguards already, because they didn't interfere.

"I'm . . . in rough shape, to be honest. Full doses of serindalla always makes everything hazy."

"I can tell." Kallen angled himself so that anyone coming around the corner wouldn't see Elenor, placing her back against the hedges. At that angle, she had to crane her neck up to look Kallen in the eyes. "Elenor, are you seriously going to give Lirin up for the life of a bodyguard? I don't know what Enica and Navarl will find in that contract, but I am certain it will not be in our best interest. I did not expect you to announce the engagement tonight."

"I didn't have a choice."

Kallen frowned, but didn't chastise her further. Instead, he leaned in. "I know it might not feel that way, but you do. I can help you, Elenor. You promised me you would consider me as a spouse, but I realize now that I never gave you sufficient reason. Let me fix that. My informants tell me that the Miri have an armada just out of sight of shore. I suspect that they plan on invading if you don't do what they want, but that doesn't have to scare you. I have the power you need to tell them to leave and never come back, Princess. House Drego has been supplying the army with weapons and men for decades. We have rifters, too—many of them, all outside the reach of Tirit Mindel. It would be bloody, but with my help, you could be free of the Miri for good."

"And what about Seehana? If I break this engagement now, wouldn't they turn against us too?"

Kallen shook his head. "I don't think so. Seehana's military isn't as strong as it was in generations past, after their last war with the Mondaer. They can't afford to take Lirin by force. Besides, nothing unites a country like a war. Lirin being attacked could help secure your rule, as long as you have the resources to win. Your father's grasp was always tenuous because he could never count on the West, but you can. You've made friends out of the Ondai and Enicas, and I still have good relations with most of the rest." His eyes were shining in the moonlight, excited and animated.

Elenor shifted uncomfortably, having a hard time following his impassioned, hurried arguments. "What about Paul?"

Kallen's smile faded. "There are many skilled doctors I could call from Tirit Mindel, and I have contacts elsewhere too. We would do our best to save him. I can't make promises, but if he loves you as he seems to, do you think your *doena* would truly wish to be the reason you spend your life under the thumb of Miriel? You are going to be our Queen, Elenor. Sometimes ruling requires sacrifice."

Tears sprang to her eyes. Kallen brushed his thumb over her cheek as one rolled down her face. "Elenor, you're sick, you're in over your head, and you're tired. I can see that. Let me take care of all of this—the Iamings, the Miri, this murder charge. I have the money and the connections to make them all go away. I know you haven't known me long, but in that time I've come to care about you a great deal. Lirin needs a ruler as compassionate as you are. Let me serve you. All I need is for you to give me the power to do it. Cassian Iaming can't help you save our country. I can."

"I can't talk about this right now, Kallen." Elenor tried to duck out of his reach, needing space, but Kallen grabbed her arm, pressing her further into the foliage.

"You've been saying that for days, and yet today you agreed to marry someone else without so much as talking to me first, when you promised to seriously consider my suit. Every minute we delay makes this harder to come back from." He leaned in, eyes bright and focused. "Let me make your enemies stop hurting you and our country."

His thumb trailed down her jaw, face inches from hers. Elenor opened her mouth to tell him to give her space, but then his lips pressed against hers. They were soft, yet demanding, the taste of peppermint lingering on his tongue. At another time the sensation might have been pleasant, but not right then. The branches of the shrub were digging into her back, making her oversensitive skin shriek with pain. Elenor's hand shook as she lifted it to Kallen's chest, pushing to give herself more room and breaking the kiss. "I said *I can't talk about this right now,* Kallen."

"Elenor—"

Crack!

"Get your fucking paws off my lover, Drego. You better not be the reason why she's crying."

"Claire," Elenor called, as Claire, Gabriel, and Tomaz appeared in the darkened garden no more than a dozen paces away. Both Gabriel and Tomaz looked worse for wear, bent over and gasping. All three were soaking wet and covered in what looked like sand. Claire, though, was staring right at Kallen with fury in her eyes.

Elenor ducked under Kallen's arms and ran for Claire, throwing her arm around the other woman. "I've been so worried about you. What happened?"

"We got the contract, but not the antidote. I'm sorry." Claire wrapped her arms around Elenor, hugging her tight and burying her face in the crook of Elenor's neck.

"I'm just glad you got out. You had to use your Gift?"

"About a dozen times. It kept dropping us in the wrong places. I'm sorry it took us so long to get back."

"How did you know where I'd be?" Elenor asked, stepping back to look Claire up and down, ensuring for herself that she really was fine, other than some damage to her wardrobe.

"I didn't. My Gift seems to like dropping me near you, though, when it's not trying to drown me, or bury me in sand."

"We . . . Mondaer . . . fucking giant abandoned city," Gabriel gasped, still bent over. Seeming to lose the fight with gravity, he sprawled onto the grass, panting hard. "Never doing that again."

"Never," Tomaz echoed, coughing and wheezing.

"So what did you find?" Kallen asked, crossing his arms. He did not seem pleased by the interruption.

"Nothing good," Tomaz said, reaching into his coat pocket and handing Elenor a drenched, but still legible, slip of paper. "Look at the last few lines. That's why I stayed. I abbreviated where I could."

On the bottom, a messy, scrawled script said:

I, E. L., f/t good of my people & country, agree to leave Lirin & live in Seehana, naming my first cousin Silla Miri as regent, to rule in my stead for life, so I may better focus on the duty of producing and mothering an heir fit to take the thrones of both Lirin and Seehana, & all conquered lands.

Elenor held out the note to Claire, then each of the others in turn. When it returned to Tomaz, who placed it back in his pocket, they all turned to Elenor.

"They're taking everything from me," she whispered, voice haunted and distant. "They're taking it all, even my right to rule my people, and I signed it all away without a fight. They won before I even knew what the battle was about."

CHAPTER TWENTY-TWO
Seven Rivers
GABRIEL

I don't know what to do, Warren. I'm scared. If Mark realizes I've been lying to him about the baby, I'm worried that both our lives might be at risk. I shouldn't have kept it. This was a mistake. I feel like I'm losing my mind, and keep waking up with nightmares of Sianta figuring it out. She can count. She's not stupid, and, as gullible as Mark is on matters he cares deeply about, he's not either. They're going to figure it out. What do I do? I feel so alone.

—From a covert letter to Warren Miri, from Lilian Lirion

IT WAS WELL PAST MIDNIGHT. Gabriel watched Elenor's eyelids sink lower and lower. With the way her limbs twitched every few seconds, however, he knew sleep would be long in coming.

He, Elenor, and Claire sat alone in the princess's room. It was too quiet. For almost an hour, no one had spoken, Elenor listlessly staring into the dying fire while running her fingers through the fur of her mock dragon, head resting on Claire's shoulder.

Gabriel sat on the other side of an intricately carved coffee table covered in jars and bottles of medication, interspersed with notes, discarded jewelry, and a lonely deck of cards being used as a paper weight.

Unlike the night before, Paul wasn't snoring on the couch. The *doena* still hadn't been released from the infirmary, and the last time they had checked on him, a medic had said he had been in and out of consciousness all day. At least they weren't asking questions anymore, not after Eric had made it clear that no word of his condition was to be spread around.

Gabriel carefully unwound one of the bandages from his

hands, then flexed his fingers, examining both sides. A few faint lines remained, but little else to show for the explosion of gold just that morning.

He reached for the deck of cards, shuffled them a few times, stretching each finger and checking the range of movement, then set the deck down on the table. "Seven Rivers?"

Elenor looked away from the fire, glassy eyes full of unshed tears. "I'm not in the mood for games."

"El-belle, it might take your mind off . . . " Claire didn't need to finish. There were simply too many things wrong. "Go on. Trouncing someone at Seven Rivers will help."

Elenor's shoulders slumped, but she nodded.

"You in?" Gabe asked Claire, who shook her head.

"I'm still not sure what exactly my Gift perceives as danger. I don't want to accidentally disappear because I'm in danger of losing a game."

"If I hadn't seen you do that and gone along with you, I don't know that I'd believe it. Even Tirit Mindel only has one or two Gifted. Elenor, are we playing standard or a variation?"

"Standard."

Gabriel dealt three cards from the deck to the princess, who reached forward to pick them up with stiff, jerky movements. He carefully set the Hardor card in the middle of the table, and placed three barge tokens each on it. He put the Writ deck faceup, then drew his own hand.

Elenor frowned, cocked her head to the side, discarded, drew, then placed a canal card north of Hardor and moved one of her barges on to it.

"Bottlenecking the whole north off from Hardor in a succession play? Bold opening move." Gabe studied his cards. A river and two barges. He traded in his barge cards for barge tokens, then set a river card down south of Hardor, turning east.

Elenor raised her eyebrows. "Not playing off of my canal? I was gambling that you would trade in any rivers in your opening hand."

Gabe shrugged, the motion tugging at the worst of his remaining injuries, as he moved three barges onto his river. "And force me into playing through a bottleneck from the start? No thanks. Besides, no one plays a canal first round if they don't have a second one to work on an outpost. You have a city in your opening hand."

Elenor scrunched her brow, traded in some barge cards, set down a city, and moved all her current barges onto it, securing it unless Gabe wanted to outbid her.

The game continued for a few rounds, the object to place seven Writ cards down faster than one's opponent. That was hampered by long, winding rivers, robber cards, the special powers of each Writ, and by the fact that to win most games, one usually had to take at least two cities from the other player.

Within ten rounds, Claire was leaning forward, staring intently at the unfolding game. "Wow, you're actually keeping up with El at Seven Rivers, Gabriel."

"Actually, he's soundly beating me," Elenor said, biting her bottom lip. "He's expanding in three directions at once, and has twice the draws I do every round now that he has four Writs to my two."

"So, what are you going to do about it?" Gabe leaned forward.

"Probably lose," she muttered.

Claire poked her. "None of that, love. I know you're in a bad place, but I've seen you turn worse games around."

"My aunt's got me pinned into a corner too," Elenor answered, placing another river card in her dense, well-controlled northern river system. It was a solid play, but safe and slow, just like her whole game until then.

Gabriel reached forward, picked up the card, and handed it back to her. "Then stop playing the same losing strategy."

Elenor frowned at the card. "Any river I put down this turn anywhere other than the north, you'll move right on to. You have more barges than I do."

"And?" Gabe asked. "You're playing conservatively. I'm playing aggressively. Aggressive expansion will win every time if you sit back and let it."

"To stop you now I'd have to dismantle my whole strategy up to this point and leave my cities defenseless. You'd take both of my Writs in a couple moves."

"That depends on whether you can make me sweat about mine by then. Try it. What have you got to lose other than a card game which you're already behind in?" Gabe challenged.

Elenor tilted her head and narrowed her eyes, then started picking up barges. She gathered every single one she legally could, other than three she had placed over her first canal.

"Good. That hampers any invasion unless I have a robber free, but you know I just played both of mine, so they're in the discards. Assuming you've been counting robbers."

"Of course I'm counting robbers," Elenor said, gaze roaming around the table.

Claire rolled her eyes. "You've read books on this game too, haven't you, Gabriel?"

Gabe smiled slightly. "My mother loved Seven Rivers. We played almost every night growing up, and when I got to the Island and found out there were actual books on game strategy, I think I inhaled every single one over about six months. Almost failed a political science class because I used that hour to read."

Claire shook her head. "No wonder you're good at it. Looks like you've got a real challenger at last, El-belle."

Elenor didn't respond, still studying the board with her now-bulging handful of tokens. It all came down to this turn's placements. If she didn't break his monopoly on at least one river system and challenge a Writ, he'd win the game in three rounds.

Her shortest and most direct path was to Gabe's Ondai Writ. Elenor's eyes, though, fixed on the Tellen Writ: the core of Gabe's barge production empire.

"You don't have enough barges for that," Gabe warned. "You're down two, even if you pulled your canal blockade."

She looked up, and her lips twitched. She tipped her chin toward the draw pile, which only held two cards. "Clearly I've been counting better than you. One of those is a robber. If I sacrifice two barge cards, I'll definitely draw it."

"You need at least one of those barge cards if you want to make it to Garendor," he warned, smiling. "If the second card in the deck is a river, you'll be short."

"Garendor is too close to your other Writs. You'll crush me if I take it," she said.

Claire snorted. "That's a bit too apt. The last time a House other than the Ondai took Garendor for real, they were almost wiped from existence. Good thing we Enicas don't hold grudges."

Elenor snorted. "Have you ever once passed up a chance to pull a prank on Eric and use that as an excuse?"

"Yes. Exactly once. We were fifteen, remember? I *didn't* put a snake in his bed, when you asked nicely," Claire replied, as Elenor discarded two cards to pick the last two of the deck.

She peeked at them, and smiled.

"Robber and a barge?" Gabe asked.

"Sometimes a gamble is worth it." She picked up one of Gabe's river tiles, and swapped it out with her barge-laden canal, making a shortcut he hadn't seen coming

Gabe swore.

It took Elenor about a minute to dismantle Gabe's biggest river system. After that, it was a battle of attrition, with the princess holding a densely-packed bunch of barges in the very center of Gabe's empire of convoluted rivers, and expanding out in brutal, quick bursts. Gabriel still squeaked by with a win, but it was mostly luck, with three barges and a lucky last-round robber as the deciding cards.

Slapping his remaining cards down, Gabe sat back, rolling his neck. "I don't think I want to play with you when you're no longer sleep deprived. I'm pretty sure you could wipe the floor with me."

"No. You have much better strategy. You would have crushed me half an hour ago if you hadn't prompted me to go on the attack. And there were at least three times where I just drew better than you near the end. I got lucky." Elenor leaned back too, gingerly turning so she could extend her legs. The mockling stretched and turned over, belly up and snoring.

"Have you decided on a name?" Gabriel asked, starting to gather up the cards.

"Daemon said to give her a name with a double vowel, specifically Ee," Elenor replied, through a yawn. "I think I'm going to call her

Reeza, like that fox character in the story Paul used to read us about the little girl who lost her shadow."

Claire's face darkened. "That's a pretty name, but I don't like that Daemon keeps showing up, El. He's dangerous. I don't trust him."

"Neither do I," Gabe added. "He's been very helpful, and if I learned anything at Tirit Mindel, it's that people don't help for free."

Elenor shrugged, closing her eyes. "So I'll pay. It can't be worse than what I'm already paying, and I need all the powerful allies I can get. He *is* powerful. No one can deny that."

Gabe crossed his arms, but didn't argue the point. It wasn't his place. He could aid her with Lirin and play a game of Seven Rivers to help her relax, but, unlike Claire and her friends, he didn't actually know Elenor. Not well enough to voice an objection over who she spent time with. After all, Gabriel *had* held her at knife-point once, and now he owed her his life. Even if he'd felt able to press the point, though, he wouldn't have. Despite Daemon's shawl, sweat still beaded on her skin, her light nightgown and loose hair clinging to her. She didn't need another fight.

"Cool shower?" Claire asked, clearly just as worried.

Elenor shook her head. "Too much energy. And my legs hurt so much. They're numb but burning. I may have pushed too hard today."

Her lover rolled her eyes. "You think?"

Elenor poked Claire in the side. "Shush."

"I'd tell you to make me, but you'd embarrass yourself," Claire teased, and Gabriel was hit with a pang of melancholy that might as well have been a physical blow for how much it hurt. When was the last time he had been with someone he knew well enough to tease that way?

I need to get out of here. I need to find out where Fay and Fedrik went, and get a message to them. Elenor needs allies she can count on, and Fay can get what's left of the Rebellion on her side.

Elenor whimpered and closed her eyes, snapping Gabriel out of his thoughts. "You should try to sleep. We could try patience and dacel, if you're ready."

The princess shuddered. "Do you have any idea how . . . torturous it is to be stuck between sleeping and waking, unable to consciously move but with every muscle in your body twitching uncontrollably? That drug combination is horrid."

"But you would eventually sleep," he pointed out gently. "And you need sleep. It's been days. Your body won't recover if you don't rest, and if you can't manage it unassisted, it's going to have to be the patience."

By the scrunched up, resigned look on her face, Elenor clearly knew he was right. With a groan she sat up fully. "Claire, will you make sure this little one is let out in the night, and stay with me? I don't want to go through this alone. Not without Paul."

Even saying his name made her tear up. Gabriel's heart broke for her, and he was glad when Claire leaned in to give her shoulders a squeeze—firm, to avoid the worst of the fever-induced oversensitivity.

"Of course I'll stay, love. You never have to worry about being alone."

Far from reassuring the princess, that seemed to cause her more distress. Her whole face fell, whatever composure she had regained during the game crumbling. "Even though I'm engaged?" Elenor asked. A momentary pause followed, as she hung her head, then in a rush, "Even though I'm a broken mess? And I'm a murderer? And that I can't . . . can't protect the people I love the most?"

"Oh, sweetheart," Claire murmured, pressing a kiss into the princess's hair as her shoulders started to shake. "There we go. About time. Cry it out, love."

And cry she did. With each broken, raspy sob, Elenor seemed to collapse in on herself more. He'd seen this almost every day in the wasting fever wards. Even when patients didn't have a kingdom riding on their shoulders, the sleep deprivation was enough to drive almost anyone to tears. He'd seen a mature, confident business woman sob uncontrollably over a cup of spilled tea, and a stoic woodsman bawl for his mother.

Like he had then, Gabriel felt utterly helpless as she fell apart. Was there someone he should call for? Perhaps one of her other friends? Except, most of her little group hadn't known why she was sick until that day. It had been as new to them as to Gabriel, which hinted that perhaps Elenor was a little more isolated than she appeared. Gabe might not know what it felt like to be told he would lose a kingdom, but he knew a thing or two about feeling alone in the world, and about the pain of losing those he loved.

Standing, he went to get Elenor a glass of water from a nearby pitcher, then sat down on her other side.

The mockling woke up to the noise and jostling, and wiggled between the princess and Gabe, smacking him in the face with a pointy wing as she did. The little creature butted Elenor's hand with her black nose, which only elicited more tears. Carefully, Gabriel reached forward to take the hand she had jerked away, pulling it back into the dragon's soft fur. "You're allowed good things, you know? Even in the midst of pain, and sadness, and guilt, you are *allowed* to have moments of calm and of joy without guilt. It's all right to be conflicted and to have complicated emotions."

Elenor seemed to hesitate, then with another soft sob scooped up the mockling and hugged the squirming creature to her chest, burying her face in its fur.

Claire looked up over Elenor's head and gave Gabriel a small nod of thanks. Aloud, she said, "El, it will take more than a bullshit contract and a bit of danger to get rid of me. And you're not broken, you're ill. Really, really ill. You've gone through too much, and you need sleep, love. It will be better after, I promise. Right, Gabriel?"

"Right." He placed a hand on Elenor's back and, when she leaned into him rather than pulling away as he expected, he wrapped his arm fully around her. "You'll have a rough hour or so, but then you'll wake up feeling rested."

"I can't. Not without Paul. He . . . he stayed up and read to me every night until I was actually asleep. I-I could concentrate on his voice. But he can't—"

"I can read to you," Gabriel offered. "Come on. Let's get you into bed, give you your medicine, and I promise I'll read for as long as you need."

She hesitated, then gave a little nod.

Together, Claire and Gabriel helped her up. Elenor's legs wobbled, but with two people bracing her, she managed to get into bed. Gabe had already poured the dosages for her earlier in the evening, having been ready to force the medication down her throat if necessary. She took them without protest, then climbed under the sheets. Claire pulled off her bathrobe and followed suit, lying down, then nodding to the empty space on Elenor's other side. "If you can, do that thing you did earlier with the magic while you read. To cool her down. She said it helped."

"I'm not sure I can replicate it, but I can try," Gabe said, as he kicked off his shoes and sat beside Elenor on her large bed. "Right, what would you like me to read?"

"The rest of the document we found," Elenor said, eyes closed.

"Are . . . you sure? Don't you want to wait until—?"

"I'm awake enough to have a panic attack? No, I don't think so. Let's get it over with. I need to know what all of this is about," she interrupted. "It's in my nightstand."

"I don't know that this is a good idea, El. What if you can't sleep after because of what it contains?" Claire warned.

Elenor yawned, pulling a pillow into a better position with a wince of pain. Gabe reached over to place a hand in her hair, closing his eyes and focusing on the heat there. At once, with hardly a thought, his magic flared to life and hungrily sucked that warmth in. Elenor let out a relieved little sigh, and curled up closer to Gabriel.

Claire snuggled up on her other side. "I'll tell you if she's getting too cool."

"Thank you. So, the document or not?"

"'S fine. Read it after I'm asleep and tell me in the morning, then. You'll tell me the important bits, right, Claire?"

"'Course I will. Gabriel, there should be a book under the pillow behind you. Why don't you read that until she's out?"

After a little shifting, Gabe held a battered and well-worn copy of *Fables of the Blue* with several earmarked pages. Gabe wrinkled his nose. "Never heard of a bookmark, I take it?"

"Keep losing them," Elenor muttered, the twitching in her limbs dulling a bit. "Besides, I've spilled tea on that book and dropped it in the bath so many times that it's already pretty shabby."

The pages were, in fact, stiff and crinkly, as though they had been submerged in water at least once. "You're lucky it's not *Fables of the Black*. I'm pretty sure the God of Scholars would smite you for treating a poor, innocent book this way."

Claire chuckled. "I am afraid to say that the fate of that volume was far worse than this one. El forgot it out in the rain when she was about fifteen, and we found it a week later in the blackberry patch at Tellen Manor. It was basically sludge."

"What were you doing reading in a blackberry patch?" Gabe asked, as he flipped through the pages for a story that looked good.

"Best place to eat blackberries," Elenor replied matter-of-factly. "And no one but Paul, Fed, and Claire knew to look for me there. It was peaceful."

"Fedrik gave her that set of books for her birthday," Claire supplied.

Gabe smiled. "You know, I think I remember him buying them, now that you mention it. We went book shopping in the Night Market and he spent about four hours waffling between a set of Ionist Fables and a collection of murder mysteries. It took him so long that we had to sneak back into the Academy after curfew."

"It's a little surreal still that you were in school with him," Claire said. "He was always so quiet about his time on the Island."

"I don't blame him. We spent most of our education planning to overthrow the Lirinian government. Can't imagine rants about ending the crown's overarching power and moving to a constitutional democracy would have been welcome at high society parties," Gabe said.

"Wait, I thought your whole plan was putting Wilam on the throne?" Elenor mumbled, words slurring.

"It changed after we met Wil and brought him on board, but only because he agreed to shifting at least some power away from the Writted Nobility, and that he would consider a constitution. It was a compromise we were willing to make because backing Wil would have been significantly less bloody than overthrowing the government the old-fashioned way. Our first priority was always getting the Miri out. What happened after was more debatable. Some of the Rebellion wanted the Lirion back in power, some wanted to cut off their monopoly at the Water Race, so that the ruler of the country would change with the times between the Writted Houses, and a section of us wanted to give power to the people. Fed was pretty entrenched into that ideology."

"And you?" Elenor asked.

Gabe looked down at her. "I just wanted the man who killed my family to not be able to hurt anyone else. After that . . . I'd like to see a fairer system where fewer suffer. I don't think there's just one way to get there. It's why I was willing to die clearing the way for a Lirion to take the throne back from the Miri, even though I didn't know what kind of ruler you'd be. When you heard what he had done to my family, you cried. That was all I needed to know."

"Guess we'll never know what kind of ruler I'd be," Elenor said, then yawned as the strong sedative began its work.

"We will if I can help it," Gabe promised. "And I think you'll have more allies than you believe. I don't know how much of the Rebellion is still out there, but there is no way they will sit still for a blatant Miri coup. We're going to get through this. Now, why don't you try to get some sleep?"

When she didn't argue, Gabe opened the book and started reading a fable about a moral dilemma featuring a talking turtle and a mock dragon. The little white mockling jumped up onto the bed a few minutes in and curled up on top of Elenor's lightly twitching feet, lying outside the covers.

He read for over an hour, one hand combing through Elenor's long hair and drawing magic into his well. It was hard to concentrate on the book with the delicious tingle of power tickling through his veins and fixing more of his injuries, but the quiet room and crackling fire helped keep him focused.

Elenor whimpered and moaned in pain every few minutes, eyes squeezed shut as she rode out the conflicting mix of sedatives and serindalla. Claire gave her a little squeeze each time a tear rolled down her cheeks, face drawn with worry and not at all sleepy. Gabe's chest was tight with concern too, having heard stories of the horror of being trapped in a body screaming with pain, but unable to move. The wasting fever patients he had treated in school had said that it was the worst part of surviving the disease, and what filled their darkest nightmares.

At last, though, Elenor's breathing evened out. Gabe kept reading for a good half-hour, then carefully put the book aside and looked over at Claire. "She out?"

"I think so, though it's hard to tell. Ready to find out what else is in that document?" she asked, not moving from where she lay spooning the princess. "And ease up on the magic. She's nice and cool at last. Would you mind staying here with us tonight, though, for when she warms back up again? I think it's really helping."

"Of course I'll stay. Besides, I was planning on remaining awake for as long as possible. I can't say I trust that no one will try to kill her in the night with everything that's happened over the last few months."

"Probably not a bad idea, especially without Paul," Claire replied, pressing her lips into Elenor's limp, sweaty hair. "Wake me when you get sleepy, and I'll take the next watch."

Gabe reached over and pulled the thick bundle of papers from the bedside table. "Alright, let's see how much work we have to do."

The first few pages were primarily a list of the titles and assets that would be passed to Elenor upon the day of her marriage or twentieth birthday, whichever came sooner. There were concessions to make sure the three Miri children would be comfortable and taken care of, but other than governorships, all Miri power would be vested in Elenor.

It was on the fifth page that Gabriel stopped. "Claire . . . she was engaged before tonight. This document includes a betrothal."

"Excuse me?" Claire had been lying with her eyes closed, but wiggled up to a seated position at that. "Give me that."

He handed it over. She skimmed down the page, then looked back up at them. "Who the fuck is Alexander James Silvarin II? That family hasn't existed in centuries."

"Does it matter?" Gabe asked, a nervous flutter in his chest and slight hitch to his voice the only outward indication of what that last name meant to him. "If this comes out, doesn't it supersede the contract with Seehana? Wouldn't it render it null and void?"

"Tomaz is the lawyer, not me. We'll have to find out. But even if it does, that doesn't save Paul, or Lirin if the Miri decide to invade. This document won't change any of that." Claire handed it back to him and lay down with a sigh. "She's still stuck, and once she's married and Silla named regent, it won't matter. We only have four weeks. What are the chances we can even find out who that is, let alone find him? And even if we did, how could we trust a stranger?"

Gabriel didn't disagree with her analysis, but reached a different conclusion. One that made his heart race faster. He squeezed his eyes shut to keep from smelling smoke. "We . . . need to talk to Robin Tirition. If he wrote this and is looking for it, he knows more than we do. The Island still recognizes the Silvarin Empire. If anyone of that line survived, they would know where they are."

"If Sianta knows about this, it's no wonder she's pushing so hard. If Elenor marries Cassian she'd be signing away *both* countries, not just one, and Elenor and the South never would have known until it was too late. This needs to come out, but until then, not a word."

Gabe carefully got up, hands shaking as he gingerly slipped the document back into its envelope. "Where do I put it?"

"Back under the wardrobe. Paul kept it hidden there for years. And you speak of this to no one, got it?" Claire's voice was ice. "Not your Rebellion, not the others. This *must* remain a secret."

Gabe turned to her, annoyed. "Of course it must. What do you take me for, a fool?"

"An unproven ally."

"I'm not going to sabotage her, Claire. She saved my life," he said. "Besides, as you demonstrated today, you have the ability to drop me in the middle of the ocean or in a spooky abandoned desert city. I think you're someone whose good side I'd prefer to be on."

"Smart boy."

"I'm older than you," Gabe pointed out. "By at least five years."

Claire waved that off. "Irrelevant."

He shook his head, then hurried into the other room to hide the document again. By the time he returned, the little mock had taken his spot. Gabe picked her up, careful of the wings, and settled next to Elenor again.

Neither he nor Claire spoke for a few minutes, then Enica said, "If that becomes public, it's going to be war with Miriel, Gabriel. And it will mean Paul is going to die. We need to find a way to get him out of danger, or she'll never take the necessary steps. I know her. El's lost too much, too recently, and she'll freeze. The next month will pass before we know it, and then she'll lose it all."

"I wish we had found that antidote," he replied, leaning back against the headboard. In his lap, the mockling stretched and rolled over, belly-up and snoring. He reached down to pet her.

"I didn't want to say this while she was awake, but I don't think it will be that easy. Sianta is probably carrying it with her, and if this is the game she's playing, there will be a backup plan. Everyone close to Elenor needs to start watching their backs, because my bet is that at least one more of us is going to be compromised before the end. Eric, Beth, Tomaz, and I are well-known as her friends, and I'm sure by now Kallen and you are on the list as well, as is everyone on Elenor's staff. We need to be as paranoid as Fedrik used to be, because if another one of us falls, she might topple too. You are the only rifter who probably isn't playing your own end game. Kallen certainly is, and Daemon is dangerous to Elenor. Neither of us knows how our powers really work, but I have to believe that it's not an accident that we're both here. So I really hope you're telling the truth, and that I can trust you, because if I'm being honest, I'm terrified that I won't be enough to keep her safe all alone."

Gabriel met Claire's eyes. "You can trust me."

She held his gaze for a long time, then let her head rest on the pillow. "Wake me when you get tired, or if anything strange happens. And if that Daemon man shows up again, tell him to go away. I'm willing to give you the benefit of the doubt. Him, not so much."

INTERLUDE
The Queen's Memoria
RIONA

RIONA NAVARL SAT ON ONE SIDE of a wide desk as a woman with light blonde hair was cuffed to the seat opposite her. The room they were in had no windows and only one door, the light coming from a circuit lamp above them. Riona wasn't sure where they were, only that Robin had led her deep within the All Gods Temple of Hardor and through many labyrinthine passages to reach it.

Riona still couldn't believe she was in *Hardor.* Sure, she had read novels where people could go from one side of the continent to the other in the blink of an eye, but Riona always thought that was a bit of a deus ex machina and made for poor fiction. She had never expected to do it.

Then again, she had never expected to meet a half-dragon, but the small woman with delicate draconic wings and long tail who had greeted her upon arrival was real too. Riona was sure of that, considering Ara had let her touch the tail.

The little half-dragon stood in the corner of the room, directing two men in black uniforms securing the elegantly dressed woman to her seat.

"Make sure not to touch her skin," Ara repeated, as they carefully tightened the restraints around the prisoner's wrists and ankles. "She nearly escaped last time by erasing the minds of the silverguard assigned to it."

Riona shifted uncomfortably in her seat, but didn't say anything until the two guards left the room. The bound woman remained silent but finally looked up. Her eyes were gray like the storm clouds that often hovered over the Garendor harbor in the fall, and heavy with reproach. It was hard to believe that the Queen of Lirin was really right there in front of Riona.

"You have children doing your dirty work now, Robin?" Lilian Lirion asked.

"Miss Navarl is weeks away from coming of age. She is hardly a child. Trust me, I know. I do run a school."

"Not lately," the Queen said. "Lately all you're doing is meddling in my country's succession."

Robin made a small gesture of concession, then turned to Riona. "Ara and I will wait outside. You know your task. Please knock twice when you are done, or if you need anything. And remember, do not touch her. You have thirty minutes, unless she talks."

"I remember," Riona said, shifting in her seat and adjusting the stack of blank paper and her favorite pen. "I can't begin until you're gone, though."

With a bow, Robin escorted his wife out of the room. The lock clicked, and Riona was left alone with Lilian Lirion.

The Queen of Lirin stared at Riona with a blank, bored expression that made her squirm. "So, you're his latest tool? What great Gift do you have, girl? By the last name, I take it that you are related to that boy Robin is championing?"

Riona inclined her head. "I've never met my brother, but I've been learning about him. He's not why I'm here today, though, and while I am a rifter, I have no particular power."

"What, then? They hope I'll talk to a child? They should have brought in a six-year-old. That has always been my favorite age," Lilian snapped, tugging at her bindings, which secured both wrists and ankles to the heavy chair.

"I'm a *memoria*, a memory-taker. I'm here to record your life story, so it may be remembered by the Gods."

All the blood seemed to drain from Lilian's face, and she stopped struggling. "Am I to be killed in this damnable tower, without ever being able to see the light of day again, or say my farewells to those I love?"

Riona didn't have an answer to that, so said nothing.

The Queen shook her head, letting out a bitter laugh. "You know nothing of taking memories, girl, and are not prepared for the ones I have stored in my mind. Let me live on in the recollections of those who have known me in life. I will say nothing to you."

"That's fine," Riona replied, setting down her pen.

"Is it? I didn't realize Robin's minions gave up so easily."

"I'm a *memoria.* I don't and can't force you to share more than you wish. My service is to the dead, not the living. If you do not want to confide in me, then I will not force you, but I will be available to you at any time if you change your mind, and when you pass, whenever that may be, I will share anything you tell me with those who you wish to be remembered by." Riona did her best to keep her tone calm, like her teachers had taught her. Even her choice of words was more formal, though it always made her squirm to be so . . . apocryphal. "You may also ask me questions, if that will put you at ease."

Lilian's brow furrowed, and her look of skeptical disbelief could have given Mindellion Katrin a run for her money. "I am not about to hasten my own death by telling you a damn thing. Robin wouldn't have sent you if he wasn't after specific information. Let me guess: he's looking for the missing copy of a document."

"Yes, he is," Riona replied. "He said there were three copies, one of which you burned, a second that likely ended up in your sister's hands long ago, and a third that was lost."

A small gasp left Lillian's lips. "So that's what he meant when he said he had lied. A third copy. I should have guessed it. Those who believe in the Silvarin always did fetishize the number three."

Riona allowed the Queen a moment to regain her composure, then continued. "He doesn't think you know where it is, but hopes you might have a clue as to who has it, since your burning of one copy would do nothing if you couldn't confirm that the others were no more."

"Untie me, and maybe I will tell you," Lilian challenged.

It was Riona's turn for skepticism. "I may be young, but I'm not stupid. They told me what you can do, and had me meet one of the men you stole memories from. He has no recollection of even seeing you, let alone trying to take you prisoner. Though why stop there? Is there a limit to your, um, Gift?" Riona hoped she had the right word. Robin had explained Gifts to her the night before over dinner, but Riona wasn't entirely sure she had wrapped her mind around it.

Lilian pressed her lips together.

Alright, then. "Maybe asking me some questions might put you at ease?" Riona asked, settling in more comfortably.

"And why," Lilian said, voice dripping with condescension, "should I, the Queen of the most powerful country in the world, trouble myself with some child Robin has decided to use in his meddling?"

"Well, for one, if you don't start talking to me, we have only thirty minutes before I'm supposed to leave you here alone for the foreseeable future, thinking about your life choices in solitude and darkness. From my understanding, no one is going to speak to you, or interact with you in any way. I think that's needlessly cruel, but I'm not running this show, so all I can do is offer you a few minutes of conversation while you can still have it. We can talk about anything."

"Are you Lirinian?"

"I am. I grew up in Garendor."

"Then what you *should do* is untie my bonds and help me escape from here. I can offer you anything your heart desires, and you will avoid being an accomplice in the death of your ruler. What ever happened to patriotism?" Lilian asked, drawing herself up to look as regal as one could while bound to a chair.

"Frankly, loyalty to Lirin has never been high on my priority list to begin with, and I recently found out that you stood back and let your husband slaughter my village and family, so I'm seriously thinking of moving away from this shithole of a nation. Beggin' your pardon for the language, Your Majesty," Riona said, then took a deep breath to quell the anger that had slipped in. Continuing with less of her natural Garendaren accent, she said, "Forgive me. A *memoria* is supposed to be open and impartial. I let myself go where I should not."

"So that's why your brother did it. I always thought it had been Robin who set him on that path, to put pressure on me. Fitting, that you and Gabriel were both products of my weakness, the same as my daughter."

"Would you like news of your daughter?" Riona asked, picking up on the slight quiver in the Queen's voice on that word.

Lilian stiffened, and if Riona had to guess, a battle of pride and need took place, until she finally whispered, "Yes."

With a smile, Riona pulled a folded stack of newspaper pages out of the large pocket of her dress and spread them out on the table, where Lilian could read them.

"She's alive," the Queen gasped. "Thank the White."

"And regent. Also quite the good writer, if she penned these editorials herself—"

"No, she won't have. She has friends who will be helping her. Of that, at least, I made sure. The western nobility has been instructed quite forcefully by my allies to support her, if something were to happen to me. I knew I was unlikely to survive much longer than this. I just always thought my sister . . . " Lilian said no more, and Riona didn't push, especially when they were finally getting somewhere.

"Would you like me to get any messages to your daughter? I may not be able to deliver them until I'm out of Robin's employ in a few weeks, but if there's anything you want her to know, I'll see it done."

Lilian clenched her jaw and said nothing, causing Riona to sigh. "I know this must be frightening, but I *am* trying to help you. I want your story to be remembered the way you wish it told, instead of the way others will tell it."

"You really think that *you,* a child, could even *begin* to fathom what I have gone through and the choices that have defined me? I suppose I remember the foolishness of youth. No, Miss Navarl. I do not wish to speak to you. If I could not tell even my own children the truth of my life, why would I ever confide it to the minion of a man I have come to hate over these past few days?"

"Honestly?" Riona asked. "Because if not, you may never get a chance to say your goodbyes. I lost my family, and I believe your parents, too, were taken from you young, and without warning. So we both know the agony of not being able to say our farewells. And as much as I may blame you for my own family's loss, I have no such antagonism towards your daughter." She was proud of how many official-sounding words she'd stuffed into that sentence. As Riona caught and held the Queen's gaze however, she dropped the formality. "I don't want another person to spend their lives wishing they had one last word from their mother to cling to."

The Queen did not speak, but she did squeeze her eyes shut, and then, as slow as the waters of the Garendor bay, a tear formed at the corner of one eye and rolled down her cheek. "I was so close. I had almost done it, almost saved my daughter. That's all I've ever wanted. To save her, and to save as much of my country as I could."

"So, how can I help?" Riona asked softly. "I can't help you escape, but tell me about your dreams, and your ambitions, and I can pass them on to people who will care about them as much as you do."

A knock came at the door.

Riona sighed. *Great timing, Robin. Really excellent.* She considered asking for another half hour, but Lilan hissed, "I'll talk. I'll tell you what you want to know, but I need you to do something for me first."

"A message for your daughter?"

"No," Lilian said, "I need you to go to the home of Eric Ondai, tell him my situation and have him put pressure on my daughter to marry into the Iamings as I set up for her to do, but also tell him to pass on a command for his grandmother: that the plan must move forward, with or without Elenor and me. It's too late to divert resources into saving us. Do that, come back here without ears at the keyhole, and I'll answer all of your questions."

The door opened.

"Did she tell us what we needed to know?" Robin asked.

Riona shook her head. "Not yet, and I don't think she will today. I'll try again in a few, after she's had time to think."

Gathering up her things without looking at the Queen, Riona deliberately left the newspaper pages. Hopefully, they would provide some little relief. Riona had been locked in her room plenty of times to know how loneliness and boredom could eat away at a person's soul.

At the doorway, she turned back, catching the Queen looking straight at her. Minutely, Riona nodded.

She didn't speak much on the way back up to the ground floor of the Temple, especially since she was surreptitiously counting turns. Much like on their way down, they stopped at the top of a long flight of stairs. Robin beckoned Riona forward and held out a pin to her.

"As I instructed earlier," he said, gesturing to a copper plate on a smooth segment of wall. Riona pricked her index finger with a small wince, then pressed the droplet of blood to the copper plate. With hardly a sound, a doorway slid open in front of them, leading into a wine cellar in the basement of the Temple Tower.

"Are you going to tell me why my blood opens that door?" Riona asked for the second time, not expecting an answer.

To her surprise, Ara, not Robin, gave her one. "You're a keyholder. There aren't many with enough of your bloodline anymore to unlock these passageways. It is part of the reason you are so precious, though not the greatest one. I cannot wait for Gabriel to see you."

"I look forward to it as well."

Robin gestured up the final set of stairs. She had to blink a few times in the morning light as they reached the sunny storerooms of the Temple Tower's graduate housing wing. Back on familiar ground, Riona almost asked to go for a walk, so she could see about finding the Ondai residence in Hardor, but bided her time.

In fact, she waited all the way through breakfast with Robin and Ara.

It was only when Ara was busy writing on a lap desk, and Robin was going over his long and exhaustive checklists before his meetings, that Riona coughed. "I was hoping to go out this morning. I've heard that there's an early Harvest festival in one of the nearby parks and I wanted to go see it for myself."

Ara looked up, smiling. "Do you need money? Company? I can't go out much normally without drawing attention, but Harvest is one of the few times of year when no one blinks at my wings and tail."

"Maybe tomorrow? I was hoping to wander a bit. I've always dreamed of seeing Hardor," Riona said truthfully.

Robin frowned. "We should still send you with an escort. You're not of age yet."

"Weeks away, love. She's plenty old enough to take a walk on her own in the middle of the morning. Just don't leave the Old City," Ara said, reaching into her pocket to extract a wallet. She handed Riona a sizable stack of banknotes. "And be careful."

"Will do," Riona said, not liking the way Robin was still squinting at her.

She gathered her coat, walked out of the Temple at a meandering pace, and set off straight for the park mentioned on all the flyers for the fall festivities. Out of the corner of her eye, she thought she saw a figure peel off from the security detail in front of the Temple and follow at a distance. Other than to keep track of them, Riona paid the tail no heed until she heard the sound of music and laughter up ahead.

The festival was set up between the trees of a beautiful park. Little booths dotted the paths, and people danced and made merry on the grass, even though it was starting to drizzle. Many of them wore masks or colorful costumes. Riona stopped at the first mask stall she found and bought the most boring, common mask she could, donning it as soon as she had pocketed the change. She wandered through the crowd a while longer, genuinely enjoying the jugglers, musicians, and dancers performing.

At last, she spotted what she needed. A cloak, lying unattended on a bench. Riona squeezed her way between them, and without breaking stride, snagged the cloak. By the time she was on the other side of the crowd, it was around her shoulders and covering her hair.

She zigzagged and wove through the festivities, at one point having to step off the path entirely as a trio walked by. Riona averted her head as one of them—a redhead wearing a guard's uniform—looked her way. As she passed them, she heard a snippet of conversation: "You worked for the city watch, right, Jo? And I spent most of my life *avoiding* the watch. Either side of trouble we might find, one of us will be equipped to handle it. More people would draw attention, and so will talking about it. Come on, this way."

Deciding she wanted no part of any trouble, Riona hurried off as fast as her legs could take her. It wasn't until she was pretty sure she had lost her tail that Riona scampered down the first alley she could find after leaving the park. Up she went, clambering to the roof using the drain pipes and window sills, and finally she was in her natural habitat.

Leaping from chimney to rooftop dovecote, Riona remained in the shadows. She didn't know the Ondai residence's exact location, but she was sure it would be close to the Palace and that she'd know it when she saw it.

It took a little longer than she would have liked, but eventually a tall townhouse painted in garish colors drew her close enough to see the Ondai name printed on the gate. There were sentries in Ondai blue, white, and yellow on either side of it. Riona backtracked so she wouldn't climb off a roof in sight of them, then approached.

"Who goes there? Move along, now."

Riona didn't budge. "I'm here to see Lord Eric Ondai."

One of the guards, a tall, skinny man with chain armor hanging off his shoulders like a windless sail, laughed. "Unless the Queen Regent is hiding under that hood, you can't just walk up to the gate of the Ondai Townhouse and demand an audience with a Writted noble. Shoo, before we make you."

"I think he's going to want to hear what I have to say," Riona said, crossing her arms.

"I doubt it," the other guard scoffed under his breath, then said, "please feel free to go to the House Ondai offices with a note *like the public is supposed to.* They will set up a meeting, if it is deemed necessary."

"Don't have time for that. It has to be now."

"I told you," the first one barked, patience seeming to be wearing thin. "No one just—"

"Repeating yourself will just make me do the same, so can we skip ahead to the point where you get someone above your station for me to talk to? Or do we have to play this whole thing out?" Riona asked, using the this-isn't-going-to-go-your-way expression she had practiced daily while standing up to Katrin Mindellion at the Temple, every time she'd tried to get Riona to follow yet another rule.

The shorter of the two guards placed a hand on his sword hilt. "You're trying my patience, girl. You have until the count of three."

"Alright. I'll count it out. You have three seconds to let me in, or when I do eventually speak to Eric Ondai," Riona said, smiling widely, "I'll tell him that you two were the ones that stopped me from telling him where the Queen of Lirin is. One, two—"

The gate opened, and Riona stepped through.

PART FIVE

CHAPTER TWENTY-THREE
Xirra
DAEMON

The problem with Xirra has never been her ideals or dreams, but what and whom she will sacrifice to see them fulfilled. As such, though we may partner with her or her minions when our goals align, you must never trust them.

—from a letter to Robin Tirition, from Zorbennen the Black Dragon.

THE COLD MOUNTAIN AIR WHISTLED through ivy-covered ruins. Between the burned and crumbled husk of buildings, an overgrown road wound down the long valley of Nillenia from its narrow entrance to a lake at the base of a towering rock face. Long grasses swayed in the breeze, growing from cracks and crevices at Daemon's feet where he stood atop what had once been a small shrine to the Blue.

As he waited for his patron to arrive, Daemon looked over the dawn-lit valley. At the far end, a deep blue lake reflected the mountains and sky. He had already double-checked and yes, there on the banks were his and Claire Enica's footprints from when he had tested the limits of her power. Her Gift had brought them here on the last jump of their escapade. It could not be a coincidence. She had also taken him to the location of the Red's death days before she had died. There was more to be discovered about her power, but Daemon was too tired and emotionally worn out to ponder it.

He shouldn't have stopped by the Palace on his way back from the desert, but he hadn't been able to resist. Earlier in the day, Daemon had stood in the back of the room when Quindo Deil had announced the death of the Red to the *daradeio*. Their shock and mourning had been more painful than he had anticipated, drawing up feelings he had tried to bury.

While the Mondaer had cried for their dead Goddess, Daemon had fought back tears for another loss. For the home he had built, and the last remnants of the family he had loved. The rest of the day was a blur, not returning to clarity until he'd found himself outside Elenor's room. He hadn't expected the emotional blow of what he had seen, or how close to home it had hit. A Lirion, a Silvarin, and a woman of Jia heritage, all cuddled up on a bed. The arrangement was different from Cianira Marzi, Alexander Silverin, and Gabril Lirion, but it was too reminiscent not to set off alarms.

Kennotoza had said it outright: Gabriel and Elenor were going to mean something to each other. It was her one certainty, and to see it happen before his own eyes made her other predictions feel like a noose. He could still remember that empty chamber where all futures ended, and her words of caution: if Daemon remained close to Elenor, their future would end up there. Though he hated to admit it, Elenor and Gabriel's growing friendship also gnawed at another old wound: at the envy for the way Alexander had always triumphed when Jac had lost. And here he was again, getting mixed up with the Silvarin family when they had never brought him anything but pain.

Daemon took a deep breath and tried to clear his mind of too many things. All he had learned in the desert was mixing with the mystery of Elenor, his guilt about Alehan, and his hatred of Alexander. He needed to push it away, or Xirra would notice. Life would get infinitely more complicated if she did.

So instead of his problems, Daemon focused on the landscape. On the destroyed village, covered in new growth, and the mountain peaks dusted in early snow. Despite the rough beauty of the soaring cliffs and the swaying wildflowers in the meadows, his eyes kept being drawn back to the large pile of long-decayed bones in the center of town.

"Regrets?" Xirra asked from behind him.

Daemon did not turn at once, closing his eyes and breathing in deep as her presence washed over him.

"Did you know, seventeen years ago when you asked me to plant information about rebel activity in this village for Mark Lirion to find, that Gabriel lived here?" he asked.

"They thought they were clever, hiding him right under my nose. They underestimated me. As soon as I felt that power grow and looked closer, their lies did not survive."

"But *he* did." Daemon turned to her and stared at the uncanny beauty of the Blue Dragon, where she stood in all her elegance and grace atop the rubble of her shrine. "I told you, when I entered your service five centuries ago, that I would kill for you. I drew only one line: children. You knew, and yet you used me to hunt a child."

"I used you to plant information. I never made you raise your blade against the boy. Not until he was full-grown."

Daemon's hands balled into fists, but he did not contradict his Goddess. "A technicality. My actions still could have resulted in the death of a Silvarin child, and did result in his suffering and the death of many others. Don't do it again."

"So grumpy of late," she scoffed.

Daemon ground his teeth. "What comes now, Lady? Fulsixia is dead. The others plot against you."

She nodded, her silky mahogany hair swaying in the breeze. As always, Xirra was dressed in flowing blue silk, the fabric hugging her perfect curves like a second skin. This close, Daemon could feel the same pull that first drew him to her like a heartsick moth to a flame. It swirled around her like a physical presence, a dark ripple of power deeper than he could fathom, yet even as it tugged at him, something about it felt hollow.

Thump, thump, thump.

Against his finger, the ring that connected him to Elenor beat slowly, but it was the broken, fast-then-slow rhythm of someone not at rest. She had to be in pain. Casually, Daemon slipped that hand into his pocket where he could brush his thumb over the warm metal without attracting his patron's attention.

Xirra stepped close to Daemon and surveyed the landscape, gaze rising up the craggy side of the mountain far above: her lair.

"Have you heard yet that a golden Dragon was spotted in the sky? As I predicted, Sarthia has already made her move, so it is at last time to carry out mine." She turned her eyes to Daemon, the setting sun reflecting in those sapphire depths. "Are you ready to learn about where you came from, and the truth the others decreed I never tell you?"

At what cost? Daemon asked himself, but knew better than to voice it aloud. Besides, when had he ever been able to turn down the lure of a mystery? "Yes, Lady."

She placed her hand on his and transported them to her lair. Even after so many years, it still made him twitch in surprise. Most days, the Gods traveled the way Daemon did, but that was by choice, not necessity. They could simply wish themselves elsewhere between one blink and the next.

Xirra's cavern extended into the shadows as far as Daemon could see, constellations of twinkling lights dotting the inky blackness. The bright specks swirled around them like swarms of fireflies. His and Xirra's bodies cast shadows that shifted with the lights, dancing and warping together before falling apart, much as Daemon's life had in her service.

Xirra lifted one hand and the lights pirouetted around it. "It begins with the Gifts."

The Gifts? Daemon's pulse pounded in his ears, the hand in his pocket clenched so tight his nails dug into his palm. Five centuries of trying to weasel any information he could get about the Gifts from Xirra, the other Gods, Tirit Mindel, and the Gifted themselves flitted through his memory, as far back as his first meeting with Xirra.

"Serve me and I will answer every question you ask and teach you all I know of magic, but there are three topics you must never ask about: the Gifts, the Stormwall, and what came before the Empire. I can give you the world: access to every library, a seat at any table, a window into any room, but it comes at the cost of those terms and an eternity of service. Do you accept?"

Daemon's attention snapped to the present as Xirra waved her hand in a swooping gesture. The lights swirled into the forms of eighteen people. They lacked much definition, but as more lights flitted in to fill the gaps, he recognized a few of them.

Xirra the Blue, features unnaturally perfect in every way.

Zorbennen the Black, light-strewn face shifting with each breath.

Kennotoza the White, tall and angular, hair elongating and moving without wind.

Gullien the Green, winged, huge, and imposing beyond the confines of mortal men.

Fulsixia the Red, hundreds of eyes blinking upon her face.

But there were thirteen others. Some—like Gullien or Fulsixia—had clearly inhuman features. One sported wide, feathered wings. Another had six arms, and one floated as a disembodied swirl of vaguely humanoid light. Only one, like Xirra, did not have an instantly recognizable air of Godliness, and yet . . .

"Who are they?"

"The Pantheon of Holders, or, as you call us, Dragon Gods," Xirra replied. "One for each of the eighteen Gifts of Dracona."

"There are . . . Eighteen Dragons?" Which could have just as easily been: '*There are eighteen Gifts?*' The first statement had just left Daemon's mouth before the second.

Xirra inclined her head in assent, then another flick of her hand and all but seven vanished—the five he knew, and two standing on the other side of what had been the circle. "Each Gift comes as part of a pair, and the Gods are no different. Zorbennen the Archivist who remembers the past and Kennotoza the Bode who predicts the future are one such pair. I am the Gatekeeper and I destroy. My other half, the," Xirra snorted, "*light* to my *darkness,* the Goddess of creation itself, is the Gold. Her name is Sarthia, and her Gift is that of the Incarnate."

Incarnate.

Daemon had heard that before—just hours ago in the desert, in fact. It seemed like everyone had this mysterious Gift on their mind. Perhaps Xirra would be more forthcoming than the Mondaer.

Xirra walked towards the woman she had indicated, and Daemon followed. Up close, the lights formed into clear, glowing features. She looked young, innocent, beautiful. From her hands, flowers bloomed, more entwining in her flowing golden hair.

"Sarthia the Gold was a child when she created the world. Foolish and selfish, she tried to do it alone. She made this continent and filled it with powerful, magical people who worshiped the very ground she walked upon. She controlled every aspect of their lives and when they fought back against her tyranny, she destroyed them. In her rage, Sarthia wiped out all but the smallest remnants of her first people, crushing their cities and laying waste to their histories."

"The Eldel," Daemon said under his breath.

Xirra nodded. "The Mother in Gold they so worship first tried to eradicate and then abandoned them. She created a new land far across the sea, and there she welcomed us, the other Gods, to join her in creating the world anew. But it was an empty promise. She had not learned wisdom in her first failure. Instead, she believed that even more stringent control was needed. She made human magic weaker and less plentiful, breaking or enlisting those born with power to use toward her ends. She filled the sky with her mock dragons, each a pair of eyes and ears for her to spy on us."

"Wait, mocks are *spies?*" Daemon spluttered, worry suddenly filling his chest. There were a few blue mocks on Ayre. Did Xirra know he had kept the island from her?

"Only gold ones, and none of those have flown in our skies for as long as I have lived on this continent."

Daemon tried to contain his sigh of relief, lest she wonder what he had to hide. To keep her on topic, he asked, "So she controlled everything?"

Xirra nodded. "Yes. Her priests monitored every moment of every life and we, who should have been Gods by her side, were relegated to honorary figureheads." She walked around the youthful Goddess to stand behind her. "I should have been her other half. I am the destruction to her creation, the bringer of metamorphosis. Of progress. But she did not want that. She wanted stasis. Perfection. A world where no one struggled, which meant a world where no one *changed.* In her perfect society, all advancement was viewed with suspicion, all differences looked down upon as sin, and all infractions punished with death."

Daemon shuddered, the urge to hug himself too strong to resist. "What did you do?"

Xirra finished her circuit of the Gold and came to stand before the other God on this side of the circle. She reached up, fingers brushing the androgynous face made of silvery light. "We had a plan, my Harrodorin and I. They were the God of Weavers, with the power to unite those who were divided. We gathered together four who we thought would listen—dear, trusted friends. The Red joined us because she abhorred the way Sarthia treated her rifters and Gifted, giving them no choices other than service or having their magic broken. The Green because he would not stand for the way she abused her power over those who could not resist. The White, too, had strong reasons to help. When she first came to be, she had a vision of a being made of golden light destroying our world—"

Daemon let out a startled gasp without meaning to. Xirra stopped mid-sentence, peering at him with narrowed eyes. "Yes, Daemon?"

He dared not lie to her. She was the Goddess of Honesty and Justice. She had caught every lie he had ever told her, which was why he had learned to always skirt around subjects he did not want to discuss. It was like tossing that coin, except that unlike Kennotoza, Xirra was staring straight at him.

His patron's hand shot out without warning, grabbing him by the wrist. She pulled his hand up, trailing a long nail across his palm to the ring upon his finger.

"Sweaty. You're hiding something. Does it have to do with this old relic? Am I wrong in thinking this is the same ring you made for Alexander Silvarin as a wedding present?"

Daemon jerked his hand out of her grip. "It is. I retrieved it from him on the day of his execution at sea."

"Mhm. And who wears the other half?"

Daemon pressed his lips together.

"I see."

Xirra stepped away from him. A second later, pain shot through his body. Though Daemon had braced for it, no amount of self-discipline or practice could lessen the anguish of feeling a God press down on his well and capacity. His knees dropped out from under him, but he hardly noticed; he was being crushed and torn open at the same time. The doorway connecting him to magic, to the

Plane—to his very immortal existence—strained, hairline cracks appearing. Each was a gaping, blistering cut to his very soul.

Daemon screamed.

The pain ended.

For several long seconds, the only sounds in the vast chamber were Daemon's gasping sobs. Then Xirra knelt by his side and brushed his hair off his forehead. "I thought you had grown past these childish antics, Daemon. You know that every piece of information you collect must come to me. I am trying to save the world. You have lived under my protection for five hundred years, and that is the cost of your safety. Why do you still struggle against it so?"

Because I never would have sworn myself to you if I had known the cruelty that existed beneath your grand ideals.

But instead he rasped, "Forgive me, Great Dragon."

"Don't think I didn't notice that you just avoided my question again. Do not fear, though. I will not punish you for having private thoughts, even if they are less than complimentary. I am not a vain creature, Daemon. What I am is efficient. When I cannot trust my sources of information, my plans grind to a halt. So once again, who wears the other half of that ring's circuit, and why were you hiding it from me?"

Daemon squeezed his eyes shut, pressing his face against the smooth ground. "A girl. She's not important to your plans and I'm still getting to know her. I didn't want to bring her into this side of my life yet. I'm sorry."

Technically, it was the truth. Xirra had yet to give him any instructions regarding Elenor. It was as close as he could get to the truth while not naming names. All he could do was pray she didn't press. "What happened when you turned against the Gold?"

"Changing the subject so soon, Daemon? Alright. I won't insist *yet,* but I need your full focus right now. If I catch you becoming distracted because of something as insignificant as love for a woman who will be dead and burned in less than a century, there will be consequences. Understood?"

"Yes."

Xirra stood, and, much less gracefully, Daemon followed. Every muscle in his body was sore and tight, and his magical capacity felt brittle. That would fix itself in time, but it made Daemon want to go hide in a cave until it did. Having been recently reminded of what a broken capacity looked like, he wanted nothing to do with it.

"Where was I?" Xirra asked, as if she did not know. Though his patron did not have Kennotoza or Zorbennen's powers of seeing into the past and future, she was still one of the sharpest minds Daemon had ever encountered. He had no idea if that came from her godliness or simply who she was, but it put him to shame.

"You were explaining about how the others were recruited to your uprising."

"Yes, right." She turned back to the androgynous, strong-looking figure of light that she had named Harrodorin, the Silver Dragon. "The plan was simple at its core. We were going to kill Sarthia the Gold, and Harrodorin would temporarily step into her shoes, uniting those of us who remained until we could form a consensus for how we would lead this world *together*."

"What went wrong?" Because something obviously had. The Five Daemon knew certainly were not friends, and the Silver was dead instead of this Gold Dragon.

Xirra's hand dropped from Harrodorin's face and she turned away from them. For the first time Daemon could ever remember, his Goddess showed unabashed grief as tears formed in her eyes. "I could not kill Sarthia with my own power. We were too well balanced. She could no more destroy me than I could her, but I thought I had a work-around. Gods are made of the same energy as magic, and what anchors us to mind and body follows its laws. Just as a rifter can break, a God can too, except we have nothing holding us here if we do. While she could counter me by simply creating the replacement power I could destroy, a single, concerted blast, aimed straight at the core of her magic, should have been enough to kill her. Harro created a device that would allow hundreds of rifters to join together in order to kill her."

Daemon shuddered, but his attention also sharpened. A machine to kill a God was . . . promising. After what the White had done to his villa, Daemon wouldn't really have a problem tossing a rifter he didn't like into a God-Killing machine. Or, better yet, the whole Mother Rock. It was his, right? There had to be the equivalent of millions of rifters' worth of power stored in that gold.

While he considered that, Daemon asked, "Did it malfunction?"

"Yes and no." The Gods disintegrated in the air around them, reforming as a group of people connected by thick wire. "We needed hundreds of rifters, and the Gold was always thorough in her purge of them. Hiding out in the most secluded locations we could find, we worked and worked to save enough people, but it was for nothing. We did not have enough unless they would have been willing to have their capacities broken, setting off the sort of explosive chain reaction that might have amounted to a sufficient power surge. Fulsixia, though, forbade it. So we looked further. Specifically, the White did. For over a century, she looked for ways to kill the Gold, searching the future while the rest of us fought for the lives and rights of our flocks. Our armies grew, bolstered by the people but shunned by the other Gods. They called the war the Great Strife, but really it was . . . the death knells of freedom. We knew we could never win as long as the Gold lived."

The crowd of people vanished one by one, extinguished like candlelight as Xirra continued her tale. "We were losing by the time Kennotoza returned with a plan. There were two Gifts, she said: the Incarnate and the Gatekeeper—mirrors to mine and Sarthia's powers. Either of them individually might be able to take down one of the lesser Gods, but together they *might* be able to kill the Gold, assuming she was already pushed to the limit. We did not have many rifters left by then, but it was our only shot."

Xirra led him forward until they reached a small table set with two elegant goblets and a bottle of wine. He knew better than to expect her to pour, so rushed to do it as she took her seat. It was only when he presented his Goddess with her drink that he again asked, "So how did it go wrong?"

With a long sigh, Xirra leaned back in her chair. "A betrayal. We were ready. Fulsixia and Gullien searched out the Incarnate and Gatekeeper, and Harrodorin was there to bring peace between them. We had gathered our remaining rifters and all waited as I brought Sarthia into the trap. Fulsixia, Gullien, the rifters, and I all cornered Sarthia and weakened her. Then, just as the Gatekeeper and Incarnate prepared to strike, Kennotoza and Zorbennen arrived. Instead of aiding us, Zorbennen killed the Incarnate. This stripped the Gift from the Gatekeeper as well, but in the burst of energy that came from that breaking, the Gatekeeper turned to the nearest God and, whether out of grief or by accident, killed my Harrodorin."

Xirra took a long sip of wine, then set the glass down, the sound ringing through the cavern. "After that, we knew we had lost. Kennotoza and Zorbennen—the traitorous cowards—surrendered and begged for forgiveness. Kennotoza claimed that she misunderstood her vision, and that her powers had deceived her. I managed to twist the events enough that Sarthia believed that Harro had been there to save her, instead of part of the plan, hoping to spare their family from the fate facing us. I expected a wholesale slaughter, but such . . . straightforward mercy has never been Sarthia's way. Instead, she exiled us here. She sent us to these shores which she abandoned and created the Stormwall, trapping Gods and mortals alike inside it, never to return until we all united under the family of the God we had killed: the Silvarin."

Daemon sat, digesting all that she had said. "Why don't we Carinnians remember this?"

She laughed. "That would be me. I had a Razer in my employ at the time. I chose to erase your origin from all who came here. You see, while the others saw this exile as a punishment, I did not. This is a land where Sarthia does not rule. It was a clean start; a place where I could bide my time—build up our power and knowledge without the Gold breathing down our necks. The others, I'm afraid, disagreed. Zorbennen has worked since the beginning to fulfill the terms of the exile; he feels responsible for Harrodorin's death, and believes that the Silver will be reborn if the Silvarin come to lead us and fulfill Sarthia's stupid, made up prophecy. The White still has not apologized for her betrayal and has mostly kept to herself except for a brief return to sanity when she had the Lirion family help me destroy the Silvarin back in your mortal days."

Xirra got a far-off look, and Daemon waited, trying to hide

his impatience until his patron finally continued, "Sarthia must be growing restless. She wanted us punished, but she is clever and political. She will take the Red's death as an excuse. The war I have been expecting is coming, whether the others wish it or not. Which means," she said, turning her gaze on Daemon, "that I have a new mission for you."

Daemon's heart sank all the way to his navel.

"Only one Gift I know of could have killed a God. It is why I sent you to the Mondaer—to find the man or woman who ended the Red and confirm my suspicion that they are a Gatekeeper. For where there is a Gatekeeper, there is an Incarnate, and if we can gather both along with a Silvarin to break the seal placed around this continent, then when the time is right . . ." Xirra took a sip of wine. "We will be ready to kill her. And this time, I refuse to fail."

"So that's my mission? Gather together a Gatekeeper, an Incarnate, and a Silvarin, then bring all three to you?" he asked. At least she no longer wanted him to kill Gabriel. It made sense that she had hunted down the Silvarin when she wanted to keep them from rising to power again. Now, the sword had been temporarily lifted from over their heads. And if it descended again . . . well, Daemon could always throw North at her.

Xirra smiled. "That, and the heads of all three of the other Gods of Carinn on a platter before me if they get in my way. This time, I kill the Gold, and I will let nothing and no one stop me." She leaned forward, her piercing gaze pinning Daemon to his seat. "Don't disappoint me this time. No mistakes, no diversions, and most of all, Daemon, *no lies.*"

CHAPTER TWENTY-FOUR
The Blackberry Bush
ELENOR

Elenor won't be home tonight. She and Fedrik fell asleep in the blackberry bushes again and it's a pleasant evening. I don't want to wake them. We'll be back for breakfast.

—From a note sent up to the Palace by Paul Marek

ELENOR AWOKE TO A SHARP RAPPING on the door and her back pressed against a broad, warm chest that definitely wasn't Claire's. Opening her crusty eyes, she realized Gabe was still sprawled on her bed on top of the covers, a throw blanket over his legs and one arm around her waist. Claire was sitting up in bed on Elenor's other side, fully dressed and with a lap desk covered in scribbled-on pages.

She looked over at them when Elenor stirred. "It's just past seven. I told the staff not to wake you until eight."

"Could it be one of your friends? Or news about Paul?" Gabriel asked, his voice as groggy as Elenor felt.

Sleep tugged at her eyelids again and she snuggled into the pillows. Gabe's arm tightened around her waist a moment later, blissful cold following. She pressed in closer, willing the rest of the world to go away.

"I'll go check," Claire said. "She's been sleeping comfortably for the last few hours, so don't you dare move, Gabriel. If there's any chance we can buy her another hour, we're going to. " Claire set the writing desk aside and slipped out of bed. She padded over to the door and cracked it open. Despite her desire to sleep, Elenor peeked over to see who it was.

Claire's hand moved a second later, as though to slam the

door shut. Before she could, it was pushed open by the least welcome sight possible.

"Navarl, get out of my fiancee's bed if you know what's good for you, or Gods help me, I will make you regret it," Cassian Iaming snarled, striding into the room as though he owned the place.

Gabriel started to sit up, but before he could make it to his elbows, a ball of fluff and teeth appeared from under the blankets and hissed loudly enough to make Cassian stop dead in his tracks. Reeza extended her tiny wings as far as they could go and let out another shrill shriek.

Elenor was as shocked as Cassian, since she hadn't even noticed the mockling asleep atop her feet.

Gabriel extricated his arm from under Elenor and surged out of bed. The moment his bare feet hit the floor, he pointed at the door. "Out, Iaming. You can see her when she's ready for visitors."

The dragonette screeched in agreement, fur puffing to twice her usual size.

Elenor pushed herself up with a hiss as she put weight on her injured wrist, nightgown falling off one shoulder and hair a disaster. Moving made her joints ache terribly, skin so sensitive even the brush of her messy curls seared. "Prince . . . Cassian? Am I late for . . . something?"

Ignoring Gabriel, Claire, and the hissing mock, Cassian took another step forward. "You never returned to the pyre last night. You asked for a few minutes then disappeared without so much as a goodnight after publicly accepting my suit. If that were not insult enough, I find you like this? Seriously? *The night of our engagement?*" He gestured from Elenor's disheveled state, to Gabriel's wrinkled suit, to the clothes Claire had worn the night before drying over a chair. "Why would you agree to this alliance if you intend to flaunt your disrespect for it before our union is even ordained?"

"Oy, you don't talk to her like that," Claire said, stepping between Elenor and the furious southerner. "Want to talk about disrespect? Who's the one barging into a Queen Regent's chambers like they own the place, without so much as a by-your-leave?"

"When I correctly suspect breaches in the contract she *just signed,* I have every right to investigate them. My country's future is on the line here. I have no intention of standing aside and letting Lirinian superiority make me a cuckold before I am even a husband."

"Oh for fuck's sake, Iaming," Gabriel snarled, taking a few steps forward and gesturing around. "Read the room. Does this look like the aftermath of a night of wild sex?"

Elenor winced. Cassian clenched his jaw and his fists, but his eyes did track over the bottles of medicine scattered around, the crutches and canes propped up anywhere Elenor might need them, the papers covering most flat surfaces, and Gabriel's rumpled but still present clothes. As he seemed to take it in, the prince's eyes narrowed further and further. "So perhaps she's just a sickly cripple with no sense of decorum, not an unfaithful slut."

The words hit like punches. Elenor couldn't breathe, but Cassian wasn't done. "That doesn't change that things are being concealed or that rumors will spread. The South will not stand for this, not with how much we risk with this alliance."

Elenor wanted to say *good. Leave. Lirin doesn't want or need you here,* but she didn't for the same reason that all the blood left Claire's face and Gabriel went from looking furious to concerned: Paul's life hung in the balance of this arrangement with the South. If Cassian walked before they could find a solution, Paul would be as good as dead.

"Claire, Gabriel, would you see to my *doena* please," Elenor said, reaching forward to pick up her mockling and handing her wordlessly to Gabe.

The armful of wiggling dragon seemed to distract him enough that he wasn't able to argue before Claire dragged him out of the room and into the garden behind Elenor's suite.

The door closed behind them, leaving Elenor alone with Cassian. She reached up to rub the sleep from her eyes. "Would you give me a few minutes to change? I'm in nothing but my nightgown."

"That didn't seem to bother you a moment ago," the prince said, gesturing at the door through which her friends had left, "and the last time you wandered off you never returned, so I think not. I'll be seeing much more of you than this within a month."

Elenor flinched. Given the way Cassian's expression went from chilly to icy, he must have seen it. Her aunt's orders from the night before rang in Elenor's ears. *"That southern boy does not look happy, Elenor. Fix that. Make sure by tomorrow Cassian Iaming thinks it's because you were instantly taken with him."*

Fighting back the desire to point out that where she went and whom she saw in her own home were none of his business, Elenor managed to stutter, "As you wish. I swear to you this isn't what it looked like. If I could just explain—"

"I wish you would," he said, crossing his arms.

Elenor tried not to grind her teeth at the pointless interruption. Instead, she pulled the sheets up higher. "I felt unwell last night. I should have returned to the gathering to tell you I was going to retire, but if I'm being honest, I hardly made it back as it was. These last few days have been strenuous. Please forgive me."

"You think an apology is enough for leaving me to explain why my *fiancee* disappeared moments after the engagement was announced, or for putting me in a position where I had to represent you at *your father's own Passing?*" Cassian's scowl deepened, eyes scanning the room. They passed over her wheeled chair, her crutches, the bottles and jars of medication. Each time he stopped to look at something, Elenor's tension grew. "So you really are a cripple. I had hoped the disclaimers in our marriage contract were worst-case scenarios, but I should have known my sister would push for me to have a wife just like her."

While she had never met Nora Iaming, the Princess of Seehana had written her letters for much of Elenor's life. The first letter had come months after she had fallen ill. The last, about a year after she had returned to court. They had never been deep or personal, but Elenor had always had the suspicion Nora had written because she, like Elenor, had felt lonely in her illness. To hear Nora's own brother speak of her disability that way cut deeper than Elenor wanted to admit. "Prince Cassian, I truly am sorry for disappearing. It really was because I felt ill, though. I know you think that—"

Again, he didn't let her finish. "Whether you fucked that Enica strumpet wouldn't matter if you had an ounce of sincerity or discretion. The fact that every time we talk you lie to me half a dozen times, though, makes me disinclined to believe anything that comes out of your mouth. Let me be blunt: the woman I agreed to marry was described as honest, obedient, and healthy enough not to *look* like an invalid. So far, you have failed to live up to any of those descriptions, and seem to have no interest in making this alliance work, despite having signed the contract. We did not come here to be made fools of by a nineteen-year-old girl with blood on her hands, especially not in front of not only Lirinian nobility, but other visiting royalty. I gave you a chance to tell me what's wrong last night, and you did not take it. I am not in the habit of making such offers twice, but since we are to be married and I do still want this union for my country, I will give you a chance to make amends."

Make *amends* for not trusting him when he was allied to her aunt? When she couldn't be sure he wasn't part of the blackmail plot that threatened to take everything from her? He'd had time to read that damnable contract, and had signed it even though it took everything from his wife to be. The presumption in that '*offer*' made Elenor want to gag.

Paul's life depends on this man's happiness.

Elenor's fists clenched around the sheet as she forced her eyes down and her voice into the quiet, demure tone she had heard from her mother her whole life long. "I don't seek to make you look a fool, and I . . . sincerely apologize, if I am less than you hoped I would be. How . . . how can I convince you of my good intentions?"

The tension in Cassian's shoulders eased. He stepped forward, and gestured to the rumpled bedsheets. "You will start by never sharing a bed with another. You will not when you are my wife, so you will begin now. I will have one of my retinue's maids spend the nights here, to ensure your compliance. It is beyond insulting that I am forced to do this, but I'd rather solve the problem than argue about whether it should have arisen in the first place."

"As you wish," Elenor replied, using the way her loose hair fell across her face to conceal the tears of frustration and helpless rage forming in her eyes. "Is that all?"

"No." Cassian approached closer, until he was standing by the end of her bed. "Look me in the eyes and explain your behavior."

Was he serious? She wasn't a petulant child who had stolen a pie off a windowsill. Yet at the same time she thought that, the memory of Paul's pallid, pained face flashed through her mind. She had lied for years to protect the reputation of her family. Surely, she could do so again to save the man who had raised her.

Slowly, Elenor tilted her head up until she could look Cassian in the eyes, hoping he'd misinterpret her tears of frustration for ones of remorse. "I've been very ill. A . . . relapse of wasting fever. I had it as a child. Between that, the worry for my mother, my father's death, and the pressure of your arrival, things got . . . out of hand."

"Wasting fever? Show me your legs." Cassian gestured for her to sit on the edge of the bed. Once she was, and without asking permission, he pushed her nightgown up to her hips. Elenor let out a startled gasp, which Cassian raised an eyebrow at. "Don't pretend to be demure all of a sudden. Not when you've openly admitted to at least one lover."

Just because I let Claire touch me doesn't mean I want you to.

Cassian knelt down, examining her knees. "Scarring from braces. Bet that gave Navarl quite the thrill. He's always had a perverse fondness for unfixable problems, especially wasting fever."

"Despite what you might believe, there is nothing between Gabriel and I. He was in my bed because he fell asleep reading to me. He's been helping treat me, nothing more."

Cassian continued his examination of Elenor's legs. "Well, he won't be doing that either from now on. I'll have the Mindellion doctor traveling with us tend to you until you can hire a competent medic of your own. At least I'll take comfort in the fact that you don't look crippled, except on close inspection. In my country, physical prowess is as important as mental acuity to rule. It is expected of royalty to be as comfortable on a battlefield as on a throne. As long as you dispense with canes in public and medicate yourself so as not to show the pain, it will do."

He stood, hands returning to her nightgown to pull it down. "That is, *if* you become my wife. I'm still not convinced you're being honest with me. Why did you sign the contract so quickly? What is your family playing at? Most importantly, *where is your mother?* She was supposed to be here to negotiate, and her absence is most troubling."

"You don't think it's troubling me, too? That I don't want her back? I don't know where she is. I have people looking, but no one has seen her. Trust me, no one would be happier than I if she walked through the gates this very minute." If she did, Elenor could return to just worrying about her own mess, instead of having the whole country on her shoulders too. "None of this is an elaborate plot, Prince Cassian. At least not on my part. I'm just . . . trying to survive it."

He crossed his arms, looking down at her. "I asked you last night if you needed assistance, and you told me no. I will ask again. Do you need help? I *want* this union, and all that rides on it. I was told you wanted that too."

No, all I want is for this to be over. But she couldn't say that. "Marrying you would create a lasting peace throughout three-fourths of Carinn and bring prosperity to my kingdom. Those are both important to me."

Cassian raised his eyebrows, pausing for so long that it made Elenor squirm. At last, he said, "So you *do* understand what's at stake. I had started to wonder if your mother hadn't even bothered confiding in you."

An intense flash of curiosity almost made her ask what he meant, but she didn't dare, not when he had finally started relaxing.

More gently—and unfortunately more painfully, as the soft touch of his fingers was agonizing against her feverish skin—Cassian took hold of her chin. He turned her head one way, then the other. "At least you're as pretty as your family led me to believe. That will help sell this to the people. As a whole, most are more willing to trust in grand visions when they're spoken by someone who looks innocent and sweet. It will be useful."

Elenor wanted to gag, but bit down on the impulse. Thinking back to the etiquette lessons her mother had insisted on, she finally settled for a stomach-churning, "I'm glad I meet with your approval."

He smiled.

Dread settled in the pit of Elenor's stomach, but she knew what she had to do. Her aunt had made her point clearly enough.

She turned her head, lips pressing against the palm of his hand. Even with her eyes closed, it was hard to imagine it was Claire's. His fingers were too broad, calloused more than she would have expected from a prince. When she looked up at him, his smile widened, and his other hand rose to run through her hair.

"May I," Elenor swallowed back the creeping bile, "show you how much I want this union to work?"

Cassian cocked his head to the side. "Brazen little thing, aren't you?"

No, I'm really not.

"Please," she managed to say, and hoped he heard the desperation in her tone as an invitation, and not the cry for this nightmare to stop that it was.

"We really shouldn't until we're wed. Though I am tempted . . ."

"Please." *Go away.* But she didn't say the last two words aloud; she was sure her aunt had people watching her door, and Paul needed the first dose of the antidote she had promised. "I feel terrible about last night. Let me make it up to you."

Even the thought of going through with this made her body scream in protest. Every inch of her skin was on fire from the fever, her muscles aching all the way to the bone and joints stiff and inflamed. But he couldn't know that. Couldn't find out just how sick she was.

I've hidden it before. I can again.

The way Cassian was staring down at her made it hard to breathe in all the wrong ways. Intent, fascinated, hungry. His hand in her hair tightened, making Elenor whimper at the pain and clench her hands around the sheets.

"I suppose if you're to be mine in a month, there's no harm in enjoying the benefits early. It would certainly make this stay more enjoyable."

Elenor closed her eyes as his lips found hers so he wouldn't see the panic hiding behind them, and did what she always had when her body wasn't a place she wanted to be in anymore. She pictured the blackberry patch on the grounds of Tellen Manor, warm summer sunlight falling through the leaves and brambles. With meticulous care, she tried to recall every brick in the wall the vines had engulfed, and the sound of the bees buzzing from flower to flower.

She was distantly aware of moving, of being laid out on the bed, of words whispered and clothes discarded, but Elenor tried to disconnect from it as much as possible. It was hard when Cassian's every touch sent pain racing down her nerves, but it had been hard to ignore when Djina had made her walk with braces digging into her knees and thighs too.

So she had learned to run into her own mind. To the time before it all went wrong.

"What are you thinking about, Ellie?" Fedrik's voice drifted out of memory, except not like it had been then, when they were children. Instead it was in the deep, soothing tone she'd come to treasure when he'd lived at the Palace.

In her imagined hideaway, she lay with her head against his shoulder, his hand listlessly playing with her hair. She could smell the sandalwood scent he favored, hear the steady beating of his heart.

"I'm thinking that I'd give anything to be able to spend the day hiding in these blackberry bushes with you again, like we did so long ago, when everything made sense."

"With me, not with Claire?"

"I can't think about Claire right now. If I do, I'll cry, and I can't cry."

She wanted to cry. It hurt enough to cry. But not in the blackberry bush.

"Then stay here with me until it's safe to go back. Stay as long as you like. You know I'll always be there for you, just as you've always been there for me."

CHAPTER TWENTY-FIVE
Blind Trust
FAYRIAN

Dearest Pheebs,

I wanted to be the one to tell you, before the news arrived some other way. Harrison is gone. We don't know if he's dead, or if he left and doesn't want to be found, but when Robin went to check on him, the boy in his care was missing, and so was Harrison. They say the boy was discovered to be Gifted and put to death. My guess, however heartbreaking, is that it was the final straw for our dear friend. You know how much guilt he's always carried for every Silvarin child he failed to save. Between Alaric's loss and the news that the other one, too, is presumed dead, it was probably too hard a blow. As much as I wish to believe him to be alive out there, I doubt any of us will see him again. I admit that I may be reaching my breaking point too. Maybe I'll take you up on your offer after all. Would there be a place for me, still, among your people, if I left the Island for good?

—From a letter to Phoebi Deil, from Denzel Tirition,
Weapons Master of the Academy of Tirit Mindel.

FEDRIK WAS RUBBING AT HIS TEMPLE while looking northeast when Fay found him early in the morning, sitting on a bench outside their room.

"Couldn't sleep?"

He shook his head. "I woke up tasting blackberries. And that made me think of *her*. I feel sick."

"Murderous?" Fay asked, keeping her distance just in case.

"Heartsore." He still hadn't turned to her, but one hand was bunching the fabric of his pants. "Like part of me is shriveling and dying. We grew up together and I loved her. Throughout our whole childhood, when one of us was scared or upset, we used to fall asleep in the blackberry bushes behind my house. No one knew to find us there. And the fact that I can't do that now when all I want to do is run from this pain is tearing me in two. I hate her so much . . ."

"All the more so because you need her right now?" Fay ventured.

"More than ever."

She extended a hand to him. "Then we best get started so that maybe one day you'll be able to be near her again. Suela and Master D are waiting for us to begin."

Fedrik took her hand, but still looked so sad. "I don't know how they plan to help me. Even when I miss her, I still want to rip her apart."

"Why don't we go find out."

"Your training will consist of three parts," Suela said, as Denzel wrapped a sash around Fay and Fedrik's wrists. "The first is to work out how your Gift activates and flares, and what, exactly, it does. The second is to figure out if and how Avilor's Gift can suppress it, and the third is for you to learn to move as a team, since Avilor's Gift requires direct skin contact to work. We will begin with that, because the first two will not matter as much if they cannot be implemented."

Fayrian rolled her eyes, mostly for Denzel's amusement and to try to lighten Fedrik's miserable expression. "Good thing this is old news, right, Master D?"

"In your Academy days, I gave you a full three feet of rope. It was downright easy," the old weapons master reminded her, though he did smile as he tugged the knot on the sash tight. "When you're comfortable moving as a unit, the sash will come off, and we'll practice transitions to swap hands or other body parts."

Fedrik snorted, which was the first display of anything but serious concentration Fay had seen from him since waking. Her companion was near-vibrating with nervous energy, and from a man who had always been a little too composed for his own good, it was worrisome.

"Right, what do we do first?" Fay asked, ready to get moving. Maybe some exercise would help Fedrik as he fought off the worsening effects of his Gift.

"Navigating difficult terrain. You see that broken path over there? I want you to climb up and over that building, then back down the other side. Then go down the stairs, over that wall, and back up through that house."

Fay looked over at the obstacle course and shrugged. "Easy."

"Not so much," Suela said, clicking her tongue. "The Gatekeeper will be blindfolded."

"Why?" Fedrik demanded. "My Gift isn't like yours was. My eyes don't activate it."

"As far as we know, but it doesn't matter. Seeing your Incarnate will still potentially make you lose your self-control, and there may be times when you are not in your right mind. You must trust your companion to guide you when that happens, so we practice here, where it is safe and you are as calm as possible. When it must be done in times of great stress, you will be prepared."

Denzel pulled a second sash from his pocket and wrapped it around Fedrik's head, blocking his eyes. As he did, Tellen whispered, "If you make me run straight into a wall and break my nose again, Avilor, I'll return the favor."

"Haha," Fay said drily. "You'd never catch me. I'm faster than you."

"I have longer legs and am not afraid of heights. I'm sure I could catch you."

"In your dreams, pretty boy. Come on." Fay entwined her fingers with his and took off at a slow walk. Despite the teasing, she had no intention of running. They would take their time. The last thing they needed was for her or Fedrik to be laid out with an injury, especially when Fay's leg was only just starting to feel normal. Suela had warned them that once the Mondaer found out what Fedrik had done, they had to be ready to move out with little notice. She was sure they would have to take a risk or two in this training, so why add unnecessary ones?

"Rubble ahead, put your other hand on my shoulders," Fay said, as they reached the tricky bit. Going first, she carefully led him through the scattered rocks and debris. "I wonder if this happened naturally, or if a Gatekeeper before you blew it up?"

"Or punched it down," Fedrik muttered. "I can hardly focus today. Talk to me while we do this. All I can think about is—no, I don't even want to say it."

Fay reached back and patted his hand where it rested on her shoulder. "Well good, because I don't want to hear it. What do you want to talk about?"

"Lirin. What are you going to do when we go back?" he asked.

Fay helped him up and over a large piece of broken wall, then answered, "I want to find Gabriel first and shake him for that stunt he pulled with the engagement bracelet in the fucking suicide note. That's first."

Tellen chuckled, then swore as his foot slammed into a protruding rock. "Ow. A little warning next time, Avilor?"

"Sorry. Right. We're almost at the wall we have to climb. I'm going to have you give me a boost, then I'll lean down and guide you up," she said.

"Do you still have the bracelet?" Fedrik asked, picking up the other conversation. "Or did you lose it with the rest of our gear when we got on that wild mock?"

"It was in my pocket. I still have it," Fay said, then added. "I keep thinking about it, but I haven't put it on yet. It feels wrong."

"Why? No offense, but you and Gabe have basically been married for years. The only thing missing has been the legalities," Fedrik said, stopping where Fay indicated and hoisting her up. She put a knee on his shoulder, hand attached to his placed atop his head. Her other hand barely skimmed the flat roof of the single-story building.

"Higher."

Fedrik huffed under her weight but adjusted his grip so she could plant a foot on his shoulder and hoist her torso over the lip of the roof. It sent shooting pain along her ribs, but only for as long as it took to hook a toe in a crack and roll over the ledge, bound arm twisted at an awkward angle. After repositioning, she leaned over as far as she could and gripped Tellen's wrist. "Right foot on the windowsill in front of you, and free hand a foot above it. There's a missing brick you'll be able to reach with your left foot once you're up. Give me your other hand when you've found it and push up. I'll pull."

And pull she did, once he was in position, straining under his weight and leaning back with her feet braced against the lip of the roof. Tellen grunted as he over the ledge at an inelegant angle. He wiggled, and Fay heard his boots scraping against the stone walls. Then, without any warning, he toppled over right on top of her.

"Real graceful," she wheezed. "Why do you have so many angles, Tellen?"

"The better to leave you bruised and grouchy, my dear," he answered, then smiled and didn't move. "Not that I'm complaining about this."

"You're asking for another broken nose," Fay said, but without much bite because his comment mostly just warmed her, and not for the reasons he might think. Not that it was unpleasant to have his body covering hers after weeks of not nearly enough physical contact, but mostly because this whole situation—Denzel setting them on an obstacle course, jumping between topics, grumbling and teasing and threatening each other bodily harm—was strangely nostalgic.

"Worth it," he said, then rolled off her and helped Fay stand. "I'm thoroughly turned around. Which way were we going? And you haven't answered my question about the bracelet."

"And here I'd hoped that your perverted mind would have forgotten that, what with the pinning me to a roof with your knee between my legs." Fay turned Fedrik in the direction they were going, and led him forward.

"I can multitask."

Fay rolled her eyes. "You're really annoying. Fine. I haven't put it on because I wanted it to be him. I wanted a proper, Gabe-like, overenthusiastic proposal. He'd been carrying it around for months, and obviously I knew he was waiting for the right moment. My guess was whenever we managed to actually off Mark Lirion. You know as well as I do that Gabe wants the whole deal: children, a home, a proper family. We couldn't have that until the job of freeing

Lirin was done, so I was happy to wait. What I got . . . it wasn't that. He put our dream before our relationship, and while I might have done the same if the circumstances were reversed, now that I know he's alive, I'm kind of angry at him," she said, warming to the subject as they wove around old, sun-bleached and disintegrating roof furniture. "And on top of that, I'm pissed because I feel like I might have somehow missed my window. Robin never said it outright, but he always hinted that while it was fine for me to warm Gabe's bed, a marriage wouldn't be permitted. He's too important, and I'm . . . well, I'm fucking no one, right? Gifted, useful to have around, but certainly not fit to found an Empire with him. For all I know, he's already betrothed to some stuck-up noblewoman. That's exactly the sort of long-term game Robin enjoys."

She paused as they had to climb down the other side, which proved to be much more difficult than the way up. They were both panting by the time they made it to the ground. Fay leaned against the side of the building, taking a quick break since their three caretakers couldn't see.

"You know that wouldn't matter to Gabe, right? You're his whole world," Fedrik said.

"Might matter when he finds out I've been lying to him. And even if it somehow doesn't—because you and I both know he's loyal to a fault—how the fuck am I supposed to marry and have a family when I'm literally tied to you? Possibly for the rest of our lives." Fay held up their bound arm.

Fedrik blanched.

"Didn't consider that, did you, Tellen?"

"I hadn't. I haven't been thinking further ahead than a few hours. Fay, you don't—"

She elbowed him in the ribs to shut him up. "You might not have been, but I was. Gabe isn't the only one who is a self-sacrificing idiot."

"Giving up your dreams for other people isn't a competition to see who can do more of it, you know," Fedrik grumbled, rubbing at the spot she had hit.

"Have you met me, Tellen? Everything is a competition."

He smiled, then rested his chin on Fay's hair and ran his fingers through her curls. Despite herself, Fay sagged into his touch, happy to be close to him after fearing she'd never see him again. Being alone wasn't something Fay dealt with well.

"Avilor, you said it yourself: you've spent most of your life watching out for Gabe and trying to fix Lirin. Now you're jumping in to helping me and the Mondaer without stopping to breathe. In other words, prioritizing everything and everyone over yourself. You're *allowed* to have some strong emotions and ask for help with them. You know that, right?"

"Pah, I don't know what you mean." Except that even as she said it, Fay gave Fedrik a grateful squeeze, which he silently returned. "Come on, you overemotional beanpole. We should get back to it."

After a morning of running around the Sandhewn City and a hearty lunch of stewed lentils and flatbread, they moved on to the next of Suela's tasks.

Fedrik was told to sit cross-legged in the middle of a large terrace with Fay on the outskirts., "Every Gift has a range," the old ex-Gatekeeper instructed. "Fayrian, you said you can sense and absorb magic through your skin. We need to find the edges of his power. Boy, you are to try to pull your Gatekeeper aura in as far as you can. This may be impossible, but you will still attempt it. Fayrian, you are to walk as far as you need until your Gift activates, then return and see if you can spot the edge. When you do, see if your Gift will affect it. Denzel, you go in the other direction, and Phoebi, fly up. I want to see the shape of his Gift, not just how large it is. I studied one Gatekeeper who had a similar aura, but it went straight up instead of out.

"Wait, you're Gifted too, Master D?" Fay asked, surprised, though she didn't know why. These people had controlled the Incarnate Gift for centuries.

"Indeed I am," the old man said, walking backwards to stay facing her. Fay did likewise, as Phoebi took to the sky on her white mock. "Trueborn Sunder."

"Trueborn? Like me and North?"

"You're not Trueborn, girl," Suela interrupted. "I had one of my assistants look you up in Sidian's chronicle of Gifts. He gave you yours at the age of five at your father's behest, on one of Sidian's visits to Lirin."

"What did you say?" Fay stopped in her tracks. "You mean I got this shit *on purpose?*"

Mind reeling, Fay wasn't sure if anger or shock was prevailing, but they mixed together uncomfortably in her chest. Why would her *father*—who had always preached that every man and woman was equal to all others, no matter their magical status or accident of birth—want Fay to have a Gift?

"He wanted you protected, according to Sidian. I do not know the details. I would guess the Ghoster Gift was chosen because of how subtle and easy to hide it usually is. Now stop dawdling; I want to hear footsteps. We don't have time to take this slow." Suela clapped her hands, clearly intending for the talking to end.

Fay ground her teeth and turned away, cursing under her breath with a particular emphasis on the word *fuck* just to spite the old woman.

She got three blocks away before she felt her Gift flicker and her awareness of the ambient magic return. "Here!" Fay called, hoping the others would be able to hear her. The white mock was flapping in the air at about the same distance from Fedrik, and a few minutes later, Denzel's distant cry came.

Fay turned back in Fedrik's direction, closing her eyes. She took a half step forward, then another.

Her Gift flickered and went out. She stopped, adjusted her position, then tried again. The same thing repeated, again and again, despite her efforts to somehow get a grasp on the edge of Fedrik's Gift. It was slippery like an eel, seeming to retreat and dance at the edge of Fay's Gift's range.

Almost an hour later, she was no closer to success but was much closer to punching a wall out of frustration, sweat rolling down her neck and making her red tunic cling to her back.

By the time Suela called her back at around the ninety-minute mark, Fay's mood had gone from bad to deplorable. It only got worse when she saw the other four sitting and drinking water together.

"So I see I'm the only one actually *working* here," she snarled, stomping across the terrace to them and snatching Fedrik's water cup out of his hand.

"None of us can do what you can," Phoebi said gently. "Why don't you sit for a little in the shade and cool down?"

Fay scrunched her sunburnt nose. "I don't need your fucking pity."

"Language, Fayrian. If not *decent* language, at least inventive," Suela said, calmly.

"Don't you 'Language, Fayrian,' me. I've just spent an hour and a half pointlessly doing the same thing over and over again. I thought you said we were in a hurry."

"We are," Denzel replied, "but some things cannot be rushed. Remember when I first taught you to shoot a bow? You were determined to get as many arrows into that target as you could, as fast as you could, and how was your aim?"

Fay bared her teeth, so it was Tellen who answered, "Terrible, if I recall."

"Exactly. This is like that. We must identify how the Gift works, then practice each part of it slowly and steadily, so that one day you may do it fast and efficiently. I've had mine since the day I was born, and I'm still learning new things it can do."

That was the last thing Fay wanted to hear. She sat down with a huff. "Except in this case people could literally be coming here to murder Tellen *right now,* and if we have to run, we'll be potentially putting him in reach of others he could hurt. I think fast and dirty might be in order. Not that you'll listen to me, you old fossils."

Denzel chuckled. "If your attitude continues to age this badly, I pity the world when *you're* as old as we. Does it not occur to you that we may have a tad more experience in this area than you? I have been a teacher for most of my life, and Phoebi has studied more about Gift lore than anyone I know. Suela bore the Gatekeeper Gift for years. We know what we are talking about."

"So about all of that bullshit," Fay said, raising three fingers. "One, you skipped out on teaching half-way through our finals, leaving us dangling, so fuck you, Master D. I didn't even know you *were* Gifted, and I worked at your damn yards to offset my tuition for literal years. Two, bookworm in the glasses there has yet to contribute anything useful, and three, this one had her eyes gouged out so she wouldn't be able to do what Fedrik has to. He doesn't have that kind of shortcut. So maybe you could all take it down several notches."

Phoebi began to laugh. "You were right, Denzel."

Fay crossed her arms, not at all liking the idea that she had been talked about behind her back. "About what?"

"That Robin was a fool to try to use you as a tool," he said.

Her whole world lurched sideways.

Fedrik must have seen her blanch, because he reached out to place a hand on her knee, and responded when Fay was unable to form words. "You knew about what Robin Tirition was doing?"

"'Course we did. Pheebs and I joined the True Project just after our graduation. Do you think you're the first Gifted or noble to get tangled up with Tirit Mindel's obsession with the Silvarin? Because I promise you, that is not the case. They've been trying this for generations."

"If you're going to waste time with stories from outside the desert, I am going to lie down," Suela said, laboriously getting to her feet and leaning on her cane. "Wake me in no more than one hour. We have much still to do."

No one spoke while the old woman hobbled away, leaning heavily on her cane.

"She looks so tired," Phoebi whispered, when Suela was well out of sight, giving Denzel a telling look that Fay couldn't quite decipher. Not that she really cared to try.

"Explain," Fay said.

Denzel turned to Fay, reaching up to tug at his goatee. "Impatient as ever."

"If it has to do with Robin and the Silvarin, you better bet I am. And if you're about to tell me that my favorite teacher at the Academy was in league with the people manipulating and blackmailing me, I am going to be fucking pissed."

"We quit," Phoebi said. "When Robin decided that kidnapping

babies and blackmailing children was a line he was willing to cross, each of our little group of friends broke from the True Project."

"Who else was fucking involved?" Fay asked. She had always thought of Robin's organization as some shadowy, basement-dwelling cult of weirdos, like the dean's half-dragon wife. It had never even occurred to Fay that other teachers might have been involved. Especially not the one she had actually cared about as a friend, not just a mentor.

Denzel held up his hands. He was missing several fingers, but he still counted down. "It started with me, Pheebs, Elehanna Ondai, Amandine Taberlin, and a man named Harrison. We were inducted by our Core Six instructor, Corinne Daran, because of Harrison. He was our generation's Gabriel, as it were."

"Excuse me?" Fedrik asked.

Phoebi clarified. "The Island has been trying to recreate the Empire basically since its collapse. Infighting between the Colleges about who should control the puppet strings, however, means that most candidates end up dead, if they show promise. The True Project was created to unilaterally protect the Silvarin and let them return to power and rule *without* strings. Or at least it started that way. Honestly, none of us cared about Empire building. In fact, it sounded terrible, but Harrison's siblings and half-siblings were in danger. He wasn't a viable candidate because he had . . . badly burned-out while in school. Too much pressure, too early. He ended up blowing up most of a building and almost taking me with it."

"Was that why Gabriel always had extra classes?" Fedrik pressed. Clearly, while he had understood Fay's story, he hadn't spent much time *thinking* about it. Not that Fay could blame him for it.

"Yeah," she said. "It was why I was always pissed at Robin whenever he pushed Gabe to take yet another elective. It was an underhanded push to try to get him 'ready' for leadership. Total bullshit."

"It was brutal to watch," Denzel agreed. "And I fought Robin about it every step of the way."

"You did?" Fay asked, incredulous.

Denzel nodded. "From the start. As soon as Robin told us about you two, and the deal he made, I started advocating for Gabriel to be told everything and for you to be released. Robin has too powerful an ally for me to take action on my own, but I made sure to get in his way wherever I could, and offer you as much of a safe haven as possible."

Fay crossed her arms. "You could have said something."

"So could you, to Gabriel," Denzel pointed out, eyebrows rising.

Well, that hurts like a kick to the gut.

Fedrik squeezed the hand that still rested on Fay's knee when she rocked back. "Fay was a child, Master Denzel. That's not a fair comparison. And if you cared so much, why did you leave?"

The old weapons master reached up to run his fingers through his coarse gray hair. "I left because I couldn't watch any longer, if I'm honest. I'd seen it too many times before, and seen the Project destroy too many of my friends. Do you remember when you requested your deferment near the end of your last year, Avilor?"

Fay did. It had been when she found out that her father was sick, and only about a month before Denzel had been thought to have died at sea. Those two events in combination had nearly destroyed her. "What does that have to do with it?"

"I spoke to Robin. Offered to get out of his way for good, if he would give you two a chance to do what you wanted out of life for ten years. I had hoped that before your time ran out, you would have done exactly this." He gestured around to the desert. "It's why I mentioned the Mondaer to you so many times. I had hoped you and Gabriel would finish what you had to do in Lirin and run south, where the Island wouldn't be able to touch him, and where you could both be free."

"As slaves," Fay muttered.

"As *daradeio*," Phoebi objected.

At another time, Fayrian would have argued, but honestly . . . she was rather touched that her teacher had done that for her. It would have been helpful if he had *told her* the plan, but still. No, actually, fuck it. "Why not just tell me?"

Denzel's bushy eyebrows crept higher. "You don't know, do you?"

"Know what?" Fedrik asked, sounding as annoyed as Fay felt.

"The Island," Phoebe said. "It's the home of one of the Gods."

Dead silence. Finally, Fay asked, "What?"

"A God. Zorbennen the Black. He's the one pulling Robin's strings, and he's the Archivist. Everything that happens in his domain, and I mean *everything,* becomes part of his memory. There is no such thing as a secret on the Island," Denzel said.

"Or off of it, for the most part," Phoebi added. "Anywhere where there is copper, there is an ear for Tirit Mindel through a reverse sending rift. Zorbennen the Black might not be able to sift through every single word spoken or written across the world, but Tirit Mindel is *always* potentially listening, and both God and Island share their information with Robin Tirition."

Fay sat in stunned silence. *Another* God? More importantly, another one who had actively fucked-up her life? No wonder Robin had always known every time Fay had gotten close to telling Gabriel. He had made her believe that he would simply *know* if she broke her promise, and proven it enough times that Fay had wholeheartedly believed him.

"What do you mean where there's copper Tirit Mindel has an ear? There's copper everywhere. For goodness sake, we have copper *coins,*" Fedrik pointed out.

"Exactly," Denzel said. "Copper is a magical metal. Tirit Mindel has very publicly stated that reverse sending—where a rifter can transport soundwaves from far away to them—is impossible, but it's not. It just needs a source of copper and the right circuit. They've made sure to keep copper coins in circulation even after banknotes were introduced exactly so they could have an ear in everyone's pocket. The Island hears all. That is, and always will be, the greatest threat it poses, and why I couldn't tell you any of this."

"That's criminal," Fay exclaimed. "I'm never fucking touching a piece of copper ever again."

"Won't do you any good if the Black focuses in on you. The only way to be absolutely sure no one knows what you do is to never speak it, never write it down, and find . . . alternative ways to get information to those who need to know it."

Fay's eyes went wide. "Like forcing me to take a class on Mondaer politics, so I'd know this was an out."

Master Denzel inclined his head.

“But . . . How can the Island have kept this a secret? How is it that no one knows that copper is—”

“Oh, there are plenty of people who know,” Phoebi interrupted. “But the Island sells information, and those educated enough to realize how they get it are usually already dependent on the Island in one way or another. Those who stir up trouble end up in more of it than they can handle. Most just go about their business, and know not to wear copper when they take a long walk in the woods to meet with their allies. The only place that I am certain is absolutely free from eavesdropping from outside is the Hardor Palace. I’m sure that’s at least part of why rifters and circuitry have been heavily monitored in Lirin.”

Fedrik and Fay exchanged a puzzled look. “I don’t understand. There’s plenty of copper at the Palace,” Fedrik said.

Phoebi’s eyes lit up and she leaned in, conspiratorially. “There’s also a great deal of circuitry in and under there, just as old and sophisticated as any the Island controls. While the people who care for it have some goals in common with the True Project and Zorbennen the Black, they are pretty antagonistic to Tirit Mindel’s current political position in the world. We don’t have time for it now, since we really should get back to work, but remind me some time soon to tell you about the time we went spelunking in the Hardor Palace basements. You won’t *believe* what’s down there.”

CHAPTER TWENTY-SIX

Return To Ayre

NORTH

What if this is why I was rendered immortal? I never thought I'd feel joy again, not after what I did to Alehan, but today, watching the first child born free on the shores of Ayre Island, I did. This little girl would never have been born if not for the safe-haven I have created. I saved both her parents from the clutches of people who sought to use them. I have watched them build a family, heard their laughter carry over the waves. For so long, I thought everything I ever touched would be cursed, but maybe not. Maybe this city is building me back up as a different man as much as I am building it, brick by brick. All I know is that I would protect these people and this city with my life, even from the Gods themselves if needs must.

—From an early journal of Daemon Indigo

THE SUN HAD RISEN ABOVE THE HORIZON and the chill of the night was fading from the stone of the Mother Rock. North stared out across the desert, enjoying the companionable silence with Tsiihsi and Obri. They had spent all night on the top of the mesa, feet dangling off the edge and Bard incessantly getting reacquainted with two of his favorite people.

"Daemon will be back soon," Obri said, leaning forward on the railing that kept the unwary from falling to their deaths. "He said he'd return right after his next meeting."

"And has he told you what he's going to be discussing during this meeting he was *required* to go to alone?" North asked, trying and failing to hide the derision in his voice.

Tsiihsi and Obri exchanged a knowing glance.

"What?"

"There are things that we can't tell you, North," Obri hedged.

"You're really still intent on keeping his secrets? Even after he proved himself perfectly willing to let me die of thirst in the middle of the Mondaer desert, and bullied his way into another culture's most sacred space to interrupt them in their time of grief? He's not a man worth following," North rebuffed. They had danced around this all night. North had asked them about their mocks, and Tsii's studies. They, in turn, had asked him about his life here with the Mondaer and all he had seen. The one topic that all three had avoided was Daemon. With the end of this uninterrupted time together looming, though, it was almost a relief to broach it.

"The Red named him as her successor. Doesn't the faith of a God make you trust him?" Tsiihsi asked.

It was a good point, except for one detail. "She knew he might not be trustworthy. Besides, I am not sure how much faith I can put in her judgment when her messenger is Moe." Not to mention, the message that the strange man had left him with was as baffling as it was troubling.

"Who *was* he?" Obri asked. "Is he a Schism? The way he moved through space wasn't like Daemon, but he also seemed to have predicted when we would arrive like a Bode. That's impossible, though. No one can have two Gifts."

North didn't have any of those answers. "I don't know. When I look at him, my Gift malfunctions painfully. He's *wrong.* Like he doesn't belong here. All I get are jagged flashes."

"I don't suppose you'll tell us what he told you?" Tsiihsi asked, looking hopeful. Knowing how curious she was, North was sure the mystery was eating her alive, but he had no intention of *ever* repeating the words Moe had spoken in his ear, especially not to people who still counted themselves friends of Daemon.

"Sorry, Tsii."

He had been about to say more, when someone coughed behind them. All three swiveled around to see Daemon leaning against a low wall, hands in his pockets as though he had been waiting there a long time. "You sure about that, North? Has it ever occurred to you that I might need that information to do good?"

"No," North replied, getting to his feet and crossing his arms. The movement drew Bard's attention to Daemon's arrival. He perked up, looked around, and saw Daemon.

Three seconds later, Daemon was on his back, face being aggressively licked and nuzzled by the mockling. "Oof, you're getting heavy. Bard—ick! Don't stick your tongue up my nose."

North didn't call his dragon off. Maybe Bard would squash Daemon. Tsiihsi, though, ran forward to pull Bard away from him. The mockling launched himself upward, flapped into the air, and did a happy spin, leaving Daemon clutching his midsection in pain. Good.

"How'd your meeting go, Daemon?" Obri asked, also standing.

"About," the immortal rifter wheezed, "as expected. Which is to say, badly."

Daemon got to his feet with Tsiihsi's help, then leveled a chilly stare at North before looking to Obri. "I'm sending you back to our Hardor headquarters. I want you to get our rifters and Gifted ready to come here, and assemble a team of circuitry adept to help me on Ayre. Tsii, I want you with that group. North, since I'm stuck with you, let me make something abundantly clear: what you are going to see is a secret that's about to become quite public in a way I have been trying to avoid for centuries. I'm in a bad mood. So watch if you must, report back to your minders if you have to, but keep your mouth shut unless you're going to say something useful or productive. Got it?"

North ground his teeth, but nodded. "I'll get Leo."

"Make it quick. I have a lot to do." Daemon flicked his hand. A doorway to a room full of people opened. Obri rushed through, Tsiihsi on his heels. Who were the others? Before North could get a good look, Daemon snapped it shut. "I'll be here when you get back."

North glared at him, but turned on his heel and stalked off. Bard stayed behind, still delighted by Daemon's presence. Traitor. Good thing the dragon was so cute.

North found Leo where he had left him in one of the many rooms filled with beds that any *daradeio* could use while staying at the Mother Rock. Kaedy's face was nestled up against Leo's neck, both of them fast asleep with Kaedy's son snoring between them. For a second, North hesitated, not wanting to wake Kaedy, but he didn't trust being alone with Daemon. Not because he thought the rifter would kill him—Daemon wanted something from North—but because the Mondaer would probably be more inclined to listen to one of their own.

Kneeling down, he shook Leo's shoulder. "Hey, it's time to wake up. Daemon is back."

Leo's red eyes blinked open, curly hair falling across his forehead. There were tear streaks on his cheeks and crusted in his lashes, as though Leo had finally had a good cry at some point in the night. North was probably due for another one, but too much had happened in the days since the Red had died.

"Did you sleep at all?" Leo asked, quietly so as not to wake Kaedy.

North shrugged. "Only a little. How's she doing?"

"Cold all the time. She was shivering in her own bed, so I came to keep her warm. I don't think it helped much, but every little bit is better than nothing, right? Should we bring her with us?"

"Quindo said not to leave her alone until we know she's not a danger to herself. Unless we find someone in her family to watch her . . ." Unfortunately, North wasn't sure who that would be. Both her brothers were broken too, as were many of her parents. Quindo was busy leading the Mondaer through the loss of their patron God, her grandmother Phoebi had left with Suela and Fayrian, and Akaaron was busy getting another expedition ready to find the new Incarnate. Besides, North had a strong suspicion that Daemon would behave much better if Kaedy and Daari were with them. Broken rifters and children were a sore spot North was not above poking.

Leo shifted enough to press a kiss to Kaedy's brow. "Wake up, *liuda*, we have people to see and places to be."

North didn't recognize the Eldel word. As Kaedy blinked awake, he asked, "What does that mean?"

"It's a familial endearment for those who are family but not related by blood. Like 'beloved one of my heart.' Our *doenas* have been friends for many, many years, as have their families. Kaedy was one of the first people I met when I came to the desert as a child. She used to tease me about my Eldel pronunciation all the time. Do you remember?"

Kaedy, who had her eyes open but hadn't moved, pressed her

face more firmly against Leo's chest. Her hand found Leo's and squeezed. Daari, who was also waking, stretched. The little boy was too young to really understand what was happening around him, which was probably for the best. As Leo sat up, North smiled at the toddler. "Remember me, Daari? I'm North. Do you want to go on an adventure today? We're going to an island. It's a lot of fun, and you can sit with your mama on the beach while your uncle Leo and I do things. Does that sound good?"

"Yah!" the little boy exclaimed, then looked to his mother and held out his arms. Kaedy picked him up, burying her face in his wispy black hair.

It broke North's heart that even with her son in her arms, Kaedy couldn't muster a smile.

Twenty minutes and a quick trip by a kitchen later, they made it back to the roof. Daemon had been busy. A huge portal stood atop the great mesa, large enough for adult mocks to fly through. On the other side was a beach North had never thought he'd see again, palm trees swaying in the breeze. Quindo was up there, along with dozens of other *daradeio*.

As they approached, North heard Daemon explain, "I'll be moving cabling through all week. Have you mapped the copper and gold veins? It may take me a few days to get my circuitry reconfigured as a defensive weapon, so whatever information you have to speed it along would help. I'll probably need to drill into some of the walls, too. From my meeting this morning, it sounds like conflicts between the Gods are inevitable at this point. We'll want to be ready without drawing too much of their attention."

"I am not sure how comfortable I am with this," Quindo replied as people North didn't recognize stepped onto the beach through other portals.

"I won't connect anything up until your rifters get a chance to check it all over," Daemon assured. Then he caught sight of North.

"Ah, there are my minders. I'll be off, then. You two, through here and either pitch in or stay out of my way." He gestured to North and Leo, but bowed his head respectfully to Kaedy, eyes settling on the little boy in her arms. "And who's this?"

"My son Adaariol," Kaedy replied, her voice weak, tired, and hoarse. So unlike the vivacious young woman she had been when North had first met her. "I hope it's alright if I bring him. I don't—"

"Of course it is. I have a nice shady area where you can get comfortable and nap if you need to, and there are plenty of people in my crew who would be happy to sit with you, or entertain your boy if you require some time. We are at your disposal." The kindness in Daemon's voice as he spoke to Kaedy was jarring, as was the smile he directed at Daari, who was peeking up at him from behind his mother's legs. Daemon made a goofy face at the little boy, who giggled.

That levity left Daemon's gaze when he caught North staring. "What are you gawking at? I told you, go through."

Leo grabbed North's hand and dragged him forward. The young man's eyes were wide as he took in the shimmering portal. At the threshold, Leo poked a toe through, then his head. "Wow. This is incredible. How is it done?"

"None of your business," Daemon muttered, passing them.

Sand crunched underfoot as North stepped onto the beach of Ayre Island. He inhaled deeply, closing his eyes as the scent of salt water and plumeria filled his lungs. Bard was already in the water, splashing around with Kita and Edan. The sun was shining in a clear sky, but unlike the desert on the other side of the portal, the air was pleasantly humid.

"Is this the Island Union?" Kaedy asked, as she cautiously stepped through the doorway, Leo still examining it while muttering exclamations of delight and disbelief.

"It is. I can't tell you exactly where in it, but far south," North supplied. He offered Kaedy an arm, walking her along the beach. After a few yards, Leo ran to catch up, the three of them and Daari following behind Daemon. The little boy was pointing at the mocks, the monkeys, the birds overhead, and all the other wonders of the tropics. His chatter was nearly unintelligible to North, but Daemon, who was walking a bit ahead, turned to them at one point.

"If you like dragons, kid, you'll love what's coming. Tsiihsi, you ready up there with the disconnect? We have to power down before we can do anything else," Daemon yelled ahead.

From beyond the foliage they were headed towards, Tsiihsi called back, "Almost. This lever is corroded shut. We're working on it."

They emerged onto an outcropping of rock North had never noticed, tucked around a corner and through a thick patch of trees and lianas. North had to let go of Kaedy to get through, reaching back to lift Daari over a fallen log. In a small clearing overlooking a cliff and the open southern ocean beyond, a pile of rocks had been moved aside. Tsiihsi and three others had their sleeves rolled up. They knelt next to a huge copper lever coming out of a thick metal platform that looked like it had been buried. Tools were scattered around them, and one of the group was using a hammer and a wrench to try to undo a corroded bolt.

Daemon crouched down next to the man, touching his shoulder. "Let me do that, Trevor. Can you brace me?"

"Yup." The man, Trevor, who North's Gift identified as coming from Miriel's capital Gilde and being a Type Three rifter, knelt and pointed both hands out in front of him. "No one get between me and that rock wall. I'm going to be pushing kinetic."

Daemon wedged a copper plate against the wrench, then placed a boot against it, sitting back-to-back with Trevor. "Two hundred pounds on three. One, two, three."

North couldn't sense the magic, but he saw the effects. The foliage growing out of the rocks Trevor was pointing at flattened. The rifter slid a few inches, back thudding solidly into Daemon, as Daemon moved in the opposite direction, boot pressing hard against the wrench. Three or four seconds of pressure, then the bolt twisted.

"Stop," Daemon called. The pressure pushing the two men together vanished, and both slumped a little, taking a gasping breath.

Tsiihsi, who had moved out of the way, asked, "Opposed kinetic pushes?"

"Does the trick, if you trust the other person to hold their own," Daemon replied. He started twisting the bolt off. "Trevor, I want you with the team swimming down to the perimeter. I need the circuits directing the copper pulled up and brought to shore, so I can modify them, and you're one of the only ones who has the well and capacity to absorb the blowback if one of the circuits is too far gone."

"That's going to be an all-day job, at least," Trevor griped, wiping grease off his large hands. "I'll need people to pod with."

"Bring in as many as you require. Time is of the essence. If this takes every rifter we have, so be it."

Who was he talking about? Who *were* these people? North had only ever seen Obri and Tsiihsi . . . except for that one time in Daemon's house. There had been a map with hundreds of names and faces on the wall. But where had Daemon been hiding them?

"Righty-ho, boss. I'm on it." Trevor headed off the way they had come.

Daemon finally turned to acknowledge North's existence. "You really don't deserve to see this, but at this point it's not like I'm going to be able to keep it a secret. If you get in my way of protecting it, though, I'm feeding you to a mock." With that, he grabbed the large lever with both hands and, putting his back into it, pushed. The metal groaned and creaked, then gave.

The subtle buzzing that had always filled the air on Ayre and that North had grown used to while living there stopped. Across the water from them, a whole island appeared. It was several times the size of the one where they stood, and on its slopes and beaches was the city North had once seen sketched onto a piece of paper on Daemon's wall.

Beside him, Leo's hands went up to cover his mouth. Kaedy gasped, her son staring at the island in wonderment. Mocks flew above it, mirrors and mosaic walls reflecting the early morning sunlight. It was . . . beautiful. Far more so than anything Daemon had a hand in should be.

Slowly, he turned to Daemon, who instead of staring at the island was looking right at North. "I told you I protected what was mine, did I not? Did it ever occur to you that perhaps that was a little grander than a few huts on a beach, and that there were more lives at stake than just my own?"

No, it had not. North wasn't sure what to say.

With a sigh, Daemon turned back to the city. "Alright, Tsiihsi.

Let's get to work. Time to figure out how to connect Ayre to the Mother Rock. Nothing like taking apart five centuries of circuitry to brighten one's day. It's going to be *quite* the endeavor."

North sat on the beach, wiping sweat off his brow as he tried to regain enough breath to gulp water. Daemon hadn't exaggerated when he said that connecting Ayre Island to the Mother Rock would be an endeavor. Despite only having been sent to watch Dameon and make sure he wasn't up to anything nefarious, North didn't have it in him to observe people doing hard manual labor and not pitch in.

He, Leo, and eventually even Kaedy, had spent the early hours of the morning hauling endless coils of copper wire onto the beach. Daemon's people—who all wore a medallion around their necks or on their belts but otherwise seemed to be made up of folk from all over Carinn—had worked below the surface of the ocean, dragging identical devices onto the beach from all around the much larger island. According to Daemon, they had only pulled up a tiny percentage of the massive underwater circuitry control units, and it would take weeks to finish.

With the sun beating down on them fully, though, the pace of the work had slowed. People still labored, but in shifts. Those taking a break lay in the shade on the beach, hydrating or eating breakfast. Leo was lying next to North, panting. His red linen undershirt was drenched in ocean water from a quick dip, curls glistening where they were not coated in sand.

"Have you two eaten?" Obri asked, walking by with a basket of rolled flatbreads, stuffed with something that smelled strongly of garlic. "We have a worksite kitchen set up on Ayre proper. They've sent me to make sure no one is working on an empty stomach."

Leo pushed up onto his elbows, sand clinging to his entire underside. "I am hungry enough to eat a mock."

"Don't say that around here. People have been parted from their mocks for days. It's been a rough transition. Almost everyone on

Ayre has one." Obri handed Leo a wrap, a banana leaf folded around it as a makeshift holder. The second one was offered to North, who took it with a nod of gratitude while trying to catch his breath.

"How'd you . . . end up . . . handing out food . . . instead of . . . hauling cables?" he asked, halting every few words to suck in another strained lungful of air.

The Bode chuckled. "Seniority has its perks. I'm babysitter for the new arrivals until Daemon and I decide to let them in on Ayre's secret. Means I don't get to spend much time on Ayre proper with my family and friends, so that everyone else can live in safety and tranquility. That earns me a few perks."

"Babysitter," Tsiihsi scoffed, thudding down between North and Leo. "I still cannot believe I lived here for over a year and never knew that there was a whole city not a mile away. I thought all Daemon's rules were just eccentricities. You could have mentioned *something* before last week, O."

The Bode rolled his eyes. "'Go take Edan swimming,' I said. 'I wonder what those copper wires coming off the island are?' I said. 'Oh, what must this picture of a city on Dae's wall be?' And did you ever go exploring on your own? No. It's not my fault you follow rules unless dragged into breaking them. Most new arrivals end up breaking into Daemon's villa within the first two months, and bumping into Ayre city in six months tops. If he hadn't pissed Daemon off, I bet North would have gotten there." As he grumbled, Obri handed Tsiihsi a wrap, then looked to Kaedy. "Will she want one? Or . . . anything else?"

Kaedy was kneeling in the middle of wires she had been asked to braid together, crying at the mess of tangled copper in her lap.

"I've got this," Daemon said, appearing behind North through a portal. "I've dealt with broken rifters before. They'll literally fall apart over spilled milk. She needs something that is no longer hers to use, and there's nothing that can fix it."

He walked towards the sobbing young woman, hands in his pockets. Leo waited until he was far enough away, then leaned in to whisper to North. "That's not entirely true. Some Gifts can fix broken rifters, or at least give them a new way to access power, but until we find . . . well, it might be awhile."

"I hope she makes it," North said, with a sigh. "One of us stays with her at all times, alright? I've seen this too, on North Island. When rifters were broken so they could stay with their families instead of being executed or exiled . . . well, they rarely survived a full year."

On the beach, Daemon knelt next to Kaedy. With motions far slower and gentler than North had seen since the day Daemon had helped him with Bard's hatching, the rifter pried open Kaedy's hands and removed the wire from them.

Bringing her knuckles up to his lips, he spoke in a soft voice that did not carry. At first, whatever he was trying didn't seem to work, but then she let out a snotty laugh and leaned into Daemon's shoulder to have another good cry. He rubbed her shoulders until it was done, then motioned Leo over.

North went too, unsure of what to think of this unexpectedly nice Daemon. The older rifter ignored him, but patted the sand next to Kaedy for Leo. "Let's put your magic to good use, instead of trying to fuck with mine. Her capacity is broken, but her well is still full and filling as ambient magic suffuses her body. It feels like being nauseated but unable to vomit, and starving but unable to eat, all at the same time. She's coming off a lifetime of being addicted to her magic. She needs to have her well emptied and weaned off of the need to use magic. You can help with that, Leo."

"I don't think I can. We have tried to find a way to—"

Daemon was shaking his head. "The Mondaer are great at *using* magic in big, impressive ways, but you keep Tirit Mindel and their innovations out. I'm sure you have your own researchers, but I promise you don't know how to do what I do better than me. I literally wrote the book on podding, though don't look for my name on the cover." He let out a bitter laugh, as though it was an old joke that he had never found funny.

Leo—who had crossed his arms—huffed. "We know about podding. Lots of escapees from Tirit Mindel come to the desert and are among the *daradeio*. It cannot be done with the broken. They cannot connect their magic to that of another."

"True . . . and false," Daemon said, giving Kaedy's hand a squeeze as she let out another whimper. "She will never be able to join a pod on her own, but they can be . . . forced."

"Of course you'd figure out how to force something," North said, though he wasn't entirely sure what a pod was, only that it had something to do with joining magically with another person.

Daemon leveled him with a cold stare. "I am getting tired of this petulant antagonism. It's not like I tried to purposely figure out how to pod someone against their will. Alexander and I discovered it by accident, while developing our theory of podding while on Tirit Mindel."

"You mean Alexander Silvarin? The Last Emperor of Carinn?" The man whose son he had murdered? North's scowl deepened.

Daemon inclined his head. While Leo was busy gaping at him, and even Kaedy's tears stopped, he added, "And the man who took all the credit for *my* research. He was a fucking asshole even before the war. But we were friends while in school, and were among the original three people to figure out podding. We decided not to include how to force one in our published work because of how much potential it had for abuse, and how hard it is to teach. Others have happened upon it over the years, but I hunt them down and either bring them here, or kill them. It's not something I want spreading around."

North crossed his arms, staring pointedly at Daemon, who shrugged and ignored him, turning his attention to Leo. "I'm going to show you how to do it. If I ever catch you doing it for any reason other than helping a broken rifter or saving others from a critical break, I'll snap your neck. Got it?"

"Why would I use it for anything else, if it's so bad?" Leo asked, eyeing Daemon with obvious nerves. His hand found North's, and squeezed tight.

"I don't know. People change once they have power—I know I did. Alright, I'm going to show you by doing it to you. It's the easiest way. You need to make physical contact with the subject's skin, then it's quick." Daemon placed a hand over Leo's forehead. "You turn your magic into the shape of a needle; thin, but sharp. Shove it through their capacity, and pull it back without ever letting go, snagging your subject's power on the way. You'll *want* to let go, since their well will try to dissolve your magic and make it theirs, but hold on tight. It takes some force to push through in both directions, so it's easiest if you do it fast and hard."

Leo let out a startled cry, back arching. Before North could react, though, Daemon had rocked back and Leo sagged, panting. "I . . . You're . . . In my . . ."

"Yes. I have control of your well. I can empty it," Daemon said, holding up a hand over which a flame appeared, and making Leo shake in the process, "or fill it from mine," again, Leo spasmed, but this time in what seemed like pleasure. "And let it go at a distance, if need be."

North jerked to catch Leo as he swayed then collapsed, like a puppet with a cut string. He looked up at Daemon. "You're a sadistic asshole."

"No, I'm not. I'm teaching him in the gentlest way it is possible to do. This is just an uncomfortable process. It would be better to have someone like Fayrian Avilor do this for Kaedy, but she doesn't seem to be in the Mother Rock anymore, so we're left with my method. Now Leo, I'm going to pod with you the normal way, if you know how. I want you to feel closely as I go into Kaedy's well, and how I do it. With your permission, my dear?"

Tsiihsi had joined them by then, and asked to be connected too. North wasn't sure exactly what happened magically once they started, but his Gift did not like it. Their magical statuses got fuzzy and blurred, as though they were caught somewhere between Daemon and Tsiihsi's Type Threes and Leo's Type Two. Kaedy—who didn't read as magical at all anymore—lit up like a circuit lamp to his Gift when Daemon placed a hand on her bare shoulder and forced his way into her magic.

"I can feel it!" she exclaimed, a smile brightening her face. "I can feel my magic."

"It won't last, I'm afraid, but if your friend here learns to do this trick, he can stay connected to you this way when you need it. Be careful, though. Podded rifters are much more fragile and easy to break, so only do it when you are safe and undisturbed. Now, I'm going to siphon off the excess magic in your well to make you more comfortable. Leo, Tsiihsi, watch how. She doesn't have a capacity, so I am having to use the thread of magic I've placed to connect us like the needle of a syringe. It's going to seem incredibly slow and cumbersome, but don't push it too fast or hard. Without a capacity, the structural integrity of her well is at stake. If that goes too, it could be deadly not only to Kaedy, but to anyone in the area. This process won't fix a broken rifter, but it may take the edge off."

In the end, it took most of an hour to teach Leo and Tsiihsi how to drain Kaedy's well. In that time, Kaedy went from a crying wreck to more relaxed than North had seen her since the death of the Red. The other, less fortunate, consequence was that Leo had started staring at Daemon as though he held the answers to all the questions in the universe. He'd seen Tsiihsi look to Daemon that way often during their time on Ayre, and North found it bothered him to see it happen once more to someone he considered a friend.

Near the end of the impromptu lesson, Daari ran up, flushed and laughing from playing in the surf with Bard. Kaedy gave him a genuine smile, but was yawning and getting sleepy.

"Mama, come play with us," the child exclaimed, pulling at his mother's shirt.

"I've got him," Daemon said, giving Kaedy a little smile. "You should eat and rest."

"I don't know if—" North began, worried about Daemon having access to a child after everything he knew about Alehan, but Obri, who had finished handing out food, interrupted.

"Don't worry, North. Daemon is great with kids. He's godfather to three of mine."

"You have *children?*" North asked, incredulous. Obri had *never* struck him as the type to settle down or want a family. "But you spent all your time with us on this island."

Obri laughed. "Daemon left a portal between the two islands open inside my hut, behind a wall hanging. As soon as I heard your snores, I'd sneak home and spend my nights with my wife. Our fourth is due by Midwinter."

In the time it had taken North to absorb the incongruity of

Obri being a husband and father, Daemon had introduced himself to Daari and offered to show him how to make castles in the sand.

As Leo escorted Kaedy somewhere comfortable to rest, North watched first in apprehension, then bewilderment as Daemon rolled up his pant legs, flopped down in the wet sand by the shoreline while completely ignoring the giant circuitry project he had started, and spent a full hour making drip castles with a two-year-old.

A few other people came to sit around North with their breakfasts. The man from before, Trevor, thudded down quite close and shook his head. "Oh no, who handed Dae a kid this time? We won't get him back to work ever again."

"Don't you worry about him? Or don't you know who he is and what he did?" North asked.

A few people shrugged, others looked at him questioningly. It was Obri who answered, "North, we've been over this. Daemon's past is his own. What we know is his present. Everyone here's either been raised on Ayre or brought in the way you were. We've all gone out with Daemon from time to time. We all get the talk and see his bad side, but we also get to know him as a person. Worst or best, though, he *never* hurts or involves children. The kids of Ayre island are the safest in the whole of Carinn."

But he tortured a child to madness to get all this, North wanted to retort. He bit it back, though, gaze returning to Daemon, who had just hoisted Daari onto his shoulder and was running along the beach with the boy, chasing after Bard.

"How do you stand the dissonance? He's a murderer."

Obri opened his mouth to answer, when a deafening boom sounded over the whole island. Every eye turned upward, where a giant White Dragon had just appeared in the sky, outstretched wings casting a shadow over the beach.

It opened its mouth and in a thunderous voice cried, "Jac Drego, *where is my property?*"

CHAPTER TWENTY-SEVEN
What The Walls Hide
GABRIEL

As I watched Cassian Iaming pack his bags for his one-year suspension, I wondered if there was more I could have done to make peace between him and Gabriel. It occurs to me that never once, in the five years I had them both as students, did I look at this proud, talented prince and see the pain he was hiding. I see it now. Raised in the shadow of a sister who was better in every way but one, knowing that the only reason he was the Heir of Seehana instead of Nora was her ailment, would have twisted any child. But then to arrive on Tirit Mindel, eager for a fresh start only to see Gabriel, who came from nothing, rise higher and faster than Cassian in every way . . . I should have seen Cassian's tendency to bully and provoke for what it was: a cry for attention. I have failed him as a teacher, and it is, I fear, too late for me to fix it.

—From the journals of Robin Tirition

"YOU'RE . . . LEAVING HER ALONE WITH HIM?" Gabriel hissed, as soon as the door to Elenor's suite closed behind him and Claire. Reeza struggled out of his arms and bounded across the lawn, right into the fountain with a loud splash. Gabe paid the baby dragon no mind, much more focused on the way the curtains had been pulled shut, blocking their view.

"Absolutely," Claire said, tugging Gabriel to the right. "She's perfectly capable of handling herself and doing whatever she thinks best for the future of Lirin. What could he possibly do to her that's worse than she's already survived? We have somewhere more important to be, on her orders."

"Where?" Gabe asked, as Claire hooked a foot on the vines on their side of the wall and started climbing up the way he and Elenor had snuck in, what felt like a lifetime ago.

"Antidote for Paul. Murder Auntie told her that he'd get his daily dose as long as she made the South happy. Well, she's alone in a room with him, which Elenor just decided to take advantage of. I'm pretty sure that will be good enough to count, if I spin it right. Come on. You're my security detail."

A soaking wet mockling landed on top of the wall, spraying Gabriel and Claire as she shook herself.

"She can come too. Maybe she'll bite Sianta's ankles," Claire added grimly.

"I don't trust Cassian," Gabe panted, as they dropped to the ground on the other side. It didn't hurt as much as he'd expected, though. Rolling his shoulders, he found his back sore but no longer stinging.

"He's not going to physically harm her, is he?"

"Well, no—"

"Then the worst that happens is that she calms him down by fucking him like Murder Auntie wants. Not ideal, but politics have demanded worse," Claire didn't look happy about the prospect; her jaw was clenched and Gabriel got the distinct impression she was trying hard to put on a brave face. Though the thought of Elenor having to appease Cassian Iaming for invading *her* privacy burned, Claire did have a point. She would survive it.

Losing her *doena* would be a much worse blow.

Claire led the way back around and past Elenor's bedroom door. Gabe couldn't hear anything, which was either a good sign or a very bad one. A few turns later, they came to the guest wing, Reeza trotting along behind them. Before turning the last corner, Claire swiveled around. Gabe nearly ran into her.

She reached up, running her fingers through his messy hair to get it to lay straight, and brushed the wrinkles from his shirt. "Try to look like the super-powerful and scary rifter you are, instead of the surprisingly nice and helpful person you're turning out to be, alright? It would be for the best that Sianta gets it through her head that if she takes Elenor down, she'll have to deal with you, whether that's true or not."

"It's true. I haven't fought my whole life to kill one Miri trying to destroy Lirin, just to bow to another."

Claire patted his cheek. "Good boy. Now, scary face."

Gabe wasn't sure how to make one of those, but he did his best to lean into his worry and anger about leaving Elenor alone with Cassian.

He followed behind Claire as she crossed the hall, ignored the guards at the door to the Miri suite, and knocked. A few seconds later, a servant answered.

"I'm here on behalf of Her Highness the Queen Regent to speak to Her Majesty," Claire said, usual attitude vanishing and a polite, polished intonation taking its place.

"And who asks for me?" a woman said from inside. Behind the servant, the Queen of Miriel appeared, standing tall and proud, and already fully dressed.

Claire curtsied, though she was once again in a well-tailored suit instead of a more customary noblewoman's dress. "Claire Enica, newly appointed Heir to House Enica, in the process of petitioning for my Writ."

When had that happened? He had thought Claire was one of the youngest of the Enica daughters. Gabe made a mental note to ask Claire about it, but didn't let his surprise show on his face.

Sianta looked Claire from head to toe, her lips turning up in a sneer. "And you are bothering me because . . . ?"

"I'm here on the Queen Regent's behest, since she's busy . . . entertaining His Highness the Crown Prince, and may be busy for some time. I believe there is a certain brew she said you offered, to help her *doena* while he recovers from his newfound heart condition?"

Sianta's face broke into the smallest of satisfied smiles, and Gabe felt sick. "I'd be delighted to provide it, but I believe I was specific about the fact that I would only hand over that medicine to my niece herself, lest it not make its way to the correct recipient in a timely manner. She can come to me when up and about. Considering how early and abruptly she retired, I do hope she got a good night's sleep. She looked quite . . . worn, last night."

Behind Gabriel, Reeza hissed, expressing Gabe's feelings perfectly.

Claire, though, never broke her facade. With a small bow, she said, "Forgive me, Your Majesty, but the Queen Regent insists that I not leave without it, as she has a busy day ahead and wants to make sure that this matter is taken care of. If you are worried about me being delayed, you are welcome to send one of your men with me to the infirmary. But I promise I will be well protected in my task, since Her Highness kindly lent me the services of her rifter."

She gestured at Gabriel, who tried his best to imitate the stony expression of the imposing bodyguard who had appeared behind Sianta and was glowering at him.

The Queen of Miriel shook her head, then reached into a pocket Gabe had not noticed, and pulled out a small vial. "She so quickly forgets the ethics her parents tried to instill in her. Not a good look, for someone on trial for murdering one of them. Here you are. It is to be injected via syringe. Tell Her Highness that tomorrow it best be her at my door, unless she begins to show herself to be a more amenable hostess.

"As for you, Lady Enica, I wouldn't bother with that Writ. I believe your chances of marrying into the throne have sailed away, if they were even there to begin with. Enjoy these last few weeks of elevated status. Power attained through deals with rifters and murderers will never pay dividends, no matter how skilled one may be in . . . more intimate arenas. Those of Jia heritage might be pretty, but your . . . kind should never have been allowed to infiltrate the ranks of the nobility. Have a good day, Lady Enica."

The door shut in Claire's face.

Gabriel saw the smallest quiver in Claire's bottom lip. The noblewoman inhaled deeply, exhaled, balled her fists, then turned and marched away. They were halfway to the infirmary before she burst out with, "I really, *really,* hate that woman."

"I can see why," Gabe said, watching Claire's shoulders shake, then offered, "Need a hug?"

"So fucking much."

He stopped, and a second later had an armful of noblewoman squeezing the life out of him as though he were a suitable stand-in for strangling Sianta Miri to death. Gabe just wrapped his arms around her in return and stayed there until she stopped vibrating.

"Thanks," Claire muttered, pulling away and wiping her eyes. "I hate everything about this week. This should be the happiest damn time of my life, now that Elenor's a breath away from the throne and free of her parents. Yet it feels like all we're doing is struggling vainly against the tide washing her away. I'm trying to hold it together for El's sake, but fuck . . . Do you have any idea how hard my family and the Tellens have fought to be respected? I'm as Lirinian as that bitch is, but I still have to put up with the *looks* every single fucking day. It's *exhausting.*"

"I bunked with Fedrik for six years. I've heard a few stories." He smiled down at her. "And held a punching bag plenty of times as he worked out his frustration. If you ever need me to do the same, just let me know." Then he gave her a nudge. "Come on, we should get to Paul, then hurry back to Elenor. The sooner we do, the sooner we can kick that bitch and all her minions out of our country."

"Right. Yes." Claire nodded, straightened her blouse, and set off again. Reeza was still following, although the walk across the Palace on very little legs seemed to be wearing the baby mock down.

At the infirmary, Claire handed Gabriel the vial and picked up the yawning dragonette. "I don't know how to use a syringe, and I don't want to leave this to a doctor we don't trust. I have no clue how many people here might be in Sianta's pocket. I'll wait in Djina's old office so Reeza doesn't wreck anything."

Paul was lying in a bed near the end of the long room. Some of the medics and attendants looked at Gabriel askance as he walked toward the *doena,* but a barked order from Claire made them scuttle away.

There were fewer filled cots this time. Gabe just didn't have the nerve to ask whether that was because survivors of his magic had been discharged or . . .

"Where's Elenor? How is she?" Paul asked, as soon as Gabriel reached his bedside. Talking made him cough and clutch at his chest, but he still managed to wheeze out, "Is she taking her medication? Are my shifts being cover—"

"We've got this," Gabe said, pulling up a stool. "I've been dosing out her serindalla myself, and she slept last night. Claire had extra guards posted, and we have what you told us to find well-hidden and secure. You need to focus on resting, or it will upset her."

Paul seemed to relax a little, slumping back against the covers. "Send me that prison guard, Jozen. She's the only one I can think of who probably hasn't been contracted by the Miri. Too new. She should take over for me until I can return to work."

Every word seemed to tire the middle-aged man. Gabriel looked around and spotted a cabinet of medical supplies. Grabbing a bottle of spirits, gauze and a sterilized syringe, he got to work. Though Gabe hadn't done much with his medical training in years other than patching up cuts and bruises, his hands remembered. Unencumbered by bandages and broken bones, he was done in under a minute.

"There we go. Hopefully you start to feel better soon, at least for a little while. We're working on a more permanent solution," Gabe said, unwilling to mention that their only attempt to do so had failed terribly. He did pocket the vial, though, a sheen of the antidote still present. He didn't know how to begin to identify it, but maybe someone else would.

"How is Elenor?" Paul asked, voice low and worried. "Honestly."

Gabe looked down, then reached out to squeeze the *doena's* hand. "She's overwhelmed, but as stubborn as any Lirion I've known. I'm sure she'll come to see you soon. Her fever is under control, and it's not getting worse as far as I can tell. Textbook flare."

Paul nodded, then coughed. "Listen carefully, boy. You owe her your life, and you're a big part of the reason she's in this mess to begin with. I've never met a rifter with one-tenth the power you have . . ." He trailed off, once again struggling to breathe.

Gabe gave Paul's hand another squeeze. "I've already had this conversation with Claire. Yes, I'm going to stay close to her. Yes, I'll protect her. I know what she did for me, and for people I care deeply about. This was never where I expected to be, and fucked if I know why I have all this magic, but I'm not going to sit on my ass when there's work to be done."

Paul gave him a grateful nod, then closed his eyes. "Good."

Gabe waited until the *doena's* breathing evened out into the gentle rhythm of sleep, then stood up to fetch Claire from Djina's office. When Gabe slipped into the room, she left him with Reeza and went to check on Paul herself.

Since the dragon seemed quite happy curled up on a chair, Gabe took the moment to stretch and shake out the stiffness in his shoulders. The last of the bandages were itchy against his chest, so he spent a few minutes removing them and examining the skin beneath. Not so much as a scar marred it, other than the long-healed ones from his childhood burns.

He needed to find out why and how. The next time Daemon appeared, he would shake it out of him, if needed, because Gabe could remember attending to the doctors treating some of the most powerful rifters on the Island, and even they didn't heal as quickly or fully as he had, and definitely not in such a short time.

Claire came back as he was buttoning his shirt. Her eyes were red. As soon as the door was shut, she collapsed against it, running a hand over her face. "Seeing him like that . . . It reminds me of Elenor. When she first got sick they took her away and wouldn't let me see her. When I finally did, I remember crying until Djina taught me to take a pulse, because I was sure she was dead. She would be so still for so long, except for this . . . fluttering and jerking every few breaths. There were days I could only sleep if I had my fingers on her wrist, making sure she was still alive."

Gabe pulled up a chair for her, but Claire shook her head. "No. I don't want to sit. I sat for years, listening to her parents come in and tell us that no one could know that she was ill. *A bad fall that led to infection,* they said. *Playing in the garden with Claire. It happens. They're children.*"

Her shoulders shook. Gabe wasn't sure if it was out of grief or anger, not with her hand still hiding her face. All he could do was say, "Well, we know why Sianta Miri would want to kill her. If that document comes to light, all that is hers would revert to Elenor. But why would Elenor's parents go along with the ruse?"

Claire looked up at him through her fingers. "Don't you get it?"

"No."

"Because politics meant more than people to them. Both of them. Because Wil and El were nothing but tools, and broken tools aren't useful. There's nothing more complicated going on. I . . ." She pushed off the door, walked to the desk, then looked up at him. "I wish Fedrik had just taken her and run. Every day, I think about doing it and hate that I care more about her happiness than her safety. She's so . . . so damn stubborn about duty to this mess of a country when it has done nothing but hurt her over and over again. She heaps so much on her shoulders and I'm scared that one day they'll just . . . snap. I was almost sure it would happen when the Tellens were killed. I didn't dare show her how much I was hurting over that because I knew that in her head, she was already flaying herself with a decision *her father* made. My every tear would have been another lash. Even if I took her to the ends of the earth, she wouldn't stay put because her parents somehow convinced her that all of this mess is hers to solve alone and it makes me so fucking angry that their decisions are *still* hurting her. Everything they've done, she's found a way to take the blame. Even now, when one of them is missing and the other is ash. *It shouldn't be this way.*"

Claire grabbed a copper paper weight and threw it with a grunt against the closest wall. The mockling jumped straight up, puffing and snarling. More alarming, sparks leapt off the wall, the bright flash imprinting itself on Gabriel's retinas before he could squeeze his eyes shut.

Crash. Bang. Hiss.

He raised his arm to shield his face, but nothing hit it. Seconds later, the tinkling sound of metal shards falling to the floor filtered through the ringing in his ears.

"What happened in there?" someone called from outside.

"Claire, are you alright?" Gabriel asked, coughing as smoke swirled through the cramped office. No one answered. Looking around, he realized Claire was gone. Damn it.

He coughed again, the smoke thick and sulphury. The moment he thought it, a strong breeze burst out of Gabriel in every direction, sending him and the mockling stumbling. Furniture and loose items alike went careening around the enclosed space. Belatedly, he realized he was channeling magic and tried to pull it back. The kinetic push slowed, then stopped.

Around the room, everything not bolted down had crashed to the floor and bashed against the walls. Reeza righted herself and gave Gabriel a disgruntled look.

"Listen, I don't know what I'm doing any more than you do," he whispered, not caring one bit that he was talking to an animal. He'd raised goats smarter than some people before Nillenia had been destroyed, and mocks were definitely smarter than goats.

Pounding started at the door. "Lady Enica? Are you alright?"

Oh shit.

Even though he knew she had disappeared, Gabe looked around anyway. How was he supposed to explain Claire being gone? Gabriel wasn't sure *he* even understood it all the way, and he doubted Elenor would want her lover's ability to become public knowledge.

His gaze continued to dart about the room, as though an idea might be hiding in a corner, then jumped. On the wall the paperweight had hit—which had previously been covered in tiny jars and bottles—a strange-looking panel was hanging open. It was still smoking, copper and gold wires twisted around lumps of molded cerulean. It took a second for his shock-addled brain to recognize what that meant, but it was definitely and recognizably a magical circuit.

What is that doing in the Palace infirmary?

"Lady Enica, I insist that you open the door. We heard an explosion," an authoritative voice called.

Shit.

Someone tried the door, rattling it, but Claire must have locked it. Gabriel had just started to really panic when a familiar voice broke over the others on the far side of the door.

"Let me through," Tomaz Catoali said. "Claire, are you in here?" The shadow of the nobleman replaced the others through the opaque glass.

Gabe stepped up close and in as low a voice as he could use and still be heard, said, "It's Gabriel. Claire's a little . . . indisposed? Like she was last night. Could you get us some privacy?"

A pause, and then the noble said, "Back to work everyone. I'll take care of this."

Gabe flipped the lock and let Tomaz slip into the office. He looked around, black eyes moving from the panel of circuitry on the wall, to the debris scattered around the room, to Gabriel. They stopped on Gabe's face, and Tomaz muttered something under his breath. Louder, he asked, "Claire's gone?"

"Into thin air."

"Then we best hurry. Don't want you anywhere near here. You're already in enough trouble without another noble's disappearance. Better that they think they just missed seeing you leave along with Claire." Tomaz ran his fingers through his short, loose curls, then let out a curse under his breath. "This is a mess."

Gabe opened his mouth to point out that the only way out of the room was through the door, when Tomaz seemed to come to a decision and marched to the panel by the wall.

"Over here. And grab the dragon," the nobleman ordered. "Hold out your hand."

"What—"

"Shh. We have to be fast. People will be coming on the other side, too. Shit. It will take me hours to explain showing you this."

"Showing me wha—"

Tomaz pulled a pen out of his pocket. He took Gabriel's offered hand and without warning stabbed the nib straight into Gabe's thumb.

"Ow!"

"Shush," Tomaz repeated. He yanked aside a tapestry, trailed a finger up and down as though counting bricks, then pressed Gabe's bleeding thumb between two of them while whispering, "Please work, please work, *please* work."

A line of copper lit up like it had in Elenor's bedroom when Gabriel had bled on it. Tomaz leaned forward, pressing on the wall. It slid back smoothly on a set of tracks, exposing a narrow and dark passageway behind it.

"Go that way. Turn left at the first intersection and you'll find yourself at a dead end. There will be a triangular panel on the wall. Smear some blood on it and push if it lights up. If it doesn't, the gold is out of power and you'll have to throw some magic at it. The door should open into a linen cabinet. Stay there until I come get you. *Don't* stay in the tunnels. *Don't* make noise, and for the sake of all that is holy *do not* go down the stairs. If you hear voices coming, run."

"What—" Before he could finish, the unimposing and usually soft-tempered noble pushed Gabriel and Reeza into the space between the walls and pulled the doorway closed behind him, casting the tiny hallway into darkness.

Gabe's head was spinning. He stood still, arms full of wriggling dragon. Through the wall, he heard Tomaz's muffled voice say, "Busted circuit lamp took out part of the wall. Damn things are a menace, aren't they? No need to disturb the court, though. I'll have one of my family's construction crews here within the hour, but until then, best not to come in here, in case any of the broken bottles were dangerous."

After that, his words became too muffled to understand. Gabe looked around, but he might as well have had his eyes closed. Despite knowing he wasn't in the Subterranea, that dark, rancid cell closed in about him once more. Only Reeza, still struggling to get free, kept Gabriel grounded in the present. He pulled her up higher, pressing his nose into her fur and inhaling deeply. She smelled of the grass that she had rolled in outside Elenor's room, still slightly damp from the fountain. Not rotting human flesh.

"Alright, little one. Questions after we get out of here." He turned in the direction Tomaz had pointed—or hoped he did. Extending his left hand to the wall so that he wouldn't miss the turn, he edged forward.

The air was stale and sweltering, the strong scent of mildew and dust hanging suspended in the humidity. Inch by blind inch, Gabe slid his feet along the stone floor. Distant echoes seemed to carry down the passage, but he couldn't work out from which direction they came, let alone if they were inside or coming through the thick palace walls.

There was some kind of metal band at shoulder height with regular outcroppings—maybe lights?—but Gabe didn't dare take the time to examine them. Not when Reeza was kicking him in the stomach to be let down. The last thing he needed was to lose Elenor's pet in a dark passage inside the walls.

What *was* this place? And if Tomaz knew of it, did others? If Fed had, and Gabriel ever saw him again, they would have words. This would have been perfect for hiding rebels in the Palace. Surely Wil—

His attempts to distract himself failed as his shoulders started to shake and beads of sweat appeared on his brow, panic creeping higher. Every step got faster and more desperate, each breath a struggle. *I'm not back in the dungeons. I'm not stuck in the wall in my cottage. There is no fire. Mark Lirion is dead.*

It didn't help. Gabe's body seemed determined to panic whether his mind agreed or not. He almost missed the turn when it finally came because he was stumbling along so fast. When his hand ran out of wall, though, his balance failed. Gabe went sprawling. He twisted so as not to land on the baby mock, badly bruising both a shoulder and a knee for his troubles.

Unsure his legs would support him, Gabriel grabbed Reeza by the scruff and guided her along at a crawl. It was only a few yards further until they met a dead end. After a few minutes of desperately feeling about in the dark, Gabe's fingers found a smooth triangular panel. The moment his blood touched it, the metal glowed faintly. With the light, so came a little relief from the anxiety squeezing his chest, enough to remember Tomaz's instructions when the wall did not immediately budge. Pulling as little as he could from his well, Gabriel channeled magic into the metal plate.

It lit up as bright as a winter fire and, with minimal grinding, the wall slid open. Reeza bounded ahead into a cramped linen cabinet, Gabe following close behind. He pressed the door closed with his foot, then lay back on the stone floor, one hand flung over his spinning head.

He was still lying like that ten minutes later when Tomaz found him. "What happened to you?" the nobleman asked, stepping into the cabinet.

"Dark, enclosed spaces aren't my friends," Gabe said, cracking his eyes open. "What was that? Escape tunnels, or something?"

"Or something," Tomaz muttered. "Up you get. Claire hasn't returned yet, so we best get you back to Elenor. I don't like the thought of you wandering the Palace alone."

That got him moving, a different kind of fear rising.

Tomaz didn't lead him back to the princess's chambers the direct way. They took half-a-dozen roundabout turns until they got to what seemed like the accepted back-door into Elenor's suite.

"Up and over the wall with you. Duncan Eurieha is back at

court today and ranting and raving about the presence of an unregistered rifter in the Palace. *Don't* go anywhere alone, Gabriel. Understood? The best place you can be is right next to Elenor, for both of your sakes."

Gabriel wanted to ask more questions, but his worry over the princess alone with Cassian won out. He clambered over the wall, reached down for the dragonette when Tomaz handed her to him, then let Reeza soar down to the grass.

The back door was cracked open. No sounds came from within. Gabe crept forward, then peeked inside. Relief flooded him when he saw Elenor sitting on the edge of the couch and Cassian nowhere to be seen, but it vanished as she turned to him, face ashen.

"What happened?"

Her arms reached up to hug herself, and she shook her head, lips pressed tightly shut.

"Did he break off the engagement?" he asked, honestly not knowing which answer he hoped for. Yes, would mean that Paul likely had less than a day to live. No, meant Elenor was still stuck under the thumb of the Miri and about to lose everything. There was no good outcome.

She shook her head again. "I told him what he wanted to hear and did what my aunt wanted me to do."

It was only then that Gabriel noticed that under her robe, she was no longer wearing her nightgown. He clenched his teeth, but tried not to let his anger at Cassian or this whole fucked up situation show as he carefully knelt in front of Elenor. "What do you need? How can I help?"

"I . . ." Her shaking was getting worse, eyes staring through Gabriel. Dissociated, dazed, miserable. "I need out. I need air. I can't . . . can't . . ."

Keeping his movement slow and deliberate, he took her hands and gave them a squeeze. "Then I'll get you out of here."

CHAPTER TWENTY-EIGHT
Visit From The White
DAEMON

Are you sure about this? While I trust my powers, I know how long it can take people to live up to their names. If I die too early, are you sure he can be trusted? I am not certain that I am comfortable leaving the Mondaer an ally that, by your own words, "will use every tool at his disposal to fulfill his own agenda." What if his agenda doesn't line up with ours? Will you watch over him, Moe? I hesitate, because you could be described much the same way.

—From a message to Merihem "Moe" Crystal, from Fulsixia the Red

THE MASSIVE BULK OF KENNOTOZA THE WHITE in her draconic form loomed over Ayre Island. She was lithe and lean, with the body of a snake, the maned head of a lion, and huge wings that billowed like silk in the gale of their beating.

"Where are you, Jac? How *dare* you steal from me?"

Her voice boomed so loudly that Daemon's ears popped and the boy on his shoulders clasped his pudgy hands over his own, crying out in pain. Dae swung him down to his hip, previous experience with the Gods in their true forms giving him enough wherewithal to not drop the child. Barely.

Around him, people were screaming and scrambling for the treeline. Only Kaedy was heading in Daemon's direction, face a mask of distraught horror.

Daemon held out a hand to her. "Stop. I'll bring him to you."

Kaedy stopped, one bare foot on each side of the thick wire cables that Dae had been working on all day. The cables ran into the ocean on one end, and through the portal to the Mother Rock on the other, the two ends disconnected from each other until Daemon could finish building the circuitry controls.

Looking up at the Dragon, he used magic to send a message to her, since there was no way she would be able to hear him yell over the wind from her wings. **I'm sure you're angry, but let me give this child back to his mother before you eat me.**

The Dragon roared in response, but she didn't launch forward to bite him, so Daemon took that as consent. He backed up, each step careful. Daari was clinging to Dae's shirt and bawling. Doing his best to keep the worst of the blowing sand out of the boy's eyes with his other arm, Daemon's gaze never left the Dragon.

Out of the periphery of his vision, though, he saw his people racing for the various open portals. Some were pulling out coins, like Daemon had instructed them to do in this situation. Others were pushing the Mondaer back onto the Mother Rock, or pulling those too stunned to move toward safety. If the White was here to break the Accords, he had to buy the people of Ayre enough time to scatter.

"How dare you come into my home? How dare you take that which is mine?" the White screamed, her voice loud enough to make the sand and water vibrate. It was a physical force, a battering ram of noise that caused Daemon's feet to stumble.

Centuries of learning to keep calm under pressure, though, gave him a small advantage.

The thick copper cables glistened in the sunlight. He had set up the end of the circuitry that connected to Aina Brisbhan himself under dozens of watchful Mondaer eyes. It didn't reach down into all the veins, but it was hooked into the large one that striated the roof and that Quindo was letting him experiment on. Would that be enough to kill a dragon?

Daemon had no idea, but it didn't matter because there was no cerulean circuit hooked up to it, nor was it yet connected to the copper ring around Ayre. It would need something or someone to channel that magic, and that much of a load was sure to break whoever tried it . . . if it didn't kill them outright. This close to Aina Brisbhan, the explosive release of magic from a broken rifter could trigger hundreds, maybe thousands more. It would be catastrophic.

"Don't you dare—" Kennotoza began at the same second that Daemon launched himself toward the thick copper cable. He skidded on the sand, twisting to keep from crushing Daari. The Dragon lunged, but she was too late.

His fingers wrapped around the cable.

The Dragon stopped mid-roar. Then she transformed. In the place of the enormous beast, Kennotoza the Bode stood on the beach in her human form, luminescent hair and white robes billowing around her. "Stop!"

Daemon's lungs weren't expanding correctly. Adrenaline thundered through him, mixing with bowel-loosening terror. Moving at a glacier's pace, he got to his knees, then his feet. "Kaedy, take your son and back away slowly."

Not that it would do much good.

The young woman's hands were shaking as she wrapped them around Daari's waist and pried the child's death-grip from Daemon's shirt. He didn't turn to look at her, but he did wait until the crunch of her retreating footsteps had grown distant before speaking again. Hoisting the heavy, unwieldy bundle of copper wires against his hip, Daemon looked Kennotoza squarely in her multi-colored eyes. "Take one more step toward me, or threaten any of my people, and I'll discharge this vein of gold to break my capacity. That might not be enough to kill you, but the chain reaction when every rifter on this island and in the Mother Rock blows probably would."

Kennotoza put up both hands. The placating gesture was enough to give Daemon a jolt of confidence in his half-assed plan. Her words, less so. "That's not a future you want, Jac. You wouldn't survive it."

"But neither would you, right?"

"Innocents would die."

Daemon let out a bitter, high-pitched laugh laced with panic. "When's that ever bothered you, or do you forget the scores of Silvarin children murdered on your orders? I'm serious. It's not a ploy. I *will* end you, Kennotoza." Visualizing the rift he needed and pulling power from his well to activate it, Daemon held up one hand, fist clenched. "Even if you kill me, you'll go out with me. I've set a rift to the kinetic motion of my hand. If the fingers open, I release the whole vein of gold instantaneously. Look into the future, if you don't believe me."

She closed her eyes. Through her translucent eyelids, though, Daemon could see her pupils moving in quick, jerky motions.

An interminable fifteen seconds later, Kennotoza's eyes snapped open. "This is not a wise course of action, Jac. My death would be catastrophic for our world."

"I'd be dead. Why would I care?"

The last few people had retreated through the doorways. Daemon snapped most of them shut, leaving only the one to the Mother Rock. Selfish, definitely, but the Mondaer at the Mother Rock would have a slightly better chance of surviving than the people of Ayre. If a rifter was clever enough and had gold at their disposal, they could ride out a magical explosion by channeling everything that came at them into the gold. They *might* make it. "You took all that I had left of my family, and you didn't predict that I'd be willing to die to avenge it? Some Bode you are, Kenny."

If the nickname bothered the Goddess before him, she did not let it show. She stood perfectly still, and Daemon got the impression that while her eyes were fixed on him, they were still looking into the future.

"I saw many things, Jac Drego. Some of them good, most bad. I will tell you what will happen if you set off the Mother Rock, though. First, you will die. It will rip through your capacity and explode your well. The open door to the Plane at the center of your being will be burst wide, and magic will flood this place. There are a dozen or more rifters within the first hundred feet of that blast who will suffer the same fate. Their detonation will carry further still, and in a single selfish act, you will strip the Mondaer of almost all the rifters that live in and around their capital city. If I die too, that might be enough of a backlash to set off the Mother Rock in its entirety. Where the Mondaer Desert stands, a crater will remain. Do you care so little for human life that you are willing to take that risk for revenge? I know your plan, Jac. I know you intend to use the circuitry around your island to catch the burst of power from a dying God and safely contain it. I also know you have not yet finished your work, nor do you yet have the information needed to make a circuit on that scale work. Are you prepared to be the cause of hundreds of thousands of innocent deaths trying?"

"Are you prepared to make me, just because I broke into your house?" Daemon retorted, knuckles of his clenched hand white from the pressure he was exerting upon them.

"You had no right to steal one of my dragons."

"You had no right to take what little I had left of my family or fuck with my life. I'm not your creature. I'm Xirra's."

Kennotoza bared her teeth. "And clearly just as bad at listening as she is. I showed you what's at stake, did I not? What I am working to prevent? I'm trying to save the world. *You keep interfering with my plans.*"

Daemon bared his teeth right back. "I've seen what you've chosen to show me, and heard what you've decided to tell me. I have no way to know if any of it is true, and definitely don't believe that you're working in any of our best interests. I heard the story of what happened from Xirra. How you betrayed her. It hasn't filled me with overwhelming confidence in your trustworthiness."

Kennotoza shook her head, translucent hair swaying in a rainbow of colors. "That's not . . . It was different then. I didn't understand the future like I do now. There's more to this than Xirra has told you, Jac. So much more."

"I know there fucking is. I heard you. You mentioned *Alehan Silvarin returning.*" His voice broke on the name, a touch of hysteria entering his tone. "What do you know? What aren't you telling us? If you have any intention of walking out of here alive, you better start talking. I'm no longer in a mood to be toyed with."

Kennotoza's eyes flew wide, and he thought he heard her mutter, "Here we go . . ." before she squared her shoulders. "I am not toying with you, Jac Drego. I'm trying to save the world. Every time you interfere with my plans, it narrows the already minuscule margin of error I have. Fulsixia never should have left you the Mother Rock. I should have watched her more closely. It worries me that even after her death, she is somehow pulling strings. It makes me think she's allied with a force I have long feared, and who has a history of wrecking chaos across a multitude of worlds. If you continue down the path the Red set before you, Daemon, you will lose so much more than you already have. I see you here, on this island, staring out into an empty sea. Alone, powerless, after having lost everything you ever cared about. That is the end of your path if you continue like this."

"I asked about Alehan, not your vague mumblings," Daemon snapped, refusing to let her distract him. He'd seen the millions of threads in her cavern. She had said it herself that the future was not set in stone, so why should he give any credence to her predictions?

Kennotoza crossed her arms. "The future is no laughing matter."

"Do I look like I'm laughing? Talk. And if I don't like the answers, don't think I won't blow us both skyward. Why should I hang on to this fucked-up immortal life when you destroyed the things that helped me remember Aislin and Julian? Do you have any idea how hard it's been not to forget their faces? The way they spoke? The things they did? So many people from back then are nothing but vague ghosts, and it gets worse with every year. You stole my family from me all over again, so don't test me, Kennotoza."

A flash of genuine fear rippled across the Goddess's face, the ethereal wind moving her hair and clothes diminishing. "Perhaps doing that was a mistake. I reacted in anger, and to keep you away from my family. Fulsixia's death threw so many wrenches into my plans that I may have miscalculated."

"You think? At least you can admit when you've been a petty bitch," Daemon snapped. "Now if only you would *stop wasting my time.*"

He could tell he was getting under her skin. Kennotoza had always been proud. Out of all of them, only Xirra was more of a stickler for decorum than the Bode. It was why they had worked together from time to time, while his patron refused to *ever* have dealings with Zorbennen the Black. Knowing what he did now, though, the fact that Xirra and Kennotoza had allied briefly during the fall of the Silvarin didn't quite line up. There was something more happening with the Gods, and Daemon was going to find out what it was . . . if he survived this encounter.

"Alright, Jac. I will speak, but know that I do not like being threatened, and I will not forget it."

"Don't worry, neither will I," Daemon snarled. "Talk."

"Alehan is alive."

Daemon almost dropped the coil of wires. "Impossible."

"Is it? You're alive too, are you not? The day you became immortal, you did it by yanking both you and the boy into the Plane. What happened to you happened to him as well. He lives, though no longer on this continent. When he and his family were sentenced to a watery grave, the Stormwall parted for him. He has been in the care of the Gold ever since, alive as you are. Xirra has told you about the Pantheon by now, right?"

Daemon took an involuntary step back. "Wait. No. He can't also—"

"He is. Between Zorbennen and I, we have charted his course. He has been kept alive because of what you did—what you made him, and what he made you. Because neither of you should exist. You trouble us greatly."

Daemon's head was spinning. He almost released the pressure on his upheld fist, dooming them all, but stopped himself at the last second. Legs too unsteady to hold him up, he sat down in the sand with a thud. He could still remember watching from the Garendor pier as the boat containing Alexander, Cianira, her brother Mathe, Alehan, and a repentant Gabril Lirion had disappeared into the Stormwall. That had been the day he had permanently abandoned the name Jac Drego and become Daemon Indigo, servant of the Blue.

Alehan couldn't still be alive.

"Jac, if you do what I've told you, you need never cross his path. Walk away from all of it. From Xirra, from Elenor, from Gabriel. Ignore what the Red left you. Step away entirely from the political arena and this crisis may yet be averted. Alehan is coming, Jac. He will be brought back to our shores by the Gold and if you do not remove yourself from this mess, you will face him again. But this time he will not be a powerless boy, but a man willing and able to destroy far more than I have taken from you, and doom us all in the process."

"If I step away, Xirra will kill me." He lived by her pleasure, just another one of her playthings. That was a fact he could not escape.

"There are places you could run where she cannot follow. Places deep within the Plane. You could leave this world behind and never look back. If you do not, you will suffer far more than you can imagine. Do you think it gave me pleasure to destroy your home? I do not give warnings lightly. I am trying to save our world."

"If I'm so dangerous, why not kill me?" Daemon demanded. "Because we all know the Accords are going to fall, and soon."

Kennotoza shook her head. "Trust me when I say that I would be delighted to. If I am the one to break the Accords, though, retribution would strike down my family. Elenor must survive now that this nightmare has begun."

"Which means you're going to back the fuck away and stop bothering me after today, because I am not hampered by that concern. If you're telling the truth, all you're doing here is having a hissy-fit, and there's no bite to your bark. So get the fuck off my island and out of my life. I'm going to do what I want, when I want to, and with whomever I want to, under the rules of the Accords. My people aren't ever going to be in one place long enough for you to kill them, and if you destroy my city like you did my house, we will rebuild it. I started from nothing, and will again if need be. If you tell Xirra about us, it will be the last thing you do." Just to make his point, he added, "With how much the Gods and their other minions have been pissing me off of late, it would be my pleasure to go on a killing spree the likes of which this world has never seen."

Kennotoza studied him, then shook her head in disgust. "You really are her creature. You think the solution to every problem is destruction, and it has blinded you to the cost of that belief. You take lives without care, destroying every possible future they could have lived."

"Oh, spare me the high-brow lecture. You slaughtered an entire family down to the last baby you could find. The Silvarin Massacre was *your* fault, as much as it was Xirra's, and it was your family who benefited from it. Now get the fuck off my island, you hypocritical lizard."

"Jac, I am one of the Gods of your world. You don't speak to me that way, or so help me, I will—"

Daemon twitched his fingers. "One."

"You must listen to me—"

"Two."

Giving him a glare that made his blood run cold with the certainty that she was going to kill him one day, the White Dragon vanished.

Daemon waited a whole minute, every muscle tense to see if she would return. Then, with extreme care, he released the rift he held in his mind, relaxed his cramping hand, and fell back onto the warm sand.

A twig cracked. His eyes, which had closed, snapped open. Instincts that had once been honed by combat had him twisting about, one hand still on the bundle of copper, the other pointed at the source of the noise.

A pair of brown eyes stared out at him from between two trees. At first, he let out a relieved sigh thinking it was Kaedy. Then he recognized the face and his lips pulled back into a snarl. "I see you there, Claire Enica. What the *fuck* are you doing on my island, and what did you overhear?"

CHAPTER TWENTY-NINE
Streets Of Harvest
ELENOR

Harvest for the comfortably wealthy is a time of celebration. Of plenty. Of indulgence. I remember when I saw it that way. Now, after years living by the whims of the earth and sky, I see Harvest as the last gasp of air before the plunge into deep waters. One final prayer that spring will come again, and the currents won't have pulled us too deep to see it.

—From a letter to Robin Tirition, from Talia Navarl

ELENOR WASN'T ENTIRELY SURE how Gabriel had gotten her out of the Palace. Everything had been a fuzzy daze until he'd helped her out of a carriage in front of the All Gods Temple. Gabe had walked her through the large room with the hood of her coat up over her head and Jo following close behind, only to walk right out the other side and into the streets of Hardor.

At any other time, Elenor might have questioned where they were going. She might have worried about the lack of escort, or what would happen at the Palace when they realized she was gone. None of those thoughts penetrated the numbness, though, as they walked along a rain-swept street and into one of the city parks.

"How are your legs holding up? Do you need a break?" Gabriel asked, brow scrunched in worry under his own coat. The pitter-patter of raindrops on leaves muffled some of the sounds of the city, but the drizzle wasn't nearly heavy enough to keep the citizens of Hardor off its streets. The park was full of booths, canopies up to protect wares and customers alike from the weather.

"I'm fine," Elenor whispered, voice hoarse.

Gabriel reached down to take her hand. "If you're not, that's alright."

She couldn't bring herself to answer.

They walked further into the park, past a covered pavilion where people were watching a Harvest play. On stage, dancers in colorful, flowing silks were performing a mock fight in front of a backlit rice paper screen, shadow puppets creating the appearance of a mighty battle. The orange and red lights flashed before her eyes to the staccato rhythm of the ornamental swords. Each clip and clap of wooden blades pounded against the empty hollow shell Elenor couldn't seem to break free of, a numb curtain separating her from the teeming life outside.

The smell of green tea and spices drifted in steaming clouds from tents where people gathered around Seven Rivers tables while waiting out the rain. Beyond them, children played between the trees.

"I love how the city comes alive the weeks leading up to Harvest," Jo said, sidestepping a group of youngsters as they raced by. One of them hit a puddle just right, splashing water up at Elenor and drenching the bottom of the simple blue dress she wore. Jo swore, then yelled after them. "Oy, watch it."

"It's alright, Jo. They're just children," Elenor managed to say, "and just some water."

"But you're—" the guard stopped herself, leaned in closer, and said, "Really, really not supposed to be out here. Are you sure this is wise, Your Highness? I feel like your *doena* wouldn't—"

"Paul used to take me out into the city all the time. He didn't like me going without my guards, that's all. We used to put on masks and ride down on the trams at festival time, and when I couldn't do that anymore, Paul would carry me to the gates of Tellen Manor for the parades, so I could sit on top of the walls and watch."

"Guards *plural,* is the point I'm trying to make," Jo said, but Gabriel cut in.

"You worked for the city watch, right Jo? And I spent most of my life *avoiding* the watch. Either side of trouble we might find, one of us will be equipped to handle it. More people would draw attention, and so will talking about it. Come on, this way." His hand was still tight around Elenor's as he led her onto a side path, dodging around a cloaked woman hurrying in the opposite direction. A few turns later, they were out of the park and onto the Silverway.

"Where are you taking her?"

"Almost there."

"That wasn't an answer," Jo complained.

Elenor didn't chime in. In truth, it was restful not to know where she was going, nor have to decide what to do. She could just watch the world go by and focus on putting one foot ahead of the other. The pain and disorientation of the wasting fever flare didn't seem so bad when all she had to do was follow.

They finally stopped at the covered stoop of a small seamstress shop, tucked between two other cramped, colorful storefronts. Three wood mannequins stood in the window, wearing dresses that were pretty, but nothing a fashionable lady at court would be caught dead in.

"Tammy?" Gabriel said, as he pushed the door open. "You here?"

A head of riotous brown curls and a pair of huge round spectacles with thick wood rims popped up from behind a pile of fabric bolts. *"Gabriel?"*

The woman who rounded the counter at a run was short and plump, with a long tape measure draped around her neck and bits of thread sticking to her dress. She launched herself at Gabriel, giving him a hug that sent him stumbling back into Elenor and Jo.

"Easy, Tamara. Let us in before you maul me. It's raining."

"Oh. Yes, of course. Who do you have with you? And how are you here? Gods above, we all thought you were back in jail when you didn't make it out with the rest. Mum said—"

"So Mari made it here?" Gabriel asked.

"Mari Baker?" Jo added from behind Elenor, while closing the door. "They didn't catch her again?"

"Blessed Red no. She's fine. Well, as fine as can be expected with what happened to Pa. She's right upstairs," the seamstress said, then her eyes fell on Elenor and widened to large brown saucers, magnified as they were by thick lenses. "Oh dear. Is that . . ."

"Tamara, this is Elenor Lirion. Elenor, this is Tamara Baker, the daughter of one of the women you freed, skilled seamstress, and all around treasure of a human being," Gabriel said, reaching forward to pinch Tamara's rosy cheek.

The young woman batted his hand away. "Goodness. You couldn't have given a girl some warning before bringing literal royalty to her door? Welcome to my humble shop, Your Highness." Tamara curtsied and nearly knocked over a mannequin in the cramped space.

"I'm not here as royalty. You don't have to do that. In fact, I'm not sure why I'm here at all . . ." Elenor said, sinking back into her hood. She had thought Gabriel was going to take her somewhere quiet, where she could come out of this fog without her aunt hovering over her shoulder. So why were they in a shop talking to the family of someone her family had imprisoned and tortured? How was that going to hel—?

Tamara reached forward and took both of Elenor's hands, squeezing them tightly between her warm, calloused ones. "Then you are all the more welcome, especially coming here with our Gabriel. Come in, come in. Mum will want to see you. And you. Are you Jo?"

"You . . . know my name?" the guard asked, looking alarmed.

"'Course I do. You only came into the bakery pretty much every single day. I did work there on the weekends, you know. Mum said you slipped her extra food and were always talking to her while she was in that hellhole. Says you kept her sane. Now, flip the sign closed and the lock for me, will you? Let's go upstairs, and I'll get the kettle on. Coats?" Tamara asked, all in the same breath. Before Elenor knew it, her coat was hanging on a hook by the door, and Gabriel was leading her up the most cramped, steep staircase she had ever seen, into an equally tiny apartment.

The room couldn't have been larger than Elenor's bathroom, but it had a wood stove, several plush armchairs, a table, and a couch crammed in. A woman of Tamara's same build but with gaunt cheeks and no hands was sitting in one of the armchairs. She had been staring out the small window, but when Gabriel made it to the landing she stood and gasped. "Gods be praised."

"Mari." Gabe sighed happily in return, running forward a few steps to give the middle-aged baker a fierce hug.

Elenor just stood there, not sure what she was supposed to do until Tamara squeezed by her. "Right, tea all around. Do you take milk and sugar?"

"Ah . . . both. Would you, um, like some help?" Elenor stared at the cast iron stove with apprehension, but offering seemed like the polite thing to do.

Tamara laughed. "The Queen Regent of Lirin helping me make tea. I'll be telling my grandkids that, if I ever have any. Mugs are over on that shelf. Would you get five down?"

Elenor hadn't expected to actually be put to work. The rush of relief as she moved about following instructions, however, was so intense that some of the fog over her thoughts started to clear. By the time steam was rising from the cups and ginger biscuits had been stacked up onto a chipped plate, her ears weren't even ringing with Cassian's—

"Come here, child. Let me look at you," Mari said, beckoning Elenor over and interrupting her train of thought before it could spiral back to what had happened.

She scooted around Gabriel's knees, where he reclined on the worn couch, then sat on the edge of it, squeezed in next to him. She would have remained standing, but with the slope of the roof, that would have ended in disaster.

Mari Baker's had been one of hundreds of faces Elenor had not known during the prison break. If not for Gabriel's attention, she doubted she would have remembered it. What she did recall were the stumps where hands should have been, and Jo's story about the fish pies.

"I'm so sorry for what you went through, and what you lost, Mrs. Baker," Elenor began, though it didn't feel like enough for the magnitude of what she had allowed to happen to her people, while turning a blind eye to her father's cruelty.

Mari reached up and touched Elenor's cheek with one of her bandaged stumps, tilting her head to the side. "I got your nose wrong."

"What?"

"Years ago, when your return to court was announced and there was a city-wide celebration for it, I made cookies with your face on them. From the picture in the papers, you know? I got your nose wrong."

"Mrs. Baker, you don't need to make small talk," Elenor tried to say, but was shushed.

"I'm not. I take pride in my work. I want to make sure that next time, I get it right," Mari said, then looked down at the bruises still fading on Elenor's neck, and her arm in a sling. "Were you hurt for what you did for us?"

"I was hurt that night, but it wasn't as a punishment. Besides, it's nothing compared to—"

"Suffering isn't a competition, so I will have no more of that, child. What happened to me has no bearing on the fact that a young lady should not be walking around with bruises and eyes so sad, especially not when she's brought hope back to so many."

Before Elenor could protest, Mari pointed at a stack of newsheets piled up on the tiny coffee table. Elenor reached for them, and saw the Ondai Tribune's heading. "The article you released about the events leading to your father's death is all anyone's been talking about. There was cheering in the street when we heard you'd been made Queen Regent and reversed the taboo on your brother's name."

Elenor hung her head, setting the paper back down. "I'm not the one you should be thanking or cheering. It was Gabriel who suggested freeing all the prisoners, and Beth Rinelisi who drafted most of that article. I just gave them the story. You're assigning me credit for things I do not deserve."

Mari looked over at Gabriel and Jo, shaking her head. "I see what you mean."

"Excuse me?" Elenor asked. What had they said about her while she had helped Tamara?

"They're worried about you, dearie," Mari said. "Specifically about how little you seem to expect from others, when it comes to basic compassion and kindness."

Elenor had no answer to that. She hid her confusion in the flurry of activity as mugs were passed around. Wrapping her chilled hand around the warm ceramic, Elenor took a sip, made a face, and reached for the sugar bowl at the exact same time as Gabriel did.

"You first," he offered with a smile. "I keep forgetting that you like as much sugar in your tea as I do. Fedrik used to complain about it constantly."

Elenor let out a hoarse chuckle. "Yes, he did mention a classmate who also 'ruined his beverages' a time or two as well."

"Sweet drinks are a comfort no one should be denied when heartsore," Tamara stated, smiling as she dipped a biscuit in her cup and popped it in her mouth.

The warmth of the cup was seeping into Elenor's skin and up her arm. She leaned back onto the couch, pressed between the armrest on one side and Gabriel on the other.

After taking a sip, she asked, "Forgive the question, but why am I here? I understand why you'd want to come, Gabriel, but why bring me?"

Gabe looked at her in consternation. "Because you said you needed out and have been through a hellish few days. I thought you could use a warm cup of tea where no one would know to look for you, and to hear and see for yourself that your actions are having a positive impact. Not to mention, Mari here has the best head on her shoulders and the most strategic mind of anyone I've ever met. It might help with figuring out our next move. Besides, I knew she would want to see you."

Elenor very much doubted that last one. She certainly wouldn't have wanted to see someone who had sat on their hands doing nothing while their father was killing and terrorizing family and friends.

Mari, though, was nodding. "I've been trying to find a way to get a person into the Palace to check on both of you ever since our escape. Daren's been raising a stink against you, your Highness, but the Rebellion doesn't like that the Miri are here one bit, and want to help boot them out. As soon as we saw the papers and the way you lifted the taboo on Wilam's name and told the truth about your father, most agreed that if Gabriel really was backin' ya like rumor claimed, we'd have to find out how we could help. *Are* the rumors true? Are you really marrying the South? Does that mean you intend to turn Lirin into a parliamentary monarchy like they are? Are you considering a constitution? Do you—"

The ringing started up again in Elenor's ears. Gabriel held up a hand to keep Mari from continuing. "One thing at a time, Mari. It's more complicated than that." He pulled the mug from Elenor's fingers as it started tilting dangerously. "And she's had a very bad morning."

"What happened?" Tamara asked, leaning forward with a look of such genuine, uncomplicated concern that Elenor didn't know what to do with it, other than answer truthfully.

"I had to convince my fiance that I'm worth marrying or . . . someone I loved would have been hurt worse than he already has been. I . . . Cassian . . ." It was caught in her throat, and Elenor had the violent urge to run to the nearest source of water and scour every inch of her skin clean. Instead, she leaned back, and when Gabriel wrapped a comforting arm around her shoulders, Elenor leaned into it, shaking.

No one hurried her, so after a few ragged breaths, she managed to continue. "It hurt so much more than I thought it would, and the whole time, I had to pretend to be enjoying it. Pretend I was the besotted idiot my aunt wants me to act like. I don't even know that it was enough. He . . . when he was leaving, he said that if I was willing to p-part my legs for him, he couldn't trust that I wouldn't for others. He's going to have one of his retinue spend the nights in my suite and wants me to send Gabriel and Claire away."

"That fucking rat-bastard," Gabe exclaimed under his breath. Jo had turned a little green, and both Tamara and Mari were looking at Elenor with wide eyes full of pity. Usually that might have pricked at Elenor's pride, but there wasn't much of that left these days.

"Oh, you poor thing," Mari murmured. "Giving yourself to another should never be a decision forced on you. No wonder you look like you've seen a Forgotten ghost."

"No, that's the fever. Her wrist is still healing and she's been sick for days, on top of it all," Gabriel said. "Cassian should have known. Should have felt that you were feverish, at the very least, and put a stop to it. With how oversensitive your skin must be, I can only imagine . . . What kind of man doesn't question—? No. That's exactly the kind of entitled prick he has always been. If he thinks he gets to isolate you, while taking advantage of your desperate situation, then he has another thing coming. I have no intention of leaving you alone to deal with this mess, and Claire doesn't seem like the type to give up without a fight, either."

While he spoke, Tamara had gotten to her feet to go rustle

through a cabinet. She returned with a bottle and small cup, then poured a dark liquid that smelled herbal and handed it to Elenor. "First thing's first, drink up. For contraception."

Elenor hadn't even thought about that. She took the cup and downed it without hesitation, grimacing at the bitter taste and washing it down with a mouthful of tea. Usually, she would have worried about poison, but this wasn't court, and Gabriel seemed to trust these people. Not that he hadn't once poisoned her, but that had been a very different situation. "Thank you," she said to Tamara.

The young woman waved her thanks away. "None needed. I wish I could help more. That sounds like a dreadful experience. You're not going to marry him after this, right?"

Elenor bit her lip. "I may not have a choice."

"Aren't you a Queen?" Mari asked.

"Queen Regent, and only until I take my Water Rite, or my mother is found," Elenor clarified. "And if I don't get hanged for my father's murder, after the trial."

Mari huffed. "Hypocrisy, there. He murdered your brother in front of a room full of onlookers, and not one noble made a fuss. If your account of the events in the paper is true, you also defended yourself and your country when he was killed, and yet you are being tried as a criminal. Why is that, I ask?"

That was actually a surprisingly good point. "I . . . don't know. Because they think there's something to be gained?"

"It's because you're," Jo gestured to Elenor, "well, you're not a big, imposing man with a sword who they're scared of. This happened all the time in the watch. I had to work ten times as hard as any of the big guys to get the same level of respect. People used to getting their way will take advantage of any perceived weakness, real or imagined. You've been mostly just reacting to things others have done since the breakout, and letting them corner you into tighter and tighter spaces. Eventually, you'll have nowhere left to retreat. At some point, you have to stand your ground against bullies and thugs of any ilk and bloody their faces."

"What about Paul?" Elenor asked. Because that was the crux of it—the linchpin Sianta had carefully placed in any plan Elenor might be able to concoct, so that she could pull it out at her convenience.

"Who?" Tamara asked.

Gabe summarized the situation with Paul, the contract, and the split in allegiances between the nobles of Lirin. By the time he was done, Mari had lost any semblance of a motherly smile and was dead serious.

"This was before most of you were born, but I remember the day Lilian Lirion's pronouncement of regency put your father in charge of our country, Your Highness. I was in the crowd just close enough to get a glimpse of her face, and she looked a lot like you do today, Miss Elenor. She stood there behind her husband, clutching little Wilam close like she couldn't believe what was happening, but didn't have a way to stop it. That night was when I joined the Rebellion, back when it was just a few people getting angry at the Miri around the table of a pub."

"Told you that some of the rebels were Lirion loyalists, didn't I?" Gabriel asked, flashing Elenor an encouraging smile.

"I admit I hadn't quite believed you."

"I know," he said, giving her shoulders a squeeze, then added, "I've been watching you for days, and the thing I've noticed the most is that you don't seem to open up much, even to those closest to you. I think your family has very systematically convinced you to trust nothing and no one, and to expect and accept a frankly appalling amount of coercion and abuse. Mari, you remember the first night Wil came to dinner, right?"

"I'll never forget it. Only time anyone has ever cried into one of my fish stews," Mari said, shaking her head. "Poor lad didn't know what to do with affection that wasn't transactional or conditional. He deserved better than the fate he got, as did so many others." Her tone turned sad as she said that. Mari reached up and brushed a tear from her cheeks with the bandages covering her wrists. "My Kyle did like him so."

"I'm so sorry," Elenor said, bowing her head.

"Whatever for, child? You rid us of the man who killed him, didn't you? And you freed me on top of it, even though I had spent decades fighting against your government. Both Kyle and I knew it would be over if we were found out. Everyone who joined up understood the risks they took and accepted them. Our agency is not your responsibility, Miss Elenor. This is our country. If we want it to be better, we must work and sacrifice for that dream. That is true as much for me as it is for you."

Elenor looked over to Gabriel. What was this all about? He knew what was in that contract—that unless she was willing to sacrifice Paul, she was going to lose Lirin even if everything went her way in the trial and Water Rite. Was this some sort of new form of punishment the Gods had chosen for her? Revenge for what she had allowed to happen to him and Mari?

"Princess," Gabriel said, interrupting her spiraling questions. "I didn't bring you here to make you feel worse. I wanted you out of the Palace before you saw this, because it's more important than ever that you know."

From his coat, he pulled out a bundle wrapped in cloth. As soon as he unwrapped it, Elenor recognized the document Paul had kept hidden. She had a vague recollection of asking Gabriel and Claire to read through it, but had completely forgotten about it after Cassian's incursion woke her. Her gaze flitted up to Gabriel, who nodded minutely, then turned to the other women in the room.

"Would it be possible to have a moment alone in your bedroom, Tammy?" Gabriel asked.

It took some scooting around legs and furniture, but soon enough Elenor found herself in a closet-sized bedroom, sitting on a neatly made bed while Gabriel pulled a curtain between the rooms. He knelt in front of her, and brought her hand up to his lips. "Feeling steady enough for this?"

"How bad is it?" she asked. "It worries me that you thought you had to bring me all the way here to tell me."

"That's not why I brought you here. I did it because you were scared, hurt, and asked me to get you out. This would have been my destination whether you had been the lowliest of servants or the Empress of the whole damn world. Everyone needs some warmth and comfort from time to time."

Elenor let out a hoarse chuckle. "My track record of keeping the people who offer me those things alive is pretty abysmal. I wouldn't try too hard."

"By that logic, neither of us deserves a lick of compassion or affection, and that's just patently untrue." Gabriel's thumb was running circles over her palm as he spoke, massaging away a little of the constant ache the fever always brought on. "Elenor, the way your family has treated you isn't normal. Parents aren't supposed to threaten their children, or force them to keep silent when a family member literally tries to kill them. Aunts and cousins aren't supposed to try to steal everything you have, while blackmailing you with the safety of one of the few people who has been a constant in your life. This morning never should have happened, and it's everyone's fault but yours. You understand that, right?"

Did she? Honestly, Elenor wasn't sure. She had been the one to agree to see Sianta in private, wasn't she? It had been stupid, and Paul was paying for that decision. The same way turning in the Tellens had been her own foolish choice. Maybe she deserved this.

Gabriel must have noticed her hesitation, because he shook his head and gave her uninjured hands a firm squeeze. "Clearly we have a lot of work to do on your mental health when all this is over. You're expecting me to tell you something terrible and catastrophic, aren't you?"

Elenor raised her eyebrows, then with a sigh admitted, "You're not wrong. But isn't it?"

"No. Well, maybe not. It's too early to tell." He let go of her and picked up the document again, from where it lay beside Elenor on the small bed. He set aside the first few pages, then pointed to where she should read. "Take a deep breath, because this might knock your feet out from under you."

"So, my normal," Elenor muttered drily.

Gabriel let out a surprised laugh, then looked down at the old, crinkling pages. Elenor inhaled deeply as he had instructed and, unable to put it off any longer, turned her eyes to the text. Almost a minute later, after having entirely forgotten that she was holding her breath, it burst out of her in a wheezing cough as the whole world started to spin.

"Woah, easy there," Gabe exclaimed, catching the papers as her hands went slack.

Like a swift autumn wind, the words on the page started stripping away the fog that had clung to her thoughts for days. The fever remained, but a small break in the clouds opened up. "I was already betrothed? To a," her voice stuttered on the Forgotten name, "Silvarin? Does that mean—?"

"We don't know anything yet, but we'll find out. We'll . . . talk to Robin." That seemed to be hard for Gabriel to say. In fact, his whole posture was tense, though Elenor wasn't sure why. Did he suspect Robin of something? Before she could ask, Gabe continued. "This might be a way to get Tirit Mindel on your side. With the Island, even if the South protests, they would never dare rise against you." Gabriel's smile returned, encouraging and reassuring. "That just leaves Miriel, and guess what? That's a pretty even fight. Which is why we're here. You're going to need people willing to take up arms to back you up. Mari and I can get you that quietly, while you focus on saving Paul. Your aunt wouldn't be rushing this union with Cassian if she wasn't scared. She's terrorizing you to keep you distracted, but she wouldn't need to do that if her position were as secure as she has implied. That means there's a way you can win."

Elenor's head was spinning, but for the first time since the Miri had arrived, it wasn't out of panic. "Right. *Right.*" Another perusal of the document, a deep inhale, then Elenor looked back up at Gabriel. "What's our move?"

She made to rise when the air beside the bed shimmered and parted into a doorway. Gabe twisted to get between it and Elenor, but before he could, Daemon stepped through, one hand around Claire's upper arm and a look of supreme annoyance on his face.

"Don't come to my home uninvited again, Enica, if you know what's good for you." He tossed Claire onto the bed, then looked to Elenor, shook his head as though trying to clear something from it, and gritted his teeth. "Not now," he muttered. Taking a step to the side, Daemon gestured to Gabriel, then to the doorway. "You. Through. I can feel the excess magic coming off you like a fucking wave now that you're mostly healed and this one—" He glared at Claire, "—said you've been stupid enough to *absorb* more energy helping Elenor. It's a fucking miracle you haven't blown already, so git."

Gabriel did not look inclined to move, eyes narrowed and jaw clenched. Elenor placed a hand on his shoulder, then looked up at Daemon. "Now's not a good time. We were in the middle of—"

Daemon held a finger up to quiet her. He shook his head again, like a dog with water in their ears. "Please don't speak, Elenor. I have some things I need to discuss with you too at some point, but I need to stay on task today, and have already entertained too many distractions. We'll talk when I come back with Gabriel."

"I'm not going anywhere with you until—"

Daemon interrupted Gabriel by moving forward a step and grabbing him by the arm. Half a second later, Gabe gasped and bent over, eyes wide and chest heaving as though he couldn't get enough air.

"What did you do to him?" Elenor demanded, worry cutting through her shock.

"Nothing permanent. I forced my way into his magical well and am draining off the excess. I don't feel like accidentally dying if I annoy him, because I intend to do that quite a bit. Princess, Enica, have a good day."

Elenor tried to grab Gabriel, but Daemon had already yanked him to his feet and tossed him at the doorway. Gabe stumbled through, boots crunching on sand.

"You can't just take—" Elenor tried to say, but with a tip of a non-existent hat, Daemon stepped through after Gabriel and slammed the magical portal shut.

The afterimage of the glowing door still floated in her retinas as Elenor turned to Claire and asked, "What happened?"

Claire, who had laid back and was staring wide-eyed at the ceiling took a second to answer, then slowly turned to look at Elenor. "I . . . need a minute to process that. You first. Where are we?"

"Seamstress's shop off the Silverway."

"*Why?*"

"I asked Gabriel to get me out of the Palace."

"Did he tell you what else was in the document? About the betrothal?" Claire asked, still without having blinked once, and with almost no intonation in her voice.

Elenor ignored the questions, far more worried about that blank look on her lover's face. "Claire, *what happened?*"

Slowly, Claire turned her head to face Elenor. "You know how the fact that your dad wasn't your dad, you're the heir of Miriel not just Lirin, and you're technically betrothed to someone from a family presumed dead for five hundred years is all earth-shatteringly big news?"

"Yes . . ." Elenor trailed off, unsure of where Claire was going.

"Well, I think it might actually be very, very small in comparison to mine. I . . . I think I saw a . . . ah . . . God. A golden one. And I think she's planning to kill us."

CHAPTER THIRTY
Letting Loose
GABRIEL

The one irrefutable fact about podding is that it must be voluntary. To enter another's well without permission is impossible, but even if it were not, it would be an unforgivable violation of self. This is why the study of it has been deemed forbidden.

—From A Theory of Podding and Associated Circuits,
by Alexander Silvarin (with contributions by Jac Drego)

GABRIEL STUMBLED AS HIS FEET HIT THE SAND. Heat, blinding sunlight, and humidity assaulted his senses, but they were secondary to the feeling of someone else inside his well. The tall, scowling rifter walked past him. Before Gabe could regain his balance, Daemon grabbed him by the arm and pulled him forward.

"Of all the asinine idiocies I've ever heard of, not training you magically as a child has to be up there with the best. Robin is a fool; it would serve him right if I let you blow up Hardor. As if I didn't have enough on my plate. You, stay put."

Daemon dragged Gabriel to a log and pushed him down, then stalked off, still muttering to himself.

Gabriel tried to call after him, but he could hardly gasp in air, let alone make words. His well of magic, which had been brimming with delicious power for days, felt as though it were being siphoned. Magic was pouring out of him, but it wasn't under his control. Cold sweat broke out on his forehead. A few seconds later, his stomach seized, and what little he had eaten that morning came up.

As Gabe knelt in the sand, heaving and with his vision spinning, Daemon strode along the beach, opening portals in the air and shouting through them.

"Yeah, it's all clear. I don't think she'll return. We have a lot more work to do and I have another problem on my hands, so get everyone gathered back up. Now where the fuck are those two idiots who are supposed to be watching me? Someone go find them, so I don't get in trouble with the Mondaer for trying to save their hides."

Gabe squeezed his eyes shut. The noises of crunching feet and other voices were each a blow to his spinning head, making the nausea worse. Magic was still pouring out of him. It felt like it was being drawn from his very flesh, not just his well. The letting of a substance he needed as much as blood.

"Oh dear, what happened to you?" someone said, walking over.

Gabe cracked his eyes open long enough to glimpse a woman with dark skin and curly hair, then had to close them again, the light far too bright.

"I'm draining his well the not-so-fun way, because he hasn't been doing it. I need you here, Tsiihsi. Contact everyone who scattered and is wearing an amulet. And find me North and Leo." Daemon stomped back over, grabbed Gabe by the collar of his shirt, and hoisted him back up to sitting. "You probably won't be sick again, now that you don't have excess magic literally leaking out of your pores. Think of it as a very quick detox. You'll feel like shit for a few minutes, but the clamminess and nausea will pass. Obri, send North through to the big island when he gets here. And whoever finds Kaedy Deil and her son, a cup of tea might be in order. They had quite the fright. I'm going to be working with an untrained rifter, so Gifted and non-rifters only on the big island."

"Got it, boss," a tanned man with a mop of black hair said, before going back to jogging along the beach.

Daemon waved his hand, a glowing doorway to a city square appearing. Half-pushing, half-pulling Gabe through, Daemon marched them all the way across the tiled plaza to an overhang. Chairs and tables were laid out in front of an empty cafe.

In fact, all the buildings seemed empty. They weren't like any Gabriel had seen before. Tall, ornate towers rose in every direction, painted and decorated in enough bright colors to make him feel at home. Unlike Garendor, though, this city didn't feel crowded. The buildings popped up with no clear organization, trees and rock formations poking between them. From the top of some of the taller towers, mock dragons stared down at him, their scales and feathers glistening in the midday sun.

"What is this place?" he asked, when he finally found his voice.

"Nowhere on a map, and none of your business." Daemon, who had once again disappeared into a new doorway in the air, returned with a large brick of gold. "Why haven't you drained your well into the gold I left for you?"

"I tried. It blew up."

That stopped Daemon in his tracks. He turned around, ran off, then returned with a bizarre device the size of a briefcase. "So, a large capacity, not just a big well. *Splendid*."

Setting both the gold brick and the device on one of the spindly wrought iron tables, the rifter went back to ignoring Gabe while he flicked switches and connected wires.

"What did you do? How are you in my magic? I can feel you pulling it out of me like you did in the dungeons," Gabriel said, leaning forward as another wave of nausea hit him.

"It's called podding."

"I know what podding is. I had to read a whole book about it," Gabe snapped. "It was very specific about it being voluntary."

"Was it *A Theory of Podding and Associated Circuits?*"

"Yes. How did you know?"

"It's been in the Tirit Mindel curriculum for centuries. Every few decades I go in, create a persona for myself, and publish a new edition. So since I *literally wrote the book* on podding, and you're an uneducated buffoon when it comes to magic—by no fault of your own, to be fair—perhaps we should establish some ground rules. The first: forget everything you've ever read about rifting. The Island keeps most of its discoveries secret. Second rule: no questions. We'll revisit that when you've mastered the basics."

Daemon stepped away from the device on the table. Fully set up, it consisted of a box with a copper handle on one side, a thick copper cable coming out the other, and a windmill-like contraption set atop it.

"You expect me not to ask questions when you've appeared out of thin air, again refused to give me any explanation as to why, and took me away from Hardor when I'm needed?" Gabriel asked, irritation making its way through the miasma of discomfort and bewilderment.

"Yes, because for some inexplicable reason, I'm actually taking the time to beat some magical training into your head. If you make that more of a nuisance than it needs to be, I'll be inclined to get rid of the problems you're causing me by killing you, instead. But you know what? Fine. No *stupid* questions." Daemon pointed to the copper handle, as he wrapped the cable around the bar of gold. "We're going to measure your capacity. That's done by pushing pure magical energy through this device for one second with all your strength. It will measure how much comes through, and give us a rough estimation as to how much magic you can use at any one time."

Gabriel crossed his arms, not taking the handle. "You told me last time that you would explain what is happening to me—why I have all this magic. I would like that explanation before I do anything. I'd also like to know how you do that thing with the doorways. Is it like Claire? A Gift?"

"No." Daemon tapped his foot, then with a huff pulled up a chair, turned it around, and sat down straddling it. The pull on Gabriel's magic lessened, then stopped altogether. "Wow it's hard not to be annoyed at you when I'm in your magic. Do you have *any* idea how long I've wanted to get my hands on a rifter of your abilities? It irks me to no end that you're the one who finally shows up."

"Why? How are you connected to any of this? You've helped both Elenor and me over and over again, but neither of us knows anything about you. Frankly, that doesn't make me inclined to trust you." Gabriel still did not take the handle of the device.

Daemon raked his fingers through his smooth black hair. "You'd think doing nice things for you like saving your life would make you grateful, instead of suspicious. No matter. I am not going to be the one to explain why you're important. Go to Robin for that mess. What I will say is that Gifted and rifters are a particular interest of mine. As for Elenor, well, she's a mystery I'm trying to solve and someone I've begrudgingly come to like. But don't ask me why I keep helping the pair of you, because I honestly have no idea. That's much of the reason why I'm in this bad of a mood."

There was Robin again. Ever since Djina had mentioned that his mentor was in Hardor and asking after him, Gabriel had thought it odd. To have this mysterious man refer to the Tirition too made Gabe's curiosity spike and a sense of old, half-forgotten dread settle at the base of his stomach. It was the same unease he'd felt reading Warren Miri's document, and each time someone asked about his green eyes.

He would have to find a way to talk to Robin. A more urgent matter, though, was before him. "What do you know about my magic?"

"There, at least, I can answer your questions. You are a vital rifter whose power has been magically suppressed for most of his life."

"How?" Part of Gabriel wanted to dig in his heels and tell him that was impossible, but then again . . . hadn't he felt the vast depths of his current power? And hadn't he struggled for years with magic that seemed to sometimes be there, and sometimes not? But how and who would have both the motive and the way to keep him from his magic? More pressing: why?

"Unimportant. What *is* important is that because of this, you are coming into your full potential now, instead of during your adolescence. Instead of a steadily growing amount of power you can adjust to, you're being hit with the whole package." Daemon gestured at the machine. "I want to measure how much magic we are dealing with so I can teach you to safely contain it. You've been very oversaturated, but not feeling it as much as you should have, because the magic has been diverted into healing your injuries. Since you're looking almost back to normal, that state will change. Oversaturation leads to recklessness, mania, impulsivity, and a compulsion to rift. With power like yours, that could be catastrophic. I drained some of your well because, while oversaturated, stray thoughts or annoyances can turn into explosive bursts of magic, and I didn't want you to accidentally kill me or someone else while we were doing this. I'm going to release the pod now. Before I send you back to Hardor, I'll show you how to empty your well safely. It is essential that you do so any time oversaturation creeps up on you, because having an overfull well is addicting. It feels fantastic and draining it is unpleasant. This has sent many a rifter into a spiral of abusing their own magic like one would any drug. You'll be more prone than most, since you've had no time to adjust."

That caught Gabriel's attention. He gave Daemon a solemn nod. "Understood." He could still vividly remember the one time he had been coming off serindalla. It had been a struggle to quit, even with all his medical knowledge telling him why he had to. The last thing he wanted was to have to deal with that again, but with a substance that he couldn't hand off to Fedrik or Fay for safekeeping.

"Good. I'm going to release the pod now." Daemon closed his eyes for a brief moment, then the pressure on Gabriel's magic vanished.

Gabe gasped in relief, reaching up to massage the back of his neck as though Daemon's grasp on his well had been a physical claw digging into his flesh. "Thanks."

"We may not get to it today, but eventually I'll teach you to pod the normal, voluntary way. It is much less painful."

"That would be appreciated. I do feel . . . lighter. My body hurts more, though."

"Without the excess magic giving you a high, it will. You can still direct power into any still-healing injuries, but it will be controlled instead of an overabundant overflow." Daemon pointed once more at the device. "Take the handle. The circuit connected to it will channel any magic you use into the device, so you don't have to worry about accidentally causing an explosion or starting a fire. When you're ready and centered, pull as much from your well as you can in one burst, then stop."

Nervously, Gabe took hold of the cool copper handle. "Will the gold disintegrate?"

"No, there's an overflow circuit. Any extra will be released into the ambient magic in the air." Daemon got up and went to stand directly behind Gabriel, one hand on his shoulder. "If it's more than I can channel, I'll have to pod with you again or risk injury, but hopefully it won't come to that."

Licking his lips and inhaling deeply, Gabriel closed his eyes. He hadn't actually felt around for the extent of his magic since being released from prison. When learning from Paul, he had been so focused on pulling threads that he hadn't even considered using all he could.

Gabe's senses expanded into the core of his being. And expanded. *And expanded.* "There's so much."

"Mhm. Being podded to you feels like teetering on the precipice of a canyon. Not infinite by any stretch, but far more than any one person should have. I've felt a few like you over the years, though you'll be amazed how quickly even that much power can be used up when you're trying to do something." Daemon's hand on his shoulder tightened. "Make sure not to push more than you can comfortably. We're trying to find out what your range is, not how far you can stretch it in a pinch."

When Gabriel thought he had a handful of magic that felt *right* in a way he could not put into words, he tensed, exhaled, and rifted. The rush burned through his body and soul, sizzling, raw, and ecstatic. Every ache and pain vanished, replaced with blissful energy.

On the table, the device whirred, filling the air with a high-pitched whine. Daemon gasped, stumbling. Half a second later, the earth itself shook, sending chairs and tables toppling.

Pain seared through Gabriel again. Instinctively, he fought against the incursion, but Daemon was too quick.

The magic stopped. Control was yanked out of his grasp so abruptly that Gabriel jerked, head thudding back against Daemon's chest.

"Holy fuck. You have some serious oomph, don't you?" the rifter gasped, sounding winded. Bending over and letting go of Gabriel, Daemon braced his hands on his knees. "Ow."

Gabriel shared the sentiment. His head was throbbing worse than the first time Daemon had podded to him that day. In the aftermath of all the power, the absence made his bones feel brittle and lungs hollow.

They both spent a minute or two catching their breaths, then Daemon released the pod again. "Well, I'm fairly certain you channeled too much for this machine to measure, but we'll see."

A bit of fiddling later, Daemon pulled a small notebook and stub of a pencil from his pocket. He scribbled some numbers down, frowning. "Just over the limit. If I work backwards from how fast you filled this weight of gold, I should have a rough estimate. Good news is that your capacity seems to be proportional to your well, which means finding a balance of output is possible. I once met someone with a well as large as yours, but with a minuscule capacity. He could channel his maximum amount of magic all day long and it wouldn't have been enough to keep him from oversaturation. The only way he could empty his well was if he podded with someone else."

"What happened to him?" Gabriel asked, still rubbing his throbbing temples.

Daemon shrugged. "He was what we call a magical anomaly. Most of them die. I think he made it to nineteen before running straight into a battle without armor or weapons, because he was high enough on his magic to think he didn't need it. Got killed by an archer. Rifters are pretty dumb." Winding the wires on the device back up, Daemon gestured to Gabriel. "I only have an hour or two today to work with you, so we're going to concentrate on giving you the tools you need not to blow anyone up or be oversaturated."

Moving hurt, but Gabriel followed, shaken by how much magic he had channeled. It made Daemon's caution feel less frustrating and more reasonable. It also filled him with more burning questions . . . which the strange rifter probably wouldn't answer.

Daemon opened a doorway in the middle of the plaza. With the sun beating down on their heads and his too-warm clothes, Gabriel let out a happy sigh when a gust of frigid air blew through it.

On the other side was snow as far as the eye could see. The sun shone there too, reflecting brightly off the blindingly white glaciers in the distance.

"We're going to talk about heating and cooling as a way to drain your well," Daemon explained, straddling the doorway and beckoning Gabriel over to do likewise. "Releasing pure magic like you just did is the most effective way of ridding your body of excess, but it could have the unintended effect of breaking someone's capacity if they are close-by and you release too much at once. With how big of a well and capacity you have, I don't want you to ever do that unless you are under my supervision or it's a matter of life or death."

"So how do I?" Gabe asked, nerves returning as the throbbing in his head died down.

"Well, you clearly have a knack for sucking in heat, if you've been doing it for Elenor. The fact that you haven't accidentally turned her into an ice-cube tells me that you also have a fair amount of precise control. I expect it's because you've been fighting for whatever dregs of power you could get your whole life. Let me guess, you use magic to cool your food when it's too hot, yes?"

"Um... yeah." Gabe said. "And to cool myself down if I'm too warm."

"Practice makes perfect. Here's the thing with magic: what works for one person won't work for everyone. We're going to eventually find out the best way for you to learn to rift, but for now we'll work on building on what you can do already. Muscle memory is your friend." Daemon held his arms outstretched, one hand in the warm sunlight of the tropics, the other gathering a dusting of snow. "Making things colder gives you power. Making them hotter uses up power. So how would you use that to drain your well?"

Gabriel hadn't expected the question, but years at the Academy had prepared him well. "You'd heat something up. The air, maybe?"

"Good boy. Got it in one. I'm glad to see you're not all magical muscle with no brain behind it. Now, what problems can you see with that course of action?"

Gabe scrunched up his nose, thinking. "Well, you wouldn't want it to get so warm that it could hurt someone, for a start. And I'd imagine that the air near you would heat up fast, so you would need some way of circulating it. Maybe walk while you do it?"

Daemon nodded. "Very good. One more problem, though not one you will probably ever have to deal with: the more heat you introduce to the environment, the more power another rifter might have to absorb if you get into a fight. But as I said, not as important for you."

"So how do I keep from toasting anyone?" Gabe asked, which made Daemon chuckle.

"Like so. With one hand, touch something warm, like your own skin, or the stones above a fireplace. When you rift to heat the air, set that temperature as your upper threshold. The rift should be phrased in your mind as 'heat the air to the temperature of my hand.' Does that make sense?"

"What braid should I use? Not the one for fire, right?" Gabe asked.

"Braids," Daemon scoffed. "Tirit Mindel's obsession. They're useful as a training tool—a mnemonic device as it were—but mostly a waste of time for vital rifters like you and me. You didn't use a braid to absorb heat from Elenor, did you? You just focused your intentions and concentrated on exactly what you wished to happen. Same thing here. The clearer and simpler the thought directing the magic, the better. Don't overcomplicate it. The more you get in your own way, the worse it goes and the longer it takes. In a magical standoff, the person who wins is the person who goes first. That's the advantage people trained my way will always have over Tirit Mindel."

Gabriel shifted uncomfortably, but did as instructed. Focusing on his hand in the balmy air of the island, he held out the other one and rifted. At once, the air on the other side of the doorway became blistering. Snow melted, condensation puffed around them, billowing up toward the clear blue sky.

"Too hard. More focus on your warm hand. Really concentrate on how it feels. Instead of actively rifting, try to just loosen your control over your magic. It will flow into the space of your intention on its own, if you let it," Daemon corrected. He flicked his fingers. A gust of wind picked up, pushing the heat away from them. "Try again."

Feeling silly and sure he was about to stand there like a fool, Gabriel tried to do as Daemon instructed. He focused on the sun beating down on his hand, and the humid air brushing over it. At the same time, he attempted to relax his hold on his magic.

After five minutes where nothing happened at all, Daemon grumbled something that sounded like, "Robin, you little fucking shit." He motioned for Gabriel to stop. "Well that's a problem. I think you might be holding on to your magic too tightly for that method to work. Makes sense, I suppose, since you've had to conserve every scrap for so long. That might also explain why you *haven't* exploded yet. Guess there are pros and cons to anything. Let's try another way."

Daemon reached into his pocket and extracted a small spool of silvery-blue wire. Unwinding a segment and cutting it off with magic, he twisted it together into a thicker band, then wrapped it around Gabriel's wrist.

"Cerulean can hold commands. One command per piece of cerulean, though the command *can* be rather complex if you know how to phrase it with proper syntax. We're going to break our process down using this. I want you to concentrate on your warm hand, focus on the cerulean, and think 'heat the air around me to the same temperature as my left hand, then stop.' One sentence, and as I said, the syntax is important. Don't fuck it up."

"Will that really work?" Gabe asked, incredulous.

Daemon shrugged. "Yes and no. That small piece of cerulean isn't enough to overcome your thoughts if you decide to push, but it will be enough to direct them if you don't. I would offer to make you a more permanent circuit, but I'm busy and this is easy, so I'd rather you learn to do this for yourself. Almost anyone can learn single-metal circuitry, it's when you start combining them that it becomes complicated. This should be within your skillset, as long as you concentrate."

Gabriel scowled. "You know, I'd probably be able to concentrate better if you hadn't yanked me away from Hardor during an important conversation. Elenor is in the middle of the city. I should really be getting back to her."

Daemon hesitated, then shook his head. "She has Enica. They'll be fine. If danger comes their way, it won't catch them. But I promise I'll get you back shortly. As soon as you learn this rift, in fact."

Gabriel didn't like that answer, but despite his worry for Elenor, he really did need to learn this. So he gritted his teeth and focused on the cerulean bracelet. "How will I know if it worked?"

"You won't. That's the annoying part about cerulean. You won't find out if you did it right until you push power through it. That's how most circuitry builders burn off their eyebrows or get shrapnel embedded in their hands."

Charming. More nervous than he had been, Gabe repeated the command to himself three times, hoping he was doing it right. He supposed they'd find out soon enough. By the time he was ready to go again, Daemon and the northern wind had circulated the air enough for it to be icy. Counting down from three under his breath, Gabe reached for his power. This time, he tried to use only the amount he had with Paul, when charging the gold.

A tingle ran down his arm, and the air on the other side got slightly warmer. Nothing exploded, or overheated.

"Good. That's very good. Keep going until the cerulean activates," Daemon encouraged.

Thread by thread, teeth clenched with the effort, Gabriel kept at it. He could feel Daemon's watchful gaze on him, even though he had closed his eyes. Tension was radiating off the other man, as though ready to launch forward and force his way into Gabriel's magic again.

The momentary flash of annoyance had unintended consequences. His magic flared hot. For a second the air around his outstretched hand burned, then without warning his power cut off.

"Perfect," Daemon whooped. "That worked exactly the way it should have. Excellent. We'll make a non-death-trap rifter out of you yet."

Daemon was halfway through explaining how to create a breeze with kinetic magic to dissipate the heat when a noise caught Gabriel's attention. A man and a woman had walked through the doorway that still stood open on the other side of the plaza. The man was tall and powerfully built, with shoulder-length brown hair and a thick beard. Gabriel thought he recognized the woman, but it took him a while to figure out from where. Akaaron's apprentice? Yes, that was it. How was *she* tangled up with Daemon?

"Leo is taking Daari and Bard back to the Mother Rock. Kaedy wanted to stay to thank y—" the man said, before cutting off abruptly.

Kaedy. That was it. She looked a little different than last time, but maybe that was because Gabe had never seen her not smile.

"Gabriel?" the man asked. There was shock in his tone, whole posture changing from angry to surprised. "Daemon, what are you doing with him?"

"Teaching him to rift, ye of little faith," Daemon drawled. There was a dangerous glimmer in his eyes that made Gabriel step back. "North, you will not interfere with the lesson. I'm supposed to let you watch me, but I don't need your input. Kaedy, dear, if you go into the cafe there, there should be a cold-box in the kitchen. I'm sure there's some chilled ginger wine. Help yourself and please, no thanks needed. Those who I *invite* onto my island are under my protection."

What had this North done to piss Daemon off? They were staring at each other with looks that could kill.

"You can't expect me to—"

"Shut up and do as you're told? No. You're very bad at that, even when your life is on the line. However, since many more lives than yours are at stake here, I hope you'll consider refraining."

"But he—"

What did Gabe have to do with this argument? "Um . . . maybe I should go?"

"You can stay right where you are until you can both expel heat and circulate the air. I don't want to have to come dispose of crispy bodies."

That made Gabriel blanch, the burn scars on his arms, chest, and shoulder throbbing in remembered pain. It also seemed to shut North up, though he glared at Daemon the entire way to the cafe.

When he and Kaedy had gone inside, Gabriel turned to Daemon. "What was that about?"

"North and I do not get along. He likes poking his nose in other people's business, and passing judgment over things he does not fully comprehend. I am sure he thinks you're in quite a bit of danger from me."

"Am I?"

"Not anymore. Not that I won't kill you if you ever seriously threaten to blow magically, mind. But that's not specific to you. Killing one rifter to save hundreds or thousands is a choice I will always make, no matter who that person is," Daemon replied.

Gabe gulped. "You said not anymore . . . were you once?"

A slight nod.

"Why?" This time, he didn't intend to let Daemon brush the question off. "Is that why you left me to rot in that cell when you could have taken me through one of these doorways? Because I haven't forgotten that."

"I'm sure you haven't," Daemon said, slipping his hands into his pockets and stepping fully into the icy tundra. "But I don't owe you an explanation. My business is my own. I would remind you that you offered me *anything I wanted* if I set you free, and I did not take you up on it. I could have had you and all your magic at my beck and call, and am instead teaching you without asking for anything in return. Consider that before getting up in arms about my methods, or my motives."

Gabe hadn't thought of it that way. It was enough to shut him up through another round of lessons. This time, he was aware of eyes on them. The two sitting in the cafe were speaking quietly to each other, but North's gaze never once left Gabriel and Daemon.

Once Gabe could kinetically push the air gently enough to not send Daemon sprawling into the snow, they moved on to combining the two techniques. Gabe was sweating with the exertion of using that much magic by then, but so elated he didn't mind. Every time he pulled from his well, his aches and pains would fade, replaced by a blissful sense of power. It was invigorating.

"Wash that grin off your face, boy. This is as basic as basic gets. You have a long way to go before you should be smiling," Daemon grumbled. "But you've done well enough for today. Better than I expected with how behind you are. How's your well feeling? When it's getting low it will feel like a different kind of hunger."

Gabe searched within himself, more aware of his reservoir of power than he had been before spending the last hour or so working with it. It no longer ached or threatened to overflow, but magic still swirled within it, sizzling and vast. "It doesn't feel low."

"Then let's fix that. I can estimate approximately how fast you refill by the timeline of your captivity with the Lirion. It's not wildly fast, so that's the first and only plus in this mess. I want you out of my hair for at least a week. So turn that way, away from my island, and really go for it. There's nothing and no one out this far north, not even white mocks, so let's see how big of a boom you can make."

"Are . . . you sure?" The smile faded from Gabe's face as his nerves returned tenfold stronger.

"Yes. I'll catch you in a pod if you do anything wrong. Just don't use kinetic energy, or if it hits something solid you'll be the one who goes flying in the opposite direction. I'd suggest fire."

"I don't like fire," Gabe said, shuddering.

"Even better. You won't accidentally make it too close to us. A bit of fear is healthy for a rifter. The fearless ones end up dead." Daemon stepped behind him, turning Gabriel by the shoulders to point in the right direction. As he did, Gabe noticed that North had sidled closer, standing just beyond the threshold of the doorway.

"So how do I do it?" Gabe asked, a slight quiver to his voice.

"The parameters you want are fire, direction, and duration. First two are easy. The last should be: ten seconds, or until I want to stop. Without a size parameter, your magic will default to whatever a comfortable draw through your capacity is. Keep those three elements in mind and relax. Let all other potentially intrusive thoughts go away, then when you are calm, rift."

"Just like that? You do realize that it takes *three years of study* on Tirit Mindel before students are allowed to do more than light candles, right?" Gabe pointed out.

Daemon chuckled. "Tirit Mindel has many reasons to be overly cautious, and while a few of them have to do with students in the past blowing up buildings by accident, most of them center around how many claws they can dig into you before handing you the keys to power. They like loyal minions who are well-trained, and for everyone else to flounder."

Gabe licked his lips and shifted into a more stable stance, snow creaking under his boots. *Fire, ahead of me, for ten seconds or until I want to stop.* It seemed like too little. No complicated braids to memorize and visualize, no weeks of practice.

"Relax your shoulders," Daemon instructed, placing both hands on them. "The stiller and calmer your mind, the clearer your parameters will come through. It's why rifters who are of average skill can look like masters on the battlefield when they get enough adrenaline pumping, and why people who have trained their whole lives can fumble if they've got a lot on their mind."

"It would be easier to do that if I had an instructor who actually answered my questions, and whose motives I trusted," Gabriel grumbled, causing Daemon to laugh.

"Tough luck, kid. You're not the one I made a deal with to

answer questions. If I do that twice in one decade, my reputation will be ruined."

From the doorway, North snorted, arms crossed and glaring at Daemon. "He does like keeping his secrets. And when he doesn't, you often wish he had."

Gabe wasn't sure what to make of that, but looked over his shoulder at Daemon. "I don't suppose your many secrets include why there are tunnels inside the walls of the Hardor Palace, do they?"

Daemon raised his eyebrows. "I might know a thing or two about that subject, yes. Why do you ask?"

"Because I was shoved into one today and thought I heard voices. My blood has activated what looks like magical circuitry multiple times. Magic seems like it's your area of expertise, so I thought you might know something about it. With the Miri in residence at the Palace, I don't like the idea of people being able to move around in the walls."

"Voices? Interesting," Daemon said, eyebrows pulling together. "Now stop overthinking this. I'll count down from three."

Gabe sighed regretfully, not having expected anything better.

He turned toward the glaciers, clearing his mind as best he could. He rolled his shoulders, trying to relax his muscles as he raised his arms. *Fire, ahead of me, for ten seconds or until I want to stop.*

"Three, two, one, rift."

Fire burst from Gabriel's outstretched hands. It filled the skyline, a wall of roaring flames as high as a mountain. The heat hit a second later. It barreled into them, making both Gabriel and Daemon stumble back. Ice cracked and sizzled. The wind sent waves and eddies of sparks flying into the sky. Higher and higher the fire grew, turning white, then blue at the center of the raging inferno, until it blotted out the sun, casting a shadow upon them.

Through the roar, Gabriel thought he heard Daemon laugh. Gabriel might have too, if the trilling bliss had allowed anything as pedantic and shallow as laughter.

CHAPTER THIRTY-ONE
A Different Strategy
ELENOR

Pass it on and find Fayrian Avilor: The Miri are blackmailing the Queen Regent, but she is on our side. They have come for Lirin. We will not give it to them. Gather arms, gather men, and prepare to fight. This time, the Lirion are with us. We will take our country back, whatever it takes.

—From a note to the rebel network from Mari Baker.

"TELL ME AGAIN EXACTLY WHAT YOU SAW," Elenor said, as Claire wheeled her down a hallway toward her father's old office. Her legs had needed a break after her excursion out of the Palace.

Jo was off carrying out her part of the plan Mari had helped devise, so they were flanked on either side by normal guards. On Elenor's order, they were giving the two women a wide enough berth so they could speak without being overheard.

"I appeared in some sort of massive golden temple, and there was a huge dragon. Like a mock, but a thousand times the size. She was talking to a group of strange-looking people and said something along the lines of, 'If the families of the Exiled Gods have not changed their ways after this long, then there is no redeeming them. Now another heinous crime has been committed, and I don't care who's responsible. They had their chance. Why should I give them another?' or something like that. I was panicking, so can't quite remember word for word," Claire recounted.

"And the man she was talking to begged for more time, right? And to save someone named what, again?" Elenor said.

"Alehan, I think? My Gift activated again not long after, so I was a little discombobulated. I ended up on a tropical island."

"Where you ran into Daemon?" Elenor asked, to confirm the order of events Claire had first explained on the carriage ride back up the hill.

"Yes. Well, after a lot of false starts. I got stuck in some sort of jungle by a warehouse for some time, then a damned glacier, then another stop in the desert by this strange ravine city where I've been before, but yes, after a few more hops I got to a tropical island. He was talking to a really strange-looking woman, but she left before he noticed me, and I didn't catch anything other than a mention of God killing. It worries me that I seem to have gone from a conversation about a God wanting to kill people to one about Daemon wanting to kill a God. That seems too neat and connected to be a coincidence. My Gift is taking me to particular places, but I can't figure out why, or how it chooses."

"We'll prioritize that as soon as we can."

"Not until Paul's life and Lirin aren't on the line, we won't."

As Claire wheeled her past the hallway damaged from the fight with the King, Tomaz walked out of a room Elenor was fairly certain had once been a linen or storage closet of some sort. He stopped dead in his tracks, then jumped and rushed over. "Oh. Exactly who I was looking for. Can I walk with you?"

"Why were you in there? Isn't that where we keep excess chairs?" Elenor asked.

Tomaz reached up to twist a strand of sable hair around his finger. "Yes it is. I sometimes go in there when I need some quiet to get work done. It has surprisingly good lighting and, well, chairs. People almost never go in, either. I needed somewhere to run numbers. My family took the contract to repair the damage to the Palace, so I wanted to get all the paperwork for it sorted as soon as possible."

"You're overseeing that in person?" Claire asked. "I thought you were working on Elenor's defense. A bit of plastering can wait, Catoali."

Tamaz waved Claire's grouchy words off. "That's not what I needed to talk to you about. It's about your trial. The date has been set for September the 21st at noon. I tried to find you as soon as I found out, but you weren't in the Palace."

Eighteen days. Which put it one week before her wedding day. That wasn't much time at all, especially since she'd have a better chance at the tribunal if she had already passed her Water Rite. Swallowing back the panic that had been her constant companion, she reminded herself that she and her allies had a plan. This didn't change it, it just gave them a timeline.

As she opened her mouth to thank Tomaz, the closet door swung wide again, and Gabriel and Daemon walked out. Tomaz jumped, eyes bulging. She had to assume they had not been in there a moment ago.

"Don't worry, Tomaz. Daemon likes appearing out of thin air, though how you always manage to know exactly where I am is disconcerting," Elenor said, crossing her arms. "I'm irritated at you."

Daemon, who, like Gabriel, smelled a little smoky and seemed . . . singed, tilted his head. "Irritated? That's such a pleasant change of pace. Today most people have been furious at or terrified of me. Irritated is *charming*."

"Who's—?" Tomaz asked, but Gabriel interrupted.

"Don't try. He doesn't answer. And trust me, Elenor, I'm irritated too. Though I think I've learned more about magic in the past two hours than the entirety of my Tirit Mindel education."

He was bouncing on his tiptoes, his wrinkled shirt sweat-soaked, and hair a sandy mess.

"Oh, I'm so glad you had fun. Meanwhile, I was left basically alone in the middle of Hardor to figure out how to save my country from Miri rule. Daemon, if you're here for that chat you wanted, I don't have time."

"It can wait," he said, with a short bow. Then he turned to Gabriel, poking him firmly in the chest. "Do what we practiced and *nothing else*. Got it?"

"Yes. You've repeated yourself many, many, *many* times," Gabriel said, with a scowl.

"Good." Daemon turned to go, but looked back over his shoulder at Elenor.

"Yes?" she asked, tapping her foot against the rest of her chair.

"You wouldn't happen to know where your mother is, do you?"

"Are you *serious*?" Elenor gestured to the coronet in her hair, then around the ruined corridor. "If I knew where the *rightful* ruler of this country is, do you think I wouldn't be asking you to take me to her right this second? What business do you have with her, anyways?"

Daemon shrugged. "Oh, nothing. Just wanted to ask her a question or two. She seemed particularly good at keeping secrets, and it got me wondering about something. But no matter. Good day to you all."

He strolled off, leaving Elenor fuming, Gabriel still bouncing with energy, Tomaz pale, and Claire vibrating like a teapot about to whistle.

Elenor opened her mouth to ask Gabriel what that was about, but then three of the seven nobles she had asked to meet her rounded the corner. If it had only been Kallen and Eric, she would have spoken freely, but the current stand-in for House Tellen was there too.

"Queen Regent," all three said, bowing.

"My Lords," she replied, trying to regain some composure.

"On your way to the meeting?" Kallen asked.

Elenor nodded. Turning to Gabriel and Tomaz, she added, "Tomaz, I'll speak with you later. Gabriel, brush that sand out of your hair and come with me." Elenor motioned Claire forward.

Eric caught up with her a few steps late. "Elenor, we need to talk in private."

"I can give you five minutes before the meeting begins."

"I would like the same," Kallen said, taking the spot on her other side. Elenor thought she could hear the sound of Claire's teeth grinding over the creak of the wheels.

Elenor looked up at him, squinting. She hadn't forgotten that the last time they had been alone he had tried to push her into agreeing to marry him and kissed her without her consent. At the same time, she desperately needed his help if she wanted any chance at the plan that Mari had helped her put together. "Five minutes. That's it. Eric, take Claire's spot. Claire, catch Gabriel up. Kallen, slow the others down until we reach the office, then you may have your five minutes before the meeting begins in earnest."

Shortly thereafter, she and Eric were far enough ahead to speak without being overheard.

"Elenor, I know where your mother is."

She twisted in her chair to look back at him. "You do? Where? How long have you—?"

"She sent someone to deliver a message this morning. I came to find you as soon as I could, but you were gone."

"You should have requisitioned the Palace Guard and—"

Again, her cousin cut her off, expression grim. "It's more complicated than that, Ellie. It's Tirit Mindel. They have her."

Robin. As soon as Eric mentioned the Island, Elenor had no doubt it was him. He had dodged her questions about the Queen when they had met. She had thought it suspicious at the time, but in light of this information it was damning. Eric was right, though. It made things much, much more complicated. "Are you sure of the validity of this informant? Could it be someone trying to throw off the trail, or cause dissent? I have to be sure before I start making demands of the Island."

They turned a corner while Eric said, "Who the informant is, I have no idea. She wasn't in our employ, to be sure, but the information is genuine. Unless they have convinced her to divulge very sensitive plans, the message is from the Queen."

"What did it say?" Elenor asked eagerly. "A way to help her? Or maybe where in the city she is?"

"She wants me to put pressure on you to marry Cassian Iaming and leave the country. And Elenor, I think she may be right. Drego updated me on what was in that contract. We simply don't have enough time, if we are being realistic, to get out of it without ruining Lirin's relations with both the South and Miriel. I want the Miri out of our hair as much as you do, but this is a coup, and one that they seem to have been planning for some time. A few weeks won't stop them, not with half the nobility against you, and Tirit Mindel getting involved."

"What about an army?" Elenor asked, remembering what Kallen had said to her about Drego forces united with the West.

"Armies take time to muster, and the Lirion army may not follow you at all if you are convicted of killing your father. Ellie, your position is too precarious. I'd much rather see you leave the country, get somewhere safe, and help you plan your return, than have you die trying to win a fight where the odds are stacked against you."

Squinting, Elenor stared up at her cousin as he continued to push her along the hallway. "You can't expect me to up and leave. Lirin is in shambles. I'm not going to let Silla Miri sit on the throne my family has held for five centuries. You have to know that, so what aren't you telling me?"

Eric avoided meeting her eyes. "My grandmother Elehanna is up to something. I don't know the details, but from the message I got, I'm guessing your mother was involved. Gram is the canniest politician I know and hates the Miri. If she wants you to marry the South and go along with this charade, I have to believe it's because it's part of a plan."

Elenor wasn't sure she agreed, or that she could take that risk. Their time to talk in private, though, was up. As the doors to her father's office and the adjacent meeting chamber for the King's Council came into view, the rest of the people following her caught up. Elenor told Eric they would talk more later while motioning for Kallen to follow her into the office.

"Five minutes," Elenor said, as he closed the door behind him.

Kallen was as impeccably dressed and groomed as ever, but there were dark circles under his eyes. "Thank you, Your Highness. I wanted to apologize for my behavior the night of your father's Passing. I didn't mean to pressure you, and am not sure what possessed me to do so. I've been up most of the night thinking about it."

Some of the tension left Elenor's shoulders, and she sagged against the woven back of her chair. "Thank you. I appreciate the apology, and harbor no ill will. It was a stressful night all around. As it so happens, your proposal of marriage is actually what I was hoping to discuss."

"It is?" he asked, head snapping up from the contrite half-bow. "Are you considering it?"

"I am." Elenor's stomach knotted itself, but she, Claire, and Mari had discussed it at length. "I recently found a way to potentially invalidate the contract I signed with the South. It might mean marrying someone I don't even know exists, but I *might* be able to use it to simply free myself. If that's possible, I'll need to make some alliances very quickly, including with the Island. I would like to know exactly what's on the table, Kallen. Saving Paul's life and keeping Lirin safe and on good terms with Tirit Mindel are my non-negotiable terms. If you can show me that marrying you includes those things, then," she took a deep breath, "all things being equal, I'd prefer to marry you than Cassian, and truly do believe you have Lirin's best interest at heart. You were right last night, Kal. I do need help, and so far, yours is the only offer that I am fairly certain is driven solely by ambition, instead of an international agenda. I won't lie and say that I am thrilled by that, but I can respect it. You've been a good ally to me over the past few weeks. Find me a way out of this mess, and you'll have the crown you want."

"Blunt, honest, and to the point, as befitting a follower of the Blue. This is why I respect you, Princess. I admit I had not expected this when I walked in here, but I am pleased. I'll have my lawyers draw up an alternate marriage contract and send it to you for your perusal while I work on the matter of your *doena*."

Elenor let out the breath she had been holding. "Thank you. Now, was there anything else you wished to speak to me about?"

"Yes, there was. I take it you've heard your trial has a date, right?" Kallen nodded at one of the chairs in front of the desk and Elenor inclined her head, giving him consent to sit. "I have been talking to the Houses that opposed you all morning, to try to bring them around . The Lavarin will not be convinced, but while speaking to the Amad, I discovered that the Miri had been talking to them as well. Some inquiries with my contacts at the bank tracked down a large payment sent to the Amad from a Miri account several months ago. I got suspicious so looked further, discovering that your father signed the rights to the Sailon mines over to them shortly before his death."

"What are the Sailon mines, and why are they pertinent to our current dilemma?" Elenor asked, not for the first time wishing she had paid more attention to politics before becoming heir.

Kallen looked around, then reached for a rolled up map at the corner of the desk. Laying it flat on the smooth wood surface, he pointed to a spot north of Hardor, right on the border between Lirin and Namnia. "The town of Sailon sits there and is contested land between Namnia and Lirin. Both kingdoms believe it to be theirs, and it has been traded back and forth for centuries. It used to belong to the Taberlin family, but the town became a self-governing commune about fifty years ago under Namnian occupation. I wouldn't have made note of Amad's interest in it, if not for what Navarl found in that contract with the South, about Seehana no longer giving military aid to Namnia. The reason Lirin hasn't retaken Sailon or held it for good is because war with our Northern neighbors has always been risky, and Sailon historically sells to both nations, no matter who owns the land. The North-South alliance between Namnia and Seehana has meant that if Lirin were to attack either, the other would retaliate, and we'd be stuck with a war on two fronts."

"So once that isn't the case, and with the Miri backing the Lirion, you think the Miri have paid the Amad to take this town from Namnia and what? Start a war to the north?" Her head was starting to throb, but Elenor did her best to ignore it.

Kallen nodded. "Exactly that."

"But why? What makes Sailon special?"

"Cerulean." Kallen gestured to the entire continent of Carinn. "It's one of the three magical metals, and one could argue the most important because of its rarity. Almost all the cerulean mines in the world are in Miriel, except for Sailon. It produces a massive amount, though. This keeps cerulean prices steady, which Tirit Mindel likes. Without Sailon, the Island's power would diminish for a start, and Miriel would emerge as the new financial and magical leader of the world."

Elenor was already shaking her head. "My aunt hates rifters as much, if not more, than my father did."

"Hates, yes. Has uses for, probably also yes. It's Miriel, Elenor. 'Magic and Might' is their motto. But that aside, what all this comes back to is that this looks like empire building to me. As soon as you marry Cassian Iaming, the Miri sweep in here with their appointed regent, a war starts with the North that we will win handily, and Tirit Mindel will be forced to either fold, or fight without access to cerulean. It would be devastating."

To hear him spell it out made her heart sink, yet at the same time it firmed Elenor's resolve and simplified what she had to do. "Well, we won't let that happen, will we?"

"I know you don't want to hear this, Elenor, but one man's life is not—"

Elenor held up a hand. "You're right. I don't want to hear it. I have until the end of the month to figure out a way to save both Paul and Lirin. I'm not a fool; I know I may not be able to do both, and if it comes to a choice between them," she swallowed, then finished, "I know where my duty lies. But if you think I'm going to give up on someone else I love without a fight after everything that woman has put me through, you have a lot still to learn about me, Lord Drego."

With a grunt of pain, she pushed herself to her feet, brushing the wrinkles out of her dress. Rounding the desk toward the door that connected to the meeting chamber, Elenor gestured Kallen through. "Go keep them busy organizing what their sources have told them so far in the search for my mother." That should keep the nobles distracted and out of Elenor's hair for a few minutes, especially since, thanks to Eric, she didn't actually need the information they might have.

Elenor hadn't even made it back to the desk when a soft knock came at the door. A young man with spectacles and arms piled with folders elbowed through.

"Good afternoon, Your Highness," he gasped, his load teetering.

Taking pity on her secretary, Elenor motioned him forward.

When the documents were safely on the desk, Uriah pushed his glasses up his nose and shook out his arms before bowing. "My apologies. I didn't have long to gather up what you asked for, but I believe it is all accounted for."

"Thank you, Uriah. Please, step outside and ask for Gabriel, then take a seat."

When Uriah had pulled up a chair, he reached forward, starting to organize his pile. "The pardons you requested are here. I think this is the complete list of individuals, but some of the names were a little hard to read, and the broader categories are still in progress. I'll have another batch for you later today." He pulled out the folded piece of parchment Elenor had sent up the hill earlier in the day with Jo, Tamara's messy handwriting covering every corner.

The stack of documents Uriah presented her was several inches thick. Elenor shook out her hand and reached for a pen. "And the proclamation?"

"That all of this is in celebration of your upcoming wedding? Being drafted. I'll bring it by as soon as it is done, and we've scheduled a time for you to speak to the city."

"Thank you, Uriah." She continued signing, each paper bearing the name of someone in the Rebellion that her father had arrested in the last few years, and who had not yet been executed. There were also pardons for all those accused of water tax evasion in the last three months, to help conceal the rebels she was releasing. "What of the other matters?"

As she said that, Gabriel slipped into the room. "Claire just told me you're pardoning every known rebel in custody?" he asked, as soon as the door closed behind them.

"I am. I need you to go to Mari a few nights from now. She's arranging a meeting with the rest of your forces. There is a Lirion warehouse near the river that happens to be full of supplies meant to go to the army. I'm ordering a routine cycling of staff and replacing them with people who were loyal to Fedrik Tellen or that Mari indicated were rebel infiltrators. You can use the space and equipment to regroup your operation. I can't make any overt moves to build up a fighting force, but I can clear the way for you to."

"So we're fighting?" he asked, brows furrowing.

"We're preparing for every eventuality, including one where we have to push the Miri out by force. I think we're safe to assume that as long as I look like I'm going along with them, Sianta will make sure I'm not convicted for Mark's death. It wouldn't benefit her plans. So we wait, hold, and prepare until then. As soon as I walk out of that tribunal, though, we end this." Mari had pointed out that angle not long after Gabriel had left, leaving Elenor cursing herself for not realizing it before. She had been so focused on not swinging for her father's death that it hadn't even occurred to her that she wouldn't be able to marry Cassian if she did. Sianta would not let that happen, which, for once, meant that Elenor had the upper hand.

Gabriel's eyes flicked to Uriah, then back to Elenor.

"He can be trusted. He's Djina's nephew. Uriah Grau, meet Gabriel Navarl."

Uriah, who had been staring wide-eyed at Gabriel, pulled another sheaf of papers from the pile. "Your gift to the citizens of Hardor."

Elenor glanced down at the page, checking over the details. "Good, I'll announce this shortly to the nobility, but it is going to the papers first, so they won't be able to stop it."

She signed the bottom of the page with a flourish, handing it to Uriah. "Go to the Hardor Gazette and Ondai Tribune yourself. I want this in circulation by the end of the day. The article should read something along the lines of 'to honor the upcoming union of Seehana and Lirin, and a new era of peace and prosperity with our Mirielee allies, and to begin to mend the division that led to the tragic deaths of Wilam Lirion and Mark Miri, a month of festivities is being called,' etc. It has to come off as a celebration. That should cover most of the movements we need to make in and out of the city. Gabriel, I'm counting on you to make sure your network knows to get to Hardor."

"Got it." Uriah stood, collecting his stack again. "I'll be back as soon as it is done."

She turned her attention to Gabriel, holding out a sheet of paper she had reserved. "Your official pardon for the accusation of attempted assassination of Mark Miri and Lilian Lirion. It turns out it was all a bad misunderstanding, don't you think? And since that misunderstanding resulted in significant pain and distress on your part, I am granting you a royal boon, in the form of a court position of your choice. May I *strongly* suggest the recently vacated position of private physician to the Queen and Queen Regent?"

Gabriel's throat bobbed, as he took the paper. "Understood. Yes, I would be honored. Though I don't think this is really a request, is it?"

"No, it's an order, but it's polite to frame such things as requests. I need you to be able to stay close to me without overt suspicion or public scandal. As my physician, it will not seem untoward for you to be alone with me from time to time, and to remain close in case this flare worsens, or other threats to my health pop up. With the Miri here, that's rather important. Included in that document is your registration as a rifter, with full authorization to be in the Palace and use magic within its walls, dated two months ago. Seems like there was a paperwork mix-up in all the chaos."

Gabriel was shaking his head, smiling. "I see you're not wasting any time today. Good to know bureaucratic minutia and manipulation is as alive and well as ever in Lirin."

"Would it even be Lirin if it were not? You play Seven Rivers—sometimes, to win, you need to arrange the landscape to your advantage long before making your move. Before you go, Gabriel, I've asked someone here to see you."

Jo had, in fact, just knocked on the door, Elenor's cue that her next item of business was here. "Let him in."

The door opened, and Robin Tirition strode in. Elenor stood, motioning the tall man to a chair. Robin didn't seem to notice, gaze fixed on Gabriel.

"Master Robin," Gabe said, running his hand over his messy hair as though the sight of the Tirition had reminded him that he was still covered in sand and lightly singed.

"Gabriel." The open relief in Robin's voice seemed too sincere to be a manipulation.

Elenor sank back into her chair, some of her apprehension about this meeting leaving her now that it had begun. "Thank you for coming up the hill at such short notice, Master Robin. Please, have a seat. Gabriel, you as well, if you wish. We don't have long, so I would appreciate getting down to business. We can arrange for a longer visit at a later date."

Robin hesitated, as though about to protest, but he did not. As both he and Gabriel sat, however, he clasped the younger man on the shoulder. "I cannot tell you how pleased I am to see you alive and well, my boy. I have been worried."

"Thank you. And thank you for trying to help me while I was imprisoned. I heard from both Elenor and others that you advocated for my release," Gabriel replied, smiling at the Tirition with genuine warmth.

It made Elenor queasy, knowing what she did of the lies Robin had spun around Gabriel. This, however, was not the time to discuss that. "Master Robin, you asked me to find a document, and then bring Gabriel to you for one hour. I don't have that hour today, and wasn't sure Gabriel would be here to join us until a few minutes ago since he was with Daemon—"

"You were? Are you alright?" Robin asked, shoulders visibly tensing.

"Fine," Gabe replied, reaching up to rub the back of his neck. "Confused, but fine. Elenor, do you know how he does that thing with the doors in the air? Or who he is, for that matter? He helped me a few times while I was locked away, and now he's teaching me how to use my magic, and I still have no clue as to his motivations."

Elenor raised her eyebrows, staring straight at Robin. "Care to elaborate? I'm guessing you may have more answers than I do."

Maybe it was wrong to take pleasure in the uncomfortable way Robin adjusted his posture, but Elenor did nonetheless.

"Daemon is a . . . colleague of sorts. One could say we're in the same field. He's a dangerous man to have as an ally, but it's better than having him as an enemy. I'm glad to see he's helping you."

Elenor crossed her arms over her chest, lips pursed. From where she sat, it seemed as though the same could be said about Robin, and so far Daemon had proven much more useful. "I asked you here to request some assistance from Tirit Mindel. As you can see, I'm keeping my end of the bargain we struck. I'd like to test our . . . friendship, before I hand over what you want."

She felt bad waving Gabriel in front of Robin's nose this way, but it was unavoidable. The Tirition was a key player in this game, and Elenor needed the upper hand.

"And what is it that you want, Miss Lirion?" Robin asked, eyes finally turning from Gabriel's very confused face.

"You told me once that you could sway public opinion against me with the snap of your finger." She was paraphrasing. To be precise, Robin had threatened to tear her kingdom apart and blame it all on Elenor. "I'd like you to spend the next few weeks doing the opposite. I have a trial coming up in eighteen days and much to do before then. I'd like for you to ensure that the nobles of Lirin understand that Tirit Mindel would be *displeased* if things don't go my way."

"Oh, is that all?" he said, drily.

"No, actually. I'd also like what you took from me back."

Robin froze in perfect neutrality. It was enough to confirm Eric's source. Tirit Mindel had Elenor's mother. "I'm sure I don't know what you mean, Miss Lirion."

"I think you do."

"Even if I did, I don't believe we're good enough friends yet for that sort of discussion. Not while you, too, still retain control of that which I seek." Robin didn't look at Gabriel, but it was clear what he meant. Her mother wasn't going to be returned to her until Gabe was in his custody. "But perhaps that friendship can grow. Did you find what I asked you to?"

Elenor nodded, patting the pocket hidden in her dress.

Robin smiled. "Good. I hope it was illuminating. How about this? I promise to work on your popularity problem. In return, to cement this friendship of ours, do try to schedule that hour to talk as soon as possible, and try to come into it with an open mind. As a friend."

Well, fuck you too.

Her lips never budged from a smile. "That sounds perfectly acceptable. Now, if you will excuse me, I have some of the most important people in Lirin on the other side of that door, waiting for me. Master Robin, my personal guard will escort you out so you don't run into any trouble. Things are a little tense when it comes to Tirit Mindel, with my aunt in residence. Gabriel, go take that paper to the Palace infirmary and they'll get you outfitted in the correct uniform. Check in on Paul for me while you're there. I'll be over to see him as soon as I'm done here."

Gabriel gave her a brief—if not particularly elegant—bow. "I will."

She waited until both he and Robin were gone before rising once more and walking into the adjoining room. The King's Council was gathered, with several other noble representatives from the lesser houses there too, along with the Miri and the Iamings.

Elenor walked over to the head of the long, semi-circular table and sat in the ornate chair her father had claimed for the entirety of Elenor's life. There were chairs around the perimeter of the chamber for those whose houses had not ranked high enough at the last Water Race to have their voices heard. All were full.

The hum of conversation died as Elenor sat, motioning her council to do the same. "Lords and Ladies of Lirin and honored guests, thank you for your patience. We have much to discuss, principally the continued disappearance of the Queen. But before we begin, I would like to officially introduce you to my fiance and soon-to-be King Consort of Lirin, Cassian Iaming, and invite him to be part of today's discussions. I would also ask my honored aunt, Sianta Miri, to sit in lieu of House Lirion's second Writ, and invite King Jonah Iaming to join us in an advisory capacity as befits visiting royalty."

Chairs had already been set for them, since Elenor had sent orders ahead as soon as she and Claire had returned to the Palace. There were a few minutes of shuffling. Cassian took the seat to her left, smiling pleasantly at her. "Thank you for including me, Your Highness. It is an honor. I was concerned when I heard you had left the Palace; is everything alright?"

Elenor did her best to smile back, though inside she recoiled from his touch as he placed a hand over hers. "It is. I simply wished to visit the Temple. As we spoke about this morning, these last few days have been . . . trying. I needed to clear my head, and find myself much refreshed. I hope I'll have the pleasure of your company at dinner?"

"Naturally."

Turning back to the gathered nobles after that tortuous bit of necessity, Elenor stood. "I will shortly be calling on Lord Eurieha to update the Court on the state of the search for Queen Lilian. Prior to that, however, I would like to announce that I have, as tradition dictates, enacted a period of celebration within the city and country ahead of a royal wedding. As you know, it is customary for the nobility of Lirin to allow the people to join in our joy, with festivals, pardons, and gifts of rice and wine. This is no normal royal wedding, however. Lirin is uniting with our southern friends and allies, cementing a bond of peace from the sunny coasts of Seehana to the far northern reaches of Miriel. I, for one, am honored to be a part of such a visionary and important moment in our country's history. On a more somber note, though, this nation has suffered great division and strife of late, so I have decided to take these next few weeks to make a show of unity, peace, and healing."

Murmurs were starting around the room, but Elenor had eyes only for Sianta. Her aunt had asked for a besotted young woman, had she not? Elenor had every intention of giving it to her in such overabundant waves that Sianta would choke on it.

"Those who have recently been deemed Forgotten, including my late brother Wilam, Lord Sebastin Tellen, and Lady Alessia Tellen, have had their names returned to the Hall of Memory. They, along with our late King, will be equally celebrated in the coming weeks. It's time to put the past behind us, and embrace the new beginning we have been granted by the Gods. To do so, I have chosen to pardon all those imprisoned in the city for paltry offenses." By the time anyone noticed that the list also included suspected rebels, the orders would already have reached the watch. "In addition, I have chosen to make a gift to the people of Hardor. From today until the last day of Harvest, no water taxes shall be collected, and all those who come to the doors of the Palace will receive, beyond the usual rice and wine, a purse of coin enough to join in the Harvest Festivities and bolster local business. I will also be donating heavily to many of our local institutions that help the most struggling and downtrodden of our citizens, so that those who need help will receive it, and all may rejoice together." Hopefully, no one would notice until too late how many of those charities were fronts for rebel activities.

Murmurs spread through the hall. No doubt, every noble there was doing the math, trying to figure out how much of a dent this would make in Lirion coffers.

Elenor sucked in a breath, then dropped the core of her plan. "I ask that all the other noble and Writted Houses of Lirin join me in my gift to the people within your home provinces, so the whole country may unite in remembering the past and celebrating the future."

Immediately, people started talking. Elenor raised her hands before the protests became shouts. "A moment, please. I know the next Water Race is coming, and everyone is tightening their purse strings. I ask nothing of you that I am not willing to do myself. This is why House Lirion will be *matching* all your generous acts over the next four weeks, mark for mark. If you wish to do nothing, it is within your rights. I force no one to give what they cannot part with to help the citizens under their care."

Dead silence. Elenor tried not to smile as her eyes tracked from face to face, watching as each noble in the room realized what Elenor had done. By not ordering their cooperation, she had challenged them to a month-long game of financial one-upmanship. The people in their provinces and cities would hear about Elenor's proclamation, and know that if food, money, entertainment, and resources did not shower upon them as they would the people under Elenor's direct control, it would be because *their* provincial Lords and Ladies had chosen not to participate, even with a boon from the Crown. It would be a disaster.

Arguing against it, even more so, because they would become easy targets for accusations of putting their finances ahead of the people they had been entrusted to govern. Besides, it was also a chance to dent the financial control the Lirion family had always maintained. Every ten years during the Water Race, a handful of games and a financial audit determined the rank of every Writted House. With the next Water Race only a year away, if a Writted House could do better than the Lirions during the Water Race audit, they would take the throne. Therefore, it was suddenly in their best interest to make Elenor spend as much as possible, as swiftly as possible.

Thank you, Mari. This may come to bite me if I survive to the next Water Race, but if I do nothing, I certainly won't.

Her gaze fell on her aunt, who was staring at Elenor through squinted eyes. Elenor would have given all the gold in the Lirion treasury to know what was going on in her aunt's head. Sianta had ordered Elenor to appoint her to the Council, make preparations for the wedding, and entertain the Iamings, had she not?

Elenor just hoped that the Queen of Miriel saw this as her bending over backwards to follow instructions instead of the calculated risk it was. As Mari had pointed out to her, though, when Elenor had hesitated on the way out the door: "*Blackmail has two sides. If she lets your guardian die, she loses her leverage over you at a time when she needs it to further her plans. Push a little today, under the parameters of what she wants. You might find you have more power than you think, if you don't let her terrify you into inaction.*"

She'd get on her knees and beg forgiveness to save Paul later if Sianta tried to deny him his next dose of the antidote, but Mari was right. Elenor had to know how much she could get away with, and how much her aunt needed *her.*

Until then, Elenor settled back into her chair and motioned Daniil Eurieha forward. "Now that that's taken care of, I invite Lord Eurieha to give us his update on the search for the Queen."

CHAPTER THIRTY-TWO
Gatekeeper Talks
FEDRIK

I want this power gone. That, more than anything, drives my need to kill Sidian. I want it gone. It is a curse that's eating me up from the inside. Please, Lady Red, kill me. Let another carry it.

—From a letter to Fulsixia the Red, from Suela Alveara.

FEDRIK SAT ON THE EDGE OF A TERRACE, the first rays of the rising sun shining on his upturned face. His eyes were closed, hands clasped loosely in his lap, but while outwardly he was making an effort to appear calm, inside a storm raged. He'd woken up to another dream of *her*.

This time, Elenor had been standing by the edge of the water, a white shift swaying in the current around her knees and skin flush with fever. The wind had whipped her loose golden hair into a frenzy, each strand set alight by the rust-hewed brilliance of dusk. Her eyes were focused on the far bank, determination and fear etched in the furrows of her brow.

"Eighteen days. I have to make it across by then." The words had been spoken under her breath, followed by the litany of the Blue. Each syllable had twined through Fedrik's soul, a noose tightening and pulling him toward his Incarnate.

He had woken with Fay's sleeping body nestled against him, yet all he had been able to see was that river and how easy it would be to shove Elenor into the water and hold her down. Fedrik's arms had acted on their own. One moment Fay had been fast asleep on their mat after a grueling first day of training, the next she had been flying across the rough stone floor.

"I hear you tried to remove all the skin from my apprentice's left side. I must admit, I find the cursing marginally less irritating when she has legitimate reason to complain. I think it time you and I have a private talk. We haven't had a chance since our arrival."

Suela's cane, then her feet came to rest near the railing Fedrik was propping his elbows on. He looked up at her, having to squint against the sunlight to do so. "I have a question, and it's not a stupid one."

His head held a bruised spot from the number of times Suela's cane had come down on it the day before.

"I will be the judge of that."

"How often do Gatekeepers die?"

"Thinking of flinging yourself off the edge?" At least there was no cane whack, so the old lady must have deemed it a worthwhile conversation.

"Sometimes."

"I tried."

He hadn't been expecting that, so didn't know the right words to reply. Suela did not take that as a deterrent. "A few months after a knife and fire pot were placed in front of me and I took my own eyes, Sidian came here. We knew he was safe from my Gift, as was the world, so it should have been easy. So many Gatekeepers can't be controlled by something as *easy* as mutilation, yet still found a way to find peace with their Incarnate. Everyone said we would be no trouble in comparison, especially with the bond he and I already shared. I cared for Sidian like a mother cares for a son. I gouged out my eyes for him without hesitation, because I *believed* in my culture's faith and that it was the right thing to do.

"But it wasn't easy. Or perhaps it was, but it didn't feel that way. I went to bed every night covered in bruises from the guards our overseers had brought to tackle me to the ground if I so much as twitched. I woke up each morning screaming because in my dreams I had succeeded where I could not while awake. I felt alone in a darkness that never ended, without even the comfort of the desert sun. Not a minute passed when my mind did not conjure another way to tear him apart, but when I would wake with his imagined blood on my hands it was always grief that consumed me. I didn't want him to die. Just as strongly, I needed him to."

Fedrik's insides churned. Oh how he knew that feeling—that ceaseless gnawing guit wrapped in fury. "So you tried to end it?"

"Then? No. I got through the training eventually. It took months, but in time I learned to touch him without trying to kill him. Once I did… it was peace. I cannot explain it and perhaps it is nothing more than the normalcy that was stripped from us feeling all the more potent for being restored. Be it as it may, the moment I could touch Sidian, it got easier. Finally, we were deemed ready to go out into the world to do the work of Gatekeeper and Incarnate.

"The night after leaving here, we stayed at the home of an almond farmer. She had a large family with many rifters and several *daradeio*. Throughout dinner everyone was polite to us both, but when the laughter and song began, the attention of the group shifted. One by one, starting with the rifters, people drifted over to Sidian. Within an hour, everyone was laughing and enjoying the night near him, caught in the pleasant aura of his presence. Meanwhile, I had been utterly ignored. I don't think it was malice, but when they looked at me and my bandaged eyes and dark robes, they saw something *other*. Foreign and dangerous, despite the fact that I had been born in the desert and Sidian still longed for the kingdom of his birth. That was when I realized that while I was struggling and changing myself to constrain my Gift into a form society would recognize as useful, Sidian had done none of those things.

"Where I got suffering and an endless uphill battle, always destined to be treated with apprehension, Sidian was greeted with adoration by every rifter who passed. His power was praised for its ability to give Gifts, while mine was seen as monstrous. He never once woke covered in cold sweat and vomited his guts out because of the death toll our Gifts had caused and the fear that he wouldn't be strong enough to keep it from happening again. The privilege and status he enjoyed came directly from my ostracization and labor, and there was nothing I could do to change it."

Fedrik looked away from her, the constant throbbing in his head a pounding accompaniment to Suela's far too relatable words. "Did you hate him for it?"

"Every day."

"But you didn't kill him?"

With several creaks and groans, Suela sat down beside Fedrik. "I did not. The night after our stay with the almond farmer I decided to take a different life. I was numb, exhausted, and all I wanted was to look out over the desert and see the moon shining upon the sand. Yet my eyes were gone and my heart ached for what I had been forced to give up for this cursed existence he had given me. I wanted it to be over. So I had loaded my pockets with stones and was standing by the edge of the oasis when Sidian found me.

"I told him to stand back and not interfere. That I wasn't strong enough to endure any more of this constant torture. I didn't want to spend the rest of my days working so hard only to be feared. My words were cruel. I screamed at him, cried out my fury and grief that he had it so easy while I had worked night and day. Since I could not see his face, I can't tell you what he was thinking or feeling as I ranted, but he let me finish without saying a word.

"Only when I fell silent did Sidian take my hands and tell me that I was right. That it wasn't fair, that I was justified in my anger at him, and that it was wholly wrong that people feared me when I had succeeded in controlling my power and given my life to better our desert, but not him. I remember his words as though it were yesterday. 'I asked a rifter to take off his sandals at noon and walk a mile on the burning sand,' he said. 'And at the end of that mile, with bleeding, blistered feet, he thanked me for it. They look at me and see a legacy of pride in our desert and its Gifts, and you as the unfortunate price we must pay to achieve it. Yet between the two of us, it is my Gift that is the monstrous one. I'm more of a danger than you will ever be, and much more likely to be corrupted by the power I was granted. I can't do this without you, Suela. I need to know that you are there, ready to stop me if I stray from the path of morality you taught me to follow.'

"Then Sidian sank to his knees and swore me an oath. He promised to be my eyes, if I would be his voice. To speak for him so that his Gift could not twist the minds of those around us; to choose for him, so that his will did not blindly become law. In return, he pledged to remain by my side always, and share with me the honor and trust our people placed in the First and Last Gift. To look out across the desert for me each morning and tell me of the beauty we were working so hard to protect. Most of all, he promised to let me decide the day we passed on our Gifts and became free, so that I would never again feel like I was trapped."

Suela stopped, a wistful sigh passing her cracked and wrinkled lips.

Fedrik's heart was aching so badly that he could hardly breathe.

"Hold on tight, El, and keep watch. I'll be your legs if you'll be my eyes. If my parents catch us climbing up to the roof we're going to be in so much trouble."

The snippet of memory broke through the blinding rage he usually felt. It was followed by another, one which he hadn't thought about in years: the first night at the Palace after killing Cornen.

"I don't know what's wrong, Fed, but I know you're hurting. You don't have to tell me why, just know that I'm here for you and always will be. Whatever you need, whenever you need it, today and for the rest of time. We're family. I love you."

Elenor had held him for hours while he cried and never once demanded a reason for his tears. He had woken the next day tucked into bed with a fresh evergold flower on his pillow and a cup of steaming tea by his bedside, as though she had only just left. As though she had spent all night watching over him to keep his demons away, just as he had once sat by her sickbed holding her hand through the pain.

"Did Sidian ever do something so bad that you thought you could never forgive him?" Fedrik asked in a quiet voice.

Suela let out a chuckle. "Often. But then again, I made my fair share of mistakes and bad decisions too. That's what being human means. The trick wasn't to expect perfection; being perfect isn't achievable. What was under our control was holding each other accountable for our choices, and forgiving once we had done our best to make them right."

Fedrik remained quiet for some time before speaking again.

His eyes drifted over the stark, vertical landscape, taking in all the beautiful details he hadn't taken the time to notice. "The sun is coming up over the canyon. There are striations in the red stone that shimmer when it touches them, like embers in a fire that has mostly burned out. The stream is still in shadows, but the flowers growing by the bank are starting to open. They are white and pink specks nestled in pockets of green. The lizards are gathering in the sunny spots near the top of the city, and up on the edge there's a wild red mock sunning its wings. It's beautiful."

Suela turned her face up, the sun rays touching her wrinkled skin and bandaged eyes. "Thank you."

Fedrik got to his feet, then bent to press a kiss into her crinkly gray hair. "Thank *you.* I'll see you in an hour for practice. Time to get Fayrian up. I think I'm ready to get to work."

EPILOGUE
The Gold's Will
ALEHAN

THE CURTAINS OF THE CATHEDRAL BILLOWED in the hot wind off the mesas. From where he stood, Alehan could see the light of Gold City begin to shimmer as the sunset turned the western sky pink. A seagull swept past the window and out towards the distant coastline and the freedom that would never be his.

Beyond that horizon—though Alehan could not see it—was the Stormwall he and his family had been sent through more than five hundred years before.

He shivered.

Sometimes, when he closed his eyes, he could still see his mother's head disappearing under the choppy waves. Still hear his father cry out to him before Alehan, too, went under. Before Aleh drowned, but didn't die.

Now, if the Gold wished it, Alehan would be going back. Back to the land that had scarred him, murdered his family, and destroyed his childhood. Back to where the forces that had orchestrated all his suffering had taken control.

Around him, several Gods and priests milled. Some of the Gods were in their draconic forms, towering over the mortals but still dwarfed by this immense chamber. Most, however, had chosen to don their more human form, talking quietly with their retainers.

Alehan remained quiet in the shadow of Sel'Caronock's mighty feet. His scales were of labradorite, shimmering each time the light touched them or Alehan tilted his head. It should have made him feel safe, but nothing could have done that.

He was not safe.

The only comfort he could take was that Raiyana was there too, and staring at him with her usual predatory hunger. Maybe she would convince the Gold to let Alehan stay. She would, he was sure, delight in experimenting on him for the rest of time. That might be better than going back to Carinn.

A gong sounded, and the doors at the far end of the hall opened. All conversation stilled, every eye turning to the two lines of priests dressed in golden silk who were filing into the room. The floor shook with each rumbling step of the creature in the darkness beyond.

A spotlight appeared, pointed at the threshold of the open doorway. Alehan despised the theatrics, but even though he knew exactly what she was doing, it still worked. His breath sped up as the footsteps drew nearer, then caught as the shimmering golden head of a mighty Dragon entered the beam of light. The refracted brilliance was so blinding that he had to look away. Around the chamber, God and mortal alike bowed.

Alehan refused to. It wasn't as though Sarthia would be able to see his defiance with that glaring spotlight in her eyes, so what was the point? This was all smoke and mirrors.

She did not fully enter the hall. Her bulk remained in shadows, only her head and occasionally the tip of a razor-sharp claw or mighty wing entering the beam of light.

Her voice, when it came, filled the cathedral, booming off the walls and making every human flinch. "The exiled mortals of Carinn have deepened their sins. Three days ago, they killed our fallen sister, Fulsixia the Red. For this, they will be punished. Many of you gathered here have pleaded for mercy. For one final chance to redeem themselves. I am a kind and benevolent Mother, and have listened to your pleas. I will give those who rose against me one final chance to find redemption, and send unto them a prophet to bring them back to my fold."

Every gaze shifted to Alehan. They all knew. *Well, fuck them.*

Alehan straightened his shoulders and walked forward. He stopped where the Gold could see him, then said, "No."

At first there was dead silence, then the whispers started. Out of the corner of his eye, Alehan saw Nash's face pale where he stood among the Gold's priests.

Even the Goddess he had defied seemed momentarily blindsided by his refusal, for it took several seconds for her to reply. "Perhaps you do not understand the path I am offering you, Alehan Silvarin. You have been spared the pain of exile for five centuries and allowed to live in my light. You are being offered a chance to share that same redemption to all the wretched, lost souls of Carinn, in place of the extermination they are due for killing a God."

Alehan's mind buzzed with retorts. The 'redemption' he had been granted amounted to confinement, isolation, and experimentation. If all of Carinn's people truly deserved death, one man's action couldn't change that. He had no responsibility to the descendants of people who had killed his family. He forced himself to relax his fists and focus on the part of this that actually mattered. "Punishing them is your choice, not my responsibility. I am not going back."

"Clearly, you have grown brazen in the light of my favoritism. You seem to need a reminder of what proper deference looks like." A single claw extended from the shadows, pointing straight at Nash.

Alehan steeled himself. *This is her decision. I am not culpable.* Maybe, if he said something, Sarthia would spare Nash. But he had never seen Sarthia spare someone she had marked for punishment.

Nash hobbled forward, leaning heavily on his cane, until he stood before the great Dragon. There, he sank to his knees, prostrating himself. His voice shook as he recited the litany of the Gold. "I am no longer my own, but thine. To thee who gave me life, I surrender this mortal flesh, this sinful heart, this hopeful soul. Let thy will chart the course of my days, let it flow through my veins, and give me wings of golden fire. All that I was is gone, all of my secrets bared, all my desires relinquished. Thy servant I am and will remain 'til mountains turn to dust and all the stars are dead."

The last word still hung in the air when a giant gold-taloned foot descended upon Nash, crushing him like a bug.

Alehan flinched as a spatter of blood coated his shoes. He knew Raiyana's eyes would be on him, anticipating how the sight of viscera and broken bones would make him feel when Sarthia moved her foot away from the mutilated corpse. He looked at the Gold's face instead, even as his hands shook at his sides and his throat tightened. He couldn't allow himself to be cowed. "I will not go."

"Refuse, and you die alongside them. Your years here and family name will not spare you." There was an ominous rumble in the Gold's voice. A promise of violence and death. There were good reasons why people never spoke against her, reasons Aleh had carefully considered before this meeting and chosen to ignore.

Almost, Alehan laughed. It would have been a bitter, ugly sound, but he kept his composure. Did she think that was a threat? He had died before. If she knew of a way to make it permanent, a part of him would welcome the release. But he couldn't lose track of his argument. "Your decision about what the people of Carinn deserve has nothing to do with me. If you want to spare them, spare them. If you want to punish them, punish them. If you want to—"

Sel'Caronok stepped forward, the rumble of his footfalls interrupting Alehan. The Labradorite Dragon bowed low before the Gold. "Forgive the interruption, My Lady. From my own studies around the anomaly of Alehan Silvarin, and those of the honorable Raiyana, I do not believe threats to his life will be sufficiently motivating."

Sel'Caranok had been the one to pull Alehan out of the Plane the last time. In moments of vulnerability, he had shared things with his patron that he had shared with no other Dragon or human. Things that even Raiyana hadn't been able to torture out of him. If any of them understood Aleh's relationship with death, it was him. Yet still, Alehan was just a curious object being bartered, his most private emotions merely another point of negotiation, because Sarthia wouldn't take responsibility for her own actions.

Sarthia's gleaming golden eyes narrowed. "And what, in your estimation, would be *sufficiently motivating?* I am curious to know, and especially curious about the validity of your opinion when you did not know this boy well enough to prevent his cowardly escape attempt."

From behind him, Alehan heard a self-satisfied huff from Raiyana.

Sel'Caronok simply deepened his bow. "It was that very attempt that convinced me that he would rather lose all that he has gained in his time here than be sent back into Exile. His deepest desire, My Lady, is for freedom. Death is one type of freedom, but less motivating than what he has shown he is willing to risk everything for. I believe that if you wish him to be the voice that brings the Exiles back into your light, the motivation he needs is the freedom to chart his own course. After all, is devotional work not at its purest when it comes from a place of willingness, not fear?"

Alehan looked at the massive, radiant form beside him. Sel'Caranok had said he would have asked the Gold to spare him, but this . . . it took a moment for Alehan to process what was being asked. His first reaction was betrayal that his patron was arguing in favor of sending him to Carinn. He tightened his hold on his emotions. It was too easy for him to lose track of his goals and argue against the details. If he accepted that any terms were worth considering, it would legitimize that Sarthia had a right to demand anything of him at all.

She will demand it whether or not I acknowledge her right.

Sometimes Alehan thought of himself as a person unable to die. More often, he considered those times he had ended up in the Plane as true deaths, which he was cursed to always come back from. He had made his peace with death, but he was still scared of what Sarthia might do to end his existence. If she failed, he would suffer her attempts and then be given to Raiyana. Even if Sel'Caranok successfully advocated for him, the best he could hope for was a continuation of his current miserable life.

Sarthia had no right to demand anything of him, but he was not so idealistic that he thought he could convince her of that. The goal of his arguments hadn't been to make her spare him, but to assert his own agency.

Sel'Caranok's unexpected words brought him out of that single-mindedness. His principles demanded that he not give her an inch. The utilitarian part of him knew that there was no way that he would be left out of this, and that he had an opportunity to get what would have been impossible otherwise.

Alehan's eyes finally lowered to Nash's body. He had made his peace with losing every person he would ever know, but he hadn't seen one die so brutally since he was a child. He didn't owe Carinn anything. Every one of those people would be dead in a hundred years with or without Alehan. But he could deny Sarthia the satisfaction of their deaths.

The situation crystalized in his mind. Sarthia wouldn't negotiate with him—that was beneath her—but she might agree to his terms to avoid prolonging the discussion and looking weak. He had one chance.

Before Sarthia could respond to Sel'Caranok, Alehan spoke. "If you truly want me to go back, then I'll do it. But first, you must grant me self-determination. Immunity from the demands and manipulation of any God or their servants, on this continent or Carinn." He looked back at Raiyana, making his point. "Immunity that is not contingent on the Gods' cooperation. Not even your own. I will carry out your orders for this single goal. I will act as your prophet and unite the peoples of Carinn. But I will not do it while under your control. My success or failure will be my own. Their life or death will be on my shoulders, not yours . . . Great Dragon." Those last words were a struggle to force between his teeth, but he didn't dare omit them as he sank into a bow.

Alehan didn't breathe. Whatever Sarthia said, Alehan could either agree or forfeit this chance for a future not ruled over by the Gods. She would not argue minutia in a room full of onlookers.

"You are bold, but so was the God of your family. So you will need to be, to save those who think they can kill one of our own with impunity. I accept your request, Alehan Silvarin, for the sake of Harrodorin, who sacrificed their life for my own. And only for Harrodorin. Such impertinence will not be forgiven twice. You will do my bidding. While you do and if you succeed, no God will determine your destiny. But if you fail," The Gold waited until Alehan peeked up from his bow to say, "You will die. And if you do not stay dead, I will kill you again and again from that day until the end of days, if necessary."

Alehan's gaze fell once more to Nash's remains and steeled himself, deepening the bow. "So be it. How long will I have to prepare?"

The great Gold Dragon's eyes narrowed, but since Alehan had not asked *whether* he would have time to prepare, it would make her look petty to make him go at once. A huff sent searing air rippling over Alehan, fluttering the silk of his clothes. "In my infinite mercy I will grant you eighteen days, one for each of our Gods, to devise your strategy and gather what you believe you require."

"And how long will I have to bring them into your light?"

It wouldn't be long. She wanted him to fail. It would allow her to wipe out a troublesome continent and blame it all on Alehan.

"The day you arrive, the Harborstone of the Red will fall. Each year thereafter, another will. When none of the six remain, I will come to end the Exile . . . one way or another."

THE END

Solace of Memory

A LAST GIFT NOVELETTE

Dedicated to all the lives lost and remembered in 2020
and all those who fought to save them.
May your memory be a blessing.

DENIAL

The rattling gasps woke Gabriel from a fitful sleep, where he sat on a stool in the corner of the ward. The smell of death and smoke hung like a shroud over the sweltering hospital room, even with the windows flung wide and a circuitry-powered fan moving the stagnant air.

Gabe blinked away the drowsiness and looked around, trying to find the source of the noise. Eight beds had been crammed into the room that had once held four. On each, a patient lay, the youngest a child of ten, the eldest in his seventies. It was that man who was gasping for air, back arched off the bed in a posture Gabriel had become far too familiar with over the last month.

Getting to his feet was hard. Everything hurt, and his head was pounding. The stimulant drug that was keeping him from catching wasting fever had allowed for little sleep, even when he'd had the opportunity to lie down. Each step pressed against the blisters on his feet, but despite the discomfort, Gabe crossed the room as fast as he could.

"I'm here. Let's get you sitting, Tom. You'll be able to breathe easier," he said, reaching the bed. The old man grasped at his hand when Gabe offered it, staring up at him with wide, panic-filled eyes as his mouth opened and chest spasmed, with no sound but the wheezing escaping his blue-tinged lips. Gabriel knelt on the bed, using what leverage he could to pull Tom gently upward. The man let out a gurgled scream, limbs going rigid in pain.

Head turned so his patient could not see it, Gabriel squeezed his eyes shut. He managed to keep his voice steady as he rubbed at Tom's back. "Concentrate on each breath, my friend. I know you're scared, but we'll get through this. Breathe with me. In.... and out...."

GABRIEL WALKED TO THE ACADEMY through the snow, each crunching footfall slow and tired. His bag was slung over his shoulder, and though it had been days since he had left Miriel, he just hadn't found time to remove the medic patches from his coat.

A carriage passed by, headed into town. Through the window, he saw students packed in like sardines with cases piled on their laps. The last boat to the mainland had to be leaving soon.

With a sigh, he bent his head and continued to walk, his hope that he would catch Fedrik or Fay before they left for the holidays growing dimmer along with the setting of the sun. He should have saved up enough for the coach ride back to the Academy, but like all his fellow student medics, he had donated the substantial paycheck from Tirit Mindel to help the victims of the wasting fever outbreak. Gabe didn't regret it yet, but he was sure he would when the day of Remembrance came and for the first time ever, he'd be alone. A last kiss from Fay would have certainly helped balm that pain.

The gates of the Academy were flung open, wrought iron dusted in snow.

"Hey, Navarl, I didn't realize you'd make it here the holidays. Didn't you go straight home?" One of the Silverguard watching the gate said, waving at him.

"Need to get caught up on schoolwork," Gabriel replied, trying and failing to conjure a smile. "Finals don't stop just because plagues start."

"True that. Glad to see you back safe. I'll catch you later."

With a last wave, Gabriel turned to the path. Coming in from the south the way he had, the Core Six dorms were clear across the grounds. He rounded the library and the temple, took the long way around the Silverguard barracks to avoid the mud near the training yard, and finally got to junior housing.

Gabe nearly cried as his building came into view, a fire lighting the windows and candles flickering on the sill. The snow on the front steps had been swept away. As expected, no one was in their living room, but there was a pot of what smelled like mulled wine by the hearth so *someone* had to still be there, even if it was only Master Robin.

After setting his pack down on the nearest chair, Gabe bent to remove his boots. The last thing he needed was a lecture about tracking mud into the house. That might be the straw that broke the thin veneer of alright that he had scraped together on the boat voyage back from Miriel. As he worked on the icy laces, he groaned, every muscle sore and in need of a hot shower. Should that come first, or dinner? The loud growl from his stomach answered that. Stopping for a minute to warm his hands by the fire on the way, Gabriel crossed over to his bedroom door.

Huh…

Fedrik must have forgotten to make his bed before leaving. That was unlike him, but he did always get excited near the holidays. To keep his friend from getting in trouble with Robin, Gabe dropped his pack on his own bed, shrugged off his coat, and fixed Fedrik's covers. As he did that, he noticed the suitcase that usually sat tucked between the bed and the dresser was still there.

Gabe tilted his head to the side. Had he gotten the dates wrong? Fedrik should have left earlier, and Fay would have had to leave that morning at the latest to make it home in time to celebrate with Cornen and the Rebellion. Midwinter was their organization's biggest and most important season, a time to help the families of those the Lirion had forgotten, and a time to recruit. She never missed one.

"Gabriel," Robin's voice came from the doorway. "You're back already? I thought you weren't due until tomorrow morning. Welcome home."

"Thank you, Master Robin. We had the wind with us, and made good time out of Miriel. Have the boats to Lirin already left?"

"Aye, they have. Were you hoping to make one?"

"Not this year," Gabe replied, shoulder slumping. Even if he had wanted to go home with Fay, he couldn't have afforded it. Since he was making some money of his own, he refused to let Cornen foot that bill again. The Rebellion needed the funds more than Gabriel needed to be in Hardor for a few days. Even so, his heart ached for it—for the smell of Mari's baking and for late nights of playing Seven Rivers with his friends and Wilam, if he could get away from the Palace long enough.

"Well then, let me know your plans. The teachers and students who stay here over Midwinter tend to have a gathering of our own for Remembrance Day. You are welcome to join us," his teacher said.

Gabriel gave him a nod of thanks. "That sounds great. Do you mind if I lie down for a few hours? I'm exhausted."

"Of course, of course. I'd like to hear of your time in Miriel, but only after you've had a chance to rest. Though I thought you'd want to see Miss Avilor and Mr. Tellen first."

Gabe had gone back to making the bed, but his head snapped up at that. "Wait, they're still here? But I thought you said the last boat to Lirin had already left?"

"Yes, it did, but neither of them was on it. Both chose to remain here for the holidays, hoping you would be back. I believe they are at the practice yards at present."

Gabe was already squeezing past Robin toward the door by the end of that sentence. Before he could run out into the cold again, though, his teacher caught him by the back of his shirt.

"Perhaps a shower, first, Mr. Navarl? Before you go running around my Academy with dirt smudges on your nose?" Then, with a twinkle in his eye, he added, "I am certain Miss Avilor would appreciate it as well"

A hasty shower and change of clothes later, Gabriel raced toward the training yards as fast as the slushy snow permitted. He was still several turns away when he heard Fay's voice ringing through the crisp air.

"If you keep telegraphing your attacks before you make them, of course they're going to kick our ass. Will you please stop smiling before you swing high? It's basically the same as fucking shouting it. A five-year-old could predict what you're about to do." She sounded out of breath and quite cross.

"Says miss always-follows-a-side-step-with-a-faint. Learn it before you teach it, Avilor. And for the record, in what twisted reality would I be fighting a five-year-old?" Fedrik's deeper voice countered. "Let's go again, if you two are willing?"

"Actually," Gabe said, stepping out from around the armory with a wide grin, "I think practice is done for the day."

Fay and Fedrik were standing in the middle of one of the fighting rings, him with a practice sword and her with a stave. They were tied together at the waist, with about six feet between them. Two older students were catching their breaths across the muddy ring. Unlike Gabe's friends, they were not bound to each other. Denzel Tirition, the weapons master, had originally forced Fay and Fedrik to fight tied together to get them to cooperate, but Gabriel suspected these days it was because they worked better as a team than on their own.

"Gabe!" Fay cried, swivelling around. Her staff dropped to the ground and she raced straight at him.

"Woah there, Avilor. Oof!" Fedrik yelled, as she jerked him—still attached to her—right into the fence around the training yards, as she vaulted over it to throw herself into Gabriel's arms.

Gabe might have felt sympathy for his friend, but he was a bit too busy falling backward into the slush with an armful of curly red hair and exuberant energy on top of him. Not caring one bit that mud was soaking his freshly washed hair and seeping into his uniform, Gabriel squeezed Fay in the tightest hug he could manage and buried his face in her curls.

"Hey there, beautiful," he whispered.

Her lips found his in a long overdue kiss, and the last month faded away in a rush of relief and joy.

"Are you going to drown the poor man in a puddle right after he makes it back, just to have your wicked way with him, Avilor? Shame on you," Fedrik said. He had made it over the fence, rubbing his chest and busy untying the rope that still connected him to Fay. "Welcome home, Navarl."

"I wasn't expecting either of you to still be here," he replied with a laugh, as Fedrik offered him and Fay a hand each to get up. Once Gabriel was on his feet, the tall nobleman hugged him too. Both of his friends were already covered in mud splatters from practice, so it wasn't as though a little extra dirt could hurt.

"And leave you all alone with *Robin?* He would have made you study to catch up all the way through Midwinter," Fay said, shaking her head and beaming up at him. "Besides, Tellen has been pining for you. Staring out the window all day long, waiting for you to return."

Fedrik snorted, the red and black beads at the ends of his dreadlocks clinking together as he shook his head. "Mhm. Absolutely. That was definitely me and not you, Avilor. Though truth be told, I have been pining for some actual interesting company, instead of a brutal taskmistress who drags me out here every chance she gets. She delights in leaving me bruised and bleeding, I tell you."

Fay smacked Fedrik on the arm, scrunching up her nose. "I wouldn't have to if you practiced fighting when left to your own devices, instead of burying your nose in your poison and politics books. If I'm going to be literally tied to you until graduation, you're going to have to keep up with me."

"I've missed you both so fucking much," Gabe said, pulling his friends in for another welcome and sorely needed hug. It was so good to be home.

ANGER

"I want more of the medicine. The one tha' makes the pain go away and my breathin' better," Tom wheezed, when he was finally able to, and Gabriel had settled him back into bed. "You gave more to Ito, and he got better."

Gabe let out a sigh, eyes rising from the clipboard he had just picked up. "If I give you more now, there would not be enough later. Ito got more because his family paid for more. It shouldn't be that way, but last time you talked me into giving you extra, I got the lecture of a lifetime. There's only so much serindalla to go around in the general supply. If you get extra, someone else won't get a dose."

"I don't give a rat's ass 'bout anyone else. No'n ever's given one for me," the old man grumbled.

"That might be because you're a cranky old scarecrow," Gabe said, with a smile that Tom returned after rolling his eyes.

"Yer not wrong, but don't think I won't be reporting ya. No way to speak to a dying man. This whole system's fucked, and fuck you too for workin' for it. If ya'd have an ounce of decency, you'd give me the drugs. How much sicker's a man got to get before he gets some proper care?" In contrast to his words, Tom patted the bed beside him, then sank further into his pillows, as though the simple motion was all he could manage without getting winded. "Sit with me, will ya? There's a good lad. For fucks sake, you re'lly are a kid, aren't ya? I'd ne'r noticed, but in the light, yer all baby-faced. Young and healthy and all fancy in that Tirit Mindel uniform. Fuck you."

"I turn eighteen this spring." Gabe sat, the cot creaking. He really ought to do his rounds again, but no one was crying out, and he doubted Tom would be with them much longer. Gabe hoped he passed before one of the attending physicians decided they were wasting medication on him. There had been one of those patients the week before in bed three, and Gabriel still woke up with her screams ringing in his ears. "And my uniform isn't fancy. It's covered in sweat and your piss. Still think you missed the bed pan on purpose, you perv."

Tom laughed, which turned into a cough, which turned

into his chest spasming as he gasped for air. "Tryin' to kill me, you are. Should be mad, but I'm too tired for it. Would ya... would ya just sit with me, for awhile? Until I can sleep again? You're shit company, but it's better than nothin'..."

Gabe gave his hand a gentle squeeze. "Of course I'll sit with you, Tom. I'll be here as long as you need me."

"SO, HOW WAS IT?" Fay was the first to broach the subject. They were sitting around the hearth in their dorm, drinking mulled wine. Robin had left after dinner and no other classmates were staying over, so for the first time Gabe could remember, the three of them had the place to themselves.

Each building in Core Six housing was set up the same: a living room, a small classroom for study with their live-in teacher, and six bedrooms. By their final year, only Fedrik and Gabriel were still sharing a room, four of the ten students they had started with having dropped out or fallen behind over the course of the previous years.

"Worst thing I've seen since Nillenia," Gabe answered, chin resting on the top of Fay's head and an arm wrapped around her waist. They had dragged pillows and blankets into the living room and were sitting on the floor, leaning up against the nearby armchairs. "The pyres were going around the clock, and they ran out of dry wood, so the smoke was so thick it blotted out the sun some days. By the time I left, they were running so low on fuel that they were digging mass graves."

Across from them, Fay's feet in his lap, Fedrik shuddered. "That sounds horrific. I thought the mortality rate of wasting fever was starting to come down, what with that new early treatment protocol you were talking about before you left."

"It is," Gabe replied, after taking a long sip of his mulled wine and tamping down the burst of annoyance. Fedrik didn't know how many times his patients had asked that question, and how hard it had been to not be able to give them the answer they wanted. It wasn't his friend's fault that it poked at a bruise Tellen didn't know existed. "The new protocol is complicated and takes a lot of attention from the doctor overseeing the physical therapy and drug regime. It's expensive, too. Even if it wasn't, though, there weren't enough medics to give that kind of care to everyone who needed it, not when hundreds of new infected showed up every day. It was starting to finally slow when I left, now that the colder weather is here and the mosquitos are dying off, but if the Miriel government doesn't shell out the funds for daily serindalla treatment for at least a year, it will just happen again next spring."

Fedrik was already shaking his head. "There's no way Miriel will do that. Even with how much money the Lirion are funneling into the country, it would be too sizable an amount. Especially with how high serindalla prices are these days."

"Yeah, I know." Gabe closed his eyes, shoulders tensing. The tapered down dose of the drug Gabe had taken with dinner was making him jittery, but the alcohol helped. It had been the only way he'd managed to get a few hours of sleep each night, the last week of his posting. It had dulled the desire to give the medicine away to those who needed them more, even though it was the only thing keeping him safe from the fever."And it makes me so fucking frustrated, because it means everything we've done, all the lives we saved and all the ones we couldn't, won't change a damn thing. Everyone who caught the fever will relapse as soon as they can't afford the serindalla, and more will be infected every summer. The nobles up north are safe, so why would they spend the money? It's not the fault of the people who are suffering that their government isn't taking responsibility for this mess, but they're the ones dying." He had to fight hard not to let his hands ball up into fists, yet the desire to vent a month of repressed fury at the injustices he had witnessed was hard to subdue. "It's criminal."

"That's always the case," Fay said, taking his hand and kissing the palm, as though she could feel his need for a calming touch. Bless her. Somehow, she always seemed to know. "But you did make a difference, Gabriel. There are people alive today who would have died if not for you, right?"

"Not enough." The need to move was making his legs twitch and heart race, but Gabe stayed put. With Fayrian leaning against him, it was a little easier to keep the despair that had been his constant companion over the last month at bay. It had been there, tangible like the smoke hanging low in the muggy air, shadowing his every waking hour and haunting his sleep. He had seen it bow the shoulders of every doctor and nurse fighting against the endless tide of incoming patients, and felt it weigh down his feet as he ran from bed to bed, choosing who would get the life-saving drug and who would die without it. The fact that Tirit Mindel had reserved so much serindalla to keep their own staff safe when it could have saved countless more lives was as frustrating as it was sensible.

"Gabe, no offense, my friend, but you don't look so good. Is there anything we can do to help?" Fedrik asked.

With a shake of the head to clear it, Gabriel realized he had fallen silent. He drained his cup. "Do we have something stronger than wine? I'd like to say I'm fine, but... I'm not. Even after everything I've seen in Lirin, this was different. It was… the worst part, I think, was how slow it was. I had time to get to know them all, before they died. And it was so painful. When we've dealt with the razed towns and villages in Lirin, most people are already dead, or their wounds take them quickly. This disease isn't like that."

"No, it's not." Fedrik grew silent for a while, staring out the window as though thinking hard. Then he clambered to his feet. He returned a minute later with a bottle of brandy. Gabriel gratefully let him add a hefty splash to his glass. When Fedrik had returned to his spot on the floor, he said, "I've seen it, you know. A family member of mine caught wasting fever when she was little. She survived the initial illness, but had a rough recovery. I'll never forget the way she would cry and scream for hours. I cannot image what a whole ward of that must have been like."

"Like a nightmare," Gabe supplied. "We didn't even have enough cots for everyone. There were people lining the hallways and not half-enough doctors to tend to them. On my third day there, they enacted field triage protocols. Those who didn't have a good chance at recovery were all placed in one ward and offered nothing but palliative care. I did a few shifts there and…" He couldn't make the words move past the lump of anger and grief in his throat. It was in the shape of a three-letter word. Of a name. Gabriel *wanted* to tell them about the face that haunted so many of his nightmares, but every time he let his thoughts drift to that wizened visage, all of it threatened to come back. The death. The pain. The helpless horror of realizing that his best would not be enough.

Fay gave his leg a squeeze. "You don't have to talk about it, if you don't want to. Maybe you should take a break from working at the clinic, love. Sounds like you could use some time off."

Gabe shook his head. "Can't afford to. I donated my pay."

"*Again?*" Fedrik asked. "Gabriel, you need money. You're in mountains of debt to the school, and while I'm happy to help out while we're here together, I'm not continuing on to the Colleges. You need savings."

"Maybe I'll get a scholarship," Gabe ventured, though without much hope. "And if I don't, I can always keep working nights."

"And burn out like you did at the end of last year?" Fay chided. "If you'd let Dad keep—"

"I'm not going to take money from the Rebellion when I'm capable of working, Fay," he snapped. "We've been over this. Your father and Mari covered over three years of my expenses. That's more than generous enough."

He couldn't see her face, but Gabe just *knew* that Fay rolled her eyes. "They think of you as family, idiot. They're still putting the funds aside each year, even though you refuse to take them."

"Yeah, well, when they need them for something, they'll still be there, untouched. Besides, after this last month, I'll likely get a promotion at the clinic. I should be able to put enough aside by the time term ends to make it home with you for the summer. If I need to work for the Island while we're in Hardor to keep my loans from coming due after graduation, I can do that alongside helping with the Rebellion. I'm used to pulling double duty."

"Too used to it," Fay muttered. "I wish Robin hadn't convinced you to take more classes this year. I feel like I never actually see you."

"But when you do, aren't you happy that it's my favorite time of day?" he asked, with a smile.

She gave his knee a firm smack. "Don't think being sweet will make me less annoyed at you. You were supposed to only be away two weeks, if you recall." Before Gabe could reply, Fay added, "though I knew that was a lie even before you left. You have no self-control when it comes to volunteering for more than you ought to handle."

Fedrik snorted. "As opposed to you, Avilor? Who, if I remember correctly, spends all her evenings planning to overthrow whole monarchies on top of her schoolwork at *the most prestigious and difficult school in Carinn.*"

"Yes, well, not everyone can be as good as me." She grinned, raising her glass and giving Fedrik a light kick with her bare foot. Gabriel nestled his face into her curls and closed his eyes. There was just something about holding Fayrian that always made him feel so relaxed. With the weight of the last month and their uncertain futures on his shoulders, he planned to enjoy it for as long as the winter break allowed.

On the first day of Midwinter Black's three-day festival, Gabriel awoke in Fay's bed. She was still sleeping, her naked body pressed up to his on the narrow mattress and her breath warm against his chest. Snow was falling outside the window, the house quiet and the world still.

It surprised Gabriel that he had actually slept, considering he was still on a sizable dose of serindalla, but the nightmare that had woken him tugged at Gabe's consciousness. His head was pounding from the brandy he had kept drinking until it put him to sleep. Yet still, the faces of the dead and the cries of the dying were there. *He* was there, bitterly asking why Gabriel hadn't saved him.

Every time Gabe closed his eyes, every time he stopped moving, the question returned. What if he could have done more?

To keep from pondering it further, Gabriel kissed his lover's forehead. "Good morning, beautiful."

Fay scrunched her nose and pulled the covers up higher, pressing her face into the crook of his arm. "Must you be so chipper in the mornings?"

"Must you be so grumpy when it's almost time for *breakfast*?"Gabe asked, willfully pushing the lingering weight of the dream away.

Fay snorted, then stretched with a groan. "You expect me to want to move when we don't have classes to get to and the boy I rather enjoy spending time with is naked in my bed? You know, some girls would be hurt to have their partner leave for a month right after the first time they had sex," she said, jabbing a finger into Gabe's chest, then kissing him to soften the barb. "It's almost like you're a good person who puts other people before himself, or something. Super annoying."

"Mhm, that's me. A veritable beacon of perfection."

That earned Gabe a snort, and a naked young woman straddling his hips. "Sure you are."

A loud knock came at the door.

"Go away, Tellen," Fay yelled.

"How did you even know it was me?" Fedrik's muffled voice replied. "Could have been Robin coming to ground Gabriel for about a year for falling asleep in your room."

"Because you *always* have the worst timing."

Gabe tried and failed to suppress a laugh. Fay glared down at him, and mouthed, "what, do you want him walking in?"

Eyebrows rising, Gabriel's smile only grew. "Are you saying you'd complain?"

She shook her head, curls bouncing. "I never should have told you I find him attractive. You're insufferable."

"What are you two talking about in there? Can I come in?"

"No!" Fay shouted. "Not unless you want to see us both naked."

"I see you naked all the time. We have communal showers, Avilor. But point taken. Just hurry up, yeah? I want breakfast."

As Fedrik's footsteps faded, Fay looked down at Gabe, lips pursed and eyes sparkling with mirth. She trailed a finger down the light brown skin of his scarred chest, rolling her hips in a way that made him groan. "*So*, are you going to hurry up or what? You have an anniversary to make up for, and I'm charging interest."

Gabe laughed, pushing up on his elbows to kiss her. "Of course you are."

"Are you *serious*?" Fay asked, as Gabriel dragged her into the library. "You *just* got back, and you want to *study?* We're not even *supposed* to be studying. It's a religious holiday."

"I'm an atheist," Gabe pointed out, as he and Fedrik led the way toward their preferred nook in the expansive building full to bursting with books. "And I'm a month behind. Contingent early acceptance letters to the Colleges are going to arrive any day now. If I have a shot at the College of Science scholarship, I'll have to be in the top 5% of our class."

"And I have to get through the lessons I would have been taking during break, if I had been home," Fedrik said, hefting the large bag of books to make his point. "I don't know when my parents plan on me picking up one of their Water Writs, but when they do, I have to be ready for it. I'll be the head of my House one day."

"Yeah, yeah, we know you're important. No need to rub it in, Tellen," Fay complained. For all her griping, though, she settled in with a book on military tactics without much fuss once they found their spot.

Unfortunately, studying wasn't as easy as Gabriel had expected. Every time someone cleared their throat, or footsteps came their way, his whole body tensed, all focus vanishing as adrenaline coursed through him. Frustration mounting higher and higher, Gabe grit his teeth and jabbed his pen down harder each time he dotted an i.

At one point Fay actually reached over to loosen the grip on his pen. "Are you sure you don't need more of a break?"

"I'm fine," he muttered, stretching to try relaxing his tense shoulders.

Gabe had almost finished writing up his report of the last month when Robin appeared between the stacks. "Ah, exactly who I was looking for. How are you three this morning?"

"Quite well, Master Robin," Fedrik answered, emerging from behind a thick tome on Lirinian law. "It's nice to be here without classes."

Their teacher chuckled. "Yes. I remember that feeling after

graduating from Core Six, and before I started my College days. It was relaxing. Fayrian, do please take your feet off the table."

Fay gave Robin an unexpectedly cold look and didn't budge. Huh… What had Gabriel missed? He would have to ask her about it later. She'd always had a contentious relationship with their Core Six instructor, but this was colder than her usual sizzling annoyance.

Robin, meanwhile, was shaking his head, but didn't push, turning instead to Gabriel. "I took the liberty of compiling the assignments you missed while in Miriel. I'd suggest starting on them over the break, so you aren't too far behind when next term begins."

Damn it. Gabriel tried to suppress a sigh, but didn't quite manage it. Before he could take the pile of papers Robin had pulled out of a satchel, though, Fayrian slammed her book down. "He's already decided he's going to Science if they'll have him. Why keep pushing Diplomacy and Discipline on him? He already hardly has time to breathe between classes and work, and just came back from the front lines of a damn epidemic. Doesn't he deserve a few fucking days rest?"

"Fay, I'm fine," Gabe protested, squashing down his own frustration since it would only fuel Fayrian's. Trying to put on a brave face, he took the folder. Gabriel had hoped Robin would give him a pass this once, since he had been working for the Island, but apparently even plagues didn't stop schoolwork. "Thank you for putting this together, Master Robin."

"Are we forgetting last year during finals when you literally worked yourself so ragged you collapsed? Because I haven't," Fay snapped, still glaring at Robin. "Or the year when you only had five minutes between classes for ten hours straight every day? He's putting too much pressure on you. Not even stopping for Midwinter is an insult, and a disgrace. You ought to get the same vacation as anyone else."

"Miss Avilor, could we have a word in private?" Robin said, tone even and patient, despite her obvious animosity. Fay gave him a curt nod and they walked away together.

As soon as they were gone, Gabe leaned over and asked, "What happened there?"

Fedrik shrugged. "I have no idea, but they've been prickly at each other ever since your letter saying you were extending your stay in Miriel by two weeks arrived. I've tried to get why out of her, but she won't spill. I wouldn't ask about it if you value your longevity. Every time I've brought it up, I've had something chucked at my head, though she might be less likely to do that to you."

"Doubtful," Gabe replied, brows scrunching with worry. Why would his decision to stay in Miriel longer affect Robin and Fayrian? To distract himself, he set Robin's assignments aside and asked, "Game of Seven Rivers for ten? I think Fay will need some fresh air after this, so I don't really want to start another project."

"Sure."

They cleared off the table and were over half-way into the card game when Fay returned. She stomped over and thudded down on the couch next to Gabriel, letting out a loud huff. "Don't ask about what happened. I don't want to talk about it."

"We weren't going to," Fedrik said.

"Good." She rested her head back on the cushions, let out a long sigh, then sat up straight. "Right. Who's winning?"

"Who do you think?" Fedrik asked, with a groan.

"You shouldn't let him play a defensive game, Tellen. You know he'll always wipe you out in the second half if you do."

"Yeah, well, I didn't *mean* to, but Gabe got a Drego Writ early and cut off all his cities from Hardor," Fedrik explained, pointing at the cards placed in the ever-expanding grid on the table between them.

Gabe smirked. "It's called the succession play. If you had stopped me from making this one-way corridor out of Hardor early on, I couldn't have done it." As he spoke, he placed yet another city, moved the small barge markers over, and bought another Writ, taking his total to six out of the seven he needed to win the game. "You should probably concede, Tellen. You're done for."

"Rub it in, why don't you?" The nobleman did, however, put down his cards and hold out his hand in surrender. "Game's yours. I swear, it's getting expensive to be your friend, Gabriel."

"That's why I no longer play him for money," Fay said, starting to gather up the cards. "You know, Gabe, you could probably make more playing pickup games in the Night Market than you do in the clinic. I mean, I know you won't because you have to be dragged out of the clinic kicking and screaming most days, but it's a thought."

It was. Gabriel yawned and stretched. "Want to go tonight and see?" It had, after all, been a long time since they had gone on a nighttime excursion together. It would be nice to use up some of the excess energy the serindalla was giving him. Hopefully, if he wore himself down enough, the nightmares might leave him alone.

BARGAINING

"No, ya can't take me," Tom cried, though it was hard to make out the words through the screaming. The old man was clinging with all his remaining strength to the side of the cot where he had lain for over a week, as medics trying to be gentle were attempting to move him onto a stretcher. "That's where they take ya to die."

"We're sorry, Mr. Riell, but this bed is needed for someone else. We'll take you somewhere where you will be comfortable. Please don't struggle so. You'll hurt yourself," one of the medics said, then she looked to Gabriel, who had been collecting Tom's things. "What are you standing around for? That can wait. Get his legs. He'll only hurt himself if he makes us drop him."

There was a familiar exhaustion and frustration in her tone. Gabe had heard it growing in all the doctors and in himself with every day that passed. Yet it was the panic in Tom's gnarled face that tore at Gabe's soul and weighed down his shoulders.

"Ya can't let them take me, Gabe. I'm getting better!" Tom screamed. Across the ward, it woke one of the children, who started to cry.

"Mr. Riell—"

"Shut the fuck up. Gabe. Please. Don't let 'em take me. I won't ask for the medicine again. I won't curse or anythin'. Don't—" but Tom had to stop to cough, his whole body seizing as his muscles contracted around joints the fever had wasted away. With Tom unable to resist, the two medics finished moving him onto the stretcher. Gabe saw tears in their eyes, and when the first one stood, her skin was as pale as a sheet.

"Does he have family we need to notify about the change of room?" she asked.

"No. He's…all alone." Gabe replied, fighting hard to hold it together. "Tom, I'll be by with your things, alright? I'll come see you as soon as my shift's done."

Tom did not answer, probably in too much pain to hear

him. The second medic sighed, and looked up at Gabriel. Quietly, he warned, "I wouldn't go there if you want to retain any shred of your sanity, Navarl. It's not pretty. The best we've been able to do is keep them sedated. Not that we're given the supplies to do so often enough to matter. Do yourself a favor, and say your farewells now. I know it's hard when it's the ones we get attached to, but we can't save them all. Focus on the ones you can."

"TELLEEEEEEEEEN," GABE COMPLAINED, as Fedrik once more put down one set of books and picked up another. "They're both good choices. Make up your damn mind. I'm hungry."

"I was hungry this morning while you were busy getting laid. Payback's a bitch," the nobleman grumbled, hefting the collection of Ionist fables as though trying to guess their weight. "She'll like these, but the murder mysteries are fun too."

"Do you really want to get a Lirion a book about how to murder people?" Fay asked, from where she was leaning up against the shelves of the cramped Night Market bookstore.

"Elenor wouldn't murder a fly," Fedrik muttered, eyeing the other boxed set of books.

"If you change your mind one more fucking time, Fedrik, I swear to all that is holy that I will bite you," Fay warned.

"Promises, promises, Avilor." Fedrik flashed Fay a grin, then set the mystery novels on the shelf with a long, drawn out sigh. "The fables it is. You have sharp teeth."

Ten minutes and a sum of money that made Gabriel cringe later, they were out on the street. The Night Market wasn't as packed as it usually was, with so many students having gone home, but it was still bustling with locals. The smoke and steam from the hawker stalls that lined the main thoroughfares hung in the air, blurring the outlines of the taller buildings. Gabriel inhaled deeply. Smells of food from all over the continent mixed together in a pleasant, unique way that always made him feel at home. It helped ease the distant, echoey way his surroundings got sometimes, when his mind would wander back to Miriel. The hospital had smelled of death, not frying garlic and grilled meats.

Except as soon as he thought that, all he could smell was the smoke. Shaking his head sharply to clear it, Gabriel turned them in the general direction of their usual favorite haunts. "Where to for dinner? You're buying, Tellen."

"Why thank you for asking, Gabriel. Yes, I would be happy to buy you both dinner at the establishment of your choice," Fedrik grumbled. Gabe elbowed him, nearly sending Fedrik tumbling into a display of pounded copper circuit jewelry.

"Oy, watch it!" The proprietor yelled.

"Sorry," Gabe called, as Fayrian snickered and hooked an arm through each of theirs.

"*Boys.* I'll get them out of your hair, Howard. Sorry for the commotion." True to her word, and despite being shorter than either Gabe or Fedrik, Fay dragged them along. "I want fish pies. If we're not going to be in Hardor for the holidays, I at least want to eat like we are."

Walking three-abreast was a challenge in the Night Market, but that didn't stop Fayrian. Gabe looked over at Fedrik rolling his eyes. Fed grinned and mouthed, "Business as usual."

The stall they finally stopped at fronted a bakery. Fedrik took care of ordering, and before long, they were sitting on an icy stoop, holding steaming pies. Gabriel was the first to dare take a bite of the flaky crust, his stomach rumbling. Remembering the last rifting lesson Robin had given him in his teacher's nearly six-year quest for Gabriel to work on the tiny amount of magic he could use, Gabe absorbed a smidge of heat from the pastry. He converted it to magical energy, refilling a bit of his reservoir of power while cooling the pie. It made the gravy just shy of tongue-burning, so he took a large bite.

"You're cheating again, aren't you?" Fedrik asked, cracking the top of his with his fingers and blowing on the thick gravy and chunks of fish inside.

"Having and using magic isn't cheating. Especially when it's hardly enough to light a candle."

Fay muttered something, face turned down into her thick scarf.

Gabe could only conclude that she agreed with Fedrik. Leaning in, he pressed a kiss to her flushed cheek. Her smile in return warmed him from the top of his head to his toes.

"That love-struck grin is going to make me lose my appetite," Fedrik said, but added, "But damned if I didn't miss it. It really is nice to have you back, Gabriel. It hasn't been the same here without you. And I'm not just saying that because of how much more agreeable Fayrian is when you're around."

"How many times must I tell you that I hate my full name?"

"At least once more."

They left the Night Market well past two in the morning, Gabriel's pockets full of coins and small banknotes and head spinning from probably a few too many drinks. It had eaten up more of his earnings for the evening than he should have spent, but it had made the crowded, smoky bar bearable.

"I told you you'd make more playing Seven Rivers than at the clinic," Fay said, as all three of them leaned on the rails of the ferry, watching the small island that held the Night Market fade into the mists.

"Only because the regulars weren't expecting me to win. Now that they know my skill level, I won't get away with half as many easy victories," Gabe countered, his gloved hands rubbing Fay's to keep them warm.

"I'm just glad you finished that last game quickly. I wouldn't want to walk home tonight. It's freezing." Fedrik was on Gabriel's other side, coat collar up against the chill wind, and scarf and hat leaving only a narrow slit for his brown eyes. "I hate the cold."

"You don't say," Gabe said. "I rather enjoy it. Better than the summer mugginess."

And with no more warning than that, memories from Miriel crashed into him. He tried to push back the sticky, miserable humidity inside the clinic, heavy with the smell of vomit and death, but the smell lodged in his nose and wouldn't budge. Fay must have noticed how still Gabriel had become, because she gave his hand a tight squeeze.

"Hey, you alright, love?"

Lips pressed tightly together, Gabe nodded. He didn't want to worry her, not over something as little as a stray memory. "Just tired."

"Are you still due for another dose of serindalla tonight, or did you already take it? I hope you sleep better this evening," Fay said, leaning into his shoulder. "You were tossing and turning all of last night."

"Already took it, but I doubt I'll rest well until I've titrated down significantly further. Even when I can sleep, it's light, broken, and, well… I have a lot of shit my subconscious likes throwing at me. I'm sorry if I kept you up too."

"Yeah, that drug is horrible. I can't believe people take it for fun," Fedrik said with a shudder.

"I can," Gabe said, trying to smile and managing a weak one. "The first day I was on it, on the way to Miriel, I was bouncing off the damn walls. It was pretty exceptional. I'm kind of happy the side effects are so nasty and it's so expensive. If I can't get my eyes closed tonight, I might borrow that bottle of brandy again, Tellen. If you don't mind, that is. I'd rather be a bit hungover tomorrow than get so worn out I crash."

Fedrik gave him a worried look. "You already had quite a bit, Gabe."

Gabriel waved it off. "You know I metabolize things stupidly fast. I'm hardly feeling it. The serindalla makes it hard to sleep, that's all. I'll be off it by the time term starts up again. An extra drink or two while on break can't hurt right? Aren't you two always the ones telling me to relax a bit?"

"If you're sure," Fedrik said, though he didn't sound convinced.

"Tirit Mindel *is* covering the serindalla, though. Right?" Fay asked. "Since it was obligatory. I don't know the cost of it through the school, but I know the price on the black market is off the charts right now. Had a kid try to sell me some for finals last semester and I had to laugh in his face."

"Yes, they're footing the bill. They know they'll never get what I owe them out of me if I die. I don't even have family to inherit my debt." He gave Fay's hand another squeeze as they both sighed.

Fedrik patted Gabe on the shoulder. "Let me guess, you two not planning on being one of those insufferable couples who get married right out of Core Six?"

Fay's eyebrows rose to the bottom of her wool hat. "With how much we both owe the school? Not in a million years. Maybe when the Rebellion actually succeeds, but until then I refuse to saddle Gabe with my debt if I end up dying for the cause."

"And vice versa," Gabe added. "But it will all be worth it. We'll have time for all of that when Lirin is in good hands again."

Mail was waiting for them on their beds when they got to their dorms. Fedrik had a box from his parents, and Gabe a sizable pile of letters from the last month. As Fay went to change into something cozy, Fedrik unpacked books, holiday sweets, and unfathomably, a ceramic frog painted in bright colors.

"What… even is that?" Gabe asked, sorting through his mail as Fedrik started laughing.

"Elenor and Claire's idea of a joke. El *hates* frogs, and when I was little I used to make fun of her for it. She and Claire decided to get back at me by dropping a dozen or so frogs in my bathtub. It was supposed to just startle me, but the kind of frog they got was mildly toxic and I ended up covered in a rash from head to toe. Unfortunately they had handled them too, so their hands were as red as I was, which made finding the culprits quite easy. It was a very itchy week all around."

"So they were caught *red handed?*" Gabe asked, chuckling.

Fedrik snorted and placed the frog on his dresser. "Exactly. So, whatcha got?"

"Bills, mostly. Housing costs didn't stop just because I wasn't here." Gabe said with a sigh. "I'll deal with them tomor—" A thick, bulging envelope caught his eye.

On the front was the seal of the College of Science, embossed and painted red like the Patron Goddess of that branch of Tirit Mindel. "Fed," he held it up, hands shaking.

"Shit, is that…?" Fedrik hurried over, sitting down next to Gabriel on his bed and staring at the letter. "Go on, open it."

"What if it's—?"

"Denial letters are thin. That one's huge."

"If I got in but didn't get the scholarship—"

"Then you'll be in two lifetimes worth of debt instead of one. Plans the same either way, right? Die trying to fix Lirin, or work for the Island for the rest of your days so they'll forgive the debt when you retire. This could be your chance to get into the branch you want, Gabriel. Open it," Fedrik encouraged, then shouted. "Avilor, get your ass in here!"

With trembling fingers, Gabriel cracked the wax seal and extracted the papers within. He squeezed his eyes shut, held his breath, then unfolded them in a rush. "Read over my shoulder. Tell me—"

Fedrik's whoop of triumph was so loud it made Gabriel's ears ring. "You did it!"

"Really?" Gabe's eyes shot open. There, on the top sheet, in neat handwriting, were the words *Congratulations on your conditional acceptance to the College of Science with a full tuition scholarship.*

"Woah, there," Fedrik said, as Gabriel swayed.

"I can't… fuck. I… did it."

"Yes, you did. See? I told you that you had nothing to worry about. Didn't you have, like, a solid inch-tall stack of letters of recommendation when you applied?"

"Yeah, but—"

"But nothing. Congratulations, Gabriel. Really. For all that Avilor and I tease, I'm so damn proud of you. And I know your family would be too." Fedrik's arm around his shoulders squeezed tight.

Tears sprang to Gabe's eyes, but he blinked them away to read the letter again, still not quite believing the words. "I'm going to be a Tirit Mindel certified doctor like my mother."

"Master Gabriel Mindellion, here we come. And more immediately, maybe this will convince Robin to drop his endless campaign to get you into Diplomacy." Fedrik grinned at him, ruffling his hair, then once more yelled, "Where are you, Avilor? Get in he—"

Fay pushed the door open. She, too, had a letter in her hand, but far from pleased, there were tears streaming down her cheeks. Gabriel sprang to his feet. "Fay, what's wrong?"

"It's my dad," she said, quietly.

Worry pushed out all elation faster than someone blowing out a candle. "Did something happen? Was there a raid? What—" but her shake of the head interrupted his questions.

"He hasn't been feeling well for a few months and Mari finally convinced him to see a doctor. They aren't sure and won't know for certain until it advances, but they suspect it's a cancer of the liver." Her voice didn't shake or falter. It was emotionless and subdued, which from Fay worried Gabriel far more than shouting and screaming would have. She looked up at him, eyes reddened and bottom lip wobbling. "Gabe..."

He wrapped his arms around her. A moment later, Fedrik joined him, both of them holding tight as Fay began to sob. Gabe wanted to read the letter, to ask a thousand questions, to find out what they knew and how much time Cornen had, but with the way Fay was bawling, he knew it would be more bad news. He pressed his lips into her hair, whispering words of love and comfort until her sobs turned to sniffles.

"They say he might still have a year or two, but there's not much they can do." Fay straightened a little. She didn't resist when Gabe pulled her down onto his bed, Fedrik on her other side.

"I know it sounds callous at the moment, but would money help? Better physicians? If there is anything my family or I can do, it's yours," Fedrik said, face drawn with worry.

"I doubt it, but thank you. If there is, I'll let you know," Fay replied, rubbing at her dripping nose. "Why is this happening? Haven't we lost enough?"

Even though she'd asked it to the room at large, Gabe knew it was directed at him. Because of the homes they had both lost to the Lirion, Gabriel's family and Fayrian's mother, dead and deemed Forgotten, and the countless friends who had perished in the Rebellion's push for a better Lirin. To lose Cornen too, especially to something as… meaningless and random as disease, was cosmically unfair.

"We should go back to Hardor," Gabe said. As he did, he surreptitiously slipped the papers with his admittance to the College of Science under his pillow.

"He said that under no condition were we allowed to run home before graduation. He knew we'd want to," Fay said, handing the letter to Gabriel. "He's right. We can't leave this close to the end of our studies. Not without giving up everything we've been working towards. Having Tirit Mindel graduates leading the Rebellion is too big of a boon."

"Fayrian, you don't have to be sensible right now. You're allowed to just want to go home and be with your dad, instead of putting the Rebellion first," Fedrik hedged.

She shook her head forcefully. "No. I'm not. He w-wants me to take over for him. Mari can't deal with the responsibility, and my sister hasn't ever wanted anything to do with it. Daren can hold us together for a little while, but he wants full-on revolution, not to work with Wil. It has to be me. Which means that whatever I'm feeling right now has to come second to what must be done. Otherwise, what kind of daughter would I be to Cornen Avilor?"

"Then we finish out the year and come with you to Hardor," Gabe said, in a tone that brooked no argument. Fedrik eyed him questioningly, but Gabriel shook his head. No, he didn't want to talk about what that would mean for his own news, because Cornen had raised Gabriel like a son, and Fayrian was going to need his support. He could do his own grieving in private, both for the man whose time was limited, and for the opportunity he could feel slipping through his fingers even as he clutched Fay's tightly. "You'll need a second you can trust."

Turning, Fay wrapped her arms around him. "Thank you. I didn't want to ask—I know how much you love it here—but I don't want to face this alone. You and I both know that my sister won't be there."

"Yeah," Gabe agreed, drawing the word out to hide his bitter displeasure at Fay's sister, and because it gave him time to push his own, more selfish grief further down, dreams of becoming a doctor slipping through his fingers.

"And you know you'll never be rid of me, Avilor. We're stuck together as long as Master Denzel is alive and has rope. At this point, I don't think I would even know what to do with myself in a fight if I weren't literally tied to you," Fedrik said, ruffling Fay's curls.

"You'd get your ass handed to you, that's what," Fay said, in a vain attempt at a joke. None of them laughed.

DEPRESSION

It was late and Gabriel ought to have been sleeping, but instead he slipped into the dimly lit room that had once been the hospital cafeteria. The tables had been dragged outside to make room for pallets filled with patients. Only two doctors moved between the hundred or more beds, never dispensing more than a sip of water or handkerchief to wipe away sweat and tears.

These were the people who were too poor to afford care, and too sick for Tirit Mindel to 'waste' charity on. Most were either children who couldn't be past six or seven, or gray-haired grandparents who would nevermore be able to lift them into their arms again.

Even with the windows thrown wide, the lack of a breeze kept the room sweltering. The air stank so badly that Gabriel—even used to the stench of the pyres and the sick—had to cover his nose with his sleeve. Eyes watering, he looked around, squinting through the dimness.

Was he too late? Gabe walked between the rows of dying wasting fever patients, searching for Tom's scraggly gray beard and tangled, wild hair. At last, in the far corner, he found him.

Tom lay in the curved, tilted posture so many adopted, back arched up and legs locked into a rictus of agony. He needed physical therapy, herbs to relax his taut, degrading muscles, and ice to soothe the inflammation. Instead, he had been given a bucket to puke into, and a meager tray of food that lay untouched.

Gabe knelt down next to Tom, placing a hand over the old man's where it clutched at the blankets. "Hey there, grumpy pants. How are you feeling?"

Tom opened his eyes, red and clouded. For a moment, it seemed like he would not recognize Gabriel, then his face contorted into a sneer. "I thought I'd finally been rid of you, when they brought me to this fine, upstandin' guesthouse. We don't want yer kind here muckin' up the place." The last few words were interrupted by coughs that brought up blood, spattering onto Tom's already dirty skin as he covered his mouth with his inner wrist. Collapsing back, he fixed Gabriel with tearful eyes. "When will it be over, do you think? These useless idiot's be avoidin' all my questions, but you'll give it to me straight. Right?"

Gabriel wanted to look away, to hide the pain in his gaze, but didn't. Tom needed the truth. To others, the platitudes of the healers might be calming, but Gabe could understand the desire for honesty. "Not for another week or two. Wasting fever kills slowly. That's the worst part of it. I don't... think you'll make it to Midwinter, though."

"Ha. Don' think you get to decide wha's the worst, when you aint got it. It's not bein' able to take a piss without someone helpin' me that's the worst. Didn't mean this when I used to say I wanted a sweet young lady to touch my—"

"Keep going like that and I'll remember you as a real creep," Gabe warned, forcing a smile. The joke, as strained as it was, did not seem to amuse Tom. It did make him take Gabe's hand in his frail one, though.

"But ya will? Remember me, that is? Don't think anyone else will. No one's left... I had a family once, but they all died too. One by one, like this. For so long I thought I'd been better, been stronger, than all them others who got the fever..." Tom's voice wavered, then a tear rolled down his smudged cheek, and in a wheezing whisper he croaked, "I'm... I'm all alone. Please. My name's Tom Riell. T-o-m-r-i-e-l-l. I know I ain't done nothin' to deserve it. I don't do my devotions or give to them's less fortunate, but you're a smart and healthy lad. You'll make it out. Please remember me. I don't want my soul to die too, if I ain't gonna make it. Please."

GABRIEL STARED DOWN AT THE PILE of schoolwork Robin had given him and felt tears bead at the corners of his eyes. What was the fucking point? He had been at it for nearly four hours, tucked into an out of the way corner of the library where he went when even Fay or Fedrik's presence was more than he wanted. That had happened more and more the last few years, as his course load grew ever heavier.

All for nothing.

The pile of assignments taunted him. Rifting, diplomacy, medicine, history, even a damn course on Mondaer culture that their weapons master had inexplicably insisted on. Almost six years of working himself to death in and out of the classroom and doing his homework in the clinic's breakroom, and for what?

Why was it that every time Gabriel got the least bit ahead, the world found a way to knock him down? Why was Mark Lirion, a man who slaughtered his citizens, still healthy and alive when Cornen Avilor, a legitimate hero of the people, was dying?

And why was Gabriel doing fucking schoolwork? Tirit Mindel had the money and medicine to fix Miriel's wasting fever crisis even if the government refused to, but they didn't. They could have aided the Rebellion in Lirin, but they wouldn't. Gabe had once hoped to use his in with the Island to help people. The bitter truth was that it would never be enough, because the system was broken and the universe existentially unfair.

Why am I here? I should have stayed in Miriel to help. They still needed people. Cornen needs people. This whole place is a fucking waste of time.

That didn't stop him from continuing to write. Page after page, Gabe read, took notes, answered questions, and laid out arguments for future essays. The whole while, he itched to pull out the jar of serindalla from his pocket, but didn't. It might have helped with his shifting focus, but he couldn't *fucking afford* to get hooked on the drug. Not when he'd have to start paying back his loans on an Academy graduate's potential salary, instead of that of a fully accredited Island doctor.

It was nearing dusk when he returned home, his pack heavy with books he needed to get through in the coming days. He's intended to drop it off, then head straight to dinner. Instead, he found Fay waiting for him in his room, holding his admission letter. "Gabriel James, we need to talk."

Here we go.

With a slump to his shoulders and a heavy heart, Gabe shut the door and steeled himself for the fight he could see brewing behind Fayrian's tearful, determined eyes.

"How are you holding up?" Tellen asked, sitting down in the living room next to Gabe, who was carefully measuring out his nightly dose of serindalla from the tiny jar. He was down to nearly a quarter of what he had taken in Miriel, and was tempted to go up again, just this once. He wasn't going to sleep anyways. The soothing relief it provided to both physical and emotional pain sounded great right about then.

"Like shit, to be frank. Fay finally asked about the admission letter, and spent the last two hours trying to convince me she doesn't need me to watch her back in Hardor, and that I should stay." Gabe pushed the golden sap around in the jar, teeth clenched. Fayrian had gone to talk to Robin about making arrangements to withdraw her applications to the College of Discipline half an hour before, but their disagreement still hung in the air. "And I wish she wouldn't. It makes it harder."

"Have you considered that she might be right? Fay's a survivor. She *would* be fine, and I'd be there to keep an eye on her. If you were in the Colleges, you could always take a semester of leave once things get… bad. They're way more lenient after Core Six about how long your studies take you," Fedrik prompted, using the exact same logic Fay had tried.

Gabriel shot him a nasty glare. "Stop it. I've made up my mind. Honestly, maybe this is for the best. I love this place, and it's blinded me to the whole reason I came here to begin with: to learn enough to defeat Mark Lirion. I'm not going to do that by becoming a doctor."

"The Rebellion would be rather fucked without doctors. Don't sell yourself short," Fedrik replied, not rising to the bait of Gabriel's anger. "Have you considered that your role might not be on the front lines?"

"No." Annoyance flaring hotter, Gabriel took his previous full dose of serindalla, plus whatever clung to the measuring spoon, and pushed the jar away, slumping against the couch. Fuck it. Today was not the day to cut back.

"Gabe..."

"I said no, Tellen. You don't get it. Lirion didn't show up one day to slaughter your parents and everyone you knew and cared about. He didn't leave you an orphan on the streets with a baby sister to take care of. Yes, I want to continue in school. I want to be a doctor like my mother, but I'll do it after Mark Lirion is fucking dead and buried. I'm not going to put all that responsibility on Fayrian while I stay here with my nose in a book." Gabriel reached for the glass that still held a finger's worth of brandy, and downed most of it to clear the sticky, sappy taste of the serindalla from his mouth.

Fedrik reached forward and snagged the bottle, placing it on the floor out of Gabriel's reach. "Say that again when you aren't relying on serindalla and alcohol to hold yourself together. Fay might be too distracted to notice how much you've been drinking since you got back, but I haven't been. I don't think you're in a clear enough mindframe to be making these kinds of decisions. Why don't you put it off until you're done with the serindalla and have actually dealt with whatever you're trying to drown out?"

"Fuck off, Tellen."

"Can't do that. You're my best friend," the nobleman said.

"Fine, then I will." With a huff, Gabriel pushed up from the couch and slipped on his boots. Without bothering to tie the laces, he grabbed his coat and walked out the door.

Fedrik didn't follow, and Fay was still with Robin, so after stomping around through a fresh dusting of snow until his annoyance had cooled off enough, he headed in the direction of the clinic. There was probably work to be done, and he could use something dull and repetitive right about then. Maybe that would ease some of the built up energy coiled in his every muscle and let his mind find a little peace.

Unfortunately, not two minutes after walking through the doors of the building that had been his workplace and refuge for nearly six years, Gabe had to walk right out again, eyes stinging after one of the senior physicians congratulated him on his early admittance to the College of Science.

In the end, after a long walk, he ended up at the mock dragon yards. There were always young mocks in need of flight practice and exercise, so when Gabriel asked if he could go flying, the stable master pointed him at a black female dragon and a saddle. It took a few minutes and a fish from the feed bin to make introductions and get the skittish creature to let Gabriel saddle her, but after that they took to the air.

The moment they were up, Gabe let go of the reins, leaned back on the dragon's scaly spine, and closed his eyes. The frigid wind whipped at his hair and exposed skin, every snowflake a stinging projectile as the mock picked up speed. She soared up, jostling Gabriel in the saddle with every powerful wingbeat, until they broke into the low-hanging clouds and started to soar.

Everything went silent, other than the quiet rustle of cloth and open, leathery wings. Gabriel extended his arms, flexing every finger wide. Melting snowflakes beaded on his cheeks and caught in his lashes, steam from his breath billowing behind him. He breathed in deep, held it, then exhaled.

His mind stilled.

I'm going to miss this.

"Were you flying?" Fay asked, when Gabriel snuck past Robin's door and into her room well past midnight. "Aren't you freezing?"

"I needed to clear my head. A lot has happened over the last couple days." Gabe pulled his sweater off, then sat down on the edge of her bed. "How was your talk with Robin?"

Fay shifted to pull her knees up to her chest, resting her chin on them. Her eyes were dry but red, as though she had been crying earlier. A pang of guilt shot through Gabriel for not being there.

"He's going to look into a deferral for both of us on our loans. He said he couldn't guarantee it, but that he'd try to give us at least a little time. He was really upset, though," she said.

"I should have gone with you to talk to him." Gabe scooted in so he could rest against the wall and pull Fay close.

"It's fine." She leaned her head on his shoulder, then let out a long breath. "Gabriel, I'm sorry. I'm not going to try to talk you out of this again, but I'm sorry. For so much."

"Yeah, me too."

They sat in silence for a time, each lost in their own thoughts. At last, Fay said, "Fedrik mentioned that you were in bad shape earlier."

"Of course he did."

"He's watching out for you, Gabriel James, that's all. And I think he's right to worry. I know you've not been sleeping well ever since coming back from Miriel. I didn't want to bring it up because, well, I know you'll tell us when you're ready. I just wanted to let you know I won't break or anything if you do. You've been very supportive and sweet, and I appreciate it, but I love you. It's fine if we're both a mess. You don't have to be alright."

Gabe snorted. "When did you get to be so mature? I distinctly remember when you used to yell at the world any time you had a strong feeling, instead of actually talking about it."

"Yeah, well, the world yelled back, didn't it?" Fay poked him gently. "Gabriel, you're deflecting."

"Mhm. Yes, I am. Thank you, though. You're not wrong, and neither is Fed, much to my chagrin. I'll talk when I've sorted this mess of feelings into words, but that hasn't happened yet. I was really counting on this week being a reprieve from the bad and an opportunity to process. That didn't exactly happen."

Fay pulled the blanket up over both their laps, fussing with it a bit. "Tomorrow is the Day of Remembrance. I know you don't usually come to the Temple with us. Even if it's coming to an end, this place has meant a lot to you, and it might do you good to be able to leave something of yourself and those you remember behind."

"We'll see," Gabe replied, after a moment of thought. He didn't dismiss it out of hand like he might have at another time, which surprised him enough to add, "I suppose it might not be the worst idea to visit a Temple. I don't know that what I saw in Miriel strengthened my belief in the Gods, because what sort of benevolent being would allow so much suffering to occur? It's a fucking joke. But...I did see how much people cared about being remembered. It brought them together and gave them a reason to speak about their lives." He had learned so many things about his patients, about their families, their hopes and fears. It made it hurt worse when they went, but it was also beautiful. They took comfort in their Oaths and their devotions, even while they were dying. With a sigh, Gabe leaned his head against Fay's. "Sometimes… I wish I could believe that way."

Fay squeezed her eyes shut. "That's… that's what I want to do with my dad. I want to be there, so I can ask him to tell me all his stories one last time. I'm going to write them down, if I can. If we don't manage to fulfill my dad's goals by the time he… leaves… I at least want him to be remembered after. I want his dreams to keep living. Maybe then it won't feel like he's really gone." She turned to face Gabriel, pulling both his hands up to her lips. "I love you, you know? I think you're an idiot for giving up so much to come home with me, but I am so, so grateful that I didn't have to ask, because this is going to hurt more than I know how to express. Pointless or not, though, I need to say this once. Gabriel, as much as I want you with me, you don't *have* to come."

He shook his head, a sad smile turning up only the corner of his lips. "I would never forgive myself if I did not. The Academy will always be here when the time is right. The Rebellion and Cornen are the only reason I'm alive, though. It's time to show my gratitude and give back what I can. We always knew where we were heading, my love. This is just sooner and for a sadder reason than expected."

ACCEPTANCE

"It will be today," said a medic who had spoken to Gabriel a few times while he came and went, visiting the old man holding onto life with an iron grip. "I've arranged for someone to cover your shift. I know we're told not to get attached to them, but it happens to the best of us."

Gabriel had wondered how she had known death was upon Tom. Until he saw him, that was. The gruff vagrant lay still on his cot, only his chest rising and falling in shallow flutterings, like the wings of a drowning moth. His legs had wasted away to half what they had been four weeks earlier. Beneath his sunken eyes, Tom's cheeks were hollow, dark brown skin sallow, bruised, and graying.

His lips moved, muttering the same hoarse words over and over. His name: Tom Riell.

"He's been doing that all day, every day. He can't sleep at night until we've repeated it back to him a dozen or more times," one of the new nurses said. She had not yet developed the haunted, haggard stare of those who had been there longer.

Gabe knelt by Tom's cot, nodding in weary thanks to the nurse. "Hey there, old man."

Tom barely managed to crack open his eyes. His lips moved, only nothing but raspy, rattling breath came out.

Gabe took his bony hand, squeezing it tight. "Guess what? I finally talked them into getting you some more medicine. It's the good stuff, too. You'll be high as a kite and giggling in fifteen minutes tops."

Tom coughed in what might have been a chuckle. He cracked his mouth open as Gabriel pulled a small bottle of laudanum from his pocket. It didn't have much left in it, which was why he'd been able to filch it without anyone noticing, but hopefully it would be enough so that Tom wouldn't be in so much pain as he passed. He shouldn't have taken it, and would probably get in trouble if they found out, but Gabriel had honestly stopped caring about how this trip would affect his career. How could one stare at devastation on this scale and think of anything so small?

The old man swallowed and smacked his lips, making Gabe chuckle through the tears running down his cheeks. "Glad you're enjoying yourself. Probably delighted that I'm here crying like a baby, right?"

Tom inclined his chin in a nod.

Gabriel rolled his eyes. "Knew it."

The old man tried to speak again. Gabe leaned close, and through the wheezing made out, "Gotcha." Then, a few breaths later. "I'm dyin', aren't I?"

Gabe squeezed his hand. "Yes. I think this is the end of the line, but I'll remember you, alright? Tom Riell, the gruffest, most ornery patient I ever had the privilege of calling a friend. I'll remember you."

"Will it hurt?" he asked.

"I don't know, Tom. But I don't think so. The medicine I gave you will make you sleepy. At some point, it will just... end, and the pain will be over for good. You'll be at peace."

"Thank you." Tom closed his eyes. "Will you be here? I think... I think I'm ready, but I don't want to die alone."

Gabe wiped away the tears blurring his vision and leaned down, pressing a gentle kiss to Tom's forehead. "I'll stay for as long as you do, and carry your memory with me when I leave. You won't be alone. Not ever again."

DINNER BEFORE THE VIGIL OF REMEMBRANCE was every bit as joyous as the night would be somber. Despite everything that had happened, Gabriel found it hard not to laugh and smile as the handful of students from all the different grades joined their teachers in cooking and eating a veritable feast.

Peeling potatoes right between a Master of Diplomacy and a first-year student was bizarre enough to delight him. That they all knew their way around the kitchen was the thing he loved most about this Island. Everyone started at the bottom. No graduate had gotten there without their share of scrubbing pots and mopping floors.

Some of the rifters who had stayed on rolled up the sleeves of their gold uniforms and performed magic tricks for the younger students and teachers' children. Fay and Fedrik pulled out their instruments and played a handful of rambunctious tunes, and Master Denzel, the weapons master, told a story about when he had accidentally convinced a ship full of pirates that he was a sea god while traveling during his younger years.

Mulled hard cider was passed around amongst the adults, and Robin had rolled his eyes and nodded when Fay, Fed, and Gabriel had sidled up to the pot. "Go on then, it's not like your whole class hasn't been sneaking liquor into the dorms since fourth year. Don't think I don't know about it."

So it was full, light-headed, and happier than he had any right to be that Gabriel skipped toward the temple, arm in arm with his two best friends. Fay let out a giggly shriek as she half-tripped, causing both boys to stumble to catch her.

The group walking over was spread out, but boisterous. As the lights of the cafeteria faded behind them, though, the levity seemed to drop away with every step. First the laughter died, then the discussions, too, faded.

From inside the tall temple tower, the haunting hymns of Remembrance carried through the still, cold air. Fay leaned in closer and Fedrik and Gabriel joined hands, the crunch of their footsteps the only other sound in the stillness of the night.

The stairs up to the door were covered with lit candles, and people sat upon them, sipping hot beverages or staring out into the darkness. Some had tears rolling down their cheeks, and a few spoke to each other. No one, though, talked above a whisper.

Within, even more had gathered. Gabriel recognized vendors from the Night Market and locals from the town of Tirit, scattered about between people in the gray robes of the College of Theology.

He shivered as he passed over the threshold into the echoing vastness of the temple. Other than for classes, Gabriel had rarely entered the sacred space, preferring to leave it to the people for whom it meant something. That evening, though, the cool temple air seemed to clear the lingering smoke from his lungs.

The statues of the six Dragon Gods worshipped on the Island were lit by more candles, each one placed on the divot created by a carved stone scale. In the center of the six-sided cathedral, an altar held a shallow, intricate carved golden bowl, as wide as Gabriel was tall. Fay led them towards it slowly, careful not to disturb or get in the way of anyone on their knees in prayer.

The music drifted down from the walkways and balconies high above. Gabriel didn't immediately recognize the words, though he'd heard the tune from afar every Midwinter. Fedrik must have noticed his concentrated frown, because he leaned in to whisper, "They're reciting the names of the dead. The song starts at dusk and continues until dawn each day of Midwinter. It's everyone who the Island has been asked to Remember, so their souls may live on."

At last, they reached the altar. Fay gave Gabriel's hand a squeeze, then let go in order to walk forward, bow her head, and take a slip of green paper and a pen from a stack that lay above the carved oath of Gullien the Green. Fedrik, likewise, picked up a white piece of paper and used the altar as a writing surface to scribble something down.

"I'm surprised and pleased to see you here, Gabriel. I had not realized you intended to join us in our devotions this year," Robin said, catching up to him. The Tirition Master wore his most formal robes, the long black vest of the College of Academics brushing the floor.

Gabe looked up at his mentor, shifting uncomfortably. "I'm still not sure. I was thinking about it, though."

"Would you like to share your thoughts while we walk? This might take some time. I know Miss Avilor, especially, has many names she writes down each year, along with her devotional pledge," Robin offered.

Gabe nodded, and together they started winding through the temple. The Tirition was quiet, and Gabriel had studied under him long enough to know that he was waiting for his student to decide where to begin.

After some time, Gabriel asked, "Do you actually think that souls live on after death, Master Robin?"

The middle aged man seemed to ponder the question, then replied, "That is a difficult one to answer, because it is so multi-faceted a topic. Do I believe that those who pass from this world retain a consciousness after death? Perhaps. I suppose we are doomed never to know until it is our time. Likewise, I often wonder whether we make too much of the distinction between burning and burying, for surely our ashes return to the earth too, and in time, they are buried under loam and plants, nourishing the land the same way as those who are buried and Forgotten. However heretical, I doubt anyone who has heard of someone innocent who has been buried has not questioned that part of our faith."

Robin's pointed look had Gabriel glancing down, color rising to his cheeks. "I admit, that is part of the reason I've fought so hard not to be part of… all this."

"And understandably so. For if the priests are correct, many you have loved are stuck in limbo, unable to find peace, but also unable to visit those who remember them at Midwinter. I am sure that must make those who loved them all the more prone to disbelieve anything the Ionist faith teaches. If the priests are wrong about that, after all, perhaps they are wrong about all of it. Am I getting close?"

Gabe nodded. "That, and my mother didn't believe."

"No, she wouldn't have," Robin said.

"Why do you say that?" Gabriel's parents had lived in a remote village halfway across the world. Was it because Nillenia had been so close to the Mondaer that Robin thought that? "Most of my town was Ionist."

"I didn't mean to cause offense. I simply meant that not many twelve-year-olds arrive here with an active antagonism to the Gods. Usually it comes from a parent," Robin explained. "But you asked me about whether I believe souls live on after death. Let me try to answer the actual question instead of talking in circles, as your Fayrian so often accuses me of."

Gabe reached up to rub the back of his neck. "Yeah… I keep asking her to be more polite, but if it hasn't stuck yet, I doubt it will."

"Her stubbornness is part of her strength. However frustrating it can be, she is who she is because of it. The Oath of the Green fits her well. She is a person that requires clear rules to her world. As such, on this day every year, you will always find her as she is now, writing down the same list of names and once more dedicating herself to the belief that if she does her best and works her hardest, she will make a positive impact in the world. To her, I expect, the souls of those who have passed before her are another in a long line of responsibilities. Their afterlives literally depend on her remembering them. With this news of her father, I am sure it is a comforting faith. It is not one I share, though. The Black Dragon's whole Oath is about remembrance, if you look between the lines. 'I build with strong foundations, stone by stone. In questions, not answers, will my wisdom grow, and in listening, not speaking, will it expand. I dedicate my life to the pursuit and sharing of knowledge, so that when my days come to an end, others may follow in my footsteps.'"

"So you do think you'll live on with every new generation that learns what you've researched?" Gabe asked.

Robin nodded. "I hope so, but as I said, I don't know that I believe I will retain consciousness. More that, as long as that which I have taught lives on, I will still be with all those who learn it. My own, personal faith is that the dead we remember live on *in us,* not *with us.* Their lessons, their wisdoms, and yes, even their faults and follies. They are all lessons, and so long as we remember them and learn from them, in a very real way, those we lost do live on."

Gabe pondered that as they continued walking through the vast cathedral, weaving around people in prayer. Finally, he said, "And what about those who no one remembers? While I was in Miriel, a man with no family was admitted to our ward. He was poor and alone, and the whole time he was dying, what concerned him the most was that no one would remember him. He made me repeat his name back to him, over and over again. It was the only thing that soothed him in his last few days. Do you think his soul would have been lost, if he had died in his home instead of making it to the clinic where I could learn his name? Because so, so many died like that. During the worst of it, they were finding bodies on the street so wasted away from the fever and bloated by rot that they could not identify them."

With a long sigh, Robin bowed his head. "The teachings of the church would make us believe his soul would have been lost, if his name is not remembered tonight and every future Midwinter. Fortunately, Ionism also embraces the questioning and analysis of their dogma. So what do *you* think? Would this patient of yours have been forgotten, if you had never met him? Would his soul be lost if he was among those buried instead of burned, as I know many have been each year that wasting fever ravages Miriel when they run out of wood?"

"No," Gabe said, without hesitation.

Robin quirked his eyebrows, a cue to explain his reasoning.

"Even if I hadn't known his name, I don't think I'll ever forget the toll on human life, and neither will any doctor who worked there. I might forget the individual faces one day, but I'll never forget that each of them *was* an individual person, not just… a number. The same with every war, or famine, or… slaughter. Even if I didn't know anyone involved, their deaths still affected history. They still mean something *to me*, and deserve the dignity of being remembered. They're as important as the movers and shakers of the world, as far as I'm concerned. Possibly more so."

Robin gave Gabriel's messy hair a fond rustle. "Good answer, though it saddens me that you've seen so much loss and injustice in your young life that you have already come to that conclusion. It takes many people decades to look beyond themselves and their own loved ones, and have enough compassion to care about those who are forgotten, not just those who are remembered. More importantly, to listen to what their passings can teach us."

They walked on in silence, returning to where they had started eventually. Fay and Fedrik were still at the altar. Gabe hesitated, then asked, "So how do I do this? I don't have a God I'm devoted to."

"Pick the one who speaks to your heart the most today, and worry about a lifetime devotion when and if that will ever serve you. I am, of course, biased toward the Black in matters of remembrance, but perhaps the Red's oath would better serve you? It is, after all, the one the College of Science has embraced."

Gabe glanced toward that side of the altar, where the Oath of the Red was carved. *Though born a seed, I will sink roots and rise towards the sky. No storm can break me, for always will I bend and grow. May all be welcome in my shade, where side by side we craft a better world. Let our names live on in our creations.*

"No, that doesn't quite fit me. I don't want to build a better world, just help fix the one we have," Gabe said. "The Green and the Blue are both good, but don't… speak to me, either."

"The White, perhaps? Like Mr. Tellen? Altruism, fortitude, and humility are all traits I think you demonstrate often, and make me very proud to know you," Robin said, with a small but warm smile.

Gabe blushed, but shook his head. "Not the White, either. God of the Lirion and all that."

"Ah yes, quite right. Then I suggest, despite your general antagonism to the church and College of Theology, to perhaps consider the Silver That Was? 'The forgotten, I will remember. The lost, I will lead. The suffering, I will comfort. I shall not fear failure, for though I may fall, I will rise stronger. May my triumphs make me brave and my trials make me kind.'"

Gabriel thought about it for some time. Finally, he nodded. "Yes. I think I like that one better. Thank you, Master Robin."

"Think nothing of it, Gabriel. It's my honor and privilege to educate, and to see my students learn and grow. Go on, take a piece of paper and write down what you wish to be remembered in the coming year. If you wish it, consider also adding a devotion. It is good, sometimes, to have a task to guide us—something that can lend us strength and focus in hard times, and for which you wish to be remembered after death. Even if this is the only year you ever do, it might bring you some peace."

Robin gave Gabriel a little push forward. With careful steps, he approached the altar. Awkward and unsure, he shifted his weight from side to side as he waited for his turn. At last, Gabe was able to take a piece of gray paper.

Not wanting to take up space at the altar when it didn't mean as much to him, Gabe retreated to a quiet corner of the Temple to fill the sheet out, using the base of a column as a flat surface to write on. He pulled out the nub of a pencil from his pocket, set it to the sheet, took a deep breath, and in a careful, neat script, began to write, each letter meticulously neat and legible.

Tom Riell

The piece of gray paper Gabriel brought back to the altar was so covered in writing it looked black. Tom Riell's name had been written in large letters in the center, the only one Gabe had intended to jot down, but once he had started, he'd found himself incapable of stopping. Every patient whose name he could remember had joined Tom's. Then, like a dam breaking, other names too. His parents. His brother. The baker who had made every loaf of bread he had eaten until the age of eight. The childhood friends whose faces would never age along with him. Even his favorite goat from their herd, though he doubted the church would appreciate it. It didn't matter. Gabriel wasn't writing it for the Temple, or the Gods, but for himself. A reminder of what had been lost.

Tears coated his cheeks in salty trails and stung his eyes as he placed the folded sheet of paper in the basin. It slithered down the pounded gold side to join thousands of others, many as full as his own.

He looked down at the words carved on the altar where he stood. Some of those around him were murmuring the litany of their God, renewing their devotion for another year. Gabriel had not included a devotion on his list of names to be remembered. It had felt hollow and selfish, somehow, to ask that the Gods and church remember him for his deeds, when Gabriel did not worship them. Yet as he stood there, part of him regretted it.

Wouldn't it be simpler to believe? To imagine his family was still there, watching over him? That Tom was floating around with them, getting into a row with anyone who would listen? The dead were supposed to be closer to the living than ever at Midwinter, the veil between them thin enough to feel their love as an ephemeral caress against one's soul.

If he could will himself to have faith that there was a greater plan, would Cornen's impending death be less painful? Would the prospect of leaving this place he loved be easier to swallow? It comforted Fay. He knew that. He'd seen her recite her God's oaths each time she had to really dig deep, and stick to her convictions. It gave her strength. So why couldn't it give Gabriel any?

Maybe it was something that grew over time. He didn't believe, and wasn't sure anything would ever change that, but perhaps it was worth at least… having a focus. Words he could cling to, when lost. Or at least try. Breathing in deeply, he quietly recited, "The forgotten, I will remember. The lost, I will lead. The suffering, I will comfort. I shall not fear failure, for though I may fall, I will rise stronger. May my triumphs make me brave and my trials make me kind."

Fedrik and Fay were waiting for him by the doors of the Temple. Fay held her arms open to Gabriel, and squeezed him tight when he hugged her. When they let go, Fedrik wrapped an arm around his shoulders. "Let's go somewhere we can be alone to light our candles and hold vigil. Temples are always too crowded."

Gabriel was only too happy to comply.

Even before Fedrik took the first turn, Gabe knew where he was taking them. There was a sandy little beach, tucked away by the lake and too far for most Academy students to bother with. Fay and Gabriel had found it first year, while wandering through the woods on a plant identification assignment, and had claimed it as their own. Unbeknownst to them at the time, it was also where Fedrik ran off to when he was frustrated with the other nobles always peppering him with questions about the princess living with his parents.

They had run into each other one day, and it had been the first time the three of them had really talked. Fedrik had been a wreck, though he had never explained why. Gabe had offered to play him at Seven Rivers, and Fay had talked them into a swim. Within a month, the three of them had been fast friends, although it had been awhile longer before they ever acted like it anywhere other than by the lake.

The beach was dusted in snow and fallen leaves when they arrived. The willow tree stood naked and curved, like the back of an old man, casting a mosaic pattern of waving shadows in the light of the moon. Fay went to collect wood for a fire, which Gabriel lit with a tiny rift that exhausted most of his magical reserves. Fedrik pulled out a flask of spiced rum.

They sat shoulder-to-shoulder against a fallen log, staring out over the darkened water and passing the flask around in silence. After some time, Fay laid her head against Gabriel's upper arm. "I'm going to miss this place."

"But at least we're leaving together. It wouldn't be the same without you two," Gabe said, glancing over Fayrian to smile at Fedrik. "And it's been a good six years, right?"

"Best of my life," Fedrik answered. "May the next few be even better, sadness and all."

"I hope so." Fay sighed, then looked up at Gabe. "Robin approached me while you were working on your list of names. He's talked to the dean. They're going to give us a deferral on our loans and your scholarship. I was expecting a few months, but they're giving us ten years."

"What?" Gabe's eyes flew wide. "That's…"

"Long enough. Hopefully. I… when I met with Robin, I told him how much this opportunity meant to you. I asked him if he would be willing to ask the College of Science to hold your place. It took some doing, and I had to renegotiate my loan interest significantly to get us the deferment, but he did it. He's giving us the time we need to fix Lirin, and after… you can return here, Gabriel." She was smiling, but her eyes were sad. "I couldn't let you give up everything for me. It wasn't right."

"When you say renegotiate significantly—" Fedrik began, but Fay shushed him with a shake of her head.

"I'm never getting out of debt to the Island anyway. It doesn't matter. Besides, I'm counting on Gabriel becoming a Mindellion and happily working as a doctor in some fancy hospital until we're old and gray and our debts are forgiven. I'm not entirely impractical and generous, you know."

Gabriel was still too stunned to speak, so he kissed her instead. When he pulled back, he managed to murmur, "You… are a marvel, Fayrian Avilor. Thank you."

"If you're willing to give all this up for my sake without me even having to ask, the least I can do is make sure that one day you'll get it back. I have a condition, though. I'm keeping you off the front lines of the fight so you can actually survive to return. You can work for the Rebellion as what you are: a medic. That's non-negotiable. I won't lose you to the fight too."

"I... can deal with that," Gabriel said, head still spinning. "I love you, Fay."

"I love you too. Both of you."

"Oh good, because I was starting to feel like a third wheel in this conversation," Fedrik teased. "And am rather cross, because I was half-way through writing a long entreaty to my parents to match Gabe's scholarship if he ever came back, since he's losing out on it to join the cause. You've taken the wind right out of my sails."

"It's well known that everything you try to do, I can do better, Tellen," Fay said, with a grin. Gabriel, meanwhile, was back to speechless, tears welling up even though he had thought himself cried out.

"I don't know what I did to deserve you. Either of you."

"Eh, mostly be cute," Fay said.

"Put up with me," Fedrik said, at about the same time. "And never once complain that I snore in the five plus years we've shared a room."

All three of them laughed, and then they cried. There wasn't much else to say. They sat around the fire until the flask Fedrik had brought was empty, then Fay pulled out three small candles. "Shall we?"

After hunting around for driftwood and affixing the candles to three nice-sized pieces, they lit them off a branch from the fire and walked to the edge of the lake. A thin crust of ice had formed by the shoreline, but it was only a foot or so wide. One by one they knelt, and set their candle on the calm water, sending ripples and reflections dancing across the surface.

They stood together, arm in arm, as the lights bobbed and swayed, slowly drawn out into the lake by the current of a nearby tributary. Fay was the one who started the recitation. "I remember my mother, Sarah, and my grandmother Fatima. I remember those who died in the razing of Delford, and all those who have lost their lives trying to make Lirin a better place. May your memories guide me and be a blessing to all those who remember you."

Fedrik took over. "I remember my grandparents, Federica and Shawn, and my ancestors before them as listed in the Book of

Names of houses Tellen and Sivannah, and my cousins of Houses Lirion, Ondai, Enica, and Circada. I remember my tutor Liam Arlen, and Atticus Oswald, who died in service to the next King, my friend and cousin Wilam. I remember all those who died in the Western Revolts, and who passed away without being able to see their children one last time." Fedrik finished, tears in his eyes, and turned to Gabriel, who usually did not light participate.

Gabe cleared his throat, a lump of emotion making it hard to speak. "If the Gods are real, they know who I remember, but there is someone I do need to talk about. It might take some time, though, and I may be a mess after. Is that alright?"

"We have all night," Fedrik encouraged. "Take your time, Gabriel. Is it about Miriel?"

Gabe nodded, tilting his head up to look at the sky. It was full of clouds, not smoke, but he could still see the glow of the pyres from the day before his departure when they had burned the last of the dead Gabe had tended to. Tom's body had been one among dozens on the fire, unrecognizable once the flames had devoured his wispy gray hair. "I haven't wanted to talk about it. I still don't want to, but I think I need to start, or it will keep haunting me. I'm glad I went, and I'm glad I saw what I did, but it was the hardest four weeks of my life. Even after Nillenia, I had anger at Mark Lirion to hold me together, but there… it was just grief and despair. We were fighting a force of nature, and we were losing. It didn't matter how many we saved because the beds always filled up again. It didn't matter how hard we worked, because there wasn't enough serindalla, and there weren't enough doctors to make a difference. I'd feel so much guilt every time I'd take a dose and every time I closed my eyes, because what if that would have been the difference between someone's life and death? They warned us about it on the way over, but nothing could have prepared any of us for it. I had thought I was ready after visiting the razed villages…" Gabriel looked back down at the candles, drifting further and further away. "I wasn't."

"I'm sorry," Fay said, placing a hand on his elbow. Gabe covered it with his own, squeezing tight. "Do you regret going?"

"Not for a moment. It's what I'm meant to do, Fay. I know that. It was horrible, but it reminded me of the world outside this island. These years have been precious, but part of me is glad we get to leave, especially if it's not forever. The world is broken out there. Really fucking broken. Bad enough that it got to me, even after everything I've gone through. I really hadn't expected that." He rubbed at one of the old burn scars that covered most of his right side, still feeling the phantom pain of the fire, even though it had been a decade since he'd been caught in those flames. "I don't know how, but we need to fix it. The fact that doctors and nurses were working so hard to stop something that the powers on high could have mitigated is the same as the issues facing Lirin. Disease, famine, war, they're all facets of each other, aren't they? They all cost lives that will never be remembered as more than a number. Killing Mark Lirion is how we can start fixing that, but it's only the beginning. I want to find a way to do more. To actually *make a difference* every single day, for the rest of my life, even knowing the cost."

Fedrik wrapped an arm around Gabe's shoulders. "If anyone can, it's you, my friend. And we'll be right by your side like always, right, Avilor?"

"Right. Lirin first, the world second, if we make it out alive." Fay leaned in too. "And fuck anyone who tries to stop us."

"That's the Fay we know and love. I was starting to worry for awhile there, with all this newfound thoughtfulness," Gabriel teased, then pressed a kiss into her curls.

"So who's this person you want to tell us about? One of your patients?" Fedrik asked, turning to lead them to their seats by the fire.

Gabriel waited until they were once more seated, watching the dancing flames, and cuddled close between his two best friends. He stared out over the lake, thinking about all the ways this place had shaped him, and all the memories he'd carry with him when they left. Neither Fay nor Fedrik hurried him, minutes passing to the metronome of lapping waves and wind crying through the trees. Finally, Gabriel looked into the fire, and said, "His name was Tom Riell, and he was a friend of mine."

THE END

THE STORY THUS FAR

AFTER THE DEATH OF PRINCE WILAM LIRION during a failed coup, his younger sister Elenor becomes the Heir of Lirin. She is swiftly escorted out of the Palace by Fedrik Tellen for her own safety, and taken to the Rebellion. There, they meet Fayrian Avilor and Gabriel Navarl, the leaders of the resistance against Elenor's family. Gabriel was poisoned during the coup attempt, and Fedrik bargains for safe passage with the Rebellion in exchange for the antidote. All of this is watched over by Daemon Indigo, whose conflicting orders from the Gods to kill Gabriel, save Gabriel, and not harm Elenor in any way give him quite the dilemma.

When Daemon's actions lead to the Rebellion being discovered, Fay and Fedrik end up separated from Elenor and Gabriel. Gabe takes Elenor to a safehouse which turns out to be Tellen Manor, where Elenor lived while she was sick as a child. He proceeds to hatch a plan to infiltrate back into the Palace to kill the King and Queen. This attempt is thwarted by Elenor, leading to Gabriel's arrest.

Meanwhile, it is discovered that Fay is in trouble with Tirit Mindel, the island that runs the banks, temples, and schools around the continent. Fedrik keeps her from recklessly going after Gabriel, and takes her out of the city kicking and screaming. Daemon, meanwhile, lurks and considers his options, while North Hillman, a Namer living on his island, finds out that Daemon is immortal.

Several days later, on the road south, Fay is apprehended by Tirit Mindel, but Fedrik saves her before she can be taken back to the Island. He finds out that she has the Ghoster Gift and has been suppressing Gabriel's magic. By letting him get captured, she angered Robin Tirition, the dean of the Academy of Tirit Mindel and the man pulling Fay's strings. Together, they decide to run south to the Mondaer desert. While they do, Fay's Gift is acting erratically, and Fedrik is having bad headaches.

In Hardor, Elenor turns the Tellens in for being rebel sympathizers and finds out that they have been killed without a trial. This shakes her deeply. She also finds out she is to be married. Deciding she needs more information, Elenor goes down to the subterranean dungeons to talk to Gabriel, and discovers that her parents have been mismanaging the country and torturing him. She meets Robin Tirition who asks for her help in freeing Gabriel, and tells her about his magic and Fay's role in suppressing it. When she does not immediately agree, he threatens to turn Tirit Mindel against Lirin if she does not play along with him, which would be devastating for her kingdom and family.

Daemon continues to lurk and starts getting attached to both Elenor and Gabriel. He witnesses Elenor's lover, Claire, develop a Gift, and discovers that Elenor's mother, Lilian, is able to erase memories with a Gift of her own. Meanwhile, his relationship with North is disintegrating. After hearing the story of how Daemon became immortal by torturing a child names Alehan Silvarin to madness, North tells him off for his lack of morality and Daemon angrily sends into the desert to die with his baby dragon.

On the night of a ball at the Drego estate, Elenor's new acquaintance Kallen Drego gives her evidence that one of her parents is funding the Rebellion. She also meets Daemon, striking an immediate connection. Meanwhile at the Palace, Gabriel explodes magically and blows up a guard during a torture session, getting locked behind an impenetrable magical barrier to starve to death. Elenor's father finds out she has been seeing Gabriel and kills Djina, Elenor's doctor, in front of her to teach her a lesson. Far to the south, Fedrik and Fay make it to the desert atop a wild mock dragon.

Branded as slaves, Fedrik and Fay end up meeting North at an orientation point for new arrivals. He confirms for the Mondaer people that Fay is Gifted, and discovers that Fedrik is as well. His Gift is somehow blocking other people's and draining magic from rifters. This makes the Mondaer people very excited.

North, Fedrik, and Fay are taken to the Deil family estate to meet the Veiled Wanderer, otherwise known as Fulsixia the Red Dragon. While there, they find out more about Gifts, and it is postulated that Fedrik may have the rare Gatekeeper Gift, which would mean that somewhere out there, he has an Incarnate: the Gift that gives Gifts.

In Hardor, Daemon takes Elenor to Djina's passing ceremony, and then to see Robin. She makes it clear to RObin that she will not abide his threats but will assist him for her own ends, then hatches a plan to free Gabriel with the help of her friends. Daemon is visited by the White Dragon and finds out that Elenor and Gabriel have a future together, and that if he continues to remain near her, she may destroy the world. The White then threatens him and his island home if he interferes in her life. It is discovered that Daemon has hidden a whole city on Ayre Island, one where rifters and Gifted can live in peace and without being drawn into world politics. He begins evacuations, aware that the White Dragon is a real threat.

Elenor, meanwhile, is told by her mother that she was the one funding the Rebellion. The Queen makes it clear that she's been periodically erasing Elenor's memories for some time and that she's working for the White Dragon, but then makes Elenor forget about it with her Razer Gift.

In the desert, Fay and Fedrik forgive each other for mistakes made long ago and finally accept that they are in this together, confronting their feelings for each other. Fay is brought before the Veiled Wanderer and made daradeio. While this is happening, Elenor starts her jailbreak and is found by Lord Eurieha, her father's adviser, who turns out to be working for Elenor's enemies and responsible for warning the King about the coup Wilam died in. Fedrik feels it when Eurieha tries to strangle her, and the connection between them as Gatekeeper and Incarnate is established. In the rush of pain and magic, Fedrik kills the Fulsixia the Red Dragon, which breaks most of the rifters around him.

Elenor succeeds in freeing Gabriel by causing a mass breakout of prisoners. A guard, Jo, helps her do it. On their way out, they are cornered by her father and Eurieha. The King threatens to use Elenor's loved ones as leverage to keep her in line. Elenor decides to finish what her brother started and poisons her father with her ring.

A fight breaks out. Daemon runs in to help save Elenor's life, and Gabriel is mortally wounded. Daemon and Elenor get to him in time and help him turn his explosive magic inward to heal himself, instead of outward to destroy the city.

After returning to Ayre, Daemon is called to a meeting of the remaining Gods and their minions to discuss the death of the Red. He and his God—Xirra the Blue—break from the others. Daemon returns home to find out that the White destroyed his villa and all that he had left of his wife and son. He vows vengeance.

Elenor has a moment of catharsis while dancing in the rain as she comes to terms with everything that has happened. Fedrik is flown away to the Sandhewn City, separating him from a distraught Fay.

Later that night, Lilian and Robin talk about the cost of their lies, and Robin gives Lilian a document she has been looking for since the start of the story. It is discovered that it names Elenor as heir to both Lirin and Miriel, and that Robin is angling for a union between her and Gabriel, who is a Silvarin and therefore descended from the line of deposed emperors that once ruled the whole continent.

Lilian throws the document into the fire. She wants her daughter safe, not powerful. They part ways no longer as allies.

ACKNOWLEDGEMENTS

IT'S BEEN TWO CRAZY YEARS since I published *Where Shadows Lie,* and the world is unrecognizable. We have all endured fear and confusion, and many of us have suffered or died of a disease we could not escape. While I always knew that Elenor's illness and Gabriel's love of medicine would play a major part in this book, I did not expect to be writing about it while surviving a pandemic.

These two years also saw other tumultuous events rock my life, mainly the fight and ultimate failure of my disability case. It has left me confronting a lot of hard feelings about pain, fear, and uncertainty. Writing was a way for me to pour my worries, heartbreak, and doubts into my work.

Through it all, what kept me going were the people around me. My parents, husband, and friends supported my dreams and accepted the times when I had to hole up in the attic and cry over my keyboard for a few hours or day. My co-authors graciously let me rant at them about the struggles with this book and it's sequel until I could see their eyes glazing over, yet never once complained. My team of editors and proofreaders went above and beyond the call of duty, helping me make the difficult decision to split the book in two.

No book is a singular effort, but these feel like a community picnic. There are so many talented hands and minds involved in Project Ao, and while sometimes things get sticky and the jello has some ants, I couldn't be prouder of what we have accomplished.

So to Justin, Erica, Danielle, Chris, Tobias, Lisa, Jessica, Lene, Dash, and Rachel, thank you for being on this wild ride with me. To Lorie, Becki, August, and all my fabulous beta readers, thank you for making this book the best it could be. To my wonderful father John, Ailish, Marian, and Owen, thank you for making it beautiful and bringing it to life, and finally to my friends and family, thank you for putting up with this insanity. I love you.

But most of all thank you to you, for giving these crazy books a chance.

The adventure has only begun.

MAJOR PLAYERS

REBELS

Fayrian Avilor - Leader of the Rebellion and daughter of its founder, graduate of the Academy of Tirit Mindel.

Gabriel Navarl - Second in Command of the Rebellion, graduate of the Academy of Tirit Mindel.

Daren Ito - founding member of the Rebellion and ambient rifter, best friend to Sidian Tailor.

Mari Baker - Retired founding member of the Rebellion and owner of The Merry Baker, married to Kyle Baker.

Tamara Baker - Seamstress and daughter of Mari and Kyle Baker.

LIRINIAN NOBLES

Elenor Lirion - Heir Presumptive of Lirin, scion of Houses Lirion, Miri, Ondai, and Tellen, and second child of Lilian and Mark Lirion.

Wilam Lirion - Crown Prince of Lirin, bearer of House Lirion's second Water Writ, and eldest child of Lilian and Mark Lirion. Now deceased.

Markus Miri Lirion - King of Lirin, father to Wilam and Elenor, younger brother to Warren Miri, the King of Miriel. Now deceased.

Lilian Lirion - Queen of Lirin, bearer of House Lirion's first Water Writ, mother of Wilam and Elenor, older sister to Sianta Lirion-Miri, Queen Regent of Miriel.

Sianta Lirion Miri - Queen Regent of Miriel, mother of Jasper,

Silla, and Catya, younger sister to Lilian Lirion, Queen of Lirin.

Silla Miri – Second-born child of Sianta and Warren Miri.

Duncan Eurieha - Chief adviser to Mark Miri-Lirion, leader of House Eurieha.

Daniil Eurieha - Son of Duncan Eurieha, and priest of the Orthodox Ionist Church of North Island.

Sebastin Tellen - Deceased bearer of House Tellen's first Water Writ, leader of his House, and father to Fedrik.

Alessia Tellen - Deceased bearer of House Tellen's second Water Writ, official Tellen representative on the King's Council, and mother to Fedrik.

Fedrik Tellen - Scion of House Tellen, and graduate of the Academy of Tirit Mindel.

Kallen Drego Mindellion - Bearer of House Drego's first Water Writ, leader of his House, and official Drego representative on the King's Council, graduate of the College of Finance.

Eric Ondai - Bearer of House Ondai's second Water Writ, official Ondai representative on the King's Council, and husband to Bethany.

Bethany Rinelisi - Scion of House Rinelisi and wife to Eric.

Claire Enica - Schism, scion of Houses Enica and Tellen, best friend and lover to Elenor.

Tomaz Catoali - Student of the Hardor University's School of Law.

STAFF

Paul Marek - *Doena* to Elenor and ambient rifter.

Djina Grau - Retired medic, in service to Lilian, Wilam, and Elenor. Now deceased.

Garnet 'Jo' Jozel - Prison guard at the Hardor Palace.

Lawrence Darling - Butler to Sebastin and Alessia.

TIRIT MINDEL

Robin Daran Tirition - Dean of the Core Six Undergraduate Program at the Academy of Tirit Mindel, Master of Diplomacy, graduate of the College of Academics.

Ara Daran Tirition - Archive Director at the Academy of Tirit Mindel, Dual-Master of Magic & Science, graduate of the College of Discipline.

AYRE ISLAND

Daemon Indigo - Previously Jac Drego Tirition, Master of Rifting, graduate of the College of Discipline. Vital rifter and owner of Ayre Island.

North Hillman - Previously Alaric Nameh. Namer and ex-resident of Ayre Island.

Tsiihsi Lark - Vital rifter and resident of Ayre City.

Obri Larson - Bode and resident of Ayre City.

MONDAER

Akaaron Tieko - Namer, *daradeio* and merchant of Mondaer cloth and household goods, friend to Gabriel and Fayrian. Previously, apprentice to Quindo.

Kaedy Deil - Ambient rifter, now broken, *daradeio* and apprentice to Akaaron, mother to Adaariol, daughter of Quindo.

Quindo Deil - Archivist, *daradeio,* and part-owner of Akaaron's business, parent to Kaedy.

Tavea Longuu - Ambient rifter, now broken, *daradeio* and Mondaer border-crossing overseer, mentor to Leo.

Leo Baotiste - Ambient rifter, *daradeio,*and apprentice to Tavea.

Suela Alveara - Ex-Gatekeeper, *daradeio,* and companion to the Veiled Wanderer.

Sidian Tailor - Previously Ian Taylor. Ex-Incarnate, *daradeio,* rebel, and companion to the Veiled Wanderer. Now deceased.

Phoebi Deil - Wife of Quindo Deil, Master Mindellion of the College of Academic, Gifted Razer.

Denzel Tirition - Master Tirition of the College of Discipline, Gifted Schism, ex-weapons master of the Academy of Tirit Mindel.

HISTORICAL

Alexander Silvarin-Tirition - Ambient rifter, last Emperor of Carinn, Master of Discipline from the Academy of Tirit Mindel, and father to Alehan. Deceased.

Cianira Maarzi - Ambient rifter, last Empress of Carinn, and mother to Alehan. Deceased.

Mathe Maarzi - Brother to the Empress. Composer and musician. Deceased.

Alehan Silvarin - Vtal rifter and illegitimate child of the Emperor.

Gabril Lirion-Mindellion - Last Triumvirate Third of Carinn, Master of Diplomacy from the Academy of Tirit Mindel, and traitor to his liege. Deceased.

Aislin Silvarin - Ambient rifter, cousin to Alexander, wife to Jac, and mother to Julian. Deceased.

Julian Silvarin - Son of Aislin and Jac. Deceased.

GLOSSARY

ELDEL TERMINOLOGY

Aina Brisbhan - The Eldel name for the Mother Rock. It is the home of the Fulsixia the Red Dragon and the capital of the Mondaer Desert.

daradeio - Eldel word that means "dragon-found" and given to those Mondaer who lead the desert. All daradeio have red eyes.

doena - Eldel word that means protector, teacher, and/or guide. The word was co-opted by the nobility of Miriel and given to their close bodyguards. These men and women are usually rifters and assigned to a child a birth to protect and help raise them.

Eldel - The language of the Eldel Nations.

Eldel Nations - The people who were on Carinn before the Exiles arrived. Currently comprises the Mondaer, the Jia, and the Tekomii peoples and the territory they control.

Exiles - The Eldel name for the peoples of the five Dragon Gods, who came from beyond the sea and who currently live in the four kingdoms of Lirin, Namnia, Seehana, and Miriel.

liuda - Eldel term of endearment for one who is family but not by blood, used equally for romantic and non-romantic roles in one's life.

talidaar - Eldel word that means cherished one, and/or apprentice. The words was co-opted by the nobility of Miriel and given to the charges of their doenas.

LIRINIAN TERMINOLOGY

constituent nobility - The noble houses that have enough wealth to compete in the Water Race as constituents of a Writted house.

Crown Prince/Princess - The bearer of the second Lirion Water Writ, after the successful completion of their Water Rite.

Forgotten name - A name that has been deemed taboo. It is not to be spoken, written, or remembered in any ceremony. Speaking it has serious consequences if caught by the law.

heir presumptive - The heir of a Writted house who has begun the process of petitioning for their Water Writ, and is training for their Water Rite.

Water Race - The decennial tournament in which the provinces of Lirin are redistributed among the Writted nobility.

Water Rights - The set of rights given to the Writted nobility which grants them control over a section of Lirinian rivers, as well their tributaries and watersheds.

Water Rite - The ceremonial crossing of a river by a person petitioning for a Water Writ. To successfully complete it, the petitioner must swim across the largest river their family controls, with no assistance.

Water Writ - The document that gives power to the two leaders of each of the writted noble houses, acquired after the successful completion of a Water Rite.

writted nobility - The eight Lirinian houses that hold Water Writs: Lirion, Ondai, Drego, Tellen, Enica, Amad, Petrona, and Lavarin.

MAGIC TERMINOLOGY

ambient rifter - A rifter who does not have access to the source of magic, and who must refill their well by absorbing magic or energy from their surroundings.

capacity - The maximum amount of magic a rifter can use at any one time. If strained too far, the capacity can break, destroying a rifter's ability to ever use magic again.

critical break - When the well and capacity of a vital rifter shatter at the same time, creating a magical explosion.

Gift - One of eighteen magical Gifts, each of which is a very specific and unique power.

Gifted - A human who has one of the eighteen Gifts. Gifted cannot also be rifters.

magical circuit - A device made of the magical metals that performs a rift.

magical metal - Refers to cerulean, copper, and gold, which can be used to create magical circuitry.

oversaturation - When a rifter's well is overfull and the excess is metabolized by the body. It creates a state of heightened energy, impulsivity, and euphoria.

podding - The process of combining the wells of up to five rifters under the control of one.

rift - The specific formula or instance of using magic.

rifter - A human who can rift.

rifting - To turn magical energy into physical energy, or vice versa.

sending - A simple rift that allows the rifter to project their voice to a piece of copper away from themselves.

the Plane - The source of magic, a place outside of reality where anything is possible.

vital rifter - A rifter who has direct access to the source of magic, and whose well refills naturally.

well - The reservoir of magic within a rifter.

SCIENTIFIC TERMINOLOGY

dacel - A plant used to make sleep aids, which are often paired with patience in surgery. It produces a deep, dreamless sleep.

evergold - A common vine with yellow flowers that bloom year round. All parts of the plant have painkilling properties, ranging from mild to strong.

half-dragon - The child of a Dragon God. They are rare and usually sport some combination of wings, scales, and a tail.

mock dragon - A dragon-shaped animal of similar intelligence to a dog or horse. There are five varieties, one for each of the known Gods of Carinn. They are trainable and large enough to be ridden by between one and two average size people.

patience - A paralytic commonly used in surgery or to poison a weapon. It creates a detached, dream-like state and loss of muscle control.

serindalla - A powerful stimulant drug from the rainforests of Miriel, derived from the sap of the Jiakappa tree. It is a highly addictive substance and the only known way to control wasting fever.

wasting fever - A mosquito-borne illness from the tropics in southern Miriel, which causes a high fever and damage to muscles and nerves, usually in the lower extremities. Can be deadly, and cannot be cured, only controlled.

TIRIT MINDEL TERMONOLOGY

the Academy - Refers to the Academy of Tirit Mindel, the most prestigious school in Carinn. The Academy has two branches, one in the city of Tirit and one at Mindel. Students accepted into the program alternate between both locations.

Colleges of Tirit Mindel - Refers to the six Colleges of the Tirit Mindel Academy: Theology, Finance, and Diplomacy based in Mindel, and Discipline, Academics, and Science at Tirit.

Core Six - Refers to the initial six years at the Academy, a program that covers the basics of all six Colleges of Tirit Mindel. Students must graduate Core Six to be accepted into a College.

Council of Ten - The ruling body of Tirit Mindel, which includes the dean of each of the Colleges, the dean of Core Six, the two heads of the Church of the Five, and the leader of the Silverguard.

Master Tirition/Mindellion - A Tirition or Mindellion who has completed a Master's Thesis and had it accepted by the Council of Ten.

Mindellion - A fully accredited graduate of the College of Theology, Finance, or Diplomacy at the Academy.

Silverguard - The private and highly-trained militia of Tirit Mindel.

the Five - Refers to the five Dragon Gods of Carinn: Kennotoza, Zorbennen, Fulsixia, Gullien, and Xirra which are worshiped by the church of Tirit Mindel as it presently stands.

Tirition - A fully accredited graduate of the College of Discipline, Academics, or Science at the Academy.

LIRINIAN NOBILITY

WRITTED NOBILITY

HOUSE AMAD
THE OTTER
CERULEAN, GREEN, BROWN

mining, precious minerals, and magical metals

HOUSE DREGO
THE KINGFISHER
BLUE, BLACK, COPPER

military supply and circutry goods

HOUSE ENICA
THE SEA SNAKE
GOLD, GREEN, BLACK

medical and botanical supplies and services

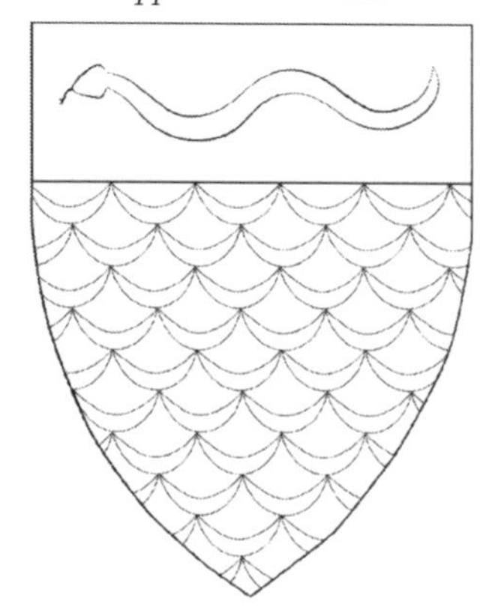

HOUSE LAVARIN
THE KOI
PURPLE, RED, WHITE

livestock and related products

HOUSE LIRION
THE HERON
WHITE, RED, GOLD

water monopoly and legal services

HOUSE ONDAI
THE OCTOPUS
GOLD, BLUE, BLACK

trade, spices, salt, and news

HOUSE PETRONA
THE DOLPHIN
WHITE, BLUE, GREEN

agriculture, primarily rice and other staple goods

HOUSE TELLEN
THE SALAMANDER
RED, BLACK,COPPER

transportation and communication

CONSTITUENT NOBILITY

Family Name		**Symbol**
Arlen	-	Frog
Bandeca	-	Jellyfish
Catoali	-	Whale
Cobe	-	Crab
Dirin	-	Beaver
Eurieha	-	Turtle
Maritanu	-	Sunfish
Quillibee	-	Shark
Rinelisi	-	Nautilus
Sivannah	-	Seahorse
Taberlin	-	Barracuda
Torien	-	Seagull
Watts	-	Clam
Zitaro	-	Walrus

THE GIFTS

Gifts Of Taking	**Gifts Of Giving**
Razer (Lies)	Namer (Sees)
Archivist (Recalls)	Bode (Predicts)
Ghoster (Absorbs)	Cede (Releases)
Cipher (Hides)	Schism (Finds)
Sunder (Divides)	Weaver (Unites)
Lusion (Obfuscates)	Lucent (Illuminates)
Fathom (Deconstructs)	Forge (Constructs)
Quell (Dampens)	Echo (Enhances)
Gatekeeper (Destroys)	Incarnate (Creates)

CONTENT WARNING

Whispers of Stone contains several sections and themes that could be triggering or difficult to read. I don't want to accidentally cause a reader any discomfort, so please be aware of the following:

Whispers of Stone contains graphic violence, mild gore, sex, swearing, character death, and non-graphic mentions of child abuse and domestic abuse. It also contains sexual situations that involve lies, blackmail, and coercion, as well as extensive and deliberate character gaslighting. In addition, it deals with the topics of slavery, death, ableism, racism, torture, drug dependency, starvation, disease, and abuses of power by people in positions of privilege.

I did not want to write a story about these dark subjects that skirted around the horrifying reality of our own history. As such, I tried to explore the dark while clearly painting it as such. These acts of evil are never glorified, and the characters who suffer through them are given chances to rise beyond their trauma.

However, I accept and acknowledge that many people read to get away from the darkness around us or do not wish to explore these difficult and potentially triggering subjects, so please proceed with caution, and stay safe and healthy.

ABOUT THE AUTHOR

Allegra Pescatore grew up in a small village in northern Tuscany as the daughter of a marble sculptor and a collage artist. She was raised on the works of J.R.R Tolkien, C.S. Lewis, Phillip Pullman, Frank Herbert, and many others, all read aloud to her while she drew and played make-believe. She began to write at the age of eight and hasn't stopped since.

Her many years of international travel have given her a well-rounded view of culture and a passion for creating unique and engaging fantastical worlds. As a disabled woman and staunch LGBTQ ally, Allegra hopes to write engaging, diverse, and representative Fantasy and Science Fiction, where people who do not often see themselves center stage get the chance to shine.

Email: authorallegra@gmail.com
Website: www.authorallegra.com
Facebook: facebook.com/authorallegra
Twitter: twitter.com/AuthorAllegra

Made in the USA
Monee, IL
05 April 2022

6981e4f6-a440-44c5-9596-dae625c8dfb4R04